JORGE AMADO was born in 1912 in Ilhéus, the provincial capital of the state of Bahia whose society he portrays in such acclaimed novels as GABRIELA, CLOVE AND CINNAMON; DONA FLOR AND HER TWO HUSBANDS; and TEREZA BATISTA: HOME FROM THE WARS. His father was a cocoa planter, and his first novel, CACAU, published when he was nineteen, is a plea for social justice for the workers on the cocoa estates south of Bahia. The theme of class struggle continues to dominate in his novels of the Thirties and Forties; but with the Fifties and GABRIELA, CLOVE AND CINNAMON (1958), the political emphasis gives way to a lighter, more novelistic approach. It was in that novel, published in the United States when Amado was fifty and enthusiastically received in some fourteen countries, that he first explored the rich literary vein pursued in DONA FLOR AND HER TWO HUSBANDS. Highly successful film and Broadway musical versions of DONA FLOR have brought to wider attention the colorful and extravagant world of Brazil's foremost living novelist.

Other Avon books by
Jorge Amado

TIETA

JORGE AMADO

THE GOAT GIRL, OR THE RETURN OF THE
PRODIGAL DAUGHTER, A MELODRAMATIC
SERIAL NOVEL IN FIVE SENSATIONAL
EPISODES, WITH A TOUCHING EPILOGUE:
THRILLS AND SUSPENSE!

*Translated from
the Portuguese by*
BARBARA SHELBY MERELLO

 A BARD BOOK/PUBLISHED BY AVON BOOKS

Originally published in Brazil as *Tieta do Agreste* by
Livraria Martins Editora S.A., Rio de Janeiro.

AVON BOOKS
A division of
The Hearst Corporation
959 Eighth Avenue
New York, New York 10019

First Bard Printing, July, 1980

BARD IS A TRADEMARK OF THE HEARST CORPORATION
AND IS REGISTERED IN MANY COUNTRIES AROUND THE
WORLD, MARCA REGISTRADA, HECHO EN U.S.A.

Printed in the U.S.A.

For Zélia, with her grandchildren around her.

For Glória and Alfredo Machado, Haydée and Paulo
Travares, Helen and Alfred Knopf, Lucía and Paulo
Peltier de Queiroz, Lygia and Juárez da Gama Batista,
Lygia and Zitelmann Oliva, Toninha and Camafeu de
Oxossi, and Carlos Bastos.

"A good place to wait for death."
(*A traveling salesman's opinion
of Sant'Ana do Agreste*)

" . . . people who turn the sea into a garbage can . . . "
(*Judge Viglietta, the Italian judge who sentenced
the directors of the Montedison corporation to prison*)

"Hurrah for the flowering cunt-tree!"
(*What Goatstink sang out
when he saw Tieta for the first time*)

TIETA

Silence, solitude, and the river flowing swiftly into the boundless ocean under a burnished sky, an end and a beginning. Towering dunes, dazzling mountains of sand, and a girl darting like a goat to the top, the bright heat of the sun and the hum of the wind in her face, her bare flying feet widening the distance between her and the strong, powerful, middle-aged male pursuing her.

The man clambers up the steep slope, puffing, clutching his hat in his hand to keep the wind from whirling it away. His shoes sink into the sand at every step; the sun's glare blinds his eyes like a honed razor blade; the wind lashes his hide; sweat pours from his body; he is bursting with desire and rage—"Just wait'll I catch you, devil-gal, I'll bust you wide open and kill you."

The girl turns to gauge the distance between her and the peddler, shuddering with alternate fear and desire: if I let him catch me he'll put it in me—with a quiver of fear; but if I leave him behind he'll give up—oh no! not that! he can't give up now even if he wants to; it's time.

The man stops too and shouts words that are lost in the sand, blown away by the wind. She can't hear them but she guesses what they mean, and this is her answer:

"Maaaaa!" like the bleat of the young goats she herds.

The challenge strikes the peddler in the face like a blow and pierces him to the balls. His strength redoubled, he clambers on. The girl watches and waits. She stands facing the ocean, the river at her back; her young eyes drink in the vast landscape and make it her own. At that moment of eager, painful expectancy, the girl fixes in her memory the dazzling immensity of the bridal bed lying before her. Beyond the sandbar, in the state of Sergipe, lies the noble expanse of Saco Beach, cradled in a sea of gentle waves, and its thriving fishing village, really a town, with a grocery store, chapel and school. The mountainous dunes where she stands invade the water on the other side, thrust themselves into the ocean and are forced back by tremendous breakers in a fierce, never-ending tug-of-war. Here the wind leaves a daily deposit of sand, polished white and fine-sifted to form Mangue Seco Beach, unique and incomparable in the world, where the convulsive union of the Real River and the sea gives birth to the state of Bahia.

A dozen or so ramshackle huts, leaning this way and that at the will of the wind and sand that sweep over and sometimes half bury them, house the handful of fishermen who live on this side of the bar. During the day the women fish for crabs on the mudflats, while the men cast their nets in the sea. Sometimes they set out to catch bigger fish, recklessly crossing billows as high as the dunes in the only boats that can defy them, and put out to sea for a rendezvous with a ship or a schooner on a pitch-dark night to bring back a cargo of smuggled goods.

The so-called peddler comes in a motor launch to pick up the boxes of liquor and perfume, the spices, the bales of Italian silk, cashmere and English linen, for which he pays a small sum in cash—just enough to keep the fishermen in flour, coffee, sugar, rum and tobacco. Once in a while he brings along a hooker with nothing better to do, and while the boxes and bales are brought out of the huts and stowed in the launch, he takes her up on the dunes to pass the time on a palm-frond bed. A real he-man, the peddler; the fishermen like him. After all, he's gone out with them in the boats more than once to where the ships and the sharks are waiting, as if the breakers were ripples.

The girl waits until the man gets very close, then turns and is off like a shot up the sandbank. When she reaches the top she sings out the longing, fearful call of the nannygoats. She knows no other expression, no other word, no other sound for love. She had heard it that very day from a she-goat in first heat when the ram Inácio, patriarch of the flock, advanced toward her swinging his prick and balls. The peddler had shown up and the girl said yes when he invited her for a ride in the motorboat, twenty minutes on the river, five on the choppy sea, and then the glory of Mangue Seco. How could she hold out and say no thanks, I can't go? No, that's a lie: it wasn't the run down the river that tempted her, or crossing that piece of ocean, or even the dunes she had loved since she was a baby. The girl hadn't tried to play innocent. She had refused such invitations before; the peddler had had his eye on her for some time. Well, this time she had said yes, let's go, knowing what was in store for her.

Now that she feels his heavy hand on her arm, fear sweeps over her from head to foot, but she doesn't show it; she grits her teeth and doesn't try to run away.

The man throws her down on some palm fronds, pushes up her skirt and pulls off the dirty rag of her pants. Kneeling above her, he buries his hat on the sand where it won't spin away and opens his fly. The girl lets him do as he wants; it's what she wants too. The time has come for her as it comes for the young nannygoats, the fearful, longed-for, implacable hour of the ram Inácio, whose balls are so big and heavy they almost drag on the ground. Her hour has struck. Doesn't blood flow between her thighs every month now?

On the sand dunes of Mangue Seco, Tieta the goat girl finds out what a man tastes like, the mixture of sea salt and sweat, sand and wind. When the peddler forces her open, she bleats as the nanny-goat had bleated, in fulfillment and pain.

FIRST EPISODE

🐆 🐆 🐆

Tieta's
Death and Resurrection
or
the Prodigal Daughter

WITH AN INTRODUCTION AND BROAD HINTS FROM THE
AUTHOR, UNFORGETTABLE DIALOGUE, PERCEPTIVE
PSYCHOLOGICAL DETAILS, LANDSCAPES SKILLFULLY PAINTED
IN A FEW BRUSHSTROKES, SECRETS AND RIDDLES, BESIDES AN
INTRODUCTION TO SOME CHARACTERS WHO PLAY A
PROMINENT PART IN THE PAST AND FUTURE EVENTS
NARRATED IN THIS EXCITING NOVEL—DOUBT, MYSTERY, VILE
TREACHERY, SUBLIME DEVOTION, HOPE AND LOVE ON
EVERY PAGE.

*Preamble, or introduction, in which the
author, the rascal, tries to shirk any
and all responsibility and ends by
rashly challenging the reader
to a duel of wits.*

Reader, I'm telling you straight: I take no responsibility for the truth of the story related here. I'd have to be crazy to put my hand in the fire. It's not just that everything I'm telling you happened more than ten years ago; the real reason is that every one of us has his own truth and his own sense of right and wrong, and in this particular case I don't see how there can be any compromise or agreement between the opposing views.

This incoherent tale, this confused episode full of absurd contradictions, somehow managed to travel all the way from the forgotten little town on the border between the states of Bahia and Sergipe, to the capital of Bahia—the 270 kilometers of bumpy asphalt over a secondary road and forty-eight kilometers of first-class mud or super-class dust, a red powder that no fancy soap can rub out of your skin once it's ground itself in—to find an echo on the sounding board of the metropolitan press.

At first it was just a hot little news item, but when it began to rouse strong feelings of patriotism and cupidity, the little item very quickly turned into full-page ads.

A certain weekly with a doubtful reputation—no, that's not the right adjective; nothing doubtful about it—stuck out its chest in a front-page editorial with a bold crimson headline, threatening to send a reporter and a photographer to the back of beyond to investigate the grave accusation, the monstrous conspiracy, the appalling danger, and so on and so forth. This self-righteous indignation lasted for just one issue before the fearless editor gulped and passed along the hot potato. Still a youngster, though a veteran of skirmishes in the world of the Bahia press, who belched radical ideology and explosive principles, all for the public weal, of course, but *sotto voce*, Leonel Vieira drowned his threats and protests in real Scotch, provided, along with luscious ladies who displayed as much zeal as they did skin, by that well-known PR man and agreeable host, Dr. Mirko Stefano. Correction: two of the most shapely girls wore long filmy tunics with little or nothing underneath, more exciting to connoisseurs than short shorts or skimpy bikinis. A friendly argument between Mirko and the journalist on this point, as they sat at ease in the poolside bar, was their only difference of opinion. On all other points they were in perfect agreement. As for me, if I may be allowed to express an opinion, I definitely prefer those long transparent garments that reveal such interesting highlights and shadows. But what I think doesn't matter. What I think, or you or anyone else, pales to nothing before Dr. Stefano's forceful arguments, couched in the strongest foreign currency, whatever difference of opinion there may be as to whether he used dollars, West German marks or both. Such irrefutable dialectics on the part of the friendly company man had earned him the flattering sobriquet of Mirkus the Magnificent from that sprightly social columnist Dorian Grey Junior. Nothing but a front man for unknown masters, as the weekly had hinted in the daring and exclusive editorial (exclusive, daring and very well paid, besides being a guarantee for the Left); after all, what other publication had the courage to stand up and be counted just then? Here was a clear and well-defined position, proof positive if proof were ever needed. And you never knew when it might be: just look at Portugal. Who could have foreseen what was going to happen there? Besides, the ideological convictions and solid principles of such upstanding yet open-minded journalists are hardly to be overthrown by a mere check, even a fat one, or a few bottles of Scotch or a pretty piece of PR lady. Leonel Vieira surely has strength of character enough to swallow it all, checks, whisky and luscious little girls, and still keep his ideology and principles intact. He pockets the check, guzzles the whisky, drools over tits and cunts and pulls his newspaper into line, all the while proclaiming—in a low voice—his radical principles. Pretty smart.

As to the big bosses, they don't show up in bars, don't waste their time on venal two-bit journalists, and they like their women nude, in privacy and comfort, far from the public eye. Oh, if I could only dare to hope that at least one of the lordly creatures might appear in the pages of this clumsy tale! What higher honor could a humble scribbler aspire to? But I'm a realist, with my feet planted solidly on the ground, and I have no faith in such a miracle. What power on earth could drag a foreign mogul through the mud and dust to the godforsaken scene of my tale? If all goes well, and the project is approved, the industrial complex installed; if progress comes in on clumping asphalt feet, with two-lane highways, motels, swimming pools, girls in transparent caftans and security police; then maybe we'll have the privilege of glimpsing one of these lords of creation, with our very own eyes, wrapped in glittering gold.

Well, I'm going ahead anyway, knowing full well that some of what I'm about to tell is hard for anyone with any sense to believe. It would take a Russian hammer and a nail as big as a spike to make it stick, as old Dona Milu used to say whenever Barbozinha the seer and bard expatiated on the past or eloquently unveiled the future in his mellow, low-pitched voice—low and well pitched because an embolism felled him years ago and almost carried him into the other world. While it didn't quite do that, it effectively removed him from the rolls of the municipal bureaucracy in the state capital, where he had functioned as a moderately capable though rather careless bookkeeper. It sent him back to the bucolic streets of Sant'Ana do Agreste, whose little cultural world gained much by his return, for Barbozinha—Gregório Eustáquio de Matos Barbosa— was the author of three books published in Bahia, two volumes of poetry and one of philosophical maxims.

There will be more about all this as we go along. My aim just now is to decline all responsibility and to keep my nose clean. I'm just telling the facts as they were told to me by people on both sides. If I put my oar in every so often and air my own doubts and opinions, it's because I'm only human and I don't claim to be in- different to the "social turmoil, the whirlwinds of the century convulsing the world . . ." (Matos Barbosa, *Maxims and Minims of Philosophy*, Dmeval Chaves, Publisher, Bahia, 1950). I'm careful, that's all, and being careful nowadays is neither a virtue nor a merit, only a vital necessity.

There is one thing I would really like to be sure of when the time comes to write finis to this story, and I'm counting on you readers to help me do it: tell me, if you can, who the heroes are in this story and which of the characters fought for the country and the people. Everybody claims to speak for Brazil and the Brazilians, each one louder than the next; but in the long run we may find that money has found its way into the pockets of those who are smart, and the country and the people be damned.

Who, in this tangled plot whose knots I'm only now beginning to unravel, deserves his name on a street, avenue or public square, laudatory essays, public tributes, titles, keys to the city, a hero's fame? You tell me if you can. Those who fight for progress at any cost, who pay the price, whatever it may be, and never complain, like Ascânio Trindade? The price would have been no higher if he had paid with his life. If they aren't the heroes, who is? Surely not Barbozinha or Dona Carmosina or Dário, the skipper with no troops to command, much less Tieta, or I should say Madam Tieta. Words are worth money too, and "hero" is too noble a word to be spoken lightly.

I'll be grateful if anyone can enlighten me when we reach the end of the story together, and the moral has been read. If there is one, and I'm not sure there is.

Ceremonious chapter in which we make the acquaintance of three sisters, one poor, one fairly well off and one rich, the last having been away for no telling how long, and learn about the letter that comes every month and the check ditto, both of them anxiously awaited, especially the check, of course; and about small slings and arrows and faint hopes on a sultry afternoon: in which, in a word, a disturbing question raises

its head: is Tieta dead or alive? Is she sailing over
the bounding main in a cruise ship or lying in a
cemetery in São Paulo?

Sitting bolt upright in her chair, hands crossed on her bony
chest, in unrelieved black from her shoes to her shawl, dressed in the
same heavy mourning she had donned when her husband died,
Perpétua lowered her voice and ventured a gloomy speculation.

"What if something's happened to her?" She thrust her head
forward, closer to her sister, and hissed, "What if she's kicked the
bucket?"

Her sibilant voice, rasping even when she whispered, grated on
the ear. "What if she's dead?"

Elisa shuddered and dropped her dishtowel, assaulted by a dire
presentiment that left her no peace, robbing her of sleep, keeping
her nerves constantly on edge. For two days and two long nights
she had been trying in vain to get it out of her mind.

"Oh, my God!"

Perpétua uncrossed her hands, smoothed her stiff grosgrain
skirt, and emphatically nodded her head; she had not asked a question, she had said it was so. And it was so. And it was easy enough to
prove.

"Here it is the twenty-eighth already, practically the end of the
month. The letter always comes around the fifth, never later than
the tenth. If you want to know what I think, I'll tell you: she's
kicked the bucket."

Untidy as she was on a housewife's workday morning, Elisa
was a graceful girl with a pretty face, a pale-skinned brunette with
full lips and melancholy eyes. Despite the crumpled, faded dress and
shabby slippers, her body was erect and slender, haunches high,
breasts firm. A flash of curiosity lit up her frightened eyes. Elisa
scrutinized her sister's face for some sentiment besides concern
about the money, and found none. Perpétua was not grieved at the
thought of Tieta's death, she was only worried about the money.
Not that the prospect of losing the monthly check didn't frighten
Elisa too. They would not only lose what would now be almost
impossible to do without, they would have to support Father and

Mother too; and where on earth was the money to come from? God help us, it was too awful to think about!

It was awful and no doubt about it, but there was more to it than that, something even worse. Elisa's fearful shudder was followed by heartsick desolation. If her sister was dead, then everything was over, not just the check, but Elisa's faint hope; only emptiness would be left. That sister Antonieta (half-sister, actually, since Elisa had been born after old Zé Esteves' second, unexpected marriage), whom she couldn't remember at all and knew almost nothing about, was Elisa's reason for living.

In the last few years, especially after she was married, she had begun to idealize the absent woman as a kind of good genie or fairy godmother, a fleeting, unreal image which took solid form in the monthly stipend and occasional gifts. She had pieced together what little information she had—the telling of old tales, remarks made by Father or Mother, the big round handwriting in her letters—to form a picture of her absent sister in her mind. Those notes were brief and contained little news, only the same inquiries after everybody's health, her parents, sisters, nephews; but they were not cold or dry either, for she sent hugs and kisses, as well as the check—and the perfume came swirling out of the envelope, even after all those days on the way. There were the bundles of used clothing, too, really hardly worn at all and good as new, her husband's papal title, and the photograph in a magazine. Out of all these things Elisa created an imaginary Tieta: a merry, good and beautiful fairy who was living happily ever after in a rich and fortunate world. Such was the vision she conjured up to help her dream of another life beyond boredom and weariness. If Antonieta was dead, what would Elisa have left? Nothing but the picture magazines. Oh God, not even that! Where would she scrape up the nickels kept back from the household expenses to buy them with?

Elisa was overwhelmed with sorrow at the thought of all she would lose, the money each month, the presents, the reveries and daydreams, but she simply felt grief for the death of her sister, too. Was there anyone she loved as she loved that half-sister she didn't even know? She shook off her grief, out of need to hold onto a little hope at least. Perpétua was just like a big black vulture, always expecting the worst.

"If she was dead we'd know about it, wouldn't we? Somebody would have found a way to let us know. She has our address at home. After all, she writes us every month. Somebody would have told us. . . ." For the last two days, at her housework or tossing sleepless in her bed, she had been repeating those arguments to herself.

"Who's going to tell us? Not unless her husband and his family have lost their minds."

"Lost their minds? I don't see why."

Perpétua studied her sister in silence, wondering whether to tell her or not, and finally made up her mind to do so. She'd find out sooner or later anyway.

"Because if she dies we'll inherit part of what was hers, that's why. The three of us are her heirs. The old man, me and you."

Elisa picked up her dishtowel again and started drying. Where on earth did Perpétua get that crazy idea of an inheritance?

"The heir would be her husband, with his title and all. Why should we inherit anything? Oh, she might leave Father something. After all, she's been a good daughter, too good really. But to us? Why should she? I wasn't even a year old when she left home. And you, wasn't it your fault she ran away?"

"She ran away because she wanted to. It wasn't my fault."

"Wasn't it you who told on her to Pa? You told on her and he beat her black and blue and threw her out of the house, didn't he? Mama told me about it, and Pa said that was how it happened. It was your fault."

"That's what they say now, to get on the right side of her. Once she started sending money she turned into a saint. Why didn't your mama feel sorry for her at the time? Who was it who whipped her and put her out of the house? Me or the old man?"

Elisa spread a tablecloth stained with olive oil, beans and coffee —Astério was all thumbs, he couldn't reach for anything at the table without spilling the soup or the sauce, confound him. She shrugged her shoulders and ignored Perpétua. Let her father and sister fight about whose fault it was, it certainly wasn't hers. She had been less than a year old when the accusation, expulsion and flight took place.

Perpétua half closed her greenish, glassy eyes. Why did Elisa insist on bringing up the past? Hadn't Antonieta herself forgotten those old grievances and injustices a long time ago? Didn't she send them money and gifts? Didn't she help them pay the bills? And besides, all's well that ends well, isn't it? If she hadn't been put out of the house and home, instead of going south to marry well and have a lot of money and live happily ever after and be the toast of São Paulo, she would have been poor and miserable all her life in this hole where she could never expect to be engaged and married because the affair of the traveling salesman would soon have been common knowledge. She would have had nothing to look forward to except being a servant to her father and stepmother all her life.

"If *she's* forgotten all that, why do you have to remember it for her?"

"I didn't say it out of meanness. I just wanted to show you why she hasn't got a reason in this world to leave anything to the two of us."

"It doesn't matter whether she wants to or not." Perpétua opened her eyes, smoothed her skirt and flicked an invisible speck from her blouse. "When she dies, her husband gets half her fortune, and since she has no children, her kin gets the other half. Her close kin—that is, her father and her sisters. Us."

"How do you know that?"

"Dr. Almiro told me."

"The district attorney? You mean you went and asked him?"

"No, I didn't go and ask him. Not on purpose, anyway. He was talking to Father Mariano, and I and some other ladies from the Altar Guild happened to be where we could hear them. They were talking about Seu Lito's inheritance. He left all his money for the Father to say masses for his soul at St. Anne's. Well, it's been more than six months since he died and the Father has yet to see a penny of it. It's all in escrow in Esplanada, they said, because his kinfolk are suing for it. They've brought in a lawyer and everything. Dr. Almiro says half of it's lawfully theirs. So I spoke up and asked a few questions, as if it didn't concern me much."

"You mean to say that when a person dies he has to leave half of what he's got to his kinfolk?"

"That's right." Perpétua rummaged in her skirt pocket for a handkerchief to wipe the fine perspiration from her forehead. When she fished out the handkerchief, a rosary with black beads came along with it.

"You mean to say if you die, Pa and me get half of what's yours?"

"Oh, you don't listen right! That's only when the person who dies has no children. Tieta hasn't got any, but I do. Whatever I

leave when I die will be divided between Ricardo and Peto, my sons
and heirs. That was how it was when the Major died"—making the
sign of the cross, she lifted her eyes, murmuring, God give him
eternal rest—"the inheritance was divided in two parts, half for me
and half for the boys. Dr. Almiro—"

"You mean you asked about that too?"

"It never does any harm to ask."

"You think she died and her husband is keeping quiet about it
so he can have it all?"

"I wouldn't be surprised. Why didn't she ever give us her
address? She had us write her at a post-office box. Who ever heard
of such a thing? It was her husband who told her to, so we wouldn't
find out. Do you know his last name? It's Comendador this and
Comendador that, and that's the only name she ever calls him by.
Why is that? You don't notice things like that, but I've given it a
lot of thought and now I'm sure."

Elisa had thought there was something funny about it, too; but
to her way of thinking the lack of an address and surname or any
details about her sister's life and family had another meaning: Antonieta had forgiven the old grievances and didn't hold a grudge,
but she hadn't forgotten the past and she didn't want to be too
chummy with her kinfolk. They were unimportant small-town folk
and there was no place for them in her marvelous world. She helped
her father and sisters make ends meet, as a daughter who has risen in
life should. Her duty was done, her conscience was easy, but she
kept her distance.

And quite right, too, to Elisa's way of thinking. That was all
there was to it, and Perpétua had just made up the rest: her noodle
was chock full of hexes and bad luck. If Antonieta had decided to
leave something to her father and her sisters, she would have
planned ahead and seen to it beforehand.

"Well, I don't believe it. If she was dead we'd know about
it."

She finished setting the table and stood gazing into space.

"She's on a trip somewhere having a good time, that's what.
Everytime she goes someplace the letter comes late. Late, but it gets
here. You remember that time she went to Buenos Aires and sent
that pretty postcard? Now that's a life worth living: trips, holidays,
parties. Tieta's a good sister to think about us when she's having so

much fun. If it was me, you'd never, and I mean never, hear from me again."

She turned to look at Perpétua, who was telling her rosary.

"I'm going to tell you something, and you can believe it or not. Even if I was the one to inherit every bit of that money and didn't have to divvy up, even then I wouldn't want her to die."

"Who does?" Perpétua stopped praying, a black bead between her fingers. "But if the letters stop coming, it's a sign that Antonieta's dead. And if she is, I'll move heaven and earth till I find her husband and get my share."

"You'll get bats in the belfry if you don't quit thinking that way. She's off on a boat somewhere, I tell you. Why can't you hope for the best instead of the worst? The letter's sure to be here tomorrow."

"Well, I only hope you're right. I stopped by the old man's and he's fit to be tied. You know what was preying on his mind? He wanted to know if Astério hadn't got hold of the money to pay off some debt with, like he did that other time. The old man thinks we're stealing him blind." She began to finger the rosary again, the unpainted lips moving in silence.

With Perpétua it was an eye for an eye, every time. Elisa had brought up the scandal that had ended in Antonieta's leaving home, and Perpétua had managed to give as good as she got by unearthing the unfortunate five-year-old affair of the overdue bill Astério had paid. Elisa retorted in a weary voice, her heart not in it, "You know good and well the store would have gone bankrupt if Astério hadn't paid off that debt. You know it, Pa knows it. . . ."

She continued in the same tired monotone, "But as for stealing people blind, oh, we do that all right! It's no use your sitting with your rosary in your hand, mumbling 'Our Father' with that sanctified look on your face."

"I never touched a penny of the old man's."

"Fat chance he'd let you. It's Tieta we all steal from. Why do you think she sends us a check every month?"

"To keep the old man out of the poorhouse."

"Yes, and what else?"

"To help pay for the children's education."

"That's right. To help pay for the children's education. My boy died before he was two and I never got pregnant again. Never again. Seems like God doesn't want me to. . . ."

Her eyes strayed from the dining room to the bedroom; she could see the unmade double bed through the open door. Was it God who didn't want her to? Astério couldn't even do that much. . . . The toneless voice went on.

"And what about you? You never told Tieta that Peto's in public school where you don't have to pay a cent, did you? Or that Father Mariano saw to it that the Bishop got Cardo into the seminary free? I know what you told her: how much Dona Carlota's school and the tuition at the seminary cost. You told her that much, all right, and kept mum about the rest. Why did you bring up that old story about Astério using the money to pay off that debt when you know good and well we've all done her dirt?"

"It was the old man who brought it up. I'm just telling you what he said."

"One of these days I swear I'll get up the nerve to write her the truth: that I don't have any children, that the only baby I ever had got sick and died, but that we need the money so much I couldn't bring myself to tell her about Toninho's death. She might have felt sorry for me and started sending even more, but I didn't have the guts to risk it. . . . Perpétua, why are we the way we are? Why are we so lowdown and mean? That's the reason she won't have anything to do with us and won't tell us her address, but just helps us all stay alive and keeps as far away from us as she can."

Her voice became heavy and strident, almost as hard on the ear as Perpétua's.

"And she knows what she's doing, because if I knew where she lived . . ."

Her eyes stared into space.

"Oh! If I only knew where she lived I would have gone there a long time ago!"

Perpétua reached the end of her beads and kissed the little cross.

"Nobody'd take you for a grown married woman to listen to you saying things you've got no business saying. What you ought to do is to help out in the church instead of sitting home reading magazines and listening to the radio, wasting time on that trash."

Elisa's arms dropped to her sides, her voice a monotone again. "When the bus gets in tomorrow I'll stop by the post office and the letter'll be there, you wait and see."

"Well, I hope to goodness it is. Lula Pedreiro didn't pay the rent for three whole months with the excuse he was sick; and now he's sent me the key and gone to live with his son and left the house like a pigsty. If I want to rent it to somebody else, I'll have to give it a coat of whitewash at least."

"I don't know what you're complaining about. You live in your own house and have two more to rent and your widow's pension besides. Look at us! If it wasn't for the money she sends for our little angel, we couldn't even go to the picture show."

"Be sure and let me know tomorrow whether it comes or not. If it doesn't, I'll have to think about ways and means."

"You might as well stay for lunch. Where there's enough for two there's enough for three."

"Me eat meat on a Friday? You know good and well it's a sin. That's why you never get ahead. You don't obey God's law."

She stood up and put the rosary back in her pocket. A stern-faced, pious and virtuous widow, all in black, with a long-sleeved, high-necked blouse and a mantilla covering her topknot. As the cathedral bells pealed at noon, she crossed herself and went out the door. Astério's footsteps echoed in the deserted street. The hot glare rose from the ground and sank heavily down from the sky. Elisa sighed and went into the kitchen.

Of Elisa before her looking-glass, too pretty to live, and her husband Astério, who plays a mean game of pool—a chapter in which nothing happens.

The next day when Jairo's *marineti* honked at the curve just before coming into town, Elisa, sitting at the rickety old piece of furniture, possibly a valuable antique, that served her as a dressing table, had just put on lipstick and smiled at the image reflected in the cheap mirror hanging on the wall. She looked pretty to herself, with her wild black hair carefully combed and lying loose on her shoulders, framing her pale face, her languorous eyes, her mouth with its sensuous lips outlined with lipstick. "Too pretty to live"—that was what the famous radio announcer Mozart Cooper (she knew how to pronounce it: Cuuperr), "the velvet voice of the Hertzian waves, bringing balm to lonely hearts," was always saying about some movie or radio or TV star.

Miss Lonely Heart, too pretty to live.

For a few minutes Elisa forgot all her troubles as she rehearsed poses and coy expressions like the pictures in her magazines: pouting lips, an ardent gaze, a tempting smile, a passionate swoon, the tip of her tongue showing red and moist between the lips parted to receive a kiss. Who'd kiss her? She gave a weary shrug and her eyes clouded over. She remembered the letter and tried to still her uneasiness: it's in the mailbag coming in the *marineti* right now, it's bound to come today. But what if it didn't come?

At lunch the day before, Astério, eating greedily with his mouth full of words and beans, had repeated the same old question and lament. "Why d'you suppose it's taking so long? And wouldn't you know it would happen in November, when there's hardly any business. What the dickens could have happened?"

Elisa had shut her lips tight, knowing that her husband would fly into a panic if she breathed a word about the suspicion gnawing at her vitals. Faint-hearted by nature, incapable of effort and hard work, he spent his days leaning on the counter of his store waiting for a customer to happen by, roused to animation only when one of his partners at pool—Seixas, Osnar, Aminthas or Fidélio—turned up to chat about tricks and bets; if Ascânio Trindade were in form, Astério would have a foeman worthy of his steel. Osnar, who didn't have to work for a living, lounged around the store with a cornhusk cigarette hung on his lip. He never missed a Saturday, when trade always picked up because it was market day. Once the farmers had sold what they'd brought to the market—flour and jerky, beans and fruit and grain, and earthenware fired in primitive ovens (little pots, water jugs and pitchers; figures of horses and oxen, soldiers, backlands bandits, village priests and sweethearts holding hands)—the whole family would crowd into the store to buy yard goods, shoes, drawers, shirts and trousers, and once in a great while a pocket radio or other little luxury. Osnar, teetering on two legs of an old chair, appraised the young farm girls in silence, engaging them in conversation when he thought it worth the trouble. On Saturday young Sabino earned five cruzeiros for helping out by waiting on the backwoods customers—five cruzeiros and what he could skim off the change.

If Elisa told Astério what Perpétua had said, sure as fate Astério would have one of the tiresome spells that came over him whenever they were strapped for money or he had trouble with a supplier: cold sweat, legs buckling under him, writhing and vomiting fits. He would go to bed shaking and shivering, teeth chattering, and leave the store to Sabino. Osnar was the only one who could get him out of bed and off to the poolroom in Manuel the Portugee's Azores Bar.

At pool he was transformed into another man entirely. Laughing, joking, swaggering, recklessly betting, challenging Ascânio, sure he would win. A fast man with a billiard cue. "That's the only cue he ever picks up, Astério and his Golden Cue," Elisa surprised herself by muttering. What deplorable grumbling, what wicked thoughts! They had just popped into her head, confound them, and now they wouldn't go away. God have mercy.

Her musing face looked back at her from the mirror. Too pretty to live, and growing old all alone in this stick-in-the-mud town, waiting for a letter and a check. If it weren't for the radio and the magazines, what would become of Elisa?

If she told Astério the reason for Perpétua's visit, the possibility—the certainty, in her sister's mind—that Tieta was dead, he would throw up everything he had eaten, beans, rice, meat, pieces of mango, right there on top of the table. If you took away his pool he was nothing but a lazy slob; no spirit, no ambition, no cheerful good nature and nothing to say for himself. If he ever did talk or laugh it was at things he had heard in the bar, risqué stories his partners told. Sometimes it was Seixas or Aminthas who told them; once in a while Fidélio, who cultivated a natural reserve; but usually it was the well-to-do, loose-living womanizer Osnar. Osnar's stories, including the remarkable affair of the Polish prostitute, always made his hearers split their sides. They usually had to do with the remarkable size of his own penis. "He has a stallion's prick," Astério declared, separating his hands to show its amazing size: "This big or bigger."

The tired electric generator went off at nine in the evening, time to go to sleep, as the cathedral bells ordained. Astério would finish his game, rest his cue, pay or collect his bets and make his way home. Once in a while, if Elisa hadn't fallen asleep, Astério would remark as he was undressing, as a prelude to telling one of these stories, "Heard a good one at the bar just now."

Whether the protagonist was Osnar or Aminthas, Seixas or Fidélio, one of the four friends or a fellow townsman, the story was almost invariably obscene and the subject was nearly always a woman in bed—in bed or in the bushes down by the river. Elisa would listen tensely, in silence, only rarely plucking up courage to ask for the explicit details she needed to build the imaginary world in which she had shut herself up in order to survive. Every detail was important: Antonieta's grandeur, the postcard from Buenos Aires, the perfumed envelopes, Seixas and his plots, Fidélio's secrets, Aminthas' rascality and Osnar's anatomy. During the day, with the radio always on, Elisa ironed and mended clothes, washed dishes, cooked, read the same magazines over and over, visited with Dona Carmosina at the post office, and after dinner was over, listened resignedly to the droning of her neighbor Dona Lupicínia, whose husband had made his escape to the southern part of the state some five years before and was not expected back anytime soon, maybe never.

Too pretty to live meant pretty enough to die. What was the use of expecting anything else? The mouth before the mirror opened greedily for a kiss. Whose kiss? Elisa stood up. Oh, if she only had a full-length mirror! Too pretty to live and dressed up fit to kill.

"Why do I bother?" she wondered as she shrugged again. Why did she spend so much time making herself up, combing her pretty black hair and making herself as elegant as she knew how in the remodeled dress, a present from Tieta like all the dresses she owned, each one of better style and quality than the last—secondhand but hardly worn at all, almost new? Why did she go to so much trouble with her makeup, why did she put on the low-cut dress that displayed her lovely shoulders and high rounded breasts?

To walk down the deserted streets where she hardly ever met a soul. Sometimes she'd feel the weight of Chalita the Arab's heavy gaze, fat old Chalita, owner of the movie theater and the ice-cream parlor next door, with his big sultan's mustache, invariably needing a shave, with a toothpick between his teeth; or, without seeing it, feel the sly, knowing look of young Sabino fixed on the undulating hips of his boss' unattainable wife; or hear a low whistle from Goatstink, the pestilent bum, drunk and beggar, who was so far down in the gutter he could with impunity be as impudent as he had a mind to be. Those three wretches, and that was all, except for a "Good afternoon, ma'am," and a hat raised in silent greeting, the Father's blessing and the ill-concealed envy of other women she met: "You look like you're all dressed up for a dance, honey."

Proper and discreet, Elisa the honest and virtuous wife gathered to her low-cut bosom the Levantine's cupidity (no doubt she reminded him of better days and other women's bodies) and swiveled her hips for the horny young man (Sabino will dream about me tonight). She did not even scorn the whistle of the beggar who reeked of cheap rum. As for the women's envy, that was worth something too, and it tasted sweet. Elisa would answer modestly, "My sister Tieta sent me this dress. She *does* have good taste, doesn't she? I can hardly throw it away, can I?" Then would follow a chorus of praise for the absent Antonieta, the generous sister, the exemplary daughter, the unfailing monthly check, the queenly gifts —yes, they were fit for a queen: every one of those dresses cost an arm and a leg!

Elisa told little Aracy to mind the house, closed the street door and headed for the post office. She would cross the marketplace and pass by the Arab, the scrawny youth, the half-crazy drunk, the gossiping women in the church porch. Her face was grave, as became a matron, a proper married lady. Her heart beat painfully, in the deep-down certainty that the letter hadn't come.

Brief explanation by the author for the benefit of those who search an elephant for fleas.

The critics have already started in on me, and my tale is hardly begun. One Fúlvio D'Alambert (José Simplício da Silva in private life), a close friend and colleague in *belles-lettres*, in which he toils in bitter anonymity as I do, has first crack at my manuscripts. He usually returns them with praise that is very agreeable to hear and with one or two minor corrections in spelling or grammar— commas, periods, verb tenses and such. This time his criticisms went further, too far, to my way of thinking; and while Elisa is on her way to the post office, I intend to answer them without losing any time.

Fúlvio thinks it ridiculous to use the old-fashioned word *marineti* to describe an automotive vehicle used to transport passengers. "Omnibus," "long-distance bus," "interurban bus" would be the correct, modern, appropriate terms for the changing, developing times in which we are fortunate enough to live. He accuses me of having an underdeveloped mentality and argues well. At a time when new highways in no way inferior to the best in other countries are slashing their way across the landscape; when industries are springing up all around us; when the trumpet call of progress is awakening a new northeast, redeemed from droughts and epidemics, the age-old curse of starvation, and, last but not least, illiteracy, now speedily being eradicated; when the press, radio and television are standardizing customs, manners, mores and language, sweeping away regional habits, expressions and diversions like so much rubbish; when monumental skyscrapers unify the city landscape, rising from beneath the rubble of history and old houses with pretensions to artistic value; when at last our popular music is based on universal, especially Yankee, tunes and themes, abandoning the rhythms of our own wretched Brazilian folklore; when Hindu and kindred mysticisms illuminate young minds amid the swirling fumes of marijuana from Alagoas; when the more advanced ideologues among us do their best to stamp out miscegenation and inculcate white, black and yellow racism until we catch up to the truly civilized nations and violence marks our face, wiping it clean of the old Brazilian cordiality, a sure sign of backwardness; when a more self-conscious art ignores the land and people of its birth and becomes concrete, abstract and objective like European, North American, or Japanese art; when we are creating a new language for literary men to write in, esoteric but extremely revolutionary in form and content, the less intelligible the better; when censorship and the policemen's nightsticks are creating a true democracy for us to replace the old kind that was always dragging Brazil to the brink of the abyss; when we are entering a period of miraculous prosperity to the drumbeat of the wealthy nations, the producers of petroleum, wheat, the atom bomb, satellites, whisky and comic strips, the apex of all literature; when we are beginning to take our proper place among the great powers and produce Brazilian motor vehicles in our own factories—Mercedes Benz, Ford, Alfa Romeo, Volkswagen, Dodge, Chevrolet, Toyota, and so on and so forth—how dare a Brazilian author call the bus that takes passengers from Sant'Ana do Agreste to Esplanada and back again a *marineti*? How hopelessly fuddy-duddy and square!

Well, forgive me, D'Alambert, and may the eminent university critics with master's degrees and Ph.D.'s forgive me too; but in this particular case, what we are talking about really is a *marineti*, last of a dying breed, named for the futurist Italian poet because they were a symbol of all that was modern in their day. It may well be the last one in existence, fit companion for the droughts, epidemics and obstinate hunger that still stubbornly and subversively linger on in the backlands, holding out against the patriotic articles and speeches launched against them.

If this *marineti* is the last to ply the back roads of Brazil, it plies them bravely. Its maximum speed is thirty kilometers an hour, which is what it averages on the six-kilometer stretch of good road that cuts across Colonel Vasconcelos' fazenda outside Esplanada. For the other forty-two kilometers it creeps and bumps and jolts along. The road is barely passable, and no modern vehicle would be foolhardy enough to venture onto it. Only long-established custom makes possible the daily miracle—Monday through Saturday, with Sunday a day of rest—performed by Jairo's *marineti*, familiar as it is with every crater, mudhole, moldering cattle guard, and improbable hill and curve. This *marineti* dates from the Second World War, when it was a modern vehicle with bouncy springs and comfortable seats and the windows actually had glass in them. In those days, incredible as it may seem, the bus actually made the round trip, Agreste-Esplanada-Agreste, in a single day, leaving early in the morning and returning just as it was getting dark.

The doughty vehicle is still worth seeing after all these years. It's a real museum piece; everything in it is a spare or a patch or a substitute for something else. In its motor and chassis coexist parts of every brand and exotic provenance, including a Russian radio. Ingenious makeshifts, mechanical innovations, bailing wire and pieces of string abound. Old newspapers are useful as window screens when the dust is too thick to breathe. Experienced passengers take along pillows for the hard benches, and hearty snacks and bottled soft drinks for the road.

This invincible old rattletrap, this last and everlasting *marineti*, sets out from Agreste every Monday, Wednesday and Friday and makes its way back from Esplanada on Tuesday, Thursday and Saturday. Puffing, coughing, sputtering, stopping—especially stopping—forever threatening to give up the ghost but never quite doing it, carrying on as a tribute to Jairo's skill and his pleas, oaths and flattery. Jairo treats the ramshackle jalopy with the tenderness of a lover, for that *marineti* is his breadwinner, all the property he owns and the only link between Sant'Ana do Agreste and the world.

When all goes smoothly the trip takes three hours, at the optimum speed of sixteen kilometers per hour. In winter, when it rains, the journey is longer and less predictable. It always leaves exactly on time; Jairo makes a fetish of punctuality. Jairo's *marineti* has occasionally spent all night on the road stuck in the mud, waiting for a team of oxen to pull it out. On such occasions Jairo is ready with a fairly good repertory of jokes suitable for family ears and the uncertain collaboration of the Russian radio. Nasal, cranky, indolent, moody and unpredictable, this remarkable contraption helps to pass the time with fragments of music and news, punctuated with whistles and volleys of static. But the business of spending the night on the road is unusual; you could count the times it's happened on the fingers of both hands.

A good, fast, comfortable trip; at least that was the opinion of Colonel Artur da Tapitanga, the octogenarian manioc planter, goat breeder and political boss, who had not set foot off his native plantations and corrals and the Agreste streets for more than thirty years. After nearly seven hours on the road (the *marineti* had broken down three times) the old planter declared as he got to his feet:

"That's a speedy little critter, that *marineti* of Jairo's. We sure did make good time."

"Speedy, Colonel?"

"In my time it used to take us two days on horseback if we was lucky."

Droughts, smallpox, malaria, leprosy and hunger, children dying right and left just like the good old days—I know there's still plenty of that out in the backlands. But *marinetis*? I doubt there's a single one left except for Jairo's. He calls her countess, my little pickaninny, morning star, yum-yum, Mae West, Agreste beauty, my love and my darling. When she gets temperamental and acts up, he loses his temper and calls her every cussword he knows, from whore on down.

In which we make the acquaintance of that important citizen Dona Carmosina, the postmistress, and receive news of Seu Edmundo Ribeiro the tax collector's son and daughter, to make up for the nonreceipt of any check or letter from Tieta, about whose state of health there is growing alarm.

Long before she reached the post-office door, Elisa read proof in Dona Carmosina's attitude of what she already knew: no letter had come. Arms drooping at her sides, small squinting eyes half-closed and a grave expression on her face, the usually cheerful and active civil servant had taken to heart the drama of this inexplicable delay in the mails. Elisa's face grew even paler, her feet more leaden, her voice a faint, all but inaudible moan:

"Still no letter?"

Dona Carmosina, fiftyish, light-skinned and freckled, with a broad face and husky voice, waved toward the day's meager mail spread out on the counter.

"Not a thing! There were no registered letters today at all. I went through the mail sack a letter at a time, just in case. Everything that came is over there, and it wasn't much. None of it's been delivered yet; you're the first one to show up. Oh, some newspapers and magazines came; today's Saturday." She observed her friend's pallor. "Would you like a glass of water?"

"No, thank you." The words came out in a strangled voice.

"Sure is taking a long time, isn't it? In all these years it's never been as late as this before."

"It's been more than ten years," Elisa groaned.

"Eleven years and seven months," Dona Carmosina corrected her, scrupulous as to details. "I still recollect that first letter as if it was yesterday. I could smell it as soon as I opened the mailbag, 'cause she used stronger perfume then than she does now; it like to have filled the whole room. Now what can that letter be? I said to myself and just glanced at the name and return address. It was addressed to your daddy or any member of the Esteves family, and the person who sent it was Antonieta Esteves, Post Office 6211, São Paulo, S.P. Now I'm going to bring you a glass of water, it's so hot and no letter, you poor little old thing. . . ."

While Carmosina had her back turned as she filled a glass from the water jug, Elisa stole a look at the mail. Not that she had any hope, but she could not bear to leave any stone unturned.

"I put a couple of drops of rosewater in it, it's good for the nerves."

As Elisa sipped the water, Dona Carmosina resumed her narrative. "That pretty pink envelope! I can see it just as clear. I sent poor Seu Lima, who was still alive at that time, with a message for your husband at the store. You all hadn't been married very long. He came with Osnar, and I handed him the letter right here at the counter. Such a nice letter, asking for news of your daddy and you and your sister, how everybody's health was and all, and if you needed any help. I helped write the answer, remember?"

"Yes, I do . . . the Major was alive and he copied it out."

"He was dumb as a doorknob but he sure could write a fair hand. Yes, he copied it out, but I thought up what to say. And all this time she's never missed once. Every single month without fail comes a letter and a nice little check."

Carried away by her subject, Dona Carmosina was oblivious to the sultry, asphyxiating heat coming in at both doors. She stared pensively at Elisa.

"It never came this late before. . . . There's something mighty peculiar about it."

Elisa, sensing disquieting signs of alarm in her friend's voice, tried to reassure Carmosina and herself.

"One time when she was on a trip to Buenos Aires—"

"That letter came the seventeenth: February seventeenth, to be exact. Today's the twenty-eighth of November. How do you account for it? Is she sick, do you think?" Dona Carmosina's little eyes observed Elisa as she clutched the empty glass. A sob stuck in Elisa's throat and she found nothing to say in reply.

Luckily Seu Edmundo walked in just then. Edmundo Ribeiro

the tax collector, formally dressed in coat, hat and necktie, wished them good afternoon.

"Anything for me, Carmosina?"

"Two letters, one from your son and one from your son-in-law." She laughed, her colorless lips parted in amusement. "Bet you anything they're both asking for money."

Seu Edmundo took the letters and squinted at the envelopes held against the light. Dona Carmosina knew and talked about everybody else's business, and there was nothing anyone could do about it, since every letter and telegram that went in or out of Agreste passed through her hands and under her eagle eye. "Carmosine, lean and mean, speckled bean, eye so keen, what you've seen!" ran a little verse that Aminthas, her second cousin and frequent dinner guest, often recited. Dona Carmosina had a good hand with seasoning and was as famous for her brown sauce and manioc cooked in milk, not to mention her couscous and cornbread, as she was for her eye so keen.

"They think all I have to do is put my hand in my pocket," sighed Seu Edmundo, in no hurry to open the envelopes despite his natural desire to know how his children were getting along. He turned to Elisa. "Your father, Zé Esteves, is the lucky one, Dona Elisa. He's got a wealthy daughter who sends him money instead of asking him for it. It's the other way around with me."

Dona Carmosina darted a questioning glance at Elisa, then told him the news.

"This month's letter hasn't come yet. Funny, isn't it, Seu Edmundo? We can't imagine what's holding it up."

The tax collector, an open letter in his hand, looked up in surprise.

"What, not here yet? Why, Dona Elisa, what could have happened?"

"I just don't know, Seu Edmundo. I guess she's off on one of those trips she takes every year, in a boat—"

"On a cruise ship," Dona Carmosina corrected her, but the eyes under the sandy eyebrows were skeptical. Seu Edmundo, finding nothing to say, turned back to his son-in-law's letter.

Elisa took her leave, her legs almost buckling under her like Astério's.

"Thank you anyway, Carmosina."

"Don't expect anything before Tuesday, honey." To raise her

spirits a little and not let her go so dejected, she added, "You look precious today. I hadn't seen that dress before."

"Tieta sent it to me."

Seu Edmundo looked up from his letter, out-and-out vexation in his voice.

"Suzana's expecting again."

Elisa pulled herself together.

"Congratulations, Seu Edmundo. When you write Suzi, be sure and send her a kiss from me."

"Let's see, now, this is the fourth baby, isn't it? You're mighty young to have so many grandchildren already. Now I call that real nice." Was Dona Carmosina's hoarse voice sincere or gently ironic?

"Oh, you call it real nice, do you? Well, I don't. It all comes out of my pocket. No common sense is what I call it."

"Oh, I know kids cost plenty. . . . And it's so easy not to have them nowadays, with the pill. You can buy it in any drugstore in Bahia without a prescription. The church says it's all right, too. . . ."

Carmosine, wit so keen.

Elisa said her goodbyes and crossed the bustling marketplace to Perpétua's house. Today she felt no Arab's gaze, no insolent youth's burning eyes on her swaying hips, no beggar's whistle to wound her ears. Tieta must be sick, Carmosina had hinted, thinking something worse. Yes, she was dead; Elisa had to face it. Perpétua was right.

Dona Carmosina, postmistress for twenty-three years, was used to pronouncing definitive judgments on both people and events.

"Now there goes a real good girl, Seu Edmundo. I've known Elisa ever since she was a little bit of a thing, and she's always acted just the way she should. Everything she does, she does well. She works hard, keeps her house as neat as a pin and always dresses well and fixes herself up, not like other women I could name who let themselves go. But now, poor little old thing . . ."

Seu Edmundo broke off his reading of the letter from his student son to pay more attention to what she was saying.

"How do you account for such a long delay?"

"If Tieta isn't dead, she must be at death's door. You'd think her husband would let us know, but then he never wanted anything to do with her kinfolks here. I'm going to tell Elisa or Perpétua they'd better send a wire."

Returning to his letter, the tax collector exclaimed, "The young fool! That's all he's good for."

"What's Leleu been up to this time, Seu Edmundo?"

"Gone and caught himself a dose of clap, that's what. Sorry, Carmosina, I mean gonorrhea. And now he wants money for a doctor and medicine in a hurry."

"Two shots of penicillin and he'll be as good as new. It doesn't cost much and he won't even have to see a doctor."

Dona Carmosina read all the newspapers before distributing them and she kept abreast of what was going on in the world—films, scientific discoveries and current events—as befitted the news agent for an afternoon paper in Salvador da Bahia and several magazines published in Rio and São Paulo.

"Poor Elisa, she was so upset she forgot to pick up her magazines. I'll take them over to her later on."

Seeing Ascânio Trindade on the other side of the street, she picked out a letter addressed to him; it was from Máximo Lima, a friend of his in the capital, and contained nothing of interest. Ascânio's correspondence used to be so romantic when Astrud wrote him love letters and Ascânio filled pages and pages with yearning vows in reply. A natural poet, that Ascânio; what a shame he didn't write poetry, it would be lovely if he did. Carmosina returned to the subject of Tieta's silence.

"Do you want to know what I think, Seu Edmundo? Antonieta's departed this wicked world."

In which Ricardo, nephew and seminarian,
lights conflicting candles at the feet of the saints:
a chapter bathed in tears. Some of them
crocodile tears.

"Well, where is it?" Perpétua challenged Elisa defiantly and answered her own question, galling though the triumph was. "Bye-bye letter, bye-bye check, Miss Bahia!" she said, pouring over her sister the bile that tasted bitter in her mouth. "If I was Astério you wouldn't go around in that indecent dress with half your bosom hanging out. All that's over now, anyway; you won't have any more dresses to show off. It's all over. We're going to be poor from now on."

Elisa fell into a chair and covered her face with her hands. If she'd had the heart, she could have reminded Perpétua that she never criticized the clothes when it was present-dividing time but tried to get her hands on the best and sexiest ones to sell them at an outrageous price to rich women in Aracaju. She wished she could cover her ears; the words sounded even crueler in her sister's vinegar voice.

Elisa had stopped by the general store, which was already full at that hour, with Osnar lounging as usual in his chair. She only exchanged a glance with her husband, but it was enough to make Astério drop the measuring tape and white cotton cloth. Osnar stood up. "Good morning, Dona Elisa."

"Good morning, ma'am." Sabino took quick inventory from cleavage to hips; hurray for whoever invented those tight slinky dresses that show everything a woman's got, even the crease between her cheeks; now that's what I call high style. How'd my stupid boss get so lucky?

"Give me three yards, please," said the customer impatiently. She had noticed Elisa's elegance, too; now that's what I call really good fabric.

Astério, hardly able to hold the tape measure and the scissors steady in his hands, fumblingly measured out the cloth.

"I'm going over to Perpétua's. I'll send Aracy with your lunch in a few minutes," said Elisa. "Goodbye, Seu Osnar, please don't get up."

She could hardly keep from crying on the way. Every word she had said in the store had cost her an effort of self-control. Now she collapsed in the chair under the lash of Perpétua's voice criticizing her low-necked dress, as if it wasn't bad enough that she had no letter and no check in her hand.

"She's kicked the bucket, I tell you. Do you mean you still don't believe it?" She was hissing and shaking her finger.

Elisa uncovered her face and shook her head, defeated, letting the tears flow. But what was the good of crying? Tears wouldn't solve any of their problems, wouldn't take the place of the check, wouldn't raise the dead, wouldn't help them decide what to do. Perpétua, however, knew and respected the proprieties and was a stickler for tradition. She retrieved a handkerchief from the pocket of her black skirt and touched it to the corners of her eyes. Her tears might not be visible, but they were tears of mourning just the same. Injecting a dolorous accent into the harsh tones of her voice, she cried to her elder son, "Cardo! Come here quick! Oh, God have mercy!"

She raised the handkerchief to her eyes again, so that Elisa might see and bear witness to the painful sentiments she felt now that her theory was confirmed and there was no question but that Antonieta was dead. May God have her in His keeping and forgive her her trespasses; she had helped support her father and her sisters, and that would surely be counted in her favor on Judgment Day.

A perspiring, barefoot young man rushed into the room, a tall, husky, good-looking youth with his seventeen years breaking out in pimples on his face. Over his smiling lips was the shadow of a mustache. He had been kicking a soccer ball around the yard and was dressed in nothing but a pair of shorts.

"Did you call me, Mother?" He caught sight of Elisa and added, "Your blessing, Aunt Elisa."

Exuding good health and animal spirits, the boy at first took no notice of the funereal atmosphere in the room. For the benefit of her son, Perpétua produced the handkerchief and wiped away a few tears she'd managed to squeeze out. The boy saw them and turned serious at once.

"Is something wrong with Grandpa? I saw him buying some things at the market real early this morning, when I went to serve at the mass, and he looked fine."

Perpétua peremptorily cut him short. "Go get a blessed candle and light it in the chapel. Your poor Aunt Antonieta—"

"Aunt Tieta? Is she dead?"

Defeated but not convinced, Elisa raised her chin rebelliously. "We don't know a thing yet for sure . . . not a blessed thing!"

Perpétua didn't trouble to answer but repeated her command. "You just do as I told you. I know what I'm talking about: a candle at the feet of Our Lord Jesus Christ for Antonieta's soul. Then you take a bath right away and put on your cassock. Play is over for today. Where's Peto at?"

"Gone fishing down by the river."

"You tell him to come on home. We'll go talk to Father Mariano right after lunch." She sighed, laying one hand on her bosom to quiet her beating heart.

Ricardo, numb and speechless at the news, still lingered in the room. He turned to Elisa, whose bent shoulders deepened the cleavage of her brown breasts. Despite his mother's constant hail of criticism, the boy had never noticed how stylish his aunt was. For the first time he realized how well she dressed and fixed herself up; she looked like a saint sitting there so downcast and forlorn, refusing to accept her sister's death and obstinately rebelling against the evidence mirrored in his mother's face and gestures.

In his aunt's voice was a plea, a supplication choked by tears. "Can't we wait to talk to the Reverend Father until we know for sure? Why be in such a hurry?"

Ricardo did not understand the reason for their disagreement, and though the full impact of his aunt's death had yet to hit him he felt sorry for Aunt Elisa, sitting as disconsolate as the image of St. Mary Magdalene in a niche of the seminary chapel.

Perpétua was not moved.

"It's never too soon to ask for good advice. Cardo, what are you waiting for? Didn't you hear what I told you to go do just now?"

"I'm going, Mother."

He longed to add something that would be appropriate now that his mind had turned to his unknown aunt, whose presumptive death seemed to be such a bone of contention. Her name always figured in his prayers, of course; she sent them money every month. And when he had gone into the seminary—he was still a little boy then—hadn't he received a package from São Paulo with a sumptuous breviary in a red velvet case, with a gilt spine and fine paper and illuminated letters? What a fine gift Aunt Antonieta had made to the future priest, who hardly had a chance to see and touch the precious thing before Perpétua presented it to the Bishop, Dom José, through Father Mariano's good offices. She had sent him that Number Five soccer ball, too. Without his mother's knowledge, Cardo had written a letter to his aunt, begging her to send him the ball and to keep it secret: "If Mama ever hears about it she'll have my hide." He got the ball, and a shirt and shorts in the Palmeiras team colors besides. The two of them had a secret of their own, he and Aunt Tieta. He raised his head and faced Perpétua.

"And I sure do hope it isn't true."

He went out to get the candles, not feeling happy any more. His eyes were burning even if he couldn't squeeze out any tears, and he felt something like a pimple swelling in his heart, every bit as uncomfortable as those on his face. He would light a candle of his own at the Virgin's feet and promise her a five-chaplet rosary, prayed kneeling on kernels of corn, if the bad news turned out to be a false alarm.

Silence fell over the two sisters in the parlor, and over the other sister too—the room was full of her face, her gestures. She had been a bold and handsome girl, braving her wrathful father and tattletale sister: "You're jealous, that's what, 'cause no man ever looked at you, you skinny old witch!" She had had a bold and sassy tongue in her head from the time when she herded goats as a little girl in the sandhills on Zé Esteves' barren land; and when she was a little older she used to jump out the window at night to meet men. The traveling salesman hadn't been the first, Perpétua was sure of that. Reckless and heedless of God's commands, she never went to church except to flirt. Finally, she had gone off laughing, a cynical smile on her pretty face, with a truck driver going to Bahia, and was gone for good. Then she had become the rich sister, wife to a Comendador, who sent money to her father and nephews from São Paulo every month; the sister deserving of every consideration, her ugly past forgotten, her wild adolescence dead and buried; the aunt to be remembered in the children's prayers and praised by Father Mariano; the good generous fairy of Elisa's daydreams, the fortunate benefactress, the anchor of hope, looked up to by all as a model daughter and sister, a shooting star, a legend and an inexhaustible subject of conversation.

Once the ritual was over, Perpétua put away her handkerchief and got down to business. "Where's Astério?"

"I just went by the store. He knows the letter didn't come, but today's Saturday and he can't even get away for lunch. That reminds me: I've got to go home and get his lunch pail ready."

"Well, I'll go over to your place tonight and tell you what the Father thinks we ought to do. Then we can make up our minds."

Elisa stood up with a shuddering sob. "Oh, why can't we wait until the end of the month?"

"Because we've waited too long already, that's why. We've got to decide what we're going to do. I'm not going to sit on my hands and do nothing, I tell you! I want what's mine." Without further tears, sighs, or lamentations, Perpétua exchanged the handkerchief for her rosary. Prayers were worth more than tears.

Elisa had used up all her arguments but one. "Maybe the letter got lost on the way."

"Registered letters don't get lost. Did we ever lose one, in all these years? That's just foolishness. You tell Astério not to go out tonight. He can live without his pool for one night. With his own sister-in-law dead . . ."

"What about Pa?"

Perpétua began telling her beads.

"We can tell him tomorrow."

"He may have a stroke or something."

"Who, the old man? He'll be fit to be tied. One thing for sure, he'll try to do us out of everything we've got. You'd better gird up your loins, sister Elisa. Good times are over."

As Elisa passed through the hall, she saw candlelight shining on the saints in the chapel down the hall, one at the feet of Christ crucified, for the dead woman's soul, the other at the feet of the Virgin, for Aunt Tieta's life. She could hear the lad's voice chanting, "Salve Regina, Mother of Mercy."

God have mercy on us!

A chaste, devout chapter of prayer for the health
of an elderly and unknown aunt.

". . . Hail Mary, our life, our sweetness and our hope!" The words of the prayer welled up, sincere and heartfelt, from that throbbing ache, that nebulous sorrow. Mechanically said, they left Ricardo's thoughts free to fly to his aunt in her death throes or even now lying in her coffin. He knew so little about her, practically nothing in fact.

"São Paulo aunt, our life, our sweetness and our hope, don't let her be dead like Mother swears she is—Mother sees everything in black. Let Aunt Elisa be right and the danger be past, to thee we pray, sinful children of Eve. To thee we cry out in our affliction and offer for Aunt Antonieta's health a rosary prayed kneeling on kernels of corn." What a stingy promise, what a miserable offer to make for such a prodigious miracle. Ricardo saw this and went too far the other way, augmenting the promise to include a whole week of rosaries and sore bruised knees, groaning and weeping in this valley of tears, to save Aunt Antonieta from death.

What sickness was it that had killed or was killing her? This was the first he'd heard of any illness. Mother and Aunt Elisa must know, surely, but they kept mum about it, it must be some dreadful disease it was better not to name, like consumption or cancer. How did they get the bad news—in a letter, a telegram? When Austragésilo's father died, the first telegram said he was in a critical condition and spitting blood. Two hours later the seminary principal brought the second telegram himself, the fatal one, and added some consoling words. He had patted Austragésilo on the back and spoken about the Kingdom of Heaven. And now the first telegram had come telling them she was sick and the outlook wasn't good. That must be it. And Mother, with her knowledge of the ways of the world, had known it wasn't the whole truth but just a way of preparing them for the worst. Aunt Elisa won't give up hope until the second telegram confirms the dreadful truth. "Be our advocate in this valley of tears and come to our aid; for thee, oh Mother of God, there is nothing impossible: thou canst stop telegrams and revoke death sentences, thy Son grants whatever boon thou askest." With a contrite heart Cardo renewed his vow, now increased sevenfold, a magnificent vow indeed.

About the disease he knew exactly nothing, and about Aunt Antonieta nothing times nothing, only vague, slippery bits of news; she was an unknown aunt to him, almost an abstraction. And yet there was no one so near and palpable and indispensable in the life of each and every one of them as the moneyed aunt in São Paulo.

To Ricardo she was only a name, a childish nickname, Tieta, mingled with vague but enthusiastic hints of a millionaire husband honored by the Pope, the monthly letter and check, the presents, the Number Five soccer ball, to give some shape and solidity to her image—but what did she look like?

"Turn thy merciful eyes to us in this valley of tears, poverty and limitations." All he could see was the patron saint, the protectress who made it possible for them to have an occasional treat and for his mother to deposit something in the savings bank toward the day, still so far off, when he would celebrate his first mass, and for Peto's studies if he ever made up his mind he wanted to study someday. When Cardo thought of the aunt he had never met, he compared her not to the Virgin to whom he prayed for her but to Our Lady St. Anne, patron saint of Agreste, protectress of the Holy Family and all other families. In the candlelight he could see the old lady's image, the gentle face, the generous hands, the sweet patron saint.

Was she a frail old lady like St. Anne or still vigorous and full of life like his mother? Which of them was the firstborn? No one had ever told Ricardo how old his aunt was, and his mother always lied about her age when anyone asked. The aunt who went away was probably much older, then; after all, she was the wealthy, powerful one, the philanthropist, the real head of the family, whom even his grandfather looked up to in awe. His mouth was generally full of cusswords, grumpy complaints and mumbled threats, but the old man magnified Tieta whenever her name was mentioned—"God give her health and increase of wealth; such a good daughter deserves it." Was she an old lady with faltering steps and white hair— or did she still dye her hair the way she used to? In the flickering candlelight Aunt Antonieta's hair was white.

He knew her schoolgirl handwriting well, the big, unsteady letters filling the page with a few words. Sometimes the stationery was blue, sometimes peach-colored or pale-green, but always elegant. And it was scented too, an exotic fragrance to nostrils accustomed to the reek of burned-out candles, the odor of mildewed furnishings and faded flowers, the dreary odor of sacristies and sweaty classrooms, the stifling fumes of incense. When she sent Cardo the football she had scrawled a note to go with it: "For my loving nephew, a little remembrance from your Aunt Tieta." He was so pleased he had slipped the lavender paper folded in four between the pages of his missal and inhaled its perfume on the sly. In a fit of pride he showed the perfumed greeting to Cosme, his deskmate, bosom friend and comrade in devotions and spiritual retreats. The ascetic Cosme refused to smell it; he saw sin and temptations of the devil everywhere. Perfume? Why, that was a mortal sin; for God's servants, incense ought to be enough. The Father Confessor soothed Ricardo's guilt anxiety: there was no sin, whether mortal or venial, in the chaste perfume of an elderly aunt.

"Turn to us thine eyes of mercy"—what were Aunt Tieta's eyes like, and her face? Austere like his mother's, strict, devout? Restless and melancholy like Aunt Elisa's? Or like his grandfather's, with its tough old *caboclo*'s scowl? Once, years ago when he was only a young squirt, he had caught a glimpse of his aunt's picture in an illustrated magazine from Rio, but once Elisa got her hands on it, no one ever saw it any more. All Ricardo remembered about it was her fair hair, fleecy golden ringlets, which puzzled him in a family full of brunettes. That was when he learned that some women bleached their hair and even painted it a different color, because his mother and Aunt Elisa had had an argument about it. To Perpétua it was a fad to be condemned: God decided what color hair everybody should have and no one had the right to change it. Elisa retorted that her sister was hopelessly old-fashioned and a churchmouse. Ricardo could remember nothing about her eyes or mouth, only those dazzling golden curls, looking white now in the candlelight. That was ever so many years ago, when he was only a boy; now he was a young man.

"And when our exile is over, show us Jesus, the blessed fruit of Thy womb"—how many years had his aunt been in exile? Tieta had already been gone a long time when Ricardo was born and he never heard his mother, his Aunt Elisa, his grandfather or his second wife, Grandma Tonha, mention other relatives at all; for a long time he never heard her spoken of by her real name or nickname. He only discovered that he had an aunt in São Paulo after her first letter came, and to this day he knew almost nothing about her except that she was rich, kind and old.

If the Virgin saved her, maybe she'd come up for a visit someday, a real flesh-and-blood aunt, a lovable old lady, so old she'd be almost a grandmother. Ricardo had never had a real grandmother. The one on his mother's side had passed away before Perpétua's late marriage with the Major, whose parents were already lying in Quintas Cemetery in Bahia when the retired army officer turned up in Agreste by chance and recovered his strength and cured his asthma in the twinkling of an eye in that health-giving climate.

Aunt Antonieta took the place of his grandparents. She was St. Anne the matriarch, protectress of the family. If she did get well, if the Virgin restored her to health, Ricardo, after fulfilling his vow, planned to write her another letter, this time asking for a fishing rod and reel with a nylon line and artificial lures, like the one he had seen in *Fishing and Hunting* magazine, the one he had looked at in the post office with Dona Carmosina's permission. He would beg his aunt to keep it a secret—if Mother found out about it she'd be bound to raise the roof. That wasn't too much to ask in return for sore knees and a whole week of prayers: fishing rod, reel, line and lures, and another secret for the two of them to keep. It felt good to have a secret. Until he had shared a first secret with his Aunt Antonieta, the only confidantes Ricardo had had were a few of the saints, the Virgin and above all St. Rita of Cassia, for whom he felt a special devotion.

"O clement, o holy, o gentle Virgin Mary, pray for her and for us so that we may be worthy of the promises of Christ. Make aunt get up from her sickbed or her coffin, o clement, holy, gentle and forever Virgin Mary."

The flame of death on the candle his mother had ordered him to light at the feet of Christ for her sister's soul flickered and went out. Ricardo's eyes widened at the miracle. Only the other candle, the flame of life, was still burning! "O mighty and holy Mother of God, amen."

In which Dona Carmosina reads an article, solves a crossword puzzle and other puzzles concerning Tieta's situation, a deduction worthy of the most sagacious sleuths of the detective-story genre; in which we make the acquaintance of Skipper Dário de Queluz, and in which Barbozinha (Gregório Eustáquio de Matos Barbosa), the bard with the broken heart, makes an appearance at the end of the chapter.

"Oh, good for you! That's the way! Pack them off to prison," Dona Carmosina exclaimed aloud in her enthusiasm. Here was an independent judge worthy of the name at last, with the spunk to make the right decision and put the rascals in jail, where they belonged. "That gang of thieves and murderers!"

Alone in her office in the early afternoon, Dona Carmosina had no witnesses to her enthusiasm and indignation. But Skipper Dário would jump for joy when he heard. He always got so riled up whenever they discussed pollution. "Every one of those blackguards ought to be behind bars, my good Carmosina; they're destroying human life." Maybe the Skipper was a little too oratorical; he did love to turn a phrase. Baroque, was Barbozinha's poetic term for him.

She tore out the page for the Skipper to read. Never mind that the paper was addressed to Colonel Artur de Figueiredo—old Colonel Artur da Tapitanga, who had subscribed to the *Estado de São Paulo* forever: since 1924, to be exact; Dona Carmosina had looked it up. For decades the *Estado* had kept the prosperous landowner informed of what was going on in the world, but now he only remembered to send for the pile of newspapers cluttering the post office every month or so. He didn't even bother to read them anymore, though Dona Carmosina did, to her great satisfaction and profit, but he always renewed his subscription before it expired. His status and lineage demanded that he subscribe to the great São Paulo newspaper, and Dona Carmosina, in whose best interest it was to remind him, never failed to do so, praising with equal lavishness the paper and the Colonel's goats.

One page more or less, one supplement more or less, made no difference to the octogenarian; he would celebrate his eighty-sixth birthday next January 18, as Dona Carmosina could have told you. He didn't much care anymore what went on in this crazy world of wars and revolutions, hate and violence and sensational out-and-out lies like that tall tale about a man riding to the moon on a rocket— nothing but a bedtime story for suckers. "It's in the newspapers, you say, on the front page of the *Estado?* Well, Carmosina, I say it's a big lie. I may be getting on in years, but I've still got all my faculties and these old antlers aren't worn down to a nub yet." Although the gate of Tapitanga Fazenda was less than twelve hundred yards from where the city pavement ended, the Colonel rarely appeared at the meetings of the Sant'Ana do Agreste Town Council, over which he theoretically presided as councilman, elected and reelected countless times, as well as former city manager and mayor. When he did come, though, he never failed to visit the postmistress.

"All right, Carmosina, what have you been reading in my paper? Don't you tell me any fibs now, mind!" And he would shake his stick at her; he still enjoyed a joke.

He told his bodyguard to stack the newspapers in the cart.

They came in handy in all sorts of ways: for wrapping packages, lighting fires, wiping off his bum in the privy. The Colonel's goats had been known to consume whole editions of the paper at a time, and while they didn't get fat on it, at least it didn't do them any harm.

Dona Carmosina folded the sheet carefully so that the story was on top; a lead article at the top of the page with a headline in bold type: "ITALY JAILS OCEAN POLLUTERS." This would be a red-letter day for the Skipper. Barbozinha, too, had taken an interest in the problem, lamenting "the baneful and inevitable side effects of progress," while Skipper Dário made no bones about damning "this madness labeled progress which is poisoning the human race and threatening to put an end to life on earth, my good Carmosina!" Waving his arms dramatically in the air: "If somebody doesn't put a stop to it, it won't be long before our children have cancer when they are born! Just look at Japan. . . ."

It was to escape from the grimness of cause and effect, to enjoy the genuine pleasures of life while there was still a time and place for them, that he had abandoned a promising career in the navy. He had hung up his uniform in a closet in his bungalow, simplifying his dress to shorts and navy T-shirts and the evening luxury of pajamas at the house at the beach and sports shirt and trousers in town. This was the life for him! All he wanted was to live in Agreste's blessed climate and enjoy the unparalleled beauty of Mangue Seco Beach—Paradise.

"That'll teach 'em a lesson!" Dona Carmosina muttered to herself again before settling down to her crossword puzzles and word games.

Great was Carmosina's thirst for knowledge and many and varied were the subjects that interested her, from politics to science, from the gravest problems of our times to the sex life of the current idols of the masses, from the UN to the OAS, from the CIA to the KGB, from NASA to UFOs, not to mention all the acronyms of all the Brazilian government bureaus and departments. She had them all down pat.

From among the circle of friends and admirers who frequented the post office to fill the empty hours (and there were plenty of them) with argument and conversation, Dona Carmosina found partners to share her every enthusiasm. She talked music, composers and performers with Aminthas and Fidélio (but Fidélio didn't really know much); tourism in Bahia and the world with Ascânio; and traded the latest rumors about the stars in our glittering artistic sky with Elisa. With Barbozinha there was vast scope for dialogue and polemics, from the most delicate wildflower of poetry to the arcanum of philosophic spiritualism, for the bard was a theoretical spiritualist and seer and she a scoffer who denied the reality of incarnation and reincarnation alike, an impious soul who mocked Heaven and earth and gloried in her atheism. "You're not an atheist, Carmosina, you're a pantheist, a worshiper of the Great God Pan," protested Aminthas, thinking he was being very clever.

No less wide-ranging were the topics she discussed with Skipper Dário: all the contemporary problems of suffering humanity, from atomic explosions to the population explosion, from pollution creeping over Los Angeles, and São Paulo, Tokyo and Rio de Janeiro smothering in a pall of smog, to the colonial war waged by Portugal; of a probable Third World War and the secret plans of the leaders of the powers and the superpowers—"You mustn't forget China, my good friend"—and the Middle East and the fate of Israel, Arab oil, and the Palestinians, and an analysis of every novel, detective story and science-fiction tale they had ever read. The Skipper enjoyed the science fiction best because it took him out of his familiar universe to unthinkably far-off planets, while Carmosina preferred detective novels, especially the classic ones like Agatha Christie's, which challenged the reader's astuteness and defied him to discover the criminal. Dona Carmosina boasted of always guessing right, of always knowing who the murderer was before Hercule Poirot's little gray cells could work it out.

The post office was the unrivaled center of culture in Agreste. When Giovanni Guimarães, the well-known columnist from Bahia's evening paper *A Tarde*, was invited to Agreste by Barbozinha the poet, his former companion on bohemian wanderings through the streets, bars and brothels of the capital, he came every afternoon without fail for a good long chat. He dubbed the post office the Areopagus, and the name had stuck. It frequently happened that the three luminaries, Dona Carmosina, the poet and Skipper Dário, were there at the same time, and then the Areopagus really caught fire, with their scintillating talk drawing people from the bar and shops to listen. Chalita the Arab was one habitué who hung on every word; he couldn't understand a thing they said, but how well

they said it and how he loved to listen to them! It was swell entertainment, and free besides.

Osnar was the only one with whom Dona Carmosina found
nothing to talk about. From his boyhood Osnar had been interested
in just three things in God's wide world: beer, women and pool.
The circle of women who aroused Osnar's interest was catholic
enough; he was neither squeamish nor dogmatic. Unfortunately,
however, Dona Carmosina was not among that happy band of objects of desire, many of whom were already bought and paid for.
Osnar admired her intelligence but not her looks. "I can't get it up
for that one," he was heard to remark. To be brutally frank, Dona
Carmosina had never yet been known to arouse desire in any man.

Synonym for concupiscence in four letters—Dona Carmosina
bit her pencil and rummaged in her memory. She had it: desire. No,
desire had six letters and she only wanted four; four, let's see now,
what could it be? Lust, of course! Dona Carmosina's little eyes,
fringed by sandy lashes, gazed out into the street with its Saturday
market-day bustle of carters spending their hard-earned coins in the
modest business district with its few poorly stocked shops. Lust was
a strong word.

When Perpétua married, Dona Carmosina had felt a brief surge
of hope. But that is another story. This is a good place to stop for a
rest, dividing the chapter in two right here and letting the reader
get his breath.

*While the reader gets his breath, the author
seizes his chance and makes the most of it.*

A good idea that! It has merit. Long chapters are tiring and make
the story too heavy and tedious; they may even make the reader lose
interest and drop off to sleep. And then, a pause gives the author the
time and space for necessary explanations of details that the characters may try to twist, change around or simply cover up, to suit
whatever confessed or hidden motives move them. The reader has a
sacred right to the whole truth; after all, he pays plenty for a book
these days.

Carmosina is an old hand at keeping secrets, covering her tracks, and keeping certain news items partly or wholly out of circulation. She is, therefore, a menace to the newsmongers on the church steps and to Agreste's population as a whole; for is there anyone alive who doesn't meddle in his neighbors' affairs, who doesn't ask questions, tell tales and put in his two cents' worth? If there are exceptions to the rule I have yet to meet them. Discussing other people's business is the principal amusement in Agreste. Some do it baldly, crudely, and maliciously; others raise it to a subtle art. Goatstink, scum of the earth, rotten inside and out, is an example of intolerable crudeness. On the grand weekly bender in which he indulges on Saturday night and Sunday, after begging all through the heat of the day in the marketplace, this malodorous piece of human refuse weaves and stumbles down the street sullying the honor of distinguished families with his unspeakable insults and slander. Unfortunately, they almost always turn out to be true.

"Better take a look at your horns, Chico Junior, they're getting mighty long. That woman of yours, Ritinha, spends more time playing around on the riverbank than she spends at home. . . . I won't say who she's playing with; I ain't the kind to rat on my neighbors."

He ain't the kind, neither am I, so where does that leave us? There is a subtle art in the voice and words of old Dona Milu, Carmosina's mother, and who ever denied she's a saint?

"They do say Ritinha's sweet on Seu Lindolfo, but there ain't a word of truth in it; you know how people love to talk. It's the price Ritinha pays for being so openhearted, maybe a mite too much sometimes . . . but that's her nature. She just can't help it."

Everyone in town knew good and well that Ritinha and Lindolfo, the municipal treasurer, were in the habit of meeting in the coves down by the river. Chico Junior's philosophy is best: Turn a deaf ear to the gossip you hear. Who cares what Goatstink says, anyway?

However. To return to Carmosina and Skipper Dário, there's collusion between those two. No, it isn't what you think. As Osnar says, using the Skipper as an example, nothing in Creation is perfect. Through the chinks of half-open windows or jalousies, languid or burning glances, depending on the age and ardor of their owner, follow his rolling sailor's walk as he strides through the streets of Agreste, a fine-looking man, all muscle, with a youthful body and the face of a mature man who has lived hard, topped off by a rebellious thatch of gray hair. Able to indulge himself in the luxury of taking his pick, he wastes the privilege and ignores them all, even Carol, Modesto Pires' mistress, a masterpiece of God and the mingling of many races. A confirmed monogamist, the Skipper, fair and square: he loves his wife, Dona Laura, and Carmosina is his faithful friend. Faithful friend, there's the nub of it. For the benefit of my readers, I will use this pause in my story to explain the riddle.

I won't beat around the bush. What is this personage's military rank; how many stripes does he sport on the naval uniform hung in the back of a closet and forgotten? Nobody knows; the title of Skipper is enough for his friends, and that is exactly what Carmosina told him when this honest, humble man said he thought he ought to tell them the truth. It's her responsibility that he hasn't. Sometimes she talks, sometimes she buttons her lip; it all depends.

That Dário de Queluz, a valiant son of Agreste, once belonged to the Brazilian Navy and added new luster to the honor of his native place, who can doubt? Proof is everywhere. One bit shines beside the Skipper's coconut carvings on top of the desk in his bungalow; a gold medal for bravery in action gleams under its glass dome. Everyone knows he joined the navy as an able-bodied seaman, a youth who ran away to sea because he couldn't find a job on land. That he rose step by step through the ranks, by dint of hard work and study during his twenty years of military service, is also public knowledge; but how high did he rise? There's the rub: when he put away his uniform and returned to breathe his pure native air again, he was addressed as Admiral. He refused the title and the flattery.

"Me? I never climbed that high up the ladder. Besides, there aren't any admirals in peacetime."

So they called him Skipper instead, and if any of them felt any curiosity about his naval rank they didn't say so; Dário was an athlete and inspired respect. Skipper was the perfect title anyway, whatever his rank had been.

A subtle art, this matter of other people's business. One day when the two of them were chatting together in the post office, Carmosina remarked casually, as if it had just occurred to her, "Skipper, please enlighten me. Can an enlisted man get to be a naval commander?"

Dário saw that his friend was consumed with curiosity; he

knew what she was hinting at. Like the kindly man he was, he answered promptly, his smile frank and aboveboard. "I didn't rise that high, my good Carmosina. I only made—"

She covered his mouth with her hand.

"Hush, don't let anyone hear you."

"Why not?"

"Because the others think you did rise to the highest rank and they're so proud of you. Why disillusion them? Skipper's all they have to know."

She listened closely, heard what she wanted to hear, and that was the end of it. The Skipper was commanding the sea and the winds on the dunes of Mangue Seco without benefit of work details, charts or epaulettes. Carmosina knew, and that was enough. She did not betray the Skipper's confidence, not even to her mother. Tell old Milu? What are you thinking of? By the next morning everyone in Agreste would have known.

Well, that's the story. The cards are on the table. I've taken advantage of the interrupted chapter to write another one almost as long, for which I apologize, but I've told my readers what I wanted to tell them. What rank *did* the Skipper reach, you ask? Ah, I can't tell you that. Carmosina is the only one who knows, and she's so selfish she keeps her mouth shut and won't tell. If any of you ever do find out, I'd appreciate your letting me in on the secret.

Interrupted chapter (continued).

When Perpétua married, Dona Carmosina felt a thrill of hope. If Perpétua, who was older and uglier (yes, uglier; niceness counts for points in beauty contests too) with that perpetually constipated face of hers, if that charmless sourpuss could find someone to cherish her and ask for her hand in marriage and take her to the altar in a veil and wreath (of all the ridiculous sights!), then Carmosina, who was younger, more intelligent, more gifted, oh so gifted! and friendly and good-humored and a very good cook besides, had certainly not lost the right to dream.

Alas, there was only one Major Cupertino Batista, and miracles don't happen twice. Retired in his fifties because of heart trouble, short of breath and short of brains, stubborn, obtuse, an oaf in fact, he was not a catch to be looked down one's nose at for all of that. As a bachelor he had been thrifty of his financial and physical reserves; when he entered the Kingdom of Heaven he left Perpétua well provided for, with two sons and three houses, besides his pension and the interest-bearing savings. The inheritance meant nothing to Carmosina, but—she sighed—for six years and a month, or seventy-one months, or 2,221 nights counting leap year, that hag, that undeserving wretch—that lucky, blissful woman!—had slept in a marriage bed with a man beside her under the bedclothes, a husband who was good to the last drop, for Perpétua had a miscarriage not long before the Major saluted for the last time and the party was over.

Carmosina wrote LUST a letter at a time in the squares of the puzzle, her thoughts winging from Perpétua to Elisa (poor thing, she was in such a state she had forgotten to take her magazines with her); and from Elisa to Antonieta.

Now Antonieta really did deserve her married state and fortune; she was gay, amusing, good-natured, kind, a delightful creature altogether. She had almost lived at Carmosina's house when they were schoolmates. Dona Milu had been especially fond of her and always took her part when wicked tongues browsed over the girl's innocent or perhaps not so innocent flesh. The good women were always gossiping about her.

"That young'un lost the stopper to her bottle a long time back. . . ."

"That little gal's set her foot on the road to hell. . . ."

"Little gal, you call her? She's a little tramp, that's what she is. Gives away free samples to everybody and his brother."

Dona Milu knew how to put an end to such talk in a hurry.

"Whatever she's giving away, it's hers to give, and I never knew of her sleeping with a man for money. Her natural cravings won't let her be. That's the way it is with her and plenty of others, ain't it, Roberta? The difference is the others won't give it away, they keep that honeypot shut up tight 'cause the rest don't matter, does it, Gesilda? The boys can paw over all the rest, from neck to fanny, as long as they don't get into that honeypot!"

She seemed to change the subject:

"What a pretty nickname the boys have given your twin girls,

Francisca. Oh, hadn't you heard? Well, I'll tell you: Gold and Silver Hands, ain't that pretty?" Dona Milu was a caution.

When Antonieta, whipped and turned out of doors, left town in the truck, Carmosina was the only one to see her off. "You go tell your friend goodbye," ordered Dona Milu. The marks from the beating were visible: some of the blows had fallen on her face and there were purple bruises on her legs.

Tieta did not complain. "Maybe it'll be for the best," she said. And she was right, it was.

During the last eleven years and seven months, a day hardly passed that Dona Carmosina did not think of her friend. Ever since the arrival of that first letter, she had read all the correspondence between Sant'Ana do Agreste and Box 6211 in São Paulo, S.P. She was privy to more than Tieta's own sisters, much more, through firsthand knowledge, plus the powers of deduction.

She had seen the check grow larger as time passed, thanks to the devaluation of the cruzeiro and the sisters' laments about inflation. She had corrected—rewritten actually—the letters Elisa wrote (grammar was not Elisa's forte), and had read all of Perpétua's letters and the others'! After the Major's death, the sisters had shared the duty and pleasure of writing to their sister, just as they shared the contents of the boxes that arrived by parcel post with dresses, nightgowns, blouses and skirts inside. When it was Perpétua's turn to write, she brought the envelope already sealed, the silly thing! Dona Carmosina would not have been worth her salt and her privileged post if she had not been an expert at steaming open envelopes, reading the pages at a glance and putting them back just as she had found them. The only hard part was refraining from correcting the mistakes in Portuguese.

Besides the unfailing blessing from old Zé Esteves, "God bless and increase you, my child," every letter complained about the cost of living, thanked and praised their dear sister, and contained many curious questions from her sisters and brother-in-law. Antonieta replied in short notes—big letters on fancy stationery embossed with a gothic A—which Elisa and Dona Carmosina feasted on together, right there in the post office.

Dona Carmosina had read Ricardo's letter too, Ricardo's and others'. It was, by the way, the boy's naive epistle asking for his aunt's blessing, a football and discretion, which . . . never mind, that's of no interest to anyone. Dona Carmosina put the thought away and went back to her puzzle. Brazilian fruit of Asiatic origin, five letters. That was too easy.

That such a long correspondence should come to an end for no good reason, unless, indeed, Tieta was gravely ill or dead, reminded her that there had been other curious features about that correspondence. To begin with, the lack of a return address in São Paulo; no street or apartment number was given, just a cold, anonymous post-office box. Agreste was no bigger than an egg and everyone knew everyone else, yet Perpétua and Elisa took pains to include the complete name and return address. Perpétua Esteves Batista, Judge Oliva Square No. 19; Elisa Esteves Simas, 28 Rosário Street; and even their father did the same: José Esteves, Blood Alley, no number.

And her husband? He was ageless, faceless, impalpable, nothing but a first name and a papal title, vague business firms, distinguished white hair in the magazine photograph. Dona Carmosina had devoted a good deal of time to analyzing this absorbing enigma. She gathered data and clues and made her own guesses.

The Major, who was still alive at that time, had assumed responsibility for the initial reply, but he could never have written a persuasive letter without Dona Carmosina's help. She set down the items of news in orderly fashion, emphasizing the most important points. It was a long letter, a narrative covering fifteen years of events.

There was detailed news about everyone in the family: Tieta's father, Zé Esteves, who was getting along toward eighty but holding his own pretty well, and Tonha, his second wife (younger than Perpétua, Tieta's age in fact, but worn out by poverty and neglect, and a mere appendage to the old man). The couple lived on the charity of their daughters and the daughters' husbands, possessing nothing of their own, neither property nor income. Zé Esteves was always trying to outsmart others but failed so miserably that he had managed to do himself out of his flocks of goats and fields of manioc, his own house, everything he owned. He sent his daughter his blessing and forgiveness and asked her for charity. Dona Carmosina changed the wording, the form and the contents; instead of Zé Esteves forgiving Tieta, he asked her to forgive him, spoke of his old age and poverty and hinted that her help would be welcome; a father can ask for forgiveness, but he can't beg his children for alms. This part of the letter, enhanced by the Major's beautiful handwrit-

ing, was so touching that it could not fail to melt Tieta's heart;
Dona Carmosina's own eyes were moist. She had always had a talent
for writing; talent and will, but not courage.

Then followed an account of Perpétua's marriage, her husband's name and title, Major Cupertino Batista, a retired officer of
the State Military Police, a brother-in-law at your service. God had
blessed the marriage and given them two sons, Ricardo, five years
old, and Cupertino, called Peto, who was not quite two. And now
Perpétua's womb had quickened again; she was expecting a child who
would have been the third. Yes, the Major was quick on the trigger
and didn't hold his fire, Dona Carmosina could see that; but she
didn't touch that part of the letter, not wanting any trouble with
Perpétua. She did take charge of describing Elisa's wedding,
though. Elisa had been the prettiest bride ever seen in Agreste when
she married Astério Simas, son and heir of Seu Ananias, who had
owned the dry-goods store on the Rua da Frente (now Rua Colonel
Artur de Figueiredo). Too bad the store wasn't what it used to be.
Business in the remote, decaying town of Sant'Ana do Agreste had
dwindled by half during the past fifteen years. The population had
dwindled too; now the old people were in the majority, for the
climate was as fine as ever, prolonging the lives of those who hung
on despite poverty and the lack of resources and prospects for the
future. If people didn't starve to death it was only because the river
and the mangrove swamp provided abundant fish, several varieties
of crab and remarkable clams all year around, and there was always
more fruit than they could eat: bananas, mangoes, jackfruit, sweet-
sop, soursop, pineapple, guavas, strawberry guavas, sapodilla fruit
and watermelons, besides endless groves and coconut palms which
belonged to no one.

After the news came the questions: And how was Antonieta
herself? What was her address? She must tell them all about her past
and present life, everything!

Within a month the answer came. Antonieta sent a check made
out to the Major, asking him to cash it and give the money to Zé
Esteves; she wanted to help her father and stepmother pay their
monthly bills. Father could count on a check every month from
now on. The amount was surprisingly large, large enough to arouse
their greed. This was big money, much more than the couple needed
to pay rent on the tumbledown house they lived in even if they paid
all the back rent they owed, plus their food and a small amount for

rum, an indispensable item in Zé Esteves' diet. Perpétua had hinted at a division of the spoils, but one glare from the old man, brandishing his shepherd's staff and ready to go on the warpath, was enough to quell that idea. Seu Modesto Pires, the owner of the tannery, kindly cashed that check and all the others that followed, so that the Major would not have to go all the way to Alagoinhas to the nearest bank.

As for their curiosity, it remained unsatisfied. Antonieta merely informed them that she was in good health, thank God, and happily married though she had no children. About her husband—his name, profession, age—she said not a word. Address? The quickest and safest address was Box 6211; a letter sent there would be sure to reach her.

During the ten years or more that followed, the correspondence between Tieta and her family continued with the regularity of clockwork: one letter per month on each side, never more than a few lines from São Paulo, on tinted, scented stationery. The color varied from year to year, but the perfume had changed only once. The one she used lately was lighter and more discreet, probably imported.

The amount of the check increased, and not only because of inflation. When Elisa's baby was born and Dona Carmosina spoke rather frankly of Astério's difficulties, Tieta added a fixed amount each month for the baby's milk and his future education, and she did the same when Perpétua wrote her dramatically, and for once in her life sincerely, of her grief at the death of the perfect husband who had left her a poor penniless widow with two babes in arms. Not a word, needless to say, about the rented houses or the savings account in the bank, but Tieta must have realized already that one sister was much better off than the other, for she sent the same amount to each: Perpétua had two children, but Elisa's hardships were greater. Then the parcels of used clothing, the Christmas and birthday presents began to arrive, but the family still knew almost nothing about either Tieta or her husband.

Almost nothing, but enough for Dona Carmosina to put two and two together and solve the conundrum.

About nine years before our story takes place—nine years and nine months to be exact—Dona Carmosina recognized Antonieta, in spite of her bleached hair, in a picture in the Carnival issue of *Manchete* magazine showing "some revelers whooping it up at the

Carnival ball in São Paulo's Excelsior Theater." There she was, right in the middle of the picture, snuggling contentedly in the loving arms of a distinguished-looking white-haired man. Unfortunately, nothing of the gentleman could be seen but his back. They were dancing, and Tieta's laughing, mischievous face was turned toward the camera. She was now an attractive and charming woman, and no longer the harum-scarum girl Carmosina had watched ride away from Agreste on the front seat of a truck. Her beauty had ripened into opulence, but then there had never been anything skimpy about Tieta's good looks.

Dona Carmosina called a family conclave, and the photograph caused a sensation. Perpétua nodded in agreement. Yes, it was Antonieta, all right; she had put on flesh and was dyeing her hair. Old Zé Esteves recognized his daughter too:

"Sure does look swanky, don't she? And her hair dyed in the latest style. God bless you and keep you, my child!" with his eyes on the other two sisters, daring either of them to say a critical word. Neither of them did, at least in his presence.

Elisa was thrilled to the core. She had had no idea what her sister looked like, and from then on she could see her in her mind's eye in her glamorous harem costume. The news that they had seen her picture in a magazine, disclosed by Elisa in a letter, gave Carmosina her first clue: in her reply Tieta revealed her husband's Christian name. The man who held her in his arms to the rhythm of a Carnival samba was her own dear husband Felipe—Felipe who, she did not say.

Not long afterward, in a letter postmarked Curitiba, she said that they were there on business because Felipe was an industrialist with business connections in Paraná. On another occasion she apologized for the check's being sent a week late, explaining that the Comendador had been ill and that she, like the devoted wife she was, had not left his sickbed for a moment. So Felipe was an industrialist and had been given a title by the Pope.

That was quite enough to satisfy Perpétua. The check was enough to satisfy her, to tell the truth; she didn't care about the rest. Elisa, on the other hand, longed to know more, much more. She speculated endlessly with Carmosina about her sister's reserve— "She's ashamed of us, or afraid we'll take advantage of her. Tieta's avoiding us, and she has a perfect right to." How good a right, Dona Carmosina knew better than anyone else. Tieta had been driven from her home—"I ain't running no whorehouse!"—and beaten black and blue because her older sister had told on her. "She's too good, that's what she is—to forget how she was tattled on and shamed and beaten and to help her family the way she does."

"Yes, she's an angel and too good to live," Dona Carmosina agreed. As for the real reason for Tieta's reticence, the postmistress had mapped out a theory of her own about it, but she kept her own counsel.

She went on gathering data, hints and clues; here was a mystery worthy of Hercule Poirot. Dona Carmosina solved it to her own satisfaction when the stylish dresses, the skirts and blouses of good quality and varying sizes began to arrive via parcel post. Antonieta had explained the reason for the different sizes in a few words: "I'm sending some dresses of mine and my stepdaughters' that are almost as good as new." Stepdaughters, note that well: Comendador Felipe's daughters but not hers, because she had none. It was clear as daylight to Dona Carmosina Sherlock Holmes. Who in Agreste can equal, much less surpass, her when it comes to brains?

Dissolution of conjugal ties with separation of bed and board, seven letters! Divorce.

Separation would be a better word; there was no divorce in Brazil. Lord, what a benighted country! And that was the only true and correct explanation: no other fit the facts.

Here we pause for a little more of the suspense typical of this kind of cheap entertainment. We'll be back right after the station break, as the announcer says when he breaks into a soap opera on the radio just at the most exciting moment, to tout soap powder or cigarettes, leaving poor Elisa all tremulous and keyed up.

Here's that bore again, just when we thought
we were rid of him.

A quick parenthesis—it'll only take a minute—to reveal damnable deeds, light up dark corners with the pitiless glare of truth and unmask Miss Carmosina Sluizer da Consolação once again.

You mustn't think I'm persecuting her, or that I don't appreciate her. Quite the contrary: I admire her virtues and have nothing but praise for the generous and noble motives that led her to violate the laws of man and God. As for persecuting her, who in Agreste would dare? Not even Colonel Artur da Tapitanga, nor Ascânio Trindade, who is such a stickler for the law. She and Ascânio are cronies, forever writing letters to newspapers in the state capital and petitions to the state government demanding all kinds of help for Agreste, but the petitions are as futile as the letters.

More than fifteen years ago—she has been postmistress for twenty-three—Carmosina worked out a nice little scheme with her quondam fellow post-office employee, Canuto Tavares, by which Canuto runs a repair shop in Esplanada, and makes a good living at it too, being a handy sort of man. Realizing he would never amount to a hill of beans if he stayed in Agreste to vegetate on his meager salary as a telegraph operator in a backwater post office, he decided to pack up his tools and ambitions and leave for good. When he told Carmosina of his plans, she proposed a clever arrangement that would be to the advantage of both: Canuto could go tend to his repair shop in Esplanada with an easy conscience, and in exchange for half his salary, leave his colleague in full command at the post office of Sant'Ana do Agreste, a responsibility which did not, after all, involve any very backbreaking labor. For Canuto, who had been all set to resign, half a salary was so much gravy, while the extra income enabled Dona Carmosina to maintain a household in greater comfort. Dona Milu was getting too old to contribute much; she was a retired midwife who only rarely brought a baby into the world these days. So Dona Carmosina was left as sole and unchallenged mistress of all letters, telegrams, parcels, magazines and newspapers, and thus of the doings of Agreste and the great world. The arrangement had been working well for over fifteen years (she could have told you exactly how many years, months and days) and at no time did it so much as cross anyone's mind to call the attention of the authorities to Dona Carmosina's brazen flouting of the law in dispatching the official time and attendance report to Esplanada each month via personal courier (Jairo) for Canuto to sign. Who would have dared?

The only thing about Carmosina that I disapprove of is that she's biased. I wonder what her advice would be if one of Perpétua's sons were to die and the mother wanted to keep Antonieta in the dark to make sure the monthly stipend kept on coming as fat as

ever. I wonder if she'd do what she did when Elisa came to her at
the post office in despair after Toninho died. Dona Carmosina had
tried to console her by telling her that the poor innocent babe
would never suffer any more. He had been sickly since the day he
was born. Dona Milu had been frightened when she had drawn him
from Elisa's womb; he looked like an unformed fetus, and the only
wonder was that he had lived so long. The doctor and the medicine
that Tieta's checks had paid for had done no good, and neither had
the trip to Esplanada to consult the baby doctor, Dr. Joelson. The
pediatrician had shaken his head; there was no use even writing a
prescription. The poor little thing can rest now and so can you;
how long has it been since you had a good night's sleep? But Elisa
refused to be comforted.

Besides losing Toninho—however ailing and puny, he was her
child and her consolation—she would lose the money from her sister, which should have gone for milk, medicine, doctors and her
nephews' future education, not for cosmetics, magazines, weekly
tickets to the movies and batteries for the radio. All those goodies
bought with the leftovers from Tieta's charity would go a-glimmer-
ing with Toninho. "Oh, Carmosina, what shall I do?"

The little squinting eyes gazed at Elisa. Carmosina had watched
her come into the world. Dona Milu, practical nurse and midwife
emerita, had taken her daughter along to help her when she was
called urgently in the middle of the night to attend Tonha in the
pangs of childbirth and had found her blowing into an empty bottle
as Zé Esteves had ordered her to do. Carmosina and Tieta had
boiled water and helped with the delivery, while squeamish Perpétua shut herself up in her room to pray. Everyone helped the best
she knew how.

As a teenage girl Elisa used to stop by Dona Milu's on her way
to school for the midwife's blessing and some of the caramelized-
sugar, guava and coconut candy she could never get enough of. It
was Carmosina who had first reminded Elisa that Tieta was alive;
her family never mentioned her. She was a scandalous topic, but
Carmosina found occasion to talk about her friend. She would mention her nickname and good looks: your sister Tieta was with me
that time; she was such a pretty girl it was a joy to look at her. Elisa
too had grown into a pretty girl whom it was a joy to look at, and
had married and had a child. Just think, Carmosina had watched her
being born. She looked so elegant in Antonieta's dress, and yet she

was in despair. She didn't even have a sick child to take care of any more. What on earth was she going to do? Pitiful, that was what she was.

Carmosina went up to her and murmured, "Don't tell her anything about it."

"What?"

"Just go on as if Toninho were still alive."

"But what if Perpétua lets on? You know what a tattletale she is; she always says she can't tolerate a lie."

"If she threatens to tell on you, you threaten her right back. Who's got the most skeletons in the closet? You don't think she lets on to Tieta about those houses she owns or the money the Major left her, do you? Does she tell her she takes the money Tieta sends her for the children's expenses and deposits it in the savings bank because she doesn't need it? Like fun she does."

It should be plain enough by now that Carmosina lacks a moral sense. By advocating untruths and blackmail to a friend in need she shows her want of honor, too: her familiarity with the contents of Perpétua's letters through an abuse of power gives her no right to misuse her ill-gained knowledge. But Carmosina doesn't care a fig for moral precepts or the rules of honor. Not content with giving advice, she takes over and directs the plot. "You leave Perpétua to me. I'll talk to her myself."

Perpétua lifted her eyes to heaven and beseeched the Lord for forgiveness, then unclosed her lips.

"She won't find out from me. After all, if Antonieta cuts off her allowance, it'll be me who'll have her and her husband hanging around my neck."

Now that was good reasoning, and well put. Perpétua was nobody's fool and was not about to be blackmailed. Carmosina giggled, the laugh of an innocent child.

"Well, for whatever reason you do it, the main thing is to keep your mouth shut."

Just one more thing and I'll be off. Do you remember Ricardo's letter asking for a football and begging his aunt to keep it secret? When she thought of it, Carmosina was tempted to reveal that she too had written to Antonieta, reminiscing about their friendship and the far-off days of their girlhood and sending her affectionate regards from Dona Milu. And a request: could Antonieta buy a good rhyming dictionary, the best she could find in the São Paulo bookstores, and send it to her and let her know how much it cost? She didn't want to order one from Aracaju or Bahia because people would talk. The book arrived promptly, inscribed "To my good friend Carmô, this little remembrance from your friend Tieta."

Far into the night, by the light of an oil lamp in the stillness of early dawn, Carmosina writes poems and counts syllables, rhyming shame and aflame, fire and desire, afar and Osnar.

Well, now you know as much as I do. I'll take my leave of you in the post office—Areopagus, rather—and say *au revoir* for now.

End of a twice-interrupted chapter, oof!

The riddle was so easy, and it had taken her so long to solve it! She had lacked sufficient data and had had to piece it together bit by bit.

Desquite, separation without remarriage: one of the most damning proofs of Brazil's backwardness and underdevelopment. Many were the long and heated arguments Dona Carmosina had had on the subject with Father Mariano, Carlota Alves the school-teacher, and Dr. Cáio Vilasboas—how a doctor with a diploma from the medical school could be such a reactionary! To think that two people were tied together for the rest of their lives, even after they were legally separated, and forbidden to marry anyone else! Dona Carmosina had read statistics on the number of couples living in concubinage—what a nasty word!—in Brazil. There were liter-ally millions of them, accepted as married couples and received in society as Mr. and Mrs. Alves, Lopes or Silva, but with no legal rights. You weren't a wife, you were a concubine. Dona Carmosina had solved the riddle at last. It was so simple. With a minimum of data and her own powers of deduction she had found the answer. Antonieta was living with a man who was rolling in money, just as though she were married to him, but she wasn't. She was accepted by his family, even by his daughters—she had mentioned her step-children and the Comendador's nieces more than once—but they couldn't make the union legal because he was divorced. Tieta, who had firsthand knowledge of Agreste's prejudices, was keeping mum about it and shrouding husband and marriage in mystery and silence. She couldn't have forgotten her father, waiting for her in the dark beside the open window with a shepherd's goad in hand, and the beating that followed and woke up the town. Saying nothing about her marital status was the most sensible thing she could have done.

Several years before, a revenue agent had come to live in Agreste with his wife, a distinguished, pleasant, very refined lady and the mother of a pair of twins. They were well received at first, until the woman naively disclosed that both she and her husband were divorced and had been living happily together for the past ten years. Doors were soon closed to them and smiles turned to frowns. Eventually they had to leave town. In Agreste you were either married by priest and judge or you weren't married at all. Antonieta was quite right to live her own life and keep her distance from the wagging tongues in town, beginning with Perpétua. Dona Carmosina would have given anything to see Perpétua's sour face the day she found out. She'd swallow her own tongue.

To Dona Carmosina's mind, the only thing that mattered was whether a couple got on well together. Priest and judge, veil and wreath could be dispensed with. She herself had put all such mental reservations behind her a long time ago. She would settle for a husband, legal or not, bachelor, widower, divorced or married with a wife and children. As long as he was a man who had his eye on her and was ready for action, Dona Carmosina wouldn't say no to a featherbed or a riverbank or the bushes. If she had her choice, Osnar would be the lucky man. Failing that, any other man would do. Unluckily for her, it was not to be Osnar or any other man.

Catching sight of the Skipper coming home from market, she forgot love's disappointments and the problem of Antonieta's long-delayed letter. She ran to the door, waved the newspaper and called excitedly as soon as he was close enough to hear:

"Come and read this! I've kept it just for you."

Skipper Dário took the page and Dona Carmosina pointed to an article. He read in silence, then, stirred by the subject, began reading aloud: " '. . . the political transformations that have recently taken place in Europe have all but overshadowed an event of great importance to defenders of the environment everywhere in the world: the sentencing to prison of the president and four members of the board of directors of the largest chemical firm in Italy, the

Società Montedison, for the crime of polluting the waters of the Mediterranean. . . .' "

A broad smile appeared on the Skipper's face.

"Now that's the kind of judge I like! An Italian judge with guts!" He went on reading: " '. . . the bone of contention is the titanium-dioxide factory in Scarlino, initially hailed with enthusiasm by the impoverished inhabitants of this Tuscan province but beset by strikes and work stoppages by its five hundred employees since it opened its doors. . . .' "

Barbozinha the seer came in during the reading and stayed to listen. The Skipper insisted on reading it all over again from the beginning so that his friend would not miss a single detail: in Italy, at last, a judge with balls!

"Now listen to this: 'Attorney Garaventa, one of the lawyers for the defense, contended that the company's board of directors had always required legal permission from the authorities for everything they did. If they were prosecuted, what would public opinion have to say about the administration that gave them permission?' "

"That's a good point!" put in Barbozinha. "They were acting legally, they had permission from the authorities—"

"Legally, my foot! It's the authorities that ought to be in jail. They were in cahoots with those bloodsuckers the whole time. Let me finish: 'Judge Viglietta, however, was not impressed by this argument, since he belongs to a new generation of young magistrates who are not intimidated by wealth and power.' Bravo, Your Honor!"

"But if they hadn't broken the law—"

"Oh, hadn't they? Here's the law the judge slapped them with; just listen and don't interrupt, we can argue about it later if you want to: 'He based his decision on an Italian law dated July 14, 1965 . . .' " The Skipper interrupted himself to remark: "A brand-new one, you see? It's about time a few good laws were passed." He went on reading: " '. . . but rarely invoked, which stipulates penalties for anyone who willfully throws any foreign substance into the ocean that is toxic to fish or is likely to provoke chemical or physical changes in the water itself.' "

As he finished reading the article, Dona Carmosina listened with rekindled enthusiasm and Barbozinha with half an ear. " 'Judge Viglietta intends this verdict to be a warning to all those who use the sea as a garbage can and threaten to turn the Mediterranean into a dead sea.' ...

"Now there's a judge for you! Sure do wish we had one like him in São Paulo! Barbozinha, we don't know how privileged we are to be living in this little piece of God's paradise that men forgot!" He turned to Dona Carmosina. "May I keep it, Carmosina?"

"I tore the page out just for you."

As the Skipper was folding it carefully, Barbozinha inquired of Dona Carmosina, "What do you know about Tieta? I've been told she's departed this world."

Reminded by his question of the magazines Elisa had left behind, Dona Carmosina fetched them and laid them beside her purse.

"I surely hope not, but it certainly does look that way."

"Who?" the Skipper wanted to know.

"Antonieta, Tieta. You know who she is, don't you?"

"Why of course. What's happened to her?"

"I'm awfully afraid she's dead. We don't know yet for sure."

"I wouldn't be surprised if she had died of cancer in that polluted São Paulo. All those cars belching gases and carbon monoxide ..."

He took his leave: Dona Laura was expecting him at home.

"Thank you for the story, Carmosina. It did my heart good to read about that judge."

Carmosina prepared to close the post office for the day. She would have to stop at Elisa's house before supper and try to cheer the poor girl up a little. Barbozinha, downcast, remote, was staring at something on the horizon that was invisible to Dona Carmosina. Barbozinha was a seer.

No one knew—it was a secret that had never been revealed, not even to the postmistress—that Tieta was the muse who had inspired the finest poems in the two published and five unpublished books, seven volumes altogether, by De Matos Barbosa the poet. And now Antonieta Esteves, his devouring passion, his *femme fatale*, had taken leave of the flesh and was an incandescent star on another astral plane. He would write her one last poem: death is not real, my beloved, the body is naught but a husk to be cast off, and I shall meet you once again and you will be mine at last, for I desired you as a slave five thousand years ago, I knew you as a Mayan princess and that love cost me my life; I tried to rescue you from a convent in the Middle Ages and was thrown into a dungeon, loaded down

with gyves and chained to a rock; I followed your footsteps by the
rivers of Hindustan and my flesh rotted away and floated on the
waters; until one day I found you again, a goat girl leaping on the
hills.

Of picture magazines and proofs of friendship:
a comforting chapter to set the stage for an epic
family battle.

"You forgot your magazines." Dona Carmosina dropped them on
the table and pulled up a chair.

Twilight tints and a soft evening breeze enfolded Sant'Ana do
Agreste. In Barbozinha's paraphrase of the Portuguese poet's lines:
Where are the artists who should be painting this heavenly land? He,
De Matos Barbosa, had done his duty by composing more than fifty
poems and sonnets dedicated to the scenic beauties of Agreste: the
Real River running down to the sea, the dunes on Mangue Seco
Beach where he had declaimed for Tieta, on a distant bureaucratic
holiday, ardent verses blown away by the wind. Barbozinha left
Dona Carmosina at the door; no, he wouldn't go in. Steeped in
sorrow, mumbling a poem, he turned in the direction of the Azores
Bar.

Elisa sat insensible to the cool freshness of late afternoon, blind
to the rich shades of yellow, violet, red and blue glowing in the
firmament as the river waters drew the sun onward until it dropped
into the sea behind a horizon of sharks and the moon rose behind the
dunes. There was going to be a full moon that night. Dona Carmosina was shocked to see Elisa so undone. Her eyes were swollen
with crying. It was a terrible blow to her and Astério, there was no
denying that. How would they ever be able to balance their household budget without her sister's help? I'll end up supporting them,
Perpétua had prophesied the last time Elisa was in despair.

She sat drooping forlornly without even glancing at the magazines, Elisa who couldn't wait to find out whether her favorite
celebrities' love affairs had flourished or languished that month,
what weddings and divorces, breakups, and big parties had taken

place—everything that was printed about the world of the movie, radio, theater and television stars. Magazines? Perpétua would never give her the money for a single one. "That trash! Men without a godfearing bone in their bodies, hussies showing all they've got in those indecent magazines of yours. I wouldn't have one in my house. If I was Astério . . ." Fortunately she wasn't, so Elisa could stay abreast of society scandal and pore over movie magazines to her heart's content.

Elisa's expertise was limited to Brazilian celebrities; they were her specialty, so to speak. She did not pretend to the world view of Dona Carmosina, whose erudition in this fascinating subject went far beyond the borders of Brazil. There was nothing, however trivial, that she did not know about the Beatles, before, during and after the formation and dissolution of the group. All that erudition, knowledge, curiosity for the sheer intellectual pleasure of knowing and correcting Aminthas, who was mad about the Beatles and every other rock group, crazy for contemporary sound. Aminthas owned a record player and a tape recorder and spent every penny he earned, and more, on records and cassettes.

When it came to music, Dona Carmosina, a romantic at heart, preferred traditional melodies like "The Caboclo's House" and "Western Moon." Now that was music with a tune to it, and feeling, and not that senseless racket the longhairs made. She enraged Aminthas by debunking idols—"That awful-looking Yoko doesn't know any better than to have her picture taken nude. Look at her, will you; you can't tell her face from her fanny."

"I'll go get the money for them." Elisa's voice was toneless, her eyes still wet with tears.

"Never mind, it can wait."

"I still have enough money for these."

Her eyes sought those of her bosom friend, with whom she had shared such cozy long talks about the radio and TV stars. Elisa had never seen television but once, when they had gone to Bahia for three days so that Astério could consult a doctor and have an X-ray taken. Luckily it was nothing serious, only a bad scare and a lot of money wasted. The one small luxury in the modest hotel near the highway was the television set in the front room for the entertainment of the guests. Elisa's eyes were glued to the set the whole time she was there—that wonder of wonders. And now she wouldn't even have the magazines. Tears sprang from her eyes and she sobbed out the words.

"If it turns out to be true after all, I'll have to stop subscribing after this month. You'd better take my name off the list."

"What, cancel all five?" Dona Carmosina knew the answer, but she asked the question anyway. How could Elisa live without her movie magazines?

"Yes, all five."

Dona Carmosina rose magnificently to the occasion. These were the times that tried the soul of a true friend.

"No, not all five! I'll pay for two of them anyway, out of my commission. I won't have you going without a single one."

Elisa was touched by the gesture, but reality broke through.

"Thank you, Carmosina, you're so good. But in the first place I can't let you do it, and in the second place you're not so rich you have money to throw away."

"This is all guesswork anyway. Why, Tieta's probably just as alive and kicking as you or me." Dona Carmosina, inwardly relieved, quickly substituted encouragement and hope for the rash promise of weekly magazines.

"That's what I tell everybody, that she's just away on a boat trip like she was that other time—"

"A cruise," Dona Carmosina corrected her for the second time.

"But I don't really believe it myself. I can't help thinking she must be dead."

"The worst of it is that the news is all over town. Nobody's talking about anything else. Poor Barbozinha's inconsolable. He was sweet on Tieta before she went away, you know, but he thinks I don't know anything about it. . . ."

"Seu Barbozinha, as old and worn-out as he is?"

"Well, that was almost thirty years ago . . . he was a fine-looking young man then; it's true he was a lot older than she was, and frail. He was never strong. . . . Tieta hadn't any use for boys her own age." She sighed. "How time does fly! You mustn't give up hope. Where's the proof she's dead? I'll have to have proof before I believe it. Well, I'll be going now." She hesitated, her mouth itching with a question. "Are you going to the picture show tonight? I'll come by for you if you like."

"Not tonight. Perpétua's coming over to talk to Astério and me. She's made up some crazy story about an inheritance, but that isn't why I'm not going. . . . You know, I just don't feel like going tonight somehow. I wouldn't enjoy the movie."

"I know what you mean. . . . Inheritance? What on earth do you suppose she means?"

Elisa caught her hand beseechingly. "Oh, Carmô, if you could go to the movies tomorrow instead and come back here tonight, I'd be so grateful! I think we all would, even Perpétua. You know about these kinds of things."

"Well, I will then, if you want me to. I'll gobble my supper down and see to a few things at home and be back in a jiffy."

She certainly would! No film was worth missing such a treat. What on earth could that story about an inheritance signify? Perpétua was no fool. Besides, her duty as a friend demanded that she be at Elisa's side in her hour of need. Duty and pleasure were thus agreeably combined; Agreste was short on entertainment, even for the postmistress.

Too bad it was Saturday and movie day. The films came from Esplanada in the *marineti* and were shown on Saturday night and twice on Sunday, with the matinee at three o'clock. The Saturday showing was attended by the best people in town. Some of them had their own places staked out by custom, and no one else ever sat there; the chairs in which Modesto Pires and his wife, Dona Aida, sat, for instance, and Carol's, two rows behind them. The matinee, full of screaming children, was impossible: every time the sheriff shot or punched somebody there was a deafening roar, and every time the hero kissed the girl he brought the house down. At the Sunday-evening show the din was just as loud. That was the third and last showing, for which Chalita the Arab peddled tickets according to what he thought the film was worth. If the public had been indifferent the day before, he sold admission for almost nothing; at the box-office successes you paid plenty even if you had to stand up. Friendship had its price: tomorrow Dona Carmosina and Dona Milu would brave the Sunday-evening session, with its screeching and clouds of smoke.

Astério, hangdog and whey-faced, came in straight from the store. On Saturdays he always bathed and had his dinner before going off to play pool at the Azores Bar. Today he would have Perpétua for company instead of Aminthas, Seixas, Fidélio and his pal Osnar, a poor trade. Dona Carmosina gazed at him pityingly, thinking what a dishrag he was.

"How are you this evening, Astério? I'm going home now but I'll be back for the debate."

"What debate?"

"About Tieta."

"Oh, yes! Tieta! It's all mighty peculiar if you ask me. I just can't figure it out."

The light from the street lamps, which had been lit at dusk, barely reached the sidewalk, but the full moon drenched Agreste with honey and molten gold, shining on the streets and the river, the road and the paths, and the last market-goers on their way home to their little farms.

Of the sensational clash between Perpétua and Carmosina, with the former holding her own in the first round.

"You say it was Dr. Almiro who said it? Well, he ought to know. I never would have thought of that." Astério pricked up his ears and began to pay attention to the talk, his aches and pains soothed and his stomach appeased.

He was lying stretched out on the couch, and if his sister-in-law and Dona Carmosina hadn't been there he would have been in bed with the covers up to his chin; he had been feeling bad ever since Elisa made a sign to him in the store and he understood there was still no letter and no check. He felt so sick he hadn't touched his rice or fried banana, nothing but coffee with milk and a thin slice of bread and curds. Stomach cramps hurt him so much he could hardly stand it.

Perpétua arrived a little before seven, leaving Ricardo at his homework. On Monday the boy would go back to the seminary to take his written and oral exams. At the end of term Father Mariano, who had gone to Aracaju for a few days, had brought his godson back for a weekend at home with the proviso that he study hard for his exams. If he failed, that would be the end of his free schooling, Perpétua had warned him for the umpteenth time before she went out. As for Peto, he had sneaked out and gone to the movies, the limb of Satan. He saw every single movie three times and never paid because he helped the Arab sell tickets. There's no such thing as censorship in Agreste; anyone of any age can see any film. Mothers nursed their babies right in the moviehouse, where Peto, who had yet to reach his thirteenth birthday, was learning more than seventeen-year-old Ricardo would ever learn in the seminary classrooms. He picked up information at the movies, on the riverbank where he spent most of the day fishing and watching what went on, and at the Azores Bar, where he was a one-man claque for his Uncle Astério in the evenings. When Osnar won he treated the boy to *guaraná* or ice cream or Coca-Cola. Peto could already handle a billiard cue. Osnar, the wag and rake, liked to tease him. "What about that other stick down there, Sergeant Peto? Can you get off a good shot, do you think? It's about time you learned."

No sooner had Perpétua taken a seat in the rush chair, the best in the room, than a loud clapping and Dona Carmosina's sonorous "Yoo-hoo!" resounded through the house. Perpétua scowled. What had the postmistress forgotten that was so special she was willing to miss her sacred Saturday-night picture show? Pushing herself forward where she wasn't wanted, putting her oar in, with her reasoning and her hunches and her canny shrewdness, the smarty-pants. Elisa rushed to welcome her friend.

"Perpétua just got here."

Without waiting for an invitation, Dona Carmosina took the floor and launched right into the matter at hand.

"It's all over town; nobody's talking about anything else. Just as soon as I got home Mother asked me, 'What's all this about Antonieta? I heard tell she's dead.' 'Nobody knows a thing,' I said to her, 'just that the letter with the money she sends every month hasn't come yet.' Mother opened her eyes wide, I can tell you. 'It hasn't? Then she's dead sure enough, she'd have to be not to keep her word. I knew that girl as well as I do you, and once she made her mind up no advice, threat or punishment could make her change it. You take my word for it; if she's stopped sending the money it's because she's no longer in the land of the living. You go on over there, child, and give them my condolences!'" There was a pause. Dona Carmosina added, "The buzzing in the streets is getting louder and louder."

Why, that snoop had come on purpose; she'd rather gab than go to the movies. In fact, Elisa had probably asked her to come.

Perpétua bit her lip and touched the crucifix of her rosary in the pocket of her black skirt. Never mind, maybe she could help; the hateful thing spent the whole day doing nothing but reading magazines and newspapers, whole long articles; she knew all kinds of things and showed off all she knew. Well, Perpétua had no doubt about what had happened.

"She's kicked the bucket! I've been telling Elisa that ever since yesterday, but she wants to fool herself and other people too."

"She's ignoring the evidence, you mean," Dona Carmosina corrected her.

Perpétua would not stand for such exhibitions of superior wisdom. All that restrained her was a wail from Astério, huddled in the depths of the couch: "Oh, no! Are you folks saying she's dead? Antonieta's dead? Oh, say it ain't so!"

Elisa felt sorry for her husband; the poor devil had had such a shock. This was the first time the possibility of his sister-in-law's death had occurred to him. He had thought of a letter gone astray, of temporary financial difficulties—even the wealthy have their ups and downs—of Elisa's plausible explanation of a trip. Sickness and death had never crossed his mind. Perpétua's statement fell on top of him like a ton of lead.

"Arrgh!" he moaned, clutching his stomach, his face a grimace of pain.

"You're the only one in Agreste who doesn't know she's dead, and your wife's the only one who doubts it." Perpétua's rasping voice turned the knife in the wound.

Dona Carmosina jumped again into the fray.

"We haven't any proof yet. Only suppositions."

Perpétua, a pitiless adversary, flung Dona Milu's ammunition in her daughter's face:

"What more proof do you want than the fact she hasn't written? Didn't you hear what your mother said? She's right: when Antonieta makes up her mind to do something, she does it come hell or high water. I ought to know."

"There's no question about that," Dona Carmosina conceded grudgingly. "Suppositions backed up by facts, but suppositions nevertheless."

"This'll be the end of us," moaned Astério, as the dimensions of their misfortune began to sink in. "What are we going to live on, if she's dead?"

Elisa, struggling to hold back her tears, went to fetch a glass of water and a pill.

"Take this, Astério, it's your stomach medicine."

"Oh Lord, what are we going to do?" The pill fell from Astério's hand. Elisa and Dona Carmosina scrabbled on the tiled floor and found it. Elisa put it in her husband's mouth and handed him the water.

"There won't be any money for medicine, either." Astério gulped.

Dona Carmosina nodded sadly. They were in a fix, for sure. Not Perpétua so much; she had the rented houses and money stashed away. But Elisa and Astério lived from hand to mouth off the wretched stock of the little store and the meager earnings it brought in on Saturdays. Dona Carmosina tried to put these considerations aside; they were insignificant details compared to the awful looming reality of Tieta's death. They had been good friends, childhood and girlhood chums; Tieta's confidences had been whispered to her long ago. But insignificant? Not with the price of rouge and lipstick, mascara and nail polish, and five movie magazines a week—and Elisa had forgotten to pay for the ones that came today. She had talked about getting the money, but she hadn't. If it turned out that Tieta was dead, Dona Carmosina wouldn't have the heart to remind Elisa of her debt and would just have to pay for them herself. It was times like these that tried the bonds of friendship.

But now Perpétua puffed out her bosom; the bun seemed to rise higher on the back of her head and her nasal voice grew stronger. "She's dead and we're her heirs."

There it was at last—the business of the inheritance. Every one of Dona Carmosina's antennae was aquiver. Astério, writhing in agony, could not take it in.

"What'd you say? Heirs? How's that?"

His interruption gave Dona Carmosina just enough time to review her knowledge of jurisprudence and put on her lawyer's gown.

"Hum! You may be right. Married, but no children . . . the relatives inherit . . . I've read something about that, let me see . . ."

Witheringly, Perpétua explained it all.

"The other day I was talking to Dr. Almiro when he was here to see about Seu Lito's will. The husband gets half and the close relatives, father, mother, sisters and brothers, get the other half. Whether the dead person wanted them to have it or not."

It was at that point in the conversation that Astério's pain diminished and his stomach settled down. He pleaded for reassurance:

"Did Dr. Almiro say that? Well, he ought to know what he's talking about."

Of the second round, a victory for Dona Carmosina, the post-office champion.

Not even Dona Carmosina, taken by surprise as she was, could deny that Perpétua had scored a goal. She attested to the truth of the legal theory, all the while displaying the suspiciously innocent smile of one who has the deck stacked in her favor and the winning cards in her hand.

"Well, isn't that something? You'll be rich overnight. Half for Zé Esteves, half for you two girls. All you have to do now is find the husband, don't you?"

"Exactly." Perpétua was leading the discussion now, and even the postmistress listened attentively. "We never did know her husband's full name. Just Felipe, as if he hadn't had a father. Rich, that we do know, and a Comendador. But Felipe what? What kind of business was he in? Did he have a papal or a government title? I always thought that was peculiar, but I discovered an explanation for it a long time ago."

"Well, what explanation did you discover?"

Knowing they were all hanging on her words, Perpétua hid her vanity in a voice that was as sibilant and harsh on the ear as ever, overnight heiress or not.

"Her husband wouldn't let her tell us anything about him. He didn't ever want to have to account to us for anything. That was the reason; there isn't any other."

"Do you think so?" Dona Carmosina was plainly skeptical.

Elisa spoke up. "She was ashamed of us, that's what, and afraid that the more we knew about her husband, the more we'd try to take advantage of them." As far as Elisa was concerned, all the vileness and shameful motives were on her side, Astério's, Perpétua's, her father's. Tieta and her clan were rich, virtuous, above reproach.

"Maybe so." Dona Carmosina seemed to be weighing, measuring, comparing one argument with another.

"Well, for whatever reason she did it, I intend to get my share even if I have to follow him to the ends of the earth." Perpétua, looming larger and larger in her chair, did not trouble to answer Elisa. "I'll find out where he lives and burst in on him when he least expects me. Nobody's going to do me out of what belongs to me and my children."

"You went to see Father Mariano today, didn't you? What did he tell you?"

"He said not to be hasty about it, that we haven't any proof yet that Antonieta's dead, and that we ought to wait awhile. I say let anyone wait who wants to, not me! I'm going to Esplanada first thing Monday morning and talk to Dr. Rubim."

"To the district judge?" Dona Carmosina nodded in apparent agreement. Her small, half-closed eyes darted a glance at Astério and Elisa and settled on the imposing figure of Perpétua, puffed up in her chair like a bullfrog. Forgive me for robbing you of your hopes, Elisa, you and Astério deserve better, but I just can't stand the presumption of that high and mighty know-it-all showing off her secondhand knowledge another minute. "Yes, I always thought there was something funny about our not being told Tieta's husband's last name. But I came to a different conclusion from yours."

Perpétua was not daunted by the competition.

"Let's hear it."

"You, Perpétua, forgot to take certain facts, or should I say clues, into account. She told you she had stepdaughters, didn't she?"

"Yes, we know his family gets half."

"I'm not talking about the inheritance. There is no inheritance."

"What?"

"Don't say that!" implored Astério, all his aches and pains coming back.

"I'm sorry to disillusion you, Astério, but if you all will just think for a minute, if you'll use your little gray cells, you'll realize that Tieta lives, or rather lived, with this titled gentleman without being legally married to him. Just like thousands of other couples in Brazil, he's separated from his first wife and can't legally marry again. That's the only logical explanation there is, and if it's the right one, then only his legal family has a right to inherit."

"Ohh!" A heartfelt moan from Astério as he saw his dream castle crumble and his wealth fade away like the illusion it was, and himself poor as Job again.

In which the churchmouse champion rallies and
wins another round, and her adversary is
saved by the bell.

Perpétua was the only one not to change expression, unless the slight pinch of her lips could be called a smile.

"It's a clever theory, I'll grant you that. But it won't hold water."

"Do you have a better one?"

"Yes, mine is a better one, and I have proof."

"What sort of proof?"

"Proof that she was wed in holy matrimony by church and state. There's no question about it, and I can prove it."

"Let's see you do it." There was a slight note of uncertainty in Dona Carmosina's voice.

Elisa was in tears. Astério—rich man, poor man, rich man, poor—could not make up his mind whether his stomach hurt or not. From the depths of her purse Perpétua extracted an envelope, and from the envelope a clipping.

"Carmosina, you read other people's newspapers all the time, but you didn't read this one." Aid from above was worth boasting about: "When someone is devoted to St. Anne and thinks of the church more than of herself, that person can count on the grace and protection of God."

"Get to the point, can't you?" Even Astério, who was usually afraid to open his mouth when his sister-in-law was around, had had enough. "Spit it out!"

Perpétua, clipping in hand, was in no hurry:

"I went to Aracaju not two months ago to kiss Dom José the Bishop's hand and ask him about how Ricardo was getting along in his studies. Since I had to go there anyway I paid a call on Dona Nícia, Dr. Simões the banker's wife—"

"You went to sell her dresses Tieta had sent."

"The few you left for me. Better to sell 'em than put 'em on my back. Big-city women can flaunt themselves if they want to, but not here. . . . Be that as it may, Dona Nícia showed me a São Paulo paper, the society page, where they wrote about a lady friend of hers who had gone to visit some relatives. She pointed to an item and said, 'I think this is about your sister,' and then she cut it out and gave it to me."

She slowly put on her glasses and held the clipping up to the light. Astério rose from his chair. Elisa moved to a chair closer to her sister's. No one wanted to miss a word.

At that very moment there were loud voices at the street door.

"Calm down, old man!"

"Like hell I will! Lemme at that bunch of thieves and robbers!"

Old Zé Esteves strode into the room, followed by Tonha. Planted firmly on his two legs, an angry scowl on his face, he brandished his stick and bellowed:

"Gimme my money, you swindlers! Where is it? What have you done with it? Tieta sends me that money and you rob me blind! Did you think I'd believe that rigmarole about her being dead and that's why the money ain't here? You pack of thieves! I want my money and I want it now!"

In which Perpétua takes over as the head of the family, after felling Dona Carmosina with a knockout blow.

"Your blessing, Father!" Perpétua said tranquilly from her chair. "Would you be good enough to sit down, please, and Mother Tonha too, and I'll tell you the news about Antonieta and her husband."

"Is she alive or is she not? What damnfool story is this about her dying? That's all I've been hearing. More than a dozen people have come over to tell me the news."

"Everything seems to point that way, Father. And if she's dead—"

"We'll be rich, Seu Zé. Filthy rich," interrupted Astério, cured of his stomach cramps.

Dona Carmosina pulled herself together.

"Seu Zé, Perpétua was about to read a story from a São Paulo newspaper that tells about Tieta."

Tonha sat down but the old man stayed on his feet.

"Well, let's hear it then."

Holding the clipping to the light again, Perpétua cleared her throat and informed them before starting to read:

"I made a note of the date of the newspaper. September eleventh, not three months ago."

"Two months and seventeen days." No one paid any attention to Dona Carmosina's finicky exactitude.

" 'Comendador Felipe de Almeida Couto,' " Perpétua read deliberately, " 'and his wife Antonieta have invited their numerous friends and admirers to a thanksgiving mass commemorating their fifteen years of marriage, to be celebrated in the Cathedral Church by Father Eugênio Melo, the same priest who married them. That night Antonieta and Felipe will open the doors of their mansion and welcome their friends with their customary lavish hospitality. Minister Lima Filho, who was then a judge and performed the civil ceremony, will come from Brasília especially for the party. Champagne corks will pop far into the night and there will be dancing and a midnight supper!' "

The clipping passed from hand to hand and everyone heaved a sigh of relief.

Perpétua stared at Dona Carmosina defiantly. "Well, what do you say to that?"

It was Elisa who answered, her voice throbbing with hurt feelings. "You mean you knew her husband's name all this time and didn't say a word about it?" Elisa was thinking of the mass in the cathedral, the mansion, the banquet, the champagne corks popping.

"Yes, I've known for more than two months. Why on earth should I have told you?"

"I'll go with you to Esplanada to talk to the judge," proposed Astério elatedly.

"Talk to the judge? What for?" demanded Zé Esteves.

"To ask him about the inheritance. Half of it's ours."

"That's right, Father," Perpétua explained. "His family gets half and the other half belongs to Antonieta's family, to us."

"Well, I'm going too. I want to get this business straight."

"Nobody else has to go. It'll be better if I go by myself. That way I can speak for the whole family and there won't be any mixup. Then we can decide what to do, with no outside interference."

The defeated Carmosina was banished.

"Just the family." Bolt upright in her chair, bosom jutting out and topknot riding high on her head, Perpétua assumed her rightful place as head of the family.

Of Tieta's death and burial, complete with sermon and surprising revelations about Father Mariano, with Nephew Ricardo at the thurible.

Tieta died and was buried that weekend in Sant'Ana do Agreste amid almost universal mourning, although not everyone in town wept at the premature wake. The news passed the gates of Tapitanga Fazenda, and even yanked Colonel Artur from his Sunday doze and brought him out into Agreste's streets in affliction. Zé Esteves' flock had prospered and increased as long as that gal Tieta looked after it. As long as she was around those fat nannygoats were always dropping kids.

It was a time of tears and prayers, grief and threats, condolences and praise, schemes, counterschemes and ordinary townspeople paying their respects. Some spiteful folk, particularly those who still bore scars from Zé Esteves' malice and cunning, hardly troubled to hide their satisfaction at seeing the old scoundrel's undeserved life on Easy Street coming to an end.

"When he has to live off Perpétua's leavings he'll find out what's good, I *don't* think. He'll get what's coming to him now, and high time, too."

"That's what you think. *Now* that old son of a bitch is gonna be a rich man. There ain't no justice in this world."

"Spell that out for me, will you? I don't follow you."

"His family stands to inherit a big pile of money, and half of it belongs to him."

Now the old gossips, who had been around forever because death so rarely bothered to visit that remote neck of the woods, once more disinterred Tieta's lost maidenhead and other long-buried sins and peccadilloes.

"I still remember that beating. The old man lived in a house on the square not far from us. He caught her coming home just before daylight and lit into her so hard he broke that stick over her back."

"Well, if you ask me, she deserved it. She was a scandalous, shameless hussy. Even did it with married men."

"Just look at Seu Barbozinha's grieving face, the picture of sorrow."

"They say he never could stop thinking about her and that's why he never married."

"Do they? I wouldn't be surprised. And what do you all know about this inheritance thing?"

"Shh! Here comes Perpétua."

Woebegone faces and tearful eyes follow Perpétua as she crosses Cathedral Square. Bust like the prow of a ship, black Spanish comb thrust in the crest of her bun—she hadn't worn that comb since the Major's death; he had given it to her as a present—and wearing the same dress she had worn at her husband's funeral, she nevertheless looks younger than the young woman she was in her twenties. Already old in her black mantilla and already a sanctimonious old maid despite her youth, the most self-righteous prig, the most bigoted bigot, she had gone to her father and tattled on her sister: "She jumps out of the window every single night to meet that traveling salesman down by the river. Everyone's talking about it and she's dragging our name in the dirt."

They flock to Perpétua and enfold her in a chorus of praise for the dear departed, the wonderful daughter and sister who has kept her family out of the poorhouse all these years and is now going to make them rich. How many masses will she say for her sister's soul? God has certainly forgiven her for those sins long ago redeemed by charity and an honest life.

Even those who most persistently recalled Tieta's misdeeds admitted that she had the attributes of a good heart: loving-kindness, laughter and pleasure in helping others, not to mention her grace and beauty; the face of an angel and a voluptuous body, alas, made for love. Dona Milu summed it all in one sentence: "She never did a mean thing in her life, and the good she did can't be measured."

She was the good daughter, who forgot her resentment to be the mainstay of parents and sisters, even though her mother was only a stepmother and her younger sister only a half-sister—which made her conduct even more meritorious and lent added luster to each coin. And the source of all this was São Paulo, the huge metropolis where Antonieta had made good and found herself a rich, famous husband, a Comendador, a tycoon, a Paulista with a four-hundred-year-old name and money to burn. She had put Sant'Ana do Agreste on the map.

A native son who had gone to Rio de Janeiro and eventually become the owner of a bakery in Cascadura was loyal enough to his hometown and its patron saint to christen his establishment "Sant'Ana do Agreste Bakery," and he had sent his relatives pictures taken on opening day. Lots of pictures but not a leaf of the green stuff—it seemed his wife was a skinflint and wouldn't let him share. A handful of other citizens won a name for themselves in the state capital, with De Matos Barbosa at the head of the list. The poet's full name, Gregório Eustáquio de Matos Barbosa, had been shortened to Barbozinha by his fellow citizens, who took pride for the most part in the verses and philosophy of the former municipal functionary and bohemian whose memory lingered at the café tables of Salvador da Bahia until the cafés were torn down. Skipper Dário de Queluz could boast of an even richer curriculum vitae, but his fondness for the climate of Agreste and the spectacular scenery of Mangue Seco had decided him to retire from the navy early and settle down for good in his native place with his wife, Dona Laura, a fine southern girl who adapted to local ways in no time. The couple could more often be found roughing it at Liberty Hall, a rustic cabin set among coconut palms next to Mangue Seco's dunes, than in the modest bungalow in town where the Skipper's masks, boats and figures of saints and animals piled up higher and higher. As if his enviable military rank and the saga of his travels were not enough (he had even visited Japan), the Skipper had accumulated still more acclaim as an artisan and was generally deemed a full-fledged artist. He and Barbozinha were undoubtedly the *crème de la crème*. Speaking of culture, we should perhaps add Dona Carmosina Sluizer da Consolação's name to the others because she knows so much about so many different things. On the other hand, she's never been out of Agreste except for short trips to Esplanada and therefore lacks the polish that only life in a big city can provide. Among the chosen few who had done well in the outside world, Dr. João Augusto de Faria, a pharmacist in Aracaju, should not be forgotten. And that's the list, since Ascânio Trindade had quit law school in his second year and never graduated.

No one, neither poet, naval officer, pharmacist nor Rio baker, had flown so high nor triumphed so signally nor raised the name of the obscure, dying little backwater town of Sant'Ana do Agreste to such heights of fame and glory as Antonieta Esteves, luminary of São Paulo high society, the only one among them all to flaunt a fortune, spend money like water and get her name printed in the newspapers of the prosperous south.

Aminthas, Osnar, Seixas and Fidélio rested their cues.

"What did you say her husband's name was? Matarazzo?"

"No, no, no. It's a traditional Portuguese name, one of these four-hundred-year-old ones. Perpétua can tell you."

"Prado, maybe?"

"No, I'm pretty sure it's a double name, one of those first-family names."

"Astério's gonna be in clover now."

Those Paulistas don't give a damn, they'd just as soon marry a girl with a hole in her as not. Customs vary from place to place; even today in Agreste and adjacent parts, a girl had better watch her P's and Q's if she wants to catch a husband, and not many marry even so. Most of the men go south to look for work, and all that's left for the women is their churchgoing, their kitchens, their patchwork quilts and crochet, their long days and restless nights.

In Rio and São Paulo it's a different story. You don't have to be a virgin to get married, that's just an old-fashioned prejudice. And the fashion's sweeping the country; if you've got a hole, the pill will plug it up. That fashion, however, has yet to reach the banks of the Rio Real. Had Tieta stayed in Agreste she never would have caught a husband, but in São Paulo, who cares whether a girl still has her maidenhead or not? Beauty, intelligence, style, class and wit are what count down there. None of these good qualities was denied Tieta during the weekend when virtually the whole town mourned her death. You might say they made her a saint before they buried her, so to speak.

By vespers on Sunday, no one shared Elisa's frail hope that Tieta was away on a trip, having a high old time in New York or Paris or St. Tropez or Bariloche; not even Elisa. She was inconsolable and had to be supported by her husband and Dona Carmosina, one on either side. When Father Mariano blessed the people, not wishing to take the responsibility for bad news that had yet to be confirmed, he nonetheless dwelt with pathos on the sad account of Tieta's demise that was circulating in the streets. He lauded the purity of heart of one who, having won material wealth in this world, had remembered her estranged family and her birthplace.

Visibly moved, he revealed to the faithful that it had been Antonieta, and not an anonymous parishioner as he had said at the time, who had donated the magnificent plaster image of Our Lady St. Anne, enthroned with such jubilant rejoicing three years before to take the place of the worm-eaten old wooden image that he had gotten rid of as soon as the new one came.

So it seemed that Father Mariano, too, shared a secret with Tieta; and with Dona Carmosina, of course. Like the postmistress and Nephew Ricardo, he too had sent a petition by stealth. Standing beside Elisa, Dona Carmosina smiled. If she'd had her druthers she'd be back there talking it over with the boys, but friendship has its obligations. Tieta's nephew wept before the altar in his fine vestments, the white skirt and red robe, as he shook the thurible, releasing a strong odor of incense: incense was good enough for the servants of God; there would be no more perfumed envelopes for him.

"What a handsome altarboy," murmured lustful Cinira, on the verge of irrevocable spinsterhood, feeling a shameful itching in her private parts.

"Heavenly!" Dona Edna smacked her lips from a kneeling position on the other side of the church, next to Terto, who was her lawful wedded husband but didn't act like it.

Ricardo, enveloped in a cloud of incense, heard the Reverend Father's praise of his elderly aunt. He thought of her white hair, wrinkles and trembling hands; she would be more like a grandmother than an aunt. She was modest and retiring, too; the generous donor had stipulated that her name not be revealed. Only now when such mournful news was abroad did Father Mariano break his promise and speak up so that all the faithful devotees of Our Lady St. Anne might join him in prayer for the health of this pious daughter of Agreste, beseeching God that the tragic news would turn out to be a false alarm and that Dona Antonieta was enjoying perfect health.

Some of his hearers did pray for the repose of her soul; none thought for a minute that she was in perfect health.

A postscript about the old image.

At no time did Father Mariano say a word about the fate of the old statue. And that was just as well, for the new Cardinal is bent on looking into the whereabouts of the valuable old sculptured figures of the saints which have been stolen from churches or sold to antique dealers and collectors.

Who could really blame the Father, who had acted in good faith? To him that image was nothing but a rotten, weatherbeaten old piece of wood, in dilapidated condition and utterly useless; he hadn't thrown it on the dump heap only because it had been consecrated centuries before. But when the artist showed up, lured by the fame of Mangue Seco's beauty, and caught sight of the dethroned image of the patron saint lying neglected in a corner of the sacristy and offered enough money for it to buy a new thurible, Father Mariano did not hesitate for a moment. The new incense burner, a lovely sight in Ricardo's hands as the fragrant incense curled about the image of Our Lady St. Anne—the brand-new, shiny plaster image, painted in bright beautiful colors, a real work of art—had been duly bought with the money that rotten old piece of wood had brought. The artist had explained that it was a question of devotion: St. Anne was his favorite saint in all the Kingdom of Heaven, and any article that had to do with her, devoid though it might be of material value as in the case of this old image, enriched his soul, and that was why he was leaving such a goodly sum as an offering to the church. Only close friends of Carybé the artist know what a plausible liar he can be. I could tell a great many stories about him if I cared to, none of them edifying.

Today the old image, restored to its pristine beauty, is on view in the famous collection of another celebrated artist, Mirabeau Sampaio. How it came to be there I can well imagine, but would rather not say. The bargains these gentlemen make among themselves are even lower and more immoral than the one Dona Carmosina struck with Canuto Tavares, unmasked by me a few chapters back.

Of resurrection and mourning.

Tieta was resurrected at exactly five-twenty on Tuesday afternoon, and not until then did it occur to her family to put on mourning. In their preoccupation with the nonarrival of the check and their dreams of an inheritance, they had neither had time for mourning nor felt any need for it. She was dead and that was the end of it. What use would it be for her relatives to dress in black? A seventh-day mass for the repose of her soul was only fitting, of course. A thirty-day mass, even, if all that money materialized.

On Tuesday the *marineti* was late, though no later than usual; two flat tires and the motor sputtering and dying every few kilometers, nothing out of the ordinary, but it kept Dona Carmosina from opening the mail sack until late afternoon.

Perpétua came back in the same bus from Esplanada, where she had gone the day before with Ricardo, who took another bus from there to Aracaju. The judge received her after supper, and after their talk he congratulated her on her zeal in defending the interests of her children, father and sister. "I don't want anything for myself, Your Honor, but I'm ready to fight to the death for the rights of my children and my sister and my old father." So poor, so alone, yet how unselfish! The judge was impressed, and his wife, Dona Guta, was so carried away that she plied the brave widow with manioc cake and wild-cherry cordial.

Perpétua brought back with her much new knowledge and advice. In São Paulo, the judge had informed her, she could easily find a lawyer to take the case in exchange for a share of the profits; that is, if the outcome was as promising as it appeared to be. Those experienced lawyers charge an arm and a leg, naturally. What percentage of the profits? I can't tell you that exactly; it might be as high as forty or fifty percent. Forty or fifty percent? But, Judge, that's outrageous! My dear lady, since it's their own money they're risking, they want a high profit in exchange; that's only fair. Newspapers in the south print ads for law firms that bring suit on that basis. Some even specialize in lost causes, but in those lawsuits the percentage may go as high as seventy or eighty percent.

Dr. Rubim read the story in the newspaper again. "Yes, ma'am, the Almeida Coutos are a very fine family. They come of good stock and have money galore and a coat of arms."

If the facts in the case were correct, as Dona Perpétua assured him they were, a favorable verdict was a foregone conclusion. In fact, there would probably be no need to bring suit at all; people like that would rather settle out of court than be involved in legal battles. All Perpétua and her family needed was a good lawyer. "God will repay you, Your Honor, for so generously giving of your time to a poor widow; please consider me your humble servant." As soon as she got back she'd settle with the old man and Astério how much each should chip in for her trip. She'd leave Peto with Elisa and take Ricardo with her; his school holidays began in a week. In Esplanada she had made inquiries about the price of the bus trip to São Paulo and found out there was a bus that left from Feira de Sant'Ana. Neither the expense of the ticket and the journey, nor the distance, nor the perils of the great city daunted her. True, she had never gone to Salvador with the Major as they had planned—Perpétua's heart ached when she remembered that plan. Still, she had gone to Aracaju by herself to talk to the Bishop and thank him for enrolling Ricardo in the seminary, hadn't she? After that first time she had gone back more than once. It wasn't so dangerous, was it? São Paulo was bigger, a great modern metropolis, but it couldn't be *so much* bigger and so much scarier than Aracaju, which was plenty big enough.

Perpétua was still in the bathtub trying to scrub off the dust when Dona Carmosina opened the registered mail pouch. There was only one letter in it: Antonieta's. Shouting hallelujah, Carmosina left the other mail unsorted and rushed out the door and down the street to Elisa's house, waving the letter in her hand like a banner unfurled.

"Elisa, it's come, it's come!"

"Oh, thank God!"

They tore open the envelope. There was the check and sensational news: somebody *had* died, there was no smoke without fire. But it was the Comendador, not Tieta, and he wasn't any Almeida

Couto with a coat of arms and a family who had lived in São Paulo for four hundred years. He was a rich São Paulo industrialist, though: Comendador Felipe Cantarelli, "my dear departed husband, who was almost a father to me, too, and whose passing has left me an inconsolable widow." To console herself and see her family again, maybe even buy a house in town or some land on the beach, preferably near Mangue Seco, Antonieta announced her imminent arrival. One day she intended to warm her old bones and wait for death in the mild climate of Agreste. She would let them know the day and would bring her stepdaughter Leonora, Felipe's daughter by his first wife.

"She's coming, Carmosina! She's coming to see us! Isn't that wonderful?" Elisa felt reborn herself.

Hurriedly summoned, the whole family came running: Father and Tonha, Astério with his faithful cronies from the bar, Perpétua dragging Peto by the ear.

Dona Carmosina stood before them and gravely read out the letter in a ringing voice, as if she were the head of the family. Astério took possession of the check to get it cashed.

As she listened, Perpétua swallowed all the judge's information and advice, the trip to São Paulo, the inheritance; with Antonieta alive and a millionaire widow, the picture had changed and she would have to adapt. Perpétua rose from the ashes of her former plans, and staring hard at each of the family in turn, decreed, "The deceased, whoever he was, is our relative, our son-in-law, brother-in-law and uncle. We must have a mass said for his soul and put on mourning. When our dear sister arrives she must find all of us dressed in black, grieving right along with her. I know what she's going through; I know what bereavement is."

Dona Carmosina didn't know but could readily imagine. To roll over in the double bed at night and not find the comforting body of your man, the husband who had once shared your bed, what dreadful loneliness! The only thing worse was an old maid's loneliness, the loneliness without measure of not having even the memory of how good it had once felt not to be alone.

SECOND EPISODE

❧ ❧ ❧

Of Two Paulistas
Happy to Be
in Sant'Ana do Agreste,
or
the Merry Widow

WITH DEEP MOURNING, A REQUIEM MASS, A CATECHISM
CLASS, MINISKIRTS AND TRANSPARENT CAFTANS, SWIMMING
IN THE RIVER, MANGUE SECO'S BEACHES AND SAND DUNES,
DIVERS INTRIGUES, PETIT-BOURGEOIS DREAMS AND MATERIAL
AMBITIONS, THIGHS, TITS AND NAVELS, DINNERS AND
EXCURSIONS, RECIPES, THE BURNING QUESTION OF ELECTRIC
POWER, PRAYERS AND TEMPTATIONS, FEAR OF GOD AND THE
SNARES OF THE DEVIL, A CHASTE IDYLL AND ANOTHER NOT SO
CHASTE; IN WHICH WE MAKE THE ACQUAINTANCE OF AN
ANCIENT PROPHET, POSSIDÔNIO THE FANATIC. ROMANTIC
DIALOGUES AND SEXY SCENES TO MAKE UP FOR THEM.

*First fragment of a narrative in which, during
the overnight bus ride from São Paulo to Bahia,
Tieta reminisces to the fair Leonora Cantarelli
about her past life. Here is a sample; other,
more telling episodes will follow.*

"I don't think the goats even felt the heat of the sun. Not the nice warm sun we have down south but that blazing white-hot sun beating on the stones. And I didn't feel it any more than they did."

The goats stood motionless on the stony ground under the weight of the sun; they were like stone statues themselves. Suddenly they would leap and run off, first one, then another, then all of them, seeking out tufts of grass on the highest hills.

"I'd follow after, herding the goats. They all knew me; I had a name and a nickname for every one. I'd call and they'd come running. I took good care of them, too; whenever one of them hurt herself on the thorns, I'd put a gooseberry poultice on the hurt place."

"How old were you, Mama?"

"Oh, I must have been about ten years old when I started, ten or eleven. I was just out of grammar school."

She had chosen the sun baking the rocks, the dry land, the cacti, the snakes, the lizards, the frogs croaking in the creek, the bald knolls of the hills, the clumps of grass and the goats, leaving the housekeeping to her older sister.

"Perpétua was old the day she was born. I don't know how she ever got a man to marry her. She shut herself up in the church with those pious old women when she was still a teenager; when it came to psalm-singing she outdid 'em all. I was the devil in person, as far as she was concerned." She laughed. "She was right, too, I was a demon child. I had watched old Inácio the ram mount the nannies when I was just a little kid."

Serene, majestic, ungelded, the ram Inácio, father of the flock, comes stalking up with his goat stink and his flowing goatee. Lord of the herd, patriarch of the goats, with balls so big they almost drag on the ground.

Slowly, inexorably, he approaches the fidgety young female in first heat, her hindquarters wriggling as he approaches, hind legs kicking in the air, ready to be covered and quickened. Drawn by the new female smell, Inácio walks up to her with testicles swinging and lets out a sharp clarion bleat—a warning, a threat, a declaration of love.

"I didn't pay any attention to him at first, I was too young. But later on, when my period came, that bleat of Inácio's got right inside me, and I started to watch what happened next. I used to lie down on the ground so I could see better."

The she-goat takes off like a shot. Inácio does not deign to run after her but only stands still and waits. That little goat will learn. He'll let her get away with it once or twice more and then mount the runaway whenever he wants to—the master, the father of the flock.

Lying on the ground, the young girl watches fascinated, not wanting to miss a thing. Prone on the barren ground, she feels a warmth rising from her legs to her gullet, a weakness and lassitude, a pulling toward something. Inácio is a big ram and a powerful one; the female struggles when he makes her a nanny and leaves his seed inside her. One last bleat of pain and acceptance echoes deep inside the little girl's womb. Nanny and billygoat couple on the high rocks, petrified, a split rock joined together, cliff and capricorn.

"That's how I learned. But I saw more than that before I ever began. Much more."

It wasn't only the ram Inácio who mounted the goats. Hidden on the hills, she had watched young boys lying with them. Osnar, for one, and his disreputable gang. Grown men, too. Her own father, not knowing she was there.

"At home he was the strictest man you ever saw, self-righteous, couldn't enjoy anything himself or let us enjoy it either, sending all of us to bed the minute we got up from the supper table. I couldn't even talk about having a boyfriend."

"Any boyfriend of a daughter of mine is called something else, and this here's a leather strap to beat a donkey with; its full name is

quince tree branch," growled Zé Esteves. He would couple with
the nannygoats when he thought the field was clear. Some of
them liked men better than billygoats. Some she-goats couldn't get
enough.

"And I was a nannygoat, just like the rest. There wasn't a bit of
difference, the first time."

"How old were you, Mama, the first time?"

"Oh, I don't even know. Thirteen, fourteen; my blood came
early."

"And after that?"

"After that I was one of those nannygoats with bad habits who
couldn't get enough. No man could give me enough of what I
wanted."

In which the author composes a brief news story
on Sant'Ana do Agreste's past prosperity and
present-day decline.

While the townspeople talk avidly about the prodigal daughter's
imminent return, the women gossiping at church, the idlers in the
bar, excited speculation at boiling point and the post office in gala
dress, I'll snatch a moment to point out that while Tieta was still on
her way to Bahia her beneficent influence was already being felt in
her hometown and beginning to awaken it from the apathy in
which it had stagnated for so long.

The news stirred not only the townspeople but soon spread
throughout the district, arousing interest and curiosity "from the
river's peaceful banks to the white-capped waves of the Atlantic
Sea," as Barbozinha, in a poetic frenzy, proclaimed in a poem of free
verse and Attic flavor in which Venus, covered with foam and
seashells, was born again and rose naked from the waves; a very
contemporary and quite erotic poem.

There was not a soul indifferent to the news among the whole
population of several thousand—not even Dona Carmosina can tell
us the exact number of inhabitants. In the 1960 census there were a
total of 9,742 citizens, some able-bodied, some not, for there were a

goodly number over ninety years of age and many more over eighty. In the five years since that census was taken the population had gone down, due not to deaths, which were even less frequent than births, but to the constant emigration of young people seeking opportunity elsewhere.

A visitor arriving in those empty streets today, exhausted from his trek in Jairo's *marineti*, covered with dust and making his way to Dona Amorzinho's boardinghouse, will find it hard to believe that before the railroad linking Bahia to Sergipe was laid down, Agreste was a progressive, bustling place, an important distribution center from which goods were dispatched all over the hinterland of both states. Prosperity reigned in those days in what now seems like the end of the earth. The town's privileged location on a river extending to the ocean front had made Sant'Ana do Agreste the supply center for a whole vast region. Ships and schooners anchored outside Mangue Seco bar, and lighters ferried the cargo to Agreste, from where it was carried into the interior by muleback.

Today there is only one boardinghouse, Dona Amorzinho's, where at the turn of the century there were almost a dozen, all permanently overflowing with merchants and traveling salesmen. The shops and stores did so much business they couldn't replenish their stock fast enough, not to mention the bawdy houses, where the nightlife was lively and the money flowed. The best houses in town date from that time, as do the paving stones of Cathedral Square and the downtown streets. The well-to-do families ordered pianos and gramophones and colored portraits from the south to hang in their parlors. They built the two-story courthouse and the new St. Anne's Cathedral, leaving the old chapel for devotions to St. John the Baptist, whose feast day in June, preceded by St. Anthony's and followed by St. Peter's, brought the faithful flocking to Agreste from as far away as Sergipe, along with all the students on a two-week holiday from boarding schools in the capital. It was one party after another in Agreste in June, with dancing and bonfires every night after rosary or novena in the cathedral.

One of the first cities to put in electricity, Agreste was among the last to make do with the wavering, dim yellow light of a tired old generator; the town had yet to bask in the dazzling light brought in from Paulo Afonso Power Plant. It was Ascânio's grandfather, Mayor (and Colonel) Francisco Trindade, who had the generator installed and brought electric light to the then-flourish-ing community. Now his grandson was engaged in a stubborn fight to bring in the high-tension wires from the São Francisco Valley Authority, which, like the railroad and the highway, had passed the district by.

In the past few decades progress had dealt Agreste one blow after another. The first of those was also the worst: the building of the railroad from the capital of Bahia to Sergipe, to the bluffs of the São Francisco River at Propriá, bypassing our little town and leaving it bereft of rapid transportation and a railroad station where the girls could go to flirt. Agreste tried to cling to its coastwise shipping trade, but merchandise could now be transported more conveniently and much more cheaply by freight train. The muletrains were dispersed, the lighters rotted by the mangrove roots. When a ship or schooner did appear, it left only contraband and even that brought no prosperity to Agreste other than the meager profit to the fishermen of Mangue Seco, for the goods were never brought to town at all. The motor launches didn't even stop in Agreste but made straight for the port of Crasto in Sergipe. No one but Elieser anchored in Agreste after delivering the goods, and he came only because he lived there and liked to sleep at home. "Merchandise" was too dignified a name for the occasional bottle of Scotch whisky or English gin or Spanish brandy that Elieser swiped to sell to Aminthas, Seixas or Fidélio, or the flask of perfume that always went to Carol, Modesto Pires' recluse of a lady love. Now that I think of it, that girl ought to grace the pages of this novel more often for our mutual profit and pleasure.

For a long time Agreste pinned its hopes for a return to its old prosperity on a coastal highway, heralded with fanfare as the main artery from south to north. While it waited, Agreste dwindled before the townspeople's eyes and traveling salesmen were no longer seen in the streets; there were not enough orders, not enough stores in business, to justify their coming all that way. The boardinghouses closed. No one came all that distance for the June festivals any more, although the water still worked miracles, the climate was still a health cure in itself, the river still as pretty and wild, windswept Mangue Seco Beach as incomparably beautiful as ever.

The highway, as we already know, was built forty-eight muddy, dusty kilometers away. Reeling from this latest blow from progress, Agreste gave up hope of anything better and resigned itself to planting manioc and herding goats. No steam engine, no trucks, no glimmer of a railroad or bus station where the girls could go to flirt. At the anchorage were half a dozen canoes, Pirica's boat, Elieser's motor launch and a great many fat and sassy crabs. When it comes to eating, there's nothing to compare with scalded crabmeat with dark-green manioc mush—mud mush they call it around here. You've never tried it? That's too bad; you don't know what you've missed. Since the crabmeat must be pried out one claw at a time before this mouthwatering dish can be prepared, and that takes time and patience, it's served less and less often even in Agreste, where they have more time than anything else and know what's good. It's worth the trouble, though, I assure you. It'll make you lick your fingers, and it's meant to be eaten that way, with the fingers, soaking the manioc mush in the rich green sauce, the delectable crab mud.

The town's last hope was gone now, and young people began leaving home for good in Jairo's *marineti*, both young men and girls, for in the past few years women have begun to join the men in trying to find a better life where the pickings are not so slim. They find work cooking or washing or sewing or embroidering, those who don't end up in the red-light districts of Salvador, Aracaju or Feira de Sant'Ana (where they are much appreciated, it is only fair to add).

Of Ascânio Trindade, dauntless fighter and patriot, and the hard row life gave him to hoe.

Ascânio Trindade was the only man who still had the heart to fight on in hope of a miracle that would save Agreste. He loved his birthplace, to which he had been obliged by his father's illness to return, leaving law school when he had completed only half the credits for his degree. There was no longer anything to keep him in Agreste, for Seu Leovigildo had finally died after five interminable, helpless years during which he was confined to his bed, immobile except for one open eye staring into space. Ascânio was the attendant and nursemaid, the father and mother who bathed, wiped and fed the inert body, none of them easy tasks. Rafa, the old black wetnurse, would have helped if she could but was too rheumatic and feeble. Ascânio used to take his father in his arms and carry him out to the yard to lie in the sun under the guava tree, keeping him wordless company for hours on end. Ascânio was endlessly calm and patient, and no one ever heard a word of complaint about his thwarted career or his long time of trial. His father's one eye looked at him gratefully, and that was enough for the son. "The boy has already earned himself a place in heaven," said the pious old women.

After Seu Leovigildo was buried, two years before our story begins, Ascânio could have resigned from his post as county clerk, a job his grandfather, Colonel Artur da Tapitanga, had secured for him so that the penniless young man could care for his paralytic father. But then, why should he resign? To go back to Bahia and law school again? It was not so much lack of means as lack of will that held him back. Astrud was in Bahia, married now, and laughing her unforgettable, gurgling, crystal-clear laugh. "Here in my exile, staggering under the heavy cross of my calvary, I hear your crystal laugh and am filled with strength again; on the dreariest days the recollection of your green eyes sustains me and gives me hope." Dona Carmosina had shed tears over those desecrated letters. How he did love that girl!

All during the first year Ascânio thought of nothing else but going back. When Astrud abruptly announced that she was going to be married, without ever having broken their engagement, he swore an oath never again to set foot in the city where betrayal dwelt, especially after a classmate, Máximo Lima, now a lawyer with a promising career in the Labor Court, informed him that if Astrud the innocent, the immaculate, had not worn a flowing Empire-style bridal gown, it would have been plain to see from the size and roundness of her stomach that she was nearly four months pregnant. Expecting a child, and still writing love letters to Ascânio, letting him persist in his delusion of a chaste romance! The naive ingenue, the unparalleled whore! That was what had hurt him most: he had believed that her regard for him was as pure and steadfast as his own for her; she had led him on like the credulous fool he was. He ought to be wearing a duncecap.

Besides, he had grown accustomed to life in Agreste and would miss the best things about it: the water, the air, the scenery, the close companionship of friends. Yet he could not resign himself to the passive acceptance of backwardness, poverty and stagnation. His head was seething with plans that he had no intention of giving up.

Agreste was such a wretched, remote place that it did not even interest the state politicians, not that there were many of them left. Dr. Mauritônio Dantas, the mayor, a sclerotic dental surgeon whose mental vigor had been still further undermined by marital problems, kept to his house for the sake of appearances, and it was Ascânio who actually made the decisions and carried them out. The public opinion was that when the dentist gave up the ghost, Ascânio would be elected mayor for life if he wanted the job.

The undeniable truth was that Ascânio, with virtually no revenue except the county's share of the federal taxes and its meager allotment from the state, had so far managed to keep Agreste clean and its streets and alleys paved with stones carried up from the river; had opened two new county schools, one in Rocinha, the other in Coqueiro; and was endeavoring, by dint of official requests, petitions to the authorities and letters to the newspapers and radio stations, to get the São Francisco Valley Authority to lay a power line to Agreste. His efforts, unfortunately, had been fruitless. Pylons and electric lines reached the neighboring townships; Agreste was one of the few not included in the Valley Authority's latest development plan. Ascânio had not given up, though, not by a long shot. He was sure that someday the fame of Agreste's climate, its healing water and beautiful surroundings would bring tourists hungry for peace and natural beauty to its streets and shores.

There were those who smiled at his ardor, convinced that nothing would ever bring Agreste to life again, but others were carried away and shared his dream, at least for a time, accepting his fantasies as reality. Opinions about the future were divided, as usual, but as to Ascânio himself everyone was in agreement. Not a citizen in the whole district was held in higher esteem. Every marriageable girl had her eye on him. Ascânio was twenty-eight years old; why was he waiting so long to choose a bride? He couldn't very well frequent Zuleika's house after he was elected mayor.

Dona Carmosina had talked to him seriously about it in the post office more than once. So many pretty, accomplished girls in Agreste, and all of them running after you. He only smiled a sad smile. Dona Carmosina didn't insist; she had read all his letters, every line, and could have repeated from memory some of the best parts of the last missive, his reply to the news of that hussy's wedding—"Delilah, a dead man is writing you this letter, a frozen corpse, stabbed to the heart, who wishes you well from the tomb to which you drove him. May your future life be unclouded by remorse, and God grant me the boon of forgetfulness and the strength to tear your image from my breast. . . ." You're a poet, Ascânio Trindade; you could write poems just as good as Barbo-zinha's if you tried. It looks as if you haven't forgotten her and won't even think about anyone else.

He only smiled his sad smile. Another sweetheart? Never. Not even if the sweetest, most charming, most beautiful girl in the world got off Jairo's *marineti*. "Dear Carmosina, my heart is dead to love."

*Of the prodigal daughter's return to Agreste,
where the family, all in black for the
Comendador, awaits her at the bus stop,
along with the boys' catechism class, Father
Mariano, Ascânio Trindade, Skipper Dário, De
Matos Barbosa the poet, Chalita the Arab and
various other dignitaries, not forgetting the poolroom gang, still less Dona Carmosina carrying a
bouquet of flowers picked by Dona Milu from her
garden, the clergy, the city fathers and the people,
the latter represented by the young urchin Sabino
and Goatstink.*

Grouped at four or five strategic points around the moviehouse where Jairo's *marineti* let its passengers off, the crowd waited to hear its raucous honking at the bend of the road coming into town. At the church the boys' catechism class rehearsed in their Sunday clothes under Father Mariano's direction, along with Perpétua and her seminarian son with his cassock and missal, a smiling young man on holiday. At the church door the gossiping old women milled about like a band of croaking buzzards, primed for the great event, the wealthy widow's descent from the bus. They could hardly wait to see her dressed in mourning, weeping in the arms of her family, and her stepdaughter, the "foreigner," into the bargain. It promised to be a fat, full day.

Everyone in the Azores Bar, with the exception of its shirt-sleeved owner, had on a necktie. Osnar, Seixas, Fidélio and Aminthas formed an honor guard for Brother-in-law Astério, half suffocating in the black suit he had borrowed from Seixas, who was a good size or two smaller. Perpétua had agreed to Astério's simply wearing a black armband and black ribbons on his hat and lapel during the week. For the welcoming ceremony, however, she would hear of nothing but full mourning: black suit, black tie and a long face.

"You're making me do it because you don't have to spend any money yourself; you always dress in mourning anyway. Where do you think I'll get the money to have me a suit made?"

"I had to buy one for Peto."

"Oh sure, a pair of short pants!"

"Why don't you borrow a suit? Seixas has just come out of mourning."

That would have been an excellent idea if Seixas had not been a lot skinnier than Astério. He just managed to put on the trousers, with Elisa's help; the jacket wouldn't button and had split under the arms, but that wouldn't show unless he tried to raise them.

Peto escaped from church and his mother and ran to the bar. His face was clean, his hair combed and slicked back, and, an even more unwonted sight, he was wearing a long-sleeved white shirt and a bow tie, a relic of the deceased Major. The shoes were the worst, a torment to feet that always ran free on the riverbank and in the water. Osnar laughed at the fine figure the boy cut and his grimaces.

"Sergeant Peto, you're a living doll, I do declare. If I had a taste for boys, this would be your day. But luckily for you, it so happens I don't."

"Oh, cut it out."

Peto was in a high good humor though, shoes or no shoes. As long as his aunt was there he would sleep over at Astério's house in the little room at the back, far from his mother's sight and her strict timetables. He would be able to wander through the streets at night with Osnar and Aminthas, Seixas and Fidélio, on those mysterious hunting expeditions they talked and laughed about so much.

"Go away, kid, this is men's talk."

Osnar was the only one who gave him something to think about:

"One of these days I'll take you hunting with me, Sergeant. You're just about old enough now, so you be getting your musket primed."

Perpétua had decided that Antonieta's stepdaughter should have Peto's room. Like the rest of the house, it was scrubbed down with disinfectant and swept until the last particle of dust was banished, and wild-cherry leaves were scattered on the floor to make it smell sweet. All that week little Aracy, borrowed from Elisa for the duration of the Paulistas' visit, had been in the throes of a thoroughgoing spring cleaning.

The house on the corner of Cathedral Square and Tres Marías Street was a roomy and comfortable one. There would have been no need for Peto to move if Perpétua had not ignored Astério's advice to let the two guests sleep in Ricardo's room and the two boys in Peto's. But Perpétua, in an excess of hospitality (was she suffering from delusions of grandeur or hatching some plot in her head? Dona Carmosina could not be quite sure) had decided to put Antonieta in the large, cool master bedroom and actually let her sleep, incredible as it seemed, in the double bed with its fine lamb's-wool coverlet, where Perpétua had slept with the Major during her brief days of wedded bliss. If anyone else had told me I wouldn't have believed it: her room and the Major's? Impossible! Lordy, Lordy, how times change! Dona Carmosina opened her little eyes as wide as they would go in sheer amazement.

Double bed, lamb's-wool coverlet, dressing table, a huge wardrobe and heavy rosewood furniture. The Major had bought the house already furnished just before the wedding, and it was a bargain. The only heir to Dona Eufrosina when she passed away at ninety-four was a nephew who lived in Porto Alegre and had never set foot in Agreste. He had sent word that the house and everything in it should be sold for whatever it would bring in cash. And there was no other purchaser to pay either cash down or on time.

From the enormous parlor with its eight windows on the street a hallway led to the dining room, with two bedrooms on either side. The one facing the master bedroom had been turned into a study years before by Dr. Fulgêncio Neto, Dona Eufrosina's deceased husband, a famous doctor in Agreste's salad days. There was a writing desk with eighteen drawers, one of them a secret strongbox, and a bookcase with French medical tomes and the works of Alexandre Dumas and Victor Hugo. The Major left the study as it was. He liked to retire there after dinner, reading week-old Bahia newspapers at the desk or catching a few winks in the hammock. Ricardo studied there for an hour every day, even when he was on holiday. Next came Ricardo's and Peto's facing rooms, both of which had been requisitioned by Perpétua. She herself would sleep in Ricardo's room, which had an oratory, and Leonora could have Peto's. Ricardo would sleep in the study, where he kept his books. Aracy, the little serving girl, could be accommodated on an improvised pallet in the shed where fruit was stored in the backyard. Perpétua personally took charge of the housecleaning and all other arrangements connected with Tieta's arrival and sojourn.

The post office was full to overflowing. Skipper Dário and Dona Laura were there, and Barbozinha, clean-shaven in deference to his old sweetheart; Ascânio Trindade, representing the municipal authorities—Dr. Mauritônio was getting worse all the time; he saw naked women everywhere—and Elisa in a fluttering black voile dress from one of Antonieta's packages of used clothing. Its plunging décolletage had been sewn up to the collarbone in obedience to Perpétua, the arbiter of all dress and manners for the great arrival.

"Cover up your bosom at least. That outfit looks more like a ball gown than it does like mourning clothes, but since it's the only black dress you've got it'll have to do; but for goodness sake make it decent. She'll be in deep mourning, of course, and we ought to dress accordingly. Would you believe the old man wanted us to give a party and invite half the town? Mourning her husband's death and us all set for a party, can you imagine?"

Dona Carmosina placed her bouquet in a glass of water so the flowers wouldn't wilt. Impressed by Perpétua's harangue, she had had a dispute with her mother: maybe flowers weren't proper to welcome a newly widowed friend. Dona Milu wouldn't listen: "You give her those flowers and tell her they're from me. If it's all right to send flowers to a corpse, why shouldn't a widow get some? Don't be so silly."

"Oh Lord, won't that bus ever get here?" For all her efforts to be doleful, Elisa could not control her excitement, a heady mixture of joy and fear. Boundless joy that she was to meet her sister, the fairy godmother, the rich, elegant, high-toned Paulista, benefactress

to them all; fear of the consequences of her own folly and falsehood, the omission of any mention of Toninho's death so that she
could pocket the baby's monthly allowance. Dona Carmosina had
done her best to soothe her.

"When she asks about Toninho, what on earth am I going to
say?"

"Tell her the truth. Just say you followed my advice not to tell
her and leave the rest to me."

"Do you think she'll forgive me?"

"If I know Tieta, she'll let bygones be bygones. You just leave
it to me."

Another cloud cast a shadow on her joy: that stepdaughter,
almost a daughter, who seemed to hold a place in Tieta's heart that
Elisa would have preferred to have all for herself.

At the entrance to the moviehouse Chalita the Arab picked his
teeth with a toothpick, lost in recollections. Tieta was even prettier
than her sister, Astério's wife. Pretty and reckless and fiery.
Through a side door was the ice-cream parlor: a little counter, a
drawer for the money and the freezer turned by young Sabino, who
filled it daily with fruit sherbet to earn a few nickels from the Arab.
Sabino had put on a clean shirt and trousers, shoes and socks. He
would have liked to wear a black armband too—after all, he was
almost one of the family; always at Astério's beck and call, manning
the cash register, running all the errands—but he hadn't because he
was afraid of Dona Perpétua, the old witch. Goatstink sat quietly
on the curb, pickled in *cachaça*, quaffing his white lightning in
silence. He had a yen to see what this famous daughter of Zé
Esteves looked like. Goatstink had never seen her; she had already
been gone when he had come to Agreste twenty-five years before in
search of health and rum, and only a few faint echoes remained of
the celebrated beating. At the exact spot where the *marineti* always
stopped, on the sidewalk next to the streetlight in front of the
moviehouse, stood Zé Esteves and his wife, Tonha. When Elisa was
married the old man had sent his faded old blue suit to Esplanada to
be dyed black and had never worn it since. The jacket had no more
shape than a sack and the trousers hung loosely on his frame. Zé
Esteves was no longer the giant he had been, an oak tree, a fortress;
but he had been planted firmly on the sidewalk for a good two
hours, chewing tobacco and leaning on his staff. Tonha wished she
could ask the Arab for a chair, but she didn't dare tell the old man

she was tired. She was in half-mourning, a black skirt and black crepe band on the sleeve of her white blouse. She was not a blood relative, after all, as Perpétua, marking differences and distances, had been quick to point out.

After a wait of two hours and ten minutes, Jairo's *marineti* honked at the curve and there was a general scurrying around. Perpétua and Father Mariano called out their troops. As the *marineti* came into view at the head of the street, a first, premature sob was heard.

Minute description of the confused arrival of Tieta, prodigal daughter, or Antonieta Esteves Cantarelli, the merry widow.

Lined up in front were the family, mute sorrow in their eyes, in their tears, in their clothes. One step in front of the others was old Zé Esteves, chewing tobacco. Behind him, the kinfolk in black, the Reverend Father with the boys' catechism class and the town dignitaries, including Dona Carmosina, bouquet in hand, the flowers' gay colors a discordant note against the background of crepe and tears— "That creature will ride roughshod over the most sacred sentiments to call attention to herself," Perpétua muttered indignantly behind the veil attached to her bun. Behind them stood the churchmice and the rest of the townfolk.

The *marineti* approached, with Jairo at the wheel and not many passengers. A lean day for Jairo, a fat day for Agreste, a day to kill the fatted calf with bonfires and feasting to honor the prodigal daughter, if she had not been a newly bereaved and sorrowing widow. Tears, mourning and pious hymns were the only appropriate way to receive her.

The excited talk ceased and Peto teetered on tiptoe. The minute his aunt got down off that bus he'd be off like a shot and yank those confounded shoes off his feet. The *marineti* came to a stop with a tired creaking of springs. Peto counted the passengers who got off: Seu Cunha, one, a farmer and his wife, two, three, Dona Carmelita, four, her maid, five, never saw that guy before, six, or him either, seven, Seu Agostinho the baker, eight, and his wife, nine, and his daughter, ten, Aunt Antonieta and the girl are going to be the last ones. Even Jairo jumped down before they did, laden with suitcases and bags belonging to the anxiously awaited travelers. Jairo makes eleven, now it's twelve, that's her!

Was that her? Peto didn't see how it could be. His aunt should be dressed all in black, with a funeral veil covering her face like his mother's; she couldn't be in any way, shape or form that movie star, that Gina Lollobrigida. On the top step, majestically framed in the doorway, stood Antonieta Esteves—"Antonieta Esteves Cantarelli, if you please," fussed Perpétua. And she was a knockout: tall and shapely, with long blond hair escaping from beneath a red turban. Yes, red; and so was the classically cut jersey sport blouse that set off her firm, full breasts, a generous sample of which was visible at the unbuttoned neck. Blue jeans molded her thighs and buttocks, seductively emphasizing concavities and convexities. And what convexities! what concavities! Her feet were shod in fine tan moccasins. The only somber thing about the widow's outfit was the smoked glasses with square frames and lenses, chic as all get out, designed by Christian Dior. The dumbfounded silence lasted for a fraction of a minute, a very long time, an eternity finally broken by a triumphant shout from Peto.

"Aunt's not in mourning, Mother! Can I take off my shoes and necktie?"

Antonieta stood stock-still on the top step of the bus. There was the family in mourning for Felipe, her dear departed husband, and here she was in technicolor, red and blue, unbuttoned blouse and blue jeans. Oh, my God, why didn't I think of mourning? She had gone over every detail in her head and discussed it all with Leonora over and over, and then she had gone and forgotten the most important thing of all. But Zé Esteves was already spitting out his chaw of tobacco and holding out his arms to his prodigal daughter.

"Come here, child! I thought I never would see you again, but God's granted me the sight of you to comfort me before I die."

From atop the steps Antonieta recognized her father. Her father and his quincewood staff. The same, the very same staff that had beaten her black and blue that awful night. A fit of laughter shook her and she couldn't hold it back; the strangled sound burst forth uncontrollably from her lips. She had just time to cover her face with her hands before springing nimbly off the bus. Everyone ran up to console the weeping widow, the prodigal daughter smothering her sobs in her father's arms. It was a touching moment. Not even Perpétua noticed anything amiss. Elisa was crying and laughing, giddy with relief; her sister was just the way she had imagined her, the same in every way. Dona Carmosina, the only one who wondered a little at that first curious strangled noise, came up with the flowers that were so in keeping with Tieta's traveling garb.

As Tieta hugged them all one after another, disputed over by her sisters, her brother-in-law and her nephews—"Take your shoes off, honey, give your poor feet a rest"—being kissed again and again and cried over by Elisa, at the door of Jairo's *marineti* appeared the loveliest, sweetest, most charming girl in the world, the slim and youthful sylph the seer De Matos Barbosa immediately recognized and proclaimed her to be. She stood and gazed at the touching scene, touched herself. How appealing she was in her faded blue denim slacks and matching cap, around which curled an aureole of blond hair, now gray with dust. Peto recognized the heroine of every cowboy film he had ever seen. A murmur of admiration ran along the street. Tieta, disengaging herself from Elisa's kisses, introduced the girl.

"This is Leonora Cantarelli, my stepdaughter—my daughter, it's all the same."

Dona Carmosina turned to Ascânio Trindade and surprised him gaping in rapture. What now, my friend? Leonora's gentle smile broadened to include them all and lingered on Ascânio, who was staring up at her in a daze.

"Close your mouth, Ascânio, and help the girl down," Dona Carmosina suggested.

Ascânio came forward and offered the Paulista his hand. "Welcome to Agreste, its health, its beauty and its poverty, and forgive our backwardness and lack of creature comforts." Ricardo sank to one knee to ask his aunt's blessing, but she lifted him up, enfolded him in her arms and kissed him on both cheeks. "What a good-looking young priest you are!"

After some moments of understandable hesitation, Father Mariano made up his mind that all the difficult work of adapting the words of a litany to fit the occasion and rehearsing it for two weeks should not be wasted because of a mere technicality.

At a signal from the priest the children burst into song:

> *"All dressed in black,*
> *As fair as the morning,*
> *Deep in her eyes*
> *the colors of mourning.*
> *Ave! Ave!*
> *Ave Antonieta!"*

Her hand still in Ascânio's, Leonora laughed in delight. Her crystalline laughter rang out clearer—oh! far clearer!—than the lost Astrud's ever had. Astrud died and was buried at that moment in front of the moviehouse, crushed by the bald tires of Jairo's *marineti.*

Antonieta hugged them one by one.

"Carmô, you angel, I'm so glad to see you! How is Dona Milu? She's the one who picked these flowers, I bet! *Carina* . . . You see, São Paulo's made an Italian out of me, I meant to say *querida* and it came out *carina* . . ." She was the same old Tieta, jaunty, laughing, and making jokes. She hadn't changed at all, even if she did say *carina* when she meant *querida.*

"Barbozinha! Is it you? I almost didn't recognize you!"

"I've seen hard times, Tieta, hard times and grief. . . ."

"Still writing poems? You remember the ones you wrote for me? They were beautiful."

"Only and always for you. You're younger and prettier than ever."

"And you are still a liar, Barbozinha. And a flatterer."

And so she was back in Sant'Ana do Agreste, in the bosom of her black-garbed family, listening to the catechism class sing that hymn. "Thank you, Father, with all my heart." An afternoon breeze blew in off the sea to greet her. Jairo unloaded their luggage with Sabino's help. It had traveled on the roof of the bus under thick canvas, as if any covering could keep off the dust of that road.

"Let's go, child." Zé Esteves, leaning on his staff, offered her his arm.

"You'll be staying at my house." Perpétua tried to assume command of the situation amid the shattered fragments of her condolences.

It was her fault, hers and nobody else's. How could she ever have imagined Tieta in mourning for a husband? She had tried to think of her sister as an equal, as if money and high society and marriage to a wealthy Paulista with a papal title could make a silk purse of a sow's ear or straighten out a girl who was born crooked and rebellious to all laws, codes of conduct and human respect.

Antonieta Esteves Cantarelli took her father's arm, looked around and smiled at the old churchmice, at Chalita the Arab, at the Skipper and Dona Laura, at Jairo, at young Sabino, and at Goatstink, who was appraising her boldly from the sidewalk, so down and out he could be impudent with impunity. His rum-soaked voice rang out in the street in wholehearted approval.

"Hurrah for the flowering cunt-tree!"

"Hip hip hooray!" bawled the boys' catechism class.

Of doors and windows and the Sacred Heart of Jesus in the parlor, or the first few minutes in the bosom of the family.

At the corner of Cathedral Square and Tres Marias Street the cortège came to a halt.

"Well, we're home," Perpétua announced. "Let's go inside."

"Is this your house? The one that used to belong to the doctor and Dona Eufrosina?" exclaimed Antonieta. In her letters, Perpétua used to refer to "our humble home" purchased by the Major before the wedding, in Judge Oliva Square. "But this is Cathedral Square."

"Its real name is Judge Oliva Square," Dona Carmosina explained.

The doctor's house, Lucas' house. Antonieta had come prepared to face all her memories, but the surprises had begun as soon as she got off the bus and saw the old man brandishing that stick. It had never crossed her mind that she might be going to the very house where Lucas had stayed on after the doctor's death, trying to make up his mind whether it was worth setting up a clinic there or not.

Perpétua, who attributed her sister's surprise exclusively to the imposing size of the house, was torn by conflicting sentiments. Satisfaction at having such a fine roof over her head—she was no beggar woman, after all—and fear of how Tieta might react. She might think they had taken advantage of her kindness in sending money every month to rear the children. An explanation seemed to be in order.

"This house was really God's gift from heaven. The Major bought the house and everything in it for a song."

Friends were saying their goodbyes with promises to call.

"We'll come around to see you soon," the Skipper said.

"Why don't you come by tonight after dinner so we can talk?"

"Not tonight; you'll want to be with your family."

"And get the homesickness out of your system," added Dona Laura with a smile.

"Tomorrow, then."

"All right, we'll come tomorrow without fail."

If Ascânio had had his way, he would have been back that very evening. Wasn't the rest of the day enough for the family? Besides, Leonora was only a relative by marriage, she was on her first visit to Agreste, she didn't have any homesickness to get out of her system and wouldn't know or care what the family was talking about. He wished he had Dona Carmosina's nerve.

"Well, I'm coming over this evening with Mother. When I went out the door she called after me, 'You be sure and tell Tieta I'll be over to Perpétua's tonight to see her.' "

"I brought a present for your mother, just a little souvenir. Why don't you come have supper with us? May I invite them, Perpétua?"

"The house is yours. Food isn't wanting, thank the Lord."

Even before she went off to take a bath—"I need a bath right this minute, I've got dust in my very soul, we both do"—Antonieta made one stipulation.

"As long as we're living here, I'm paying the bills."

Perpétua made a halfhearted gesture of protest which her well-to-do sister cut short.

"Otherwise we'll take our bags to Amorzinho's boarding-house."

"Well, if you feel that way I won't argue with you," Perpétua quickly agreed, the heaviest weight off her shoulders. The lighter one remained: the expense that she, Astério, and the old man had gone to getting everything ready.

Even that small burden was to be lifted. Antonieta went on:

"Starting with what you've already spent getting the house ready for us."

"Oh, no! For heaven's sake!" put in Elisa. "That isn't worth worrying about. We all chipped in."

"You talk like you were rich." Perpétua had no qualms about showing her sister up; there was nothing sillier than a poor person trying to put on airs. "Are you forgetting Astério had to borrow money from Osnar to scrape together enough for your part?"

"Shut your mouth, woman!" Elisa went white with anger. Perpétua had shamed her on purpose in front of her sister and the stranger. What right did she have to let that stepdaughter see how poor the couple was?

"Perpétua's right, Elisa honey. If I couldn't do it, I wouldn't say a word. But since I can, why should you all give yourselves a hard time for nothing? Perpétua or Astério can tell me how much you all spent sometime, and that'll be that."

As she spoke, Antonieta went over to Elisa and hugged and kissed her affectionately. There was an air of kinship between the two, a resemblance of face and manner, except that the younger girl had not inherited old Zé Esteves' goatlike stubbornness and flinty hardness, so marked in Perpétua and Antonieta. But she had not inherited her mother's resignation, either.

"Honey, don't be ashamed of being poor. I'm pretty well off now, but as long as I was poor—and I've had a hard time of it, believe me—I never pretended I was rich. Who would have helped me if I had? As soon as I met Felipe, I spoke right up and asked him for a loan."

Elisa, caressed and called "honey," soon recovered her natural color along with her prejudices.

"You mean you asked your fiancé to lend you money?"

"Fiancé nothing; that was long before we were engaged. When I met Felipe I was broke. I'll tell you about it someday when we have more time. What I want to do now is take a bath. We both need one, don't we, Nora?"

"Nora?"

"That's her nickname. This is my girl. She came to live with me when she was just a little kid. I taught her all she knows. Where's our room?"

"This is yours, Tieta, the master bedroom. And that's Leonora's over there." Perpétua pointed. "Cardo, Peto, go get the suitcases. Astério, why don't you give them a hand?"

Why didn't Tieta protest politely that she would just as soon be in the same room with her stepdaughter? The window of the master bedroom looked out over Tres Marias Street, with the study door on the other side of the corridor.

"Does anyone sleep in the study?"

"Ricardo."

"I do, Aunt. If there's anything you need in the night, just call me."

Muscular, tall and dark, Ricardo in his cassock exuded innocence and good health. If he lived in São Paulo, he'd wear his hair to his shoulders, never take a bath, and smoke marijuana all the time like the children of most of her friends. Antonieta had heard too many sad stories. She smiled at her nephew.

"If the bogeyman tries to get me I'll sing out." She was touched by their attentions and kindness. "You've all gone to so much trouble for our sake."

"Too much trouble." Leonora's musical voice never rose above a minor key. "We can both sleep in the same room."

"It's too late now, everything's all arranged," said Tieta. Why did she say it? Did she sense the ghost of Lucas in the master bedroom?

Astério, Ricardo and Peto, now contentedly barefoot, brought in their suitcases and packages.

"Be careful with that box, Peto, it's breakable. I guess the best thing would be to open it right now."

Antonieta picked up the imposing parcel and placed it on the dining-room table, while the family eagerly looked on.

"It's something for the house, Perpétua."

With the skill of long experience, Astério undid the knots in the waxed string, rolled it up in a ball and folded the strong brown paper. Secondhand or not, they were quality items and would come in handy at the store. Excitement rose at sight of the showy gift wrapping and wide pink ribbon with its bow in the shape of a flower.

"You untie the ribbon, Perpétua." Astério yielded her his place.

Perpétua, trying not to show her eagerness, picked up the end of the ribbon and read the label: "Lord Jesus Shop, religious articles on installment plan or cash down. Pay for your devotion in twelve installments." Could it be, could this be the precious object she had dreamed of so long and hoped someday to order from Bahia? Could Tieta have been divinely inspired in her choice of a gift? God sometimes did use a hardened sinner as an instrument to reward the just.

When she pulled the ribbon off, a white box appeared. She took off the lid and handed it to Astério. "What's that funny light material it's made of?" Isopor, Antonieta explained to her brother-in-law. There was a general gasp of admiration, and from Perpétua's burning breast came an "Oh!" of profoundest satisfaction as she caught sight of the object of her dreams lying in the isopor box, but even bigger and more beautiful and surely holier. The bigger and finer and more expensive the image, the more miraculous it was. God must have inspired Antonieta indeed: in the box lay a plaster image of the Sacred Heart of Jesus. In the figure's hair, face, hands, garments and mantle were all the colors of the rainbow. The crimson, loving Heart lay exposed, an open wound with a drop of blood like an enormous ruby. It was an image worthy of the high altar of the cathedral in Aracaju. Aided by Astério and Ricardo, Perpétua lifted out the heavy piece ever so carefully. It was neither painting nor sculpture but a little of both, a novelty never seen in Agreste before, a three-dimensional picture meant to be hung on a wall. Strong wire was attached to it in back, and there was a wooden bracket to set it on. Even special nails were provided, big stainless-steel ones. Tieta breathed a sigh of relief.

"Thank goodness it got here in one piece. It's to hang in your parlor, Perpétua."

"Oh, it's heavenly! It's giving me palpitations. Oh, sister, I don't know how to thank you!"

Perpétua kissed her sister on the cheek, lightly and standing at a distance, as she kissed her children and the hands of Dom José and Father Mariano. If anyone had asked her what sort of kisses she used to give the Major, Perpétua would have replied that couples united in a state of holy matrimony blessed by God have a right to carnal intimacy, a right and obligation. That she lived on the memory of those kisses—that she certainly would not have said.

Peto stroked the isopor.

"Give me the box, Ma?"

"Are you crazy? You leave that box alone. Put down the paper and the string too, Astério; I may need them."

"Shall I get the hammer, Mother?" Ricardo offered, holding the wooden bracket.

"There's nothing to compare with it, here or in Esplanada. Dona Aida's and Seu Modesto's is nothing to this," boasted Perpétua.

"Ain't no other sister in the world like this one." Even Zé Esteves' compliments were rough-hewn.

Perpétua was in no mood to quibble over Tieta's virtues any more than over her faults, not even the impropriety of her conduct as a widow. The São Paulo gold, the papal title, the image of the Heart of Jesus made her perfect.

"You're right, Father. There isn't a sister in the world as generous as Tieta."

It cost her something to pronounce those words, but the future of the children the Major had left in her care was worth the sacrifice.

When Ricardo came back with a hammer his aunt and the girl had gone to take a bath. The others had gathered in the parlor. Astério held the bracket in the spot Perpétua had chosen for the divine image, between the tinted photographs of herself as a bride and the Major in his uniform, ordered from a firm in Paraná soon after they were married. Ricardo mounted the ladder and started hammering in the nails. He couldn't make up his mind which saint his aunt resembled. Before he saw her he had thought of her as St. Anne, the grandmother, the patron saint. But she wasn't like St. Anne at all. St. Rose of Lima, maybe? Or St. Rita of Cassia? Elisa held out the nails to her nephew. "Is this high enough, Mother?"

From atop his perch on the ladder Ricardo caught sight of his aunt, carrying a bath towel and soap dish, on her way to the bathroom in the backyard. But her hair was dark! Where was the long blond mane he had seen when she got off the bus? Now her hair was black; crisp curly ringlets, like the angels' hair in the seminary chapel. And the calf and thigh displayed under the negligee fluttering in the breeze were a deep toasted brown. Ricardo turned away his eyes. Perpétua looked at the wall. "A little higher, maybe; there, that's fine." She didn't see her sister approaching in her deshabille, a sheer peignoir with lace over the bosom, fastened only by a ribbon, fluttering in the late-afternoon breeze that died on the bluffs along the river. Didn't she see, or didn't she want to see? Tieta looked and said approvingly, "It'll look elegant there." Elisa left off admiring the Sacred Heart to exclaim over the peignoir.

"What a darling robe!"

Perpétua preferred to ignore the garment.

"I'll ask Father Mariano to come and bless the image on Sunday after mass."

No, not St. Rita of Cassia, not St. Rose of Lima. Which flower, then, in the garden of saints? This aunt from São Paulo, gyrating her hips on her way to the bath, what saint could she be?

Chapter of gifts, in which hearts melt and an unexpected tear is shed.

The festive gift-giving took place after supper, accompanied by much laughter and excitement. As soon as little Aracy had cleared the table, Antonieta asked Ricardo and Astério to bring her big blue suitcase, the only one she hadn't opened, from her bedroom. It was placed on the table and Astério took charge of opening it. There were nervous giggles as the family looked on expectantly and mischievous Peto craned his neck to peer inside the valise. Leonora fetched a traveling case from the room, unzipped it and held it on her lap, ready to bring forth its treasures.

To Zé Esteves belonged the prerogative of first crack at the presents, a plush box with a gold-plated wristwatch inside.

"Look at the make of the watch, Father. You always did want an Omega watch; I remember how jealous you used to be of Colonel Artur da Tapitanga's big old pocket watch. By the way, is he still alive?"

"Alive and kicking. He'll be around to see you one of these days. He's always asking about you." The informant was Dona Carmosina, sitting all dressed up next to Dona Milu.

"I ain't got no vanity left, child, no vanity and no watch either, since the one I had got busted and Roque couldn't fix it. Now I'll know what time it is for a change. I'm beginning to feel like somebody again, now you're here."

Leonora put her hand in her satchel.

"And here's a transistor radio so you and Dona Tonha can listen to music, Seu José."

"You went to all that trouble for us, little gal? A radio? Tonha's the one who'll really be happy. Ain't that right, woman? She's been plaguing me to buy one."

Tonha nodded blissfully. She had wanted a radio so much! Once she had actually dared to hint that they might buy one of those little cheap ones, but that first and last hint had earned her a terrible tonguelashing from Zé Esteves. You mean you actually want me to throw away money my daughter sends me? What if we get sick? And what'll happen when we turn up our toes? Who do you think's gonna pay for doctors and medicine and the priest and the funeral? Don't you ever ask me to throw away my money on trash again. Have you gone plumb out of your mind?

Nora slipped batteries into the little gadget and the strains of a samba, the theme tune of a radio station in Feira de Sant'Ana, blared forth.

"It's bigger than ours," Elisa whispered to Astério. "Maybe we could make a deal with Father and keep this one and give him what it cost. Tieta wants to give us back what we spent, and with what's left over after we pay Osnar back, we could . . ."

There was no need for any deal, for Antonieta next drew from her valise an imposing, sophisticated appliance with a quantity of dials, several wavelengths and a retractable antenna, and handed it to her sister.

"This is for you and Astério; it's Japanese and they don't make them any better!"

"Oh my heavens! Oh good Lord! Tieta, it's too much!" Elisa rained kisses on her for the second time, doubly grateful for the radio and her forgiveness. Dona Carmosina had assured her that the matter of Toninho's death was water over the dam, that she needn't worry about it anymore. "Does it come with batteries? I can't wait to hear it."

"I guess they're already inside. It works on electricity, too. Astério, this billfold is for you to keep your pool winnings in. And here's some more stuff for you, Elisa."

There was a complete assortment of cosmetics. Creams and colors, every kind of makeup known to woman.

"Oh my goodness, such a lot of things, I feel like I'm going to faint! This special rouge! I never saw this kind before."

"Try the iridescent lipstick," advised Leonora.

One radio station followed another: Bahia, Rio, Recife broadcasting to the world, São Paulo. "Just switch the band and listen! You can hear all five continents—what the dickens is that lingo?"

"It sounds like Russian but it's Radio Belgrade."

"What country is Belgrade the capital of?"

"Yugoslavia," Dona Carmosina told them importantly.

And so, with music, laughter and kisses, the evening got off to a good start. How had she been able to guess what each one wanted most? How did she know about Astério's prowess at pool, and Cardo's dreams of a fishing rod with a reel and nylon line and artificial lures? How had she ever guessed? Dona Carmosina smiled as the question was repeated and remained unanswered. Divine inspiration, obviously. "Bring Peto anything but schoolbooks; all he ever wants to do is loaf and dive in the river and play stickball in the streets with the other kids and watch the men playing pool; he's almost thirteen and still in grade school." Peto received a skindiving outfit with mask, harpoon and flippers. Leonora gave the two boys keyrings decorated with pictures of King Pelé, and for Astério she had chosen a necktie. Nora's gift to Perpétua was a silvery mantilla. For Elisa she had brought a chunky modern ring made of fiberglass, with a huge amber-colored stone. It was the sensation of the evening, the latest thing in the chic shops of Rua Augusta. Antonieta and Leonora had rings just like hers, only with different-colored stones. Nora went to get them. "Mine is in the jewel box on top of the dresser," Tieta called. "Jewel box" sounded well to her relatives' ears. Leonora showed them the two rings, hers emerald-green and Tieta's smoky gray. They had been created by a famous artist, Aldemir Martins, whose paintings and drawings were worth millions. He was a good friend of the Comendador, and Tieta knew him; she knew a lot of important people in São Paulo politics, business and the arts. Menotti del Picchia often went to her house. Dona Carmosina, who had read *The Masks* and *Juca Mulatto*, asked whether the poet was as romantic as his poetry. "Well, he's getting on in years but he always has a lot of pretty girls around him; he hasn't lost his taste for women," Tieta said.

Let no one think that poor Tonha had been forgotten because she was only the stepmother. Besides the radio, she received a skirt and blouse from Tieta and a blue and lavender necklace from Leonora. She was so overcome she wiped her eyes and could hardly say a word of thanks. It had been so long since anyone had given her a present. The last time was when the old man had bought her a barrette at the market years and years before. She still wore it, too; she knew how to make things last.

For Dona Carmosina there was a set of costume jewelry: necklace, bracelet and ring.

"What becoming jewelry!"

"Do you really like it?" Tieta asked.

"I love it." She also loved the ballpoint pen with different-colored refills. "Thank you, Nora, consider me your friend for life."

Dona Milu got two shiny washable plastic packs of cards to play solitaire with, and an Italian shawl for her head. Even little Aracy, peering out from behind the kitchen door, received a heart-shaped brooch for her Sunday dress. Once in a blue moon she went to the movie matinee.

"What do you think of this monstrance, Perpétua? Do you think the Father will be pleased?"

"Pleased! What a question. That's a gorgeous custodial, it must have cost the earth."

"Well, it wasn't cheap, exactly, but it wasn't all that expensive, either. I hope it'll redeem my sins." Tieta laughed and tossed her head. Ricardo couldn't imagine her committing any sins. Which saint was such a happy mixture of jollity and devotion?

"Well, now we've opened all the presents." No, wait, there was still the silver frame for Perpétua's picture of the Major, resplendent in the gala uniform of the State Military Police. The widow could not speak but made a gesture that Ricardo understood. He ran to get the picture, guarded under lock and key in the desk. Now, framed in silver on the table, shone the perennial smile (the Major's bestial smile, Aminthas had called it, trying to be funny) and frank countenance; all that was missing was his booming voice. Perpétua gazed a long time at her deceased husband, who had given her everything she wanted and two sons besides. Tieta had succeeded in touching her heart. A tear dropped from her eyes, her first real tears since she had stopped weeping after the Major's death. She raised her sibilant voice.

"He was too good for me. I had given up any thought of

marriage, much less a husband like him. I'm . . ." She hesitated over the right word. ". . . harsh by nature. Father Mariano says I don't know what pity is. Before I married Cupertino, I did wrong when I thought I was doing right. Antonieta, I hope you'll—"

Dona Carmosina opened her little eyes wide. Perpétua was going to ask her sister to forgive her. This was a historic moment. But Tieta cut her off in midsentence.

"That's all water under the bridge, Perpétua. I didn't deserve the good man I had either, and he made me what I am today. I don't let on, but you don't know how I grieve over losing him. What a shame the Major died before we could all get to know each other. But the children are still here." She opened her arms. "Come here, my darlings, come kiss your crazy old aunt."

The older one was so funny and awkward in his cassock. And the young one was a sly little imp, no flies on him. Ricardo's kiss just grazed her cheek; Peto's was warm and not entirely innocent.

Of a nightshirt, a nightgown, a jug of water and a prayer.

After the letter from Perpétua had come with the good news that his aunt was in good health and planning to visit them, Ricardo had fulfilled his vow during exam week in the seminary. Someone had died, all right, but it was the Comendador, thank goodness, and not Tieta. For seven nights Ricardo bruised his knees on kernels of corn filched from the pantry, and he fell into the habit of praying a Salve Regina for the health of his elderly aunt, his venerable grandmother.

Life holds a surprise for us at every turn in the road, Dom José used to preach in his Sunday sermons; and he was certainly right about that. Ricardo's mouth had fallen open when he caught sight of Antonieta in the door of the *marineti* and saw that she bore no resemblance to a grandmother or an elderly lady of any kind. For that matter, she didn't look like a widow either; she hadn't even put on mourning. That blond hair spilling from the turban onto her shoulders; that shapely form squeezed into a red blouse and blue jeans; the admiring exclamations she aroused. Not just the greeting Goatstink had bawled out; that was disgusting!

Ricardo had also heard Osnar comment to Aminthas in a low voice: "Wow! Get a load of that! Tits like a she-goat!" He raised his voice and called out: "Ripe fruit on the vine, that's what she is, Captain Astério. Congratulations on your good-looking sister-in-law!" (Osnar liked to bestow military titles on his friends. Seu Manuel was Admiral; Dona Carmosina, Colonel of Heavy Artillery.)

It was odd: he felt no disappointment or frustration over the brusque change in the image he had formed. That was funny, thought Ricardo as he took off his cassock, put on his nightshirt and knelt down to say his prayers and bless the Lord for making his aunt guess exactly what his heart desired. He had hidden the fishing rod to keep Peto from being the first to use it. His brother was an anarchist, had no respect at all for other people's private property. Ricardo said a Salve Regina for the health of his deserving aunt.

He stretched out in the hammock. Light shone out from the master bedroom across the hall; Antonieta was in the bathroom. Instead of an old woman, a grandmother, he had a real aunt, brand-new and cheerful. And he had thought she was older than his mother! How silly. Ricardo had overheard her tell Barbozinha how old she was. "I'm forty-four, poet. I can't hide my age here, everybody knows it. I went away twenty-six years ago, when I had just turned eighteen. In São Paulo I admit to being thirty-five. Do you think I look older than that?"

He knew his mother pretended to be younger than she was. For all her strictness and devoutness and abhorrence of untruth, when it came to revealing her age . . . Her real age was on her marriage certificate, locked up in the desk along with the deeds to the houses they owned, and his father's military commission, ID card and service commendations. His aunt didn't have to lie about her age because she was pretty anyway. No, pretty wasn't right; Ricardo groped for a better word: handsome, fine-looking. Everything about her was grand and showy. What saint did she resemble? Not any saint he knew; not St. Rita of Cassia, nor St. Rose of Lima. When Aunt Elisa had the blues she reminded him of St. Mary Magdalene. His mourning mother, in her black widow's weeds and ashen veil, was St. Helena. But that energy his aunt gave off set her apart from everyone else. No sooner had she arrived than she had them all under her spell. Oh, it was partly because she was open-handed and wealthy, but that wasn't all. There was something else, something indefinable that impressed Ricardo and left its mark, though he didn't know what it was. He saw her crowned with a luminous halo, like one of the saints. A saint? Yes, her kindness and generosity of soul were saintly. But she also had other, carnal attributes. Not carnal, human; carnal was a dirty word. Carnal sins were punished with the flames of Hell for all eternity.

He heard footsteps in the hall; it was his aunt on her way back from the bathroom. Her perfume advanced before her; the same fragrance that clung about her letters was wafted from her at every step, heralding her near approach. Thank goodness his Father Confessor had told him there was nothing sinful about an old aunt's perfume. Old? Ripe, mature.

"Ripe fruit" was the expression Osnar had used to describe her. In his first confusion when she got off the bus, everything that rake and idler said had sounded to Cardo like an insult. But now, hearing his aunt's footsteps and smelling her perfume, the image of mellow fruit, overflowing with juice and ripe for the picking, seemed right —not disrespectful, not out of place, not sinful at all. Now it *was* disrespectful to compare her to a nannygoat. Osnar was a lost sinner after all.

Antonieta was carrying a porcelain jug full of water. She trod on the tail of her long robe in the hall, stumbled, lost her balance, almost fell. Ricardo ran up in time to catch her, grabbed the jug and took it to the bedroom.

"Thank you, honey." She appraised her gangling nephew with a roguish smile. In his long nightshirt he was ludicrously tall. "You mean to tell me you still sleep in a nightshirt?"

"Next year I'll be a senior and sleep in pajamas," he told her proudly. "But Mother won't buy me any until I go back to the seminary."

Under the half-open negligee was a pink shorty nightgown that revealed more of his aunt's charms than it concealed. Ricardo looked the other way and set the jug in the metal ring of the washstand.

"Bring the washstand over here and pour a little water in the basin," ordered Antonieta, sitting down before the dressing-table mirror with her creams and lotions ranged before her. Different kinds of cold cream, flasks of colored liquids, cotton balls, a confusion of bottles and jars. Aunt Elisa didn't own half as many as that, and Mother hadn't painted her face since Father died.

He poured out the water and turned to go, his aunt watching him all the time.

"Are you going away without asking for my blessing?"

"Your blessing, Aunt. I hope you sleep well." He bent one knee. "And thank you for the fishing rod."

"No, not like that. Come here and give me a kiss."

Cardo kissed his aunt shyly, but she took his face in her hands and kissed him on both cheeks. Scent rose from her bosom. Ricardo couldn't help noticing her breasts, or rather, he sensed them pushing through her nightgown. Tits like a nannygoat's, Osnar had said.

He lay down in the hammock. The light was still on in his aunt's room; she was removing her makeup. A ray of light filtered into the study through the not-quite-closed door. Ricardo, who never had any trouble getting to sleep—his eyes closed the minute he fell into bed—was wakeful tonight. Was it because he wasn't used to sleeping in a hammock? His mind was in a turmoil, as it had been that afternoon when he had first seen his aunt in the doorway of the bus and she looked just the opposite of the way he had imagined her when they told him she had died. He'd better say his prayers. He climbed out of the hammock, knelt down and clasped his hands. "Our Father Who art in Heaven . . ." His thoughts were on God, God be praised.

In which Perpétua, the dutiful sister-in-law, takes thought for the soul of the Comendador, while Tieta and Leonora, in elegant transparent creations, dazzle the bourgeoisie and Ascânio Trindade explains the electric-power problem.

Next morning, over an abundant breakfast of yams, cassava, breadfruit and cooked bananas, and cornmeal mush sent over by Dona Milu—"How am I ever going to keep my figure? I'll soon be as big as a house at this rate"—Perpétua announced the schedule of the masses for the Comendador's soul and the consecration of the Sacred Heart; the mass on Saturday at eight in the morning, consecration on Sunday at eleven. Antonieta was alarmed. If she let her older sister go on like that she'd be spending her holiday in church, and goodbye to all her plans for excursions and lazy days on the beach.

"Mass? But we had one in São Paulo, in the cathedral. A seventh-day mass, a month's mind mass . . . every kind of mass there is."

"What difference does that make? The more the better for his soul. How would it look if we didn't have a single mass said, me and Elisa and the old man? What would people say? A papal Comendador, a nobleman of the church! Why, just a little while ago Father Mariano warned me again that we must take thought for his soul. He said all kinds of wonderful things about you because of the monstrance."

"You mean you've already talked to the Father? Today?"

"I never miss six-o'clock mass. Neither does Ricardo, when he's here. He's the acolyte."

Ricardo took the opportunity to ask permission to change into his trousers and try out his new rod and reel on the river. Antonieta quickly spoke up. "Sure you can, honey. Go have yourself a good time. And don't come back until lunchtime."

"Thank you, Aunt." He rushed off before his mother could protest.

"He's a doll, that future priest of yours. I just can't get used to the idea that he's studying for the priesthood. A cassock in the daytime and a nightshirt at night on a great big man like that, Perpétua! I'm going to buy him a pair of pajamas."

"He can start wearing pajamas when he goes back to the seminary. I made a promise to Our Lady St. Anne that if God ever gave me a son he'd be a priest. Ricardo came first, so we called him after his grandfather on his father's side. He's a godfearing boy and studious, too. I'm very pleased with him."

Tieta turned to the question of the mass.

"What a bore! I thought we'd spend the weekend at Mangue Seco. I wanted to show Leonora the beach, and see about finding a piece of land to buy. The Skipper invited us to stay with them and I was all set to make the arrangements with him today."

"I want to go too, Aunt." Peto, wearing bathing trunks and

holding his flippers and diving mask, waited for his brother to get ready.

"Don't go this Saturday. You've got to be here for the mass and the consecration! After all, you're the one who gave me the Sacred Heart. Don't you see? These are holy things. They're a whole lot more important than swimming on the beach," insisted Perpétua.

Antonieta bit her tongue and swallowed her temper. What had ever possessed her to come into town laden down with religious trophies, when she was never one to go to mass or hang around churches? It was all Carmosina's fault. "Perpétua has a Last Supper in the dining room, and if you bring her a Sacred Heart for the parlor she'll go down on her knees and thank you. Don't forget to bring something for the cathedral; Father Mariano did everything but canonize you in that sermon he preached at what he thought was your funeral mass." Well, she had followed Carmosina's advice and look what it got her: a churchgoing binge. She had been dreaming of Mangue Seco Beach since long before she got here, goddammit! She swallowed the cuss word, too.

Leonora, in shorts that showed off her long legs and rounded thighs, and a blouse knotted under her breasts, with her navel showing ("Lord, those São Paulo fads! The boys are going to lose the virginity of their eyes," muttered Perpétua as she fingered her rosary beads in the pocket of her skirt), smilingly soothed Tieta:

"We can go to the beach another day, Mama. Dona Perpétua's right, the mass is more important." She smiled at Perpétua. "Mama's been talking about Mangue Seco all the way up here. But the mass is a holy obligation."

Now that was how a good daughter should talk, even if she was a Paulista and didn't pay enough attention to mourning and the prolonged rites of death, so binding and unchanging in Agreste. If only Leonora would dress decently, Perpétua would have no fault to find with her. Why on earth did she have to show off her navel? What was pretty about a navel, for heaven's sake? Maybe Peto could have told her. His greedy eyes darted from thighs to navel to a stomach with the gentle curves of a vase.

"Nora, you're right. I'm just a stubborn old nannygoat and always was. When I go after a thing I butt whatever stands in my way. We can go to Mangue Seco next weekend."

With Ricardo as guide—"Now put on your cassock and go with your aunt"—they paid a call on Elisa that afternoon.

"Welcome, sister, to our humble home. We pay through the nose to rent it."

"Do you? If this were São Paulo . . . To begin with, only millionaires can afford to live in houses there; everybody else either makes do in a cramped apartment or rots in a slum like sardines in a can."

"Oh, but they have those wonderful apartments, don't they? Tell me about yours. . . ."

"That can wait until later; we have to go now."

"Not until you've had some fruit or preserves, a glass of cordial at least, or I'll be mad. Try these strawberry guava preserves; not many people know how to make it, and it's so good! And have some genipap cordial."

"Gosh, I'm going to get fat!" Homesick for the flavors of her childhood, Tieta drank a second glass of the cordial.

On their way back they met Ascânio Trindade, either by chance or design. Could he really leave the courthouse deserted like that? Where did they want to go? There was a lovely walk down by the river where it widened to form a little pool the women used to wash clothes in, a beautiful place called Catherine's Basin. One of the poets among Barbozinha's ancestors must have given it that literary name. Or maybe he had named it himself in another incarnation.

"Not today, we promised Carmosina we'd visit her at the post office."

"Oh, so you're going to the Areopagus?"

"The what?"

"The Areopagus. Giovanni Guimarães, a journalist from Bahia, gave the post office that name when he was here in Agreste; that's where the intellectuals meet."

"How funny!" Leonora burst out laughing, a laugh like tinkling crystal in the streets of Agreste.

A short stop at the moviehouse door to wish Chalita the Arab good afternoon.

"Do you still remember me?"

"Who could forget you, Tieta? Have some *mangaba* sherbet."

"Leonora's never tasted it before, it'll be a treat for her."

That day it was on the house; the eye-filling sight of Tieta and the girl was payment enough for the Arab. He regaled himself with a spectacle straight out of the Arabian Nights, illuminated by a ray of sunlight that filtered through the transparent caftans the women wore. Petticoat, slip? No one wears them any more, they belong in a museum. Bra? What for, if your breasts are firm and don't need any wire-and-cloth contraption to hold them up? Panties? A tiny bikini is plenty. Hurrah for civilization and come back soon (and often), implored the progressive-minded Arab.

Old maids and young girls leaned out of their windows to see better, watching every step and gesture and excitedly discussing the strangers' exotic garb.

"Would you have the nerve to wear an outfit like that?"

"Me? Not on your life."

"Well, I would if Ma would let me." Tieta had brought a miniskirt for Elisa, but she hadn't had the courage to put it on yet.

There was a commotion in the bar as the men jostled one another in the doorway. Even Seu Manuel came out from behind the bar; after all, he too was a child of God. Leonora found it all very amusing; her laughter was as free as her unbound hair. Ascânio heard crystal tinkling in the air and recalled a poem he had heard somewhere: blond as a ripe field of wheat. He was informed of the postponed visit to Mangue Seco and invited to the mass for the repose of the Comendador's soul. Tieta did not press him.

"Don't feel you have to come. There's no earthly reason for anyone not in the family to go to a requiem mass. Besides, Felipe despised anything that smelled of death: corpses, cemeteries, seventh-day masses. If I had my way, I'd go to Mangue Seco. But Perpétua won't hear of that, so it can't be helped."

Ascânio neither approved nor disapproved. He wisely refrained from taking sides when it came to differences of opinion between the two sisters, but as for the mass, he would certainly be there.

"Next Sunday? You can count on me. I'll be back by then."

"Are you going away?" asked Leonora, surprised.

"Where?" asked Tieta, interested.

"I'm going to Paulo Afonso to try to get something done about putting in electricity. They're bringing in power lines from the hydroelectric plant to just about every community in this part of the state except three, and Agreste's one of the three. Downright discrimination, I call it. I'm trying to get them to change their minds and put Agreste on their list. I've sent letters to every government office I could think of, but I've had no luck so far and some of them don't even answer. So I decided to go down there and talk to the plant director myself. If I can talk to him man to man, maybe I can persuade him to change his mind and give us a fair deal."

"Will you be there long?" Leonora's question was a plea. Don't stay away long, come back soon, I'll be waiting, said her eyes.

"Oh no, only two days. I'll go to Esplanada in the *marineti* tomorrow and take the bus to Paulo Afonso the same day. That way I'll have a whole day there and come back on Thursday. And maybe I'll bring back some good news for Agreste."

"Good for you! I like people who know their own minds," applauded Tieta. "You go fight your battle and convince your man and bring back the power Agreste needs."

"I'm sure you will!" said Leonora eagerly. "I'll be rooting for you."

"I was ready to fight before, but I'm even more ready now!"

Ascânio was transformed into an armed knight riding forth to do battle under the inspiration of his Dulcinea. When he returned victorious after persuading the distant, cold directors and technical experts of Agreste's historic importance and possibilities for tourism —he knew it would be an uphill fight, an arduous battle—he would lay the prize he had seized at Leonora's feet: the dazzling light of the Paulo Afonso Power Plant to replace the feeble, flickering illumination afforded by the generator installed by his grandfather, Francisco Trindade, in his days as mayor.

Leôncio, former military policeman and hired killer, now a civilian and a cripple on the town payroll, a jack of all trades from janitor to errand boy and guard to gardener, turned the corner and came toward them, limping. Ascânio was wanted at the courthouse.

"I'm sorry, but I'll have to go now, I know what it's about. See you later."

"We'll see you on Thursday, won't we? I'll be waiting," said soft-eyed Leonora.

"That's right, Thursday. But I'll stop by Dona Perpétua's tonight to say goodbye if you'll let me."

"You don't have to ask. Just come whenever you want to," Tieta replied hospitably.

"Yes, do come. Don't forget," the girl echoed.

At the corner of the plaza Ascânio turned; Leonora waved and he waved back. Tieta said teasingly, "Made a conquest, haven't you, nanny? He seems like a nice fellow."

"Yes, he's sweet. I really like him," confessed Leonora demurely.

Of pollution and unidentified objects, an expanded chapter, or the visit to the Areopagus.

Dona Carmosina was standing in the doorway of the post office to welcome them.

"Come on in, girls, I've been waiting for you."

Skipper Dário rose to greet the Paulistas and then went back to reading the front-page story in *A Tarde*, the afternoon paper from Bahia. He remarked indignantly, "I can't believe the government will allow anything as outrageous as this. In Italy, the whole board of directors of a factory just like this one was sent to prison. The judge over there had the good sense to put them all behind bars."

"What kind of factory? Please explain, Skipper."

"I've just read in the paper that a corporation has been formed in Rio de Janeiro to set up a titanium-dioxide factory in Brazil. It's an outrage."

"Why is that? Spell it out."

"Because it's the worst-polluting industry known to man. There are only six of those factories in the whole world, and none in America, North or South. No country wants trouble like that inside its own borders."

"Is that so?"

Dona Carmosina intervened.

"Why don't you bring that clipping from *O Estado* for Tieta to read? The *Estado de São Paulo*, you know, that scandal sheet from your neck of the woods"—she laughed in gentle raillery—"printed a story saying an Italian judge had found the directors of one of those factories guilty of the crime of pollution."

"The crime of pollution? That's what they ought to do in São Paulo: lock up a whole bunch of villains before the whole city goes down the drain."

"The worst of it is," the Skipper went on, "that the paper says the authorities have already decided not to allow the factory to be built in the south. They want to fob it off on the northeast. That's always the way it is; anything worth having stays in the south, and the northeast gets the leavings."

"The thing is, Skipper, the pollution's already so bad in São Paulo we just can't take any more."

"What's going to happen to Brazil? It's a good thing our little private paradise, Agreste, is far away from it all. . . ."

Leonora seized the opportunity to praise Agreste. "Mama always told me it was just beautiful here, but I never thought any place could be so pretty. It's Heaven!"

"You haven't seen anything yet," Dona Carmosina said proudly. "When it comes to scenery, Agreste's right up there with Switzerland. You talk to me after you've been to Mangue Seco."

"When are you planning to go to Mangue Seco? You'll stay with us at Liberty Hall, of course—Laura and I insist," the Skipper offered gallantly.

"Why, thank you very much. I'll accept your hospitality with pleasure until I can buy a piece of land and build me a little cabin," replied Tieta. "We had thought of going this Saturday and staying over Sunday, but Perpétua's having a mass said for Felipe and she's going to consecrate the Sacred Heart of Jesus in the parlor besides."

"Tieta brought Perpétua a Sacred Heart like no Sacred Heart you've ever seen. There may be one like it in Bahia, but I doubt it," Dona Carmosina explained.

"I'll see it tonight then. Laura and I were thinking of paying a call on you this evening. And consider our little house in Mangue Seco yours whenever you want it. Every day is Sunday there."

The party grew with the arrival of Aminthas and Seixas, whose covetous eyes pierced the diaphanous folds of the long caftans worn by the two elegant women. Seixas was almost drooling.

"Skipper Dário, what's this story making the rounds? I heard a flying saucer flew over Mangue Seco and everybody saw it," said Aminthas.

"Yes, I heard about it; the fishermen told me. Some of them swear they saw a strange, buzzing object hovering over the beach and the coconut grove. I thought at first it must be an airplane, but they're positive it wasn't. They've seen a lot of planes go over and they aren't likely to mistake one for something else."

"It's probably some of Barbozinha's friends from the other world come to call. He says he's in touch with outer space by telepathy," remarked Seixas.

"You make fun of Barbozinha, but at least he's sincere. He honestly believes all those things," Dona Carmosina gently rebuked him.

"Such an intelligent man." Seixas shook his head ruefully.

"If you want to know what I think," scoffed Aminthas, "what those fishermen saw was the light on some smuggler's launch. That tale about a saucer's just a cover-up."

"No," objected Dário. "Those fishermen are no fools, and why should they want to fool me? I know all about the smuggling, and they only do it at night. They saw and heard something, that's for sure. What it was I don't know, but it might very well be a flying saucer. Or don't you think they exist? I do. I don't believe in Barbozinha's spirits, but I do believe in beings from other planets. Why should life and civilization be found only on earth?"

Little Aracy came running in.

"Dona Antonieta, Miz' Perpétua sent me to tell you and the young lady that Seu Modesto's come with Dona Aida to call."

"What a shame, we were having such a good talk. Come on, Leonora. We'll expect you all this evening. See you later, Skipper. Carmô, you be sure to come."

They tripped down the post-office steps and went off down the street. The setting sun made the two women glow, touching their bodies lightly with flame and revealing their golden nudity as if the evening light had dissolved the airy fabric of the caftans, that fascinating fashion imported from the land of dreams and fantasy where Chalita was born.

Of calls and conversations, in which Leonora makes an unexpected wish.

The parlor was full of visitors that night. At Tieta's bidding, Peto had ordered plenty of beer, *guaraná* and Coca-Cola from the bar. Aunt Antonieta was Peto's new idol, having dethroned all the comic-strip heroes and the good guys in the movies. In the backyard, young Sabino chopped up a hunk of ice sent over by Modesto Pires from the tannery. Sabino was the only one who had had any real success with the new rod and reel. He brought his catch to Tieta for her to bless, while Cardo and Peto came in laden with crayfish.

The talk wandered desultorily from one thing to another, beginning with the sensation the São Paulo fashions had caused: the wigs, the sheer fabrics, the tight pants, the sandals.

Perpétua came out firmly against transparent caftans, clinging pants that squeezed hips and outlined rears, shorts that displayed bare thighs, blouses tied under the breasts and navels showing; it was all part of the licentiousness sweeping the world.

"You can call me old-fashioned all you want to. Those styles may be all right for young, unmarried girls"—this was a great concession to Leonora—"but for a married woman, I don't think they're decent. Much less for a widow. I'm sorry, Antonieta, but if I was Astério I wouldn't let Elisa wear that miniskirt you gave her."

"Sister Perpétua, you're a stick-in-the-mud," Antonieta laughed merrily.

"Everyone in Agreste is a stick-in-the-mud." Ascânio Trindade blamed the wagging tongues of the gossips on this general do-nothingness. "Even a man like the Skipper, who's seen the world, is against progress. Whenever I talk about bringing in tourists to give this place a boost, he pulls a long face."

"I'm not against progress, Ascânio, my friend; make no mistake about that. I'm in favor of whatever will be good for Agreste, but I am against whatever might rob us of our peace of mind, because that's a thing money can't buy. I have nothing against miniskirts worn by the right person, but when a woman has passed a certain age they aren't suitable anymore."

"For example?" challenged Dona Carmosina.

"For example, two of the lovely ladies present: Laura and Antonieta. To my way of thinking, they've both passed the age for miniskirts."

Dona Laura had never thought of wearing one, but she wagged a finger at her husband good-naturedly.

"I never knew you were such a connoisseur of miniskirts, Dário! Anyone would think you'd seen a lot of them. . . . Well, I'll fix you! I'll borrow Elisa's and go to town and show off."

"With me it's not my age, it's my figure. I can't wear a mini-skirt with all these extra pounds on me," lamented Tieta.

Barbozinha, smoking a literary pipe which was constantly going out, said consolingly, "Yours is the classic type of beauty, Tieta. The supreme beauty, Venus, was like you. I can't stand skeletons that walk around showing off their bones. I don't mean you, Leonora. You're a sylph."

"Thank you, Seu Barbozinha."

"Unfortunately, my poet friend, no one thinks the way you do anymore. You're the only one who'd vote for me." Tieta turned to Ascânio. "Tourists in Agreste? Is it possible?"

"Why not? The water's medicinal, we know that. Modesto Pires sent a sample to his son-in-law, who's an engineer working for Petrobras, and the results were amazing; I have a copy at the court-house if you want to see them. Modesto is thinking about bottling the water. The climate you've seen for yourself; it's enough to cure any disease. And as for beaches, where are there any to compare with ours?"

"That's the truth. I've never set eyes on a beach like Mangue Seco anywhere else. Copacabana, Santos—they're not in the same league. But that's only the beginning. . . . Well, I'll say no more, I don't want to dash cold water on your hopes. But what you want to do takes money, and plenty of it."

"I've already told Ascânio he'd better leave Mangue Seco alone as long as we're here," the Skipper said firmly.

"I want to buy a piece of land there and build me a summer cottage. That's one reason I came, to buy land in Mangue Seco and a house here in town. I mean to end my days in Agreste. Father and Tonha can live in the house and take care of it until I come back for good. I came to see about that and to get this poor girl away from the smoke and fumes of São Paulo." She pointed to Leonora. "Anemic as she is, and living in that filthy place."

"Tieta, is it true what the papers say? That the pollution in São Paulo is getting intolerable?"

"It's ghastly. There're places in the parts of town that are most affected by it where the children are dying and the adults are going blind. We can't even see what color the sky is for days at a time."

"I wish I could live there, even so," said Elisa challengingly.

Leonora contradicted her shyly in her gentle voice.

"Well, I'd love to live right here. I'd stay here forever if I could. Here I can breathe, live, dream. But not there. There all you do is work, work, work, all day and all night. Work and die."

Ascânio felt like begging for an encore. Say those words again, they're music to my ears. Ah! If only she were poor. . . .

Gazing at her, he was so carried away that he did not even hear the heated and enthralling philosophical debate going on among Dona Carmosina, Barbozinha and Skipper Dário about the UFO the fishermen had seen flying over the Mangue Seco dunes and endless palm groves. The elated Barbozinha excitedly launched into an eso-teric explanation of the phenomenon, while the Skipper displayed his vast breadth of knowledge of the science-fiction genre and Dona Carmosina spoke of mass delusions, a not-uncommon phenomenon, as they all knew. When the light went off at nine and the cathedral bell pealed out, warning all good people home to bed, the argument broke off and everyone stood up to say goodbye. But Tieta decided to break the tradition.

"Where do you all think you're going? This is no time to go home. Perpétua, can't we light the lamps? Who ever heard of going to bed at this hour? It's a good thing our young mayor's going to bring in the bright lights from Paulo Afonso and put an end to this custom of going to roost with the chickens. Let's have another beer or a soda. The talk was just getting good."

Ascânio's heart was gladdened (of course he wasn't mayor yet, just a likely candidate), and he sat down again. The Skipper and Dona Laura decided they would rather continue the conversation next day and offered to walk Dona Carmosina home. Just then Astério, Aminthas and Osnar came from the bar.

"Be careful, little cousin, don't let the bogeyman get you," Aminthas admonished Dona Carmosina.

"You mind your own business, you rude thing."

Elisa and Peto reluctantly left with the contingent of sleepy-heads, Elisa with a melancholy martyred air, Peto fully intending to sneak out later and track down Osnar, who had promised to take him hunting but never had.

Tieta invited Astério's two cronies inside.

"Don't hang around the doorway. Come on in and have a beer."

Osnar and Aminthas were nightbirds and accepted with alacrity. Ricardo had just brought in and lighted the kerosene lamps.

"Cardo, say goodnight. It's past your bedtime," said Perpétua.

"Goodnight everybody, sleep well. Your blessing, Mother."

Perpétua gave him her hand to kiss and the boy bent one knee in a slight genuflection.

"Your blessing, Aunt."

"You come over here if you want me to bless you. No hand-kissing for me, I want my kisses on the face. Two, one on each side."

She took her cassocked nephew's head in her hands and kissed him on both cheeks, two good smacks that left lipstick marks.

"You little love of a priest!"

Perpétua, too, was off to bed.

"Goodnight. Make yourselves at home. Tieta, the house is yours."

So affable no one would have known her.

"Tieta's taming the shrew," Osnar confided to Aminthas as the sisters exchanged a kiss and a hug. "Did you ever see Dona Perpétua kiss anybody before?"

"Perpétua doesn't kiss, she osculates," Aminthas corrected him.

Interregnum in which the vulgar, unscrupulous author explains his opportunistic stance.

While Ascânio Trindade is falling in love, while Elisa and Leonora dream, one of São Paulo, the other of peaceful Agreste, I'll improve this shining hour to refer to the story printed in the columns of *A Tarde* and read by an indignant Skipper Dário. "Poor northeast!" expostulated the stout sailor at the specter of industrial pollution making a beachhead on our shores. We already have drought and absentee landlords, the habit of misery, the taste of hunger and the well-known darkness of ignorance and illiteracy, once all too familiar but now almost forgotten: maybe if we don't talk about them they'll vanish in the glare of modernity. To add titanium dioxide to this heap of troubles is, in the author's opinion, not only unpatriotic but the last straw. There are those who disagree with that opinion, as we shall see; many important people in fact, some of them so influential that I hasten to make my own position clear: I am neutral. I was told about the affair when I came here, and I don't presume to pass judgment.

For instance, the corporation named in the newspaper story and editorial may be the same one that gave rise to so much argument and divided Agreste into two camps, and then again it may not; it never has been stated clearly who the corporation directors are, much less the real owners. Mirko Stefano, as we know, is merely a figurehead in charge of public and private relations—signing checks, opening bottles of Scotch at lively parties in the company of charming and compliant females, kindling hopes and ambitions, generally softening things up and applying Vaseline to make it easier for new ideas and interests to penetrate. . . .

A story came out in the paper. I take no responsibility whatever for the fact that it was printed and will not cite the name of the joint-stock company involved, nor that of any other. If the manufacture of titanium dioxide results in a saving of foreign-exchange credits for the national treasury and creates jobs for some five hundred heads of families—five hundred times five makes twenty-five hundred people dependent on the company for their livelihood—then how can we accuse those who invest their money in that industry and those who applaud them for it of being unpatriotic? There is certainly no lack of arguments to prove how patriotic and unselfish those people are; arguments of every kind, including the one that convinced our fiery Leonel Vieira, a scribbler whose ideological integrity demanded good solid arguments along with the check. The factory will be doing its bit to forge a proletariat, the class that will march tomorrow with banners and slogans unfurled, to claim its rights and inherit the earth. To a dialectician of Leonel Vieira's talents, such an argument is not to be despised. As we said before, a convincing argument can be found for every taste. For example: Without titanium dioxide there can be no progress.

The arguments of these people's adversaries, however, are no less valid, for the fumes and gases and sulfur dioxide are the very breath of destruction and death. "The presence of SO_2 in the air around the factory is extremely harmful to the health of the workers and those who live within the radius of the drifting gas," said the editorial the Skipper read. Death to the flora and fauna, death to the water and the land. Whether it seems like a lot or a little, that is the price to be paid.

It isn't that I haven't made up my own mind; I'm neutral,

which is not the same thing. Why should I bloody my nose in a fight like this? It certainly isn't up to me, an unknown writer from the quaint old streets of Bahia—tourist attractions today—a sick man seeking health in the dry backlands climate, to decide. In this pause in my narrative about the homegoing of Tieta and Leonora Cantarelli to Agreste, while Ascânio presents his case in Paulo Afonso, and before the mass for the repose of the Comendador's soul—I repeat, in this interregnum all I want to do is insert the caveat with which most books of fiction begin: any resemblance to persons living or dead is purely coincidental, not to forget that other cliché about life imitating art. While I am no artist, neither do I intend to be slapped with a libel suit or roughed up by Mirko Stefano's hired bully boys. That unctuous and mellifluous gentleman has been known to use violence on occasion when it suits his purposes.

Another part of the tale in which, during the long overnight bus trip from São Paulo to Bahia, Tieta regales the fair Leonora Cantarelli with episodes from her early life.

"I was greedy, hungry for men. The more the better. Father had a lot of she-goats but only one ram, Inácio. But I had me plenty of billygoats and I let 'em mount me anywhere—on the stony ground, on the hillsides, down by the river, on the beach. That was the only pleasure a man could give me, just that and nothing else: to lie down on the ground and be laid. At the old man's table we always ate the same things: beans, manioc flour and jerky. The man who gave me a taste for fancy dishes, the kind you can never get enough of, was Lucas, and the classroom was Dr. Fulgêncio's bed."

Dr. Lucas de Lima, a young physician in search of a practice, turned up in Agreste when he heard that Dr. Fulgêncio Neto had died. The doctor's widow put him up in the master bedroom, where she had not wanted to sleep since her husband's death. She showed him the consulting room and the physician's meticulously kept files on each patient. In the old days, before Agreste turned into a backwater, there were as many as five busy doctors in town, all earning good money, enough to build them each a fine house and a sizable nest egg. One by one they died off along with the town, and none came to replace them. Dr. Fulgêncio was left alone to make house calls, as often as not late at night, on horseback or up the river by canoe. The mere presence of the old man with his black bag was often enough to alleviate pain and heal the sick. He prescribed simple and powerful remedies: cod-liver oil, Healing Marvel, Woman's Health, Scott's Emulsion, Bromil, elderberry tea. Even these were applied sparingly; Agreste's water and air, the breeze from the river and the wind off the sea, were the best medicine. Dona Eufrosina wouldn't hear of the medical brotherhood's paying room and board and had sent to Dona Amorzinho's boardinghouse for the young doctor's bags. She cooked for him, too: nursing mother's chicken stew (Dr. Fulgêncio's favorite dish), poached shad roe and sun-dried jerky with milk mush. Dr. Lucas had no practice to speak of, but he certainly did eat well.

Not even Tieta could hold him there, in that world without sickness or vitality. He might have stayed if its natural beauty, the river, the sea, and the deserted beach had meant anything to him, but the night owl and bohemian of Bahia's bawdy houses and cabarets was used to another kind of life. It would hardly do for a doctor in Agreste to spend his nights in revelry in a house of ill repute; if he stayed, he would have to marry and settle down.

"Lucas was scared of the gossip. Every one of those old cats had her eye on him, day and night. Oh, he wanted to lay me all right. But not on the riverbank or out at Mangue Seco; it was too risky. When he told me he slept in Dr. Fulgêncio's big bed in the master bedroom, I laughed and told him just to open the window and leave the rest to me. I was real good at sneaking in and out of windows as quiet as a cat."

Before Lucas knew it Tieta was in bed with him, sinking into the lamb's-wool mattress. It was funny and soft, not solid like the ground. She stretched out and opened up for him to mount her.

"Being laid, that was all I knew. When he began to touch me with his fingers and kiss me all over with his mouth, and I felt his warm breath and his tongue like a razor blade, I tried to stop him. I didn't understand. He taught me all about the sauces and spices of lovemaking, right there in the doctor's and Dona Eufrosina's bed, and that was when I learned that a man can be more than a goat. He was the one who made a woman out of me. But I think there's still a wild nannygoat in me that nobody's tamed to this day."

Not even Tieta could hold him. Late one night she found his window shut. Lucas had kissed Dona Eufrosina's maternal face and said it was time for him to leave. He had put on several pounds, the town was beginning to agree with him, but in spite of Tieta he ran away before it was too late.

"By then I wasn't the same person any more, I had a craving for something else. It wasn't long before that traveling salesman came prowling around the house. Poor Perpétua thought he was after her, but she caught on soon enough and started spying on me. The old man beat me black and blue, so I ran away. All I could think about was finding Lucas somewhere in Bahia. I never saw hide nor hair of him again, but I went from one whorehouse to another all through the interior, back in Jequié, in Milagres, in Feira de Sant'Ana, all over. I tell you, the life of a whore in the backwoods is one hell of a school of hard knocks. That's where I really got to be good at my trade. I ate my heart out in those dumps until I got tired of being kicked around and headed south. I wanted to live like a queen and drink champagne and have a taste of every dainty dish known to man. No more beans and jerky for me."

"I wish somebody would offer me beans and jerky and a baby or two. I wouldn't wish for another thing," said lovely Leonora Cantarelli.

"We've all got something to hanker for. Not even goats all want the same thing, much less people. I know goats and I know people, and you can take it from me."

Of insomnia in Dona Eufrosina's marriage bed, strewn with feelings, memories and emotions.

The first night, exhausted after the rough trip in the *marineti* and the emotional arrival, Tieta had flung herself on the bed after wiping off her makeup and immediately fallen into a sound and restorative sleep. How many years had it been since she had gone to bed at nine o'clock? She had been used, since her girlhood, to staying up most of the night in Agreste's nooks and hiding places.

The second night was different. Long after the last visitors had said goodnight around eleven, Tieta was still wide awake. When Ascânio took his leave, she and Leonora renewed their good wishes for a successful civic mission to Paulo Afonso.

"Bring 'em back alive," said Tieta.

"And come back quick," added Leonora.

Aminthas was avowedly pessimistic about Ascânio's mission. Light from the São Paulo Afonso Power Plant? It was foolish even to think of it. The politicians had written Agreste off their books. With very few votes, no prestige, no political boss to put pressure on the board of directors or make a deal with the federal authorities, Agreste would just have to make do with the feeble light from the generator until it broke down for good. "Then we'll just have to go back to using kerosene lamps," he prophesied gloomily. "Ascânio's a great guy and he deserves all the kind words we can say about him, but he doesn't know when he's beaten. He doesn't have an ounce of political pull and that's the truth. Ascânio, am I right or am I wrong?" "You're right," admitted Ascânio, "but I won't stop trying all the same."

"Pardon me, ladies and gentlemen, but I'm agin' that Paulo Afonso electric light. It's too strong, it's too bright, and it glares down all night long," declared Osnar. "How do you think us poor nighthawks are going to manage? It'll scare away all the birds."

"What birds?" demanded Leonora.

"Oh, that's just Osnar's shamelessness, child. When he says birds he means women. He and those debauched cronies of his go out hunting for women on the streets at night."

"The pickings are slim enough already. Imagine what that glare'll do to us!"

They said goodnight, laughing. Barbozinha recited bits of his own love lyrics, all composed, he declared, for one muse alone—guess who? Tieta rolled her eyes, put her hand over her heart and sighed comically. The guests were soon lost to sight in the darkness.

Leonora said goodnight too.

"I'm about to drop. Goodnight, Mama, I love it here."

"I'm so glad. I was afraid you'd be bored."

In her room Tieta opened the window onto the narrow street and leaned out to gaze at the starry night. As a girl, she had known the names of all the stars and loved to look at them when she was making love on a featherbed or a bed of long grass by the river.

How many nights had she jumped through that window to be with Lucas?

She blew out the lamp and lay down, as wide awake as ever. Here she was, back in Agreste, in search of Tieta the goat girl. She had trudged a long and weary road, on stones and thistles that had made her feet and her heart bleed, before she had begun to rise in the world, to earn, save and invest money under Felipe's guidance, to own property and be her own mistress. During all those twenty-six years she had known she would come back to Agreste and had dreamed of this day.

A smile came to her lips when she remembered how embarrassed she had been when she got off the bus, the family all in deep mourning and she herself flaunting a bright-red blouse and turban and Leonora in denim—what a heartless, unnatural wife and child they must have looked! When they got home she had vouchsafed a brusque explanation: "I think mourning ought to be worn inside, not out; my grief doesn't concern anyone but me, and I don't believe in showing it no matter how much I miss him. That's how I see it, but others think differently, and people should be allowed to act according to their lights. And that's all I have to say, Perpétua."

Zé Esteves seconded her belligerently. "You stick to your guns, child; mourning ain't nothing but a sham. The only reason I put on this black suit was to show proper respect, but it's like you said just now: seeing as how I didn't even know the departed, why the hell should I dress in black for him? Just because he was rich?"

Perpétua assented, outwardly at least. Everybody had his own way of thinking and ought to act accordingly. Hers was to respect the old ways; she dressed in black because when she lost the Major —God bless him and keep him!—she had lost her reason for living. But she wasn't criticizing Antonieta; she respected her point of view, not being an ignorant woman and knowing very well that in São Paulo nobody followed the old ways anymore.

Poor Perpétua! The gnats and camels she had strained at yesterday and today! She was making a visible effort to be hospitable, to tolerate the invasion of her house and the violation of so many prejudices. Antonieta couldn't imagine Perpétua married; what a pity she had never seen the two together. How did she act around the Major? She would have to ask Carmosina. Did they ever kiss in public? It was very unlikely. She had overheard Aminthas whisper to Osnar, "Perpétua doesn't kiss, she osculates." Did she osculate with the Major, or did she ever forget herself and give him a good hard suck? What was she like in bed? Surely they never went beyond the classic missionary position. Or did they? The unthinkable often happens in bed, as Tieta well knew. Perpétua tangling with her husband in that bed, on the lamb's-wool mattress, must have been a grand sight to see.

Tieta laughed softly to herself at thought of the preposterous sight of Perpétua opening her legs with the Major on top of her, forgetting that if it had not been for Lucas' short stay in Agreste she herself would have known next to nothing about the pleasure a man can give. And, crazy coincidence, she had learned right there in Dona Eufrosina's and Dr. Fulgêncio's big double bed. It hadn't lasted but a few nights, every one of them a night of madness. The sky with its thousand stars had shone in through the open window, and a shooting star had exploded in her cunt.

The first time she had jumped through the window and invaded the bedroom, climbed onto the bed and pulled up her skirt, she was nothing but a man-hungry nannygoat in heat. Lucas understood and laughed. I'll teach you how to make love, he promised; and teach her he did from A to Z, including the ypsilon Y.

"You mean you don't know the ypsilon Y? That's the best one of all. Come here and I'll show you."

In all her eventful life, Tieta never met anyone else who knew the sensational technique of the ypsilon Y. She had taught it to plenty of men; it had been her irresistible trump card. She had searched for Lucas in the streets of Bahia and drawn a blank. "Do you know Dr. Lucas?" she asked everyone she met.

"Lucas who?" She had never thought to ask him. All she knew was that he was a doctor and good in bed. No one could tell her where to find him.

She had had an intensive study course in that bed of Dona Eufrosina's, where Perpétua and the Major later slept and made babies. Dumb as a stick of wood, Carmosina had called Tieta's deceased brother-in-law in her letter about the gifts. If the Major were alive you could have brought him a wooden ox yoke, that would have suited him fine. Short on brains but long on brawn, a fine-looking man: more dark-skinned than light, a military bearing, and horny! He'd have to be, to stomach that scrawny chicken-neck. With the superfluity of marriageable girls in Agreste, any one of whom would have been overjoyed to get hitched to him or anybody else in pants, the lunkhead had to go and take ding-donging, hymn-singing Perpétua to the altar, that Miss Prunes and Prisms, that tough old maid, that rag and bone and hank of hair. Still more incredible, they lived quite happily together, and there was nothing hypocritical about the inner and outer mourning Perpétua wore; it reflected her truest sentiments and deepest grief.

God had taken pity on the boys, Carmosina related in that letter report which had been so helpful. They took after their father in looks and temperament, being cheerful, good-natured and friendly, and had inherited nothing from their mother but her brains. "Perpétua has plenty of faults but she's no fool; she's scheming and ambitious, and when she makes up her mind that she wants something she usually gets it."

Tieta thought about the boys. She liked them both. When she had decided to come back here, she had expected to become attached to Elisa's little one; she loved children. But that little boy had died. In her letter Carmosina had explained the reason for her sister's silence. "It's mostly my fault, or rather it's because she's so poor. Without your help every month, Elisa would literally have nothing for herself, so she lied to you because I told her to." Tieta forgave but she didn't forget. Well, there were still Perpétua's two boys. Tossing sleeplessly in her bed, the aunt thought about her nephews.

The little one was a precocious rascal, too smart for his own good. He didn't take his eyes off her and Leonora a minute, was forever staring at the girl's bare thighs and midriff and trying to get a good look at the curves of Tieta's bosom in her low-cut dresses. He shouldn't have been old enough for that sort of thing, but then there weren't any strict rules when it came to sex, were there?

Ricardo, on the other hand, was a model of propriety and modesty, always turning away his eyes so as not to sin. The inviolate altar boy—no, not an altar boy, a seminarian dedicated to the service of God. That big husky frame in a nightshirt! Tieta bit her lips as she thought of it.

The young rooster wasn't ripe yet. A girl that age would be raring to go, but it takes longer for a man, especially if you stuff him into a cassock and castrate him with the fear of God and the flames of Hell as a threat. The little one'll catch on like a flash, but it looks like Ricardo's doomed to stay a virgin, and that's a crying shame!

If he weren't such a baby his aunt would show him what was

good. But—he was still too young and green. Tieta had never cared for callow youths; she liked her men to be older than she was. The best billygoat for a nanny is the older one with plenty of experience.

*Of the sad return of the defeated knight errant,
the telegrams dispatched by Tieta and the resulting
comment, theories and bets—both return and
telegram preceded by a dialogue between Osnar
and Dr. Cáio Vilasboas, which for its lewdness
and lack of redeeming social value has no business
in a literary work with pretensions to seriousness.*

Tieta and Leonora waited at the post office for the *marineti*. Waiting for the *marineti* and watching the passengers get off was one of the most absorbing pastimes in Agreste. When the delay was a long one, the waiting might be tiresome, but it had the advantage of being free of charge. There were always a few loafers hanging around the moviehouse where Jairo parked his heroic vehicle; others spent their days in the bar, and the elite of the town whiled the time away with Dona Carmosina.

Elisa ran into the post office excitedly. Had Dona Carmosina heard about the exchange between Osnar and Dr. Cáio Vilasboas? Astério had awakened her the night before to repeat the risqué dialogue. "That Osnar really goes too far! He has no respect for anyone!" After all, Dr. Cáio was a doctor, he owned lands and flocks, he belonged to the brotherhood of St. Anne, the patron saint of his daughter Ana, he was a middle-aged, pious, eminently respectable citizen.

Dona Carmosina knew all about it, of course. Aminthas, who had witnessed the exchange, had gone to Dona Milu's early next morning and regaled the two women with a blow-by-blow account. And the cream of the jest, to Dona Carmosina's mind, was Osnar's parting taunt. "Your respectable Dr. Cáio, my child, is nothing but a pious hypocrite; smooth shiny crust outside, moldy bread inside."

"Yes, Osnar does go too far, but every once in a while he says something that restores my soul."

Tieta interrupted, curious to know what the conversation had been about and why it had aroused so much amusement, indignation and enthusiasm.

Dona Carmosina gladly supplied details. The conversation had taken place two days before, the night that Osnar and Aminthas had left Perpétua's house late and then gone cruising up and down the streets. Coming back from the riverbank toward dawn, Osnar with a low-class hooker in tow, they met up with the austere Dr. Cáio Vilasboas returning from the bedside of old Dona Raimunda, an incurable asthmatic. If it had been some poor man on his deathbed the doctor would not have left his own warm bed, but Dona Raimunda had provided in her will for money to pay the doctor's bills when the Lord should call her to his bosom.

Observing Osnar take his leave of the wretched hag, Dr. Cáio, an amateur psychologist and born busybody, could not refrain from asking, "Osnar, old fellow, would you indulge an old friend's curiosity by answering a question if I take the liberty of asking?"

"Go right ahead, Doc, feel free to ask."

"Well, then. You're a man of means, no longer very young, but since you're still unmarried you can pass for young, of good family and clean habits. Now, you have the means to pay for a superior class of feminine company, and might frequent the establishment presided over by the woman who answers to the name of Zuleika Cinderella, where, I understand—having been there in my sacrosanct role as a physician and not as a customer, of course—that degrading profession is practiced by clean women of pleasing face and figure. Why do you seek out these miserable, filthy scarecrows?"

"First off, Doc, let me set you right on one point. I'm a steady customer of that house and, I might add, a favorite with Zuleika's girls and the madam, who's got a mighty sweet ass herself. A substantial part of my income finds its way to that den of iniquity. It's true, nevertheless, that I don't despise a low-class slut when I meet up with one on my occasional hunting expeditions. And some of them, I'm bound to admit, are in an advanced state of deterioration."

"But why? I must say this strikes me as a fascinating psychological quirk. It's worth sending off a memorandum to the Society of Psychiatric Medicine."

"Well, Doc, I'll tell you the reason, and you can write it down and send it in if you want to; I've no objection. If I lay a tramp now and then when one comes my way, I do it so as not to spoil the Father-Professor."

"The Father-Professor?"

"That's the nickname a tolerably well-preserved female hymn-singer gave him one time when we were fooling around, Doc. Just think what would happen if the Father-Professor got used to nothing but the finer things—perfumed flesh, first-class material—and took a notion he was too good for anything else. Then, one day, for one reason or another, let us say I find myself in circumstances in which I am obliged to make do with an unappetizing object, what then? My Father-Professor shrivels up and goes limp on me. No, I don't want to risk spoiling him; I just take whatever comes along, and I've known a homely gal to be worth a whole army of pretty ones. An eye-filling gal is one thing, Doc, and the taste of her cunt is something else again."

As Dr. Cáio's jaw dropped, Osnar wound up his speech with a flourish.

"I've heard about your professional calls at Zuleika's, Doc. Silvia Sabiá told me in strictest confidence that there ain't a cunt-sucker for miles around that can hold a candle to you. My sincere congratulations."

The four women were still laughing—"That Osnar ought to have his mouth washed out with soap"—when the *marineti* honked at the curve, only a measly twenty minutes late that Thursday, for a change. The passengers congratulated Jairo. Tieta, Leonora and Elisa were about to hail Ascânio when they saw him jump down before anyone else and hastily walk off.

"He's going home to take a bath. After a trip in Jairo's *marineti* it takes plenty of soap and water to make a man fit to be seen, especially by the girl of his dreams," explained Dona Carmosina. "He'll be over in a little while."

They lingered at the post office waiting for him. Aminthas joined the group and they rehashed the dialogue which had already made history. Aminthas added a final vignette: Dr. Cáio, livid in the pale light of dawn, literally speechless with rage, his eyes flashing fire. Osnar and Aminthas, fearing that the doctor would have an attack of apoplexy, had stolen away on tiptoe.

More time passed. Barbozinha appeared with a rose in his hand, a tea rose, and presented it to Tieta.

"I picked it for you in Dona Milu's garden and was about to take it to Perpétua's house when the spirits guided my footsteps here. I only regret not having picked three more as a tribute to all the ladies present."

"What about Ascânio? Is he coming or not?" demanded Elisa, who was tired of waiting.

Leonora, the girl of Ascânio's dreams as Dona Carmosina had it, waited in silence, staring out into the street. Not a sign of the town official and knight errant, dusty or bathed. "We'll have to send for him."

Young Sabino was summoned from the ice-cream parlor and told to run take a message to Ascânio: "We're waiting for you at the post office so come on over as soon as you can."

While they were waiting, they treated themselves to a dish of wild-plum sherbet served by the Arab himself. "It'll be wild-cherry tomorrow, and that's just as good. Why don't you come back tomorrow and decide which you like best?"

Finally there appeared at the corner, with hangdog look and dejected mien, their Knight of the Sad Countenance. Even before he trudged wearily up the post-office steps, the observers knew that Agreste's champion had come back defeated from the battle joined in Paulo Afonso. The battered warrior's gloomy face told the melancholy tale of a failed mission.

"Got nowhere, did you?" began Aminthas. "I told you so. You never had a chance. It's a good thing the generator's still going strong. When it conks out we'll have to go back to using kerosene lamps."

"Never mind," said Leonora consolingly. "You did all you could. What more could anyone ask? You did your duty."

"It was so humiliating, so awful. The company director, the one who lives at Paulo Afonso, didn't even want to see me. I had to beg and plead until he finally agreed to let me in his office. And the minute I began to explain what I wanted, he cut me off in the middle. Said he had better things to do than waste his time listening to me, that the decision on Agreste was no and that was that. Hadn't we gotten the official memorandum saying so? Well then? It was no use talking to the engineers. 'Agreste'll just have to wait its turn,' he said, 'and that won't be for a long time, several years maybe, when we've installed light and power in every last hump and hollow in the state. Until then you can forget it, friend. It's no use arguing, so save your breath. I've got work to do.' "

Ascânio broke off and shrugged helplessly. Where were the old enthusiasm and zest for the good fight? Evaporated, swept over the Paulo Afonso Falls, swatted down by the company director.

"And that's not all. As I was leaving he threw this after me: 'There's one way to get what you want,' he said. 'You get the president of the São Francisco Valley Authority—the president, mind you, not just another director with the same rank I've got—to tell us to install electric light in Agreste and we'll be there the very next day. So long, have a good day.' Then he laughed and turned his back on me."

A heavy silence fell over the post office. Dona Carmosina was the first to open her mouth.

"The bastard! That's why I'm against all those people."

Leonora went over to Ascânio.

"Don't take it so hard, it's not the end of the world." The soft eyes were full of tenderness.

Tieta got up from the chair where she had listened in silence.

"Just what is the name of this company, Ascânio, and who's the president? Give me all the facts."

Ascânio, still hangdog and dejected, explained what the São Francisco Valley Authority was, and the importance of the Paulo Afonso Power Plant, and then told them the name of the congressman who was acting president of the vast state project, the one who gave the orders and made the decisions, the only man who could change a plan once it had been approved. But he was inaccessible. Aminthas was right after all; it wasn't Agreste's economic unimportance that was the stumbling block, it was the lack of a political boss with clout, a man who could give an order and make it stick.

Tieta repeated the congressman's name.

"I've heard of him, but I don't know him personally. I do know everybody big in politics in São Paulo, though; they were all Felipe's friends, and they still come to my house. Carmô, Ascânio, come and help me draft a telegram. No, two."

She mentioned the names of two powerful bigwigs in São Paulo and Brasília. Dona Carmosina wrote, at Tieta's dictation, asking them to intervene with the president of the São Francisco Valley Authority in favor of Agreste. She cited the reasons given by Ascânio, adding another that would have more weight: her own interest in the matter, the great favor they would be doing her and how indebted she would be.

"That's a mighty long telegram," Dona Carmosina observed. "It'll cost you an arm and a leg."

"The town will pay for it," put in Ascânio.

"I'm the one who's sending it, kid, and I'll pay for it myself. Carmô, sign it 'Tieta do Agreste.' That's what my closest friends call me. It's the nickname Felipe liked to call me by."

By the time they got home, the news of the telegrams had rocked the town. Dona Antonieta Esteves Cantarelli had telegraphed to a senator from São Paulo and to Governor Ademar himself, both bosom friends of the deceased Comendador, and asked them to see what they could do about having an electric power line brought in from Paulo Afonso to Agreste. The excited comment this stirred up drowned out the echoes of the scurrilous dialogue about Osnar's sex life. Even if the cabled messages brought no miraculous illumination, the public weal had been served. Soon speculation was rife; could the widow really throw her weight around like that? Did she really pal around with senators and governors, or was she just showing off? What would be the consequences, light or darkness? Bets were made. Fidélio put his money on success: Aminthas was still pessimistic. "Why should the lords of São Paulo lift a finger for Agreste, the asshole of the world? Fidélio, I'll double your bet."

If they had asked her, Tieta could have assured them that the gentlemen concerned would lift a good deal more than a finger, precisely because they were lords and she was Tieta of Agreste.

To market, to market, a prophetic chapter in which the imminent end of the world is revealed.

Market day in Agreste was a weekly holiday. The first Saturday the two Paulistas were there it turned into a popular festival and came near ending in a riot.

After hearing mass for the Comendador's soul, Tieta and Leonora went home to change their clothes. They'd swelter if they went to market in those heavy black dresses; they didn't know why they'd packed them at all. Elisa, Barbozinha, Ascânio Trindade and Osnar joined the cortège. Old Zé Esteves, with his jacket over his arm, staff in hand, walked with them as far as Colonel Francisco Trindade Plaza, the hub of the sprawling marketplace. There he took his leave, promising to pick up Tieta that afternoon to take a look at the two possible houses for sale in the town among those offered.

Perpétua, invited to go with them, declined with thanks. She always went to market early, taking Peto to carry the baskets. Market day was beggars' day; Perpétua spent the rest of Saturday morning at home distributing alms, bargaining with God for a place in Paradise in exchange for her weekly act of charity. All week the families in every house on the main streets in town saved their breadcrusts, stale crackers and other leftovers like squashed or overripe fruit, and added a few copper coins for the succor of the hordes of beggars who swarmed into town on Saturdays from God only knew where. Seu Agostinho the baker sold bagfuls of stale bread as hard as a rock, big soggy cookies and moldy cakes at cutrate prices, philanthropy on the cheap. He who gives to the poor lends to God. And at such a high rate of interest, it's a good capital investment.

Some of the beggars lived in Agreste and made their daily rounds, morning and evening, at the doors of their regular patrons. Cristóvão, the blind man, for instance, sat on the church steps during mass, rain or shine, holding out his hand and reciting a singsong litany. The Blessed Possidônio, on the other hand, only came in from Rocinha for the Saturday market, a striking figure with his unkempt backwoods prophet's beard and toothless imprecations, carrying a kerosene tin and a cheese gourd, both empty. Today he had staked out a preaching place near the birdsellers, with the kerosene drum for a pulpit and the gourd for contributions—he accepted nothing but cash. The sinfulness of man was the theme of his rambling diatribes; he threatened unending woe and calamities, this prophet of a terrible, cruel and vengeful God. He quoted the Gospels, chapter and verse, damned all Protestants and Masons to Hell and proclaimed the sanctity of Father Cícero Romão. At the sight of a painted woman he would rise up and hurl anathemas at her as he consigned her to eternal damnation.

Perpétua complained shrilly about the beggars to Antonieta. She spoke as if they were her mortal enemies. Their demands were more brazen and shameless every day; the practice of charity was becoming much too onerous.

"They won't take mangoes or cashew fruit. They say nobody'll buy because there's so much of it, that mangoes aren't worth giving away! Did you ever hear of such a thing? Give them bananas, even, and they turn up their noses. 'Can't you give me some change?' It's money they want. One of them actually called me a skinflint the other day."

Leonora clapped her hands in delight at the mountains of fruit in the market. Many varieties were new to her. "What cute little guavas!"

"Those aren't guavas, they're *araçás*, strawberry guavas. That's what the dessert we had at Elisa's is made from. Look, those are the guavas over there; red ones and white ones. They don't look like much compared to the guavas the Japanese grow in São Paulo, but just taste one and you can tell the difference. The wormy ones are the best of all. And the cashews—the healthiest fruit there is except genipap; that'll even cure chest trouble. You ought to drink genipap juice to build up your strength. And good! There just isn't anything in the world as tasty as genipap. Let's buy us some right now. The more wrinkled they are, the better."

Tieta, the connoisseur, picked and chose her fruit. Mangaba plums, ambarellas, hog plums, Brazilian cherries. The watercolor tints of the many varieties of mango were splashed all over the market: rose, sword, charlotte, oxheart, bleeding heart, and many more; the beggars were right to refuse to take mangoes for alms. And the outsize jackfruit, some hard, some soft, from whose open cuts rose a honeyed aroma.

"What's that fruit that looks like a pineapple?"

"Countess-fruit."

"And that big one?"

"Poor man's jackfruit, soursop, it makes heavenly sherbet."

Leonora bent over to look at it more closely and touch it, as she did so displaying diminutive panties under her miniskirt, to the glee of the bystanders.

When Ascânio had seen the miniskirt he had almost warned Leonora not to wear it to the market, but not wanting to seem like a fussy prig and a hick, had kept his misgivings to himself. All they could do now was brazen it out and try not to see or hear. It wouldn't be easy; there was already a general buzz of excitement, and it was growing louder.

Market day in Agreste had never been such fun. Barbozinha was so absorbed in earnest explanations to Tieta of death and reincarnation and life on an astral plane, matters in which he was a past master, that he did not realize what was happening; while Ascânio Trindade, dismayed at the backwardness of his hometown, could not make up his mind what to do. Part of his distress was possibly due to a different cause: anguish at seeing exposed to the public gaze the charms that should be exclusively reserved for the happy man who would lead sweet Leonora Cantarelli to the altar. Innocent of any harm, the girl could never have dreamed she would be the scandal of the marketplace in her miniskirt, a style taken for granted in the south and elsewhere. Ascânio had seen and admired much more daring miniskirts in the illustrated magazines; Leonora's actually covered her backside as long as she stood up perfectly straight.

"She shouldn't bend over so much," hissed Osnar to Ascânio.

Not even Osnar the cynic had the nerve to tell the naive victim of local ignorance what was going on. They wended their way through the market, Leonora exclaiming and the band of urchins trailing after them, with an occasional whistle, interjection or derisive remark.

"Hey Manu, get a load of the saint in the procession."

Sacks of snow-white, fragrant manioc flour, toasted at the neighboring mills, fermented mash, tapioca, canoe-shaped tapioca scones. "Try one, Leonora. They go so well with coffee. Let's buy some. These moist ones made with coconut milk are irresistible; I'll be as fat as a pig before I know it. Well for Pete's sake, why are all these kids following us around?" Antonieta stared at the assemblage.

Why, they weren't all kids, there were grown men too; what a mangy-looking bunch. Oh, it was Leonora's miniskirt, of course; that style was something new in Agreste. Antonieta looked at Ascânio, then at Osnar; both pretended not to see the jeering throng. Barbozinha was living out his sixth reincarnation in a distant galaxy.

Tieta, arms akimbo like a marketwoman, gave the restless animals a hard look. That knowing, half-humorous, no-nonsense stare, the stare of a rich Paulista or a savvy goatherd or both, broke up the crowd except for a few of the more determined admirers. Ascânio breathed again; Osnar approved. The thing that irked Ascânio most, to tell the truth, was the presence of Osnar, with his gimlet eye and his look of sanctified bliss.

Next came two barber chairs in the open air, both occupied, and Claudionor das Virgens the balladeer, reciting verses from printed leaflets hanging on the clothesline beside him.

> *"I've had three wives in my short life,*
> *One white, one black, one half-and-half.*
> *If I take another gal to wife*
> *It'll be a shotgun wedding, hey!*
> *It'll be a shotgun wedding."*

The balladeer's voice broke off as the procession went by. Inspired by the miniskirt, he improvised:

> *"Oh I'd like to make a pass*
> *At Aurora's ass."*

"This is what we eat for breakfast." Tieta pointed to the cassava roots, yams and sweet potatoes, and green breadfruit.

Elisa noticed with alarm that the gaggle of gapers was growing again.

"Why don't we go on home now? I'm about to die in this heat."

She really was about to pass out. She had not changed after mass and was still wearing her high-necked black dress, an absurd contrast to Leonora. It was hard to tell what disturbed Elisa most, the noisy scoffing youngsters, the balladeer's taunt, or the fact that the Paulista was undeniably the center of attraction.

"Ascânio promised to take me to see the birds," Leonora piped up sweetly.

The crowd thickened as they headed for the bird market. There were the orioles, painter birds, blackbirds, cardinals, blue grosbeaks, yellow finches, parrots and parakeets, and a bellbird with its metallic, ringing cry like a hammer striking an anvil. Leonora was radiant. The crowd following them was beginning to act like a mob at a public rally, with open laughter, catcalls and wisecracks.

"I really think we'd better go now," Elisa said uneasily.

"Just a minute more. Oh, look at that darling bird!"

"That's a *sofrê*, a kind of mockingbird. It can imitate all the others. Listen." Ascânio warbled and the bird responded.

The jeering men and boys mocked them with other, coarser whistles, and the little bird hooted, *Fi-ti-o-fó*. Osnar, laughing slyly, a cornhusk cigarette in his mouth, advanced on the cut-ups and grabbed one by the ear. The others retreated, booing, and the commotion spread through the marketplace.

Nearby on his oil-drum pulpit, gourd by his side, Possidônio the Prophet announced the imminent end of the world, foretold by luminous apparitions in Mangue Seco, fiery vessels of gas bearing archangels sent by God to set their mark on the places where the sulfurous bonfires of another world would flare, transported straight from the cauldrons of Hell to consume a world given over to wickedness, license and debauchery.

Leonora, with her back to the gaunt ascetic, bent over to hold out her finger to a tame talking parrot. The comic bird said good morning, asked for her blessing, and winked at her. Versed as Possidônio the fanatic was in all that pertained to human iniquity and lewdness, those glittering eyes, scorched by the sun of the backlands, had never beheld such wantonness, such monstrous depravity. Leonora's seductive, practically nude derrière, that masterpiece of Satan's handiwork being applauded by the horde of sinners, was thrust before the prophet's mystical nostrils. An outrageous provocation!

"Away with you! Out of my sight! Back to the lowest depths of Hell, unclean woman, sinner, harlot!"

Ascânio strode indignantly over to Possidônio the Prophet. "Shut your mouth, you crazy fool!" But Tieta, shaking with laughter, seized him by the arm.

"Leave the old man alone, Ascânio. It's Leonora's miniskirt."

"What? My miniskirt?" Leonora didn't know whether to laugh or cry. "You don't mean—I never thought about it—" She turned to Ascânio. "It just never crossed my mind. I'm sorry."

"I'm the one who's sorry for the backwardness of the people

here. Someday it'll be different." Deep inside him he wasn't sure it would. Change seemed about as likely as the end of the world Possidônio preached.

They left the rest of the market for another day: the sun-dried beef, the land crabs, the earthenware pots and jugs, the clay figurines, the cane syrup so dirty and so delicious, squeezed out by primitive wooden presses. The fanatical prophet was still thundering as they left, and Tieta was laughing heartily at the incident and begging Osnar to tell her the famous story of the Polish whore that Carmosina had hinted at. A few youngsters were still keeping pace with them through the streets.

The news had preceded them to the bar and the church steps, and there was a stir as they went by, Leonora walking as fast as she could; she had never intended to bring such a storm down on their heads, much less make the world come to an end.

"Yes, it *is* about to come to an end. I was warned and I can tell you that for a fact," explained Barbozinha, for whom the secrets of the gods and the follies of mankind were an open book. "There's going to be a colossal atomic explosion. All the atomic bombs stockpiled around the world, the American bombs, the Russian bombs, the French, English, Chinese bombs—the Chinese are making them on the sly, I've been told—will explode at the same time, at three o'clock in the afternoon one New Year's Day. I don't want to alarm anyone, so I won't say what year."

Brief author's note on prophecies and sulfur.

There are those who profess to discover prophetic references to the titanium-dioxide industry in Possidônio's harangue about the near and inevitable end of the world. When, for example, the visionary prophet alludes to the hellish sulfur which is to destroy the earth and its inhabitants, is that not a clear description of the unidentified objects seen over Mangue Seco—gas ships, perhaps?

The connotations are certainly suggestive, and in these days of popular mysticism there is not much point in denying or disputing them. Radio and television prophets proliferate, but unlike Possidônio, they are not content with a few copper coins. Possidônio is just an old backwoods prophet from a semifeudal land who has never seen the wonders of the consumer society. He can't understand that miniskirts are a blessed consolation to eyes doomed to go blind from pollution. As for sulfur, it's produced in that privileged nation the United States, and there's no need to import it from Hell.

Of unfortunate beggars and ambition—a chapter about petty self-interest.

A pleased flutter of excitement swept first through the marketplace and then the whole town as the presence of Tieta and her virginal stepdaughter made itself felt. The girl's gentle ways made Ricardo think of the favored bride of Our Lord, little St. Thérèse of Jesus, despite the miniskirt, the transparent caftans, and the too-short shorts. Around the demure Leonora, even dressed in the indecent fashions of the day, there clung an odor of chastity and innocent charm.

After they got back from market Elisa threatened to put on the miniskirt Tieta had brought her. Whether her motive was to show solidarity, to avenge Leonora, or to give her some competition, Astério opposed the idea, and so did Perpétua.

"You can call me old-fashioned all you want to, but I'm against it, in Agreste anyway. In São Paulo it may be all right, but people don't like it here, they think it's immoral. So do I, to be frank." The grating, strident voice seemed to be fanning the flames of Hell.

"You don't have to worry, Dona Perpétua, as far as I'm concerned. I'll never put it on again. I don't want to be responsible for the end of the world," Leonora assured her mildly, with a fleeting smile.

"I'm not blaming you, child; it wasn't your fault."

She certainly didn't want to insult her dear adopted niece. Yes, niece; she was her sister's stepdaughter and the daughter of her brother-in-law, an industrialist with a papal title, and a wealthy heiress to boot. Too bad the boys were too young. It was Ascânio who was buzzing around the honeypot; she hadn't thought he had that much gumption.

"I know you didn't mean any harm, silly. If this were São Paulo, or the United States, or any of those places crawling with Protestants, I wouldn't say a word. But here in Agreste we still obey the law of God."

The conversation was apparently inconsequential; but behind all the joyful flutter around Tieta was a web of hopes and plans, some of them very ambitious ones. As they circled around the prodigal daughter, the Esteves clan vied with one another to flatter the two women from São Paulo, while under the cloak of family harmony was a seething effervescence of unconfessed hopes and furtive activity. Each of them eyed the others with justifiable suspicion.

As the week went by they were deluged with visitors. All the important citizens called to pay their respects: Astério's fellow shopkeepers, Dona Carlota the schoolmistress, Seu Edmundo Ribeiro the tax collector, Chico Sobrinho and his wife, Rita, who happened to be accompanied by Lindolfo Araujo, the city treasurer and town beau, who was screwing up his courage to try his luck on an amateur-hour television show in Salvador. Dr. Cáio Vilasboas appeared and explained in his stilted, circumspect way that he divided his time between medicine and farming; if he tried to make a living from his medical practice in Agreste he'd have to spend Saturdays begging. Colonel Artur da Tapitanga turned up and stayed for a whole afternoon to talk. He remembered Tieta as a girl, herding her father's goats on the land bordering his; it was his land now, he had bought it from Zé Esteves. He praised Leonora's beauty. "She's the spittin' image of a bisque figurine we had in the Big House that got broken. If I was still a young fellow of seventy summers, say, I'd propose marriage; but at eighty-six I don't reckon I ought to run the risk. She may be a good girl, good as gold, but there's always the chance she'd put horns on me." He laughed, blew his nose loudly, and puffed on his cigar.

The only notable who did not come to call was the mayor, Mauritônio Dantas. Ascânio Trindade had explained when they arrived in Agreste that His Honor was confined to his own house, having had softening of the brain after his wife left him. Dona Amélia, nicknamed Mel, was in the forefront of the sexual revolution.

Innumerable poor people came knocking at all hours, but they never got past the dining room; Perpétua reserved the parlor for important people. Each beggar had a sad story to tell, a petition, a plea. The fame of Tieta's wealth and generosity spread like wildfire, sailed up the river and traveled on muleback to the Sergipe border. Perpétua frowned in vexation; she couldn't stand being taken advantage of.

"Well, I can't stand to see anybody hungry and up against it," declared Tieta. "I know what it's like to have nothing, and I haven't forgotten."

Perpétua stopped pussyfooting and poured out her feelings for once.

"I never said you shouldn't help one or two of the worst off. Take Margarida; her husband left her on a sickbed with her belly cut open, well, all right, she can't work, I won't say a thing. But David, that gyp artist who never turned a hand in his life, what right does he have to charity? All he does is drink *cachaça* and lie on the riverbank snoring. Why, it's a downright sin to encourage sloth and idleness like that. The biggest favor you can do for those people is pray for them, pray to God to set them on the right road. I've got more charity than you do; I pray for all of them every single night. Why, just yesterday I saw you give Didinha money—a fallen woman with a passel of brats, each one with a different father, and a thief to boot. Dona Aida took her as a maid because she felt sorry for her and then caught her stealing in the pantry—"

"She was stealing beans to feed her children, Perpétua, for Heaven's sake. Do you think she ought to let the poor kids starve?"

"She shouldn't have had them in the first place. When she goes to bed with the first man who comes along she doesn't think about the future, only about her own shamelessness, God forgive me." Disgust and disapproval in the rasping voice.

"Perpétua, when a person goes to bed with a man she doesn't think about anything else, does she? Anyway, it isn't easy." Antonieta laughed. "You've been married; you know all about that, don't you?" She glanced slyly at her sister.

"Well, the money's yours and you do what you want to with it. It isn't any business of mine. But it hurts me to see you throwing it away, that I won't deny."

"She's right, daughter, they're taking advantage of you. They know you have a good heart and they take advantage. If it was me

I'd throw 'em all in jail where they belong." Zé Esteves for once was on Perpétua's side.

Every morning the old man came around to give his prodigal daughter his blessing: "God bless and increase you, daughter." He mumbled a "God bless" to Perpétua and one to Elisa if the youngest girl happened to be there. On this particular morning he glanced quickly around the room where they were talking. Leonora was lying on a hammock on the porch, listening to the trilling of the *sofrê* bird Ascânio had given her. Zé Esteves went on, staring hard at Perpétua and Elisa.

"They want to squeeze you for all you're worth, every last one of them. You better keep your eye peeled. You go on throwing your money away left and right and they'll steal you blind." Was it the beggars he was talking about? He chomped on his plug of chewing tobacco, his eyes on Perpétua, on Elisa. "You take that Dona Zulmira, oh so pious, just about lives on communion wafers, but when it comes down to saying how much she wants for that house of hers, since it's you who's asking, she hikes up the price. It's just like Modesto Pires said: highway robbery. You can't trust those churchmice as far as you can throw 'em."

Perpétua, constrained by Tieta's presence, pretended not to hear him. The old man's beginning to show his claws, she thought; it would suit him just fine if his rich daughter never gave her own sisters and nephews a helping hand. The wicked old man, wicked and ugly as necessity. Now he can't wait to move into a comfortable house in a good part of town as soon as Tieta buys one for her old age. Until she comes back for good, Zé Esteves and Tonha will have the sole use of it, that's understood. And it isn't likely that Antonieta, so good-looking and brimming over with life, will leave her exciting life in São Paulo to bury herself in Agreste anytime soon. The odds are she'll get married again, and then she'll never come back.

And in that case old Zé Esteves would be the master and live like a king, with a maid to look after the house and a comfortable allowance coming in every month—in short, he'd be living the life that he and God agreed he deserved. If he was careful and put something by every month, he might even be able to buy a little piece of land and a pair of goats and start himself another herd. "There ain't a prettier sight in the world than a herd of goats on a hill."

Of land and houses for sale, or Tieta in the world of real estate.

It was the owner of the tannery who had called Tieta's attention to Dona Zulmira's house.

Modesto Pires, with his wife, Dona Aida, on his arm, called on his distinguished fellow townsperson the day after she arrived in town. He was anxious to renew his acquaintance with the sender of the monthly checks that he cashed; he had a vague recollection of the pretty, saucy goat girl whose father had turned her out of doors for flirting. Now she had come back in triumph as a rich widow. He admired her full-fleshed figure and stately air and the elegance of her Titian wig and skirt slit up one side; São Paulo high-society refinements, no doubt. He compared her mentally to Carol; two stunning women, not at all alike except that both were ample, solid, desirable, magnificent women to take to bed.

Tieta returned the call several days later, with Leonora and the cassocked Ricardo. Modesto and Dona Aida welcomed them royally with genipap cordial, corncake, sliced banana preserves, pastry and tapioca cookies. "Dona Aida, please hide those goodies, I'm getting fatter every day. Do you want me to turn into a whale?"

"Whale nothing; you're just right the way you are."

Watching Leonora regale herself on the banana preserves, Tieta remarked, "I'll tell you later what they call that kind of candy here."

There was laughter in the room. Modesto Pires reacted like the urbane man of the world he was.

"If you want to tell her, don't be bashful, Dona Antonieta. Aida and our young priest here can cover their ears."

"No, I'm just a rattlebrained woman. Dona Aida, I apologize. The favor I wanted to ask you, Seu Modesto, is a piece of advice."

A wealthy man, with manioc plantations in Rocinha, flocks of sheep and goats, owner of the tannery and of a vast spread on the riverbank and around Mangue Seco, besides several rented houses, Elisa's among them—surely no one could give better advice than Modesto Pires when it came to houses and land.

"Well, if you want to buy land in Mangue Seco, maybe I'm your man. I own a fair piece of the coconut grove myself. We have a beach cottage, where we could take our grandchildren if they ever came."

This was a sore point with Dona Aida. Their older daughter, who lived in Bahia with her husband, an engineer with Petrobras, were the only ones who came for holidays and brought their two children. The son, a doctor with a clinic and partners in the state of São Paulo and married to a Paulista, was always promising to come but never got around to it. Neither did the younger girl, who lived in Curitiba and whose husband, a building constructor, was from Paraná. When Dona Aida wanted to see her children and grand-children, she had to take a plane in Bahia and was scared to death the whole time. Antonieta sympathized.

"Everybody's just too busy down south; they don't have any time for themselves. That's why I want to buy a house here in Agreste and some land on the coast."

There and then they settled on a lot in Mangue Seco next to Skipper Dário's, who had also bought his land from Modesto Pires. If it appealed to her, of course.

"You're going to love it. It's a beautiful place, and sheltered from the blowing sand. It's just a hop, skip and jump to the dunes, a short walk to help keep your figure trim."

"It is a pretty place," Dona Aida chimed in. "I hope you'll come often so we can have a real summer colony. We'll be going there ourselves in a few days, as soon as Marta and Pedro come." She meant her daughter and son-in-law, the engineer.

"We're planning to go out with the Skipper this weekend. I'm counting the hours. It's been more than twenty-six years since I last saw Mangue Seco."

Modesto Pires obliged her with another good offer.

"As for a house in town, I happen to know that Dona Zulmira wants to sell her house, because she offered it to me. I wasn't interested, because buying property to rent in Agreste is a los-ing proposition. Rents are low, all the houses need repairs, and the tenants never pay promptly. I have enough trouble with the tenants I already have. But that house of Dona Zulmira's is a good buy. Solid construction, with a garden. She wants to sell it and give the money to the church. She's afraid that when she dies her nephew will do the way poor Lito's relatives did; they contested the will because he left everything to the priest to say masses. I don't know whose advice Dona Zulmira listened to, but she's decided to sell her house and give all the money to St. Anne. The old lady only occupies a small part of the house, just a bedroom, kitchen and bath. All the other rooms are locked up and moldering away."

"Where is she going to live?"

"She owns another little empty house she plans to move into."

"And how much is she asking for it, do you have any idea?"

"I can tell you exactly." Modesto Pires went to fetch his portfolio and took out a piece of paper. "Here's the sum in her own handwriting."

"That's cheap, wouldn't you say?"

"Maybe it seems cheap to you. It's a fair price for Agreste. I don't say it's dear, but the thing is that houses here aren't worth anything really. If you walk down any street in town you can see how many of them are empty and tumbledown. It's as my daughter Teresa, the one who lives in Curitiba, says: Agreste's a graveyard."

"A graveyard? If Agreste, with this climate, all this fruit, all this fish and this blessed water, is a graveyard, what would you call São Paulo?"

"But Dona Antonieta, São Paulo's a great metropolis, an industrial giant. All those factories and bustle and tall buildings! What a notion, comparing Agreste with São Paulo!"

"I wasn't comparing them, Seu Modesto. For anyone who wants to make money, São Paulo's the ideal place. But to live and rest and enjoy a little leisure when you're tired of working and making money . . ."

"Is there anyone who ever gets tired of making money, Dona Antonieta? If there is I have yet to meet him."

"Yes, there is, Seu Modesto." Tieta thought of Madame Georgette's turning over the business when it was bringing in more money than ever and sailing back to France.

"Well, forgive me, but I find it hard to believe." He changed the subject. "I heard you wired to São Paulo to ask the hydroelectric plant to give us a power line."

"I cabled two friends of my deceased husband who are fond of me too. Maybe it'll do some good."

"I surely hope so. The gossip is that one of them was Dr. Ademar; is that really true?"

"Yes, it is. We're good friends, Dr. Ademar and I. I got some people to vote for him in the last elections. Felipe never would—you know what those aristocratic Paulistas are like. But they were friends, and he was always very nice to me."

"Well, if you want to know what I think," said the tannery owner, "he's a great man. 'I steal but I get things done.' If everybody did the same we would be a rival to the United States. Don't you think so, Dona Antonieta?"

"Oh, Seu Modesto, I don't know anything about the ins and outs of politics. All I know is that it's a mighty fine thing to have friends. And luckily for me, I do."

"If you get the hydroelectric plant to bring in a power line the people will put you on a throne on the high altar in the cathedral, right up there next to St. Anne."

Antonieta burst out laughing at that preposterous idea.

In which Tieta turns down Dona Zulmira's proposition and has a proposition of her own turned down by her father, her brother-in-law and Elisa, poor Elisa.

Someone, no matter who, had advised Dona Zulmira to sell her house and deposit the resultant cash profit on the altar of St. Anne, thereby guaranteeing herself a place in Heaven at God's right hand among the just. Who could say but that the same heavenly voice had counseled her to quote the rich widow from São Paulo a price that was double what she had asked from Modesto Pires? Now, for the first time in Agreste, there was a market in real estate.

If Antonieta had not known the original asking price, she might have settled for the new one without a murmur. Even twice the original sum did not seem an excessive amount to pay for a spacious, cool house set in its own grounds, with trees and a garden. Nonetheless she had a horror of being exploited; she knew the value of money, and was generous but not a spendthrift as Perpétua mistakenly thought. She had seen hard times, and the bitter aftertaste still lingered. It had taken a lot of hard work and talent and ingenuity to amass her modest nest egg, and she had no intention of throwing it away. With Felipe's death the source had dried up. She refused Dona Zulmira's first price and offered the sum quoted by Modesto Pires. Now she was waiting for an answer.

The honeymoon with the family was not quite over, but Tieta dimly perceived the hidden self-interest of each of its members, the greed that moved them all to a greater or lesser degree—all but her nephews, who still had clean hearts and remained outside the petty circle in which their elders revolved. Tieta's kinfolk plagued her far more than the beggars.

Concerned because Astério was paying rent, she proposed that once Dona Zulmira's house or another equally comfortable had been purchased, the two couples might live together: Father and Tonha, Astério and Elisa. She consulted both couples separately.

"Oh Lord, daughter, don't make me do that!" The old man struck his stick a sharp thwack on the floor and spat out a black wad of tobacco. "All Elisa thinks about is styles and dress patterns and turns up the radio as loud as it'll go, all day long. And just between you 'n' me, Astério ain't worth a fart. I got to watch him all the time so's he won't get his paws on the money you send me. 'Course, if you want it that way and don't give me no choice, why I'll just have to lump it. But if you've got a little feeling for your dad you'll spare me that grief. It might be the end of me."

Tieta had to laugh; what else could she do? That strong, healthy, willful old man in the pink of health talking so meek and weak so he wouldn't have to live with his daughter and her husband.

"What if it was Perpétua, Father? Would you like it any better?"

"Saints preserve me, daughter! I'd rather die. You may as well stick a knife in my chest as ask me to do that."

"Father, you're a varmint."

"Now, if it was you, daughter, I could live with you. You're straight, like me. The Lord made us just alike."

Astério's and Elisa's reaction was just as categorical.

"I'd rather we lived alone, Elisa and I, as long as I can afford the rent. I wouldn't mind Mother Tonha, but Seu Zé Esteves is a hard nut to crack. He's taken a dislike to me, you see," Astério apologized awkwardly. Elisa was franker.

"Father doesn't bother to act nice to anybody but you. He treats the rest of us like dirt. Can you imagine him and us living in the same house? I don't care a thing about owning a house in Agreste, sister, if you really want to know. I'd just as soon not have one."

Tieta did not ask why not. She smiled at her poor sister Elisa.

"Well, if that's the way you feel, we won't say any more about it."

Another scrap of narrative in which, on the long bus trip from São Paulo to Bahia, Tieta reminisces and recounts episodes from her past to the fair Leonora Cantarelli.

"When I realized what Jarbas wanted me to do—solicit on the street and give him what I earned so he could go on living the soft life he was used to—it made me so mad I just about choked. The worst part was the love I felt for him deep inside me, and having to pull it up by the roots. I had fallen for him so hard I belonged to him body and soul. For the first time it wasn't just fun in bed, it was the real thing. And it felt so good."

Jarbas La Cumparsita subsisted reasonably well on his Latin American, Hollywood-gigolo physique; the lean bullfighter's body, black hair slicked down with brilliantine, little mustache, manicured fingernails, long cigarette holder and oh! those fatal eyes. Unknown to one another, a whole clutch of working women labored diligently in the cooperative enterprise of keeping their sheik in funds. Threatening this one, slapping that one around a little if he had to, La Cumparsita made his rounds to collect the day's receipts. In order to ensure the best possible results, the lady-killer had to woo and win his future source of income and bring her to delirium until she said, "I'm yours, my love, do with me what you will!" Jarbas could sing tangos in an agreeable small voice and sometimes claimed to be Argentine.

When it was Tieta's turn and he swore he was infatuated and wanted only to live with her forever, boasting of his wealth and social position, it was not the prospect of leaving "the life" for a husband and children that made her fall into his arms.

"I was so crazy about him I didn't even think of that; he didn't have to make any promises to take me away from the life. If he wanted me to live with him and queen it in a house of our own, that was fine. But if all he wanted was to come and see me late at night after I was through working and lie down with me—just talk about any old thing, take my hand and say sweet words and sing in my ear and open me inside and out—that was more than enough for me. Love is blind, all right."

Once the new recruit was hopelessly ensnared by his lying talk and genuine competence in bed, Jarbas dictated the rules by which the couple's finances would thenceforth be governed, his minimum take to be seventy percent of the daily receipts. "A high-class pimp like me costs plenty, so you put your nose to the grindstone and no loafing on the job, bitch."

"I was so much in love I didn't know whether I was coming or going. I had even started to snuggle up to the idea of going to live with him like an honest woman, can you believe it? And he was just stringing me along all the time. I didn't understand why until it was too late. Just like those tangos he liked to sing about endless misery and woe, *la comparsa de miserias sin fin*. And it made me furious. I was disgusted with him and with myself. Before he even stopped talking, I grabbed his jacket and his pants and his shirt and his tie and threw everything out in the hall and yelled at him, 'You get out of here, you low-down son of a bitch!' "

Jarbas hadn't counted on rebellion and rage. Sometimes there was an attempt at refusal, a spell of crying and whining, but no woman ever held out long against his line of sweet talk and intimidation, with violence as a last resort; if his coaxing failed, his threats never did. He tried the whole gamut with Tieta, but he was wasting his time.

"First he was sweet and gentle, then he started shouting and lifted his hand to me, tried to hit me, imagine that! Me, who's tussled with nannies and billygoats, Tieta do Agreste, who got slapped around by the waves off Mangue Seco Beach until she was tough as a board. When I got my hands on his hair I realized it didn't just smell of brilliantine, it reeked. He went sailing out the door. But after I threw him out . . ."

"Yes, Mama . . ."

"I sat down and bawled like a kid without its nanny. Not at losing him so much, but at my disappointment and my broken dream. Take it from me, Nora, dreaming is the worst thing you can do."

"I dream so much. . . ."

"Well, if you do you'll pay for it. Loving's the best. I started all over again, and that's a favor I owe Jarbas La Cumparsita. I said to myself, you may be a whore but you're a first-class whore. That's when I started to go places."

"Didn't you ever fall in love again, Mama?"

"Not that kind of head-over-heels love, no. But I do like men. I think I loved Felipe."

Tieta had left Felipe's pajamas and slippers in the bedroom after he died, as if he might come back any time, unexpectedly, as he always did, for a smile and a kiss.

"It was different with Felipe; it lasted almost twenty years. I was just a young screwball when he met me."

"He was crazy about you, Mama."

"He could relax with me, and be happy, and enjoy the other side of life. I can't really say what I felt for him, either: love, friendship, gratitude or a mixture of all three. That's why I'm making this trip, because he's dead and I'm alone again, the way I was in the beginning. I want to pick up the two ends of the ball of thread and make a knot; you know, tie the end to the beginning."

"The end, Mama? When you're so young and pretty and have so many followers?"

"I don't mean that. My fire isn't out yet and I don't know if it ever will be, maybe not until I die. I just want to dive back into what I was, and see if I can find out what I'd be like if I'd stayed in Agreste instead of going to São Paulo. I want to go swimming in the river in Catherine's Basin and bury my feet in the sand on the Mangue Seco dunes, that's all. And fill your chest with clean air and cure that anemia of yours."

"Mama, you're so good!"

"Good? I'm good and I'm bad. When I get mad I'm so mean there's no living with me."

"I've seen you get mad, Mama. But the mad goes away and the kindness stays."

"I learned that the hard way. Some people lock up their hearts and other people open theirs, and I opened mine wide. Because I found Felipe. If I hadn't met him I might have turned bitter and the badness might have gone on getting bigger and fatter. To tell the truth, I don't know. People say I'm bossy."

"I think you were born the way you are now, Mama. You were born to be a shepherd and take care of your flock."

Of a swim in the river with two nephews, one precocious, the other bashful.

Tieta's nephews amused her no end. Peto, impish, knowing, devoid of scruples, buzzed around his São Paulo aunt and her shapely stepdaughter every second that he wasn't in the bar learning what he shouldn't have known, or should.

"That boy's going to be the death of me. I whip him and punish him and it ain't a bit of use. He's in the bar learning filth when he ought to be studying. . . . It makes me so mad!" Perpétua wailed, after she had shouted for the boy and found him gone.

"Filth?" Antonieta loved to tease and scandalize her sister. "For your information, they're teaching it in school; I read in the paper that it's going to be compulsory beginning in primary school."

"What's being taught in school?"

"Classes in sex education for boys and girls."

"Saints above!" She crossed herself and took out her rosary. The world was going to Hell in a handcart.

Peto emerged from the house onto the porch, grinning foolishly, mischievous eyes feasting on the half-glimpsed bosoms and generous display of legs and thighs. "You'll get indigestion if you don't watch out," smiled Tieta. He reminded them that they had planned to go swimming in the river that morning. Perpétua told Ricardo to get ready and take his aunt to Catherine's Basin.

On the way there Peto, laden with fishing gear, chatted with Leonora.

"Ma says you're my cousin. Are you?"

"Yes, I am, Peto. Do you like your homely cousin?"

In the bar Peto had heard Osnar teasing Seixas, who was always taking his girl cousins to the movies, or swimming, or out for a walk. He had a good many: my cousin Maria das Dores this, my cousin Lurdinha that, my little cousin Lalita just came in from the country. Osnar liked to warble a parody of a popular Italian song: "*Come prima . . .*" *Quem tem prima, come prima*, all about kissing cousins, only worse. The lessons learned in the bar were not lost on Peto.

"I sure do. Homely? Huh!" His bold eye pierced the beach robe. "You know you're pretty. Seu Ascânio sure thinks so."

"Who?"

"Bite here and never tell." He held out his little finger. "Say you don't know. Huh!"

An avid listener to the radio disc-jockey programs for young people, he mixed disc-jockey slang with local expressions. Tieta and Ricardo had fallen behind.

"Aunt Tieta's cool. I dig her, know what I mean?"

Catherine's Basin was a quiet cove where the river meandered and the banks withdrew to their widest distance apart. The stream wound among stones, pebbles and rocks and afforded clear water and cool shelter. From it could be seen the boat basin, where rowboats, canoes, and Elieser's speedboat bobbed at anchor. Hidden among the rocks on the bank were inviting hollows, cozy nests for courting, where the grass was bent by the press of the bodies that had lain there.

There had once been fixed hours for men and women to bathe separately at Catherine's Basin twice a day, morning and afternoon. With the appearance of bathing suits and changing customs—customs do change, even in Agreste—the separate fixed times were a thing of the past. Early in the morning you were sure to find Edmundo Ribeiro, Aminthas and Fidélio. Seixas, who was usually out "hunting" with Osnar until dawn, would turn up later with several cousins in tow. Washerwomen beat out clothes on the rocks. Catherine was a washerwoman, as the legend has it:

There goes Catherine,
With her basin,
Sweet-talkin' Massa
After her hastens.
The water's like ice,
Catherine's basin's warm,
Warm and so nice.

About six, Carol, the cynosure of all eyes, walked down to the river, in a silence that discouraged familiarity. The water's like ice, the basin's warm and nice, but only Modesto Pires dips into Carol's. It was outrageous!

Antonieta and Leonora, dressed, or rather undressed, in brief bikinis, lay down on the rocks, face down, unbuttoning their bras so as to tan their backs evenly. Rounded, forbidden masses of flesh appeared; it was well worth stealing a look. Ricardo dived into the river and swam away. Peto cast his line as close as he could, his eyes darted to and fro. The best time to swim was at night, by moonlight. When the moon waxed they would come back with Ascânio; it was already arranged.

Tieta admired Ricardo as he swam with powerful strokes, dived and crossed the river. His brown, youthful, muscular body was that of an athlete. Someone else came and lay down on the rocks nearby: Dona Edna, who wished them good morning, and Terto, her husband-despite-appearances-to-the-contrary. As Ricardo swam back toward the cove, Tieta followed Dona Edna's avid gaze as it enveloped the youth. That she-goat likes kids, look at her biting her lower lip. Can't she see he's not ripe yet? The conceited bitch. Ricardo swung himself up on the bank and sat down on the rocks next to his brother, smiling at his aunt and Leonora.

"Good morning, Ricardo," said brazen Dona Edna.

"Oh, hello, Dona Edna, I hadn't noticed you were there."

"You certainly do swim well."

"Me? Peto's a much better swimmer."

Dona Edna lowered her bathing-suit straps and Ricardo looked away as Peto's eyes weighed and judiciously compared. There was no comparison, really; his aunt's and his cousin's boobs were way out front. Tieta watched the scene, leaning on one elbow and lying on her side. Dona Edna was a married woman and a whore, and her husband a tame cuckold! Antonieta, have you turned into a puritan all of a sudden, going around defending the family and the church? Her nephew Ricardo wasn't ready for that kind of thing, that was all.

Peto, the depraved boy, touched Ricardo's arm and whispered:

"Look at aunt's hair coming out of her bikini."

"Her hair?"

"Her *pubic* hair. Take a peek."

Instead of taking a peek, Ricardo frowned at his brother, flung him a reproachful, warning stare, and plunged into the water again. The stare was lost on Peto. Either Cardo's playing dumb or he's an ass.

As he spread suntan lotion on his wife's back—a husband ought to be put to some use, after all—Terto remarked to Tieta:

"Dona Antonieta, is it true that you—"

"Yes, I sent a telegram. Have you placed your bet? Do you think the power will come in or not?"

"Oh no. I haven't made any bets; where would I get money for bets? Edna thinks . . ."

Antonieta was not interested in what Dona Edna thought, the tramp! She fastened her bra, showing firm, full, opulent breasts, not like those flabby tits Dona Edna was so proudly showing off. She stood up, dived into Catherine's Basin and swam in a graceful crawl to the middle of the river where Ricardo was. Peto threw down his rod and bait and invited Leonora in for a swim.

Dona Edna appraised the boy. No, he was a little too young to turn her on.

Of a massage with prayers.

Ricardo had plunged into the river to escape, just as he plunged into the pages of his books when it was study time after an outing; into soccer practice, fishing, and a swim every day before lunch. Coming back dripping from her bath, his aunt sat down before the mirror, loosened her dressing gown, and fiddled with her tubes of cold cream, her jars, her bottles. The perfume floated, spread, invaded the young man's nostrils.

The older nephew was so solicitous and sober, always at his

aunt's and cousin's beck and call—"Leonora is your cousin, don't forget," Perpétua reminded him—but not hanging after them, breaching depths and contours with too-knowing eyes, like the younger boy. On the contrary, he always looked the other way when a breast bobbed up or a shadow was thrown into relief under a robe or shorts.

He plunged into his books to escape into the abstractions of algebraic theorems. He had to keep his mind on what he was doing and never let it wander, because the minute it did, his eyes were drawn to the bedroom where his aunt sat carelessly primping with her door open. It would be a mortal sin to spy on his aunt, that was for sure. But what if it just happened and he saw without meaning to? However hard he tried, it was impossible not to see what was flaunted right in his face.

And thinking was worse than seeing. He hadn't looked when Peto called his attention to his aunt's hair; he had jumped into the river. But even when he was swimming in the water and not looking at all, he had imagined it. Willy-nilly, with his eyes open or shut, he thought and imagined. People imagined things without intending to; that was God's way of testing the faith and zeal of the elect.

It took a lot of self-control to keep the body tamed.

And what about dreams? People had no control over their dreams. The ascetic Cosme had put him on his guard against dreams in which men are tempted by demons and not even the anchorites are safe. You can sin and be damned in your sleep. Cosme's advice was to scatter kernels of corn or beans on the bottom sheet to mortify the flesh. But you couldn't very well do that in a hammock.

From his hammock, in the dark, he could hear and half see his aunt at her evening toilette. Closing the door didn't help; quite the contrary. All that came through the open door were faint rattlings of bottles and jars, fleeting glimpses of flesh springing out of a robe. But there were no limits to imagination, and when he closed the door, her robe opened all the way and her nightgown was so short! Only prayer could engage both his eyes and his thoughts.

Any way he looked at it, by night and by day, his tussle with the devil was no joke, and without God's help he could never prevail. In the doctor's study, before lunch, he tried to immerse himself in history or mathematics, while his aunt painted and perfumed herself in the front bedroom. Algebraic theorems, Portuguese navigators; he simply could not concentrate. The perfume that lulled him to sleep in the seminary addled his mind in Agreste.

"Cardo!"

"Yes, Aunt."

"Are you busy?"

"It's my study time. But if you want anything . . ."

"Yes, I do. Come in here."

Ricardo laid his book aside and went into her room.

"Smooth this cream on my shoulders and give me a massage. Here. Open your hand." She squeezed some of the fragrant cream from the tube into the hollow of his hand. "Go on and spread it out first, then knead it in with your fingers and your palms."

She let her peignoir slip down her bare back, then gathered it up and held it decently over her bosom with one hand, thank goodness. She bent over to make her nephew's task easier. Ricardo smoothed the lotion over her shoulders and awkwardly began to massage them.

"Now rub my back, honey."

This one had no impure thoughts, she mused; if it had been the young'un he'd have been peeking at the curve of her bosom under the lace. The youth breathed in the sweet odor of the cream and felt the softness of her skin. He could neither stop up his nose nor take away his hands. His senses were awakened against his will. The devil took possession of him through his fingers and nostrils. What to do, oh Lord? Pray, for prayer is the weapon God gave men to conquer temptation and defeat the Enemy. "Our Father Who art in Heaven . . ."

"Harder, honey."

Antonieta bent farther over, her hand no longer holding the robe. Ricardo looked away, for her whole brown, ample bosom was showing. Where had he got to in his prayer? "Lead us not into temptation . . ."

"That's enough, child, thank you very much."

As she thanked him she turned to her nephew with a smile and surprised his lips moving.

"What on earth are you doing? Praying?"

She burst out laughing and Ricardo went red with embarrassment and exasperation.

"Are you afraid of me? I'm not a devil."

"Oh, Aunt."

"And it's not a sin to massage the nape of your aunt's neck."

"I never thought it was. I'm just in the habit of praying whenever I'm doing manual labor." A lie, on top of everything else.

"Well, then, give me a kiss and go on back to work."

A kiss from the young'un wouldn't be that distant grazing of lips on her cheek. Peto was a caution. Not even Tieta at twelve had been that bold or in that much of a hurry.

Of happy, almost cloudless days.

There was no letup in the merrymaking; in fact, it increased day by carefree, happy day. There were days for jolly outings, lazy days for talking and lying in the hammock, days of birdsong and infinite peace.

Lying in the hammock on the porch, listening to the trilling of the *sofrê* bird, Leonora Cantarelli marveled that life could be so perfect. Ascânio stopped by for a minute to say hello on his way to the courthouse. Downtown, he told her, the electricity debate was at boiling point. Could Tieta, through her São Paulo friends the political bosses, get the power line brought in? Some said yes and some said no, with the naysayers in the majority. Not that anyone doubted the wealth and social standing of Comendador Cantarelli's widow, but that was not the same thing as getting big shots like the governor and senator to shake a leg. Anyway, it was an interesting subject to argue about to while the time, the slow dragging hours, away. The happy hours, Leonora thought.

After greeting the ladies and passing a few remarks on the affair of the electric light, Ascânio went off to work. Fair-haired Leonora, face flushed and laughter tinkling like the finest crystal in the young man's ears, waved goodbye at the front door. Goodbye? So long, see you in a while; for he would soon be back, a little awkward, a little afraid of wearing out his welcome. But if he waited too long Leonora would upbraid him in the sweetest way:

"Oh, Ascânio, what kept you so long?"

"I was afraid I'd be a bore."

"If you say that again I'll get mad."

Always in the midst of a jolly crowd, they went up and down the river in the Skipper's canoe, slow and sure but with a motor, or in Elieser's launch or Pirica's fast motorboat. On Saturday Tieta and Leonora were finally going to Mangue Seco as Dona Laura's and Skipper Dário's guests. The county clerk, who had recovered, outwardly at least, from the failure of his mission to Paulo Afonso, announced to the fair Leonora Cantarelli, "I've taken the proper bureaucratic steps and ordered a dazzling moonlit night in your honor. Did you know that a full moon over Mangue Seco is the most breathtakingly beautiful thing in the world?"

"Well, it better be, or I won't have anything to do with it."

"You just wait. St. George and I are pals."

Moonlight for sweethearts, she would have liked to say but didn't. Everything was so new and unexpected, an old dream all of a sudden coming true, but too late. Ascânio too would have liked to tell her he had ordered a moon just for sweethearts, but he didn't have the nerve. How could a poor, picayune small-town official dare to aspire to an heiress? Not even in his dreams. Even so, thought Leonora, thought Ascânio, these were blessed days brimming over with happiness. It was better not to think too much about it.

Toward the middle of the week they were invited to dinner at Dona Milu's. Dona Carmosina had announced a bewildering menu with a variety of the most succulent local dishes to tempt the jaded palates of the south. Most of them were delicacies that Leonora had never heard of.

In the parlor full of bric-a-brac and china ornaments, souvenirs of more prosperous days (the Sluizers' prosperity had been consumed by the deceased Juvenal Consolação, who had been fond of the finer things of life, of which only the knickknacks and the mother's and daughter's tenacious love of life remained), Leonora inquired of Ascânio, "*Tegu?* What kind of animal is that? A bird?"

"No, a big lizard."

"And you *eat* it?"

"We sure do. It's delicious. Better than capon. You wait and see."

Dona Milu came in from the kitchen, where she was overseeing operations.

"The sun-meat's almost done and so's the mashed manioc and milk. The green-cashew omelet is in the oven getting brown."

Leonora was reminded of another conversation and decided to get her own back.

"Mama, speaking of special food, what was the name of that banana dessert we had at Dona Aida's house? You never did tell me."

There was roguish laughter, Ascânio was embarrassed and Perpétua scowled. It was left to Dona Milu to explain; age had its privileges.

"Whore candy, child. They say that candy's served in every whorehouse in Bahia. Ain't it, Osnar?"

"Why are you asking me, Marshal Milu? I never eat candy and I wouldn't be caught in one of those bad houses for anything. . . . You'd better ask Lieutenant Seixas; he's a steady customer." As cynical as he was debauched.

There was a crowd around the dinner table. Besides the ladies from São Paulo, the two guests of honor, there were Perpétua, Elisa and Astério, Barbozinha, Ascânio, and the poolroom gang. The Skipper and Dona Laura were in Mangue Seco.

One dish followed another and the *maturí* omelet was greeted with enthusiastic exclamations. Barbozinha proclaimed it worthy of a poem, or at least a toast. Beer flowed and the lively talk was interspersed with jokes, laughter and a few risqué stories from Osnar and Aminthas, inspired by the air of lyric melancholy surrounding Leonora and Ascânio—dreamy on her part, eager on his. The two retired to the veranda to be alone. This touched a tender chord in Dona Carmosina, who loved the part of lovers' go-between and was ready to cheer them on to a happy ending and a wedding feast, weddings in Agreste being few and far between. How nice if it all turned out happily, if Ascânio got over the low blow struck by Astrud, the treacherous viper, and Leonora recovered from her broken engagement with that fortune-hunting cad. Blue sky, not a cloud in sight.

"Don't sit there sniggering, you idiots. Now, you tell me if that doesn't make a pretty picture. She's such a darling!" Dona Carmosina pointed to the couple sitting off by themselves, swallowing bites of *tegu* and *maturí* between sighs. "Ascânio's pulled out the winning number in the lottery of love."

"Lottery of love, you call it, vulgarly known as hitting the jackpot," Osnar chaffed her. "And we'll be losing our future mayor in the bargain."

"I don't see why."

"Colonel, for heaven's sake. . . . Where do you think the money is? In São Paulo, of course."

"Leonora's already said she wants to live here."

"That's what she says now because she's in love, but it won't last." Aminthas was a skeptic, as befitted a humorist. "That little flirtation has no future, Carmosina. It won't go very far."

"Not to mention the fact that the General wouldn't let her stepdaughter stay here even if she wanted to. If Ascânio wants her he'll have to go to São Paulo," put in Osnar. "And who'll be our mayor then, pray tell? Unless it's you, Colonel. You can count on my vote."

The General was gorging herself, vaguely listening to Barbozinha boast he was a crackerjack chef and that there was no trade, in fact, that he didn't know thoroughly, having excelled in all of them in his time. Tieta nodded and grunted agreement, as she realized with alarm that she was getting fatter every day and soon wouldn't be able to get into her clothes. She wished she had Leonora's constitution. The girl simply never got fat; she had seen so much misery as a child that now she'd stay thin for the rest of her life. Tieta looked around for her stepdaughter and saw her on the veranda, gazing meltingly at Ascânio. Poor little kid, nobody deserved happiness more. Could Ascânio make her happy? Tieta didn't think so. Even if he tried his best, it would be impossible in Agreste.

Dona Milu and Dona Carmosina came over to sit with Tieta and the poet.

"I never saw a man as much in love as Ascânio." Dona Carmosina couldn't talk of anything else. "Do you think Leonora loves him back?"

"I don't know . . . she's been through a lot. I told you about it, Carmô. She was engaged to a man who was only after her money, Dona Milu. It was a terrible disillusionment, and she's not over it yet."

Barbozinha trusted love to conquer all.

"No one dies of love, it's love that keeps us alive."

"You shameless thing! And then you try to tell me you've died of love for me I don't know how many times. But then you have a knack of putting off the flesh and putting it on again before you can say hey presto!"

"Tieta, I die for you every day. If you read my poetry you'd understand."

"Seu Barbozinha's an even better storyteller than he is a poet. He's the biggest liar in Agreste," declared Dona Milu and then turned to another topic. "What about your house, Tieta? Have you found another one you like?"

They had all heard about the astonishing hike in the price of real estate with the coming of the wealthy Paulistas.

"The nerve of those people! You'd think I really was from São Paulo the way they try to rob me, as if I hadn't been born and raised right here. But I still want the house if Dona Zulmira comes down on her price; it's just the kind of house I'm looking for. I don't like any of the others I've seen."

It was long after dinner when they left. Ascânio walked them home. Perpétua, who habitually went to bed at nine so that she would wake up in time for six-o'clock mass the next morning, was asleep on her feet. Leonora was walking on clouds, all languishing eyes and a foolish grin on her face, silly kid. Tieta shrugged. It didn't really matter; no one dies of love, it's love that keeps us alive. Barbozinha was right. Who was it who said that poets are always right? After all that had happened to Leonora, having a crush on Ascânio could hardly make her any more unhappy. A few tears on the bus going back and she'd soon forget all about him.

Before saying goodnight, Ascânio put on a solemn air to request that Antonieta agree to preside over the festive inauguration of the new pavement, garden and benches in Modesto Pires Plaza, previously known as Tannery Square because the tannery was a short distance away down by the river. This municipal project had been carried out with the help of that important citizen himself: Modesto Pires had contributed the three iron benches. With its usual obsequious gratitude, the Town Council had decided to change the name of the square. The ceremony would be held just before Christmas, with the Three Wise Men and Valdemar Coto's *bumba-meu-boi* pageant.

"Seu Modesto's wife, Dona Aida, is the one who ought to christen the square. Dona Aida or else . . ."—she laughed gaily; she had drunk a little too much and felt lightheaded—"Carol, or both of them together; that's only fair."

This upset Ascânio, who was never quite sure when Antonieta was serious and when she was joking.

"Well, you see, there're two plaques to be unveiled. One has the plaza's new name, and Dona Aida will pull the ribbon for that one. But it's the plaque on the obelisk, the one commemorating the new improvements, that's the really important one, and that's the one I wanted you to unveil. It was my idea and my godfather, Colonel Artur, who's the Town Council president, thinks it's a very good one. He told me to say the invitation came from him."

Tieta was floating after so many glasses of sugary liqueurs and so many toasts drunk to her health. It was a warm, happy, enchanted evening. Who was she to reign over unveiling ceremonies in the public square? She was touched and said yes.

"Just sending those telegrams to São Paulo about the electricity would have been a good enough reason by itself. Even if it doesn't do any good, the gesture is what counts, the good intention."

"No gesture's worth a damn if nothing comes of it, my boy. As for good intentions, what earthly use do you think they are? In this world it's results that count, make no mistake about that. Many thanks, and goodnight."

Laughing to herself at nothing in particular, she left the two young people in the doorway.

An awe-inspiring vision and an errant angel.

Tieta went to the bathroom before turning in. She felt cheerful, lightheaded and slightly drunk, almost in a state of grace. For the evening to be perfect . . . oh well, never mind.

She wandered back down the hall with a lighted lamp in her hand. She had eaten like a hog. How many years had it been since she tasted *maturi*—that green-cashew omelet? Every dish had been more delectable than the last, all lipsmacking, eyerolling good. How many second helpings had she eaten, all of them fattening? And how many little glasses of fruit liqueurs? Wild-cherry cordial—exquisite; currant brandy—divine; perfumed rose cordial, the indispensable genipap cordial, and all the others—oh, but they had gone to her head with a vengeance. To put the finishing touch to an enchanted evening . . . hush your mouth, you merry, wanton widow.

By the beam of the lantern Tieta could see the hammock where Ricardo was sleeping in the study opposite. She peered in at the door; in the darkness she could just make out the form of her snoring nephew. Did her eyes deceive her? She stepped into the room, held up the light, and saw a sight to gladden her eyes. The nightshirt had crept up to his chest, and underneath he had nothing on. Here she had thought he was green and not ready yet. Well, she was wrong and shrewd Dona Edna was right. He was ready, all right! And God be praised, he was very well endowed.

Who could the seminarian be dreaming about to give him a hard-on like that? Not about the saints, that's for sure. Here was this treasure right under her nose and forbidden to her. How unjust! She wasn't sure why it was forbidden; but she must have had a good reason for averting her eyes, turning her back, returning to her bedroom, burning, and carrying a burning lamp. What a waste!

She slept the troubled sleep of a too-full stomach. First she dreamed that Leonora and Ascânio were fleeing through the streets of Agreste pursued by the townspeople, and at the head of the lynch mob were Possidônio the Prophet and Zé Esteves brandishing his staff. The nightmare continued with Lucas teaching her sexual positions and refinements, while Ricardo in his cassock hung suspended on angel wings over the bed. Then he lifted up his cassock and displayed his prick, and Lucas vanished. Her nephew, now a fallen angel, proposed to massage her back with his magnificent tool. But when Tieta tried to grab it she couldn't lift her arms. The angel was no longer Ricardo but the ram Inácio. She was nothing but a nannygoat in heat, skipping on the rocks.

Culinary chapter in which the author tries to hook his readers by offering them a secret recipe for green-cashew omelet which he got from a blue-ribbon chef.

As my readers may or may not know, *maturi* is the name given to the cashew nut when it's still green. We Bahians, gross, sensual mulattoes that we are, brought up on yellow palm oil, white coconut milk and flaming hot peppers, use *maturí* in a rare dish with a distinctive flavor; more than one, to be exact, for the green cashew nut is equally good in fish stew and omelets.

All that concerns us here is the omelet, the savory tidbit that Dona Milu baked for Leonora Cantarelli of São Paulo to show her what first-class Bahian cooking is like. It was Nice, her cook, who seasoned and timed it to perfection on the wood stove where she's been working like a Trojan for the last fifty years; but we owe the recipe that follows to Dona Indayá Alves, illustrious cordon-bleu cook of Bahia, versed in the theory and practice of the culinary art. She gave me the recipe and I pass it on to my readers as a gift. The sense of well-being that naturally follows after eating one's fill of this ambrosia should make it easier to plow on to the still distant final pages of this already longish book. The age of propaganda and publicity is here; we all live by its rules, and one of the most tried and true of these has it that a gift for the customer is an irresistible lure.

But when I proposed to try this trick myself, my friend and colleague Fúlvio D'Alambert almost had apoplexy.

"A recipe? Just like that, plunk in the middle of a book? Dress it up, at least; give it some lively, earthy dialogue between the girl and the cook, where the cook can be teaching the girl the recipe and the girl interrupts her with questions and exclamations, or *something*. What are you trying to put over on us, anyway? A novel or a cookbook?"

"I haven't the least idea!"

Literature has its own precise canons and if we want to follow this calling we must respect them, insists the erudite D'Alambert. I doubt it; if it had them once, it doesn't any more. The other day a young theater director, a genius and the critics' fair-haired boy, explained to me that the text is the least important element in a play, that the less the audience can understand of it the better their visceral comprehension and the quality of the performance. With that I lost any scruples I may once have had, and so I transcribe, without further delay, the recipe obtained from the palm-oil-and-coconut artist.

Ingredients:

2 cups green cashews	1 red pepper
4 skewers dried shrimp	1 large coconut

4 tbsp soybean, peanut or cotton oil	1 large onion
3 tbsp Portuguese, Italian or Spanish olive oil	1 spoonful tomato paste
	6 eggs
3 tomatoes	Salt and coriander to taste

Boil the green cashews and season with garlic, salt and tomato extract. Put the dried shrimp to soak for some time, then devein and grind in mill with coriander, tomato and red pepper.

Brown chopped-up onion in cooking oil in a casserole. Add *maturí*, dried shrimp and seasoning. Let thicken. Shred half a coconut, bringing the knife toward you—this detail is very important if the mass of grated coconut is to have the consistency of smooth cream—and add to casserole with the milk from the other half, extracted from the fibers and mixed with a half-cup of water. Leave on the fire for a while and add the olive oil and three beaten eggs, first the whites, then the yolks. Add a little flour to the eggs. Taste to see if flavor is right.

When everything is cooked, turn into greased baking pan to bake the *maturí* omelet, which is then covered with three remaining eggs, whites and yolks beaten together, and a sprinkling of flour. Brown in hot oven. Leave in baking pan until cool.

There you have it, the coveted recipe. The difficult part is finding the green cashews—*maturís*—which aren't to be had in the market. If the reader goes to Camafeu de Oxossi or Luiz Domingos, the late lamented Maria de São Pedro's son, both of whom own restaurants in the Model Market in Bahia, and asks nicely, one of them might be kind enough to provide a handful or two of those green, tender, virgin cashew nuts.

The hardest part of all is knowing just when the sublime blend, the peak of perfection, has been achieved. However accurate the recipe, however strictly the laws of cooking are observed, perfection depends on the talent of the cook, the chef, the blue-ribbon master of the art—exactly like writing.

The best and surest way, after all, is to order the dish from Indayá and fare sumptuously on it when it's done. I promised the readers a present and here are two, both gratis: the recipe and the advice to go with it.

In which gentle Leonora Cantarelli announces an important decision.

Early Saturday morning Tieta, Leonora and Peto embarked with Skipper Dário in his canoe, leaving Dona Laura still asleep at Liberty Hall. As soon as she got up, she would take charge of the preparations for receiving the visitors. There would be *moqueca* for lunch, fish and palm-oil stew made from fish caught that morning.

The others would follow on Sunday; Saturday was a very busy day in Agreste. Ricardo had to stay for mass, Astério to look after his store and Elisa her kitchen, and Ascânio to be available at the courthouse until evening to see people who had come in from the outlying districts. Dona Carmosina had to wait for the *marineti* to arrive and then distribute newspapers and magazines and receive and deliver letters, some of which had to be read or rewritten for illiterate farmfolk. For the populace of the outlying villages and countryside, Saturday was not only market day but the day for complaints, demands and requests of the courthouse and the day to correspond with relatives who had gone south.

Dona Milu would go out with Dona Carmosina on Sunday, taking provisions to add to Dona Laura's for a picnic under the palms. Barbozinha would go with them if his rheumatism was better. That affliction was his punishment for the mania of staying up until all hours, scanning the horizon for flying saucers or spaceships from which beings from remote galaxies would descend, having come to earth expressly to visit the grand master of all secret societies, Gregório Eustáquio de Matos Barbosa, philosopher and seer, whose fame was renowned throughout the celestial spheres. He had lately been receiving powerful vibrations which doubtless heralded extraordinary events in the near future. Every so often, aboard a luminous saucer or in the doubtful company of Osnar, Seixas, Fidélio and Aminthas, the poet landed in Zuleika Cinderella's house of ill fame in the Beco da Amargura, where the antique phonograph squeaked out tunes of happier days and there were girls to dance with. In his literary days in the capital, in the company of his fellow bohemians Giovanni Guimarães, James Amado and Wilson Lins, in Vava's "castle" or the famous house at 69 Mountain Slope Road, Barbozinha the lightfooted dancer was much admired. Even now, old and half-crippled as he was, he still cut a dashing figure in a swinging foxtrot or a whirling waltz. And they still applauded when he got up to tango.

Tieta and Leonora watched the sun come up over the river. The girl from São Paulo sat quietly, a faint smile on her lips; the Skipper was watching her and saw that she was overcome with emotion. He, too, had been unable to keep back the tears when he had returned to Agreste and gone down the river after all those years. Tieta was silent, too, her face a mask, with an expression on it almost of pain. Only Peto cheerfully slapped the water with his hands when he wasn't helping the Skipper maneuver.

At Liberty Hall, where Dona Laura welcomed the guests with fresh coconut milk and tiny fish fried in palm oil—"And there's wild-cherry and passion-fruit daiquiris for whoever wants one"— the Skipper drew up a table and unfolded a rough sketch he'd made of Modesto Pires' lots.

"Here's our place, Liberty Hall. If I were you, Tieta, I'd buy this lot here right next to ours in the coconut grove. It's the prettiest part and it's sheltered from the sand dunes. We can go take a look at it if you like."

"Let's go right now. That's why I came."

That wasn't why she had come; she had come to see the dunes again and find her old self. But she was holding out on purpose, holding in her longing to run to the high dunes, climb to the top and look out over the vastness. She, the Skipper and Leonora went to examine the beauties of the lot firsthand. Yes, she would buy it as soon as she got back to Agreste.

"You can settle the deal right here. Modesto and Dona Aida are staying at their beach house. In fact, he's invited you over for an aperitif before lunch. They live a little farther down the beach, near the fishing village."

"Everything's so beautiful here! I never saw anything like it," said Leonora on the way back to Liberty Hall, where Dona Laura pressed her to try the wild-cherry *batida*. "Thank you, Dona Laura, I'll have one later. Right now, if you don't mind, I'd like to walk on the beach." She was a sweetheart, so gentle and polite.

"All right, but lunch is almost ready and we have to go to Seu Modesto's first. Gripa's already started on the fish stew, it's her specialty." The plump, creamy-skimmed mulatto woman in the tiny kitchen smiled complacently as she scaled the fish.

"I'll just take a quick look and come back."

"I'll go with you." Tieta's voice was hoarse.

Peto dashed out in front of them, clambered up the dunes and soon reached the top. Mounted on a dry palm frond, he slid down in a flash and waved to his aunt and Leonora to follow suit. The wind blew hard and strong, eddying the sand and swirling it in the air.

Tieta felt the sea wind blowing in her face and breathed the unmistakable sea smell. Fine sand, blown by the strong wind from the other side of the bar, penetrated her hair. The sun burned her skin. It was here that she had been a woman for the first time.

In Agreste she had asked Chalita the Arab what had become of the peddler. Oh, hadn't she heard? He had been shot for resisting arrest when the police went after him in Vila de Santa Luzia about ten years ago. It was brave of him not to give himself up; they never found the merchandise so they had no proof. Chalita stroked his big mustache.

"He liked to take tramps out to Mangue Seco. Little girls, too." The sleepy sultan's gaze rested on Tieta. For an instant, between the two of them at the moviehouse door, the smuggler came back to life.

The great dunes loomed up before them. Peto galloped down astride his palm branch. Which of these dunes had Tieta climbed on that long-ago afternoon of the peddler? Leonora looked at her inquiringly, but she shook her head.

"How do I know, Leonora? I feel so funny inside. Being here again, with that wind in my face and that ocean out there. Everything else in the world may have gone to the dogs, but Mangue Seco's still here, do you understand? When you get to the top you'll see what I mean."

They were already almost there. Peto caught up with them before Leonora could struggle to the top, the sand almost burying her feet at every step.

"God in Heaven! This can't be real!" the girl cried out when she saw the whole boundless landscape and seascape before her.

She looked around for Tieta with sun-dazzled eyes and saw her standing erect on the highest point, at the very end of the dunes where they hung over the ocean, wrapped around by the wind, beaten by the sand, a shepherdess gazing down at her bridal bed.

Leonora went up to her and said in a choked voice, "Mama, I don't ever want to leave here, never. I'm not going back to São Paulo."

Peto urged them to slide back down riding a palm branch, it was so much fun. Tieta made no reply to Leonora's mad words, and they were carried away by the wind.

"Never again!" vowed the girl.

It was far better to drown here, overwhelmed by the towering waves of an angry sea.

In which Tieta buys a piece of land in Mangue Seco and Leonora politely daydreams.

That night by moonlight, she and Tieta went back to the dunes. Leonora felt that she was floating in that enchanted scene, all at once free of the past, newly born in the magic of a full moon pouring over the dunes and the sea, lulled by the pounding waves. She had wanted to stay up there that morning and lie down on the sand and be filled with peace. But when the Skipper came to remind them of Dona Aida and Modesto Pires' invitation, Leonora, not wanting to be rude, returned with Tieta to Liberty Hall.

If she could have had her way she would have stayed there now on the dunes, under the moon Ascânio had ordered, every bit as dazzling as he had promised, and listened to the night sea dashing against the mountains of sand. She wouldn't mind being alone; she'd be thinking of him, so honorable, so zealous in his administrative duties. A decent fellow, people said of Ascânio. Decency was a rare virtue, Leonora knew that well enough. She had had to go from one end of Brazil to the other to find out what it was like. Then she realized she was being unfair; Tieta was surely decent in her way. Decency wasn't the same as dove-white innocence and chastity. A woman who'll deal with you straight and won't let you down, they called her at the Retreat.

If she were up on the dunes she could slide down on a palm-branch toboggan like that naughty Peto. She had never been naughty, nor a tomboy, nor a little girl. She had had no childhood or adolescence, had never tasted a first kiss given and received in a rush of tenderness. She had never had a sweetheart, never heard whispered, loving words. At thirteen her nonexistent breasts were being pawed.

She strained her ears to hear the harmonica; there was merry-making in the village. As they walked by they had seen the fishermen gathered around the player in front of one of the huts. The musician was none other than Claudionor das Virgens, with his accordion, his rollicking tunes, his popular songs and improvisations. He strolled from village to village, christening to christening, wedding to wedding; wherever there was a party he would know about it and turn up. When he saw the group go by he sang a greeting:

> "Hail, Master Skipper
> And hail your honored guests."

At Liberty Hall, Antonieta, impatient as always when she wanted something, arranged then and there to buy her longed-for piece of land. Leonora, who took no part in the conversation, tried to follow the jouncy tune of the accordion.

"You can take as long as you want to pay. I may be the owner, but I kid you not: land on Mangue Seco isn't really for sale. No one even knows who owns a lot of this land. It's been four years at least since I last sold a lot, and that was to a gringo who came around. Remember, Skipper?"

"Oh, yes, that German artist. He swore he was going to get rid of his house in Bavaria and come live out here on Mangue Seco."

"He paid three installments in advance because he thought it would take him three months to settle his affairs in Germany and come back here for good. Well, he never came back and he never paid the rest."

"I'll pay you now, Seu Modesto, and in good hard cash," declared Tieta, laughing.

"I can see you're no businesswoman, Dona Antonieta. With this inflation, it's always better to pay in installments."

"I don't like to owe money, that's why; but that doesn't mean I haven't got good sense. Since I'm paying cash down, I want a discount."

Now it was Modesto Pires' turn to laugh.

"A discount? Oh, all right. What do you say to five percent? Not because you're paying cash down but for the pleasure of having you as a neighbor."

They were lounging under the coconut trees, some in deck chairs, some sitting on low stools or a rustic wooden bench near the door of the house, talking comfortably while around them the moon melted into light. Peto, who was lying on a mat, had gone to sleep.

Leonora listened to the talk with half an ear. She'd buy land in Mangue Seco too if she could, not for her old age, but to live on right now. She had yearned all her life for sentiments and truths of whose existence she knew only from hearsay, through movies and soap operas. Nothing very grand, just normal human sentiments and everyday truths. Her grandmother, reminiscing about life in their Tuscan village before the crossing to America, used to speak of simple things: family, harmony, peace, love. What would love be like? In the rotten alleys and filthy slums there was no one to explain.

The lower she sank, the more defeated, lacerated, torn inside she was, the more Leonora took refuge in her modest, impossible dream: affection, tenderness, the clean love of a man. She knew a decent life must exist somewhere beyond the iron circle of sorrow and despair into which she'd been born and matured and become a woman. Walking up and down Avenida Paulista in the cold hours before dawn, bearing her heavy burden as her punishment for having been born to parents so poor in a country so rich; even then, the more her wounds throbbed, the more she dreamed. It was either dream or die.

At the last minute, when the iron circle that was her horizon became a noose around her throat and had tightened to suffocation, she had met with kindness where it was least expected and rested in it gratefully, learning new values and beginning to feel like a human being. The wild dreams of eternal love had faded, for since her new situation was not degrading, only sad, she was less in need of them. Not that she wanted nothing better; she still nurtured the desire and the intention to escape and live the life she longed for: a home, a companion (she had no hope of marriage anymore) and a couple of children. Others might crave money and fame; Leonora like her grandmother had been born to be a housewife and the mother of a family and aspired to nothing more.

Here in Agreste, this placid new world where life seemed to be more sleeping than waking, Leonora was seized with exaltation and fear. In Agreste the dream was no longer pure fantasy; it had assumed a real form in a restrained kind of courtship, was fed on smiles and glances, little courtesies, and hesitant words; grew to the song of the *sofrê* bird, the gift of the fairytale prince whom she didn't want to be a real prince, a rich man or nobleman, only Prince Charming, a decent man. Knowing as she did that he could never be her own, Leonora longed to walk up to the edge of that simple, marvelous world and touch it with her fingertips.

If she wanted to do the right thing she'd be frank with Mama, hear what she had to say and follow her advice. She was afraid, however, that Tieta would take alarm and decide to go back to São Paulo sooner than she had planned. All Leonora hoped for was a few days of tenderness, only a few, all too soon to be cut short; but knowing that we are to die does not keep us from enjoying life as it comes. Leonora only wanted the right to hear and reply to tremulous words of affection, make timid gestures of love, exchange her first kiss. What would that kiss be like?

She wanted memories to keep and store up and fill her loneliness with nostalgia. She had never felt nostalgic or homesick for anything or anyone. Everything that had happened to her on her way through life had been foul and degrading, best forgotten. And it was very hard not to have at least one happy moment, a face, a caress, a word to remember; not to be homesick for anything. Solitude becomes empty and dangerous then. So she implored the mercy of a few days' happiness, enough to fill her heart with tender moments to remember later. Then she could say, "Let's go away from here, Mama, before it's too late."

Claudionor and his accordion were still going strong at the dance; the balladeer could play all night long, night after night, and never get tired. The putt-putt of a motor boat mingled with the music down by the river. Who could it be? Leonora knew she would feel nostalgic for these minutes of anticipation. She followed the noise as it grew louder and changed tempo; the boat was battling the surf at the sandbar. The festive harmonica reigned alone again.

Then there were footsteps on the sand. Leonora rose to her feet. Ascânio appeared out of the moonlight. The girl impulsively ran to meet him.

Hands touched, lips smiled, eyes gleamed in the darkness.

"I came in Pirica's launch. He came especially to bring me here; he's already on his way back." The motor started up again as the boat met the waves.

"So you couldn't wait until tomorrow, eh, Seu Ascânio? Good for you. When someone's waiting for you, you shouldn't be late," was the Skipper's greeting.

The young man fumbled for an excuse.

"I'd rather travel at night than get up at the crack of dawn."

He wasn't sure how to act. Should he sit down and join in the conversation, or go off with Leonora? Dona Aida came to his aid.

"Why don't you take Leonora up on the dunes to look at the moonlight? It's so"—she was going to say "romantic," but stopped herself—"so lovely."

The girl quickly tied a kerchief over her hair.

"If you'll excuse us . . ."

The stir woke Peto: "I want to go with you," he said sleepily. But the Skipper, their accomplice, vetoed that.

"It's time kids were in bed."

Their forms disappeared among the palms.

"Oh, to be young again!" Dona Laura sighed. "My only regret is that Dário and I didn't do our courting here on Mangue Seco. We'd already been married ten years when I saw this place for the first time."

"It was our second honeymoon," the Skipper reminded her.

"That girl has such lovely manners . . . you can see she comes from a good family," said Dona Aida approvingly.

Tieta looked pensively after the two shadowy forms for a moment before answering.

"Leonora? Yes, she's a darling. She's just getting over a very unhappy love affair. Her fiancé turned out to be a fortune hunter of the worst kind. Luckily I found out about it in time. But the damage was done; the poor girl took it so hard her health broke down. She couldn't sleep, couldn't eat, ended up with anemia. So I thought I'd bring her with me to see if the air in Agreste can cure her."

"You did just the right thing. She'll get over it here in two shakes. There's nothing like goat's milk to help a person get his strength back," Modesto Pires assented.

"The strange thing is that Ascânio had a terrible disappointment himself. Haven't you heard about it, Dona Antonieta?" asked Dona Aida.

Antonieta had heard the story not once but several times, but she did not want to deprive Dona Aida of the pleasure of telling her own annotated version.

"No, ma'am."

"You haven't?" Dona Aida was surprised and delighted. "Well, then, I'll tell you all about it."

Of a first kiss while looking toward the coast of Africa; a dreadfully romantic chapter of the kind no one writes anymore.

They sat down on the crest of a dune with the ocean before them.

"Thank you," Leonora said.

"What for?"

"For the moon. You ordered it, didn't you?"

"Oh!" He relaxed a little. "Do you like it? Didn't I tell you St. George is my pal?"

"Thanks for coming, too."

A warm feeling in Ascânio's chest kept him from speaking. The sounds of the village festivities were lost in the thud of the waves against the dunes. Any topic of conversation was better than sitting there dumb as a post.

"Jonas, the head man of the fishing colony, is celebrating his birthday today. He has only one arm, you know; a shark ate the left one."

"Are there many sharks around here?"

"The sea's full of them out there. Sometimes they come in to shore, and they're so fierce they'll bite anything that moves. If you don't look lively you're a goner."

This was no time to think of death. Perhaps that was why they crept timidly back into their shells. Both fell silent, each stealing a glance at the other now and then. But it felt so good even so! There was the moon stuck up there, the moon he had ordered just for the two of them. A lovers' moon, and this was the moment to talk about love. Ascânio tried to say so; tried out a phrase only to have it die on his lips.

Finally he said in desperation, "Africa's over on the other side."

"Africa?"

He pointed into the distance.

"On the other side of the ocean."

"Oh yes, Africa! I know it is." She tried to keep the conversation going. "Were you very busy today?"

It was neither geography nor administrative problems that were on their minds, but where was he to muster up the courage for the ardent words that were still *de rigueur* as a declaration of love for sweethearts in Agreste?

Oh, it had been like any other Saturday: requests to pave roads, clean out springs, and make other little improvements, a cattle guard here, a footbridge there. Leonora couldn't imagine how poor Agreste really was. And to think it had been a rich community once, when Ascânio's grandfather was mayor.

"I hear you're going to be the next mayor."

"I guess I am. You know why? Because nobody else wants the job. But I'll be glad to take it. And I'll tell you something else. You can call me a Utopian if you want to, but I'm optimistic. I think everything's going to change and good times will come back. I can't stand watching this place die a slow death."

"It's good to be optimistic. You really love the place where you were born."

"Yes, I do. I want Agreste to pick itself up out of the mud, and, by golly, I'm going to see that it does!" Now he had found his voice and was eager to talk. "Life is funny, isn't it? Less than a month ago I didn't have any confidence or hope left. I wrote letters to the newspapers and requests to the government, but I had no faith that anything would happen. And now everything seems easy. After . . ."

"After what?"

"After you all got here. Everything's changed, everything's cheerful and bright. Even me."

"That's because of Mama. Wherever she is she makes sadness fly away. She's the best person in the world."

"Yes, because of her too. But for me . . ."

Leonora waited, her heart beating wildly. The wind blew up scraps of laughter, snatches of the accordion, the name Arminda shouted in the shindig. Ascânio said in a burst of feeling, "I was just a zombie before. I wasn't having any fun at all. Nothing meant a thing to me. I'd like to tell you, if you'll let me. Her name was Astrud."

He didn't need to tell her. Who in Agreste hadn't heard the tale? Dona Carmosina, who was just as romantic as Leonora, had recited the letters for her and Tieta and sighed over the sad parts. Leonora was disgusted at the way that two-timing girl had carried on. Tieta had just laughed; no sentimentality for her. "Love keeps us alive, it doesn't kill us, does it, Barbozinha?" Ascânio did not wait for Leonora's consent. She heard him out and felt indignant all over again.

She heard about his studies, his engagement, his father's illness, the letter announcing the broken engagement and Astrud's imminent marriage. Why had she kept on swearing she was in love with him when she was already in another man's arms, giving him what she had never given Ascânio and he, supposing her innocent, angelic, and saintly, had never asked for? She had made a fool of him, he confessed to Dona Carmosina, the good friend and confidante who had grieved along with him.

"Not even if a girl in the form of an angel stepped off Jairo's *marineti* . . ." he had declared, never thinking such a miracle was possible. It had happened, though. A girl in the form of an angel *had* stepped off Jairo's *marineti*.

Leonora stood up, facing the ocean, gazing into the distance where the moonlight melted into the night. Ascânio stood up too, wanting to complete his sentence: a girl in the form of an angel, and rich—oh, why? Alas for Sant'Ana do Agreste's poor county clerk and his miserable salary. Why, why did she have to be so rich?

Before he could say a word about poverty and wealth, Leonora, trembling, her eyes moist, came up to him, touched his cheek with her hand, and offered him her lips. Then she turned and went running down the dune, away from the moonlight and starlight, exalted and cast down, the taste of her very first kiss on her lips.

Ascânio did not try to follow her. He stood stock-still; when he left that spot it would be to conquer the world. Oh, yes! One day he would go to her and say: "I can't offer you luxury but I earn enough for us to live on now, and I've come for you." The moon sank down the faraway sky on the seaway to the coast of Africa.

Of how Perpétua wangles help from God to ensure the success of her diabolical plans.

Mangue Seco Beach was a lively place that Sunday with the arrival of a host of friends, Dona Carmosina, blissfully unconscious of how frightful she looked in a lavender bathing suit, in the lead. Perpétua, in her inevitable black crepe, had condescended to join the group. Dona Milu was overflowing with high spirits; she hadn't been to Mangue Seco in more than six months. Not for lack of invitations, Skipper Dário remarked. That was the truth: she had no lack of invitations and plenty of time; what she lacked at her age was get-up-and-go. They all laughed at the lie; no woman alive had more get-up-and-go than Dona Milu. "The years keep piling up and Ma's friskier than ever," Dona Carmosina affirmed.

Barbozinha had shed his jacket and tie in the motorboat, exposing himself to the wind despite his rheumatism. One night long ago he had climbed the dunes with Tieta, declaiming verses written for her and later collected in a book, *Poems from Agreste* (De Matos Barbosa, *Poemas do Agreste*, illustrations by Calasans Neto, Edições Macunaíma, Bahia, 1953). The first part of the volume, "Stanzas to an Untamed Sea," described wild waves breaking on Mangue Seco and a wild and ardent shepherdess burning with desire. Those two glorious nights of love and poetry were over all too soon, his duties as a civil servant calling him to the capital. She promised to wait for him; she always promised. A few months afterward a letter from Agreste brought the news of Tieta's departure. And now, twenty-seven years later, when he was decrepit and rheumatic, he saw her again in all her opulent beauty, a finer figure of a woman than ever, to remind him of the wild, free shepherdess and the untamed sea. She was a widow and he a bachelor. Was it because of Tieta that he had never married? He looked forward to reciting to her on the dunes, by moonlight, the great poem he had just written in her

honor, all done in the high "condor" style, so suited to public elocu-
tion. In it Tieta, apotheosized as Venus the morning star, pales with
her brilliance his feeble starlight until, once his, she causes the poet to
blaze forth like the sun as it bursts from the sea at Mangue Seco.

Aminthas, Osnar, Fidélio and Seixas came along with Astério.
Modern sounds invaded Mangue Seco, supplanting Claudionor das
Virgens's accordion while the troubadour slept off his hangover
from last night's party. But where was Ricardo? At first Antonieta
was surrounded, embraced and kissed by so many people she didn't
realize that her nephew was not among them. When the confusion
had died down a little, she suddenly missed him.

"Why, where's Cardo?"

"He couldn't come," explained Perpétua, obviously put out.
"Father Mariano's gone to Rocinha for the marriages and chris-
tenings—he goes there twice a year, in June and December—and he
took Ricardo with him. He asked for your blessing; you know how
fond he is of you. But he's a seminarian, so he had to go with the
Father."

Tieta neither commented nor replied, but Perpétua could tell
she was disappointed by the way she folded her lips together.
Perpétua rejoiced at the sight; so our rich sister's missing her
nephew? She's growing attached to the boys; that's all to the good.

"All hands in the briny!" ordered the Skipper, and was obeyed
in a flash.

Bathing trunks, bathing suits and bikinis were paraded before
the sparse population of Mangue Seco. Unlike the inhabitants of
Agreste, the fishermen were not scandalized at the lavish display of
thighs, bellies, navels and backsides. Their bronze-bodied sons
skimmed naked through the waves until the age of fifteen.

The only one who disobeyed the Skipper's command—even
Dona Milu hiked up her skirt and waded in the shallows—was
Perpétua, who walked down the beach until she found a shady
place under the palm trees, away from the sun and the wind. She
took her rosary out of her skirt pocket and began to tell her beads.
In the Major's time they used to spend every summer on the beach.
She used to brave the ocean then. In a decent bathing dress and with
the excuse of teaching her to swim, the Major would take her in his
arms and fondle her with indiscreet and knowing hands. Those joys
were gone, never to return. Now she must think of her children's
future. A widow had to be both mother and father, and it was far

from easy. Fingering her rosary beads, lips moving in prayer, she pondered the plan she had conceived and was now carrying out.

Perpétua, that devout and exemplary woman who was incapable of leaving a single religious obligation unfulfilled, whether mass, blessing, confession, holy communior. or processions; chief custodian of the church and treasurer of its congregation, was counting on the aid and understanding of the Lord to achieve her calculated ends. Her plan called for God's efficacious help and the innocent cooperation of the boys. Peto's, at least, was assured; from where she sat Perpétua could see her son swimming in circles around his aunt. That was the way to win the rich relative's heart, by perseverance and eagerness to please.

She had tried to argue with Ricardo and persuade him to come, but the boy had defeated her by pointing out that the Reverend Father needed him. Vavá Muriçoca, the sexton, had waked up sick that day and couldn't ride a horse. Perpétua was left without any arguments and had to watch her son in his cassock ride away on a donkey. After all, Ricardo was so pious and godfearing he deserved divine protection even more than she did.

She wanted both her sons to spend as much time as possible with their aunt. She had concocted a complicated plan whereby her sister would make the boys her sole heirs, by legal adoption if necessary. That was something she would have to find out. She decided to go to Esplanada and consult Dr. Rubim.

Time was getting short, and she urgently needed God's help, even with the involuntary collaboration of Ricardo and Peto, to touch Antonieta's heart and lead her to the right decision. It was up to God and the boys to transmute their relative's affection into maternal love. "You be nice to your aunt and see she doesn't get lonesome," she often enjoined them. "Help me, Lord!" she prayed. "There isn't much time left."

Antonieta had not set a date for her departure from Agreste, but she obviously couldn't stay for more than six or eight weeks. She would have to go back to São Paulo to look after her business affairs, and ten days had already passed. Astutely and patiently, bit by bit, Perpétua had succeeded in prying out of her sister considerable information about the state of her financial affairs. She knew about the four apartments and the ground-floor space downtown, all of which were leased by the month at a whopping rent. Rents were cheap in Agreste and no place else.

She still had not been able to find out what, exactly, Antonieta's business was. It wasn't factories, for the Comendador's sons ran those and Antonieta was only a silent partner. No, it must be some kind of trade; a clothing store maybe, because it was apparently staffed by women. Perpétua had surprised a confabulation between Tieta and Leonora about the girls' work. Whatever it was, this business, like the real estate, belonged to her sister free and clear, a gift from the Comendador.

Perpétua went on asking questions, picking up a crumb of information here, another there. Neither Antonieta nor Leonora talked much; perhaps deliberately, so as not to arouse their relatives' greed. One thing was certain: the businesses were large and varied and profitable, and they all added up to a fortune.

The other day Antonieta had taken a small case or portfolio (Peto, with his encyclopedic knowledge of films, would have called it an 007 briefcase) out of one of her suitcases, the one she always kept locked, and opened it up on her lap. Although it was turned away from Perpétua, she had happened to stand up just then and had seen that it was literally full of money, packets and packets of bills in big denominations.

"Oh, my God!"

Tieta explained that she had brought cash not only for expenses but to pay for land on Mangue Seco and to make a down payment on a house.

"There isn't any bank here and I don't like being in debt."

"But you've got a fortune in that valise. You must be out of your mind, leaving all that money lying around in a suitcase in the wardrobe."

"The only one who knows about it is Leonora, and now you. All you have to do is not talk about it."

"Me, talk about it? God forbid." She covered her mouth with her hand. "I won't be able to sleep at night, that's all."

Antonieta laughed.

"After I've paid for the land and the house there won't be much left."

This was real money, a São Paulo fortune, not a measly little Agreste fortune like Modesto Pires' or Colonel Artur da Tapitanga's income from goats and manioc. The important thing was to make it impossible for part of Antonieta's money and property to wind up—we all have to die someday, don't we?—in the hands of her stepchildren, the late Comendador's children, especially that prissy, mealy-mouthed Leonora. Tieta was besotted about the girl, always making a fuss over her, prodding her to eat more and making her drink goat's milk every morning. That one must be pretty rich herself, come to think of it, although when Perpétua had inspected her room and turned over everything in it, nothing was locked up or hidden but there had been no suitcase full of money. There were a few thousand cruzeiros in her purse, a lot for Agreste but nothing at all compared to the extravagant sum in Antonieta's 007. It gave Perpétua gooseflesh to think about it.

Her sister was fond of her nephews, treated them kindly and was always happy to see them; but that wasn't enough by a long shot. She would have to start treating them as if they were her own sons, for sons they must be. Both of them if possible, but one at least. Legally recognized sons. Heirs.

If Antonieta should want to take one of them with her to São Paulo, Perpétua would have no objection at all; if she chose Peto, that would be fine. He was a lost lamb going to perdition in Agreste, playing hooky and failing in school every year, hanging around the bar and the moviehouse, and he'd soon be in worse places. But if Ricardo was the one chosen to live in São Paulo and be his aunt's right arm, Perpétua would agree to that too. Peto would take the firstborn's place in the seminary whether he wanted to or not, for one of the two belonged to God. The unappetizing old maid had made a vow when she had just about lost her last earthly hopes: if God gave her a husband and children, one should be a priest to serve Holy Mother Church. God had kept his side of the bargain by providing the miracle, and she would keep hers.

There on the beach, with her eyes half-closed against the sun and wind and strong stabbing light, she struck another bargain with the Lord. If Antonieta would adopt at least one of the boys, Perpétua would commit herself to leave to the church in her will one of the three houses she had inherited from the Major, the smallest one, formerly rented to Lula the stonemason and now occupied by one of Modesto Pires' employees, Laerte the tanner. Though small, it was well situated near the tannery, in the little square where St. John the Baptist's chapel stood. It didn't look as if the Lord was going to take her up on the offer; Perpétua was on intimate terms with God and could gauge pretty accurately what reaction might be forthcoming from Heaven. She contritely withdrew the offer. The

Lord was quite right to be annoyed; a little old house that brought in such a piddling rent in exchange for Antonieta's considerable worldly goods was hardly a serious proposition. She tried to argue a little—"The square's being paved and planted, cast-iron benches are being put in, and the rent'll go up"—but soon desisted. She might incur the Lord's wrath if she persisted; she was offering a trifle in exchange for a fortune. Faith and devotion were more pleasing to God than money and property. All right, then; if Antonieta took Ricardo or Peto for her son and heir (either one of them would do), Perpétua would take both boys to the capital—"Yes, Lord God, to the city of Bahia!"—to make a pilgrimage on foot to the basilica that stood on the Sacred Hill and have a mass said there. She would leave photographs of her sons there in the Museum of Miracles dedicated to the all-powerful Lord of Bomfim. If her sister adopted both boys, she would order a high mass with singing. When considering this proposition, the Lord should not forget to take into account the fact that the children already had some legal rights; they weren't the sole heirs, that was all.

Best of all would be for Antonieta to adopt both boys and send Ricardo to one of those São Paulo seminaries where the young priests are ordained canons and bishops as soon as they graduate. What with the warmth of the sun, the rush of the wind and the pleasant mulling over of plans and promises, Perpétua closed her eyes in earnest, dozed off and had a dream. She saw herself following a procession in honor of St. Anne in a great city, bigger than Aracaju . . . it must be São Paulo . . . and before the litter with the saint's image walked a bishop in red and purple, no, a cardinal, it was her son Cupertino Batista Jr., Dom Peto! A sign from Heaven, a sealed commitment, a promise accepted, a miracle already half-fulfilled.

Of Elisa's jealousy and hopes, with a curious detail concerning a mode of address.

Elisa had never learned how to swim. The sea and the river had been banned to her in her childhood and adolescence. The lower Zé Esteves sank into poverty, the more virulent and intransigent he became. "One whore in the family's plenty," he raged, brandishing his staff. With Tieta's awful example held up before her, poor Elisa was kept on a short rein and was given a good thrashing every so often just to keep her in line besides. Catherine's Basin and Mangue Seco Beach were definitely off limits.

If she ever flirted it was at a distance, small-town'style, making eyes at the boys and watching her father shoo them off. "I don't want those silly young pups hanging around our street, not until a good prospect comes along who's willing to talk turkey; otherwise it's the convent for you," he would bluster. That threat hadn't been carried out; there was no convent for Elisa. Astério, an only son, had inherited the store where he had worked behind the counter ever since he was a boy. He was an honest young fellow and seemed like a good match, so Zé Esteves gave his consent. Elisa was married at sixteen, a beautiful bride who thought she was being set free at last. Had she known it, she had jumped right out of the frying pan into the fire.

She stayed in the shallow water, not daring to go in any deeper while Tieta and Leonora boldly dashed into the waves, surrounded by the whole lively crowd. Poor Elisa was left all by herself without a soul to keep her company. Even her husband seemed to prefer his friends from the poolroom. For whatever his company was worth . . .

Elisa was jealous. Not that her sister or the girl from São Paulo might be interested in Astério, what an idea! Leonora was sweet on Ascânio; the two of them were together all the time. And Antonieta, recently widowed, had certainly not come to Agreste to steal anybody's husband. Not that she couldn't without half trying, if she wanted to. In spite of the forty-four years she confessed to—boasted of!—the men all ran after her when she sashayed down the street with a big smile on her face. Her skin was smooth and soft and well cared for, very well cared for indeed, and her figure spectacular. "You can see she's had plastic surgery," Elisa had remarked to Dona Carmosina. Both were familiar with the life-style of film stars and socialites and knew about the miracles that the Brazilian doctor Ivo Pitanguy wrought in his own country and abroad. Tieta had probably had herself overhauled in that celebrated clinic and gotten rid of all her wrinkles and loose skin; you could tell by her magnificent breasts, full but firmer than Elisa's own.

No, Elisa's jealousy was of a different kind. She envied the wealth the two women flaunted, their big-city ways, their freedom from prejudice and limitations; she was jealous because she was not living in their world, because she was nothing but a little hick whose dreams would never come true.

She was jealous of Leonora, too, of the loving inflection in Tieta's voice when she called her by her nickname, Nora, or daughter, or fussed over her like a mother. Elisa wanted the same loving care and affection; wanted to be petted like a daughter, adopted. At times Antonieta's real fondness for her was plain. She would stroke her dark hair, kiss her on the cheek, praise her beauty—"You pretty thing!"—and affectionately call her "Lisa, child," just as Elisa longed for her to do. And yet, there were times when her sister gazed at her thoughtfully, as if she doubted the warmth of her affection. Elisa could not understand the reason for Tieta's occasional displeasure and mistrust. It was all that scheming Leonora's fault! She was trying to make trouble between the sisters, that was it. She was afraid of the competition, afraid of losing her privileged place in her so-called Mama's heart.

One day when she was alone with Tieta, Elisa tentatively called her Mama. Her sister threw her a strange look and said almost harshly, "Call me Tieta, if you don't mind."

Her voice and look hurt Elisa deeply.

"I'm sorry. I thought it would give you pleasure. I wanted to show how grateful I am for what you've done for me."

Antonieta's look and voice softened; she caressed her sister's dark head, but did not take back what she had said.

"I'm not mad. It's just that I'd rather you called me Tieta. That's what people in Agreste call me, and I like it. Mama's a São Paulo name that Nora and the other girls made up."

"You mean your husband's daughters?"

"Daughters, nieces . . . it's a big family."

That was the family Elisa wanted to belong to, the family of the Comendador, the industrial tycoon; fine people of background and achievement. She longed to rise above the mediocrity of Agreste and be rescued from its daily toil, futility and greed. She yearned after the bright lights, the bustle, the infinite possibilities and the excitement of São Paulo. In Agreste, with no beckoning horizon and no one to look up to, she was just vegetating, dying a little every day.

In a bathing suit Leonora had lent her (her own was old and out of style), molded to her splendid figure and setting off the night-black hair tumbling down her back, she waded out of the water and sat down on the beach. There was Perpétua over there asleep. Elisa knew her older sister had hatched some sort of scheme. Dona Carmosina had said so, and nothing ever got by her. Perpétua's ambition was to sell her two boys to Tieta, and for a very good price; to send them to São Paulo to be her adopted sons and heirs. Dona Carmosina had uncovered the diabolical plan, one deduction at a time.

Elisa's aspirations were not so bold. She didn't care about an old legal piece of paper; she wanted to be adopted from the heart. She was not a candidate for sole heiress; she would be content with much less. If her sister took pity on her dreary fate and that no-account Astério's, if she took them to São Paulo with her and found him some sort of a job in one of the family factories, while keeping her, Elisa, at her side as the favorite sister, almost a daughter, at least as beloved as Leonora, it would be more than enough. She had already told Tieta she didn't want a house of her own in Agreste. If her sister wanted to give her something, let her do it in São Paulo where life was worth living, where there were novelties and temptations, and somebody who was somebody to admire her beauty, not just an old Arab, a dirty errand boy and stinking beggar. She would be somebody there herself, and have a place of her own and people to show herself off to. Anything might happen in São Paulo.

Sherlocks, to your posts!

I interrupt my narrative here to make it clear that all the clues necessary to solve the mystery of Tieta and Leonora are out on the table before the reader. It doesn't take a Sherlock Holmes or an Hercule Poirot to deduce the answer. Why, then, did Dona Carmosina let herself be led down the garden path? Were her eyes so blinded by friendship that she started believing in fairy tales?

Furthermore, at no time was there ever any intention on my part to deceive the public or hide any of the facts. Naturally I didn't want to give away the ending when my story had barely begun. I'd rather let sleeping dogs lie until it's time to wake them up. A little suspense to stir up the readers' excitement and keep them guessing has always been thought an essential ingredient of threepenny novels.

There are more than enough signs and clues in the foregoing pages to enable my readers to work out the answer for themselves. Most of you probably realized the truth from the beginning, and if you kept quiet about it you were quite right not to alert the duller-witted among you. Above all, don't imagine for a moment that I invented any of the details so as to keep Tieta's reputation untarnished. If she chose to spin a web of deceit out of consideration for her family and the prejudices of Sant'Ana do Agreste, none of the responsibility and guilt is mine. For my part, I think no better and no worse of her for what she did, nor do I find her subsequent actions any the less meritorious because of her condition. Merit or demerit, it's all in how you look at Mirkus the Magnificent and his proposals. What were they? We'll find out as the story unfolds.

It was the wonderful climate, better than any health resort, that brought me to Agreste. I wasn't born here, I'm from Niterói, as the saying goes. The passions sweeping through this little burg and whipping its inhabitants to frenzy have nothing to do with me. I'm not involved at all; I'm only telling you what happened.

In which the veil covering the fair Leonora
Cantarelli's past is lifted and we learn everything,
or almost everything.

Leonora never knew anything resembling a home and family life, human warmth or true affection until she found her way to the Lords' Retreat at the age of nineteen and passed inspection by Madame Antoinette. Until then she had taken cram courses in nothing but hunger, despair and human depravity.

As a child she was used as a punching bag. When her parents skinny Vicenza and burly Vitório Cantarelli, weren't hitting each other (and Vitório didn't always get the best of it), they would hit her in the face on the slightest pretext. There were five children, four boys and Leonora, the youngest. Her brothers got out of the slum as soon as they could, to find work in the factories or take up crime. Giuseppe died before he was twenty, under the wheels of a truck one night when he was staggering home drunk. They laid his corpse on a table with his feet hanging over the edge. Giuseppe had been the only one who had any feeling for his sister, patting her grimy cheek and occasionally giving her a piece of candy. When he died she had just turned thirteen and dreaded having to go to work in a sweatshop. Everyone thought she was too pretty for her own good, and they told her so. Not to congratulate her, not as praise or a good omen, but with pity and foreboding.

"*Non sa quello che l'aspetta di éssere cosí bella.*"

"Pretty and poor, she'll come to a bad end."

They were right. Young men and old pursued her. Before she reached puberty she came near being raped on the overgrown soccer field. What's the use of bawling when it's bound to happen sooner or later? She naively told them about it at home and got a beating from Vicenza and Vitório to teach her to have more shame than to wander around the streets offering herself.

Thanks to the morning snack provided by the state, which she literally devoured in her hunger, Leonora went to primary school and learned to read and write. Seu Rafael, owner of the Etna Pizzeria, who had a belly like a woman nine months gone, regularly gave her pieces of stale pizza or tainted meat, squeezing her breasts while she wolfed it down. This arrangement lasted for months and months, during which they never exchanged a single word; the terms of the contract were agreed upon and held to in silence. One day when he saw her staring covertly at the food displayed in the window, Seu Rafael had come forward with a piece of shank meat in his hand, holding it up as if he were calling a dog. Leonora went in and he held out both hands, one dangling the tempting meat, the other groping for the nascent, still-undefined protuberances of her breasts. The girl tried to grab the shank of meat and run, but Seu Rafael held onto it, shaking his massive head; while she chewed he felt, kneaded, pinched her budding breasts. And when the ravenous girl turned her back to leave, he ran his hand down her backside. So Leonora paid for her food and her beauty from a tender age, but though she paid all she had, she always stayed hungry.

Her breasts blossomed and so did her beauty, which was striking even in her badly cut school uniform; Leonora carried herself in a way that men found seductive. At fifteen came the gang rape. It was inevitable, the neighbors said: so pretty and unprotected and overdeveloped for her age. There were four of them in the car, one older one with a beard, the other three much younger, but all waving guns around. The most brutal of them, who looked even younger than she was herself, gouged her legs and arms with a knife. The bearded one stayed at the wheel while the three teenagers got out of the car and pushed her into a dark alley. The passersby knew perfectly well what was going on, but no one came to her defense. Who was crazy enough to risk his neck around armed criminals and dope fiends? They took her, used her, beat her up and tore her dress, the only one she had besides her uniform. She went to the police, where she was treated to wisecracks and one of the cops wanted to lay her. The incident was reported in a couple of lines in the papers as run-of-the-mill news, no big deal. If they had killed her the story would have been a little more interesting. But rape, a gangbang—small potatoes. If she had ever thought of getting married she gave up the idea. All she wanted was to get out of that slum and go somewhere else, anywhere at all, with whoever was willing to take her.

She went starry-eyed over Pipo, the first boy she had ever had a crush on. She thought he was the most wonderful thing in the world, with his long hair straggling down his shoulders and already written up in the sports pages as a crack young soccer player on his way to being a star. He wowed them when he rose from the junior league to substitute for the left end on the championship team. Here, finally, was the offensive end Brazilian soccer had been waiting for. It was the beginning of Pipo's success and the end of Leonora's romance.

"Wise up, baby, and quit bugging me."

Oh, yes, he'd be around once in a while, when he could spare the time from training and nightclubbing to visit the old dump where his family lived in a slum exactly like Leonora's. But once in a while wasn't good enough; she made romantic demands for tenderness, love and affection that were wildly out of place in that heartless, sullen labyrinth.

She was still in despair when she met up with Natacha, a former neighbor who had also come back to see her folks. Leonora told her all about her love affair and how she had been deserted; Natacha already knew about the gang rape. That Pipo, who was so popular and drove around in a big car with a crowd of hangers-on, had stuck a dagger in her heart. By now the sports columnists were saying that success had gone to the kid's head and if he didn't straighten out soon he wouldn't get much farther. Natacha, smartly turned out and smelling of strong perfume, had things to tell her about the oldest profession. She didn't try to sugar the pill but said a girl could earn enough to live on if she kept away from pimps and gigolos, and it sure beat working eight hours a day in a factory or being a servant to some rich dame. The time had come for Leonora to choose: would it be the factory or the brothel?

For two years she was on her own, knocking around from pillar to post and from one man to another in cheap hotels where each windowless room was divided by a partition from the others; was arrested in a vice raid; and fell in love with Cid Raposeira.

When she met him Cid was going through a quiet phase and the doctors said he was cured; to get him off their hands, no doubt. Skinny and silent-tough, he could suddenly turn gentle and vulnerable without any warning. For a girl who had nothing, he was enough. Leonora fell for him like a ton of bricks. Cid Raposeira hated the world and everyone in it with the exception of his companion. "One of these days we'll get hitched and have a couple of kids," he'd say, but talk of marriage and children was a sure sign of crisis ahead. The seizures grew more frequent and the lucid intervals more brief. With no transition he would swing wildly from tenderness to hate. "Goddam you, get out of my sight." On those days he would curse her and slap her around, threaten to kill her, try to kill himself, and end up in an asylum or a police station. Once the crisis had passed he would come crawling back, reduced to skin and bones, starving, whining, useless. Leonora's heart would turn over with pity and she would take him back. If Raposeira had not gone off with a Bolivian drug pusher, Leonora might never have had the courage to leave him.

Again it was Natacha who changed the course of her life. They met by chance in the street early one afternoon when Leonora was looking for a pickup. Natacha looked prosperous, smart, and superior.

"I'm a call girl now in the best establishment in São Paulo, and the most expensive. It's the Lords' Retreat—haven't you ever heard of it?"

She looked appraisingly at Leonora, whose prettiness had not only held its own but grown into an absurd, translucent, virginal beauty: enormous eyes like water, golden hair, a pure, sweet face, the picture of modesty and innocence.

"Hmmn, maybe Madame Antoinette would take you on. You're the family type. I'll introduce you if you like."

Madame Antoinette, arms akimbo, scrutinized the new arrival.

"What do you want?"

Natacha spoke up first.

"Leonora—"

"I asked her, not you, nanny."

"I'd like to work here, if you'll have me."

"Why?"

"To live a better life."

"Are you married? Were you ever?"

"No. But I shacked up with a man for a few months."

"Why'd you leave him?"

"He left me."

"How come you're in the profession?"

"So I wouldn't have to go to work in the factory. I wish I had, though."

"Have you got a man? Somebody you like? A gigolo, a pimp?"

"Only the one I told you about. He was sick."

"Sick? What was wrong with him?"

"Schizophrenia. But in between times he was a wonderful guy."

"Any children?"

"No, I never got pregnant. I've been lucky that way."

"Why? Don't you like kids?"

"I love kids. That's why I said I was lucky. I don't earn enough to keep a child. Why have one if it's going to go hungry?"

"Have you ever had a disease? Tell the truth."

"You mean social diseases, venereal disease?"

"That's right."

"No. I was always afraid of catching one, so I'm very careful. I keep myself clean."

"All right, I'll try you out. You can start right now."

A few months later Lourdes Veludo, a stunning mulatto girl, one of three women who lived permanently at the Retreat, joined the cast of an all-black variety show and left the house when a

European tour materialized. Madame Antoinette, who had come to appreciate Leonora's discreet and gentle ways, offered her the vacant place. That was two years before the trip to Agreste.

Last fragment of the narrative in which, during the long bus trip from São Paulo to Bahia, Tieta reminisces and recounts episodes from her past to the fair Leonora Cantarelli.

"When I met Felipe he didn't have a papal title yet and I was still Tieta do Agreste, the name they called me back home, in Bahia, in Rio de Janeiro, and in São Paulo when I started out. Felipe had just come back from Europe."

At fifty, Felipe Camargo do Amaral had risen as high as anyone can rise in the business world. As an entrepreneur he had succeeded at everything he put his hand to, and he was equally fulfilled as a Paulista, a citizen and a man.

In the 1932 Revolution,* instead of taking the political post in the governor's cabinet to which family tradition entitled him, he marched to the front as a volunteer recruit; but when he got there he was promptly promoted to first lieutenant and aide-de-camp, as it was not fitting for a Camargo do Amaral to be a common soldier. Before long he was a major on the revolutionary general staff, drafting manifestoes and proclamations. He had been born into a rich coffee-growing family, with four hundred years as plantation owners in São Paulo. If you counted the few drops of Indian blood that stamped him as an authentic *bandeirante*, his ancestors had been Brazilian for much longer than that.

He became a captain of industry on his own; a genius at making money; president of firms, consortiums, banks, with more shares and dividends than he could count. His political career was brief. Elected deputy to Congress in 1933 after a comfortable exile in

* A constitutional revolution calling for elections two years after Getulio Vargas overthrew the government of Washington Luiz.—Translator's note.

Lisbon, he did not make a bid for reelection. He lacked the patience for boring debates and interminable sessions, preferring to apply his brains to better effect than in electoral squabbles. And so he did, as his wealth and knowledge of the world increased.

"Felipe knew how to live, and he taught me plenty. I was a maverick and he turned me into a lady. I learned the value of money from Felipe, but I also learned that you've got to own money and enjoy it, not be a slave to it."

His worldly wisdom consisted in living well. He was no slave to his business but enjoyed music, pictures, books, a good table and a good cellar, travel and women. He had explored the five continents and knew Europe and the United States backward and forward. He had bought the favors of countless women. "You have to pay for a woman one way or another," he would say, "and the best way is with money. It's cheaper, and it saves trouble in the end." A good family man, he lived on amicable terms with his wife, whom he had chosen from a coffee-exporting clan of proud lineage and substantial fortune, and he doted on his sons. One of them worked with him in the various business firms as his second in command; the other had settled down in a scientific research laboratory in the North American university where he had gone for postgraduate study and was married to a gringa. Felipe had no quarrel with life.

"The Retreat was his idea, long before he ever met me. It had a French name before."

Properly speaking, the idea had not been his. Along with a small, select group of men of the same high economic standing and equally high ideals, he had financed a worthy project put forward by his clever and charming friend Madame Georgette. One of Felipe's sons had studied in the United States, the other in Oxford, but he preferred *la douce France*, like the old connoisseur of Parisian wines, cheeses and women he was. "The more I visit other cities, the more I love Paris," he used to say. Madame Georgette had brought some highly seasoned, piquant French delicacies to São Paulo and laid in a stock of the best local products. She was an expert at picking agreeable companions for gentlemen.

Her project called for the establishment of a very exclusive house of rendezvous to be frequented by none but the great landowners and captains of industry, influential politicians—ministers, senators—and the occasional famous artist or man of letters to add luster to the house. The capable, experienced Madame Georgette outdid herself on this pet project, the Nid d'Amour, where weary gentlemen could find surcease from the stress and fatigue of their hectic lives in the youthful arms and perfumed laps of her compliant and carefully trained *jeunes filles*.

"When Felipe got back from those trips he was tired of white women. Anyhow, he had a yen for a dark, toasted color just like mine; my great-grandmother was a Negro slave. So this wild little nannygoat, sunburned since the day she was born, was served up to him with champagne."

Madame Georgette knew Monseigneur le Prince Felipe's tastes —she never called him anything but Prince—and had reserved a morsel worthy of his discerning palate: Tieta do Agreste, a curly-haired brunette, burnished to bronze by the sun of the backlands and brought up in small-town brothels; the flower of the house.

"Why he took a shine to me, I don't know. But he never let me go, and that's the truth."

"What man wouldn't take a shine to you, Mama? Besides being pretty, I bet you were lively as a red-hot coal."

"Yes, I was pretty and I was sassy. Everything tickled me in those days, I could talk the hind leg off a donkey, and when I had a good partner there was nobody as good in bed. I don't know if I caught his fancy because of that or because I knew how to cuddle him to sleep."

What had it been about her that caught Felipe's fancy and kept him faithful? The girl's chatter of the small town in the backlands and its uneventful life, goats leaping on the rocks, swims in the river? The undeniable fact that she was good in bed? Or the warmth she gave off, her vitality and love of life? In that room with Tieta he felt young again, no longer a weary man of affairs seeking refuge and rest from the everyday grind with a high-class prostitute to be used once and almost never repeated. Madame Georgette's vast stock of call girls was continually being renewed. There were innumerable telephone numbers in her little blue book, every one of them selected with a knowing eye. She had been amazed when le Prince Felipe asked for the little backwoods nannygoat again, and after a few more times, reserved her permanently. "I don't want her working any more, I'll keep her for myself."

When Felipe was in São Paulo he eagerly sought her body with its wild, musky backlands flavor, her natural coquetry, her caresses, more tender than lascivious, her soft fingers in his hair, the childlike ways she had of lulling him to sleep. When he was away he saw to it that she lacked for nothing and had money enough to remember and respect him.

"Didn't you ever put horns on him, Mama?"

"Horns? The only one who could have put horns on him was his wife, Dona Olívia, but I don't know that she ever did. I was only his kept woman. He never told me there was anything I couldn't do, except sleep with men for money. I put out when I felt like it, when I liked the man, just the way I used to back in Agreste before I was a hustler, to see if I could find some way to put out the fire that burned my tail, but I never did it for money. I was discreet about it, too. I always respected him and we never talked about it."

"And what about him? Did he have affairs with other women?"

"I never tried to find out. I never asked about the other women he slept around with. One time someone told me about one he had brought over from Sweden."

She was a knockout, the mischiefmakers told Tieta, a tall, sculptural beauty of wheat and snow. Tieta had ground her teeth but hadn't said a word. As soon as he came around again and found himself petted, charmed, amused, lulled to sleep by her fingers in his hair, Felipe dismissed the Scandinavian; or rather, gave her up graciously, in exchange for a stock of Cuban cigars, to a friend who was an importer of all kinds of foreign articles. She was secondhand goods but in very good condition, remarked Felipe good-humoredly, concluding that when it came to mistresses he was clearly a monogamist.

"I guess he stuck to me for the rest of his life because I never gave a damn about his money. I didn't care if he was rich or not; what meant so much to me was that he was always kind and polite. I never asked Felipe for a thing except a loan, twice. The first time was the day we met. I had a chance to buy a gorgeous Argentine leather coat, brand new, but I had to pay cash or I'd lose it. He gave me lots of other things, too, but it was just because he wanted to."

He gave her apartments, one after another, in new buildings as he constructed them. One day he came in with a blueprint and spread it out on the bed.

"This is going to be a twelve-story building on Alameda Santos."

"Gee, what a big one!"

"I've saved an apartment for you. They're all alike: a living room and two bedrooms, four to each floor."

"Are you out of your mind? How'm I gonna pay for it?"

"Who said anything about paying? It's a present. Pretty soon it'll be three years since we met."

With all the other things he had on his mind, Felipe remembered dates and anniversaries. He was very fond of Tieta, but she had grown even fonder of the man who gave her so much and asked for so little. Felipe's slippers rested by her bed, his pajamas under her pillow. The buildings grew taller, the apartments bigger. In the last, huge building, vast as a city, her present was a shop on the ground floor, a prime location. If she gave him affection, he paid her in cash, or in real estate, which came to the same thing. Money's best, it's less trouble and costs less in the long run.

"One day Madame Georgette called me over for a talk. She wanted to sell the business and go back to France, and she was giving me first chance at it."

Madame Georgette had deposited her savings and profits in France, bought herself a house in a Paris *banlieu* and never stopped thinking of the day when she could retire there. When she called Tieta, she had already booked passage on a ship sailing for France in two months. For the second time, Tieta asked Felipe for a loan.

"Felipe laughed. 'You still haven't paid back what I lent you the day we met. Never mind, just leave it to me. I'll arrange things with Georgette. The Nid is yours.'

"I took over more than thirteen years ago. I remodeled the whole place and set aside that ritzy apartment for me and Felipe. Then I changed the name and raised the prices."

"Why did you change the name, Mama?"

"Nid d'Amour sounded too much like a whorehouse. The Lords' Retreat is classier. And that's what all my customers are, lords. But that meant I had to change *my* name. That was Felipe's advice."

"If you want to fleece the customers in style you must have a French name, *ma belle*. Madame Antoinette goes very well with your type," he had told her.

"My color with a French name, honey? Can't be done."

"You can be a French girl from Martinique, like Napoleon's Josephine."

Customers became friends and the prestige of the establishment grew. To be an habitué of the Lords' Retreat became a privilege more sought after than membership in the Jockey Club, the Racing Society, or any of São Paulo's other exclusive clubs. In the luxurious comfort of their private apartment, Felipe's slippers stood at the foot of the bed and his pajamas lay under the pillow. He was older, a widower now, and the Pope had honored him with the title of Comendador. He still presided over his numerous business affairs but seldom traveled anymore; he was more and more reluctant to leave Tieta's warm laughter and her bed.

"As far as Felipe was concerned I never changed my name. I was Tieta do Agreste to the end."

To the others she was Madame Antoinette, a Frenchwoman born in the Antilles of the union of a *général de la République* with a *métisse*. Along with her Paris upbringing and robust charm, she had an unerring eye when it came to choosing delicate tidbits for the refined taste of her customers, the richest in São Paulo, *Dieu merci*. To the two or three girls like Leonora who lived permanently at the Lords' Retreat, she was Mama: strict and generous, feared and loved.

Of an urgent message.

At the height of the party an urgent message arrived. Lunch had been devoured, dessert repeated, and Dona Laura, Elisa and Leonora were serving coffee. It was a grand spread with a varied musical background: ultra-contemporary tapes competing with the strains of Claudionor das Virgens' accordion. The balladeer could smell out a feast, the perfume of rum cocktails and *batidas*, the scent of *cachaça*, from a long way off. Without waiting for an invitation he appeared with a by-your-leave, his accordion and a broad grin, a party-crasher who was never turned away.

While Elisa, Aminthas, Fidélio, Seixas and Peto made do with rock and roll, the others applauded Claudionor and Elieser. The balladeer's repertory leaned toward hillbilly music, while the owner of the motorboat, usually so grumbling and taciturn, loosened up after a few drinks and, at Tieta's and Dona Carmosina's urging, showed off his excellent voice in half-forgotten melodies. Tieta, sitting on a mat, her face shielded with an enormous straw hat, had a request.

"Play that one Chico Alves used to sing, Claudionor."

"Which one?"

"The one that begins: 'Goodbye, goodbye, goodbye, seven letters that make me cry . . .' "

Elieser burst into song, Claudionor accompanying him on the accordion. Tieta drifted off on the music. She was distant today, taking no part in the conversation, and that troubled Leonora. She knew Mama: when she was quiet like that it was because something was bothering her. What could it be? She didn't dare ask. It was wiser not to, better to leave her alone until the laughter came back. "When I've got the blues just let me be," she used to warn them at the Retreat. Leonora went over to sit by her in silence.

Tieta sensed Leonora's presence, turned and caressed her cheek. The girl took her hand and kissed it tenderly. Crazy little kid, thought Tieta, she'll lose her head and fall in love if she doesn't watch out. Was Leonora the only flighty one? Leonora and who else?

What inexorable obligation could have demanded Ricardo's presence at the Father's side in Rocinha? Obligation nothing! Her nephew was running away from her, more likely; he had gone with the Father to get out of coming to Mangue Seco, to keep from sullying his chaste eyes—chaste? sanctimonious!—with his aunt's splendid nudity in her skimpy bikini, the young ass! She had missed the boy these last few days when she went out walking or swimming in the river. He had even changed his study hours, so as not to have to give her another massage, no doubt. And Tieta, the old fool, dreaming of her nephew, seeing him night and day with an angel's wings and a prick like a table leg. She had never been interested in young men, much less seventeen-year-old kids; she liked grown men who were older than she was. She had had to come back to Agreste to get a crush on a hulking schoolboy, feel chills run up her spine when she thought of him, be sulky and out of sorts, feel empty because he wasn't there, sad, irritated, blue. She certainly had not counted on this. Her nephew, and a seminarian to boot. Seeing that she was far away and lost in her own thoughts, Leonora got up to join Ascânio. Tieta touched her cheek again, fondly.

"Do you know 'It Was All a Dream,' Elieser?"

"Let's see . . . I guess so, Dona Antonieta. Put your heart in it, Claudionor!"

Tieta drifted off again on the music, leading Ricardo by the hand. Osnar, sodden with beer, settled down in the shade and sucked on a cigar. Barbozinha was snoring under a coconut tree, his ambitious plans for declaiming atop the dunes forgotten. After the marathon of palm oil, pepper, coconut, ginger, *batidas*, rum and beer, fatigue began to set in as the afternoon wore on. The morning had tired them out—the vigorous swim in the ocean, battling rough waves, and then the hard clamber up the dunes under a sizzling sun. Nevertheless, Ascânio and Leonora planned to go for a walk on the beach by themselves, but later on when it wasn't quite so hot, before the sun set and it was time to go back.

Suddenly there was the sound of an outboard motor in the distance. Skipper Dário, to whom all the sounds of the sea and the river were familiar, declared that it was Pirica's boat.

It was Pirica sure enough, with a message for Ascânio from Colonel Artur da Tapitanga with the sensational news that some engineers from the Paulo Afonso Power Plant were in Agreste and wanted to talk to somebody at the courthouse. They had gone to the mayor's house, which had made matters worse. They had not been able to get any sense out of Dr. Mauritônio, who lived in a world of phantoms; the poor man had lunged at the chief engineer, mistaking him for Aristeu Regis, the agronomist responsible for the decampment of Amélia Honey Mel. Insulted and driven out of the house, they eventually located Colonel Artur da Tapitanga, the Town Council president, out on his plantation. The octogenarian had dispatched Pirica to Mangue Seco, with orders to bring Ascânio back with him.

There was a general stir and everyone begged for details at once. Pirica could add only one bit of information to what he had told them: the Colonel had been in a high good humor when he had entrusted him with the message.

"You tell Ascânio those electricity fellows are here and he'd better hightail it over here just as soon as he can."

"They've come about the power line. I've won my bet. Viva Dona Antonieta!" yelled Fidélio.

The first cheer, followed by others, resounded under the palm trees, the opening salvo in the town festivities. Agreste was going to rock with the news. Ascânio, standing very straight, walked over to Tieta.

"Dona Antonieta, allow me to be the first to thank you in the name of the people of Agreste."

Tieta held out a hand to Ascânio for him to help her to her feet.

"Whoa, Ascânio, don't belch before you've had your dinner. You go see the Colonel and get the story straight. We don't rightly know what's happened yet. A long time ago I learned that if you set off a firecracker too soon you get your hand burned. If it does turn out to be true, the one who deserves congratulations is you. You did all the work; I didn't do a thing but ask a favor."

"Gestures and good intentions aren't worth anything unless they get results; you told me so yourself," Ascânio retorted.

"You didn't just have good intentions, you fought for them. You go find out what's up, and if it's true we'll celebrate together."

"And everybody else in town with us, Dona Antonieta. It'll be the biggest party Agreste's ever had."

Enthusiasm prevailed among the merry crew. Tieta was hugged, kissed and congratulated. Barbozinha threatened to make a speech and announced that he would write a poem to the light of Paulo Afonso, the light born in Tieta's eyes. Osnar proposed that they carry her on their shoulders in triumph. "Let go of my leg, you shameless man!" Aminthas promised Fidélio to pay off his bet the minute the news was confirmed. Tieta received a warm embrace from the Skipper and ceremonious felicitations from Modesto Pires, who was overcome at the prestige of his fellow townswoman. He hadn't believed for a minute that her requests would bring any action. "They'll just ignore those cables or throw them in the circular file," he had scoffed to Dona Aida and a few friends. Perpétua puffed out her chest: "Our sister's intercourse at the cupola of state government is a source of pride to her family. Her high social position elevates all those who are kin to her." If Tieta hadn't been in such a bad mood she would have gone into a paroxysm of laughter; as it was, she smiled in Perpétua's embrace. Elisa was so excited she couldn't help crying as she covered her sister with kisses. As for Dona Carmosina and Dona Milu, they had never had any doubts; they had been counting the minutes until the answer came. Now that the engineers were actually here in Agreste, what would those of little faith find to say? They'd have to eat their words or their hats. Tieta would have liked nothing better than to take part in the general rejoicing, but the one whose kisses she longed for wasn't there, hadn't come, hadn't wanted to come, would rather ride behind a priest on a donkey, the idiot! How ridiculous she was to hanker for him! So her rival was God. Well, God had better watch out, because when it came to that particular kind of contest, Tieta of Agreste didn't like to lose.

Dona Carmosina proposed that they should all go back right away with Ascânio, and was unanimously seconded. None of them felt like hanging around Mangue Seco the rest of the afternoon waiting for the sunset when there were such goings-on in Agreste. They all wanted to see the engineers.

All but Tieta. She announced that she had decided to accept Dona Laura's and the Skipper's invitation to stay in the beach house until Wednesday, when she would go back to Agreste with Modesto Pires to sign for the purchase of the land.

While the others were getting ready, she drew Perpétua away to Liberty Hall and handed her a bunch of keys.

"I want you to do me a favor. Open the blue suitcase—here's the key—take that briefcase I keep my money in, the one you saw the other day, open it with this little key, and take out . . ." She calculated the sum aloud, just enough to make a down payment to Modesto Pires on the land and start building.

"You mean you're going to start building a house? Right this minute?"

"Yes. Right this minute. I'm going to mark off the land and begin work on a little house, just a cottage. The Skipper says he'll see to the construction work. In Saco they've got everything I'll want in the way of building materials and labor. All I need is money to pay for it. The Skipper says the building may go pretty fast. I do want to see my little house standing, at least the four walls, before I go back to São Paulo. You and the children can enjoy it after I'm gone. Elisa too." She gazed at her sister and said in a gentler voice, "I really want to do something for my nephews, Perpétua, since I have no children of my own."

"Oh, sister, how happy it makes me to hear you say that." The glassy eyes shone, the rasping voice was tremulous. She had only just now driven a bargain with the Lord and it was already working.

"We'll talk about it in Agreste."

"Who shall I send the money and the keys by?"

"By the Skipper; he's offered to take some people back in the canoe."

However, the Skipper did not have to go after all, since everyone managed to crowd into either Elieser's motorlaunch or Pirica's boat, in which Leonora and Peto as well as Ascânio found room. Tieta was upset.

"Oh, and I need that money tomorrow first thing. Just send it by anyone who's coming this way."

"Don't worry, I'll see that you get it," Perpétua assured her.

Tieta, now cheerful and smiling again, was sure she would. Her bad mood had passed, Leonora noticed as she said goodbye. When they were just about to push off from the beach, the caravan broke into noisy impromptu cheering under Dona Carmosina's baton.

"So will it be yes?"

"Yes!" the chorus replied.

"Does Tieta get a cheer?"

"Yes!"

Dona Carmosina joined in with the others:

"Hip! Hip! Hooray! Antonieta! Antonieta!"

Modesto Pires repeated a prediction he had made before:

"Dona Antonieta, if this tale about the power line is true, as it appears to be, the people of Agreste will enshrine you on the high altar in the cathedral, right next to Our Lady St. Anne. I told you before and I'm telling you now."

Tieta burst out laughing. What a funny world it was!

Of an ill-tempered question.

Back at the courthouse, the chief engineer, who was in a foul temper by now, informed the breathless Ascânio that there had indeed been a change in the plans mapped out for the running of electric power lines in the state. Agreste had suddenly, inexplicably, been included in the list of communities to receive the benefits of light and power from the plant. And that wasn't all, though that was incredible enough. Orders had come down from the very top, from the president of the light and power company, to give absolute priority to Agreste and start work immediately, on the double. It was unbelievable that they had been brought out here to this backyard of hell on a Sunday, a day of rest, and got covered with dust into the bargain, goddammit! To add insult to injury, they had already wasted several hours of their time looking for some responsible official they could talk to.

Before getting down to the nuts and bolts, there was just one thing the chief engineer and his assistants wanted to know: how the hell did a miserable, backward, half-assed little place like Agreste, whose mayor was a nut who ought to be put in a straitjacket and shipped off to the funny farm and whose Town Council president was a doddering old relic, get changes made in plans that had been approved, finalized and already set in motion? How in hell had they gone right to the top of the list ahead of rich, prosperous communities protected by well-known politicians in high places? Who had made the request? Request nothing, demand! For God's sake, tell us the name of this powerful leader, this honcho, this almighty goddam big shot who turned the trick. It has to be somebody way up there, a general, most likely.

Osnar, the bestower of military titles, called her General. But Ascânio held his peace so as not to put the engineers in an even worse frame of mind than they were in already. He smiled modestly and suggested they get down to business.

Of fear and longing dissolved in moonlight.

General? All alone on the crest of the sand dunes lay the madcap goat girl of Agreste. The sea scent and the huge tumult of the waves were music and perfume from the beginning of the world. In the sky were the moon and the timeless stars.

It was there, on the dunes with the sound of the breakers in her ears and on the bare sandy hummocks with her flock of ornery sheep, that she had grown strong and determined, learned to want things intensely and then fight to get them. The tumultuous sea and arid land were two faces of the same wilderness; harsh, poor, with a terrible beauty. She might have sprung from the very rocks where the goats leaped, from the sand masses shifted and blown by the wind. She had in her something of the land and the ocean, sweet water and salt, the river's currents and the sea's undertow. She had learned not to be afraid, not to run away but to face things and seize her chance when it came. The stars in the sky could never be counted; could she count the times she had loved, with desire in her throat, in her fingertips, in the pit of her stomach? Fleeting loves and one love for a lifetime, Felipe's. No one counts the stars; why count the urgings, the dryness in the mouth, the need that would not be denied? It wasn't the number that mattered, it was the kiss, death and life in one. On Mangue Seco on the sand and in Agreste in sheltered nooks along the river, she had been the wild goat. In a real bed, when she came down off the parched sandy hillocks and discovered the byways of pleasure, there had been only Lucas. Now she was back on the dunes again. It was like the very first time. She was tense, ready, and waiting.

A light blinked out on the river; it might be the reflection of a star. All sounds were lost in the roar of the waves dashing their heads against the mountains of sand, but the full moon shone bright and soft on the dunes. A form stood hesitating at the foot of the slope, uncertain which one to climb up. Tieta got up, looked, guessed, knew. She modulated the nannygoat's call into a gentle invitation to love, a soft, almost whispered bleat, to help him find the way up.

Aunt and nephew were face to face. Cardo was wearing the Palmeiras soccer shirt and shorts Tieta had sent him. He smiled awkwardly.

"Your blessing, Aunt. Mother sent me to bring you what you asked for. I left it down there with the Skipper."

"Is that all?"

"She told me to stay and help you."

"But you didn't want to come."

Embarrassed, the boy made a tentative gesture and lowered his eyes. Half falteringly, half proudly, he answered evasively, "They're celebrating down there because of the electricity. The whole town's dancing in the street and cheering you, Aunt. They say you—"

"You're afraid to stay here now, aren't you?"

The confusion that kept him from replying was mirrored in his frank, open face in the moonlight. Tieta went on, "Tell me about it. Is it me you're thinking about when you have those dreams? Tell me the truth."

The adolescent looked down.

"Every single night. Please forgive me, Aunt, it isn't my fault."

"And so you're afraid and run away from me?"

"It doesn't do a bit of good for me to hide or pray. Even when I'm praying, I can't help thinking and seeing."

"You think I'm pretty?"

"Too pretty! Pretty and good. I'm the one who's no good. I must be naturally wicked, or else it's a punishment from God."

"Punishment? Why?"

"I don't know, Aunt."

"If you don't want to stay you'd better go now, right this minute."

She pointed to the foot of the dunes, then lay down again on the sand, her skirt open and her blouse unbuttoned, her body in full view. Ricardo's voice reached her from a long way away, from the depths of time.

"I'm afraid of offending God and you, Aunt, but I want to stay."

"Right here next to me?"

"Yes, Aunt, if you'll let me." His eyes lit up.

Far off, rockets rose into the sky and burst in the air, fiery stars lit by the people of Agreste to praise and honor their illustrious daughter, the rich and powerful widow, the Paulista whose wish was a command.

Tieta smiled and held out her hand.

"Don't be scared. I won't hurt you, and neither will God. Come over here and lie down."

They were floating in the moonlight, in time to the music of the waves. Moon, stars and sea were the same as before. What did age, kinship, a seminarian's cassock matter? A woman and a man were eternal. Here on the dunes one day long ago, a young she-goat had gone into heat. Tieta had come back to her beginnings. Now she was a nannygoat with her teats full and rich, and she was tired of Inácio the ram. She was about to deflower a kid.

*Intermezzo in the style of Dante Alighieri,
the author of another famous novel (but in verse),
or dialogue in darkness.*

The moon, heavy with amorous sighs and moans, was far on her way to Africa when they finally paused for breath. As their clenched thighs disentangled, life and death fell apart and death and resurrection were no longer a single act. Until that moment their bodies had been fused into one, one rocket bursting high in the sky and melting into light over the waves. Until then, moonlight and sunlight were the same; no distance, no interval of time, separated day from night or the sun from the moon.

When at last they came up for air, both sun and moon had disappeared; darkness covered the world, the night shed its warmth and brightness and turned hostile and cold. Ricardo heard an accusation and a sentence in the voices of the breakers crashing on the dunes and the shrieking, sand-laden wind. Only now, beyond death, beyond life, did he realize the full extent of his crime. There was no human measure for the punishment awaiting him; eternity can't be measured. With an effort that seared his throat and chest he recovered the faculty of speech.

"My God, Aunt! What have we done? What have I done?"

Once he had made a solemn vow of chastity, consecrating himself to God. He had promised to deny himself the joys of the flesh and be a chaste son of Mary and Jesus. Well, he had broken his vow.

"I've damned myself and you too. Oh, Aunt, please forgive me!"

He heard soft laughter like a spring welling up in the heart of a storm. A sandy, windblown hand touched his guilty face, and fingers with long nails grazed his lips, smothering his sobs. Men don't cry. And after all that had happened, what was he but a man like other men, his heart branded with the mark of sin? A man like other men? No, he was worse. Other men had made no commitment and Christ's blood shed on the Cross had ransomed them all, world without end. But he had made a vow, he had promised, he had sworn, he had accepted a commitment. And then he had betrayed God's trust. In the blackness he saw leprous sores flowering into pus on his perverse, iniquitous body. Only the fingers pressing on his lips kept him from crying out with horror.

"Don't call me Aunt unless there're people around, silly. When there aren't any people I'm Tieta, your Tieta." The benighted woman was laughing! Little did she know he had doomed her to the torments of Hell. She was laughing as gaily as if she had no notion of the horrible thing they had done.

The devil had possessed him; the most dangerous, cunning, subtle devil of all, the demon of the flesh. Not content with dragging him down to perdition, the devil had used him as an instrument to tempt and corrupt his aunt, to turn an honest widow, faithful to her husband's memory, from the path of virtue and transform her into a maddened female animal in heat, moaning and howling and bleating like the goats on the Agreste sandhills. Oh, Aunt, what a terrible misfortune! The hand ran over his lips and the nails scratched the skin, then threatened to withdraw.

She too was possessed by the Evil One, the Cur. She was now beyond the pale, and it was all his fault. And he owed her so much! Gratitude, respect, the honorable love of a nephew and a protégé. Hadn't she sent him gifts from São Paulo, hadn't she brought him a fishing rod and reel, hadn't she given him money, a new shirt, and the pajamas his mother was keeping for the seminary? Hadn't she donated a saint's image and a monstrance to the church, the pious creature? Blithe, flippant, impetuous she might be, but she had a generous heart and was truly a lamb in God's flock, as Father Mariano had said. A pure soul and an innocent heart, worthy of the Lord's regard and a divine recompense, the Father had proclaimed in his sermon during the mass. She deserved his deepest respect and gratitude in return for her affection, loving-kindness and generous gifts. His mother had admonished him to look after his aunt, do her bidding and become her friend. Had he even tried to obey? Had he tried to draw her still closer to God and the Church as a good nephew and seminarian should? Had he talked to her of saints and miracles, told her wonderful things about the Lord and the Virgin, and described the marvels of the Heavenly Kingdom? No, he had not. On the contrary, he had enlisted in Satan's ranks to win his aunt's soul, skulking instrument of the Accursed One that he was. He, who had once been God's servant and consecrated angel, was now a slave of Satan, his obedient henchman, his active accomplice, a fallen angel.

"Oh, Aunt, forgive me...."

The hand stretched out to cover his whole mouth, the palm pressing down on his lips so hard his teeth bit into it.

"Don't call me Aunt, call me Tieta."

After he had died a leper's death, the first sign of Divine Wrath, eternal punishment would follow. Hellfire forever and ever with no appeal, no rest, no interval, no right to contrition, for it was already too late for repentance. Repentance? The hand covered his mouth and the nails scratched him lightly.

His sinful, putrid flesh would burn in Hell and be ever renewed for the burning throughout eternity; for whether saved or damned, the soul was immortal. He heard soft laughter born of ignorance, the laughter of one who knew nothing of God's wrath. Through the sweet contented baa he could hear the devil's sinister, triumphant, insulting guffaw: he had won two souls with a single roll of the dice, snatched away two more souls for sin and the flames of Hell. A good night's winnings indeed.

All those days, all those nights, he had battled so hard. For he *had* struggled and tried to resist. With his little strength and puny weapons, he was nothing compared to the saints who were truly worthy to serve God with all the might of the law and the Commandments. Even so he had done his best to hold out, he had entrenched himself first in the doctor's study, bent over his books, then in the river, diving into the water when Peto, inspired by the devil, told him where to look in Catherine's Basin; in his prayers before climbing into his hammock; in pleas and promises at mass: if the Virgin would only save him from temptation, he would sleep on kernels of corn every night during the school year. But the trenches he had dug were destroyed one by one by the devil. Those breasts, half-glimpsed in a low-necked dressing gown, jumped out at him whole from an algebra problem or a printed page; the hair his brother had seen through the gap in the bikini stretched out into the river, binding him hand and foot and drawing him back to the rocks where she lounged with legs carelessly sprawled, heedless of the lust she inspired. Even during the holy sacrifice of the mass, the spiraling smoke from the thurible traced the swaying curves of the round, bouncing brown rump he had seen peeking out of her shortie nightgown.

He had toiled night after restless night, seeing visions of lewdness whenever he tried to conjure up chaste images, holy lives, sanctified pleasures in his sleep. Before being lost forever here on Mangue Seco, he had been on the verge of sinning every single night, sleeping or waking, and if he hadn't it was only because he didn't know how. Hardly had he finished his prayers and closed his eyes, still with the name of God on his lips and his thoughts on the salvation of his soul, when the Accursed One would fill his hammock with breasts and thighs, buttocks and pubic hair; his aunt, all of her, stark naked.

Neither pleas nor prayers nor promises nor flight had done him any good. Almost mad with despair, he had opened the Good Book to the page that told of the flight into Egypt after God's warning to the Israelites. Taking heed, he had mounted a donkey and gone off to Rocinha behind Father Mariano instead of taking the motorboat to Mangue Seco, where he could have seen her half-naked on the beach, gone into the water with her, and saved her from certain death when she was about to be drowned in the breakers on the sandbar. He pictured himself struggling heroically against the waves, gathering her up in his arms and bringing her to shore, her inert body clasped to his breast.

He had ridden a donkey away from temptation. And what good had it done? He had her in his arms all the way to Rocinha, clasped to his breast as the animal trotted along. Whenever he grazed the pommel he was clasping his aunt between his thighs.

Feeble strength and weak will were frail weapons indeed to pit against the power and the snares of the devil. Beelzebub had used Peto to tempt him by the riverbank; and to send him to Mangue Seco, his strict devout mother, incredible as it seemed, had been the instrument. He should have argued and held out, used the late hour as an excuse, pretended to be sick. But he hadn't. His mother didn't have to ask him twice before he was off and running to hire Pirica's boat. He knew very well that the Evil One had chosen Mangue Seco as the scene of his damnation, and yet he had gone there freely of his own accord. All the way down the river he had told Pirica to hurry, though he knew that once he stepped out of that boat he was lost. And that was just what had happened: in Mangue Seco the Evil One had overthrown him and taken possession of his soul.

The fingers wandered down to his chin, leaving a taste of fresh

pulp in his mouth. Words were pulled out of his guts, choking him
and tearing his lungs:

"I'm damned, Aunt Tieta, and I'm taking you down with me to
Hell. I'm so incredibly evil that I've fallen into the pit and am
dragging you down with me."

A hand of fire splayed out from his chin to his neck, but even
flames were joy and delight at the moment of sinning; no burn felt
painful then. Hellfire was something else again, something quite
different, and eternal.

"That's right, little billygoat, you take me down with you.
You're just a little pet kid like the ones I used to carry in my
arms."

She was a virtuous widow and he had made her renounce the
decorum and virtue of the widowed state, sully her husband's memory, go out of her head and say crazy things like that with no
rhyme or reason, murmur unconnected phrases, giggle and shake
with laughter, indifferent to the fearful punishment hanging over
her head, not even aware she'd done wrong.

He and he alone was guilty, but they were both damned, and
God's wrath would fall just as heavily on his aunt's head as on his.
Neither one's soul had been able to hold out against the vile body
and the putrid flesh, but he was the only real culprit. His aunt had
told him to go away if he wanted to and had pointed to the foot of
the dunes. Well, he hadn't gone; he had stayed, knowing full well
that if he stayed he'd forget the respect he owed her, offend God,
lie and give himself over to Satan to be the willing agent of his
widowed aunt's downfall and perdition.

"Oh, I wish I could die."

"Yes, in my arms."

Her hand glided from his shoulder to his chest. Oh no, Aunt,
no. Don't you see the demon is unloosed, that he's flying over the
dunes and the sea like a great black bat, hiding the moon and making
the night inky and cold? The Tempter was there, just as he had
always been, from the moment his aunt appeared in the door of
Jairo's *marineti*. It had been the devil who had spoken out of Osnar's mouth when he compared her to ripe, juicy fruit. That was
the beginning of the struggle that he had just lost. The truth was
that it had been lost from the beginning, in her footsteps coming
down the hall at night, in the fluttering lace of her negligee, in the
brief bikini and the short nightgown, in the hands daubed with cold

cream, in the garbled words of the Lord's Prayer, in the desire-laden dreams when he held her naked in his arms in the hammock and didn't know what to do. Now he knew and would pay for his knowledge for all eternity. They would both pay, culprit and victim, he and his aunt. Or, who knows? God is just. Maybe He would take pity on his aunt and let her serve her time in Purgatory. However long it might be, even if it lasted millions of years, time was not eternity; it had a limit and an end. The day would come when the sentence was over and the condemned criminal was set free. But the torments of Hell? Ah, those would never end. "Nevermore" Hell's clock repeated at each successive second. That was what Cosme had said when they were talking about eternal punishment.

"God is good and all-knowing and He'll take pity on you, Aunt. He knows it wasn't your fault."

The gay, heedless laugh bubbled up and the hand wandered down his suffering breast.

"Don't call me Aunt, call me Tieta."

Her hands caressed his poor breast, suffocated with shame and remorse and bursting with fear. How could he ever face God on Judgment Day? The hand calmed his nightmare, transformed his feelings, untied the hard knot, conquered the shadows! But it could not put out the fire of heavenly wrath, for palm, wrist and fingers were one burning coal of divine warmth. Divine? Thus did Satan beguile men to their doom. That divine warmth would turn into unendurable pain in the depths of Hell, where sinners were consumed in its slow and never-ending fire.

"It's all my fault. God is bound to forgive you, Aunt."

"Not Aunt. Tieta, your Tieta."

Why hadn't he heard the voice of God in his aunt's voice pointing down the hill to the right road, the pathway that would lead him to salvation, to the priesthood, to Paradise?

Paradise? Which one? The hand led to Paradise too: only a little while ago he had seen all the beauty and sweetness of Heaven in every detail of the body exposed to his gaze in the moonlight. The hand played with the hair springing from the virile young chest. The Major had been proud of his hairy torso, with hair all over his chest and his back. His father had been a real he-man. His son, castrated by his own vows and his mother's promise, could never be that. But the demon had lured him to rise up against the Law, aroused his quiescent flesh to lust and perverted him, turning an innocent youth who knew nothing of desire and wicked thoughts into a gross male animal with no control over his body and soul, a randy billygoat.

Not only that, he had made use of him to ensnare his own aunt and lead her to her doom.

"Purgatory lasts a while and then it's over, Aunt. God knows it was all my fault. God is just, He won't send you to Hell."

"I'm an old nannygoat, you silly little kid. Call me nannygoat, say I'm your own nannygoat."

Now that he'd never do. Not even in the hour of sin, when you stop thinking with your head and your mouth moans and cries out almost anything at all. "Nannygoat," Osnar had said in the devil's voice when he was bowled over by her standing there in the door of Jairo's *marineti*, and the Evil One had added an indecent remark about teats with plenty of milk. And what about himself? Where had he buried his head, rested his lips, where had he frantically bit?

"Forgive me, Aunt. Swear you'll forgive me."

"Say Tieta."

Her fingers navigated and explored the firm-muscled belly. She inserted her little finger into his navel and tickled him. The live coal burst into flame, devouring the sin, concealing the crime, lighting up the moon.

"Aunt, I want to tell you—"

"Tieta."

"I want to tell you that even if I have to burn in Hell for eternity, even so . . ."

"What, little billygoat?"

". . . Even so, I'm not sorry. And even if the punishment were much worse, even then . . ."

"What?"

". . . Even so I'd want . . ."

Where was the hand? Flames licked him from head to foot and ran over his whole body; his head throbbed, his mouth opened, the Cur rose up.

"What would you want, little billygoat? Tell me. . . ."

"I'd want to be here with you, Aunt."

"Tieta."

The roaming hand found what it was looking for; felt, then grasped it. The demon grew taller.

"I'm not sorry, Tieta, oh no, Tieta!"

"Say nannygoat, my little billy."

Where were the shades of night and Hell and the fear of God? Paradise opened for the Cur under the moon, a narrow gate of honey and black roses. Well worth Hell and worse. Come on, my little billy! Oh, nannygoat, my own nannygoat, I'm a randy goat and the fire's devouring me.

THIRD EPISODE

🐎 🐎 🐎

Progress Comes to the Back of Beyond,
or
Joan of Arc of the Backlands

WITH MARTIANS AND VENUSIANS, SUPERHEROES, SPACESHIPS
AND FANTASTIC FEMALES; OF THE MANUFACTURE OF
TITANIUM DIOXIDE AND THE FATE OF WATER AND FISH, IN
TERMS OF THE DEBATE DIVIDING AGRESTE AND PUTTING AN
END TO SOMNOLENCE AND PEACE; IN WHICH WE WITNESS THE
STIRRING OF GREED, AMBITION AND A THIRST FOR POWER AS
WELL AS THE BLOSSOMING OF LOVE, BESIDES A THREE KINGS
PAGEANT, BUMBA-MEU-BOI AND OTHER TOUCHES OF
FOLKLORE IN WHICH THIS POOR LITTLE NOVEL HAS BEEN
LACKING UP TO NOW.

*In which superman and wonderwoman make their
first appearance in Agreste, interrupting a pleasant
and sinful practice during the sultry hour
of the siesta.*

The first sighting in Agreste of fabulous beings from outer space
took place early one afternoon at the heat-dazed hour when no one
willingly disturbs his neighbor's rest.

Only in Plínio Xavier's general store, open, like the others,
merely from force of habit and respect for the traditional working
hours of eight to twelve and two to six, were there certain suspicious
signs of life. Two or three times a week, always at the siesta hour
when customers could be trusted not to blunder in, the drygoods
merchant, a respectable citizen, husband and father, concealed himself
behind the flitches of jerky and busied himself by thrusting his hands
up the skirt of the overripe virgin Cinira and manipulating her private
parts with his fingertips. Facing the shelves along the wall, she pretended to see and feel nothing, all the while opening her legs to make
his task easier. Plínio Xavier too worked in silence, sweat dripping
from his face. All at once Cinira would sigh deeply, shudder, raise
her hand to where, as she knew, the coveted weapon bulged outside
his trousers, give it a hard squeeze and leave in furtive haste.

On this day, just as she was about to reach the sigh and the
shudder, a sinister, abominable roar echoed through the street,
rudely interrupting the pleasant little game. Before she knew it,
Cinira found herself running down the sidewalk and screaming in
panic as the monstrous, unknown machine bore down on her, its
enormous wheels leaving deep furrows in the road. Its exhaust pipes
and orifices spewed forth pestilent black smoke and without warning it emitted a series of piercing hoots like nothing ever heard in
those parts before. Plínio Xavier buttoned his fly and reached the

door in time to see the outlandish vehicle in front of his store. In its belly were two indescribable beings, apparently one of each sex, although it was hard to tell one from the other by either their physical attributes or the identical spacesuits they wore.

A few days before, a rumor had circulated to the effect that the fishermen at Mangue Seco had seen an unidentified object fly over the beach and the coconut grove, flashing in the sunlight, and then disappear again out to sea. Still, the town was not prepared for this new apparition, and it caused a considerable stir.

Of the spaceship in Cathedral Square and the first close encounter between spacemen and human beings, with references to hotels and paved roads, while Miss Venus turns on all the men, including Manuel the Portugee.

Cathedral Square was silent and deserted when the spaceship careened to a stop in a lurid burst of spitting exhaust and the creature who was presumably male—the long hair appearing below his space helmet and the violet shadows under his eyes caused some to dispute the point—vaulted over the door of the fantastic machine, looked all around, and saw no one. On his hands he sported thick gloves of some exotic material, and he was wearing garments of a totally exotic style, a kind of blue overalls with zippers and pockets in the legs and arms, studded with flashy metallic grommets and nailheads. On closer examination the suit turned out to be a jacket and trousers with pockets full of strange objects, deadly weapons, God knew what. The female creature, outfitted in identical style except that she stuck out more in front, raised her helmet and revealed herself as quite a dish. She drew off her gloves and with long fingers fluffed up her auburn hair, no longer than her companion's, with a platinum streak in the middle, showing that she was either a Venusian or from Rio de Janeiro, and very exciting either way.

Osnar looked on dumbfounded from the depths of the bar, where he was alone with Manuel the Portugee.

"Ahoy there, Admiral! Come and tell me if you see what I see or if all I drank at Zuleika's last night has given me the DTs."

Seu Manuel left the glasses he was sloshing around in the water—"You carry squalor a little too far, Vasco da Gama," Aminthas told him every so often, pointing to the smudges on plates, glasses and silverware—and went to the door. His mouth fell open and he scratched his chin.

"And who might these wanderers be?"

"After all Ascânio's talk about tourists, here they are," ventured Osnar. "Unless they're the crew from the flying saucer that flew over Mangue Seco."

His reconnaissance having flushed no earthlings, the being who was probably male returned to his ship and the Venusian donned her gloves; the unholy racket started up again, black smoke belched out of the exhaust pipes and orifices, and the vehicle lunged forward up a side street and was lost to sight. For some time the noise could be heard all over town, rudely awakening those who, like Edmundo Ribeiro the tax collector and Chalita the Arab, were trying to catch a few winks, and bringing the startled and bewildered townspeople to their doors. Storekeepers shut up shop on the off chance that it might be Lampião, the most notorious backlands badman of them all, come back from Hell on a motorbike. Lampião had never passed through Agreste but he came pretty close once, three leagues' march away, and the event is remembered even now.

When the space heroes, after roaring up and down every street and alley in town, zoomed back to Cathedral Square for a second landing, Ascânio Trindade, who had seen them out the second-story window of the courthouse, was already running down the steps to meet them. When Osnar said they were tourists he had been pulling his friend's leg in absentia, but if he had heard him Ascânio would have approved: yes, tourists, and why not, I'd like to know? The first to accept the invitation he had composed with Dona Carmosina's invaluable help and sent to an evening paper, *A Tarde*, in Bahia, suggesting that tourists "make a side trip from Salvador to the healthiest city in the state, Sant'Ana do Agreste, and see the most beautiful beach in the world, the sand dunes of Mangue Seco." The paper published the letter in its readers' column, lamenting in an editorial footnote that the incredibly bad state of the roads made the invitation impracticable. No tourist with any sense would be willing to risk losing his car in one of those craters that kept on getting deeper every day, just to see Agreste, "even though it is a little Paradise on earth." Anyone who came through the potholes of the main road unscathed would still have to face "the indescribable fifty kilometers of mud after leaving Esplanada."

Ascânio's face, usually so serious, was wreathed in smiles. Even if the highway was more like a ditch than a road, even with those fatal forty-eight kilometers—forty-eight, not fifty—added on, there were still brave men and women ready to answer the call.

Dusty and perspiring as they were, the strange beings waved a cordial, and thirsty, greeting. The female beckoned impatiently with an enormous leather flipper.

"Hi there! . . . Welcome to Agreste!" Ascânio greeted them cheerfully.

"*Bonjour, frère!*" answered the spaceman, taking off his glove to wipe his forehead with a mauve handkerchief. "Hot enough for you?"

"It'll cool off in a little while. It always cools down about four in the afternoon, and at night it gets downright chilly. It's a perfect dry climate, can't be beat." Ascânio already had his spiel down pat.

"I'll believe anything you say, luv, if you'll only find me something cold to drink." The voice of the female was all swooning promise.

"Oh, yes, sure, whatever you like. Let's go to the bar."

Osnar was watching from his table.

"Admiral, they're heading this way. You'd better hold me back or I'll forget myself and grab hold of that gorgeous dame right here in your bar. I always did hanker to make love to a Martian lady if I can't have a Polack—there ain't a woman on this planet or any other that can beat a Polish whore." Osnar's Polish joke again.

The little group entered the bar and sat down after good afternoons all around. Manuel served them solicitously while Osnar's eyes were hopelessly glued to the female, who, since there was no coconut milk to be had (Ascânio made a note to keep fresh coconut milk on hand in the bar), accepted *guaraná*, or passionflower juice.

"Whisky on the rocks for me," said the presumptive male. "Scotch, naturally . . . I mean *escocés*."

"All I've got is domestic whisky, but it's the genuine article," Seu Manuel told him proudly.

"No, no please! Just bring me some mineral water without gas. But ice-cold, mind you."

"Our spring water's better than any mineral water; we sent it to Bahia to be tested and it passed every test with flying colors," Ascânio said helpfully.

"All right, just as long as it's good and cold."

Seu Manuel served the *guaraná* with a straw as a special touch, and the water, iced, in a glass. The Martian approved. "This is mighty good water. Let's have a little more, please, and tell me how much I owe you."

At a sign from Ascânio, Seu Manuel bowed.

"No charge . . . it's on the house."

"Why, thank you very much. I'll accept the favor this time, but . . . Is this the only bar around here?"

"Well, there's Nigger Caloca's tavern, a kind of saloon, down in the Beco da Amargura. But you can get a slug of *cachaça* in any grocery store."

"You'll have to improve your stock a bit, my friend. . . ." (This was in English.) "Decent brands of Scotch, good wines . . . What about hotels, *frère*?" *Frère* was Ascânio, to whom he seemed to have taken a liking. "Is there a decent one in town, with private baths?"

"Not what you'd call a hotel, exactly. But Miss Lovey, Dona Amorzinho, has a very nice boardinghouse with first-class grub and clean rooms. No private bath. But the spigot in the bathroom's as good as a showerbath."

"We'll have to put up a hotel, I see," observed the male, as if building a first-class hotel in Agreste were the simplest thing in the world. Precisely at the moment that statement issued from the space hero's lips, Ascânio Trindade's daring reveries began.

"That road is a nightmare," mewed the female. "Especially the last part. . . . I never was jounced around so much or swallowed so much dust in my life." She fluffed up her dusty red hair with the alluring platinum streak. "The minute I get to Salvador I'm going straight to Severiano's for a wash and comb. . . ."

"It only needs to be widened and paved, darling. How many kilometers is it, *frère*?"

"From here to Bahia?"

"No, just the last stretch, the cattle track."

"Forty-eight kilometers."

"Baby, you're putting me on," said Miss Venus to Ascânio reproachfully. "It must be a hundred at least. I'm worn right down to the bone." She clutched her Venusian backside with one hand.

"Ay!" moaned Osnar, but if anyone heard him they didn't let on.

"No, he's right, darling; it must be about fifty kilometers. That can be paved in a jiffy."

A paved road, a hotel . . . Ascânio's heart lifted and his dreams took wing.

"Let me ask you something, *frère*: what about a motorboat to go down the river to that beach . . . what's it called?"

"Mangue Seco."

"*C'est ça.* . . . Will I have any trouble renting one?"

"Well . . . there's Elieser's launch. It's not for rent but I think I can talk him into taking you there. He's a real nice fellow."

"You can tell him I'll pay him well."

Ascânio went trotting off to find Elieser. Persuading him would take some doing; "nice fellow" was not the most accurate term for Elieser, but Ascânio had influence. He'd better not say anything about hotels and paved roads; the other man might view any such plans as a serious threat to his legitimate interests. By now Ascânio understood that the visitors were not casual tourists but entrepreneurs scouting out the possibility of investing big money to transform Agreste into the fancy tourist mecca they had argued about so often at the post office.

"There's no infrastructure at all," Dona Carmosina would say.

"There's no one with money to build one, and the county certainly can't," Ascânio would retort. Well, now it looked as if money would not be a problem.

Osnar and Seu Manuel, finding no acceptable common topic of conversation, smiled foolishly at the strangers. Aminthas soon joined them, having torn himself away from a radio broadcast of the Rolling Stones. The queen of the planet Venus gave the three humans a long, come-hither look, one after another, with a special smile for each to show there was nothing she'd like better than to go to bed with that particular earthman—"Just with you, luv, nobody else in the world." Luckily Ascânio was back before Osnar forgot where he was entirely, with the news that Elieser was ready to meet them down at the landing where the launch was moored.

"Thanks! *Andiamo, bella*, we haven't got much time. *Arrivederci!*"

How many languages did they speak in space? Osnar almost choked on Portuguese saying goodbye. The Martian held out a hand; Aminthas couldn't decide whether to risk a lethal handshake or not.

"You'd better leave your motor in the square and walk; the road's in pretty bad shape. I'll show you the way."

They all trooped out, even Manuel, leaving the bar to run itself.

"Oh, you all are so nice to us," purred Miss Venus gratefully.

On the way down to the landing Ascânio tried to learn a little more.

"Are you thinking of establishing some sort of business here, if you don't mind my asking?"

"Don't know yet. We may; it all depends on the surveys being made."

"Were you thinking about a hotel? The water here is the best anywhere around."

"Hotel? Yes, that too. You'd have to have a hotel. Water? Maybe. But those would be secondary investments, diversification of capital. The water's something we can think about later."

They had reached the landing. Ascânio meditated on these hints of ambitious projects. Tourist development on a large scale was in the offing, that was obvious. The splendid creatures stepped into the motorboat with Elieser at the helm.

"*Merci, frère*, thanks again, *Ciao!*" He waved goodbye.

"Ascânio Trindade, county clerk. Count on me for anything you need."

"Oh. You're the county clerk? Who's the mayor?"

"Dr. Mauritônio Dantas, but he isn't well. I'm taking care of things. Just talk to me if there's anything you want."

"OK. We'll come and talk to you for sure. And soon. We have a lot to talk about."

The motorboat sped off; the redhead with the platinum streak threw a kiss and offered herself with her eyes, but Elieser's scowl did not soften one iota.

Ascânio Trindade smiled dazedly, as if in a dream. The superior beings had landed at last.

Of the ensuing remarks and the first, still good-natured, argument.

A crowd was gathered in the plaza, elbowing one another to get close to the vehicle.

"Get a load of the heft of those tires!"

"Wow!"

"Did you hear the horn play the beginning of 'Rio, Cidade Marvilhosa'?"

"What'll they think of next?"

There was a great stir and bustle in the bar. Storekeepers abandoned their shops. Plínio Xavier was proud of being the first to have seen the infernal machine and caught a glimpse of its pilots.

"There I was, minding my own business, totting up accounts . . ."

Now what was Osnar laughing at! All eyes turned to the door of the church, where Cinira was standing with the pious ladies' battalion. She wasn't one of them yet but it wouldn't be long now.

"When I heard that godalmighty racket and dropped what I was doing . . ."

Astério and Elisa joined the group. He had gone running home at the hour of peril to look after his wife. He was worried about Elisa, who was out of sorts and fidgety lately and still hadn't come down to earth after her sister's homecoming. They went to the plaza together to look at the machine, Elisa so dolled up that the space queen with the platinum-blond streak in her fiery mane was hardly in the running. That platinum streak had Osnar in such a state that he confided to Seixas and Fidélio:

"I swear to God, if I could get my hands on that Martian gal I'd start licking her big toe and take a good three hours to get to her navel. . . . I'd tongue-whip her within an inch of her life."

"Filthy swine!"

Seu Edmundo Ribeiro was no Puritan, but some practices repelled him as unworthy of an upstanding macho male. To take a woman to bed and mount her was all very well. But to put his tongue . . . Kisses were meant for a mouth, and a clean mouth at that.

"Edmundinho, old fellow, don't tell me you never in your life ate hair pie . . . never sucked a honeycomb . . ."

"I'm a serious man and a clean one and I'll thank you to respect me."

At the post office another argument had reached the boiling point. Ascânio Trindade had given Dona Carmosina a detailed report in the presence of Skipper Dário de Queluz, who warned him in plaintive accents, "Ascânio, my dear fellow, you'll be sorry you ever were so obsessed with bringing tourists to Agreste. You and all the rest of us will pay dearly for it. One of these days some crazy fool's going to read that nonsense you and Carmosina keep sending in to the papers and take it seriously. They'll set up a business to exploit Mangue Seco Beach and Agreste's water and climate, and where will we be then? In Hell, that's where."

"In Hell, Skipper? In Heaven's name, why? I never heard of a watering place, a spa, a seaside resort being Hell. They're just the opposite, they're places to rest and relax."

Dona Carmosina put in her oar. "You know very well no one loves nature and defends Agreste's air and scenery more than I do. But I don't see what harm there'd be in a spa."

"Oh, a spa here in town wouldn't be so bad. But Ascânio wants people swarming all over the beach, all kinds of junk—"

Ascânio blew up. "What do you mean, junk? Summer cottages for tourists, restaurants, a hotel! Is Acapulco Hell? Are St. Tropez and Arembepe Hell? Agreste's future lies in tourism, Skipper, whether you like it or not."

"Yes, those places are Hell, and they are full of junk. Just the other day there was a feature story about Arambepe in the *Evening News*. It's turned into the hippie capital and the junkie capital of South America, in case you didn't know. Did you ever stop to think what Mangue Seco full of long-haired drug addicts would be like? Leave our paradise alone, Ascânio, at least as long as we're alive."

"What you're saying, Skipper, is that you'd just as soon Agreste went on being a good place to wait for death?"

"Yes, my boy, that's exactly what I'm saying. Death takes its time here, and that's all I ask. Pure, unpolluted air and a clean white beach."

Ascânio turned to his ally Dona Carmosina, who took up the cudgels again.

"Who said anything about pollution? I don't know about hippies, though I must say their philosophy's the same as mine—peace and love, the best thing invented in this century so far—if only they didn't take drugs. But tourists with money, Skipper? I don't see anything so bad about that. Nice summer cottages, good movies in town, shops full of people—where's the harm?"

"Skyscrapers, hotels, a land rush, no more coconut grove, no more trees, no more peace and quiet! God forbid! It's a good thing it's all nothing but a wild scheme you two have cooked up."

Peto came running in to tell them the launch was back. Ascânio issued a good-natured invitation as he left.

"Well, Skipper, I think we'll have tourism in Agreste before you know it. The 'crazy fool' has already turned up. Why don't you come along with me and meet him?"

"All right," said the Skipper, "I will."

However, by the time they reached the square the super-couple, surrounded by a curious throng, were already astride the glittering machine and ready to depart. Ascânio tried to engage them in conversation, but they were in a hurry; it would be late that night by the time they got back to Salvador.

"I'll come back soon and we can talk then. Just let me write down your name." He extracted a little notebook from a mysterious pocket in his trouser leg. The pen on a chain around his neck looked like a microphone in a spy story. A tiny, powerful camera clicked in Miss Venus' slender, long-fingered, gloveless hands.

"My name? Ascânio Trindade. This is Skipper Dário de Queluz."

"Skipper?"

"Yes, he's a naval officer."

"Retired," the Skipper informed him.

"Uh-huh." After a pause he introduced himself, "Dr. Mirko Stefano. À bientôt. So long."

"Bye-bye, luv!" cried Miss Venus, her bedroom eyes speaking worlds.

The machine took off in a cloud of dust and a roar that burst sensitive eardrums. Doctor? He looked more like an astronaut, the captain of a spaceship, one of those entrepreneurs of our time who are transforming the earth and human life. As for the vehicle, it was Peto who knew all about it. Why should he worry about getting through primary school when he already knew all there was to know about cars and racetracks? This car was a Bug, with wide-tread magnesium-wheeled tires, KITS 1600, two carburetors and a souped-up horn. In fact, everything about it was souped up, especially the engine; Peto's enthusiasm was boundless. He ran home to tell Aunt Antonieta and Leonora all about it.

They heard about the superior beings from Elieser's grudging lips.

"All that fella was interested in was the part along the river-bank, the coconut grove and the vacant land. He asked me who it belonged to and I told him it had never had an owner, as far back as anyone knew. They took a heck of a lot of pictures. And at Mangue Seco they took off their clothes and went swimming in the buff."

"In the buff?"

"Yep, both of them, just as if I wasn't there. That dame has guts, though. She went all the way out to the breakers."

"You see, Ascânio? Nudism, and this is barely the beginning. It's lucky for them I wasn't there; I wouldn't have allowed it." Skipper Dário was no more a Puritan than Edmundo Ribeiro, but he would draw the line at nudism on Mangue Seco as long as he was around.

Elieser went on before Ascânio could reply. "The guy asked me how much he owed me and I told him it was nothing, like you said. Who's gonna pay me for my time and the gas, Ascânio? You or the town?"

Osnar, who had been listening in silence, broke in, shocked to the core.

"Elieser, you mean to tell me you took a gander at that babe bare-assed and you want money, yet? I'd fork over plenty for one look at her.... You're a degenerate and that's God's truth."

*Of Tieta's light and her virtues, with
quotations in Latin.*

Not a manioc planter, farmer, goat herder, fisherman or smuggler in Agreste and the neighboring hamlets, from the banks of the river to the white-capped waves off the harbor bar, remained in ignorance of the momentous event. From Rocinha, Possidônio the Prophet thundered on about the Apocalypse and the end of the world, his two favorite themes, citing the Scriptures, notably the Old Testament, as authority.

And then, lo and behold, things began to happen in Agreste, startling the town out of its habitual lethargy, sparking discussion, provoking agitated arguments, and making the habitués of the Areopagus sit up and take notice.

In obedience to orders from above, the electric wires, strung on colossal pylons, began to stride through the backlands toward the community, at an unheard-of pace for any public work. From time to time a jeep debouched engineers and workmen into the quiet streets, and Seu Manuel's bar was now a livelier place. The chief engineer was sure the power line would reach the town in a month and a half or two months at the most; then the job would be over and a date could be set for Inauguration Day festivities. Since the community enjoyed such high standing with the federal government, some high muck-a-muck from the São Francisco Valley Authority might turn up for the ceremony. Maybe the director would make a special trip from Brasília.

The chief engineer was ready to believe anything after he was informed that it had been a vacationing widow who had used her late millionaire husband's influence with friends to get the schedule changed and Sant'Ana do Agreste put at the top of the list. It was hard to believe, but since everyone in town swore it was true, the engineer was now anxious to meet this celebrity who had been able to change plans that were already approved, dig up pylons and plant them someplace else, and dictate where light and power lines should go.

She was an outgoing, unassuming kind of person, Aminthas told him, not hoity-toity even if she was the rich widow of a papal nobleman in high society down south and very well connected; the best proof of that was the engineer sitting there in the Portugee's bar swilling beer. She had done it all with just two little telegrams and given a kick in the pants besides to that uppity director who had treated the town's official representative, Ascânio Trindade, the county clerk, as if he were a nobody and Agreste were nowhere. Ignoring Ascânio's credentials and the fact that the young man had gone to Paulo Afonso to defend his community's legitimate interests, the director had let him sit there cooling his heels before he sent him packing with a resounding no, without even listening to what he had to say. Agreste was nothing but a dried-up goat pasture, as far as he was concerned, and he had told Ascânio so. Dona Antonieta was so furious when she heard what had happened that she had sent a wire. And that was all it took.

Aminthas embroidered the tale a little when he told it to the chief engineer, and at the end of it he laughed in his face.

"Dona Antonieta Esteves Cantarelli, that's the lady's name. Naturally you've heard of the late Comendador Cantarelli, the great São Paulo industrialist."

The engineer knew when he was beaten. He concealed his ignorance. Oh yes, he said, he had heard that name in the same breath with the Matarazzos, the Crespis, and the Filizolas. He lifted his glass of beer in a respectful toast to Mrs. Cantarelli. Not only Aminthas but all those present joined in. When the grateful townspeople, who still had not recovered from the shock of this unexpected gift from Heaven, referred to the new electric light, they didn't call it the Paulo Afonso Light, or the Power Company Light, or the São Francisco Valley Light, the names it was known by to everybody else. To the people of Agreste it was Tieta's Light.

When Tieta came in from Mangue Seco the Wednesday following that festive Sunday to sign the deed for her land before the notary public, she was surprised to see a banner in Cathedral Square, hung between two of the weatherbeaten old electric light posts in the vicinity of Perpétua's house. It read: "GREETINGS FROM THE GRATEFUL PEOPLE OF AGRESTE TO DONA ANTONIETA ESTEVES CANTARELLI." There was only one thing wrong with it. At the insistence of Perpétua and Zé Esteves, the word "Esteves" had been added on after the banner was all finished. It had to be squeezed in between and above the other two names, in the middle; but that was only a little flaw, not enough to mar the imposing effect of the red letters against the white cotton cloth.

It had been Ascânio's idea and they had all agreed; to the townspeople, Tieta was the woman of the hour. True, they hadn't put her next to St. Anne on the high altar in the cathedral yet, as Modesto Pires had predicted, but they had done just about everything else. When she walked down the street that afternoon with Leonora and Perpétua to the notary's office to keep her appointment with the owner of the tannery, people came out of their houses to thank her, and some even kissed her hand. When Colonel Artur da Tapitanga heard she was back in Agreste, he left his plantation house and walked the kilometer to the city limits to embrace his meritorious fellow citizen.

"You see, child, God really does write straight with crooked lines. When Zé Esteves drove you away it was because God wanted you to come back like a queen." He looked her up and down with his lecherous old goat's eyes, showing there was still lust in his heart if no strength left in his balls. "When are you coming to pay me a call and have a look at my goats?"

Goatstink saluted her too in his way, when he caught sight of her at the entrance to the moviehouse door.

"Hurrah for Dona Tieta, the boss lady and a pretty piece of ass!"

As she passed, Tieta dropped into his grimy hand enough to keep him in *cachaça* for a week, and thinking to gladden his eyes, walked away swinging her hips like the prow of a ship in a gale.

The terms of the purchase of the land were agreed to, the deed drawn up and cash paid on the barrelhead. Before heading home, Tieta went by the post office to say hello to Carmosina and mail a letter. They were soon joined by Ascânio and De Matos Barbosa, the seer and bard, who was suffering from nostalgia and rheumatism. "Tieta, you're sunlight and medicine to me. All I have to do is look at your face and I'm cured."

Dona Carmosina declared her intention of coming over that evening for a chat. "I have ever so many things to tell you." Her eyes showed she meant Leonora and Ascânio, her favorite topic.

"But I won't be there. I'm going back to Mangue Seco this afternoon, in just a little while. I only stopped by to see you and send my regards to Dona Milu."

"You're going back today? Why in such a rush?"

"I'm building me a little cabin, and the work's already started. You know me; when I want something I have to have it right away. And I do want to see the walls standing before I go back south."

"But you can't think of going so soon. How can you do such a thing?"

"Why not?"

"Before the great day the new power line comes in? Why, people won't let you."

Tieta laughed.

"You make me feel like I'm running for Congress or something. . . . You can represent me at the ceremony." She was quiet for a few moments, lost in thought. "On second thought, though, maybe I will stay on a while longer. Not for the ceremony so much, but to see my little house in Mangue Seco finished."

"Oh yes, I'm sure you'll stay. You both will. . . ." Dona Carmosina couldn't help adding, as she watched Leonora's pensive face, "I know someone who may not ever want to leave." Her little eyes sparkled with mischief.

When they were home and she could talk to Perpétua alone, Tieta told her what a good boy Ricardo was and what a dear nephew, and how she could never have managed without him. He had taken care of everything with the Skipper's help; had crossed over to Saco village twice and hired the construction workers needed for the job: bricklayers, carpenters and a foreman, men who were used to working with coconut trucks on the shifting sand. Thanks to Ricardo everything was all set, and work had actually started the day before. She'd made him her assistant, and she'd like to keep him at Mangue Seco for a few days.

"Why of course, sister, he's on holiday. Keep him as long as you want to."

Speaking of holidays, Ricardo had asked for his school textbooks so he could keep up with his homework even on the beach. He slept in a hammock in the living room at Liberty Hall. What a wonderful boy he was! Wanting to help him, Tieta had decided to open a savings account in his name in a São Paulo bank. In that letter she had just mailed at the post office she had given her second-in-command instructions to start her nephew off with a large initial deposit to his new account (Perpétua shivered when she heard how much) and she would add a still undetermined amount each month. That way, when Ricardo was ordained, what with capital, interest and compensation for the changing rate of the cruzeiro, he'd have a nice little nest egg. Perpétua lifted her grateful eyes to Heaven, where the Lord had commenced keeping His part of the bargain. After silent but heartfelt thanks to God, she looked at Tieta.

"Sister, I don't know how to thank you or what to say. God will surely repay you." She caught her sister's hand in an unwonted gesture and pressed it to her heart, which was shielded by a brassiere of some thick stuff as unyielding as scaffolding. She wiped her streaming eyes with her black handkerchief.

After much pleading from her family, Tieta finally consented to receive a visit from Father Mariano that afternoon, before escaping from her fellow citizens' demonstrations of gratitude and taking refuge at Mangue Seco. The Reverend Father thanked her in the name of his flock for the grace of new light that would alter the face of the town and alter its customs, too. She had done the community an enormous service. In benefiting them all, Dona Antonieta had, ironically enough, unwittingly created a serious problem for the parish. The lighting system in the cathedral was on its last legs and would never be able to withstand the force of the increased power from Paulo Afonso. He had consulted an engineer from the hydroelectric power company, who had told him it was absolutely essential to replace the wiring in order to avoid a short circuit and grave danger of fire. Where to find the money to do it? To whom could they turn if not to her? The cathedral was deeply in her debt already for the new image of their patron saint and the monstrance she had brought from São Paulo, as no one knew better than the priest—but he also knew how generous Dona Antonieta was; one of the Elect and widow of a papal nobleman, who therefore had a rightful place in the hierarchy of the Church. Tieta heard him in the presence of her father, stepmother, sisters and Leonora, an equivocal smile on her face. Perpétua, thinking of the savings account, took up the parish priest's words:

"One of the Elect, Father Mariano; truer words were never spoken."

The Reverend Father could not be sure of an affirmative response from the full lips parted in an enigmatic smile; he could only note that Tieta had undoubtedly grown younger in those few days spent at Mangue Seco. She looked sleek, satisfied and prettier than ever, and the sun had burnished her copper skin with gold.

"Don't worry about it, Father; go ahead and put in the new wiring."

The relieved Father Mariano was about to express his thanks when she went on playfully, her voice bubbling into laughter, "That's to repay Our Lady St. Anne for robbing her of her sacristan for a few days. I mean my nephew Ricardo, who's at Mangue Seco helping me build my house."

Perpétua shivered. Despite her black mourning garb and the decorum she owed the priest, she could not hide the satisfaction all at once reflected on her forbidding face and beaming in her triumphant gaze. By linking her nephew to the donations she had made to the church and naming him her intermediary in her dealings with God and His saints, Tieta had taken a giant step forward on the road to adopting him as her heir. God had just been placed in her debt, having received, by way of Ricardo, the gift of new electric wiring for His church.

Father Mariano, also beaming, raised his voice in well-turned laudatory phrases.

"God doesn't forget those who aid Holy Mother Church; He repays the widow's mite a hundredfold in enduring benefits. Dona Antonieta, you can be sure the Virgin will shower blessings on you and your family"—he raised his hand to bless Esteveses and Cantarellis alike—"and I think I can speak for Our Lady St. Anne when I say that she willingly lends you her squire. Ricardo can learn and practice nothing but good in such holy company."

As he was taking his leave the Reverend Father commented on Tieta's appearance: how healthy and blooming she looked! Those days on the beach, he said, had been a real tonic to her. She was plainly overflowing with health and good spirits. Her purity of soul shone in the beauty of her face: *tota pulchra, benedicta Domini.* May God preserve her just as she was.

Zé Esteves was the only one to mumble and grumble at the importunate request and the fact that it had been granted.

"That old black vulture in the cassock is pretty smart. He's been raking in the shekels with his soft soap and his Latin for a long time now, and the suckers fall for it like sitting ducks. Forgive me, child, for speaking my mind, but you ought to watch your money closer. You're buying a house, don't forget; this is no time to be throwing money away."

Exactly a week later, as luck would have it, Tieta was summoned back to Agreste by Zé Esteves. It seemed that Dona Zulmira was willing to lower the price of her house and strike a bargain. Tieta left Ricardo in charge of the construction work, which was rapidly going forward. He would be all alone at Liberty Hall; the Skipper and Dona Laura had gone back to their bungalow in town three days before. Three days, or rather three nights, during which aunt and nephew traded the lonely, romantic sand dunes for the comfort of a horsehair mattress on the double bed in the mariner's bedroom.

That mattress had come along at just the right point in her nephew's instruction in one of the good things in life, if not the best—just when they had attained a second, higher stage in their study of the subject in which Tieta was a past mistress, a professor *emerita*, a *doctora honoris causa*, as Father Mariano might have said in Latin. She was giving Ricardo intensive classes in all she knew; that is, the entire alphabet, including the indescribable ypsilon Y.

Tieta returned to Agreste the very morning the amazing creatures from outer space landed for the first time, but she didn't see them and only heard of their coming late that afternoon when Ascânio came in bursting with enthusiasm.

"Investors from down south! And they're thinking of investing capital right here in the county and starting a tourist business. It's really a big deal. They're going to pave the road and build hotels. What do you think, Dona Antonieta? What do you say to that, Leonora?"

Tourist business? In Agreste, to take advantage of the water, the climate, Mangue Seco Beach? Well, why not? Anything was possible. She had been wise to buy that lot on the beach, and it would be wise to stop being so stiff-necked and take Dona Zulmira up on her offer; she had seen land and property values shoot up unbelievably in São Paulo and she knew it could happen here. Felipe had had a flair for buying land and more land for a song in places where no one had ever made an offer and reselling it for a fortune years later. Tieta asked Perpétua for a pen and paper, wrote Dona Zulmira a note to seal the bargain and sent Peto to deliver it.

She decided to stay in Agreste long enough to close the deal, draw up the deed and take possession of the house. Even as she felt her body's ardent, insistent demand that she return without delay, even knowing her boy would burn with the fires of Hell all through the sleepless night, she chose to attend to business. She had learned not to lose her head, not to let even the wildest, most delirious passion keep her from looking after her own best interests.

Ascânio went on outlining plans for Agreste's radiant future. The big change had started when the two Paulistas came to town. Everything would be much easier now that the São Francisco

Valley Authority had decided to include Agreste among the fortunate communities chosen to receive power from the Paulo Afonso
Falls—Tieta's Light.

A chapter in which Tieta tries to define love and fails.

Tieta left the sweethearts at the street door, alone and free to say
goodnight in their own way, but she lingered in the shadowy hall,
straining her eyes to see what would happen next—the wandering
hands, the passionate kisses, the voracious lips, the coiling tongues,
those first steps that lead to all the rest. She was thoroughly disappointed, and it made her uneasy. All she saw was Ascânio's lips
graze Leonora's cheek in a shy, hurried caress. Call that a kiss? She
was wasting her time spying on that pair of idiots. From the doorway, where she lingered until she couldn't see any more, Leonora
waved a long farewell, and Ascânio must certainly be waving back.
That was a bad sign. Tieta didn't like the direction in which this
romance was heading at all.

Leonora wouldn't run any real risk, she thought, if she and
Ascânio ended up at Catherine's Basin on a moonless night taking
their pleasure in a nook among the rocks. Later on she'd scrub out
her cunt with soap and water, and that would be that. When it was
time to go back to São Paulo she'd shed a few unhappy tears on the
bus going south, and *c'est finie la comédie*, as Madame Georgette
used to say and Madame Antoinette said too, whenever one of her
girls fell too hard for a man.

The danger lay precisely in those bashful kisses, that silly
mooning and spooning that was old-fashioned even in the sticks.
When a couple in Agreste courted like that, with so much respect,
holding their impulses in check, it was because they had engagement
and marriage in mind. And for Leonora to think she could get
married and settle down in Agreste was sheer moonshine. In a case
like this, scrubbing out your cunt won't do the trick. A separation
brings real anguish, not just a few tears on the bus leaving town.

When Tieta had come in from Mangue Seco that day, overflowing with life and full of enthusiasm about her own little house on the beach, slimmed down and with her perfect figure back, Leonora had thrown herself into her arms and whispered anxiously in her ear, "Mama, I've just got to talk to you."

During the day, though, they had no time alone. Perpétua hung around the whole time fawning on her sister; no flattery was too much for her now. Antonieta had gone straight from being a well of iniquity to a Jacob's well of mercy to the thirsty traveler, and a *turris eburnea* to boot. To extol her, Perpétua even called on the few Latin phrases she had learned by heart from hanging around the sacristy all those years and had formerly reserved for lauding God and the saints. *Turris eburnea* had so far been an exclusive attribute of the Virgin Mary, but now no praise was too high for Tieta's goodness and virtues.

At dinner the table was crowded: Zé Esteves and Tonha, Elisa and Astério, and Peto, asking for his aunt's blessing so that he could feast his eager eyes on that brown, abundant flesh. Wouldn't you know Cardo would be the lucky one. Keeping her company at Mangue Seco, he could stare his fill at everything there was to see of his aunt as she lay in that skimpy little bikini, but what did his stupid brother do but pretend to be a hermit or a mystic or something and turn around and look the other way. The big dummy probably walked around on the beach blindfolded. "What an example of God giving nuts to a toothless man," Osnar had complained. "Huh! You said it!"

That afternoon they went to Dona Zulmira's house to settle the deal, and from there to the notary's office so that the title could be checked and a day set for signing the contract. "The sooner the better," pleaded Tieta, in a hurry to get back to Mangue Seco. The walls of her grass shack, as she called her little cottage on the beach, were beginning to rise; and she wanted to watch each brick, set in each bit of mortar, in the company of her faithful nephew, whose enthusiasm matched her own. That evening too the parlor was jam-packed. Dona Carmosina was there with Dona Milu, and Barbozinha, and Astério and the barroom boys. Ascânio appeared before sundown and stayed to supper, sticking to Leonora like a leech.

Dona Carmosina too urged the overriding necessity of a long talk with Tieta in private, so they made a date for the following day. "Remember! Tomorrow without fail!" said the postmistress when bidding them goodnight. "I've got a thousand things to tell you." She glanced meaningfully at the courting couple on the couch. They were sitting a good handspan apart, the girl's face wearing a fond and foolish smile as she listened to Ascânio expatiate about Agreste's rosy future.

Perpétua had already gone to bed when Ascânio took his leave; the pious woman couldn't risk oversleeping and so missing six-o'clock mass in the morning. At that point Tieta left the lovers in the doorway for the passionate farewell that was such a flop.

While Tieta was removing her makeup, Leonora came in, sat down on the bed and opened her heart. What could she do? She was in love. This was passion, no infatuation or passing fancy. That wasn't her way, as Mama knew well enough. In three years at the Retreat no man had ever made her heart skip a beat. This was the first time, and it was love.

"Tell me what to do, and how I ought to act. Oh Mama, I can't tell him the truth!"

"You certainly can't! That's out of the question. Unless you hate me or have gone out of your mind."

"I never thought of telling him, how could I? I just don't know *what* to do. Oh, Mama, please help me out of this fix! You're all I have in the world."

Tieta left her lotions and her mirror, took the girl's hands in hers and stroked the blond mane. Her own sisters were not as dear to her as this unhappy waif she had rescued from the streets, this little Nora, so branded by misfortune and still able to dream and hope.

"I know you won't tell. I know my little nannygoats—poor me if I didn't. What should you do? Why, enjoy your holiday and make the most of it. Let Ascânio make love to you. He's a nice young fellow and good-looking too, a real hunk of man. A little too simple-minded for my taste, but a good man just the same. Go to bed with him if you feel like it. You're dying to sleep with him, aren't you?"

Leonora nodded and then buried her face in her hands. Tieta came and sat down beside her on the bed.

"Go to bed with him, flirt with him, go places with him, enjoy him all you like, but don't get hooked and don't be afraid to let him go. And be careful not to cause too much gossip. Why haven't you slept with him already? That's what I don't understand."

"Mama, he thinks I'm a virgin. I never knew a man to be so

trusting and respectful before. And I don't have the nerve to tell him I'm not, I can't find the right words. I'm so afraid he'll be disappointed in me and not want to see me any more."

"Well, he might be at that. Agreste isn't São Paulo, that's a cinch; they have a long way to go before they catch up with the twentieth century. Here you're either a good girl and a virgin or a harlot with the gates wide open; take your choice. You know what happened to me. Father threw me out of the house and told me to go and be a scarlet woman someplace else, the farther away the better. That was years ago, but I notice things haven't changed much here. There must be some way, though. . . ."

"Yes, Mama, but how? Ascânio thinks I'm a millionaire virgin who inherited Comendador Felipe's money. He can hardly get up the courage to hold my hand because he's poor as Job and I've got millions. You won't believe this, but he still hasn't said he loves me. He talks all around it, and hints and sighs, and then when it looks like he's going to come right out and say so for sure he bites the words back and grabs my hand and stops right there. I kissed him at Mangue Seco, not the other way around. And except for that one time, he just touches his lips to my face to say goodbye and that's all."

"I know; I was spying on the two of you and I couldn't believe my eyes. The poor nut must be spending all he earns at Zuleika's house to make up for it, or wearing his hand out if he hasn't got the dough." She smiled at Leonora. "You just do as I say; take things easy, give him time, and in the meantime enjoy yourself as much as you can. That way, at least you won't be bored."

"Bored? Mama, let me tell you something. These days we've spent here have been the only happy days I've ever had in my life. I'm in love, Mama, for the very first time. With Pipo and Cid it was different, not a bit like this. I told you, remember?"

To the young girl ground down by the sordid slum around her, Pipo, whose name she heard over the transistor radios and whose picture she saw in the papers, had seemed the personification of the invincible heroes of the comic strips, the adventure movies, the television soap operas. All the other teenage girls on her street had been jealous because she was his girl. When he had kicked her out of his life it had been mostly her vanity that was hurt. "We can still fuck once in a while if you want to," Pipo had said insolently, thinking he was doing her a favor. Well, he wasn't. She had wanted to be his one and only, the crack soccer player's inspiration every time he kicked a goal, and she couldn't swallow the humiliation. The whole neighborhood had made fun of her and she had cried for a week, but she hadn't missed Pipo himself very much.

When she met Cid Raposeira in a low dive where she was scouting for a john so she could eat the next day, he looked so lonely in his drug-dazed world, so pitiful with his rumpled, Christ-like head, so in need of companionship and help, that he struck a chord in Leonora's sensitive, sympathetic heart. That was the start of an interminable, despairing *via crucis* during which the rare days when Cid was tender and humbly grateful alternated with desperate insanity and violence. She had been less lover and companion than nurse and good Samaritan, a sister trying to help a brother who was even more unfortunate than she. They were a couple of outcasts ignored by the great city of stone and smoke which held no joy or happiness for them. Neither the famous Pipo nor the contradictory Cid had anything at all to do with her stubborn, persistent dream of a peaceful home, affection, love.

"This is love, Mama, don't you see? It isn't the same thing at all. All I want to do is stay right here with him and never go away."

Tieta was moved. Poor Leonora, poor little homeless nannygoat driven away from where she longed to be. She smoothed her hair and gently pinched her cheek.

"It's not that I'm against your staying, child; I just don't see how you can."

Tieta had begun to worry that night at Dona Milu's house, watching the idyll developing between Leonora and Ascânio. If it had been an ordinary love affair, with hugging and kissing and a few tumbles in the hiding places among the rocks along the river or on Mangue Seco's warm sands—perfect spots to let nature have her way—there would have been no problem but being as discreet as possible and keeping out of range of Agreste's long, sharp tongues. And if they were found out, well, it just couldn't be helped. Nora would be leaving soon for good, and she wouldn't much care what those hicks thought of her. But no, the girl wanted to settle down with Ascânio and raise a family. Once when the experienced, blasé Felipe listened to Tieta talking about her protégée's problems, her unhappiness and wish to retire from the oldest profession and trade the luxurious life she led at the Lords' Retreat for the narrow prospect of an ordinary home and husband—for love, as she passionately cried over and over—he had declared that she was hopelessly lower-middle-class.

"That's where the criminals come from, from that despairing petty-bourgeois milieu—the drug addicts, the kids who murder people for kicks or put an end to their own stupid lives. I have no sympathy for them."

Tieta listened to his arguments and shook her head. There was no point in arguing with Felipe, who was worldly-wise and knew what he was talking about. His brilliantly successful life was proof of that. And yet she sympathized with Leonora's sentimental, corny dreams. Not that she could wholly enter into the girl's restless, yearning intensity or her refusal to be satisfied with a situation that was highly privileged. Such problems had not been a part of Tieta's experience, at least not in the same way. Still, unlike Felipe, she felt truly sorry for the unhappy girl and showered her with kindness and affection. Of all her stable of very special girls, selected with the greatest care to gladden the leisure of rich, powerful old billygoats, many of whom had obsessions and peculiar tastes, Leonora was her favorite. It might have been because Tieta had affection and devotion to spare that she watched over poor Leonora like a mother over a daughter. To Felipe she was a hopeless little bourgeoise; to Tieta, a foolish, sentimental dreamer. Since she herself could not have been foolish and sentimental if she had tried, dreamer though she was, she respected all the more the girl's desperate clinging to the illusion that her life might change someday, that she might remold it nearer to her modest heart's desire.

A little while ago when she had watched the frustrated farewell from the darkened hall, Tieta had let out a sigh. God in Heaven, why did there have to be so much foolishness and futile yearning in this world? Life could be so simple and easy, so pleasant and exciting, when you knew how to live it with courage and common sense. All you needed was a protector, a man to keep you company and see to it you had enough money, a guarantee you'd want for nothing in your old age; and lovers for bed, all the lovers your lust demanded, joy and laughter unconfined. Care killed the cat, and you couldn't pay debts with grief.

In Catherine's Basin or on the Mangue Seco sand dunes, in a shadowy grotto or facing the vastness of the sea, Nora could sate her thirst for love in Ascânio's arms, just as Tieta, on the beach, or in the Skipper's bed, was doing in Ricardo's arms. She too was passionately in love in her way, never more so. Except that unlike Leonora, she didn't let her love for her nephew trouble her; it only gave her joy. It was a real passion, too. She was so hungry and thirsty for the young seminarian she was eating him up alive, and if that wasn't love, what was?

But when it was all over and the fury of desire had gone, all she had to do was scrub out her cunt with soap and water to forget, until the next time when the embers of passion were fanned into unquenchable flame. Love, lust, was there any difference between them? Yes, it had been different with Felipe. They had been happy together for so many years, he generous and superior, she wise, devoted, and knowing him through and through. They had been fond friends, passionate lovers, a lord and a serving maid. A serving maid or a queen? Was that what people meant when they talked about love? It probably was. And yet it hadn't kept her from wanting other men; she couldn't count the lovers she had had. It was a confused, complicated world, and she didn't pretend to understand it.

She fondled Leonora, whose disheveled head rested in her lap. Tieta would have to get that girl's life back on the track if her holiday was to end as happily as it had begun. She'd have to light a fire under this namby-pamby milk-and-water flirtation pretty quick and bring it to a boil on the riverbank or on the Mangue Seco dunes, so that love would be a reason for living and not a reason for dying, just as Barbozinha said it should be.

The motherly hand on her hair and the soothing voice in her ears calmed Leonora in her trouble.

"Sleep tight, little nannygoat. I'll take care of you."

Of the family gathered in the notary's office for the solemn signing of the deed.

The Esteves family turned out in full force for the ceremonious purchase of the house belonging to Dona Zulmira, which, after the legal formalities were concluded and payment had been made, would become the property of Dona Antonieta Esteves Cantarelli. The only interested person absent from Dr. Franklin Lins' office was young Ricardo the seminarian, who was vacationing on Mangue Seco and looking after things for his rich (and slightly dotty) aunt from São Paulo.

Old Zé Esteves, leaning on his staff and chewing tobacco, was about to jump out of his best Sunday suit with glee. It was way too big for him, having been tailored to measure in the long-ago days of prosperity. Originally cut from a length of good smuggled blue broadcloth, it had been dyed black for Elisa's wedding and taken out of retirement in the clothes chest for Tieta's arrival. And now he had put it on again for the second time in just a few days. He was beginning to be somebody again, and pretty soon he'd be living in a good house on Quality Street, right in the middle of town. His prodigal daughter had rescued him from the tumbledown shack in the alley, from a hovel in a shabby part of town that it injured his pride to live in.

If it were up to him he'd move into the new house this very day, the minute Dona Zulmira got her truck out of there. Antonieta, however, had decided to make some needed repairs. She wanted to fix up the bathroom and toilet, paint the walls, retile the roof, all kinds of São Paulo extravagance. He had grumbled a little but hadn't tried to argue with her; she was paying the piper and she called the tune.

Under his daughter's stewardship his life was being made over. In the registry, listening to Dr. Franklin read the terms of the contract, keeping track of the time on his new Omega watch, a sign of his renewed importance in the world, Zé Esteves could hear bleating goats skipping ever nearer over the bald crowns of the hills, land and flocks of his own. Near him stood Tonha, silent and acquiescent, a humble shadow to her man. Mean hovel or spacious dwelling, wide street or muddy alley, anything was good enough as long as she could share it with her lord and master. She had learned to obey and to bow her head to fate a long time back.

Perpétua, rigid in her inevitable mourning, was wearing an expensive dress she usually saved for St. Anne's feast day. On her head was the mantilla Leonora had given her. She followed the reading closely, ready to intervene if the contract contained a clause that might be prejudicial to her children, especially to Ricardo, the presumptive heir. You couldn't be too careful with the old man; he spent all his time buttering up Tieta, badmouthing the rest of the family and hinting that his other two daughters were out to cheat her. The very day before, he had dragged her off to one side to tell her a secret, hatching some scheme, probably, or trying to play her off against her sisters. Perpétua did not miss a single word of the principal clauses and addenda.

She held her son Peto tightly by the hand. The gangling boy, who was used to wearing open sandals when he couldn't be barefoot, silently cursed his shoes and wondered why the dickens Mother had forced him into stockings and a clean shirt, and dragged him here to stand on one foot and then on the other while he listened to Dr. Franklin drone out an interminable screed as slowly as if he didn't care whether he ever came to the end of it or not. If his aunt and Cousin Nora had at least been wearing their usual casual, tight-fitting, low-necked dresses, he could have looked at them to pass the time. But both of them were all dolled up today; he had never seen them in such fancy outfits. What a drag!

Elisa and Astério listened reverently, her adoring eyes on Tieta, his fixed on the floor. Not even Leonora, half-hidden at the back of the room, could compete with Elisa's splendor; she was stunning with her mass of black hair, high bosom and proud derrière and her half-modest, half-haughty air, as elegant as if she were about to parade down the runway in a fashion show. Anyone who wanted a house in Agreste could have one, but as for her, thank you, no. She expected quite a different boon from her wealthy and generous sister: an invitation to go back with her to São Paulo to live, she and her husband. Of course, Tieta wouldn't take her by herself but there would be a job for Astério in one of the Cantarelli family businesses and, for Elisa, a place in her sister's heart and home, perhaps the very place now occupied by her stepdaughter Nora.

All Elisa wanted was to turn her back on Agreste, shake the dust of the place from her shoes and never come back. And her wish could come true, because Tieta, who had come back to help them all, couldn't be kinder or more understanding. Besides, Elisa had had recourse to the good offices of Dona Carmosina, a trusty friend who had championed her since she was a little girl and was Tieta's close friend as well. She had begged her to intercede with her sister to make it possible for her to move. Life was waiting for her in São Paulo, real life, replete with events and sensations, not this Agreste apathy, this tedium of what one cannot change or avoid. As Dr.

Franklin enunciated with care all the legal terms, what Elisa heard was the exciting sound of traffic on streets crowded with luxurious automobiles and the thrilling, caressing male voices that hailed her as she strolled along Rua Augusta on an afternoon's shopping expedition with Tieta.

Astério listened to the reading without enthusiasm. Now his father-in-law would have a decent, comfortable place to live, in his daughter's house; it would be just like having a house of his own. Tieta certainly had a forgiving nature. Anyone else would have had a grudge against the father who had thrown her out of house and home and the sister who had told on her, but not Tieta. She had come back loaded down with presents for everyone in the family. For days and days Astério had vainly wondered why, when she was being so openhanded in distributing her bounty, his sister-in-law had yet to give her younger sister and brother-in-law anything except the presents she had brought them. They were the neediest ones, and yet Zé Esteves, though he had nothing of his own, was getting a fat monthly allowance and was spending practically none of it, since his food and shelter cost him so little, while he and Elisa had to scrimp and save and struggle along a day at a time because the store and their allowance brought in barely enough for them to live on. Perpétua needed no help at all. She was the one who had everything: a mansion to live in, the income from rented houses, her husband's pension, a savings account in Aracaju, and the protection of God. Yes, God's protection—other people could laugh if they liked—had never failed her. As Elisa had found out and informed him, her wealthy sister had opened savings accounts in the Bank of São Paulo for both nephews, but he and Elisa didn't even have a child, a nephew to stir the protective feelings of his millionaire aunt. Toninho had died, and if Miss Carmosina hadn't been so fond of Elisa, they might have lost the little they had. After all, it had been a base lie they had told, important news kept back, a dirty piece of blackmail.

Some time ago, when the prolonged bargaining for Dona Zulmira's house had only begun, his sister-in-law had proposed that the two couples, the old man and Mother Tonha and Elisa and himself, live in it together after it was hers, there being plenty of room for the four of them and to spare in that large, comfortable residence. He had not been particularly entranced by the idea and it had appealed to Elisa even less; Tieta had heard their reasons for refusing and had agreed with them. After that, Astério had waited expectantly for some hint on the part of their charitable relative that she intended to see about finding a house for her younger sister, of whom she seemed to be so fond. He had waited in vain; his sister-in-law had never mentioned the subject to them again, and it was only the day before that Astério had discovered the reason for her silence. When he came in after his nightly game of pool, he was thinking of the contract due to be signed next day and the fact that the purchase of Dona Zulmira's house was settled at last. He had said hopefully, "You never know, maybe it'll be our turn next." His wife had explained that Antonieta had said nothing because Elisa herself had shown she had no desire to own property in Agreste. From between the sheets her implacable, merciless, insensitive, almost challenging voice beat on his ears:

"I told Tieta I didn't want a house of my own in Agreste. If she wants to do something for us, I said, let her take us to São Paulo, get you a good clerical job in one of the factories and give us a room in her apartment. It's a great big one, a duplex. A duplex means it's two stories high."

Astério responded with a groan; his bellyache was back with a vengeance. Elisa's words tolled in his ears like a plainchant at a funeral. She was tearing his guts out. A job in São Paulo, in the office of some factory? God, what a prospect! Leave his peaceful life in Agreste for the hubbub of a metropolis, sit behind a desk adding up accounts or writing inventories from eight in the morning until six in the evening, with no freedom to come and go as he liked; no friends, no Manuel's bar, no pool table? He had never been threatened with such a misfortune. True, in Agreste the couple lived in poverty, for the store yielded scarcely enough for the essentials, and some months not even that. But with Antonieta's help they were at least managing to eat and pay the rent, and could even go to the movies once in a while and buy magazines for Elisa. Besides, except for a half-dozen privileged citizens, everyone in town was only comfortably well off or else downright poor, but they all muddled along somehow. He had the boy to help him at the store and Elisa had a girl to help her at home. The only real problem was the way his stomach acted up every time business was bad or he had to pay interest on a bill, but the doctor in Bahia had assured him it wasn't cancer, only nerves and nothing to worry about. Aside from that he was content with his lot, with the companionship of his cronies, pool at the Brunswick Pool Hall, the bets, the arguments, the triumphs, being called the Golden Cue, the pleasant, idle talk, the relatively easygoing life, and his pretty wife, the prettiest girl in Agreste, waiting for him in bed when he got home at night and felt like mounting her, always in the same classic position, almost with respect, as a self-respecting husband should.

As a bachelor he had been a regular customer at Zuleika Cinderella's, where one woman after another had caught his fancy, always the kind with a bouncy behind and curvaceous hips. Neither was he reluctant to try interesting variations in bed; in fact he was notorious for preferring a woman's behind to her front, as any girl who went to bed with him soon found out. Whenever he appeared in the parlor, where there was dancing, the girls passed the word along: "Watch your ass, Astério just came in." It was well known too that this penchant of his was not limited to prostitutes: he had once gloried in the nickname of Old Maids' Ass Comforter.

Once married, however, it had never entered his noggin to possess Elisa in any way but the way that was proper, in the right and decent hole with him on top and her underneath: Papa and Mama, as the hookers call the baby-making position—proper, that is, for husband and wife. It had never so much as crossed his mind to mount her from behind and make the most of those magnificent buttocks, a mare's haunches, beyond compare for miles around. Not that he didn't want to—if she were a woman of easy virtue or a free-running girl, a country gal or an old maid, he would never pass up such an appetizing morsel as that sumptuous ass, the fundamental reason for his having fallen in love and proposed engagement and marriage. Unfortunately, one's lawful wedded wife should not be desecrated, but respected and placed on an altar among the saints. The most that Astério ever permitted himself, once in a blue moon, lifting the climax to ecstasy and making of it a whole new experience, was to run his hand over his wife's behind in a furtive caress.

As for Elisa, assiduous reader of trashy, gossipy magazines about the prowess of radio, television and movie stars, she resented her husband's apparent lack of sexual interest, his methodical, bureaucratic fornication—a sexual bureaucrat, one fiery actress had called the famous comedian whom she had just divorced, in a sensational interview in *Amica* magazine—the same old way all the time, with none of the variations she had read so much about. Astério himself, when retelling Osnar's or Aminthas' or Seixas' or Fidélio's latest

good one, referred occasionally to other curious positions and tech-
niques, all of which were known to Dona Carmosina—"Only in
theory, I'm sorry to say, Elisa dear; I only wish I could tell you
about them firsthand!" Elisa wished so too, and for that reason she
was probably unfair to her husband. There was no lack of interest
on his part, only the conviction that married love should be modestly expressed, free of lust, evil thoughts and unbridled passion; in a
word, respectful. The repressed Astério was content to be the
owner of that spectacular piece of tail and get a peek at it out of the
corner of his eye when Elisa was dressing or undressing, or feel it
next to him in bed. Astério was an upright husband and he held
himself in check.

Agreste and its tranquil village life, companionship and simple
pleasures were good enough for him. He asked for nothing better.
São Paulo? A well-paid office job with strict hours? A room in his
sister-in-law's house? God forbid. The argument that night was hot
and heavy. Elisa forgot herself and accused him of being indifferent
and spineless; selfish too, thinking of no one but himself and not
even caring what she thought. This stupid dull life in Agreste might
be good enough for a dishrag like him, but she was young and lively
and she wanted something better, a big city where there were all
kinds of possibilities and life was worth living. And where Astério,
incidentally, could get ahead, earn good money, and be somebody if
he just put his mind to it. But he didn't understand her or pay any
attention to her, just treated her as if she were a stick of wood, a
rag, a useless beast of burden.

Astério fled into the living room, clutching his stomach to
assuage the pain. After a while Elisa, hearing his loud groans, went
after him and found him dizzy, pale, the color of wax, in the middle
of one of his violent attacks of abdominal pangs. She gave him his
medicine and begged him to forgive her for her harsh words. Her
bad temper had given way to tears, but she was as determined as
ever to persuade her sister somehow, some way, to take them to live
with her in São Paulo. Whey-faced, his mouth full of bile, Astério
made no reply, but between fits of retching he made up his mind to
take immediate steps to forestall any such thing. Of course Elisa
must be kept in the dark so that she would not blame him for the
collapse of her monstrous plans. As he listened to Dr. Franklin he
mulled it over in his mind and came to a decision.

The comely Leonora Cantarelli, stepdaughter of the lady who

was making the purchase, stood quietly next to a bookcase full of papers, a gentle smile on her delicate face. Of all those present it was she, perhaps, who most sincerely longed to own a house in Agreste, even a humble cottage on an unpaved street, but with a little garden full of pinks and mignonette, a palm tree laden with coconuts in the backyard, and a porch on which to recline in a hammock in the heat of the day. A nest for her and her husband, lawfully wedded or not; it made no difference as long as he was Ascânio Trindade. Mama had promised to do something about it, to take care of her; and when Madame Antoinette promised to do a thing she did it. Leonora felt comforted enough to wait. She heard out the reading with patience, a virtue she had learned the hard way.

On the other side of the partition, listening attentively to the interminable singsong reading, stood ancient Dona Zulmira like an old bird of prey, with her old-fashioned spectacles perched on her hooked nose, a rosary rolled around her skinny fist, and around her neck a locket containing a picture of her deceased husband as a young bridegroom. She smiled with satisfaction. This house, converted into cash, would go a long way toward saving her soul and would glorify St. Anne besides. Now it was safe from the excommunicated clutches of her twice-damned nephew João Felício. Satan had been foiled, and her nephew would never play fast and loose with her last wishes on earth as Seu Lito's wicked relatives were doing with his last will and testament, taking it to court and trying to rob Holy Mother Church. Father Mariano hovered around her like an acolyte. The money from the sale of the house would eventually be spent for masses at the high altar in the cathedral, before the image of its patron saint, for the repose of the donor's soul. Until then it would be left with Modesto Pires to bring in enough monthly interest to help Dona Zulmira pay her medical bills, according to the document attached to the contract that Dr. Franklin was finally coming to the end of.

João Felício, the nephew, owner of a little grocery store, waited in ambush on the sidewalk across the way. His face was very like his aunt's, with the same hooked nose and sharp chin, a hawk about to swoop down on its prey. The prey had gotten clean away from him this time, snatched up to Heaven by one of the saints those idolatrous, superstitious Roman Catholics worshipped. The comfortable house he had hoped soon to move into with his wife and little boy—"The old lady can't live forever, can she?"—would be occupied instead by that conceited, arrogant, spiteful Zé Esteves and his wretched wife. Well, he had no one to blame but himself; he had taken to wife a Protestant girl, the daughter of the pastor at the Esplanada Baptist Church, without his aunt's consent. To Dona Zulmira, an old-style Catholic who had never heard of ecumenical theories, a Protestant was as bad as a heretic; they were all enemies, all damned, and they all had cloven hooves. The "Believers" were children of Satan and good Catholics ought to deny them bread and water, since the Holy Inquisition was unfortunately defunct.

When he finished reading the contract, Dr. Franklin invited the interested parties to sign it. Astério and the Father affixed their signatures as witnesses, and everybody shook hands all around. From the deep pockets of her black grosgrain skirt, Perpétua, depositary *pro tem*, fished out roll after roll of money and passed them over to Dr. Franklin, every eye in the room following the movements of her hand. The notary counted them, one banknote at a time, before handing them to Dona Zulmira.

An apprehensive thought gnawed at Tieta as she smiled: did the land and the house, legally bought and paid for by one Antonieta Esteves Cantarelli, belong without a shadow of a doubt to plain Antonieta Esteves? The lawyer she had consulted in São Paulo before she left had assured her they did, as long as there were witnesses to the sale and the payment; in that case it would be merely an error in the name and easily corrected. It was not some little shyster lawyer who had told her that; it was the attorney general of the state of São Paulo himself, a regular customer at the Retreat and legal counsel to Madame Antoinette.

Late afternoon at the Areopagus.

After Tieta had said goodbye to her relatives and hired Liberato, who had been recommended by Modesto Pires as an excellent construction foreman, she managed to go by herself to the post office for the promised tête-à-tête with Dona Carmosina. Now the two friends would finally have a chance to catch up on the latest events.

Both were equally interested in talking and listening, both were hatching schemes, and both had ulterior motives.

When she saw Tieta coming up the steps, Dona Carmosina threw down her newspaper and exclaimed, "Alone at last!" She laughed and held out her arms to embrace her illustrious visitor. "Hail to my leader!"

Tieta was all too illustrious, it seemed. Before five minutes had passed they had company. While they were still dragging up chairs and exchanging affectionate greetings, Tieta asking after Mother Milu (she always said Dona Milu was a second mother to her), the first acquaintances appeared and a curious crowd gathered outside the door of the Areopagus. Everyone wanted to see and salute their fellow citizen, the Lady Bountiful from the empire state of São Paulo, the woman who had a say in how the federal government was run. They stood there, smiling at her. Petitioners who had not found her at home had sniffed her out at the post office, their senses sharpened by necessity. Each tale was more harrowing than the last; all of them were sad and all were true. Tieta made a date with two of them for the following morning at her house. Dona Carmosina shook her head; that would never do. At the same time her heart was gladdened by Tieta's kindness and patience as she listened to the poor wretches and thought how they could best be helped, as she chatted with idlers who only wanted to talk to her and congratulate her on bringing in the power line.

When they were gone Antonieta heaved a sigh of relief and laughed. "You know, I'm getting downright sick of hearing about the light."

"Don't talk that way, honey, they're just trying to show they're grateful. They're good people; civilization hasn't corrupted them yet."

Skipper Dário's voice in the passageway put the quietus on Dona Carmosina's hopes. Obviously their heart-to-heart talk à bâtons rompus was not to be. Every so often Tieta used a French expression; in the south she had attained a level of sophistication rarely met in that remote backwoods. That was her husband's influence, no doubt. She had made herself into a real lady, not only because she was rich and stylish, but because she knew how to use her brain. Dona Carmosina felt proud of her friend and was sure everyone in Agreste felt the same way.

The Skipper pulled up a chair and straddled it, plainly intending to stay for a chat. He inquired when Tieta planned to go back to Mangue Seco. He and Dona Laura were returning next day right after lunch; would she like to go with them in the canoe? She certainly would. Now that her house was bought and paid for and the contract signed, there was nothing special to keep her in Agreste. The old man would see to it that the house was cleaned up and painted and a few essential repairs made, especially on the bathroom, and a decent toilet put in. The bathroom fixtures were in an unusable state. Dona Zulmira must have been bathing in a basin and shitting in a chamberpot for years. The Skipper heard her list of what she considered trifling little repairs and warned her, "That'll be a month's work at least. Liberato takes his time."

"Not with Father for an overseer," Antonieta assured him. "The old man can't wait to move in. He'll keep Liberato hopping for sure."

"Did you contract for the work or are you hiring him by the day?"

"For heaven's sake, Skipper, don't forget I was born here! For the work, of course."

"A month, then. Liberato's slow but sure. You can set your mind at rest on that point."

"Skipper, isn't it funny how things turn out? Now I think Dona Zulmira's house was a good buy."

"You paid more than you should have had to here."

"Even so. It cost me a pile of money, it's a fine house and it's being remodeled, but all I can think about is my little cabin on Mangue Seco. I'm really putting my heart into that one. I won't leave until I see it standing."

"Folks in Mangue Seco take their time even more than they do here. You know what beaches are like. You can't work for very long at a time with all that wind."

"That's why I want to get right back and give 'em a hand. Cardo isn't the old man, he won't get tough with anybody. . . . That poor boy must be thinking his aunt's gone off and left him and lit out for São Paulo. He's worth his weight in gold, Skipper, that nephew of mine."

Her eyes shone when she talked about her nephew. Dona Carmosina and the sailor seconded her praise of Ricardo. God had certainly lavished blessings on Perpétua; He had not only saved her from spinsterhood, a miracle in itself, but He had given her a good husband and good sons. In a brilliant display of the subtle art of settling other people's business, Dona Carmosina and the Skipper whiled away a pleasant quarter of an hour meditating aloud on God's goodness in rewarding Perpétua's ecclesiastical virtues. Ecclesiastical? That description of Perpétua's virtues was Barbozinha's invention, and Dona Carmosina thought it was both poetic and fitting. Thus, in idle talk and laughter, the time flew by. It was no use Tieta's saying that she had come for one night and had already been in Agreste for three whole days. And just think, she still hadn't had time to discuss some urgent business with Carmô, though actually that was why she was here in the post office, in fact. But tomorrow she was going back to Mangue Seco no matter what.

The Skipper did not take the hint; he was explaining that Ricardo, on holiday in the earthly Paradise itself, could not help being happy. As she listened to the peroration of the Skipper, caught up in his favorite subject, Tieta thought of her poor little Ricardo, all alone on the horsehair mattress or lost in the wild landscape of the dunes overhanging the sea. Yes, Skipper, he may be in Paradise, but he's undoubtedly suffering the pangs of Hell! He's probably perched on top of the highest dune this minute, scanning the farthest reaches of the river for the wake of a boat, straining his ears to hear the sound of a motor. She herself longed for nothing so much as to follow the current downstream, cross the breakers at the bar, land on Mangue Seco and run to the arms of her boy; feel the hair on his muscular legs and arms and adolescent chest bristle with excitement; the warmth, the trembling thrill of his body, the last redoubts of shyness not quite overcome—then the lunge, the mast of the fishing boat raised and its sails unfurled. These last few nights, as she tossed in the big bed alone, had been sleepless torment. Finally, in search of peace, she had lain down in the hammock in Dr. Fulgêncio's study where Ricardo had slept. Looking for something to remind her of her nephew, she found evident signs of the battle joined with the devil in the hammock where he had desired her against his will, where he had clasped her naked in a voluptuous dream and could not possess her because he didn't know how. Now that was a nightmare! It was there that the virgin seminarian had begun to lose his chastity. Tieta had wallowed in the hammock, touched the white stain and moaned like a she-goat in heat.

Another person dropped in to indulge himself in a chat and postpone the essential tête-à-tête yet again. This time it was Ascânio, accompanied by Aminthas and Seixas. The Skipper lost no time in criticizing the patriotic county clerk's latest activities and his sinister plan to bring tourists to Agreste. He rejoiced that fortunately all that was nothing but a mirage.

"Mirage, nothing," Ascânio protested. "He'll be back any day now—"

"With that classy dame, I hope," Aminthas cut in.

"—to firm up the plans, I know that for a fact."

Skipper Dário threw up his hands.

"There goes our peace and quiet. Well, I'm going to Mangue Seco to dig trenches and throw up the barricades. If those nudists show up again I'll welcome them with a hail of bullets, the way Floriano Peixoto threatened to welcome the British."

"Nudists?" inquired Tieta.

"That's right. Hadn't you heard?"

"I heard about the couple who were here and went to Mangue Seco . . ."

". . . and threw off their clothes as soon as they landed and wham, went running slap bang into the water and down the beach, naked as the day they were born. Thought they were Adam and Eve, I guess."

Thinking of poor Ricardo, Tieta was shaken by an irrepressible wave of laughter. As if he hadn't been violated enough already, now he had nudists to top it all. She wouldn't put it past him to think they were devils from Hell, come to Mangue Seco for some unholy bacchanal, some black mass that would seal his soul's doom and incidentally undo all the good effects of his aunt's bracing pep talks, all her attempts to soothe his fears and restore his good spirits and self-confidence.

"Do you think Ricardo saw those people naked?" she asked, when she was able to subdue her laughter.

They all laughed, even Ascânio, at the thought of the seminarian in the company of that unbelievable couple. Skipper Dário wound up his peroration in triumph.

"That's just what I've been telling you: Perpétua, the priests,

Dom José the Bishop, you, Tieta, everybody seeking to preserve that boy's innocence, and Ascânio's friends undo it all in a single afternoon. What's the use of your watching over your nephew's chastity? Ascânio imports lewdness, hands Mangue Seco over lock, stock and barrel to the pimps, and the next thing you know we'll have white slavery out there."

Ascânio was unmoved by the tragic panorama outlined by the Skipper.

"When land values go up and Liberty Hall's worth a fortune, you'll thank me, Skipper, and so will you, Dona Tieta. You did business at just the right time; land prices are going to go up."

"I won't sell my peace and quiet at any price!" exclaimed the Skipper, equally unmoved. He turned to Tieta. "Tomorrow, then, right after lunch, about one o'clock; is that too early? Let's make the most of these last few days before Ascânio turns Mangue Seco into Sodom and Gomorrah."

"Are you going back out there tomorrow, Dona Antonieta?" asked the unrepentant Ascânio. "The plaza's being christened a week from Saturday, don't forget, and you're the godmother and have to preside."

"I'll be back in time, never fear."

If she wasn't they'd go out there and bring her back, threatened Aminthas. He and Seixas here, and Astério, Osnar and Peto, the cabin boy, were getting up a punitive expedition to kidnap her on the beach and bring her back with them. Mangue Seco was a marvel, no one could deny that; it was the best beach in the world for walks, picnics, weekends, swimming, the bar, the sand dunes, the view; but to stay there for weeks on end when you've come to Agreste for only a short visit? No, her fellow citizens wouldn't stand for that. Dona Carmosina heartily agreed and seconded the idea. "An expedition? Let's see now, what about next Sunday? What do you say to that, Seixas?"

"Oh, that'll be fine. I'll take my cousins," said Seixas approvingly, joining the conversation for the first time.

The private talk was postponed until that night. Dona Carmosina sighed, "Let's be sure we get it in this time!" If they had to put it off once more she'd pop. She was already blown up like a balloon with all kinds of serious and exciting things to talk about. It never occurred to her that Tieta was even more anxious to have that talk than she was but just didn't show it.

Of a talk by the riverside.

Tieta gazed up at the sky. The full moon that had lighted the sand hills at Mangue Seco was waning now, but there were glittering stars by the thousand, no, by the million. She could never weary of gazing at them and admiring such a firmament as no longer existed in the cities of the south. In São Paulo where she lived and labored and a pall of pollution covered everything, the firmament was black.

"I'm feasting my eyes on the Agreste sky, Carmô. There's nothing like it down there. There isn't any sky there anymore."

They had realized that the only way they were ever going to have a conversation by themselves was to sneak out of the full house where Barbozinha was dauntlessly leading a regiment of the Prestes Column across the swamps of Mato Grosso after a previous incarnation as one of the Heroic Eighteen at the Fort, the only one to miraculously escape alive (one hero more or less didn't matter, they'd still be eighteen, that was the great thing about legends).

"Poet, you'd better be careful with your tongue," Aminthas warned the heroic bard. "I guess there's no harm in your being the ninetieth or the twenty-third man of the Eighteen, aside from a slight scratch or two on historical accuracy, but if you get yourself mixed up with the Prestes Column you're liable to be thrown in jail. They've arrested people for a lot less than that in Esplanada."

When Dona Carmosina showed up for her private talk, she found the parlor full of friends and Leonora and Ascânio ensconced on the veranda. The only recourse open to them was flight. Taking her cue from Dona Carmosina ("But we can't talk here! I've got such a lot to tell you but not in public. What shall we do?"), Tieta proposed a strategic retreat. They managed to escape out the back door without anyone's noticing. Now they were following a path down to the river.

"The only thing is, though, Carmô, you can make money there. Anyone who's ready and willing to work can put something away if he puts his mind to it. Here there's just too much poverty; I'd forgotten how bad it is."

"Perpétua's not so badly off, for one," Dona Carmosina corrected her. "She puts money in her savings account in Aracaju every month. She's no fool."

"Don't think I don't know that, Carmô, I wasn't born yesterday. I know the sheep in my flock, and Perpétua's the one I know best of all. I know Ricardo studies free because the Father arranged it with Dom José; I know Peto goes to public school and doesn't pay anything. I know more than she imagines, or you either. But I'm not going to deny her my help because of that. After all, what she has is so little! It only amounts to something when you compare what she has to what the others have, which is nothing, but it won't go far in providing for the children's future. And those boys are such lambs. Ricardo's so studious, so sure of what he wants to do, so serious, and he looks so funny in his cassock, like an awkward kind of angel." She looked at her old friend. "I've opened a savings account for him in São Paulo, as you know."

"Me? Whatever do you mean? I don't know a thing about it. You never said a word, how on earth would I know?" Dona Carmosina reacted huffily, on the verge of being insulted by the hint.

Tieta let out a loud and mirthful laugh and squeezed her companion's arm affectionately.

"You know because you read the letter I wrote my manager telling her to go to the bank, open the account and make a deposit, that's how. Now, don't tell me you didn't read it, Carmô, because I won't believe you. I'd read all the letters too if I were you."

Dona Carmosina was too confused to reply at first, but her friend's laughter was contagious. She complained, half in earnest, "Well, I never saw such closed-mouth letters as yours in my life. You never said a thing in the ones you used to write to your family and you don't say a thing when you write to São Paulo. I never saw anybody so stingy with words: do this, do that, how is everything going, is the trade holding steady? Are the girls behaving themselves? I still haven't figured out what kind of business it is you're running down there anyway, except for the factories. Everybody knows about those."

"There isn't any secret, Carmô, it's just that I'm no good at writing; the less I write the fewer mistakes I make. And besides, I don't like to have everybody and his brother gossiping about my affairs. It's nobody's business how much money somebody else makes; I'm a believer in the evil eye. But I don't have any reason to hide it from you. What I have in São Paulo is a luxury boutique with very high prices for high-society customers out of the top drawer, and it brings me in very good money. The girls are the salesgirls, of course; they're pretty and chic and they earn good money too. That's why I don't want the family turning up there, because the clientele is so chic. Can you imagine, Carmô, the shop full of high-class São Paulo snobs, every one of them filthy rich, and the folks from Agreste start showing up? That's why I never sent my address. I don't care if they talk about the factories; they can make up anything about them they've a mind to. Do you know why? Because the factories don't belong to me; I don't have a thing to do with running them. When Felipe died I got the apartments, the real estate and the boutique. That was mine anyway; it was already in my name." She tried to read her friend's expression on the dimly lighted path to see whether her explanation was convincing enough.

Dona Carmosina drank in every word. Detective-story fan and admirer of Agatha Christie as she was, she felt like Miss Marple herself lost in Sant'Ana do Agreste. From one deduction to the next, using her little gray cells, starting from insignificant clues, she had reached the truth. None of what Tieta was telling her now came as a surprise to the presiding genius of the Areopagus.

"Exactly what I thought! A luxury boutique, skinning the customers alive and all the best people in São Paulo leaving their money there. You did the right thing in keeping mum about your business and the way you live. If Elisa had ever gotten hold of your São Paulo address she would have gone down there like a shot. That's all she dreams about, poor girl."

Tieta laughed.

"Can you imagine all the folks from Agreste, starting with old Zé Esteves with his staff and chewing tobacco, at my door in São Paulo, swarming into the boutique? It would be a sight for sore eyes, I'll say that. The only trouble is, it would be mighty bad for business."

As if she hadn't heard her sister's name, she did not mention Elisa, but Dona Carmosina stubbornly returned to the topic.

"Are you thinking of taking Elisa to São Paulo, her and Astério? It's the only thing she longs for in the world, and I do think—"

Tieta found the subject uncongenial. She interrupted her friend before she could take her friend's cause too much to heart.

"What on earth would I want to take her there for? She and Astério are getting along just fine right here with what the store brings in and the help I give them. The other day, out of a clear sky, without my having asked her anything about it, she told me she didn't want a house of her own in Agreste. She never stops hinting about an invitation to São Paulo, and she never talks about anything else. I might be willing to send them a bigger remittance, or help them some other way; but take them to São Paulo, that I will not do."

"Why, Tieta, if you don't mind my asking? I'm fond of Elisa and I'd like to see her happy."

"So would I. I'm fond of her too; she's my sister and I know she loves me too; she's not a hypocrite like Perpétua. But it's not just her I care about, it's Astério too, Carmô. Astério's happy enough here; São Paulo would mean going down in the world for him. I love to see people happy, it's such a rare thing in this world. I know what it's like to be unhappy; I had the devil's own time of it after I ran away from home. I was lucky; I found a good man—my husband. We're a lucky family, Carmô. Perpétua snagged a husband with that face of hers, and that's quite a miracle; wasn't the Skipper saying so today? My miracle was even bigger; I was just a little clerk in Felipe's office, and I ended up with a ring on my finger." She held out the gold wedding ring, an unusual one with deep carving on it, a piece worthy of an antiquary. "Elisa was lucky too; she got married. Astério's all right, I like him. And Astério would be a whole lot more miserable in São Paulo than Elisa is here."

"Would he?"

"Of course he would. He has friends here; who would be his friend in São Paulo? He's not the kind of man who could hold his own in that infernal rat race. And your friend Elisa, are you so sure she'd be happy in São Paulo? You know her better than I do; you've known her ever since she was born. We were both there, remember? Do you really think that once Elisa was living in São Paulo she'd be satisfied to live quietly on her husband's measly salary —because he doesn't know how to do anything, really, and he's never going to earn much—with those glamour-girl looks? Do you, Carmô? Do you know where she'd end up, with that beautiful face and figure of hers? As a call girl or a whore in a cathouse, that's where. Is that the kind of happiness you think she's looking for?"

Dona Carmosina shuddered. Tieta's words echoed inside her

skull like hammer blows. She gave up fighting for her protégée. She had promised to fight when Elisa, almost in tears, begged her, "Talk to Tieta, Carmosina. Tell her I want to go back with her, want her to give Astério a job and let us have a little corner of her duplex."

"Goodness, you're right, it wouldn't do at all. Good heavens, why didn't I think of that? You're an even better sister than I thought."

"I know my nannygoats. It's a good thing you brought it up; I've been wanting to ask you, anyway, to do what you can to get those ideas out of Elisa's head. She pays a lot of attention to what you say. You tell her that she and Astério can count on me as long as they stay here. If they go anywhere else, though, they won't get a thing from me."

"All right, I'll talk to her, but it won't be easy. But you're right, you're right, we can't take the risk. Just imagine! Oh, goodness me!"

"Life's so mixed up I'll never understand it. All Elisa thinks about is going to São Paulo, and Leonora, now, has started saying she wants to live in Agreste for ever and ever."

A smile appeared to clear the clouds from Dona Carmosina's anxious face. Now this was an inspiring theme. They were getting close to the river. The stream's music was louder as it rushed over the pebbles, the stars wheeled in the sky, and the darkness melted away.

"That's right. She told me she had decided to stay here for good. We had ever so many talks, Nora and I, while you were in Mangue Seco. She's so much in love, Tieta. It's beautiful. Two young people disappointed in love, two . . ." She rummaged in her memory for the modern phrase she had read the other day in a magazine. ". . . two affection-starved people who find each other and give each other what they need. That's why she wants to stay here."

"Do you really think she'd get used to living way off here? She's happy now because loving Ascânio makes her forget how much she's suffered, and believe me, she's suffered like a maverick kid on a mountain. But what about later on? I was born here and I want to end my days here, but I'll only come back for good when I'm old and decrepit, not before. It's not easy for someone who's used to a big city to settle down in Agreste. Even folks who never set foot anywhere else complain because it's so pokey; just look at

Elisa. If I had even dreamed this would happen I never would have brought Nora with me. She's such a starry-eyed idiot she won't want to let Ascânio go, and that's going to be a problem."

"I know." Dona Carmosina sighed, feeling the drama as intensely as a soap-opera addict at the end of an installment. "She's an heiress and he's poor! But—"

"No Carmô, that isn't it. Rich women marry poor men every day and vice versa. Do you think I'd worry my head for a minute if that was the problem? I'd be out buying her trousseau this minute."

"What is it, then?"

Tieta stopped at the edge of the path to emphasize the confidence she was about to make. A climate of melodrama and suspense still hung in the air. Dona Carmosina waited tensely, unable to conceal her impatience.

"Well, what is it?"

"You know she was engaged to a heel who was only interested in her money. He passed himself off as an engineer, talked a good line and sold us a bill of goods. Nora was so crazy about him she was all ready to finance some screwy project or other he had dreamed up. The only reason she didn't give him the money was that I smelled a rat and got wise to him in time. Just about then the police got on his trail and we found out he had a record as long as your arm. Poor Leonora took it so hard I thought she'd die, but the things the police told us didn't come as any big surprise to me. I don't get fooled very often. The minute I lay eyes on a man I know what he's worth; the cut of his jib and the size of his prick."

Dona Carmosina suddenly relaxed and burst out laughing.

"I never saw such a crazy woman in my life! You'll be carrying on after you're dead and buried. That's a good one: the cut of his jib and the size of his prick!" She could not stop laughing for several minutes. Finally she returned little by little to Nora's and Ascânio's love affair. "I already knew about that, you told me yourself. That's why I'm telling you: here are two people who have been hurt and are getting over it, two people starved for affection"— Dona Carmosina took this opportunity to repeat the phrase she had learned—"who can help each other find fulfillment. If it doesn't matter that she has a fortune and he doesn't, then—"

"But it so happens, Carmô, that she was engaged to this man for a good six months. And being engaged in São Paulo isn't like being engaged in Agreste. Engaged couples and kids going together have a lot more freedom down there. They go out partying and night-clubbing alone, go on trips that last for days and days . . . nights and nights. . . . Girls go around with the pill in their purses along with their lipstick."

"I'm beginning to understand. . . ."

"Now you see what I'm getting at? This business of a girl being a virgin when she marries was once upon a time, as the longhairs say. That only happens in Agreste. The fact that he happens to be poor doesn't matter. Nora doesn't care the least little bit about that, and neither do I. But do you really think our friend Ascânio . . ." A pause. "That's what's worrying me, Carmô."

"Now I'm the one who's worried, and how! Oh, why does life have to be so complicated, Tieta?"

"Damned if I know! And everything could be so simple, couldn't it? *Porca miseria!* as my Italian kinfolk in São Paulo would say."

They resumed their walk, Dona Carmosina trying to take in the uncomfortable revelation she had received. Lordy, Lordy, what was to be done? Tieta went on before they reached the riverbank:

"Now that I've bought the house and it's being painted and fixed up, I'll see the old folks settled, leave some money with Ricardo to finish building my cabin on Mangue Seco, take Leonora and get out of here."

"But you can't leave before the power line comes in, you really can't. I've told you that before."

"I had thought of staying, but I can't. Not for myself so much, though I shouldn't stay away too long. I left everything I own in São Paulo in other people's hands—"

"In the hands of people you trust."

"Even so. It's the master's eye that fattens the swine. I'd stay for the celebration, though, if it weren't for Nora. I've got to get her out of here before it's too late. She can't take another blow like that; it would kill her."

"Don't be in too much of a hurry. Wait a few days, and when you come back from Mangue Seco I may have news for you."

"What about?"

"Ascânio and Leonora."

"Life could be so simple. It's people who screw it up for themselves."

They had reached the river edge where the boats rocked at

anchor. A little farther on in Catherine's Basin the weeping willows leaned over the rocks, making the darkness deeper. The breeze blew a low moaning sound from that direction.

The two friends walked forward a few steps on soundless feet. There were forms in the hollows, whispers and plaintive sighs. "Life could be so simple," repeated Tieta. The two friends and conspirators smiled, the pretty one and the homely one, the one who was satisfied and the one who was starved for affection, to use the fashionable phrase Dona Carmosina liked so much.

"I've chosen a name for my little beach cottage," Tieta told her.

"What is it?"

"Inácio's Corral. He was the big old ram in the old man's flock, a billygoat almost as big as a mule. His balls were so heavy they used to drag on the ground. I learned how to want things and go after them from him."

Sighs and moans were coming from every nook and corner of Catherine's Basin. The two friends turned back the way they had come and quickened their steps down the road to the house and the living room, where Barbozinha the poet was living in another incarnation, leading the people of Paris as they stormed the Bastille and freed thousands of imprisoned patriots—a magnificent epic with swords and harquebuses, noblemen, tribunes, and the carmagnole, and no danger at all of being thrown in jail.

In which the reader rejoins Ricardo the seminarian and fallen angel, about whom there have for some time been none but vague references (mostly praise in his aunt's lascivious mouth), and how he throws himself into the sea.

From atop the sand dunes Ricardo watched the river, impatient to spot Elieser's launch or Pirica's dinghy, or perhaps the Skipper's outboard canoe, with Tieta aboard. How could he go on like this without her, with the knowledge of sin for his only companion?

That was how he happened to see the little group disembark from a canoe they had paddled down the river themselves. Not all of those who had camped near the Saco fishing hamlet had come, only two couples and a child not more than two years old.

Ricardo watched their movements curiously. The darker, straight-haired boy lifted the improvised anchor, a jagged rock tied to a rope, and threw it overboard to hold the canoe, then picked up the baby. The other young man, a tall, gawky fellow, was carrying a guitar. One of the two girls had long fair hair hanging down her back and was probably the baby's mother, since she got out of the canoe with the youth who was holding the little girl; and the other, who was fine-boned and nimble and was wearing flowers in her hair, ran off behind the fishermen's houses, pursued by the young man with the guitar. The sound of laughter rose up the dunes to where Ricardo was sitting. All five were barefoot. They headed for the prettiest part of the beach, right under the highest dune, where Ricardo was watching. It was the prettiest part but the most dangerous too; the surf was much too violent for swimming. Only those born and bred on Mangue Seco dared swim in that stretch of ocean that rose up in fury against the mountains of sand.

On their annual holidays on Mangue Seco when the Major was alive, Ricardo had sometimes ventured out into those breakers with the fishermen's children, but when his father caught him at it he had told him never to be so foolhardy again if he didn't want a thrashing. More than one swimmer had paid for his ignorance or recklessness there with his life, had been knocked down and dragged away by the violence of the waves, then thrown back and had the life beaten out of him against the dunes. This rough water was a killing ground for sharks, too. Lead-gray shadows in the roiling sea would rise sudden and arrogant in the midst of the waves, hungrily lurking just off the beach, multiplying the danger. Ricardo had caught sight of a menacing band of them a little earlier, leaping in the stormy breakers. They had gone back out to sea, though; the gray shapes of death were no longer there.

From his vantage point Ricardo saw the two couples and the little girl running and playing on the beach. They sat down on the sand, and soon twanging guitar music thrummed on the wind. Some of the broken snatches of melody sounded like hymns; they reminded him of the plainsong he had heard in the Franciscan monastery at São Cristóvão. Ricardo had heard about the hippie camp the day before when he had gone to Saco to buy construction materials and have them delivered. A group of twenty or more young hippies, men, women and children, had arrived and were causing a stir.

His aunt having bought too few bricks because of the brick-layer's miscalculation, he had gone to buy more; and the two sons of the owner of the brickyard had invited him to go and take a look.

He had heard a lot about the hippies at the seminary and in Agreste, all sorts of contradictory opinions, most of them violently critical. Cosme, the fierce ascetic, had read stories in the papers about the promiscuous, indecent habits of those enemies of righteousness, who were given over to drug-taking and loose morals and made light of the law and sacred principles—monsters of depravity. Several days later when he was in the cloister trying to comprehend the *Imitation of Christ* in preparation for his spiritual meditation the following morning, Ricardo had overheard a singular conversation. Voices were raised in argument from a nearby group composed of several priests, including the Father Superior, the Reverend Steward, Father Alfonso (the Reverend Alfonso de Narbona y Rodomón) and Frei Thimóteo, a Franciscan friar who had come from São Cristóvão to give his weekly class in moral theology at the Upper Seminary, and who was renowned for his wisdom and sanctity. Thin as a reed, with rebellious hair, a scraggly beard, eyes as clear as water and a soft voice, he was defending the hippies from the attacks of Dom Alfonso de Narbona y Rodomón, who was fulminating against them in a flinty, unmusical mixture of Spanish and Portuguese. This noble Castilian, God's soldier and defender of the Faith, watchdog of Christian morals, vicar of Aracaju's cathedral and professor of theology in the Lower Seminary, was known among the faithful by the epithet "Old Fire and Brimstone" because of the content and vehemence of his sermons.

Unmoved by the wholesale condemnation of the hippies thundered in rude Portuspanish by the doughty hidalgo of Castile, Dom Thimóteo maintained that they were not only children of God as we all are, but especially beloved children for renouncing hypocrisy, rejecting lies, rising up peacefully against the falseness and inhuman cynicism of modern society, and confronting the impiety and corruption of the world. Their weapons were flowers and songs, their emblem, that of Christ: peace and love. Was their way of life to be condemned? What would Dom Alfonso have them do? Take up arms, bombs, machine guns? They roamed through the world giving a good example of the joy of living, and they were persecuted as reformers always had been—reformers, rebels, anyone who questions the prevailing rotten scheme of things. The priests heard him out and either couldn't or wouldn't answer back; Frei Thimóteo's fame as saint and wise man made him a charismatic figure before whom the Reverend Fathers bowed when he passed and whom the Bishop, Dom José, called "my Father." Of the contradictory points of view expressed in the heated polemic, it was the serene voice of the Franciscan that resounded in Ricardo's ears, repeating the words "peace and love," Christ's message and the hippies' greeting.

Ricardo lingered with his two companions at a distance, spying on the camp, where young men and girls sat around talking in groups, seemingly indifferent to time. Some were working in metal and leather, one skinny fellow was playing a guitar, and another rested his head in a young girl's lap. All wore the same kind of patched and raggedy garments, and multicolored strings of beads around their necks like mystic symbols. Some of them were barefoot, especially the women. Ricardo was too far away to see much; when one of the boys suggested they go into the camp he refused. He had to get back to Mangue Seco, where the workmen were waiting for bricks to build the walls of that ingrate Tieta's summer cottage.

Now he watched the two couples and the little girl from the top of the dune. He recognized the lanky guitarist as the one he had seen the day before. All four lay down on the sand while the child ran to and fro, picking up seashells and showing them to her mother.

Ricardo's eyes turned away again to the faraway reaches of the river, where evening shadows were already gathering. What could his aunt be up to and why hadn't she come back? Why had she left him there all alone, bereft of the presence, the voice, the confused arguments which were somehow consoling, even so; the hand, the lips, the comforting breast, the burning womb where all problems were solved, all doubts melted away, and affliction, anxiety and torment were transformed into joy and exultation? She would only be away one night, only one, she had promised. He had already lived through two sleepless, desolate nights.

Perhaps because the music had stopped, Ricardo turned his

hopeless, empty gaze back to the beach. The two couples shed their clothes, and the youth with the guitar and the laughing girl exchanged a long kiss and a tight embrace. The dark young man and the blond young girl walked down to the ocean with the little girl, apparently with the intention of going in. The woman's hair tumbled down her back to her hips. Ricardo sprang to his feet and shouted a warning. It was madness for anyone who had not been born and raised on Mangue Seco, in the savage freedom of that wild lashing sea and wind, to confront the waves that rushed back in redoubled fury from their clash with the dunes to gather for a new attack. Bathers there were in mortal danger, even without the fateful shadow of the sharks.

His shout was blown away by the wind before it could reach the beach, where the father, mother and daughter were wading into the ocean. Ricardo was off like a shot down the sand hill. Without even noticing the other couple making love, he flung himself into the water just as an enormous billow swallowed up the bathers, knocking over the man and the girl, tearing the child from her mother's hand and dragging her from her parents' side. In a minute or two her little body would be flung by the sea against a mountain of sand beaten hard as stone.

Ricardo dived under the waves. When he emerged farther out from shore he was holding the child against his breast and using his free arm to swim. Remembering knowledge learned in childhood, he went under again to let the wave sweep him back to shore. For a moment that seemed forever, all that could be seen of him from shore was his upraised arm holding the little girl out of the water. What if he couldn't get back; what if his strength gave out and he couldn't hold his arm up any longer? No one breathed until he rose up from the foam, free of the waves.

The mother seized and clung to her child, trying to feel her breathing, trembling from head to foot. The father tried to say something, choked up, and couldn't. The other couple had stopped making love and all four were standing together, united in an agony of fear and relief; naked, body and soul.

Ricardo hardly saw them. When he heard the child crying at last, he smiled and ran off as the night fell suddenly, with no warning, a night of a waning quarter moon and phantasmagorical, faintly glimmering dunes, where demons might gather in the shades of night.

Of Hell in earnest.

Demons gather in the shades of night. During the day while he was running back and forth helping the workmen, and working beside them, sawing the trunks of coconut palms, stirring the adobe mortar, transporting bricks across the breakers from Saco in old Jonas' canoe, Ricardo could forget the open wound in his breast, his sin and his damnation. He could even find it conceivable that he might be forgiven, as if nothing very serious had happened.

Looking at Jonas' placid face during the short crossing in the canoe, listening to the monotonous voice that never rose and never fell, he would suddenly feel a renewed interest in life. Puffing at a clay pipe as he kept the little craft on course with consummate skill, Jonas spun out an account of all the interesting things that had happened in those parts: adventures with sharks, tales of fishing and smuggling, Claudionor das Virgens' mixed-up love affairs. Whenever the romantic troubador appeared in the neighborhood, you could bet your last nickel there'd be trouble; he was the worst woman chaser for miles around. Jonas puffed at his pipe and made an odd comparison: "Has a better eye for a dame than a priest."

"A better eye than a priest? How's that again?"

Jonas laughed his easy laugh. He had forgotten Ricardo's condition as an apprentice priest, but he had a good explanation and a piece of advice as well. He had grown old at sea as a smuggler and had lost his left arm hunting sharks; nothing in this world was alien or indifferent to him.

"So you're going to be a priest? Well then, you ought to know that a priest who doesn't stink of a woman is no good. How can he understand his people if he doesn't know how to make a baby? They had one of that kind at Saco, name of Abdias; he couldn't get along with anybody, the women were scared of him, and his church was empty. Now in Father Felisberto's time—he lived at Saco a good five years because of his rheumatism, and he was one of the right kind, had him a woman and seven children—everybody went to church, even us fishermen from Mangue Seco, just to hear what he'd have to say. You should have heard those new kind of sermons he preached, all about what a pretty place Heaven is, with music and good times every day—not like that other one, who spent all his time in Hell because he didn't know about women, only about wickedness. I tell you, boy, a priest who doesn't smell of cunt smells of asshole. In other words, he's no damn good."

Paying no heed to the shock in Ricardo's face, Jonas brought the canoe around and wound up his homily.

"A man can't live without a woman, it's against the law of God. Why did God make Adam and Eve if that ain't so? You tell me if you can."

The boy had no answer for him, but Jonas' hearty view of things bucked up his spirits just as the hard work of housebuilding did and gave him hope of undoing the knot of his despair.

The sharp blade of desire was enough to undo, or cut, that knot when his aunt was there with all her gaiety and folly to open the floodgates of fear and constraint in which he was drowning. Even at night, with demons at large, in Tieta's presence he was able to forget the open wound in his breast, his sin, his broken vow and his damnation. Her presence, her laughter, her warm voice, her embrace, her mouth, her hands, her thighs, her hot belly were worth risking all the leprosy, disgrace and Hell in creation.

When his aunt was away it was a different story; he was again a leper, branded with the stigma of the damned, doomed without hope of redemption. As soon as she was gone the demons took possession of him and made him conscious of his sin, exposing him for the lost, unworthy soul he was.

Ricardo sought her in the hammock. How could she stay away so long? He had abandoned the horsehair mattress on the Skipper and Dona Laura's bed; how could he lie there without his ungrateful mistress? In Agreste, when he was still struggling to preserve his chastity on those nights of temptation in the hammock slung in Dr. Fulgêncio's study, sleeping or waking he had seen and felt her naked, tantalizing him so that in his weakness he had tried to possess her without knowing quite how. All through those nights she had never left him despite his prayers, his promises, and his determination to drive back the satanic vision that was taking possession of his soul. Yet now that he knew the way and the port so well, she would not even appear to him in dreams, and when he tried to imagine her stretched out nude in the hammock, the only vision he could see was Satan and the fires of Hell.

Why did the heartless woman linger in Agreste instead of coming to his rescue? It was almost an affront to know that she was away from him in town, where the men never took their eyes off her; she couldn't cross the street without exciting comment; her swaying hips left a trail of stares and remarks in their wake. She was surrounded with an aura of repressed desire, the center of a fiery ring-around-the-rosy in which all the men he knew took part, from Osnar, with his dirty mouth and loose tongue, to Barbozinha, whose verses described her nude and shameless, clad in seafoam; from Chalita the Arab, who had known her as a young girl, to Seixas, who preferred her to his cousins; from Aminthas, who thought he was such a comedian, to Goatstink, whose vile language knew no bounds. Ricardo, walking along with his aunt and wearing his cassock, had heard the beggar's filthy remark as they passed: "Gee, I'd like to die in the shade of that big flowering cunt-tree!" Instead of being angry Tieta had smiled, while the seminarian turned away to hide his confusion. Far from his arms, caught in that circle of desire, who could say she wouldn't smile coquettishly at someone else? Which one? Ricardo made no distinctions. They all seemed equally unworthy of her, not fit to look at her, much less receive the gift of a smile, a look, the slightest gesture of interest or attention.

Who among them, though, was more unworthy of her than he, Ricardo? He was too young, he was her nephew, and he was a seminarian, with all the sworn vows and total ignorance that state implied. And yet she had noticed him, had been aroused by the eagerness devouring him and had returned his desire. True, Satan had taken a special interest in this unusual case and was particularly anxious to overthrow these two pure souls, his own and his aunt's. As for the others, they were all lost souls anyhow, from the filthy drunkard Goatstink to wayward Peto, not yet thirteen and already well on the road to perdition.

Which of them was it? All at once, on this night of affliction and demons unloosed, Ricardo forgot his sin, his fear of punishment, his awe of God and consciousness of guilt. His mind was fixed on one terrible thought that tormented him and drove all others from his mind, suffocating him and weighing on his heart: the thought that she, Tieta, his own Tieta, his mistress, his love, might be lost in another's arms, kissing other lips, stroking another breast, curling her thighs around the thighs of another man. Who was he? Ascânio, Uncle Astério, the Skipper, who?

Ricardo could not bear these thoughts. No leprosy, stigma or hellfire could be worse than this terrible emotion that flooded him with rage, gnawed at his guts and made the saliva between his teeth taste of bile. It was a sharp pain that actually tore at his balls. In a bed or a hammock, on the ground or the sand, swooning away, dying and being born with another man, oh no! If his worst thoughts came true, then he would add the crimes of murder and suicide to his sins against chastity. Ricardo knew that only the God who gives us life has the right to take it away. Well, he would rise up against God. Better to see her lifeless than fainting in another's arms; and without her he would long for death, not life.

The moon was waning on that night of havoc when Ricardo went down into Hell and was devoured by jealousy. How could it hurt so much? He leaped out of the hammock and ran to the edge of the sea. Encumbered by his nightshirt, he tore it off and flung it away, rushed into the water and swam until he was utterly exhausted. Then he fell asleep on the sand, stark naked.

Of spiritual meditation.

Before he was awake he heard the sounds of merry laughter, guitar music, and a melody so sweet and soothing that he was lulled back into a dream in which he found Tieta at last in a wide, peaceful field that ran down to a beach and sandhills. Naked and carrying a flowering staff from St. Joseph's altar, she led her frolicking goats to graze in the ocean. Her winged feet did not touch the ground, and neither did Ricardo's. Hand in hand they floated, clean and innocent in body and soul, toward the hand of God open to receive them. And God held the world in His lap: fields, ocean, seashore, goats and lovers. Then there sounded the trumpets of the Last Judgment, no more frightening than a lullaby, and the prophet Jonas, the old fisherman and smuggler, rose from the waves astride a shark and proclaimed the Lord's unanswerable truth: no man, be he rich or poor, old or young, strong or weak, can live without a woman, and no woman can live without a man, for that is the law of God. The seawalls crumbled as Jonas, the stump of his arm upraised, proclaimed that love was not sin, not even the love of an aunt and a nephew or a widow with a seminarian. A little girl came up and adorned Tieta's and Ricardo's hair with flowers and chirped, "Peace and love," like a baby bird.

The music and singing went on as he came out of his sleep, and at the touch of the child's fingers Ricardo opened his eyes. He recalled the raving jealousy he had felt the night before, his desperate swimming feat and how he had thrown himself exhausted and naked onto the sand, where he had fallen asleep and was still lying. The little girl handed him her last flower, a lily; around him was a circle of girls and young men and some children, all equally naked and smiling, singing to lull his sleep. The lullaby soothed his heart with its strange melody and words; it was a message of peace and joy, music from Heaven. The guitar twanged by the skinny young man was an angel's harp. Ricardo sat up slowly and smiled.

It didn't matter at all that he was nude, nor did he stare curiously or wonderingly, with lust or impurity, at the nudity around him. He simply looked and saw beautiful girls, some hardly more than children, and bearded or beardless youths, some with long hair down to their shoulders. Hadn't Jesus had hair like that? The curly hair of others blossomed in great unraveled flowers or tangled birds' nests. The circle went on singing and dancing, ring-around-the-rosy. Ricardo stood up.

He found that he was utterly free of fear and unconscious of sin. The dancing and singing, the calm, smiling faces of the girls and young men on the edge of the morning had restored his lost joy and peace.

Free of the bondage of time, with no hurry and no timetable to keep, they sang and danced for him in the blue mist of dawn. One of the girls, the mother of the child he had rescued from the waves, left the circle, came up to him and kissed him on the cheek and lips; and Ricardo knew the meaning and the taste of brotherhood. Then they all ran into the ocean, the children leading him by the hands.

All was mystery, fantasy, dreaming. Day broke over the peaceful waters where girls and boys clove through the gentle waves and the children gathered red, white, pink and purple shells. Several couples made love in the dawn, but Ricardo lay among them on the beach in silence, making no effort to see or sense them, surrounded by seashells the children brought him.

Later they picked up their torn, faded, skimpy, threadbare old clothes, gathered the children together, and stepped into the canoes. They did not ask Ricardo's name or anything else, said not a word to him in fact, yet they had given him a boon he had never known before, a new kind of purity to take the place of the seminary kind based on fear and punishment, there being no more sin, nor any such thing as the devil, or evil, or despair; they had been banished from the face of the earth. Forever.

Once out from shore they cried a farewell, "Peace and love," and were gone. "Peace and love, brother." Ricardo stood quietly, redeemed.

Of an unexpected confession.

As he walked down to the beach toward the canoe where Jonas was waiting to take him back to Mangue Seco with a new handsaw and several pounds of nails, Ricardo saw sitting in a deck chair, in the shade of a gnarled old tamarind tree, the figure of a man he knew well. He recognized Frei Thimóteo even in duck trousers and sport shirt, and recalled that the Franciscans of São Cristóvão had a summer house at Camp Saco.

He went up to him and asked a blessing. The friar couldn't quite place him; now where had he seen that young face before? Ricardo explained. "In the seminary, Father." He wasn't a student of his, he hadn't finished Lower Seminary, the secondary course, yet; you might say he hadn't really begun. Still, he was just about at the crossroads where he'd have to make up his mind. And he was following that path, not like a wayfarer at peace with himself but locked in a desperate battle with the devil all the way.

"Father, when can I come and confess?"

"Whenever you want to, my son; whenever you feel the need."

"Could it be now, Father?"

"If you wish it, my son."

Ricardo stood waiting for Frei Thimóteo to put on his cassock and take him to confess in the chapel. But the friar pointed to a deck chair beside him.

"Rest your bundles and sit down here next to me. We'll talk a little while first and then I'll confess you. This is such a glorious day we ought to enjoy it as God intended us to do. Men's happiness is God's chief concern. Are you here on holiday?"

"Yes, I am, Father. I mean, not here, but at Mangue Seco."

"Mangue Seco is the most beautiful place in the world. It isn't true that God rested on the seventh day as the Scriptures say." The friar laughed, as if he realized that what he had just said sounded ridiculous. "On the seventh day the Eternal Father was so inspired He decided to write a poem, so He made Mangue Seco. But He's really still creating Mangue Seco with the wind's help, isn't He? Are you here with your family?"

"Just with my aunt, but I've been alone these last three days. She went back to Agreste, where my folks are. My aunt lives in São Paulo. She's just here on vacation. She went away a long time ago. I hadn't ever seen her before."

As the friar made no comment, he went on. "My aunt's building a house in Mangue Seco. She's rich. She bought some land here, and I'm in charge of the building. I came over today to get some supplies. The bricklayer, the carpenter and the workmen are all from Saco."

"That's right, the people on Mangue Seco don't know those trades. They're born to be toilers of the sea, which is saying a good deal. They're a strong race of men, my boy."

"Father, one day in the seminary I overheard you talking about the hippies to the Reverend Fathers. You were saying there was nothing wrong with them, that they weren't bad people."

"I don't recall that day especially, but I only speak well of the hippies. They're singing birds in the garden of God, all of them, the mystics and the atheists."

"The mystics and the atheists too? But Father, how can they be? That passes my understanding."

"You can't judge the quality of a wine by its label, my boy. It's the man that counts with God, not what we call him. Do you want to leave the seminary and go away with the hippies?"

"No, Father. I don't know if I'd like to go with them or not, I never thought about it. But even if I did want to I don't think I'd go, because it would just about kill my mother. She thinks the hippies are devils; she saw some in Aracaju and she's never gotten over it. She's afraid my brother might run off with them if he ever had a chance. That's my little brother, Peto. He's going on thirteen and he doesn't like to study."

"Is that why you want to know about the hippies? Because of your brother?"

"No, Father. It's because I felt so discouraged yesterday. I knew I had offended God and I thought that was the end of my vocation. I was full of rage and jealousy, as if I had a curse on me. I couldn't get to sleep, so I swam and swam until I was tired out and fell asleep on the beach. When I woke up there were hippies all around me, singing to me. I don't know why, but they set my heart at rest and gave me the peace I needed so much."

"'Peace and love,' those are God's words that they use. I told you they're songbirds in the heavenly garden. Do you feel that you have a vocation for the priesthood, or were you sent to the seminary by someone else?"

Ricardo mulled the question over before trying to answer.

"Mother had made a promise, because of my father's health, I think. But when she told me so, I was more than willing to go; Mother's brought me up to fear God since I was a little boy."

"To fear God or to love Him?"

"Can you love God without being afraid of Him? I can't separate the two things, Father."

"Well, you should learn to. Nothing that's done out of fear is a virtue, and nothing that's done out of love is a sin. God doesn't have any use for fear or for cowards. Do you really want to be a priest?"

"Yes, Father, I do; but I can't now."

"Why not, if you want to?"

"Because I'm not worthy. I've sinned, I've disobeyed God's law, I've broken my contract and my vow."

"God isn't a businessman, my son. He doesn't make deals or bargains, and when a child of His breaks the law He has a remedy at hand, confession. You sinned against chastity, didn't you?"

"Yes, Father."

"With a woman?"

"Yes, Father. With—"

"I didn't ask you who it was with, that doesn't change the nature of the fault."

"I thought it might, Father."

"Let me ask you just one thing. In spite of your fear of punishment, do you detest your sin or do you think it was worth it, even if you have to pay for it in Hell?"

"Well, I'm scared of Hell, all right, but I just can't repent, Father. I won't tell you any lies."

The monk smiled tenderly and said, "Kneel down now, and I'll give you your penance and your absolution."

"But, Father, how can you give me absolution before I've made my confession?"

"What do you think you've just been doing? Pray three Our Fathers and five Hail Marys, and if you sin again, don't be afraid and run away from God as if He were the hangman. Just make your confession, either to a priest or directly to God."

Ricardo knelt down to receive his blessing and absolution, but he still wasn't sure whether he should enter the Upper Seminary to prepare for the sacred task of bringing God's word to men.

"Father, can I still aspire to the priesthood after what I've done? Do I deserve to?"

"Why not? Some say priests should marry and some say they shouldn't; that's a difficult question and we can't go into it now. I can't tell you which is the better priest: the one who chastises his body and steeps it in bitter desire, who punishes himself the better to serve God, mortifying his own flesh and doing violence to himself, or the one who suffers because he has sinned, the one who yields to temptation and stumbles to his feet only to fall back again. The first is a martyr and the enemy of his own body; he is strong and may become a saint, perhaps. The other sins and is weak, but by sinning he becomes more human, his heart is softened, he is not waging an eternal struggle against his own body. Which of the two best serves God and men? I can't tell you that. Do you know why?"

Ricardo looked at the old priest with the fragile bones, the luminous eyes like water, the bony hand that had blessed and absolved him.

"No, Father, why?"

Frei Thimóteo's voice was warm and paternal:

"Because I was already an old man when I was ordained, an old man and a widower. I've been married, I'm the father of four children, my body is at peace. Just try to serve God the best you can by serving men, and don't be afraid of God or of life. If you can do that, you'll be a good shepherd."

"What about the devil, Father?"

"The devil exists and reveals himself in hatred and oppression. Rather than be afraid of sin, my son, you should be afraid of virtue when it is joyless and aims to limit human beings. Virtue is the opposite of joylessness, just as sin is the opposite of joy. God made men free; the devil tries to conquer us through fear. The devil is war, while God is peace and love. Go in peace, my son, come back whenever you want to, and above all, don't be afraid."

Ricardo kissed Frei Thimóteo's hand and picked up his packages.

"Thank you, Father, I will go in peace. Now I know."

In the canoe he turned to look at the monk, at once so frail and so strong, there in the luminous afternoon. Still alive and already dwelling in the odor of sanctity.

In which the author, always the showoff, meddles in matters that are none of his business and about which he understands nothing.

Still alive and already dwelling in the odor of sanctity—I take up Ricardo the seminarian's thought on my return to the company of my readers for a few rapid but indispensable remarks through which I hope to establish a serious ideological basis for the facts and my characters' reactions to them, thus forestalling the accusation of not being *engagé*, or not being relevant, or avoiding commitment.

You, my readers, can hardly accuse me of being a tiresome meddler. Look at the number of pages we've already waded through in the third episode of this leisurely tale without my having interrupted the narrative even once! After all, I have a right to interrupt if I want to; I'm the author and I can't let my characters have everything their own way and indulge in all kinds of whims and sentiments that have nothing to do with the message I wish to convey.

This time it is Frei Thimóteo, the Franciscan monk, who nudges me to take my typewriter in hand. By all indications he must be one of those progressive priests who are trying to reform the Church on the basis of so-called ecumenical theories. They are clamoring for, nay, demanding, a militant Christianity on the side of the exploited against the exploiters, justice against inequity, freedom against tyranny. They are trying to cleanse the Church of the ancient sin of serving the interests of the ruling classes, the aristocrats and the bourgeoisie, of being the opiate of the people or the Holy Inquisition in full cry after witches.

Against these advanced priests who are striking down prejudices and reformulating doctrine, perhaps even leading the Christian faith back to its origins, an outraged counter-cry is going up. Provocative libels and politically dangerous accusations are being hurled against them; they are called subversive and are not infrequently tried and sentenced. Priests in jail for being subversive! When has such a thing been seen since Nero and Caligula?

I don't intend to get involved in discussions of dogma; it isn't my forte, to say the least, although in principle that polemic is certainly of interest. When it comes to religion I'm neutral, since I profess none and respect them all. However, I'd like to add my two cents' worth, based on the friar's understanding and Jonas the boatman's ideas, to a debate as to the relationship between chastity and sanctity which has stirred up such a fuss; and I do so with a mind free from prejudice of any kind, out of a sheer disinterested desire to shed what little light I can on the debate.

For centuries chastity was an almost indispensable element in the making of a saint, male or female. The more the flesh was mortified, the greater were the chances of beatification. That much seems well established in canon law.

I can hardly approve of the prophet Jonas, that dubious contraband prophet rising from the back of a voracious shark instead of issuing from the belly of a biblical whale, when he declares so positively, and in such vulgar language, that a priest who doesn't smell of the vagina smells of the anus, with the sly intention, no doubt, of implying that there is a connection between clerical celibacy and pederasty. Now this connection does not always exist; the connotation is both forced and improper. The rude mariner was right as rain, though, when he swore to Ricardo that sins against chastity are no impediment to a priest's attaining a state of blessedness and even working miracles.

I have no intention of analyzing moral theories or religious precepts; who am I to make the attempt? I would merely like to bolster the evidence laid out above with a few examples of my own. Let's begin with Frei Thimóteo himself, living in the odor of sanctity. He was married and fathered children; he tasted of the fruit, yet he is thought by experts and laymen alike to be one of God's Elect and is venerated and proclaimed as such. Marriage and children came before he was ordained? True enough. The example isn't valid, then? All right, I withdraw it. I don't need it, there are plenty of others. Let's take another example.

Let's take Father Inocêncio, who passed on a little over ten years ago at the advanced age of ninety-six summers, still lucid and able to tell one of his great-great-grandchildren from another. Vicar of the town of Laranjeiras for more than fifty years, he buried with tearful devotion the three concubines who had given him a total of nineteen children. God took five in their first infancy and Father Inocêncio raised and educated fourteen: eight sons, all upstanding boys, and six girls, all of whom married well except Mariquinha, who had such a marked partiality for other men that Rubião finally lost patience with her and demanded a separation. "That gal took after me," the good Father said at the time by way of excuse, taking his daughter's fault upon his own shoulders. After all, a few extra sins more or less could hardly tip the scale for one who had sinned so often. Grandchildren and great-grandchildren grew up in the spacious house, all bearing the honored surname of the Reverend Father, Maltez, and all of them blessed by God. Even after he had had several grandchildren he was still siring children of his own, and when his first great-great-grandchild was brought to him for him to bless and christen, he gave thanks to the Lord and praised His holy name, and not in vain.

On one occasion a missionary of the kind who roam the north and the northeast frightening the people, none other than our acquaintance Dom Alfonso de Narbona y Rodomón (whose Spanish accent in Portuguese was in itself a foretaste of Hell), visited the patriarch at home and found him in the company of his third and last paramour, the prettiest of the three, a young woman of twenty-some years—a rosy mullet fit for the mouth of a king, Claudionor das Virgens had sung, comparing the morning light on her face to a glowing pomegranate—and on seeing him sitting among his children and grandchildren had brandished an accusing finger and thundered:

"Have you no shame, Father, at leading such a licentious life? And, not content with sinning, at flaunting the proof of your sin in public and scandalizing the faithful?"

"God said, 'Increase and multiply,'" replied Father Inocêncio Maltez serenely, with a pleasant smile. "And I obey the law of God. I've never seen it written anywhere that God ever said a priest couldn't take a woman to wife and father children. That twaddle was invented a long time later, most likely by some self-castrated busybody like your right reverend self."

As for the public scandal of the faithful, to the missionary's mortification he could see for himself that it did not exist. Quite the contrary; the people actually rejoiced, one might say even took pride, in the vigor of their holy man, who boasted that at eighty years of age he was still fulfilling the obligations inherent in his state of concubinage. Father Inocêncio not being a man to lie, the faithful saw something miraculous about the potency thus revealed, a clear sign of divine grace.

It appears to be true that Father Inocêncio's first miracles took place while he was still alive, before God called him to the Paradise where his three wives and nine of his children were waiting for him, five dead in infancy and four adults, plus a few children and grand-children, a whole little clan, in fact. These first proofs of sanctity were nothing very grand: he cured some minor illnesses by a simple application of holy water, and he made it rain twice when Sergipe was threatened with drought.

Hardly was Father Maltez cold in his grave, to which he was escorted by the population of Laranjeiras and the neighboring district en masse, when a whole sheaf of miracles took place, each more impressive than the last. No sooner was the Father's corpse laid under the earth when, at the very foot of the final resting place where he reposes beside the mortal remains of his three late la-mented dearly beloveds, a paralytic woman invoked his name, threw away her crutches and walked forth. The news soon spread.

After that spectacular beginning the master priest never stopped his miraculous cures, which continue, ever more numerous and remarkable, to this day. Laranjeiras, a surpassingly beautiful town, had waited vainly for years, like Agreste, for the tourists who never came to admire its magnificent old colonial houses before they were obliterated by time and neglect. Now, thanks to Father Inocêncio's miracles, there is a continuous pilgrimage of the sick and the halt, who light candles in the church next to the gravestone in the cemetery where the kindly and virile shepherd of souls is there to give aid and comfort to them all. All a barren woman has to do is say a novena and tell him what she wants. If she prays extra hard, she'll have twins.

Each year on the anniversary of his death the throng of pil-grims multiplies and the petitions are in the thousands; the town begins to hum and there is much buying and selling. The pilgrims are welcomed not only by the Reverend Father's descendants but by the grateful beneficiaries of miracles past, with pious Marcolina, the first one of all, the woman who threw away her crutches on the day Father Inocêncio was buried, in the lead.

I've given only one example. I could cite many more, but I don't want to impose on your time. Before taking leave of you I'd like to say how sorry I am that Agreste lacks a priest as wonderful as the Reverend Inocêncio Maltez, the saint of Laranjeiras, to promote religious tourism in the place. There simply isn't very much to say about Father Mariano, whether because he's incorruptible or discreet I don't know. I certainly don't mean to spy on him; I don't go with him when he travels to the capital, on diocesan business no doubt, though the wagging tongues of Osnar and other evil-minded folk would have it that he goes to find an outlet for his nature. At any rate he doesn't stir up scandals or the ire of missionaries hot on the trail of sin; he has never given Agreste anything to talk about and probably never will. For one thing, the pious churchmice, most of all Perpétua, never take their watchful eyes off him for a minute.

Those watchful eyes are too much for me; goodbye. I'm getting ready to take a trip to Laranjeiras one of these days. I'm getting to that age, you all know how it is. They say you can get amazing results with a contribution for Father Inocêncio's poor; the bigger the contribution, the firmer and longer-lasting the results. Let's hope it's true.

In which the space heroes return, this time by sea. A chapter chock-full of angles and projects involving a number of different characters, including Mirkus the Magnificent, Osnar, Peto and Ascânio Trindade.

When the shining beings foretold by Possidônio the Prophet made their second appearance in Agreste from the Atlantic Ocean in a powerful motor launch—their numbers and sex had increased, for there were males, females and hermaphrodites among them—the last echoes of the scandal provoked by Leonora's miniskirt had died away. With time the pretty Paulista's demure behavior had stilled the critics' tongues and she was now in the good graces of the godfearing and straitlaced. Elisa decided not to disobey her husband but to save her own controversial mini to wear in São Paulo before they went out of style, God willing. She wasn't quite brazen enough to stare down the jeers and disapprobation of Agreste. With the second visitation from outer space, however, miniskirts became a familiar object to everyone in town.

Peto charged up from the river and galvanized the bar with the news that a whole battalion of gringas was landing. Before he could finish getting the words out the square was full of Martians. Ascânio Trindade came running from the courthouse. All the females wore plaid kilts—real Scottish plaids, Dona Carmosina registered the fact —with yellow jerseys and high black kid boots. Such an invasion of thighs and hips, exposed to the breeze and the greedy eyes of the crowd that poured into the square from all directions, might have been staged on purpose to redeem Leonora once and for all.

"They're all wearing the same uniform; must be part of an army or some religious sect."

"Too bad old Possidônio ain't here to see the wicked sight and let loose with some of his thunder and lightning." (The prophet had retired to Rocinha to meditate and lay hands on the sick.)

The long-legged, willowy redhead, battalion commander, priestess, or guru's assistant, a veteran visiting Agreste for the second time, waved to the populace and took off her dark glasses, offering her mascara'ed eyes to the public gaze. She had on a kind of doll's miniskirt that showed everything, as Osnar noted.

"It's no wider than my hand."

He advanced to greet the traveling saleslady from space and renew their old acquaintance.

"So you're back again! What an honor for the community of Sant'Ana do Agreste."

"Why, hello, baby, how about standing me to a *guaraná* or a Coke or something? We're so thirsty we're about to die, me and my staff here."

The rest of the "staff" came up, all bouncy and bubbly. Not many noticed the men; all eyes were on the women. Some of them raised dreadful doubts in the minds of the unsophisticated townsfolk: was that one over there a male or a female? And was that peculiar-looking individual as queer as he looked? They couldn't be sure.

A curtain was pushed aside in the mayor's house and the suffering face and three-days' beard of Mauritônio the dentist were thrust out of the open window. Leonora's miniskirt in the marketplace had provoked a storm of whistles, laughter, jokes and doggerel; so many miniskirts in the plaza all at once provoked nothing but dumbfounded silence. The sidewalk in front of the bar was thronged with people who had emptied the shops and grocery stores.

"They have coconut milk at the bar now," Ascânio Trindade announced, ushering the exalted being and her companions into the bar. Manuel gave them a bow.

"Oh, how efficient!" Miss Spacelady raised her voice and inquired of the others, "Who likes coconut milk?"

"Only with whisky, babycakes," drawled Aphrodite, who wore long hair to the rump, tight pants, an Indian shirt and a cascade of beads.

"Why isn't she wearing a miniskirt?" inquired Osnar, feeling cheated because he couldn't admire those promising thighs and hips.

"Because it isn't a her, darling, it's a he. I mean . . . oh, well, it's Rufo, our decorator. He's terribly popular!"

"Not with me, he ain't. Babycakes here can do without him. He ain't my type, somehow."

The visitors didn't stay long. They were just on their way back from Mangue Seco. The engineers and technical experts were still there, the new Barbarella explained. The people who were decorating the landscape were public-relations types, assistants, secretaries, contact people, a very efficient team, now quenching their thirst in the bar before going back to the launch and up the river to Sergipe.

"So the AC-DC's Rufo; and you, princess, wherefore art thou and wherefore dost thou come? From Poland, by any chance?"

"Elisabeth Valadares, Betty to my friends, Bebé to my very close friends. I'm the Ipana girl from Ipanema."

She smiled with a great many dazzling, perfect white teeth, a mouth for a toothpaste ad.

"I have a message for you, luv." Luv was Ascânio Trindade, to Osnar's disappointment. "From Doctor Magnifico."

"Who?" Ascânio was at a loss. "Would you say that again, please?"

"A message from Mirko Stefano, darling, don't you know who he is? We call him Mirkus the Magnificent too, and he really is. You'll find that out for yourself, luv. He's the good-looking guy who came with me when I was here before, remember? I'm his secretary, executive secretary, you know. He wanted me to tell you he couldn't be here today because he had to go to São Paulo for a very important interview, but he'll be coming here to talk to you in a few days to settle all the details."

"All the details?"

"Yes, honey. Every single one."

"But all the details of what?"

"Oh, I can't tell you that. Doctor Magnifico's the one who knows. This is his baby and I'm staying out of it. Discretion is my middle name. Bye-bye for now, be sure you dream about me, *petit amour*. Bye-bye to you too, you great big man."

The "great big man" was Osnar, and he ate it up. "Just let me get my hands on this babe in the dark and sparks will fly. I'll show this chick how to get a kick from a hick's prick."

"Come on, gang!" ordered the fabulous secretary.

"You mean there isn't anything else to see around here?" asked the high-strung Rufo, shaking his Mona Lisa mane.

"Not a thing."

"What a drag!"

His decorator's eye jaded but attentive, Rufo the aesthete walked past Osnar without even noticing him, but his eye lingered on young Peto approvingly and he bit a languid lip. Osnar saw the glance and gesture and thought, "You goddam fairy, don't you even respect a kid?" Kid? The little squirt was growing like a beanstalk, probably from jerking off so much. It was about time Osnar kept his promise and took him around to Zuleika's.

"How old are you getting to be, Sergeant Peto?"

"I'll be thirteen the eighth of next month."

"The eighth of January! Well, that's just dandy."

Going on thirteen, just the right age. Osnar would have to see about fixing up that party with Zuleika and Aminthas and Seixas and Fidélio. All on the quiet, of course; Astério couldn't be in on it or he'd tell Elisa and then Perpétua would be sure to find out, and there'd be hell to pay. Osnar smiled to himself. They'd have themselves a high old time.

Skipper Dário, coming in from Mangue Seco at twilight in his putt-putt canoe, had seen a schooner anchored outside the bar. Two of its boats had been let down; one had gone up the river and docked in Agreste, the other had landed men and instruments on the beach. They had gone around questioning the fishermen and then gone farther inland to the coconut grove. All of these movements struck the Skipper as suspicious.

Ascânio Trindade, absolutely certain now that a big tourist enterprise was in the offing, promised the Skipper some definite news in the next few days. The big shot had sent his executive secretary with a message saying he'd be back soon for a talk, to discuss his project, no doubt, and make sure he had support from the authorities. "And he can count on that support, Skipper." Once tourism had brought new life to Agreste, Ascânio, the man at the helm of progress, stood a chance of making his own dream come true. For the first time in many years, Ascânio Trindade felt the stirrings of ambition, a desire to be somebody; somebody who could fight for the chance to win the rich and beautiful Leonora Cantarelli. She had been unattainable before, a vision far beyond his reach. Now she was a prize to be won, a goal to be attained by a fighter with his feet on the ground, an ideal to one who had tested his mettle and proved that he had the courage and skill to win out over all obstacles and follow his star, the aspiration of a daring but clear-headed young man who was ready to pass through any and all trials to win her. Hadn't he already passed through the hardest of them all? He had wrestled with his own soul and won. All he had to do now was rise to a higher position in life so that he could aspire to Leonora's hand in marriage. She was rich and he was poor. That didn't matter any longer. He had no fortune to lay at her feet, but on the other hand she no longer possessed the most precious pearl that a bride could bring to her husband on her marriage night, her own virgin blood. Skipper Dário could see victory shining in Ascânio's face, but no peace of mind.

Of Mayor Mauritônio Dantas' suicide and Colonel Artur da Tapitanga's advice.

It would be impossible to deny a connection between the presence in Agreste of the pioneers led by Elisabeth Valadares, the last genuine girl from Ipanema, and the suicide of Mauritônio Dantas, surgical dentist and mayor of Agreste, found dead in the small hours of that night stark naked, with his tongue hanging out. He had hanged himself by his pajamas in the bathroom.

While the pioneers made their way to the bar and depleted the honest Manuel's stock of Coca-Cola, *guaraná* and beer, the theatrical mayor was seen at the window of his house in a highly agitated state, mumbling names and gazing hungrily on the display of Martian and Carioca thighs. Mirinha, his sister and nurse, tried in vain to lead him to the bedroom where he anxiously gave himself up indefatigably, day and night, to the practice of masturbation. That afternoon, when he saw that the harvest of women for whom he had been praying to God for so long had come at last, he had indulged himself at the window within sight of that sea of thighs, splendid proof of divine magnanimity.

It was generally believed that Dr. Mauritônio Dantas had begun to go soft in the head when his wife Amélia, Mel to her intimates, packed her bags and went off to join Aristeu Régis in Esplanada and thence to unknown parts. Aristeu Régis had originally come to Agreste at the behest of the secretary of agriculture to study ways to improve the manioc crop. Amélia was sick of living in that place even though she boasted the title of First Lady, the title being so much crap to her, as she said. Aristeu offered to take her away from all that, and she was quick to accept. Some of Mel's women friends and confidantes declared that the mayor's madness went back much farther than that and that it was the intolerable intemperance and abuse to which he subjected his wife that was the real cause of her flight. However that might be, the degenerative process accelerated visibly after the departure of his unfaithful wife. As Aminthas said, our esteemed civil governor administered his horns honorably and with perfect discretion as long as Amélia spread her honey around in her own hometown. When she decided to do it far from her spouse's sight and his attentions, the worthy head of the community could not stand for such ingratitude. Why had she left him, when he had never said a word against her kicking up her heels?

The first sign of dementia was seen only a few days after Mel's desertion. On Saturday the mayor received his petitioners, who had come from the farms and outlying villages with their complaints and requests, in a state of total nudity. He had kept on only his socks, so as not to walk barefoot on the cold tiled floor. From then on, whenever Mirinha dozed off, the dentist was out the door and into the street or the square, in his undershorts or without them, masturbating in public to the glee of the little boys. This painful situation, commented on in whispers, went on for months.

When Dr. Mauritônio Dantas looked out the window and saw that the celestial miniskirts were about to retreat, he would not stand for it. Sent by God in answer to the constant and fervent prayers of His long-suffering servant, how dare they leave? Interrupting his solitary and delightful occupation, he ran shouting from his home in the hope of catching at least half a dozen. He needed them to warm the bed that Mel's absence had chilled and to soften the sharp springs of the worn mattress on which he tossed sleeplessly at night. "Sharp springs, sharp horns," the implacable Aminthas said.

Half-naked and not in the pink of condition, he had gotten only as far as the bar when the kilted battalion of tourists was already vanishing on its way to the river. Manuel the Portugee, Astério and Seixas grappled with the mayor as gently as they could and restored him to his weeping sister.

At the burial Ascânio Trindade, uncontested heir to the post of the deceased, spoke words of elegy to "the chief and friend I'll miss." Although born in the capital, Mauritônio Dantas had endeared himself to all in his eighteen years in Agreste and had rendered valuable service to the community as a diligent professional and dedicated administrator.

"Diligent Amélia did her part too," murmured Aminthas to Dona Carmosina in a funereal voice. "Think of all the votes she pulled in for her husband before she left politics."

Father Mariano sprinkled holy water over the coffin, putting finis to the principal amusement of Agreste's street urchins.

The president of the Town Council, Colonel Artur de Figueiredo, succeeded to office as stipulated by law; but the lord of Tapitanga, marching steadily toward his ninetieth year, took office as a mere formality. No one was better suited to preside over the glorious destiny of Agreste in its sunset years than the real incumbent, Ascânio Trindade.

"Ascânio, I'm counting on you, son. Next time around you'll be elected in your own right. You just steer as straight a course as you can until then, 'cause I've got one foot in the next world and I'm not up to much these days except looking after my goats and my crops."

He pointed out the window with his cane.

"Agreste used to be a byword for good times. We even had fancy women from Paris who made a pretty good living in these parts. Plenty of 'em, too. All gone with the smoke of the train we never got—all gone, even the smuggling and the gringas. All that's left besides pretty scenery is the healthy climate and the water."

He looked at Ascânio affectionately.

"You're my godson, and you could have been my son if you'd married Célia instead of wasting your time with that mealy-mouthed little tramp in Bahia."

He was referring to his youngest daughter, who had been born when the Colonel had already passed his sixty-fifth birthday and had six grandchildren. He had had fifteen children by two wives and no telling how many on the other side of the blanket.

"Well, you didn't want to do it, so now I have to support a bum who spends his time beating a tomtom; I mean that no-account husband of Célia's."

"Not a tomtom, Colonel, a kettledrum. Everyone says Xisto Bom de Som is one of the best percussionists in Salvador."

"And you think that's a job for a man?"

He thought about his daughter for a minute; he was fond of her and wished she lived on the fazenda. His eleven living children were scattered all over the world, and he had ended up alone with his goats.

"You'll be mayor of Agreste. Your grandfather was mayor, and I was mayor and town councilman. All I'm asking you to do is keep the city clean. This place has been famous for its cleanness and its climate ever since the old days, when there was money to spare and everybody had a good time. You can keep Agreste clean at least, since there ain't no way to bring back the good old times."

The Colonel was mistaken; good times, of a kind, were coming, and because of them Agreste's health, cleanliness and climate were in jeopardy.

Of a hymen on horseback.

As Ricardo the seminarian left the depths of Hell by one door, Ascânio Trindade, county clerk to Sant'Ana do Agreste and star-crossed lover, entered by another, crossing the eternal flames in delirium. Freed of damnation and punishment, reborn in the song of the hippies, in the friar's aura of sanctity, in the strength of Jonas' oars, the seminarian yielded his place in Hell to a wronged and embittered man, twice victimized by professional Don Juans.

It would be hard to say which of them had found the conversation more difficult: Ascânio, watching his dream castle tumble down around his ears for the second time, or Dona Carmosina, a keen-eyed student of human beings and their reactions, but no cold unfeeling analyst. She had suffered along with her friend, inflicting as much pain on herself as she was causing him, her eyes wet with tears as she revealed the truth about the physical consequences of Leonora's unhappy engagement. Wanting to be subtle and choose her words so as to spare him as much as possible, she exploded brusquely in her distress:

"Take it like a man!"

Those ominous words were all she could utter just then. Even for Dona Carmosina, with her facile and eloquent gift for words, it was not easy to explain. Ascânio, seeing her hesitate and stammer, at a loss for words, pleaded with her like a condemned man. "Go ahead and tell me whatever it is you have to say."

He thought he knew what it was. That afternoon in the Areopagus, Dona Carmosina had taken him aside and said, "We've got to talk. Come over to my house tonight. I can't tell you here."

That must be it. His daily visits, the long talks on Dona Perpétua's veranda, his turning up on any pretext, the flowers, the *sofrê* bird, the couple riding on a donkey (an obvious hint in pottery, the bride in white, the groom in blue)—all must have prompted Dona Antonieta or the object of his wooing herself to ask Dona Carmosina to point out how disagreeable and futile his insistence was. Didn't he realize what a gulf separated him from the young lady from São Paulo? A poor devil from Agreste with no source of income but the miserable salary the county could pay him had no right to aspire to the hand of a millionaire heiress coveted by the lords and potentates of the south. Yes, that must be it.

All he wanted to know was whether the request had come from Dona Antonieta or Leonora. The dreadful consequences would be the same, but the dagger thrust would cause more suffering or less depending on whose hand dealt it. Ascânio hoped the message came from Dona Antonieta, the stepmother concerned about the future of her charge, the girl she had adopted and loved as if she were a daughter born from her womb. He could see that maternal love has its reasons, and he understood them; he would do the honorable thing and withdraw. Leonora's happiness came before everything else.

But then again, maybe she was pining for him too and grieving at the drastic step her stepmother had taken. If she was, her suffering would help him endure his own and give him strength to make the sacrifice. It was even possible—surely it might be?—that Leonora had rebelled against her stepmother's obsession with money and had resolved to take her place beside him and fight for their love. In that case, it would be up to him to demonstrate his nobility and unselfishness by giving her up and renouncing happiness, since he had nothing to offer one who had so much to give. These were exhilarating thoughts, and they consoled him through an afternoon of weary waiting.

Despite the young man's brave appeal to spit it all out and be done with it, Dona Carmosina, with a lump in her throat, was still mustering her courage while she groped for words. Unable to bear the delay any longer, Ascânio resolved to have it out. In a sepulchral voice he said:

"Dona Antonieta asked you to tell me to leave Nora alone, didn't she?"

If only her task had been so easy! Then Dona Carmosina would have given him her own opinion and advice along with the message, counseling him not to give up the fight or abandon the field of battle. Since she still did not speak, Ascânio put forward the worst hypothesis:

"Then it was Leonora who asked you to tell me . . ." he ventured in the voice of a condemned man whose petition for grace has been denied.

Dona Carmosina tried to speak, but only a guttural sound came out. Ascânio was panic-stricken now.

"Say something, Carmosina, for God's sake. Is she sick? Is it her lungs? I've thought of that, and it doesn't matter. Nobody's afraid of tuberculosis nowadays."

Dona Carmosina drew strength from weakness and finally found her voice.

"Nora was engaged, you know."

"Yes, to a low-down skunk. He wanted to get his hands on her money, but Dona Antonieta discovered what he was up to. You told me that. But I don't want anybody's money, I'm just sorry she's rich. Lots of people marry with separation of property between husband and wife."

"Some men marry widows, too."

"Widows? What's that got to do with it? I don't see what you're getting at."

Now that she had begun, Dona Carmosina went bravely on.

"You know, Ascânio, going together doesn't mean the same thing in São Paulo as it does here, especially when the couple is engaged." She remembered Tieta's words and repeated them: "Engaged couples there go to parties and nightclubs alone and come back at dawn; they even go on trips together. In the south a girl doesn't have to be a virgin to be married. That prejudice about virginity—because that's all it is, a prejudice . . . Why don't you try to think of her as a widow?"

"Leonora? That heel she was engaged to? You mean she isn't . . ."

He read the answer in Dona Carmosina's averted eyes and covered his face with his hands, all at once empty and unarmed. He felt one raging desire: to kill the scoundrel who had defiled Leonora's purity and destroyed the most beautiful dream of his life along with it. As Dona Milu came in from the kitchen with a tray of fresh coffee, cornbread and manioc cakes, Ascânio got up and left without a word.

To know that his love had been deflowered was a hard trial indeed. He entered the purlieus of Hell and the tears came, for all he thought himself a strong man and not one to cry. When Astrud's letter had come, breaking off their engagement and announcing her imminent marriage, and later when he had found out that she was pregnant by another man, he had suffered like a dog but never cried. Nevertheless, on the sleepless night that followed this poignant revelation, the burning in his fixed, staring eyes dissolved in tears. Those were nightmare hours when he wept and pounded his pillow and grappled with himself. Before hearing the death sentence from Dona Carmosina's lips, Ascânio had always been able to leave Leonora whole, pure and perfect, waving goodbye at Perpétua's door. Now that image was gone forever; he would never see her that way again. Now she was stained, penetrated, broken, dishonored, an innocent victim but nonetheless defiled. His love was weighed, measured, tested in every way it could be on that night when he fought his first battle against prejudice. Prejudice, that's all it is, Dona Carmosina had said, and she was right. At law school Ascânio had often taken part in arguments about that burning topic, virginity and marriage. In theory it was all so simple and easy: a mere feudal prejudice.

Citing the United States and the most advanced countries of Europe—France, England, Sweden, Denmark, Norway—as examples, not to mention the socialist countries, where the reactionaries had it that free love was rampant, the more progressive students, Ascânio among them, defended women's right to sex before marriage. Why should men be the only ones to have that right? That was patriarchal prejudice, machismo, the oppression of women by men, the mark of a backward society. But though one crushing argument followed another, the majority still clung to the age-old principle that a woman must come to her marriage bed a virgin and leave some drops of blood on the spotless sheet as her dowry to her husband. Even the sarcasm of the most determined and caustic debaters, who demanded to know what difference there was between going all the way and most of the way with tongue and finger, prick in the ass, prick between the thighs, etc., had little effect. What was the use of respecting a hymen and defiling all the rest? All of these arguments, though unanswerable, were not enough to persuade most of the students. These heated, incoherent discussions always trailed off inconclusively with the swapping of dirty stories without an agreement being reached.

As he recalled those college bull sessions, on that bitter, interminable night of self-questioning doubt, Ascânio remembered a surprising thing Máximo Lima had said, all the more surprising because he was the uncontested leader of the student Left and famous for his radical ideological views, expressed in fiery diatribes attacking bourgeois morality and economics. They had been close friends since junior high school, and Ascânio looked up to Máximo as the highest and most genuine type of revolutionary, free of shibboleths and conventions and clear and straightforward in his thinking. Ascânio, although he shared the aims of the student movement, was not committed to any one organization or political group and did not always agree with Máximo's views, being content to admire and defend him when he was accused by the Right of being an enemy of God, Country and the Family.

Together they had left one of these hot debates about divorce, virginity and women's rights, Máximo's eyes still flashing with the indignation with which he had defended sexual equality in every field of human endeavor.

Ascânio, just to tease his friend, inquired in a scoffing tone, "All right, old pal, now tell me the truth and nothing but the truth. If you found out someday that Aparecida"—Aparecida was Máximo's fiancée, a fellow law student who shared his political views—"wasn't a virgin, that she had had an affair, would you marry her just the same?"

"Would I marry her knowing she wasn't a virgin? Sure I would," Máximo replied without hesitation. Then he turned serious, let his arms fall to his sides, and honestly admitted, "To tell the truth, I'm not so sure. I never thought of it in personal terms. But I do know one thing for sure, Ascânio; a prejudice that's inside you is tough to kill. You believe a thing, you stick up for what you believe because it's right and you know it, but when it comes to putting your money where your mouth is . . . Sure, I'd marry her, but I'd have to get rid of my own prejudice first."

"Would you be able to do it?"

"I don't know, I honestly don't know. I couldn't be sure until it happened and I had to face the problem and take a stand."

Well, it had happened to him, Ascânio, all these years later, when he didn't have Máximo at his side to discuss and argue the problem with and to give him advice. Aparecida and Máximo had graduated from law school and were no longer the radicals they used to be. Not that they were ashamed of their youthful ideals, but he had found a place in the Labor Court where he could defend the workers and the unions, and she had hung up her diploma and devoted herself full-time to her husband and children. Ascânio would have to face his problem and solve it on his own.

Throughout that long weary night he never for a moment blamed Leonora. In his eyes she was the unsuspecting dupe of a villain. He suffered not because he thought her guilty or unworthy, but only because she had been deflowered and was no longer whole. He was torn by doubt; should he go on wanting her for his wife and dreaming of courtship and marriage, or banish himself from her sight forever? Would he have the strength of will to look her in the face, knowing she had been possessed by another, dishonored?

He wrestled with this dilemma all through the night, sick at

heart, tears winning out over masculine pride in the struggle between the forces of tenacious prejudice and those of love. The only
solution that never occurred to him at all was precisely the one
Tieta hoped for, the transformation of their chaste affair. Her hope
had been that he would exchange his dream for the real possibility
of enjoying Leonora's favors as long as she stayed in Agreste, taking
advantage of his knowledge of her condition and ending the affair at
the door of the *marineti* in a rapid or prolonged goodbye kiss.

By the time dawn came up over the river, love had won the
first battle; Ascânio could neither tear Leonora out of his heart nor
give up his purpose of having her for his wife and the mistress of his
home. The wound was raw and bleeding, nevertheless, and he didn't
have the courage to see her just then. He might not be able to
conceal his suffering, and above all he did not want her to know that
he was aware of the truth. He was not a man to hide his feelings; he
never wore a mask; everything going on inside him was reflected in
his face. Since he could not be sure of bringing his heart and his
countenance under control, and it was easy to see from his eyes that
he had been weeping, he decided to go and inspect some modest
public works—footbridges and cattle guards—that the county was
building in Rocinha. He woke up young Sabino, who was asleep on
a cot in the movie theater, and told him to tell Leonora that he had
been called out of town on urgent business and would be away for
two or three days. He had had to leave at daybreak and couldn't tell
her goodbye, but he'd be back.

He might go and see her or he might not; it all depended on
that day's cogitations and the decision he made as a result. He sad-
dled his horse—a gift from Colonel Artur da Tapitanga to the
county—and rode out into the country, bearing Leonora's ravaged
hymen on the saddle before him. He felt its presence keep pace with
the tired animal's ambling gait, stirring up guesses, troubling bits of
detail.

Only once, or often? It couldn't have happened more than a
few times before the liar was unmasked and driven away; maybe
once or twice; no, surely more than once. Oh, what difference did it
make how often it had been? The terrible thing was that she had
given herself to another and had not kept herself intact and pure.

And yet he had to remember it had all taken place before she
ever met him. In no way did she resemble the treacherous Astrud,
who had written him love letters right after rolling in the hay with

another man who had made her pregnant. Leonora had only yielded in a moment of folly, when passion had spoken louder than decorum.

Had she passively allowed herself to be taken, deceived by the bastard and his smooth-talking charm, or had she known the violent sweetness of pleasure in their lovemaking and melted into bliss?

Riding through the manioc plantations and the green cornfields, listening to farmers as they told him their troubles and asked him for help, those speculations would give him no rest, and Leonora's hymen, tied to the horse's back, was rent a thousand times in that weary tug-of-war.

Love rose victorious from that torn maidenhead. Little by little, with no help from hippies, progressive priests or prophetic boatmen, Ascânio's heart was soothed and he was able to stop crying and bury his prejudice. He began to imagine Leonora a widow, a young, lovely and unhappy widow. You couldn't beat Dona Carmosina, she always hit on the right word. No one could expect a widow to be a virgin, only loving and circumspect. He decided to follow his dream wherever it led. One day he would ask for Leonora's hand in marriage. Knowing she had been betrayed and violated made her still closer and dearer to him, more beloved than before.

As soon as he was back in Agreste he went to visit her at Perpétua's house. Leonora thought he looked discouraged—tired from the journey, no doubt, all those leagues on horseback under a burning sun in the best interests of the township. She stroked his cheek gently in an innocent caress. Yes, she had been violated, but in her candor and purity she was chaster than any virgin.

Then, with the message from the tourist entrepreneur, the mayor's suicide and the certainty of being elected to public office; with fine prospects opening up for the community and himself, Ascânio felt that he had reason for hope. The fact that Leonora was no longer a virgin actually made things easier. The young girl's value in the marriage market . . . Good God, how could he think in terms of the marketplace when it was love that was at stake, a love so strong that it could vanquish and bury the oldest, deepest-rooted prejudice of all?

He had won a victory, yes, but the Skipper was right, his mind was not at rest. Not yet. It was too soon. It would take time for a new hymen to grow over the open wound in Ascânio's breast.

In which the author tries in vain to find the
mot juste *for the Lords' Retreat.*

No, none of the classic words—brothel, bawdy house, stew, cat-house, seraglio, bagnio, house of ill fame, ill repute or assignation—is right for the Lords' Retreat, that super-deluxe, discreet and exclusive club in the capital of the glorious state of São Paulo.

Maison de repos might do if the term were not used to describe a sanatorium for mental incurables with money. Moneyed and incurable the Retreat's select clientele may be, but weak in the head they most certainly are not. Almost all of them are uncommonly well supplied with brains and have unusually high IQs; most are either shrewd financiers or wise and judicious statesmen. If the place were in Bahia it would be called a castle, which has just the right connotations of nobility and pomp. But the Lords' Retreat is in São Paulo, where it plays a positive role in the city's medical and financial health. Not only does it satisfy the sexual needs of the rich and powerful, the richest and most powerful of all; it ministers to the oddest complexes and most peculiar tastes with its own brand of therapy, ranging from Swedish or Japanese massage to sessions on the couch with irresistible analysts whose credentials, whether domestic or foreign, are irreproachable: every one of them can spell C(unt), A(ss), T(ongue), and that is only the beginning. And then it doubles, too, as the ultimate meeting place in which to talk over confidential matters in discreet seclusion and seal high-level political and business deals. High finance is argued there, banks and industries are founded, candidates for governor are chosen.

Knowledge and inspiration falter when I leave the rustic simplicity of Agreste, where Zuleika Cinderella runs a whorehouse and nothing but a whorehouse, to mingle with the great ones of the south, with the technocratic intelligentsia, the captains of industry, statesmen, generals and admirals, and the captains of the ship of state. I fear I do inadequate justice to this noble theme. What *is* the proper name for the little empire over which Madame Antoinette reigns with Gallic flair, devotion and *toute la délicatesse?*

Forgive me, but the *mot juste* eludes me. This rude storyteller, accustomed to the baked, arid ground and humdrum lives up north where money is scarce and work is hard, is embarrassed and fearful of committing an unpardonable gaffe. Besides, why must it have a name, this pleasurable place of relaxation, where our country's great men go to soothe their nerves and recover their strength? Everyone knows that big shots who can't get it up come away from the fair and experienced hands of the girls in this blessed refuge, not to mention their crimson lips, as good as new again. Oh, but it's hard to be poor and unpublished. I say unpublished, because I know the Lords' Retreat does occasionally open its doors to a fortunate and famous writer. Who knows? Someday even I may make it, with a little bit of luck. Only then may I find the proper word to call it by.

Of the first debate to decide the fate of water, land, fish and men, with a professional helping hand from Madame Antoinette's girls.

At a gesture from the Young Politician the girls stood up, naked and obedient, left off the first stimulating caresses, smiled and withdrew. One was a blonde, the other a redhead. They would wait in the next room; they knew the rules of the game. The Young Politician, who was not yet as rich and powerful as he would like, had confided to Doctor Magnifico that if they wanted to they could change partners after the first round. The blonde checked to see how much whisky was left in the bottle before she went out. Both gentlemen were comfortably stretched out in the nude, but Mirkus the Magnificent kept his black 007 portfolio by his side.

The Young Politician was a good-looking man in his forties, although not in the same class with Doctor Magnifico and his matinee-idol good looks; Mirko could have earned a good living as the star in a television serial. The Young Politician had to watch his weight; regular saunas could not quite melt his potbelly away. Greed and cunning gleamed in his eyes. Stories were whispered about him behind the scenes in the Chamber of Deputies. Not in public, of course; no one was brave enough to come right out and accuse him of anything. It was taken for granted that he was thought well of where it counted, in the rarefied circles where real power was wielded. His name was beginning to appear in the news as a candidate for higher office; his parliamentary mandate, rather tarnished of late, was no longer important enough to contain his growing prestige. He had wangled a firm promise to be included in the next class to enter the Army War College.

Mirkus the Magnificent, accustomed as he was to hobnobbing with the great, would have thought it unnecessary and imprudent to pronounce the man's name. Money was not mentioned either, but at one point in the conversation the Young Politician's calculating expression relaxed into a broad smile; profitable transactions like this one were almost becoming a thing of the past. The Young Politician, a patriot in his way, worked cautiously but skillfully with his many excellent contacts until the right bargain was struck. "Bribe" was far too harsh, too shocking a word to describe the gratitude of those who turned his talents and acquaintances to their own advantage. If a fat sum of money came his way, it was only a just reward—ah, the right word at last!—when you considered that one false step, one word too many in the wrong ear, could cost him his mandate and his career. The hardliners were incorruptible, trusted no one, and kept a sharp eye out for hanky-panky. It was a risky business and deserved a fair reward.

It would have been reassuring to look in on the two of them there as the afternoon wore away, lounging cool and comfortable on wide divans in one of the soundproof chambers that Madame Antoinette usually reserved for rousing orgies; postponing their own pleasure, sending the girls away, sacrificing their leisure to attend to higher concerns, fully conscious of their grave responsibilities.

"Don't worry, nothing we say here will get out." A new customer and proud to be one, the Young Politician touted the virtues of the Retreat, whose luxurious rooms designed for the mingling of the sexes, like those in fashion ever since the days of the Roman baths, were equally well suited to private business conclaves.

Mirkus the Magnificent opened his attaché case, took out a leather box and offered his partner a cigar. He made a point of knowing the habits and tastes of the men he dealt with and had done his homework thoroughly, amused and made queasy by turns by the Young Politician.

"Cuban," he pointed out with a smile. Since anything Cuban was taboo in Brazil, the offer was all the more tempting.

The Young Politician helped himself to three instead of one.

"I used to smoke nothing but Cuban cigars, but you can't get them these days, thanks to the goddam Commies." He breathed in the sensual aroma. "Nothing like them! When are we going to free Cuba from the clutches of Fidel Castro and wipe this constant threat of vile subversion off the face of the continent?" He easily fell into rhetorical speech, as if he were back on the rostrum of the Chamber of Deputies.

"Oh, the Americans will give him his comeuppance one of these days." Doctor Magnifico held out his gold cigar lighter. "Seriously, though, whenever you feel like smoking a Cuban cigar just let me know; I always keep a supply on hand."

The Young Politician could not quite hide the flicker of envy in his greedy eyes. Those guys really knew how to live, they didn't miss a trick, they had every luxury they craved. And this one was just a front man; imagine how the others, the bosses, must be living it up! He decided to press his luck a little further and play hard to get.

"Thanks a lot. But to get back to our discussion—we mustn't keep the girls waiting. Look, it won't be easy. There're some real roadblocks there and frankly, I'm not so sure we can get around them. Our friend tells me he doesn't want to be involved."

"That wasn't what you told me a few days ago."

"That was before the press got hold of the story. Have you read the papers lately?"

"Oh, the papers . . . they blow everything up."

"They say there are only five of those plants in the world and no country wants one. Pollution's a dirty word. It scares people. It's poison."

"Only five? I told you the papers exaggerate," retorted Mirko. "I know of at least six myself."

"Five, six, what's the difference? I'm afraid we've got to have a really good sales pitch or our friend will say nothing doing. And unless he pulls a few strings I don't see how we can get the authorization to build the plant."

Mirkus the Magnificent was no goatherd, but he, too, knew his flock; that was what he was paid for, and very well paid at that: to make a good bargain, to know when to raise the ante and when to let well enough alone.

"I understand. And yet the arguments we've given you to pass on to our distinguished friend are pretty good ones, it seems to me."

"Not good enough. Ridiculous arguments, that's what he said. 'Ridiculous' was the word he used. He can't make the final decision, you know; he's got to convince the others, and to do that he needs better arguments." He poured himself another slug of whisky. "Only five of them, six at the most, in the whole world . . . It's in all the papers. It stinks up the water, kills the fish, and poisons the air. Didn't you read that story in the *Estado de São Paulo*? You can go to jail for that, in Italy." He puffed blue smoke into the air from the subversive but incomparable Cuban cigar.

Doctor Magnifico lowered his voice, although they were alone in a private room in the Lords' Retreat where there was no danger of listening ears or secret microphones, as there would have been in a spy story about Arab oil and arms smuggling with multinational master spies and fabulous sexy females.

"My friends are willing to bring other arguments to bear." The prissy, affected voice was now almost inaudible. "How much?"

The Young Politician thought for a minute, did imaginary sums on his fingers, hitched up the price and named his figure, a high one. Mirko shook his head.

"Half of that."

"Half? Not enough."

"Not a penny more." The voice became even more affected. "I know someone who'll do it for less."

"Oh, all right. It's a deal. After all, you can't believe anything you read in the papers, and with Julinho Mesquita being so hung up on democracy and all that crap you know the *Estado* is always going to be against everything we stand for anyway. They'll get it in the neck too, one of these days."

Mirko opened his briefcase and took out a checkbook.

"Make it out to bearer," advised the Young Politician, revealing his inexperience. Doctor Magnifico concealed a mocking smile.

The Young Politician took the check, walked over to the closet and put it in his jacket pocket. The two men poured themselves another shot and raised their glasses in a wordless toast, then set a date for a second meeting to be held in a few days, same time, same place. No site could have been more pleasant, discreet and appropriate in which to discuss matters of supreme importance to national development. The Young Politician clapped his hands, the door opened, and the girls came back. There was more to life than safeguarding Brazil's best interests, after all.

Mirkus the Magnificent did not accept the other man's generous offer to trade partners. Once would have to be enough for him; he had a date in Rio and had to catch a plane. The Young Politician lingered; he was in his element. Fish, water, crabs, seaweed . . . those things were vaguely up in the northeast somewhere. Did the northeast really exist, anyway, or was it just a subversive invention of leftist writers and filmmakers? The girl beside him was as fair as a Scandinavian. In the northeast lived a dark, inferior race. The Young Politician stretched and smiled, at peace with himself and his conscience.

As he was leaving, the deputy madam came to tell him goodbye. "Are you satisfied, *Diputado*, was everything all right?" The Young Politician, a new customer, not yet an habitué, thanked her and asked for news of Madame Antoinette.

"Oh, Madame is in Paris visiting her family. Did you know that Madame Antoinette is a French general's daughter? *La mère est de la Martinique. Très chic!*" She was trying out her French, practicing up for the day when she would take over the establishment from its present owner, when Tieta got tired of it and decided to move back to Agreste for good.

À propos of microphones and spies.

Just one quick word here, an apology. You've just read, a page or two back, that there was no danger of listening ears or secret microphones, as there would have been in a spy story about Arab oil and arms smuggling, with multinational master spies and their fabulously sexy female counterparts. It's the truth; there was none of that sort of thing in the Lords' Retreat, where Doctor Magnifico and the Young Politician held their secret rendezvous.

That's a serious shortcoming, I know. It weakens the plot, diminishes the drama and greatly limits the excitement and interest of my story. But what can I do? I have to stay within the bounds of this unambitious broadside whose action takes place in an underdeveloped country. It isn't my fault if the readers are disappointed to find no fierce sheiks, romantic Bedouins, or calculating spies of various nationalities and ideologies who belong to their own countries' secret services and the enemy's at the same time; no blond, poker-faced Englishmen, no potent Americans laying six broads at a time while the spunky little woman brings up the kids back home in Texas, no bearded Russians swallowing children sprinkled with vodka at a gulp. Much as I regret it, there's none of that kind of thing in this book at all, and I'm sorry. I have to make do with smiling front men and a few corrupt home-grown Brazilians.

As for Arabs, at least one of whom must appear in every best seller this year, the only one I can offer is Chalita, the toothless old lion of the desert, since the Turkish peddler was shot and met his death like the man and honest smuggler he was. I apologize again, but that's the best I can do.

Meanwhile, back in Agreste, a chapter full of news in which Tieta holds up old Zé Esteves as an example to emulate.

When Tieta returned to Agreste with her nephew Ricardo for the civic celebration of the new improvements in Tannery Square, she asked Leonora how her love affair was progressing. The girl smiled in embarrassment and took her protectress' hands in hers.

"Mama, I don't know what happened. Ascânio went out of town for two days to have a look at some public works, and when he came back he was changed. Just as excited about the tourists, just as nice as ever, but not holding back so much. He told me that now the Mayor's dead he's sure to be elected to the job, and then his whole situation will change. He was all worked up, not like himself at all. And you know what? He even kisses me now. Dona Perpétua caught us the other day. I'm so happy, Mama!"

"Well, it's about time. It looks like it won't be long before you try out the riverbank. You'll enjoy that; it'll be a new experience for you. You make the most of it while you can, because one of these days we'll have to pack our bags and skedaddle."

"Oh Mama, I'll die the day we do."

"No, you won't. No one ever died of love. What is it Barbozinha always says? 'Men and women have died, but not for love. It's love that keeps us alive.' "

Dear, devoted Carmô! With all her cleverness she had let Tieta lead her down the garden path. To keep Tieta from leaving earlier than she had planned, she had revealed to Ascânio that Leonora had been besmirched by a scoundrel. And Ascânio had reacted just as Tieta had hoped. As soon as he heard that, he had changed tactics immediately and started brazenly kissing and hugging. It wouldn't be long before he lost the last remnants of bashfulness, forgot his plans for marrying and setting up housekeeping, and concentrated on getting his sweetheart into bed. All's well that ends in bed.

Yes, bed was a panacea. Just look at her nephew Ricardo, who had almost gone crazy with fear and remorse, horrified at what he had done, thinking he had to give up his vocation, feeling like a leper doomed to eternal punishment for having lain with his aunt on a sandbank at Mangue Seco. And now that was all he wanted to do; he would have spent all day every day fucking if he could. Fiery, bedazzled youth, limitless potency, infinite desire, sweet, potent, fiery prick. A tempest, an earthquake, a festival! Any time, anywhere, on the dunes, swimming in the ocean, he would throw her down and mount her. Tieta was exhausted, bitten all over, sucked dry, wholly satisfied, like a playful girl on holiday or a leaping kid. A kid? No, an old nannygoat who had never known what a half-grown billygoat, an insatiable young animal, could be like. Ardent and demanding, gentle and exultant, Ricardo too had changed. He had forgotten his fear and buried his remorse, while his priestly vocation still burned brightly. He had discovered the goodness of God.

Late Saturday afternoon when the workmen went back to Saco, Ricardo went with them in Jonas' canoe. When he came back his young face was full of radiant serenity. Finding Tieta on the beach, offering herself in a bathing suit that didn't cover her so much as show her off, he looked away and informed her, "I'm going to sleep in Agreste tonight. Jonas is taking me in the canoe."

"But why tonight? In just a few days we'll have to go back for good. Most of the work's done now and the Skipper can see to the rest. After that we'll come back once in a while to spend the night. Why go back now? Are you tired of me already?"

"Don't say that even in fun. The thing is, I made my confession today and want to take communion tomorrow, and if I sleep here . . . I'll be back tomorrow without fail. Please let me go."

It was a plea, a supplication, a plaintive request in the tremulous voice of a boy divided between her and God, a goat in Tieta's pasture and a Levite in the temple. It would have taken only a word, a gesture, a look to make him stay beside her and keep him from the church and the sacrament. A boy, a Levite, a sinner who was one of the Elect, chaste and lascivious, vulnerable and strong, a child of God. And hers too, her godchild.

"Go on, then, and say a prayer to God for me too. I'll eat my heart out, though. You be sure and come back tomorrow."

She didn't want to think about how much she'd miss him when she started back to São Paulo in the *marineti*; that was when she'd really eat her heart out. No, it wouldn't be a matter of shedding a few tears and washing her cunt out with soap. Oh, my boychild, Levite of God! She had taught him all about love and the taste of a woman, all the delights and refinements, and made a man of him. When she went away Ricardo would seek in other arms, another breast, another lap the sensations, the exaltation, the joy he had learned at Mangue Seco. Tieta was shaken by a sudden rage. She made up her mind to stay in Agreste at least until the electricity came in. To enjoy that outpouring of delight, that stormy sea, that howling wind for just a few more weeks. Then she would leave him to God, free of fear and the perils of chastity that lead to sorrow, melancholy and evil. Tieta should know; she had been a victim of the conspiring, overpious old witches who stank of rancid spinsterhood, frustrated, bitter old maids who hated everyone else. That was what Perpétua had been like before she had married the Major.

On Sunday morning the punitive expedition came down the river in Elieser's motor launch, filling the beach with laughter, and then gathered before the newly built walls of Tieta's cottage. Some of the roofbeams were already in place, and handy Skipper Dário had carved the name she had chosen, INÁCIO'S CORRAL, on the trunk of a coconut palm. There was a chorus of praise for the absent seminarian when the Skipper explained that Tieta had Ricardo to thank for the building's being so far along.

Later on Antonieta heard Dona Carmosina's report as they walked over to the dunes.

"I told Ascânio what you had said about Leonora . . . all that business about engaged couples in the south, how they go off on trips and the pill and all that. . . ."

Tieta affected surprise and concern.

"You mean you told him Leonora's not a virgin? Goodness me, Carmô!" And then she quickly agreed, "Well, after all I guess he's better off knowing the truth. I appreciate it, Carmô. I bet it wasn't easy."

"That's putting it mildly. . . . But I'm glad I did it. I was afraid he'd break off with Leonora, give up all his plans and not ever want to see her again, but Ascânio fought down his prejudice, Tieta. I like him for that. He doesn't want her to know I told him, and that shows he's a gentleman."

Tieta nodded, laughing inwardly. She knew very well what the gentleman wanted. Now that there was no tiresome maidenhead in the way, Ascânio would try to get Nora into bed with him, exactly as Tieta had foreseen. If he had been in love and dreamed of engagement and marriage, he had given up that idea as soon as he had heard what had happened. There wasn't a man in Agreste who would marry a girl who had already been laid, but that didn't mean he was such a fool he'd throw her over when there was nothing to prevent him from taking her down to the river under the weeping willows on a moonless night. And then Leonora's problems would be solved. All she'd have to do would be to wash out her cunt and shed a few good-bye tears. Why the devil was Ricardo so late coming back, she wondered, staring fruitlessly up the river from atop the dune for a sign of Jonas' canoe. Maybe the altar boy had seen Dona Edna, that common trash with her eyes rolling in her head and brazen open mouth showing the tip of her tongue, in church at eight-o'clock mass.

"Are you mad at me, Tieta? If I did wrong to tell him, say so."

"No, Carmô, you did the right thing. I was just thinking about that no-good hound she was engaged to. Did you get a chance to talk to Elisa?"

No, Dona Carmosina had not talked to Elisa or tried to get her to drop that nonsensical idea of going to São Paulo with Tieta and dragging Astério along with her. She hadn't got her breath back after that painful talk with Ascânio and she needed time to recover before screwing up her courage to strike another blow. Elisa would be terribly disappointed, she knew, and she was bound to take it badly. Ascânio was made of sterner stuff; he had been tried and tested by his father's illness and Astrud's betrayal. Tieta would have to be patient for a while. Dona Carmosina would bring up the subject at the proper time, when Elisa broached it herself. Meanwhile, why not let the poor girl keep her São Paulo illusions for a few more days?

It was Astério, back in Agreste, who brought up the subject with Tieta. One evening he hung around the bar until he saw Perpétua going off to vespers with the seminarian and seized his chance.

"Sister, could I have a talk with you? It's something that concerns me directly, me and Elisa. But before I tell you what it is, I'll have to ask you to keep this conversation a secret."

"Go right ahead, Brother Astério, I can keep a secret. You don't know how many secrets I've got stashed away in this big bazoom of mine." She laughed merrily, content with life.

"It's about a notion Elisa's taken. If she hasn't told you about it already, she will. She's going to ask you to take us to São Paulo, and get me a job and give us a room in your apartment."

"Well, she hasn't actually said so, but she's hinted around. Would you like to go?"

"Good God, no!" He backpedaled, not wanting to hurt Tieta's feelings. "I mean, of course I'd like nothing better than to share your company; you're more than a sister, you've saved our lives. But I don't want to live in São Paulo. It would be no good for me at all. Elisa's anxious to leave here so we can do better, but I know it wouldn't work out. I'd rather be poor here than there."

"Brother, how right you are. You can be easy in your mind, though. I won't take you with me. It isn't the right place for you at all, and a woman's place is with her husband. If Elisa asks me, I'll get that idea out of her head right quick."

"Sister, I don't know how to thank you."

"Don't, then. Elisa's my own sister and I have a duty to watch over her and help you both all I can. But here, not there."

In her whole life Tieta had rarely seen anyone as happy as Astério after their talk. She regarded her brother-in-law affectionately.

"Look, Astério, you can't just let Elisa have her own way all the time. If she starts talking about São Paulo, you just tell her you don't want to go and that's final. You ought to keep your wife on a shorter rein."

"If I tell her that, it'll just set her against me. She'll stamp her foot and cry and nag about it all day long until I give in. How can I persuade her different?"

"Ask old Zé Esteves and he'll tell you how. You ask him how he taught Elisa's mother to mind him. Maybe he'll even lend you his quincewood staff. It's a good recipe, Brother Astério. Once is enough if you do it right. Mother Tonha never raised her voice to the old man but once. As for the São Paulo business, you just leave it to me."

That night Tieta had Ricardo in the hammock just as she had planned. In the hammock where the youth had desired and not known how to possess her, she sat astride him and was mounted by him, galloping through the night until daybreak. Trying not to breathe too hard, smothering their loving moans as they tried out the ypsilon Y. Oh, the wonderful ypsilon Y!

Of how the unblemished Ascânio Trindade bent with the wind and turned liar after a private interview with Doctor Magnifico and yielded to pride as a new day was dawning, thus committing two mortal sins at once.

After conferring with Dr. Mirko Stefano, Ascânio Trindade felt like a new man. In just one hour of sincere conversation the charismatic PR man had won the trust and admiration of the upright official, an honest man and a dreamer. Mirko showed him plans and blueprints drawn up by capable and imaginative architects, engineers and city planners, threw out numbers and esoteric formulas, and used magic words like organogram, know-how, input, labor pool, marketing, and status—Sant'Ana do Agreste would be raised to the status of an industrial center. Ascânio was swept off his feet.

As he told his visitor goodbye in the doorway of the two-story colonial mansion that housed the courthouse, Ascânio Trindade was metamorphosed into an impresario; or rather a statesman. Manager and administrator of a community headed toward a glorious future of prosperity and progress. A glorious future? No, a glorious present! Today he was only county clerk and acting mayor; but soon he would be mayor in his own right, with full powers bestowed on him by a vote which bade fair to be unanimous.

At one point in the conversation he thought he detected, in the tactful and sibylline words of the envoy of the firm's board of directors, a suspicious hint at payment for services rendered. He couldn't be sure, but to avoid any possible misunderstanding he made it quite clear that his support for the grandiose project was based exclusively on the higher interests of community and country. The pure and simple truth was that no unworthy sentiment, no base ambition moved him. It was sheer love for his birthplace and concern for its development that stirred him to enthusiasm as Dr. Mirko Stefano, consultant, polyglot and artful persuader, laid the project before him. He was worth listening to, indeed.

With his negotiating skill and knowledge of human nature, Doctor Magnifico knew how and when to retreat. There was a right time for everything. "Please, Your Honor, you mustn't misunderstand me. I only meant what direct or indirect compensation the township should receive for collaborating with the corporation. There would be expenses incurred, perhaps; certainly there would be services, grants of the necessary authorization to build an industrial complex of two large, adjoining factories in one of its districts. Mangue Seco, to be precise."

In addition to the direct benefits—a large amount in taxes, an increase in the gross per capita income, and new jobs—the company would undertake to provide certain necessary improvements; they would pave the road, for example. The company would put pressure on the state governor and the Communications Ministry if it had to. "Just between us, Your Honor, prestige is one thing our board of directors doesn't lack." A hotel would be built; there would soon be regular bus service and ferryboats on the river, not to mention the area around Mangue Seco, where the new factories would become the nucleus of a modern industrial zone with literally dozens of houses for workers, technical experts and managers. The company would be glad to do its fair share and more to make this dream of progress a reality, while asking nothing in return. Its distinguished board of directors was less interested in profits than in making its contribution toward a strong Brazil that would be worthy of its glorious mission in the world. More power to them!

Ascânio, hanging on Dr. Stefano's words, could see Agreste rise from its long slumber and take its place in the forefront of the communities in the central part of the state of Bahia. As in a vision, he saw smoke from the factory chimneys rising into the sky, making up with a vengeance for the smoke from the trains that hadn't come and had left Agreste parked off on a siding. In his mind's eye those smokestacks were bringing wealth to Agreste and a spark of pride to Ascânio's heart. In the vanguard of progress, in the lead in fact, never wearying of the struggle, was the dauntless young mayor.

By the end of his talk with the representative from the board of directors, when in the name of the township he authorized the corporation to study the possibilities of installing its factories on county land, Ascânio felt the stirrings of the old ambitions of his law-school days, when he had been engaged to Astrud: personal interest linked to noble civic sentiment. Personal, not petty or dishonest, interest.

He envisioned the possibility of riding the crest of Agreste's wave of progress to a brilliant career as administrator and politician, a career that would make him worthy of Leonora. Yes, a triumphant career that would give him credentials befitting the suitor of an heiress from one of the best families in São Paulo.

Until then he had thought of her as hopelessly above him and had lived in constant terror of their departure, and with it the end of their timid romance of expectant silences, hints and unfinished gestures. Now he had a horizon and a battlefield before him; no longer did he see himself as a lowly bureaucrat in an insignificant village in its death throes. As Doctor Magnifico had so poetically proclaimed, the first rays of a new day of progress for Agreste were dawning and great events were at hand.

What a shame he couldn't talk about the miracle to Leonora or anyone else. Dr. Mirko Stefano had insisted on the utmost discretion; total secrecy until he gave the word. Only after the conclusion of the preliminary studies, which had only just begun, would the corporation be in a position to make the auspicious news public. One careless word too soon might ruin everything.

While it was true that at first glance there seemed no doubt that Mangue Seco and the surrounding region of Sant'Ana do Agreste was the ideal site for the factories, the final recommendation depended on a full assessment of all the advantages and disadvantages, as well as a series of analyses running the gamut from the depths of the sea bottom at the Rio Real sandbar to the support of the township. Another team of experts would be coming right after Christmas. All that Dr. Stefano was asking of the mayor at this point, aside from the necessary authorization and Ascânio's goodwill, was to say nothing about their plans until the complex survey could be brought to a successful conclusion. Did the land on either side of the river belong to the township? Who were the owners? One very cogent reason for discretion was to avoid a land rush which would make the whole project economically unfeasible. So mum was the word for the present; the rockets and huzzahs would come later.

Of course they could count on Ascânio's cooperation, but keeping the matter quiet was something else again. "People around here are inquisitive," he explained, "and what they don't know they invent." The worst thing Ascânio could do would be to say nothing about the interview; there'd be all kinds of rumors then. Couldn't he hint at a tourist project? Most of the speculation tended that way; it was what Ascânio himself had believed.

This notion appeared to amuse Mirkus the Magnificent; in fact, he could not help laughing. Looking out at Agreste's peaceful streets through the second-floor window of the courthouse, he agreed jovially:

"A tourist project . . . oh, by all means. That's a good one, Your Honor. C'est drôle."

Ascânio did not ask the reason for the laughter, his illustrious visitor's air of jovial complicity or the French phrase. He helped roll up plans and blueprints, insert them into a long metal tube and fasten the elegant black executive briefcase. As he went out Dr. Mirko Stefano handed briefcase and tube to a heavyweight posted as a sentinel; the bulk of a revolver strapped to the man's belt was plainly visible. Another champion of identical build, height and scowl came running from the bar, where he had been having a beer with the driver. A gun showed inside his open jacket.

This time the PR man had brought nobody with him but his driver and the pair of cutthroats from Alagoas. To the dismay of

Osnar and Fidélio, who had witnessed the arrival, not a single Martian or girl from Ipanema got out of the station wagon, only the leader from outer space, the chauffeur and the two gun-packing bodyguards. Still, this was remarkable enough in itself to provoke comment. It was years since a weapon had been seen in the streets of Agreste except for the farmers' machetes on market day and Possidônio the Prophet's maledictions and curses, the former being the farmers' everyday working tool and the latter a threat to no one but the wicked world and the devil.

Besides being armed the two men were close-mouthed. The one who went to the bar to refresh himself kept his eyes glued to the courthouse door, where he had left his partner. Osnar didn't have the nerve to ask for news of Betty, Bebé to her friends, and reacted indignantly to Fidélio's joshing suggestion. "Why don't you mosey over and chew the fat with him awhile? Tell him about the Polack, get on his good side, find out what he's here for. Go on, you can do it."

"Why don't you go to hell?"

The scowling twosome climbed into the back seat of the station wagon with the documents. Doctor Magnifico gave Ascânio a hearty handshake and grinned at him as if they were old pals.

"So long, Your Honor. *Au revoir*, my dear fellow. Merry Christmas! And that reminds me: if you have no objection I'd like to send a few Christmas gifts for the poor children."

The station wagon roared off. The little knot of onlookers lingered for a while, gaping at Ascânio as he too stood lost in reverie, ruminating on what he had heard and dreaming of the beckoning promise of a new Agreste. Christmas gifts for the poor children! That was an auspicious beginning. Osnar went over to him.

"Well, Captain, what brought the astronaut here?"

Averse to lying, esteemed by all as an honest citizen who never told a lie, Ascânio suddenly found himself obliged to lie. Well, he would abandon those principles and say anything for the greater good of Agreste. He replied awkwardly, trying to sound natural:

"Why, he's a tourist promoter, what did you think?" He proffered one detail that he didn't think was a secret. "He's interested in buying land on Mangue Seco, in the coconut grove—"

"Land in the coconut grove? Why, hot shit, Captain Ascânio, that's going to raise an almighty ruckus. Nobody's ever been able to figure out who owns the place."

Not knowing what to reply, Ascânio caught sight of Leonora in Perpétua's doorway, looking across the courthouse square. He had promised to take her and Tieta swimming in Catherine's Basin, and it was now time. He hurriedly took his leave and retreated in confusion.

Osnar smelled a rat. Now why was the county clerk acting so peculiar? Ascânio was hiding a nigger in the woodpile and no mistake. Tourist promotion, big money, big news . . . What if those guys bought up the coconut grove and all of Mangue Seco? What if they set up an exclusive club reserved for members? No, that was one thing they couldn't do. The beaches belonged to everybody. The people had an inalienable right to them, didn't they? Maybe they'd buy land and build modern hotels and shops . . . and yes, maybe Bebé would come and spend a few days under the coconut trees to see for herself what a tourist attraction the dunes could be. She could direct a publicity campaign. "Take advantage of our amazing offer. Come screw on Mangue Seco's snow-white beaches and pay later on the low monthly installment plan." Even if she wasn't a Polack, Betty seemed pretty enterprising to him.

Of the inauguration of a plaza with speeches and dancing, a chapter awash with euphoria.

At five in the afternoon of the last Sunday before Christmas, virtually the entire population of Agreste, except for the small fry who were cheering the matinee at the moviehouse, had turned out in old Tannery Square, henceforth to be known as Modesto Pires Plaza. The garden and the path that encircled it, the obelisk in the middle and the stone pavement, all embellishments planned and executed by Ascânio Trindade, reaped a harvest of praise.

"You can't keep Ascânio down."
"Just wait till he's really mayor!"
"He'll turn Agreste into a garden."

A wooden stand had been erected for the ceremony and the folklore pageant, and a concrete plaque covered with a Brazilian flag had been affixed to the obelisk. On the street corner, on a wall of the house Laerte the tanner rented from Perpétua, was a metal plaque, also covered with a flag. It was a pity that the "Second of July Lyric Orchestra" had been disbanded thirty years before after the death of Maestro Jocafí, who had conducted the musicians with an iron hand for more than half a century. Ascânio dreamed of reviving the little orchestra, which had once been famous in every corner of Bahia and Sergipe. The stumbling block was finding someone to direct it; no one in the township had ever flourished a conductor's baton.

Majestic and smiling as a real queen, or, to plagiarize Barbozinha the poet's more exalted image, a madonna transported from the Renaissance to the Agreste sandhills, Dona Antonieta Esteves Cantarelli, patroness of the new plaza, advanced toward the simple monument on Colonel Artur da Tapitanga's arm, followed by Ascânio Trindade, Modesto Pires, Dona Aida and their daughter Marta and son-in-law, the engineer from Petrobras. An attentive silence ensued and necks were craned. Dona Antonieta reached out her hand and pulled a green-and-yellow ribbon to unveil the concrete plaque inscribed with the commemorative date and the name of Colonel Artur de Figueiredo, acting mayor emeritus. Applause greeted the brief but touching ceremony. Perpétua fished out a black handkerchief from her black skirt pocket and wiped away a tear—a black mourning tear, murmured the irreverent Aminthas in Dona Carmosina's ear, saying it was his day for black humor.

The children from the grammar school tore into the national anthem. There were huzzahs for the Colonel, who acknowledged them with a wave. He was about to burst with satisfaction on Tieta's arm: the little mountain goat had fleshed out into a prime-quality nannygoat, with nice round teats that she liked to show off. Ah, if he were only young again!

Zé Esteves, gleeful at the prospect of moving into his new residence any day now, raised his shepherd's staff and his voice.

"Hooray for my daughter, Mrs. Antonieta Esteves Cantarelli!"

General excitement, one more tear from Perpétua, Elisa radiantly smiling like a movie star, and Leonora, the most excited of all, leading the cheering. Why weren't they cheering for Ascânio Trindade?

Applause for Dona Aida, to whom had fallen the honor of unveiling the plaque on the corner wall with the name of the refurbished public park: Modesto Pires Plaza (Distinguished Citizen).

"Three cheers for Modesto Pires!" shouted Laerte the tanner

from the doorway where he stood with his wife and two children, brown-nosing his boss.

Dona Preciosa and Dona Auta Rosa, principal and vice-principal of the town grammar school, had their hands full with the few undisciplined pupils they had been able to corral and drag into the plaza. It had not been easy to round up even that handful at vacation time, much less keep them in line. "Come on, you little rascals, it's time to sing the national anthem!" Blond, pretty, short-tempered Auta Rosa had more than one unconditional admirer among her pupils. Dona Preciosa, with her drill sergeant's bark and the wart on her nose, imposed discipline by main force.

"One, two, three, go!"

The Brazilian anthem rose over the square and the nearby houses on the voices of the children and others in the crowd. "If no one shouts hurrah for Ascânio, I swear I'll cheer him myself!" Leonora threatened under her breath, disgusted at such ingratitude.

Now it was Father Mariano's turn, with chivalrous, pious Ricardo in red and white as acolyte. "God bless you!" sighed Dona Edna, standing beside her putative husband Terto. Cinira's eyes were fastened on the altar boy, and she felt a familiar itching in her private parts. Tieta, too, contemplated her nephew and smiled. She had no fear of rivals; her only rival was God, and they had made a pact: his soul was for God and his body for his pious aunt.

Father Mariano blessed the garden, the obelisk, the plaza and all those present. Special blessings were bestowed on our illustrious leader, Colonel Artur de Figueiredo, on our eminent fellow townsman Modesto Pires, and on the generous, exemplary lamb of our parish, Dona Antonieta Esteves Cantarelli, and her lovely stepdaughter. "May they be blessed with God's never-failing grace, amen." Ricardo held out the stoup of holy water to the Reverend Father, and sacred drops were sprinkled on the nearest heads. Perpétua stepped forward to receive her share.

Next the engineer from Petrobras, Dr. Pedro Palmeira, spoke a few words of thanks on behalf of his father-in-law, praising the peace and beauty of Agreste and hoping it would never be embroiled in the horrors of a world of violence, pollution and war. With his black beard and modish long hair, he too aroused his share of longing looks, desire and frustration. Beside him stood his vigilant wife, who had been born and raised in Agreste and knew what was going on.

Ascânio Trindade spoke last, on behalf of Colonel Artur da Tapitanga, whose voice could no longer rise to the heights of oratorical figures of speech. Carried away and finding inspiration in Leonora's eyes, he prophesied great and glorious days for Agreste at an early date. His esteemed fellow citizens could congratulate themselves. The end of apathy, poverty and backwardness was just around the corner. There was a real possibility that Agreste would be the hub of a new industrial axis a-building in the state of Bahia, a rival to the great Aratu Industrial Center on the outskirts of the capital. "The days of plenty will return! We'll be able to hold up our heads with pride again. Our beloved corner of the world will shine like a gleaming star on the map of Brazil."

"What the devil is Captain Ascânio up to?" muttered Osnar. "He's holding out on us, I tell you."

"Oh, I don't think so. He doesn't want to give away the tourist-promotion scheme, that's all," said Dona Carmosina. "They seem to have made some pretty ambitious plans."

"But he said something about a hub of industry."

"He didn't mean it literally. You can't deny that tourism is an industry these days, and very big business, too," Dona Carmosina explained. "You've got to remember Ascânio's in love."

"He's got it bad, all right," Aminthas chimed in.

Ascânio closed his fiery and confused oration with a ringing shout of "Hail to Sant'Ana do Agreste!" From the other side of Modesto Pires Plaza came the *cachaça*-blurred voice of Goatstink with the right cheer at last:

"Hooray for Ascânio Trindade and his pretty li'l gal! When's the weddin', Ascânio?"

Leonora colored at the teasing laughter of Elisa and Dona Carmosina. With the speeches over at last, the young men and women paired off, fingers entwined, and circled the plaza, inaugurating it in earnest. Leonora looked at Ascânio and held out her hand. One more pair of lovers strolled around the plaza. Touched, Dona Carmosina sighed. From Laerte the tanner's house came a bevy of impromptu waitresses, the tannery girls, carrying trays of pastry, meat pies and cordials which they offered to the guests of honor, courtesy of Modesto Pires.

Colonel Artur da Tapitanga sat down on one of the green iron benches and confided to Antonieta, as he patted her hand and inspected her rings (were those diamonds real ones or paste? If they were real they were worth a fortune), "All this tourist foolishness is addling my godson Ascânio's brain. Do you know he came out to the fazenda the other day with a crazy song and dance about setting up factories and building a city out at Mangue Seco? He's gone plumb soft in the head if you ask me, and it's all your stepdaughter's fault." Then, changing the subject, "You still haven't been out there to visit with me and see my goats. That flock of mine is a mighty pretty sight, if I do say so. You come and bring the little gal with you. I just bought me a fine big ram you'll want to see. Paid a mint of money for him, but he's worth it; name's Branding Iron."

That night the Wise Men's Pageant and the *bumba-meu-boi*, the comic-dramatic pageant of the death and resurrection of an ox, were performed on the dais. There were three sets of Wise Men and shepherds on their way to Bethlehem, the third and best, "The Easter Sun," from Rocinha. A dozen dancing shepherdesses decked out in colored tissue paper and carrying red and blue lanterns sang at the tops of their lungs:

> "Shepherdesses from afar we come
> From the starry skies of the East
> To greet the little Lord God of love
> Lying among the beasts."

Remembering the barefoot girl who had sneaked out of her house to run after the dancers as they paraded through the streets of Agreste, Tieta was all at once overwhelmed with emotion as she followed each move of the Epiphany pageant. She had longed so to carry a lantern and be a shepherdess of the stars! But she had had nothing but goats and kids to herd all her life. It was worth coming back to hear and see this.

> "Shepherdesses of the moon and the sun
> The moon and the sun and the afterglow."

And to watch Valdemar Coto's *bumba-meu-boi* with its ox and hobgoblin and the cowboy on his horse, all dancing on the platform and chasing the small fry around the square. The one-armed, one-legged hobgoblin, a merry and fleet-footed ghost in a fluttering white sheet, ran to Antonieta and asked for her blessing; it was young Sabino. Then the *bumba-meu-boi* and the Wise Men with their cortège made their way down the main street of town, stopping at each door to greet those within and ask for permission to enter. After singing and dancing in the parlor in honor of the householders, they all partook of homemade cordials, beer and *cachaça*: cowboy, ox, hobgoblin and shepherdesses of the afterglow.

An improvised orchestra hired by the municipality—Claudionor das Virgens' accordion, Natalino Preciosidade's mandolin, and Lírio Santiago's guitar—took its place on the dais in chairs from Laerte's house and struck up a medley of dance tunes for every taste. The couples soon stepped out.

"Look who's dancing!" Astério pointed to Osnar, whose ape-like arms were clutching a flushed little country girl in a short skirt that displayed her stout legs.

"Shameless beast!" grumbled Dona Carmosina, furious because, alas, she was not the lucky creature pressed against the bosom of the shameless beast.

The impromptu hop grew more lively, with more and more couples whirling on the dais. The mandolin wept invitingly. Leonora looked at Ascânio, who smiled. She murmured in a voice like ice crystals melting, "Oh, do let's dance."

They walked up the steps to the platform as the accordion launched into a carnival march. Leonora glided into the rhythm, her eyes half-closed. Ascânio guided the girl's slender figure pressed against his own, feeling her warm breath on his cheek and her loose hair touching his face, thinking that it was a glorious night. Soon everyone was dancing in the square. Dr. Pedro, the engineer from Petrobras, and his wife Dona Marta joined the fun. With her husband's consent, Dona Edna stepped out with Seixas. Too bad for him if he played the fool and said no; broadmindedness and courtesy were the least Dona Edna expected of her husband. Seixas embraced her tightly and she thrust one thigh forward, more lasciviously every time they spun around. Get in the groove when you find one, Osnar always said, and Seixas took him at his word.

Grave and ceremonious, Barbozinha held out the tips of his fingers to Tieta. "May I have the pleasure of this square dance?" With that Elisa nudged Astério, and Dona Carmosina brought Aminthas up to the mark.

"Why don't you invite me to dance, you rude thing!"

"Come on, then, Elizabeth Taylor, but have mercy on my feet."

"Cretin!"

The Epiphany cortèges had returned to the square and mingled with the others on the dais. Fidélio was dancing with the standard-bearer from the Eastern Sun on the trail of the afterglow. The ox, the hobgoblin and the cowboy on his dark chestnut mount ran after a band of children led by Peto. Ricardo had stayed at home to keep his mother company. After they had said the rosary together he would wait in the hammock for his aunt.

Goatstink, having exhausted the available supply of *cachaça*, staggered out of the plaza, where things were livelier every minute and the dancing had caught fire.

"Hot diggity! Gonna be lively down by the river in a little while!" He steadied himself on his tottering legs. "Come on, Ascânio, be a man and jump in with both feet!"

As he staggered off and disappeared down an alley, his de-praved, mock-moralizing voice could still be heard.

"Better be careful, Terto, or you'll pull out those new electric-light wires with your horns."

Since no one ever pays any attention to what Goatstink has to say, both warning and suggestion were lost in the music of the accordion, mandolin and guitar, in the fun of the celebration, in the carefree Agreste night.

From hellfire to earthfire, an exciting chapter in which Tieta bursts into flame.

Ricardo the seminarian, newly free of the torments of Hell, was consumed with the flames of jealousy on that festive night. Punctu-ally at nine o'clock the generator went off and the dancing in Tannery Square (sorry, Modesto Pires Plaza) broke up, but Dona Carmosina thought a stroll down by the river, a sort of nocturnal picnic, would be fun. They stopped by Seu Manuel's bar to stoke up on beer, *guaraná* and the codfish balls that were a Lusitanian spe-cialty of the Portugee's.

From the hammock where he lay waiting, the seminarian heard the group on the sidewalk and recognized the voices of Leonora, Aminthas, Barbozinha being gallant (didn't the old boy know how silly he sounded?) and Tieta's laugh. He thought they would all say goodnight at the door, but the footsteps went on around the plaza and the sound died away without anyone's entering the house. Ricardo sprang from the hammock, rushed to the master bedroom, flung open the window over the side street, and saw the jolly group just turning the dark corner on its way to the river. He felt outraged, betrayed, and miserable.

As for Tieta, she would have liked nothing better than to go home. She was tired out from the long day of festivities, which had begun with an eight-o'clock mass and a long sermon by Father Mariano. When he caught sight of this magnanimous lamb among the faithful, the grateful Reverend Father had outdone himself with generous servings of Latin and quotations from the Bible. Tieta was hungry for her boy and his violent tenderness; she had seen him for only a minute during the ceremony that afternoon, looking so fine in his acolyte's robes, offering the aspergillum to the priest. Selfish Perpétua, indifferent to folklore and thinking only that she had to pray her daily rosary, had obliged her son to stay home and keep her company. Tieta's thoughts as she twirled about in the arms of Barbozinha, Osnar and Fidélio—everyone wanted to dance with her—were on Ricardo, kneeling before the family shrine and toiling through the rosary with Perpétua. She had a foolish vision of herself entwined with her nephew, still dressed in his cassock as they glided over the dance floor, romantic and very much in love, like Leonora and Ascânio. The girl's eyes had been half-closed and her head had rested on the young man's shoulder.

Tieta had seconded Dona Carmosina's idea and gone with the group in the hope that she could quickly break up the party and leave Leonora and Ascânio alone, free to exchange kisses and vows of eternal love. In Catherine's Basin, under the black canopy of the willow trees, this silly love affair might finally take the turn that Mama wanted it to take—ardent coupling and less sentimental nonsense.

They sat down on the rocks. Osnar wielded the bottle opener, Dona Carmosina undid the parcel of codfish balls, and they ate, drank and chatted under the stars. Ascânio and Leonora, hand in hand and smiling foolishly, were oblivious to the world around them. Tieta jumped up impatiently.

"I'm so tired I'm ready to drop. What do you say we—"

She wasn't given time to propose that they leave the sweethearts where they were and go their separate ways, the sleepyheads to bed, the midnight hunters to the dark streets. Barbozinha, who was standing next to her, pointed off toward town and remarked:

"What's that light over there? It looks like a fire."

It didn't only look like a fire, it was one. Great tongues of flames leaped up, burning a hole of light in the blackness.

"It *is* a fire!" shouted Aminthas.

"Where do you suppose it is?"

Ascânio stood up; he had a map of the town in his head.

"Down in the Hollow."

"Oh, my God!" Dona Carmosina moaned.

The Hollow was home to the poorest of the poor, the dispossessed, the beggars, drunks who couldn't find work, old men who dragged themselves along and whined for a crust of bread in the downtown streets.

"Come on, let's go!" Ascânio helped Leonora to her feet.

Tieta was on her way without waiting to be urged. One night long ago, from a cozy nook in Catherine's Basin with a traveling salesman, she had heard shouts and seen big flames leaping up. By the time they got to the place where the fire was, the flames had burned Dona Paulina's house to the ground and snuffed out the lives of three of the widow's five children, the youngest ones. Fires in Agreste were rare, but when there was one it invariably left victims because there was no fire-fighting equipment or any way to put it out.

The picnic broke up and the group followed on Tieta's heels, but she soon broke into a run and rapidly outdistanced them. Townspeople appeared at every corner, attracted by the sinister brightness in the sky.

Tieta was among the first to reach the Hollow. She saw that one of the houses, which luckily stood apart from the rest, was enveloped in flames. A few neighbors were standing in a circle around a corpulent girl who was crying and tearing her hair.

"She's gonna burn up, oh, poor Grandma, she's gonna die!"

Goatstink, swaying on tottery legs, explained in a thick voice that Marina Grossa Tripa, or Thickguts, washerwoman by profession and cut-rate trollop when she could find a customer, had been awakened by fire in the house and had run out the door, forgetting that her grandmother, old Miquelina, was asleep in the back room. What with the blaze eating away at the old wood and the coconut fronds of the roof, the old lady, who was scarcely able to walk, must surely be burned to a crisp by now.

Twenty or so neighbors and curious onlookers stood and watched the spectacle of the granddaughter yelling and beseeching somebody for the love of God to save her poor old grandmother, the only relation she had in the world. No one offered to do so. If Thickguts herself, whose obligation it was as a granddaughter, wasn't crazy enough to run through the fire into that inferno, she could hardly expect somebody else to do it for her. They tried to console her by pointing out that Grandma Miquelina had already lived a very long time—in fact, no one knew for certain how old she was, but plenty old enough to have had her share of good times and bad. Why not let her rest? What was the sense of running a mortal risk in a probably useless attempt to prolong her life for a few months, a few weeks, a few days?

Heedless of the neighbors' arguments and without waiting to hear the end of Goatstink's explanation, Tieta dashed headlong toward the fire, deaf to shouts and warnings. By the time Osnar and Aminthas came around the corner she had just disappeared into the flames. Men, women and children ran up from all directions, summoned by the church bell tolling out its tale of misfortune and death.

The hubbub increased when Leonora appeared, escorted by Ascânio and followed by Dona Carmosina with distress written all over her face.

"Dona Antonieta's gone inside!"

When she realized that Tieta had gone into the heart of the fire, Leonora let go of her sweetheart's hand and tried to follow her; but Aminthas caught her in time and Ascânio turned pale and clasped her in his arms.

The roof fell in and a huge flame leaped up, scattering thousands of crackling sparks. Ricardo, barefoot and in his cassock, ran all the way across town in time to see Tieta emerge from the flames, carrying in her arms the tiny form of Miquelina, alive, unharmed, and spitting with rage at her heartless, unfeeling beast of a granddaughter who had left her there to die—"You ain't no kin to me, you heartless hussy!" The fire had respected the cot where she was lying until someone came to get her and then burned it to ashes with a single lick of flame. Fire climbed up Tieta's dress and her curly head flaunted an aureole, a halo, a splendid glow of fire.

Such were the general astonishment and terror that the bystanders were struck motionless and dumb. Only Goatstink seemed to retain the faculty of reason and the use of his hands. He ran up with a pail full of water and flung it over Tieta.

Of a popular ballad and a highfalutin poem.

When Ricardo saw her stretched out on a sheet, her hair scorched and her legs and arms a mass of ugly burns, he swallowed a sob but could not hold back a tear. Mingled with its salt was the taste of pride. When everyone else obeyed Dr. Cáio Vilasboas' command to leave the room so that Tieta could get some rest, her nephew remained to stand guard and hear her say, "Come give me a kiss."

If the affair of the Paulo Afonso Power Plant, whose wires and pylons were swiftly approaching town, had made a distinguished citizen out of Antonieta Esteves Cantarelli and assured her an unparalleled place in the annals of Agreste, her daring feat in saving old Miquelina, abandoned by her granddaughter to her fate and left to die by the curious onlookers watching the fire, had elevated her to the rank of a saint. She would be enthroned on the high altar of the cathedral beside Our Lady St. Anne just as Modesto Pires, one of the first to visit her next day, had foreseen.

Poets are always right; they have the gift of divination. Gregório Eustáquio de Matos Barbosa, the seer De Matos Barbosa, praised for his verses in the literary columns of Bahia, well known in the literary cafés of the capital and an old admirer of Tieta's, composed an ode exalting her beauty and courage; her dazzling beauty, her indomitable courage. In richly rhymed verses of classical purity, he compared her to the warrior and saint who had taken up arms to save France and braved the bonfire with a smile on her lips. Joan of Arc of the *sertão*, he wrote, intrepid and victorious over fire and darkness, defying the inferno and plucking life from death.

Oddly enough the balladeer Claudionor das Virgens, taking the fire as a theme for his clothesline doggerel, had also canonized Tieta in halting verse:

TIETA

When she heard the granddaughter shout
The old lady was still inside
She caught fire but she brought her out
And set her down on the ground
With heart so brave and face so bright
St. Tieta of the sertão.

All day long there was a crowd at the door, asking for news and delivering messages, hugs and tokens of friendship. At the head of the bed next to Leonora sat Barbozinha the poet, a once-fine figure of a man, faded and rheumatic but still true to the passion of his youth, reciting the ode that proclaimed her a saint. At the foot of the bed, next to Elisa, was her nephew Ricardo, tender and robust, longing to kiss each burn, beg forgiveness for his resentful thoughts and take her in his arms. Peto brought a flower he had picked in the woods.

Lying there in Dr. Fulgêncio and Dona Eufrosina's double bed with its imperishable memories of Lucas, between the worn poet and the ardent seminarian, listening to the hum of people in the square speaking her name with praise, Tieta, the saint with heart so brave and face so bright, intrepid Joan of Arc of the backlands, was rocked on a sea of love.

FOURTH EPISODE

⁂

Of Christmas
and
New Year's Festivities
and
the Esteves Matriarchy

WITH SANTA CLAUS COMING DOWN FROM HEAVEN IN A
HELICOPTER, POEMS THAT PRAISE AND OTHERS THAT CURSE,
A TE DEUM MASS AND SKYROCKETS, A CRY OF WARNING
WHICH ALARMS THE COMMUNITY, AN INSTRUCTIVE DEBATE IN
THE PRESS ON THE PERILS AND ADVANTAGES, THE BENEFIC
AND MALEFIC EFFECTS OF THE TITANIUM-DIOXIDE INDUSTRY,
AS POSTERS AND A REAL-ESTATE MARKET MAKE THEIR
APPEARANCE IN AGRESTE AND THE IMPORTANCE OF THE
SURNAME ANTUNES IS MADE PLAIN——OF THE RITES OF DEATH
AND THE AFFLICTIONS OF LIFE.

In which Santa Claus pays his first visit to Agreste.

Ascânio Trindade, sitting behind the desk in the mayor's office, studied the program of festivities he had drawn up for the day the electric power would be switched on. The program would have to be submitted to the Town Council and duly approved at its next session. According to the engineers' calculations the line would reach Agreste in a month or so, and Ascânio meant to hold the bang-up celebration the event deserved. This power line from the Paulo Afonso Falls was the community's first symbolic step on the road back to prosperity. You never could tell; maybe someone besides the engineers would turn up for the ceremony—one of the company directors, or a big wheel in state politics or the federal government. And this would be the first step up as well for the young administrator and future mayor, the first rung up the ladder of what promised to be a brilliant career. All this called for celebration on a grand scale, the kind they used to have in the old days, when whole caravans of tycoons and politicians had come all the way to Agreste for the speeches, banquets, balls, and fireworks, and the people danced in the streets.

Where was he going to get the money to pay for it? The community coffers were empty, as usual, and Ascânio would once again have to go down his list and hustle contributions. Colonel Artur de Figueiredo, landowner, raiser of goats, planter of manioc and corn, Town Council president, and undisputed political boss for the past fifty years, always headed the lists, followed by Modesto Pires, wealthy citizen and now a public square. Those were the only two donors worth bothering about; the names of the others only revealed the parlous state of trade and the pitiful decline of the community in general.

Ascânio was determined, nevertheless, to throw an unforgettable party for the town on the night when the dazzling light from the Paulo Afonso Power Plant took over from the feeble light of the weary generator his grandfather had brought in as mayor. Maybe he could even, finally, at this time of general rejoicing, speak to the lovely Leonora Cantarelli, ask for her hand in marriage and be declared officially engaged. Ever since his return from Rocinha on horseback, when he had swallowed the bitter draught Dona Carmosina had given him to drink and resigned himself to the loss of the girl's maidenhead, Ascânio had been going around in a state of permanent exaltation. Once his prejudice had been trampled underfoot and reduced to a dull, barely noticeable ache, an evil thought that he repressed immediately whenever it cropped up, his love had overflowed in a passion of tenderness for the innocent victim of a monstrous seducer. The intimacy between the two had grown as well; prolonged, repeated kisses marked their comings and goings, kindling desire for each other and adding another and greater dimension to their love.

Ascânio hoped he could count on the stepmother's goodwill when he did propose, that she would be touched by the tributes she would receive at the ceremony. One of the items on Ascânio's program called for giving the name of the prodigal daughter to the road over which Jairo's *marineti* came into town and by which the power lines of progress—Tieta's Light, as the people had christened it—would also have to pass. This road, called Mud Lane from time immemorial, would now be formally named for Dona Antonieta Esteves Cantarelli, Distinguished Citizen. The plaque was already on order from Bahia. Although the town councilmen had not been informed of the plan, surely none of them would be so ungrateful as to oppose it. This time Ascânio had not forgotten the "Esteves" demanded by Dona Perpétua and the old man, who was insufferably high and mighty these days. But where was the money for the banquet, the ball, the music, the pennants, the streamers and the fireworks to come from? And the money for the paving stones, for that matter? There was someone who might be willing to help underwrite the cost of the festivities if he should happen to come around: Dr. Mirko Stefano, the entrepreneur who was interested in setting up an industrial plant near Mangue Seco and was therefore a legitimate representative of the forces of progress. After the interview at which he had explained some of his plans and shown

Ascânio some blueprints, the VIP had promised to return in a few days. Ascânio's hopes were pinned to that fascinating individual. All things seemed easy to Mirko; he was like an Arabian Nights genie conjured up by Aladdin's lamp. Now if Mirkus the Magnificent would only turn up . . .

And lo and behold! He did turn up, like a smiling all-powerful genie, dropping out of the sky in the company of Santa Claus. The great metallic roc buzzed the courthouse, the cathedral, and the new park with a hideous grating noise. The rustic eyes and ears of the townspeople of Agreste had never heard nor beheld a hallucination like this.

The sun shone brightly and a gentle breeze blew in from the Atlantic. It was a beautiful day, like most summer days in the dry *sertão*. At midmorning the town was shaken from its somnolence by a strange noise that soon turned into a roar. Peto ran out into the street staring up at the sky, recognized the thing and announced that it was a helicopter, a machine never before seen in Agreste but which Peto had often admired in the magazines Dona Carmosina let him look at down at the post office. Shopkeepers came to their doors. In the deserted bar, Seu Manuel left off his uncongenial task of rinsing out glasses and exclaimed, "I'll be—!" Ascânio, interrupted by the frightening noise, left his mooning and doodling and went over to the window in time to see the craft alight in the middle of the square between the courthouse and the cathedral. Father Mariano and his pious female attendants appeared at the top of the steps, crossing themselves in dismay.

Out of the helicopter, its engines still running and its propellers spinning slowly, to the wonder of the first open-mouthed rubes who went near it, descended Doctor Magnifico, sportily dressed in jeans and a colorful Hawaiian beach shirt with a splashy print of sensual women and exotic flowers. And then Santa Claus himself hopped down, the cutest little Santa ever seen; for who should be wearing a long white beard and bright-red suit but that smashing executive secretary, our old acquaintance Miss Elisabeth Valadares, Betty to her coworkers, Bebé to her intimate friends. A really good secretary can do anything in a pinch, even turn herself into Santa Claus on Christmas Eve if Doctor Magnifico, the inventive genie of the titanium lamp, asks her to nicely.

When he saw the helicopter, Santa Claus, and Mirko showing a bemused Leôncio the cargo stowed away in the interior of the air-craft, Ascânio let out a triumphant yell, a resounding hooray, before he could stop himself. Doctor Magnífico looked up and waved to the county clerk with both hands.

"I made a point of bringing the Christmas presents for the poor children personally," explained the magician, with a warm double handshake for Ascânio, who had bounded down the steps four at a time to greet the visitors and give them the welcome they deserved.

Leaving Santa Claus in charge of supervising the transfer of a quantity of gaudy little colored sacks from the belly of the aircraft to the courthouse basement, a gratifying task which crippled Leôncio performed with surprising alacrity, Mirkus the Magnificent drew the young official aside for a word or two in private. All he wanted to say was that the results of the technical studies on Mangue Seco were highly satisfactory so far.

Oh, there were richer locations in the running, with better communications and other facilities, such as Valença on the coast near Salvador, the ports of Ilhéus and Itabuna to the south, and even Arembepe on the outskirts of the capital itself, all vying for preference and offering all sorts of inducements to persuade the great corporation to choose one of them as the site. But the board of directors leaned toward Agreste, and Mirko flattered himself that he had some small part in influencing them. He had, himself, been captivated by the beauty and climate of the place and the friendly people.

Impressed, almost moved, in fact, Ascânio drank in the fair promise of these words and wondered aloud whether it was still necessary to keep it a secret. Now that a helicopter had landed with a load of presents it would be difficult, well-nigh impossible, to hide the truth any longer.

In a French vein that day, Mirkus the Magnificent nodded.

"*Alors, mon cher ami* . . . You can tell them this much: that there is a prospect of bringing into the district, in the vicinity of Mangue Seco beach, two integrated factories belonging to Brastânio —Brazilian Titanium, S.A. Actually, it's not only possible, it's probable."

He went on to explain that the final decision was still pending until the last surveys were completed and certain adjustments could be made.

"We're still in the initial stages, and there are several possible locations, as I've already told you. Agreste's chances are very good, though. *Personnellement, je suis pour* . . . but the decision does not rest entirely with *votre serviteur.*"

He lifted both arms in a rhetorical gesture to give emphasis to his grandiloquent words. "If Brastânio comes to Agreste it will transform this community into a great industrial center pulsating with power and vitality—*magnifique!*"

Ascânio hastened to strengthen Agreste's hand with the news that in a very few days, a month at the most, they would have electric power from the Paulo Afonso Falls to offer Brastânio. The mayor's office hoped to organize a really bang-up celebration to mark the dawn of a new day, but because of the Franciscan poverty in which they still—

Doctor Magnifico did not let him finish; he begged for details of the celebration and asked specifically how much it would cost. That very morning Ascânio had gone over his calculations several times and now timidly translated them into *contos de reis.* A hefty sum to him was a trifle to Dr. Mirko Stefano, whose expense account and cash contingency fund were practically inexhaustible. With a gesture he set Ascânio's mind at rest on what had been his main worry, the paving of the street, the biggest expense and the one indispensable one.

"Leave that to me; I'll see that the street is paved. Brastânio will be proud to contribute toward making the celebration a success. As soon as the Christmas holidays are over we'll have one last talk to synchronize our watches and get set to go. At least I surely hope so."

Ascânio wasn't sure whether he meant the factory ground-breaking or the celebration of Tieta's Light.

"Er, get set for what?"

"Why, get set to put Agreste on the road to progress and prosperity!" His warm, optimistic voice inspired confidence. "As for your fiesta to celebrate the light's being turned on, Brastânio will be responsible for paving the street and will take care of all the other expenses too. We'll be honored to have a part in the celebration, and I'll try to be here if I can. Brastânio's supreme goal is to serve. Brazil *über alles,* you know." When money was the subject, Doctor Magnifico relinquished diplomatic French in favor of more down-to-earth languages like German and English. "*Auf wiedersehen*. Merry Christmas, my dear fellow."

The crowd in Judge Oliva Square was growing larger. Peto, self-appointed ambassador of the children of Agreste, approached the helicopter, engaged the pilot in conversation, grinned at Betty Santa Claus and offered to help her unload the packages. He gave one or two of them a curious squeeze and felt dolls, little tin cars, two-bit stuff for the small fry. He wasn't interested. He'd be thirteen before long, a teenager, and Osnar would be taking him hunting for the first time.

Standing in the doorway of the courthouse with Ascânio, Mirkus the Magnificent gazed around at the old houses on the square and the poor people gawking at the helicopter and remarked, "Mark my words: with Brastânio here, you'll be seeing skyscrapers before long!"

Ascânio was overwhelmed. Might the angels say amen to those blessed words! He could think of nothing he wanted more. On an impulse he turned his handshake into a grateful and hearty *abrazo*.

"Well, Doctor, ever so many thanks. I'll be waiting for you."

"I'll be back right after New Year's."

Before she got into the helicopter, Santa Claus gathered the poor children's precocious representative to her bosom, though he was neither very poor nor very much of a child, and kissed him on the cheek. What soft, warm lips, what sweet-smelling breath—yummy! Peto kissed her back and snuggled up close, feeling the pressure of her breasts bobbing under the red satin tunic.

The aircraft was full of little sacks just like the ones that had been stored on the ground floor of the courthouse, where the Town Council met when Colonel Artur da Tapitanga decided to call a meeting, which wasn't often unless Ascânio, that stickler for rules, pushed him into doing it. Meetings were a waste of time anyway, since the council unanimously approved whatever the Colonel had decided, just the way Congress rubber-stamps the president.

The propellers whirled faster and the helicopter rose and buzzed off to sea. Mirko was on his way to Valença, Ilhéus and Itabuna, spreading Christmas cheer in Brastânio's name in the form of Santa Claus, tiny bags of gifts, and promises of a rosy future. He wouldn't be going to Arembepe this time. There was a proper strategy for every time and place.

Of the contents of the gift pouches, a chapter in which Brastânio hires Jesus to do its work.

Fifty-odd paper pouches, colored green and yellow like the Brazilian flag, were counted out in the council chamber and sorted into two piles. The twenty-five or so predominantly yellow ones were for the little girls. Each contained a miniature plastic doll, a tiny tin cooking stove, two balloons, a sack of candy, a snapper, and a wooden noisemaker. In the gift bags for boys, which were predominantly green, a plastic toy automobile and tin bugle had been substituted for the doll and toy stove. All fifty were stamped on one side with the national motto, "Order and Progress," and on the other with a picture of Jesus and an inscription in gold letters which read: "Suffer the little children to come unto me. A gift from Brastânio—Brazilian Titanium, S.A., an industry serving Brazil."

Peto, his last illusions gone, stomped out of the courthouse in disgust.

"Aw . . . what a lot of garbage!"

Leôncio, on the other hand, was quivering with excitement.

"Gee whillikers! Seven pretties in each little sack, presents galore. Dr. Ascânio, please don't let me down. I'm going to want three for my grandchildren, the two little gals and the boy."

Ascânio agreed that three pouches should be set aside for the old soldier, the mayor's faithful gun-toting helper, who earned minimum wages and was not always paid promptly. Besides, Ascânio hadn't the heart to deny anyone a favor just then, when his heart was light, his prospects were bright, and his cup was overflowing with unexpected blessings.

The poor children's Christmas treat, a fine solution to the problem that had been worrying him so much. He hadn't known how the cost of celebrating the completion of the power line could possibly be met. Now that splendid company, Brastânio, would pay for everything—the street would be paved, they'd have pennants, skyrockets, and music, and Dr. Mirko Stefano might even honor the town with his presence. What excited him most of all, however, was the news that a major industry would actually come to Agreste. It was practically in the bag, Dr. Stefano had said so. In Agreste; not in Itabuna, Valença, Ilhéus, or Arembepe. . . .

As to this last matter, Ascânio had some lingering doubts. Had Mirko mentioned Arembepe among the possible sites? He had the impression of having heard the name of that famous beach, which was an internationally known tourist attraction, though it didn't have a patch on Mangue Seco. He couldn't be quite sure, though, because when the magnate had repeated the names of the competing cities, he had left Arembepe out and mentioned only two in the southern part of the state and a third on the coast and Recôncavo near Bahia. Oh well, it didn't really matter. It looked as if the top executives who would make the final decision were going to cast their votes for Agreste.

Best of all, Dr. Mirko had freed Ascânio from his vow of secrecy and given him permission to tell the populace the good news. He planned to do that when he distributed the Christmas toys.

Ascânio Trindade was not a good liar. He was prone to slip up on some minor detail and let the cat out of the bag, as he had done during his speech at Tannery Square (which he had remembered just in time to call by its new name, Modesto Pires Plaza). He had blithely announced great news in the offing and hinted of a project far vaster than a mere tourist enterprise, the hub of an industrial complex, nothing less! Most of his hearers had missed the allusion, but a few of them had pricked up their ears.

Osnar had stopped him on his way down to the river. "Captain Ascânio, what's all this talk about the hub of an industrial axis? What's this cat you almost let out of the bag?"

Ascânio, arm in arm with Leonora, had evaded the question with a joke. "Pull him out by the tail if you can!"

Colonel Artur de Figueiredo, for obvious reasons—he was, after all, political boss, acting mayor, and Ascânio's godfather and sponsor—had had to be let in on the plans and projects discussed with the "big entrepreneur." Ascânio had gone out to Tapitanga Fazenda on purpose to tell him about it. But these days the Colonel was like an old buck that had lost its antlers. He seemed to have no real interest in anything but his land and his goats. He thought the whole plan was a piece of folly, or worse, a put-on.

"You call that fellow a big businessman, son? Why, he ain't nothing but a common swindler. What he don't know is he'd do a sight better squeezing milk from a billygoat's balls than trying to rustle up hard cash in Agreste. That fella took a one-way streetcar going the wrong way. A swindler and a sucker besides. Went barking up the wrong alley."

It was useless to argue with his godfather; he'd never change his mind. Yet there were the gifts, fifty sacks of toys for the poor children, and the Colonel would have to bow to the evidence. Yes, the fellow *was* a big entrepreneur, not a swindler, not a sucker, but an entrepreneur who represented vast interests, a spokesman for Brastânio, the industry that produced titanium dioxide, which was basic to national development. And that industry could be lured to Agreste, where the dynamic and competent Ascânio Trindade was mayor. Well, if he wasn't already he soon would be; the State Electoral Tribunal would be setting a date for elections any day now.

It was absolutely essential to mark the corporate gift-giving with appropriate ceremonies. Ascânio decided to set up a committee of prominent matrons and young ladies to help hand out presents as a touching gesture on Christmas Eve, which was only two days away. Thanks to Brastânio, it would be an unforgettable Christmas. He smiled to himself at the thought of his dainty Leonora scattering toys and gladness among the children like a good fairy.

He could call upon Barbozinha to thank the generous industrialists of Brastânio in the children's name. No one could equal him at touching the hearts of his hearers on such occasions and calling forth their tears and applause. He, Ascânio, would say a few words himself; he would announce to the people the dawn of a new age for Sant'Ana do Agreste—the age of Brastânio, and (why not say it?) the age of Ascânio Trindade. Yes, Leonora, Ascânio Trindade, no longer a wretched county official—hardly more than Leôncio; Lindolfo's equal—but an administrator, a statesman worthy of your hand. He trampled the thorn underfoot; virginity was nothing but a silly convention. She was a young widow from São Paulo, and beautiful, and rich.

He left Leôncio to stand guard over the sacks in his double capacity as hired assassin and army private, and set out for Dona Perpétua's house to tell Leonora and Dona Antonieta that the gifts had arrived. Tieta was still confined to her bed, but under the tender care of her seminarian nephew, scabs were beginning to form on the burns. That boy was worth his weight in gold.

Of how De Matos Barbosa the Bard composes and recites a poem which goes unheard, thanks to the all-too-popular distribution of Brastânio's gifts to the poor children. A confused and hectic chapter in which we see Dona Edna in action.

The truth must be proclaimed: the toy distribution surpassed all expectations. Instead of a lively hubbub, a bustle of girls and matrons and happy children, it was a mob scene, a pandemonium that went beyond all bounds of discipline and good manners. The fact is, all hell broke loose.

In Agreste, where entertainments and diversions were few and far between, any ceremony, from a mass to a funeral, was enough to draw an amusement-hungry crowd. The news that Santa Claus himself had brought toys in the flying machine soon made the rounds. Not even Leôncio's scowling face and fearsome reputation were enough to repress the mob of youngsters shepherded by their mothers and other adults who jumped up and down in front of the courthouse on the morning of Christmas Eve. The only reason they stayed outside was that Leôncio had locked and bolted the front door.

Not even Ascânio Trindade, for all his devotion to his job and his knowledge of the district and its problems, had ever imagined there were so many children in Agreste. And apparently all of them were poor, for even that prosperous citizen "Stale Bread" Agostinho the baker had sent his children to receive their share of Brastânio's gifts: a fat little boy and a fat little girl, with full stomachs and all dressed up. They stood planted firmly where their mother, Dona "Sour Rye" Dulcinéia, had installed them near the head of the line Ascânio had organized—an interminable line that kept dissolving and forming again. More people were arriving every minute. The children ran about, rolled on the ground and got covered with dust and generally raised hell.

"God, what a mob! Look at them," said Aminthas, peering out from the door of the bar with his cue in his hand. "Aren't you going to give 'em a hand, Osnar? Ascânio asked us to."

"When I do something stupid it's because of a dame. You go if you want to." Osnar, engaged in rubbing chalk on his cue, was surprised when Peto nonchalantly walked in and sat down to watch the next game of pool. "You here, Sergeant Peto? I thought you'd be first in line."

"Who, me? Stand in line for that bunch of junk? Huh! I've got better things to do." Having got that long speech off his chest he stuck out his pipestem legs, called over Seu Manuel, and ordered a Coke on Osnar.

In the meeting room at the courthouse the gallant ladies' committee, minus doughty Dona Carmosina, who was confined to her bed with a cold, fever, headache, cough and bronchitis, elected Dona Milu as its chief and frantically set about dividing up the contents of the sacks so that as few children as possible would be sent away empty-handed.

A few boys came to help their girlfriends, including Edmundo Ribeiro the tax collector's son, young Leleu of whom we have had earlier, venereal news. Leleu was a second-year economics student at the university; a skinny, long-haired, unshaven hippie who wore faded Levis, his shirt unbuttoned and his shirttail hanging out. All the girls drooled over him; there wasn't enough of him to go around. Seixas was there too, convoying a bevy of cousins.

"There won't be enough toys to go around even so," declared Elisa, who had just looked out the window to reconnoiter and make a rough estimate of the children outside.

Elisa and Leonora, both dressed to the teeth, were the two stars of the committee; two beauties who complemented one another and made a striking contrast, the fair-haired daughter of Italian immigrants and the dark Brazilian product of generations of mingled blood. Leleu's sly eyes rested first on one, then on the other. Both were tempting, both were already spoken for; one was the honest wife of a tradesman who was still a young man, and the other was flirting with the county clerk. A crying shame. When he turned away he met Dona Edna's melting, shadowy, insistent gaze. Leleu returned her smile and Dona Edna approached, followed by Terto, whom no one would have taken for her wedded husband but who had married her before judge and priest.

Father Mariano came into the hall to bless the gifts. Cranky old Vavá Muriçoca the sexton carried the holy water, stoup and aspergillum, while Ricardo, in a white surplice edged in scarlet, held the thurible and incense. Dona Edna hesitated. Devotion first, pleasure later: she went up to the priest and kissed his hand, devouring Ricardo with her eyes. Oh, oh, what was this? The angel didn't turn away his eyes the way he used to! For the first time he boldly faced down her shameless stare, smiling slightly as he said, "Good morning, Dona Edna." An immaculate angel but a grown man now. Good morning, my dear little altar boy. Oh, if I could only be the first!

Having done her devotional duty, Dona Edna went over to Leleu, who was trying to butter up her husband. Silly of him to bother; Terto's horns didn't need any softening up.

When she heard Elisa's comment, confirmed by Seixas, Dona Milu consulted Ascânio briefly and gave orders that all the toys should be taken out of the sacks and piled behind the conference table, around which the high-backed chairs of the councilmen formed a sort of barricade to protect the gifts and the ladies whose task it was to distribute them. Each child would receive just one present.

"No playing favorites!" warned Ascânio Trindade, half joking, half in earnest.

Dona Milu, however, was wholly in earnest and did not laugh at all as she issued her orders:

"Dolls, automobiles, bugles, stoves and noisemakers go to the needy. That line's full of kids who have no business being there. It's a crying shame. A balloon or a piece of toffee's plenty for them and they're lucky to get it! The only reason they're here is because their parents don't have the shame a cat's born with."

And so as to leave no doubt as to whom she meant: "You hear me, Dulcinéia? Your kids are standing there in line as big as life as if the bakery wasn't making money hand over fist. And so's your brother, Georgina, a great big boy like that! You ought to be ashamed of yourselves."

The instant Leôncio unbarred the door and let them in, the line broke up and the children advanced en masse. Mothers and fathers pushed the chairs aside and planted themselves in front of the table with outstretched hands.

By dint of shouts and some ear-pulling, Father Mariano managed to hold back the avalanche long enough to bless the gifts. When he had finished he launched into a homily which was soon drowned out by the yelling and tumult that ensued. Father Mariano, Vavá Muriçoca and Ricardo were swallowed in a tide of would-be recipients of Brastânio's largesse. Dona Edna, indifferent to toys but seeing her chance, took advantage of the confusion and amid screaming children, holy water and incense, managed to press Leleu's hand encouragingly and rub her backside against Ricardo's cassock; a modest feat, but pleasant and diverting.

All discipline and control soon went by the board; all attempts to distribute dolls and cooking stoves to the girls, cars and bugles to the boys, and balloons and sweets to the children of prosperous parents were in vain. The gift-giving turned into a riot, a mutiny: the ladies' committee backed up against the wall, the chairs overturned, maternal hands grabbing at the presents. Cinira the virgin turned giddy and fainted away, and Elisa rushed out for a glass of water. "Needs a man," diagnosed Dona Milu as she stopped distributing presents to pinch the greediest little arms and rap the loudest shouters on the head.

The pile of toys was gone in a jiffy. Latecomers received nothing but the colored picture of Jesus and Brastânio's pious words.

Fights broke out in the street among the parents, two women from the Hollow were pulling each other's hair, and blubbering children were hitting out at one another with much squealing and haughty words. Defeated, exhausted, their fine dresses crumpled and their hair falling down, the girls and ladies of the honor committee threatened to have hysterics. Dona Dulcinéia beat a hasty retreat after thrusting a bugle, a doll, a stove and an automobile into her children's hands and grabbing a noisemaker, a snapper, and some candy for her husband. That was why she had agreed to be on the committee in the first place, and Dona Milu could just go and preach to somebody else. Georgina sobbed into a handkerchief after her little brother had threatened, "I'll tell Papa you wouldn't give me the car or the bugle either, you dumb ass!"

Amid all the roughhousing and hullabaloo, made intolerable by the din of twenty wretched tin horns all tooting at once, our bard Barbozinha approached the speaker's rostrum to recite the poem he had composed especially for the occasion, a moving panegyric in biblical style. In vain Ascânio, Seixas, Leleu and the other young men shouted for quiet. In vain Leonora and Elisa, the two rare beauties, raised their voices and pleaded with them all to pay attention for just a minute. Little or nothing could be heard of the poem, to the bitter disappointment of the bard, who had spent two days and two nights choosing rhymes, counting syllables and doing research on titanium dioxide.

"What the devil is it, Ascânio? You ought to know."

But Ascânio had no very clear idea of what it was either; only that it was an extremely important product which would help the balance of payments if it were produced in Brazil, a giant step forward which would set the country on the road to development. As to what was actually produced, however, he was rather embarrassed to admit that he didn't have the least idea.

Ascânio decided to save his speech to the people heralding the dawn of a new era for a more propitious occasion. The people had noisily gone their way with their loot and showed not the slightest interest in either orations or poetry. The crowd rapidly dispersed, and all that was left were poor women with babies perched on their hips, shabbily dressed men leading children by the hand and older boys lounging on the streetcorners. Thrown away in the streets and trampled underfoot were the colored pictures of Jesus with the New Testament verse and Brastânio's name. As articles to be sold or traded, they were worthless.

When Goatstink asked Leôncio for a toy or a swig of *cachaça*, he was offered one of the pictures, which were all that was left.

"Why don't you give it to your mother?" was the beggar's response.

To lame Leôncio's mind the party had been one of the finest ever, and he was willing to sing Brastânio's praises anytime. The only person to receive a whole sackful of toys—not one but three, and ahead of time, too, with no pushing and shoving—he had managed to pinch a bugle besides. He handed it to Goatstink to be rid of him.

It was only a little tin horn but it made a lot of noise. Goatstink blasted away on it for all it was worth as he staggered down the street, producing a maddening, piercing, ear-splitting shriek that set the teeth on edge. When he wasn't tooting he asked everyone he met where Terto was going to hang his new horns now that there wasn't a place left on his body that wasn't taken. He'd just have to stick them up his ass. After all, they were just a kid's horns, light and easy, wouldn't hurt much. The things Goatstink says when he's stinking drunk aren't fit to be repeated, much less written.

In which Barbozinha finally gets to recite his poem and Ascânio Trindade issues a proclamation to the people of Sant' Ana do Agreste.

The soldiers of charity, a weary regiment in full retreat and badly in need of a gabfest to restore their souls, limped across the court-house square and sought refuge in Perpétua's house, where Tieta lay convalescing in a hammock on the porch. Some indignant, some laughing, they followed their leader, Dona Milu, into the house. Dona Milu announced her resignation then and there.

"Oh, Tieta, child. I don't have the strength for another chore like this one. If Ascânio ever pulls a stunt like this again, he'll have to leave me out of it."

They all drew up chairs and sat around the hammock. Tieta begged for a full account as she kissed Father Mariano's hand and feasted her eyes on Ricardo, still in his white surplice, the Levite in the Holy of Holies. The Reverend Father had only come to say good morning, but he accepted a glass of golden ambarella-plum juice before going back to the church and taking the seminarian with him. Tieta repressed a sigh. God was her partner, and they had to respect each other's schedules.

Elisa limped off to the kitchen to make a cup of strong black coffee for the injured Barbozinha. Little Aracy balanced a heavy tray of fruit juices in her thin arms: mango, mangaba plum, am-barella plum, hog plum. Seixas' cousins peered into the house; they had never been inside and wanted to take a good look while they could. They nudged each other slyly, glancing sidelong at the ham-mock where Tieta's firm and opulent flesh was set off by the décolletage of her carelessly fastened nylon negligee, a fancy yellow one trimmed with lace.

Perpétua escorted the Father to the street door, and on her return praised the company's generosity and the valuable gifts of toys for the poor children's Christmas. She had tried to persuade Peto to stand in line, but the whippersnapper had made himself scarce. She had watched it all out the window and had harsh words for the display of bad manners.

"That riffraff doesn't deserve anybody's charity. Here those men send a plane full of presents and the town puts on this disgraceful performance. . . . It's enough to make you sick."

Tieta took up the cudgels for the people of Agreste as a part of suffering humanity condemned to squalor, whose children had never had any toys but rag dolls and toy trucks pieced together with bits of wood, with beer-bottle caps for wheels.

"They're too patient, if you ask me."

Opinions were sharply divided and the argument grew heated; the battlefield of the county courthouse invaded the peaceful veranda of the comfortable house that lodged the Paulistas. Seixas, up in arms for once, took Tieta's side and defended the right of the poor to rise up in revolt. Elisa showed them her swollen foot, which had been trodden on by a powerful washerwoman determined to get her hands on dolls and tin horns for all eight of her children. She declared that there was no excuse for either the bad manners of the rabble or the defection of the poolroom gang.

She didn't mean Astério, who was on duty at the store and had to stay behind the counter—after all, you never knew when a customer might come in on Christmas Eve. But as for Osnar, Aminthas, Fidélio and all the others who had lounged around the bar with their cues and chalk in their hands instead of coming over to the courthouse when Ascânio asked them to, to help the women hold back those animals . . . "Animals, that's all they are . . ."

As president of the Honor Committee, Dona Milu should have been the most indignant and the first to condemn the atrocious display of bad manners. Quite the contrary, she spoke up for the wild beasts:

"Animals, nothing. There ain't a thing wrong with them but that they're poor. Fussing and knocking each other down over a plastic doll that ain't worth a spoonful of strained honey, or a cheap little old tin horn to give their poor little kids. And that reminds me: what an idea to throw in those awful horns! Couldn't they have found some other doodad instead?"

There was unanimous agreement on that point at least: the piercing concert of so many shrill bugles, all blown at once, had been the worst part of the ordeal. Dona Milu turned to the poet, who hadn't opened his mouth.

"I'll have to be going pretty soon. I left Carmô in bed with a fever, and when Carmô's got the flu there's no living with her. She has to be coddled day and night. But before I go I want to hear Barbozinha's poem. He couldn't say it over there in that madhouse, with the bugles blowing and all."

The bard was usually not reluctant to recite his poems, but this morning he was sulking, his vanity wounded by his fellow citizens' lack of respect. He said that he was awfully sorry, but . . .

Tieta interrupted him.

"Of course you're going to say it! Don't punish us for what happened. You were going to recite it for me anyway because I couldn't be there, weren't you?" Her mischievous eyes were on him. "How about it, old fellow? We're waiting with bated breath. Let's have it."

Barbozinha obeyed her. The amorous troubadour, submissive to the bidding of his muse, rose to his feet, fumbled in his jacket pocket and pulled out two sheets of paper covered with alexandrines, in writing that was all curlicues. Then he said "ahem" and asked for a swallow of white rum to clear his throat. Aracy went running to get it. The poet drained the glass, smacked his lips, raised one hand, and let his voice ring out.

He was the herald of good tidings announcing the birth of a poor and naked babe in a manger in Bethlehem. Let all the children of Agreste, every one, come to take part in the universal rejoicing, for this Christmas celebration belonged to them by decree of the great Brastânio, whose owners, noble and magnanimous builders of a new Brazil where justice would reign, had flung armfuls of rich toys into the lap of poverty, transmuting the crying of forlorn children into gay laughter, into chirping and trilling and birdsong.

He had found inspiration in the Bible and the beauty of the earth, the river and the sea; had dipped his pen in the profoundest sentiments of human solidarity. Thus he brought the morning star of David to shine into humble homes and compared the Brastânio directors to new Magi seeking out the rough road to Agreste and bearing gifts of gold, myrrh, frankincense and kindness. He contrasted the people's poverty with the grandeur of Brazil, the unhappy child of the Agreste sandhills with the infant King of Judea; rhymed Brastânio with Ascânio. Ascânio Trindade, captain of the dawn, battering down the walls of benighted misery and flinging open the gates of progress.

Leonora, carried away, jumped to her feet applauding wildly, and the others followed her lead; there was much clapping and enthusiastic bravos. It was an overwhelming triumph, and it made up for all his earlier disappointment.

"Come here and let me give you a kiss!" demanded Tieta, planting a kiss on the bard's injured cheek and leaving the imprint of her lips in purple lipstick on top of his wrinkles.

"Bravo, Barbozinha, that was really fine. And Ascânio deserves the good things you said about him," said Dona Milu thoughtfully. "Ascânio never gives up, and if Agreste ever amounts to anything again it'll be thanks to him. And to you too, Tieta. Seems like things started to change as soon as you got here; as if you sort of lighted us up in a flash. I'm not talking about the Paulo Afonso electric light; I mean something else, something I don't rightly know how to explain because I'm just a foolish old woman. It ain't anything you can put your hand on, but it's there, a light you brought with you, child, God bless you."

She went up to the hammock and kissed Tieta with motherly affection.

"Now I'll be on my way. Carmô must be hopping mad by now. She'll give me an earful when I get home, and I deserve it, too."

Ascânio asked her to wait a minute, just a minute, please. He too stood up and recited his proclamation to the people, heralding the new age, the age of Brastânio. He did not add his own name to that of the great titanium-dioxide industry; there was no need to. De Matos Barbosa, seconded with applause by Dona Milu, had already done that, in verses that Leonora quickly learned by heart and repeated to herself in a low voice between parted crimson lips.

"Poet, your Paradise is threatened!" A bombshell explodes in this chapter.

On the day after Christmas the newspaper story signed by Giovanni Guimarães exploded in Agreste like a bombshell—a time bomb, for it had been published in *A Tarde*, the afternoon paper, three days before Barbozinha the poet had finished penning his panegyric for the poor children's party.

It was entirely the fault of the flu that had kept Dona Carmosina, feverish and perspiring, under the covers, and not only deprived the Honor Committee of her presence on Christmas Eve but prevented that exemplary functionary from distributing the mail as usual. Dona Milu took her place, tired out from her courthouse marathon and anxious to get back to her sick daughter's bedside. She handed over their letters to the handful of customers who came in after the *marineti* arrived (even later than usual that day) and left everything else, including the newspapers, to be delivered after the holiday.

Five people in Agreste subscribed to *A Tarde*, but there were always six copies in the bundle; the sixth was addressed to the newspaper agent, Dona Carmosina Sluizer da Consolação. That day all six were left at the post office, tied up with string just as they had come. Dona Carmosina felt much too sick even to take an interest in the goings-on at the courthouse, much less in a tiring perusal of the paper.

She felt a little better on Christmas Day. The fever had gone, but she was still very weak and her body craved bed and rest. She slept nearly all morning. In the afternoon Tieta and Leonora came for a visit with Skipper Dário and Dona Laura as well as Ricardo, who was proudly wearing a handsome piece of jewelry, a wide gold ring set with a polished, oval piece of jade of a rare dark green.

It was the first time Tieta had left the house since the night of the fire. A few unpleasant-looking red scars, impervious to unguents, were still visible, and anyone else would have waited until they were healed before going out in public. But Tieta couldn't stand lying around in the hammock at home any longer, especially on Christmas.

The night before, she had organized a Christmas Eve dinner, southern style, for her family and friends after midnight mass. Barbozinha, Ascânio Trindade, Father Mariano, Osnar, Aminthas and Fidélio had come. Seixas had a date with his cousins, and the Skipper and Dona Laura were busy too. Ever since he had come back to live in Agreste, the Skipper had thrown a party every Christmas for the Mangue Seco fishermen. There were less than forty of them all told, men, women and children, and they all gathered for a jolly communal banquet that always ended in a lively dance. Modesto Pires helped with the expenses but never showed up for the dinner. He went to midnight mass in Saco Village, but his daughter Marta and her husband Pedro joined the fishermen. So the Skipper could not accept Tieta's invitation, but he promised to come to Agreste with his wife on Christmas morning in time for a lunch of the leftover turkey and fixings at Perpétua's. Carmosina and Dona Milu could not even do that; it was all Carmosina could do to get out of bed and stretch out on the chaise longue.

Tieta had been foresighted enough to bring some small Christmas presents from São Paulo for the family, but she was so grateful for the warm welcome they had given her that she also gave money to Zé Esteves and Tonha and to Astério and Elisa and savings passbooks to Ricardo and Peto, having opened accounts for both nephews in a São Paulo bank. And to Ricardo, for his invaluable help in raising Inácio's Corral, she presented that valuable ring, an heirloom that had belonged to the deceased Comendador Felipe. She and Leonora had their hands full when they knocked at Dona Milu's door.

"More presents! Wasn't what you all brought with you from São Paulo enough?" Dona Milu shook her head as she accepted the Japanese fan. "Tieta, there's no doing a thing with you."

"I declare, my flu's better already!" exclaimed Dona Carmosina, perking up as she admired her showy new costume pin.

The visitors didn't stay long. Leonora had a date with Ascânio to go to the matinee at the movies, and Dona Carmosina, with her drawn face and hoarse voice, was in no fit state to talk.

"You go back to bed," ordered Tieta. "And don't even think of going out tomorrow. I'll stand duty for you at the post office if you want me to."

The Skipper proposed a committee of five at least to share the responsibility of taking the good Carmosina's place.

"One isn't nearly enough."

"None of you has to go at all. There won't be much business tomorrow; the mail won't come in until the day after. Mother can run over to the post office for a few minutes, and that'll do fine."

Next day after lunch Dona Milu handed out the rest of the correspondence and the newspapers and lingered at the post office in case anyone came with a letter to send, passing the time of day with Osnar and Aminthas until about four o'clock. Then she locked the door and went home, taking Carmosina's copy of *A Tarde* with her. Anybody who had to send a telegram would know where the post-mistress could be found.

Dona Carmosina, still in bed but feeling much better by now, plumped up the pillows and settled down cozily for a nice read. She glanced at the front-page headlines: there was a story about the high cost of living and what a hard time people were having trying to celebrate Christmas in the traditional way. It wasn't just chestnuts, hazelnuts, walnuts and almonds that were expensive, or gourd cheese, or codfish; staples like beans, rice, and jerky were outrageously high. She turned to the inside editorial page, where the meaty stories and important news appeared along with her favorite feature, Giovanni Guimarães' daily column. To Dona Carmosina's way of thinking this columnist was unrivaled when it came to elegance of expression, while no critic could be so stinging and scornful or take such unerring aim at the follies and foibles of the consumer society.

She clapped her narrowed eyes on the headline and what did she see? In thick black letters above two columns in italics signed by Guimarães: LETTER TO DE MATOS BARBOSA THE POET. The sick woman's face lighted up and she exclaimed: "Oh boy!" But her joy at seeing her friend's name at the top of the page turned to anxious dismay as soon as she read the first line of the letter: "Poet, your Paradise is threatened!"

Sound the alarm! A résumé of the famous or infamous column.

Giovanni Guimarães was alluded to in an earlier chapter as a friend of Barbozinha the poet, a crony of his bohemian days in the "castles" and subliterary cafés, but his sterling qualities as a columnist have not been mentioned. He had been a reporter for *A Tarde* since his long-ago days as a freshman in medical school and had written a popular daily column in that newspaper for many years. His writing was almost always light in tone; but occasionally, when exposing some violence or abuse, the writer, in whose makeup there was not an ounce of pettiness, would be carried away by his subject into making a harsh denunciation of the social injustice he was describing and would exchange his usual joking good humor for honest anger.

"Poet, your Paradise is threatened!" With that clarion call of warning, the feature writer launched into a dramatic missive addressed to the "poet and citizen of the community of Sant'Ana do Agreste, Gregório Eustáquio de Matos Barbosa." Dona Carmosina tried to guess what in the world he could mean. She recalled the reporter's hearty good-natured laugh booming in the post office during his visit to Agreste. Such a cheerful, easygoing man! He had made friends with them all in no time, especially Osnar.

As it happened, Giovanni Guimarães launched into his column with a description of the visit he had made to Agreste a few years before at the invitation of the poet who, "upon retiring from the public duties he had carried out with exemplary dedication for the city government of Salvador, abandoned his hectic life in the capital, its literary milieu and the habits of a nightowl, for the healthful air and marvelous climate of his native place." He recalled his visit, so happy though so short, in "the bucolic little town, a peaceable kingdom, an idyllic corner of the world," with boating parties on the river, swimming in Catherine's Basin, and excursions to Mangue Seco Beach, "a masterpiece of Nature, a landscape from the beginning of the world; incomparable, unique." In the company of Barbozinha, the perfect host, Giovanni had known and tasted the delights of that "Paradise on earth, that Eden of harmony and beauty, where man—despite the pious old women's merciless tongues—is still a neighbor to his fellow man."

During his short stay in Agreste he had scandalized the bigots by standing in front of the church after mass and launching into a paean in praise of sin and Hell. Hell, he told them, was full of beautiful, compliant women, while Heaven signified eternal boredom in the company of bearded saints and singsong hymns. And yet not even the old hymnsingers could resist the genial laugh and human warmth that radiated from the harum-scarum fellow; they all laughed along with him. He would always end by saying that the only Heaven worth living in was Agreste, that Paradise on earth. Breathing that clear, pure air cleaned out his lungs and heart and made him feel young again. The gossips nudged one another and said what a cut-up he was.

Well, then: "Your Paradise is in mortal danger, poet. Soon the Grim Reaper will lurk in the river currents of the Real and the surf of Mangue Seco and spread his black wings over the fields and the dunes, to turn your clear blue sky into a black stain of pollution, poison your waters, kill the fish and the birds, reduce the fishermen to beggars, bring new diseases whose evil consequences are still unknown to the abode of health."

Dona Carmosina stopped reading to take a deep breath. "Oh my God," she thought, "why is he predicting such terrible things?" One day when they were chatting in the Areopagus, Giovanni had wondered aloud how much longer Agreste would be able to enjoy the delights of its perfect climate and its social harmony in peace, far from the evils of the consumer society, and had answered his own question by predicting gloomily that sooner or later the horrors of civilization would come to Catherine's Basin and the sand dunes on the beach, and then, goodbye happiness!

"Did you know, my poet friend, that there are only six titanium-dioxide factories in the whole world? And that not long ago a judge in Italy sentenced the board of directors of one of them to prison for the harm they had done to the Mediterranean, for polluting its waters and destroying the flora and fauna of the sea? Did you know that no civilized country will allow one of these monstrous factories within its borders? That the very corporation now threatening Brazil was unable to obtain authorization to build its accursed chimneys in Holland, Mexico or Egypt? '*Vade retro!*' cried the leaders of those countries, turning away a vast source of capital, not only because it was foreign but because it would pose a mortal threat to the atmosphere and water." Dona Carmosina laid down the paper on the bed to give herself time to recover. She knew some of those things already from what she had read in the papers; in fact, she had shown Skipper Dário the story in the *Estado de São Paulo* and together they had cheered the verdict of that Italian judge who hadn't let the wool be pulled over his eyes.

"Poet, before very long your wonderful poems about Mangue Seco Beach will be all that remains of the beauty of its transparent waters and powdery sand, its teeming schools of fish and the brave men who go out in fishing boats to catch them. All too soon Death will rise from the factory chimneys and extend his black talons of smoke over the dunes. The peace and beauty that you sing of in your love lyrics will rot and wither in the effluents of ferrous sulfate and sulfuric acid, sulfur-dioxide gases, pollution without end." "My God!" whispered Dona Carmosina, feeling a weight in her chest and gasping for air.

"Although they have yet to obtain authorization from the federal government for the establishment of this industry in Brazil, the board of directors of the newly formed corporation of Brastânio—Brazilian Titanium Industry, S.A., but very little about it is Brazilian, poet, except for the stooges who speak in its name—know very well that they will never be allowed to build their factories anywhere in the south. Where do they turn, then, but to the unfortunate state of Bahia, where the corporation is making a survey of four zones to determine which of them is best suited to their deadly scheme. Its agents and technical experts are fanning out on the coast between Itabuna and Ilhéus, and the vicinity of Valença in the Recôncavo, and there is some evidence to show that they are interested in a location on the outskirts of the capital as well. All signs, however, seem to indicate that the kings of contamination prefer the north shore of the state, the mouth of the Real River, and the coconut groves of Mangue Seco." All the heat of the sultry afternoon came crashing down on Dona Carmosina's head. The sky darkened outside. Oh, poor Barbozinha: his friend Giovanni Guimarães uttering his public warning at the same time that the poet himself was lauding Brastânio and the kings of contamination to the skies. "Supreme irony of fate!" cried Dona Carmosina, scaring away the flies.

"Carmô, did you call?" came Dona Milu's voice from the street door.

"No, Mother."

"The south shore of the state is wealthy, poet, and carries weight in the national economy; it's powerful enough to turn back the threat to its ocean, the Cachoeira River and the cacao crop, which is such an important source of foreign exchange. The same can be said of the Recôncavo, which though less wealthy is defended by the remnants of political prestige that the sugar barons, decadent but barons, can still command. As for Arembepe, it would be the perfect location from the corporation's point of view, no doubt; close to the capital, conveniently adjacent to the Aratu Industrial Center, with a good transportation system already in place. But no government, however arbitrary, would dare go so far as to authorize girdling the city with a belt of contamination that would put an end to the fishing industry, make the beaches unusable, drive the tourists away and turn the state capital into a pesthole. Alas, my poet friend, there remains only the community of Agreste, forgotten by God and man and abandoned to its fate. Yes, Death the marauder will be haunting Mangue Seco soon. Poet, heed my warning! The emissaries of pollution will soon be in Agreste if they are not there already, promising the moon and babbling of progress and prosperity; but it's Death they're bringing with them in their briefcases full of foreign gold."

Dona Carmosina, soaked with perspiration, read Giovanni Guimarães's column through to the end. She could hear Dona Milu's voice in the distance as she chatted in the doorway with a neighbor. She read the last few lines: "Poet, raise your voice; take up your lyre and let a cry of protest ring out; defend the peace and beauty of your heavenly corner of the world; arouse the people to wrath and keep pollution from darkening your hills and beaches, fouling your crystal waters and covering the diaphanous skies of Agreste with a murky pall." The column ended with the same grave and ominous warning with which it had begun: "Poet, your Paradise is threatened!"

With trembling hands and wildly beating heart, Dona Carmosina sprang out of bed and dressed quickly, unmindful of her flu, and without a word of explanation to Dona Milu except that she would be right back, rushed out the door with the newspaper in her hand to look for Barbozinha. The poet could usually be found in the bar at that hour of the afternoon, kibitzing at either the pool table or the game of backgammon between Chalita and Plínio Xavier. On the way to the bar she ran into Skipper Dário, who inquired when he saw her so breathless:

"Where are you off to in such a hurry, my good Carmosina?" When he approached and saw how upset she was, he remembered that she ought to be in bed and asked in concern: "Why, what's the matter?"

Dona Carmosina held out the paper.

"Read it."

The Skipper devoured it, standing in the middle of the street. When he came to the end he exploded in an oath: "God damn and blast!"

Of another discreet conversation in an elegant apartment at the Lords' Retreat: discreet despite the grossness (in every sense) of His Excellency the Governor.

"I'll say this much for you, friends, you've got a hell of a nerve. What I ought to do is have you all thrown in jail."

That was His Excellency's comment, for openers. He had removed his jacket and the naked girl on his lap was playing with the black suspenders that held up the eminent statesman's trousers and kept his well-larded belly within bounds. His Excellency's aging face was mottled with red blotches. The shrewd little eyes, the slack gestures and indolent drawling voice, reeked with vulgarity and overweening arrogance.

Mirkus the Magnificent smiled without replying, waiting for the girls to finish serving drinks and leave the room. One of them, a natural redhead, reminded him of Betty and piqued his appetite. Maybe when the interview was over . . .

The Elderly Parliamentarian did not feel at ease in the presence of the girls either. Not that he had anything against them or objected to their nudity; he had been coming to this house for ages, was already an habitué in Madame Georgette's day when the house was still called Nid d'Amour. He was partial to call girls, especially when they had no clothes on; the most refreshing eyedrops ever invented for tired eyes, he always said. Still, there was a time and place for everything, and while this place was admirably suited to the display of artistic nudes, the matter at hand was not intended for the ears of outsiders, and nothing was to be gained by mixing apples and oranges.

One of the girls leaned negligently on the elegant black umbrella belonging to the Elderly Parliamentarian. Educated at Oxford, he had taken on the habits and the features of an English lord.

He was tall and lean, impeccably shaved, and with a bristling white mustache, wore suiting from a British tailor and a boutonnière at his lapel, cultivated a phlegmatic manner. His Excellency's folksy ways undoubtedly grated on him. His Excellency was the exact opposite of an English lord, and were it not for his position—poor São Paulo!—handed to him by Getúlio Vargas on a silver platter during that other dictatorship and maintained by dint of the most varied and dubious alliances and stratagems, he would never have been given entrée to high society.

His Excellency had mentioned jail. The Elderly Parliamentarian permitted himself a slight cough to remind His Excellency that it was hardly proper to discuss matters of such grave import to the national interest in the presence of young women who, though indisputably charming, appealing and alluring, were decidedly not the most appropriate participants in a serious socioeconomic debate at this level. It was a discreet, almost timid cough. His Excellency had an impulsive nature and had been known to react with vile language when interrupted. His usual term of address for assistants, secretaries and members of his cabinet was "crook"—an appropriate term, by the way, since that was exactly what they were—and he respected neither the age nor the parliamentary mandate of his fellow party members, especially now that the legislative branch was held in generally low esteem.

When he heard the little "ahem" His Excellency scowled. It was on the tip of his tongue to tell the Elderly Parliamentarian what he thought of him and his mania for prudence and discretion, but he restrained himself. To tell the truth the old so-and-so was right: that lovely girl sitting on his lap and skillfully massaging the nape of his neck was incompatible with a business meeting. Even in a house of pleasure a statesman couldn't afford to relax. Well, he would try to wind this meeting up fast. He spanked the girl's sweet fanny and shooed her away.

"You all wait in the other room." He grinned at the other girl, the piquant redhead who had aroused the interest of Doctor Magnifico. The latter watched resignedly. Well, it couldn't be roses all the way, could it? There were plenty of other redheads around. All for God and country.

The girls trooped out cheerfully, leaving the bottles and the drinks they had poured. That particular brand of Scotch was not served even in the Governor's Palace, the Campos Elíseos; only at the Jockey Club and the Lords' Retreat. His Excellency sipped it like the connoisseur he was.

"This is what I call Scotch; all the others are dishwater. I order the best and those thieves buy adulterated whisky and pocket the difference. I ought to throw every last one of them into jail, and the three of you too. Plus the entire board of directors."

The Eager Beaver, a super-keen, rather obnoxious young man who had graduated from the famous São Paulo School of Business Administration and Economics (where he had returned to teach after doing brilliantly in an advanced executive-training course in the United States), a whiz kid and one of the brainiest technocrats of his generation, was about to open his mouth in rebuttal when Doctor Magnifico stopped him with an almost imperceptible gesture. If he said a word of protest everything would go down the drain, the front man knew; one of the things he was paid to do was keep the members of the board of directors from putting their foot in it, as they were prone to do. As technocrats they were formidable; as politicians they were a disaster. "It's not their line," as His Excellency said when referring to business executives and—but only in private—to the military.

When he saw His Excellency smile and drop his suspenders in a gesture of bonhomie like the veriest hick, the Eager Beaver mentally took his hat off to Mirko's acumen and skill. You just couldn't fault him on these missions; he came out of them with flying colors every time. Now His Excellency began presenting his bill.

"The senator here can tell you we've had our work cut out for us with this thing."

The Elderly Parliamentarian had recovered his aplomb now that the girls were no longer in the room. With proper British understatement ("his British air, his lordly London elegance," a columnist who followed legislative affairs and owed him certain small favors had written once), he nodded and confirmed His Excellency's words.

"Yes, it was a bit of a chore."

His Excellency, conscious of the girls waiting in the next room, shed his clothes as he talked.

"And the senator here can also tell you how much we had to put up."

A slight but meaningful gesture from the Elderly Parliamentarian sufficed to inform them that a vast sum had been spent. His

Excellency, stripped to his shirt and shorts, waistband doubled and straining under the bulk of his belly, raised his glass in a toast, and the others followed suit.

"Nobody's gonna do you any favors for nothing these days; it's too risky. The way things are now, nobody can be sure where he stands." He counted on his fingers. "It took time, it cost money, and it was risky. Plenty risky. But I got you the authorization for those factories just the same, on one condition: go and pollute somewhere else; São Paulo can't take any more of this smog." His greedy eyes went from Mirko to the Eager Beaver. "Nobody else could have got it for you. Only me. Know what I mean?"

"Brazil will be grateful to Your Excellency," exclaimed the Eager Beaver rashly and naively.

"Brazil hell!" His Excellency was impulsive, as we know. He glared at the Eager Beaver. Was the little twerp making fun of him? The good-natured hick made way for the Head Man, the feudal lord with the power of life and death over his vassals.

With admirable British phlegm, the Elderly Parliamentarian rested his confident gaze on Doctor Magnifico, whose mellifluous voice, pitched low but perfectly audible, switched the expressions of gratitude back on the track.

"Brazil and Brastânio, Excellency. How much did the poor children's Christmas in São Paulo cost, exactly? Do you recall, Your Excellency?"

The Eager Beaver shuddered as he heard the fantastic amount. He was about to speak up and ask that it be halved, but was stopped once again by Mirko's almost imperceptible gesture, as if to say that trying to bargain with His Excellency was futile and could be dangerous. The license had not been publicly granted and certainly would not be until everything was in order and the boodle stashed away in a Swiss bank account, just the way these things are done in those sensational pamphlets about arms sales and oil wells. Doctor Magnifico quickly asked a question to which he already knew the reply.

"The same as before?"

"That's right."

Before disappearing through the doorway that led to the room where the two girls were resignedly waiting for him, His Excellency, pointing to the Eager Beaver, remarked to the Magnificent Doctor, "I like that guy better with his mouth closed. Every time he opens it he puts his foot in it. But when you get tired of working for those crooks, you come look me up and I'll find a place for you in my cabinet."

One of the girls ran back for His Excellency's clothes. As soon as she closed the door, the Elderly Parliamentarian picked up his umbrella and cleared his throat. Doctor Magnifico understood and reached for his attaché case. There was no need to ask how much the Poor Senators' Christmas had cost; the amount had been agreed on with the Young Politician at the beginning of that long, expensive operation, right there in the Lords' Retreat.

He opened his attaché case and made out a check (to bearer, naturally). For every situation a gambit, for every opponent, a tip, fat or not so fat, but always a respectable amount. Doctor Magnifico thought of them as tips. A tip is what a servant receives, even if he dresses in black tie and tails. It was like a good chess game. Sometimes, not very often, it might end in a scandal or a trial. Or in a checkmate, not to press the analogy too far. He shrugged; it had never come to that in Brazil that he could remember. Those who wanted to live life to the fullest had to be prepared for an element of risk. Besides finding the game a stimulating pastime in itself, he enjoyed using his godgiven intelligence in maneuvering each piece on the board: His Excellency's low cunning, the Elderly Parliamentarian's hypocrisy, and the bumptious-brassy presumptuousness of the Eager Beaver. It would have been perfect if he hadn't missed out on the redhead; that was a dirty trick on His Excellency's part.

The Elderly Parliamentarian pocketed the check after glancing at the amount: exactly what they had agreed on, not a penny more. They were stingy but they kept their word. No disappointment showed in his impassive face. After all, it was His Excellency who had stuck his neck out; that was why he was getting that bundle in Swiss francs in a Swiss bank. Switzerland was a fine country, though not nearly so fine as England. As he was about to take his leave—there was another girl, just one, the Retreat's newest acquisition, waiting for him—Mirkus the Magnificent put another question which opened new vistas before him.

"His Excellency left before we could discuss the problem of where . . ."

"Well, it can't be São Paulo, you already know that. Or anywhere else in the south."

"We've already decided on Bahia. The problem is where in Bahia." Doctor Magnifico explained what he called "a small but important detail."

The Elderly Parliamentarian permitted himself a slight British smile, a shade of satisfaction on his lordly, phlegmatic face. Ah, those power-hungry industrialists would have to pay through the nose this time; they were no longer dealing with a callow, inexperienced boy like the Young Politician. "Well, gentlemen, it won't come cheap." In the first place, he knew, from a strictly confidential and very highly placed source, that His Excellency's head was on the block. There was talk of depriving him of his political rights, no less. Yes, precisely: for corruption. And if that happened, new contacts would have to be established to resolve that "small but important detail," which was neither small nor a detail. God save the King!

It was all settled with discretion and finesse, a gentlemen's agreement. His Excellency was a boorish, revolting swine, the opposite of a lord in every way.

Of *Ascânio Trindade between the devil and the deep blue sea.*

At the height of the dispute, when he had run out of arguments and had his back to the wall, Ascânio Trindade lost his usual good temper, sending to the devil the respect due his interlocutors' age, rank and social position, and shouting angrily so that everyone in the Areopagus and the street could hear:

"Just because the Skipper has a house in Mangue Seco and wants to keep that fine beach all to himself, that doesn't mean Agreste's going to shut the door to progress! We're not going to turn away industry for the sake of a privileged few! We're going to pull Agreste up by its bootstraps, and whoever doesn't like it can lump it!"

It was almost a speech, and one made in anger. Until then Ascânio, an excitable young man but frank and friendly in all his dealings, a hometown booster full of chimerical plans to raise the decaying community from the dust, which involved besieging the tourist sections of newspapers in the capital with letters about Agreste, had so far reaped nothing but esteem, support and unanimous praise from his neighbors.

Prominent citizens backed him willingly because he was always cordial and deferential when they had business at the courthouse and because they appreciated his unstinting efforts to bring progress to Agreste. In the six years he had been county clerk Ascânio had worked wonders, not the least of which was to collect all back taxes in the county. They didn't amount to much to begin with, and the few citizens who made enough money to pay taxes were chronically reluctant to pay up. Ascânio took on the cronyism of the village mayors, the supine indifference of the county treasurer, Lindolfo Araújo, who graced the courthouse with his dapper presence but was otherwise a cipher, and the reluctance of storekeepers and planters who were chronic tax evaders and liked it that way. He actually managed to collect the meager revenue owed the county without getting anybody's back up—incredible but true.

As for the poor townspeople and farmers, he had won their trust and esteem by listening patiently to every one of the confusing problems they brought to the community head man, or rather the head man's representative, in hope of a solution which was sometimes simple, sometimes problematic, and quite often impossible. Claims, demands, complaints, misunderstandings, quarrels between neighbors, fences moved during the night to change the boundaries of farms and other properties, animals grazing on other people's land—the whole range of petty problems and disputes inevitable in a poor district, most of them personal and having nothing to do with the county. Ascânio heard them out patiently, nevertheless, and not infrequently solved them. He was mayor, counselor and judge, settling cases out of court, reconciling enemies, clarifying doubtful points of law, guiding seducers of rash and foolish virgins to the altar, even prescribing remedies for loose bowels, constipation and dropsy. He gave his whole attention to a farmer's incoherent account of an ornery jackass or the misfortunes of a septuagenarian whose wife and children had left him all alone to plow a parched, bone-hard acre of land. He acted as veterinarian and agronomist, too, in a pinch.

For those with problems utterly beyond his power to solve, he found at least a few words of consolation and cheer. Although the duties of a county clerk were in theory strictly limited, Ascânio's functions as *de facto* mayor left him virtually no free time. Saturdays were his busiest day, with a never-ending throng of pilgrims besieging the county courthouse during and after market. His door was open to everyone without exception.

His conduct was ruled by no ulterior motive: he gave freely of his time and asked for nothing in return. He asked for nothing yet he received much, in the form of gratitude, respect, and farm produce. People called him "Doctor," not because he had finished three years of law school but because they thought of him that way, as a sage who was not a doctor of this or that, just "Doctor." They brought him small presents even when they had nothing special to consult him about.

It was worth seeing him walking home on Saturdays at the end of the day to where old Rafa waited for him as she smoked her clay pipe; he was always laden down with provisions enough for the rest of the week, a rich and wonderfully varied bounty from the farmhands and tenant farmers: shanks of pork and kid, fat capons—"I fattened this one up special for your broth so's to put some meat on your bones," explained the old woman who sold manioc flour and mush—sweet-smelling jackfruit, bunches of bananas getting yellow and ripe, yams and cassava root—"This is cocoa cassava, Doc, it's so soft it'll melt in your mouth," promised the smiling, toothless *caboclo* backwoodsman—sifted manioc flour, tapioca cakes dipped in coconut milk, okra, gherkins, eggplant and chayote, all picked especially for the kind, patient young man. There was enough every week for four families, so Ascânio divided the meat, flour, corn on the cob, fruit, tubers and green vegetables with lame Leôncio and dreamy Lindolfo, who one day would pluck up his courage, get on Jairo's *marineti* and head for Salvador to try his luck before radio microphones or television cameras. Lindolfo shared in his turn with the family of his friend Chico Sobrinho, in whose hospitable home he took supper on Saturday and dinner on Sunday.

In partial justification of Ascânio's uncharacteristic fit of anger, it should be pointed out that things had not been easy for him since Giovanni Guimarães's column had exploded in Agreste the evening before. Since then he had had a bellyful, to use an inelegant expression.

A Tarde had never been so popular in those parts. Everyone wanted to read the column, and there were not enough copies of the paper to go around. The only one generally available to the public was Seu Manuel's, which he left on the bar for the customers to glance at and Aminthas and Fidélio to read. That afternoon the customers nearly came to blows over the paper, which was passed from one to another until it mysteriously disappeared. Seu Manuel, on Aminthas' advice, had tried to invoke the law of supply and demand by renting the paper out, but this provoked the ire of all and sundry. Then Aminthas, changing tactics, proposed that the bar's liquid stock be socialized immediately to punish the Lusitanian's greed. The atmosphere was jocose, but nerves were on edge and the jokes were tinged with panic.

Ascânio had lost count of how many times that afternoon and evening he had had to explain that he thought it was still too early to judge, that it was unfair to jump to conclusions when all they knew—if they knew even that much—was the argument of a newspaper reporter opposed to Brastânio. Before making up their minds they ought to hear what the company's board of directors and technical men had to say.

Just at dusk, when he was on his way to his sacred appointment with Leonora at the door of Perpétua's house for their customary walk around the plaza, hand in hand, he was accosted by an almost incoherent De Matos Barbosa, clutching a copy of *A Tarde* wheedled out of Chalita the Arab, one of the five privileged subscribers. Ascânio, realizing all too well what a deplorable state of mind the poet must be in, had been trying to avoid him all afternoon.

At first the poet had been sure he was undone forever, discredited and covered with opprobrium by the poem he had perpetrated in praise of the monstrous industry denounced before the nation by his great good friend the columnist Giovanni Guimarães. And in an open letter addressed to *him*, De Matos Barbosa, poet and philosopher, in the illustrious columns of *A Tarde*. That unprecedented honor could only be eclipsed by the far greater dishonor he had brought down upon himself by those shameful alexandrines. It was a lucky thing that the accursed poem could not be heard over the bedlam the children had raised. "And what shabby toys they were, by the way, quite beneath notice, offal in fact!" the bard said (a little late, Ascânio thought). The poem had been heard, though, and applauded by the party of friends at Perpétua's house. Overwhelmed with shame, he had gone running to Tieta, who had raised his spirits with her jokes and teasing; raised him from the

dust, helped him conquer his despondency and sent him out on
another quest. Now he wanted to tell Ascânio, whom he did not
consider to blame in any way for the terrible thing that had happened, that he was restored to fight the good fight. Ascânio, no
doubt, was as innocently ignorant of Brastânio's criminal designs as
he, De Matos Barbosa, himself. But now there was no time to lose;
they must harken to Giovanni Guimarães' trumpet call of alarm.
He had beaten his lyre into a sword and was writing full tilt again, a
series of blistering Poems of Damnation in the satirical manner of
Gregório de Matos, with which he intended to deal a decisive blow
to the sinister plots of the corporation and make the name "Brastânio" anathema by unmasking the villainy and hypocrisy of its
criminal board of directors. He would be sending the first of these
poems to Giovanni for publication by the very next mail. His battle
flag was unfurled! As for that execrable earlier composition, it no
longer existed; Barbozinha had destroyed the originals and would be
grateful if Leonora would do him the favor of consigning to the
purifying fire the copy she had made after his reading.

Ascânio, tired and already late for his walk with Leonora, did
not try to dissuade the bard from penning his poetic indictment,
knowing he would only be wasting his time and his breath. He
promised Barbozinha that the copy would be destroyed, but said he
wouldn't mislead him: he was waiting until he had more information to form an opinion. What on earth did he want with more
information? demanded the poet. Whatever information he got
would be useless, set beside the unanswerable arguments of his peerless friend Giovanni Guimarães.

In this uneasy state of mind, after a restless sleep and night-
mares in which he had seen magnificent skyscrapers on the dunes of
Mangue Seco along with shoals of dead fish, and still without arguments with which to refute the columnist's assertions, Ascânio was
forced to hear the damned column all over again from beginning to
end, as if he hadn't read and reread it the night before. It sounded
even worse in Dona Carmosina's hoarse voice, interspersed with
coughing and caustic asides from her and the Skipper. When she
had finished, Dona Carmosina handed him a typed copy. She had
made three: one for him, one for the Skipper and a third just in
case.

At first Ascânio said cautiously that he intended to look into
the matter thoroughly; that he couldn't very well take the say-so of

just one columnist, even if it was Giovanni Guimarães, at face value and condemn out of hand a project of such vital interest to the community, the installation of factories for an industry of unquestioned importance in a distant, abandoned coconut grove on Mangue Seco, on land that was uninhabited and no use to anyone.

Distant, abandoned? No use to anyone? The Skipper's indignation boiled up. So as far as Ascânio was concerned, the Mangue Seco fishermen were nobody, and neither were the citizens of Agreste who owned summer houses on the beach.

At this point Ascânio lost patience. He was talking about the palm grove, of course, not about the beach itself. The Brastânio project—he had seen the plans and blueprints, he informed them—would be located much farther down the coast and farther inland, not next to the beach. Even if some pollution should result (and there wasn't any industry without pollution) it would not affect the fishermen or the summer people.

Little by little, curious bystanders started to gather in the post-office doorway and the hall to hear the absorbing debate. Dona Carmosina, inspired by the presence of an audience, forgot her flu and retorted with a closely reasoned argument: they were not talking about an ordinary industry with a tolerable level of pollution, they were talking about titanium dioxide. Was Ascânio aware of what that meant? She urged him to read the story in *O Estado de São Paulo* about the verdict of that Italian judge, Viglietta; the Skipper had kept it. A factory located in the palm grove would not only have a harmful effect on the beach, making fishing and sea bathing a practical impossibility, it would also destroy the fishing settlement of Mangue Seco by poisoning the water and the air and turning the ocean, in the words of that courageous Italian, into a garbage pail.

Ascânio, now thoroughly exasperated, replied in kind, cutting Dona Carmosina's obvious exaggerations down to size. In the first place, he said, there was no "fishing settlement" on Mangue Seco, only a few shacks inhabited by beachcombers and smugglers whose livelihood was against the law, if anybody had any respect for the law. And the "summer people" were a grand total of four or five couples; everyone else went to Saco Village, where swimming in the ocean was not dangerous and there were some amenities, such as a grocery store and a church. As for the resulting level of pollution, it was up to the experts to pass judgment, not a mere reporter with no scientific standing.

Dona Carmosina's rage drove her flu away for good. Giovanni Guimarães, she would have Ascânio know, was *not* a mere reporter but a great journalist, a man of broad culture and integrity, with a reputation to preserve. Ascânio had been away at law school when he made that unforgettable visit to Agreste, so he hadn't met him. Dona Carmosina would not have anyone belittling or casting doubt on the ability and integrity of a true friend of Agreste. What was more, she vehemently reiterated her determination, and the Skipper's too, to fight with all the weapons at their command against what they had begun to call "the death pall"—which, as Dona Carmosina, who was too precise and erudite for her own good, took the trouble to point out herself, was yellow, not black. Giovanni was wrong about that.

No sooner were the words out of her mouth than she was sorry she had shown off. Ascânio immediately pounced on the journalist's mistake. Who had pointed it out? An adversary? No. His great friend and admirer. If he didn't even know what color the smoke was, imagine how accurate the rest must be. Where could you find more damning proof of Giovanni's lack of scientific credentials? Oh, he was a fine person, no doubt, and that he was acting in good faith Ascânio had no reason to doubt, but in matters scientific he was an ignoramus. It wasn't quite enough to write spicy columns.

There was laughter at the bit about the color of the smoke. Ascânio had scored a hit, and Dona Carmosina was furious. By seizing on a trivial detail in the voluminous mass of concrete facts set forth in Giovanni's column, Ascânio was acting dishonestly. Yes, she accused him, violently and with intent to wound: "You're being dishonest!" She emphasized the rude word. "Dis-hon-est!"

To the Skipper's way of thinking it was even worse than that. He pointed out what appeared to him an unforgivable attitude on the part of Ascânio. Having been apprised of Brastânio's plans long since, thanks to his position as county clerk, he had concealed them from the townspeople; he had lied, he had let them all think it was a tourist project and had thus become a party to the criminal scheme. The Skipper found that attitude totally incompatible with the exercise of public office. It was nothing less than a breach of trust.

That was too much. Ascânio spat out all his accumulated bile in the references cited above to the half-dozen privileged people and the beautiful beach that the Skipper wanted to keep all for himself, barring the advent of redeeming industry and holding the community back through sheer selfishness. He pointed an accusing finger, at the end of an arm that was quivering with wrath.

"I'm going to see that progress comes to Agreste come hell or high water, no matter who tries to stand in the way!" he concluded in measured, belligerent tones.

He made his way through the knot of spectators and strode to the courthouse. Aminthas, a silent and apparently respectful bystander, summed up Ascânio's statement and the general situation.

"That sounds like a declaration of war!" He turned to Osnar. "The smoke war's begun, Osnar old pal. Which regiment will you enlist in, the black peril or the yellow peril?"

Osnar shook his head unsmilingly. He didn't like the way things were going one bit.

In which Skipper Dário de Queluz recruits volunteers.

Skipper Dário waited at the helm of his boat for Tieta to finish reading Giovanni Guimarães' column. He and Dona Laura had decided to spend New Year's and Epiphany at Mangue Seco, and Tieta and Ricardo were taking advantage of the ride and the company to give Inácio's Corral one last push, since the beachcombers would seize on any excuse not to work. Tieta was anxious to have her shack, as she called it, standing before she went back to São Paulo right after the power line came in. She had never intended to stay so long; she had planned on a month and had already been here almost two, which was ridiculous for someone who had business to look after. She was having a queen-size bed with a lamb's-wool coverlet made in Agreste for the Corral, and that was where she would tell Ricardo goodbye when it was time to go. Astério had ordered some camp beds and folding chairs and tables for her, and she had bought some hammocks in the market. Those would do for the guests: the old man and Mother Tonha, her sisters, her nephews and the friends who would use the Corral when she wasn't there.

Tieta's initial reaction after reading the article alarmed the Skipper. Handing the typed pages back to him, she remarked:

"Skipper, there's a lot of money to be made out of this."

"Money?"

"Weren't you the one who told me that land in the coconut grove is vacant and doesn't have an owner?"

"Not exactly. There's an owner all right, but no one can figure out who. Modesto Pires bought a piece that belonged to some of the fishermen. And he told me the only reason he didn't buy more was because the question of ownership was so doubtful. That palm grove has any number of owners, which is the same as saying that nobody owns it."

"Well, there you are, then. We buy up the land and sell it to the company for ten or twenty times what we paid for it. Felipe was a crackerjack at that kind of deal."

"For heaven's sake, Tieta! Do you think I want to make money out of my hometown's misfortune?"

"Skipper, as long as it's going to happen anyway and there's not a thing we can do about it, let's at least make a little profit. As soon as Ascânio started talking about his tourist business, the first thing I thought of was buying land out here."

"In the first place, I don't have the money to buy a dead cat; in the second place, it won't be easy to find out who the real owners are; and in the third place"—he paused before going on—"I don't intend to stand around and do nothing, Tieta; I'm going to go down fighting. I'm the most peace-loving man in the world, but those people are going to contaminate Agreste over my dead body."

The heavy canoe putt-putted leisurely down the river. The Skipper's impassioned voice captured Ricardo's attention. The seminarian had been listening to the conversation with only half an ear at first, his thoughts adrift on the stream. The Christmas holidays in Agreste had left memories, and their faint but persistent impressions had stayed in his mind and now returned to give him pleasure. For the first time he had noticed that certain women looked at him with interest, on the street and in church. Girls leaned out their windows and followed him with their eyes when he went by in his cassock to attend Father Mariano at mass, or when he crossed the square in bathing trunks and jersey on his way to the river. Cinira bit her lip when she looked at him and sighed; and as for Dona Edna, that one ate him up with her eyes right in front of her husband. Ricardo had felt Dona Edna's round backside bump into him during the melee over the Christmas toys. The most pleasurable and lingering memory, however, was of Carol, half-hidden behind the window curtain and smiling at him with full parted lips and glistening eyes. When she saw him coming down the sidewalk, Carol had retreated from the window the better to watch him and to smile—two things that were taboo for a rich man's concubine. Younger and darker than his aunt, she had the same wide bosom and strong, supple hips, the same exuberant flesh, and who could tell, perhaps the same love of a good time.

In Agreste, Ricardo had not had time to think about those smiles and swaying hips and biting lips. They had all gone up in the smoke of incense. But now, mirrored in the river, he saw faces and gestures that were not displeasing to him. That night he would hold Tieta in his arms on the dunes, as he had the very first time. When the Skipper and Dona Laura were there, aunt and nephew behaved with model decorum, she sleeping in the twin bed and he in the hammock. On the sand atop the dunes they forgot they were kin and the wind carried their love cries to the other side of the ocean. Only a few days had passed since it all began, but it seemed an immensely long time to Ricardo. How many days? How many years? He was another person now! How strange that he had never felt closer to God, never more sure of his priestly vocation. Why was that? When he asked Frei Thimóteo, the Franciscan saw nothing contradictory about it; quite the contrary.

"You've put your vocation to the test. Now you're at peace with yourself."

Ricardo came out of these thoughts when he heard the Skipper say vehemently, his voice rising:

"I'm going to fight, and once I get into a fight I don't back down!"

"But Skipper, do you think you stand a chance?" There was skepticism in Tieta's voice.

"That's what I wonder, too," put in Dona Laura in a worried voice.

"Whether I do or not, I'm not going to stand by and let them destroy Mangue Seco without a murmur."

The canoe glided through the water near one bank of the river, which was widening as they approached its mouth. The scene became more and more beautiful. They could see the ocean in the distance; the current became stronger and the boat was swept more lightly along. The Skipper lowered his voice but spoke persuasively, with passion.

"Listen, Tieta, and pay attention to what I'm about to say. If I start a protest campaign in Agreste I might as well save my breath. Oh, people will listen to me because they respect me, and some of them will agree with me, but nothing will happen. The same with Barbozinha; all those poems he's writing won't do any good. Maybe *A Tarde* will print one or two of them. So what? People may even make fun of him and call him a turncoat; after all, he did write a eulogy comparing the company executives to the Three Wise Men and then changed sides when his name came out in the paper. You can imagine what people will say."

"Poor Barbozinha! His feelings are so hurt. When he read that column he just about went out of his mind. He said he could never hold up his head any more, I had a time cheering him up, I tell you."

"He followed Ascânio's lead, and there's the result."

"It isn't Ascânio's fault, he didn't know what those people were up to. . . . What's that company's name again?"

"Brastânio."

"They talked about progress and donated the toys, and Ascânio was thrilled to pieces. It could have happened to any of us."

"I'm not denying that. Ascânio's got it into his head that it's his mission in life to do as much for Agreste as his grandfather did. You know his grandfather was the best mayor this town ever had, back in the good old days. He put in the electricity, paved the streets, and built the harbor and the courthouse. Ascânio goes wild when he hears the word 'progress.' That's why he may spoil everything we have: the climate, the beauty, the peace. I'll tell you one thing, Tieta: he won't get my vote for mayor."

"Oh, Skipper, don't say that. Ascânio really loves Agreste, he can do so many fine things for the community—"

"And so many wicked things. I never used to doubt Ascânio's integrity. But he's done a very ugly thing."

"Why, what was that?"

"He knew what those people had up their sleeves, he saw the plans and the blueprints; he knew all about it and he didn't say a word, just led us down the garden path with all that palaver about tourists."

"Poor Ascânio, he didn't know that industry was such a threat.

. . . It seems to be pretty bad, doesn't it? If you can believe what you read in the papers. . . ."

"I'll say it's bad! Nothing could be worse. All right, we'll give him the benefit of the doubt and say he didn't realize it was a threat. But how do you explain the fact that he's still defending Brastânio after Giovanni Guimarães' article came out? He insulted Carmosina and me this morning, right in the post office. I'm a man of the world, Tieta, and I learned long ago that nothing can ruin a good man quicker than a lust for power. It doesn't matter how honest he is to begin with."

He pointed to the dunes of Mangue Seco rearing above the breakers like a rampart facing the sea, a curtain of foam rising up as the great waves dashed against them. The Skipper's voice was full of feeling.

"Think of all that covered with slimy pollution! Progress is a good thing, but it has to be the right kind of progress." He gave Tieta a hard look. "To go back to what I was saying, if Barbozinha and Carmosina and I, and two or three others, are the only ones to protest, we won't get very far. But if you join us, Tieta, if you speak out against it and take the lead, it'll be a different story."

"Why me?"

"Because the people of Agreste look up to you. For all kinds of reasons: the power line, the old woman you saved from the burning house, your personal qualities, your kindness, your simplicity, your love of life. To the people of Agreste, you're just a little lower than St. Anne. What you say goes. Don't you know that?"

"Oh, I know they like me, they always did. It was the old man who drove me out of Agreste because he was scared of the pious old gossips; nobody else would have made me go. They like me, all right, but it doesn't follow that I have to get involved. Skipper, I love this place and I intend to spend my last days here, when it's time. But to get mixed up in a fight like this . . ."

"Forgive me for reminding you that it's your bounden duty. You say you love Agreste, and I know you do; you've bought a house in town and you're building another one on Mangue Seco. My only regret is that you don't settle down here now instead of waiting until you're an old lady." He smiled at Tieta affectionately. "Hasn't it occurred to you that if you fold your arms and do nothing today, then tomorrow when you want to come back none of this will be here any more and Mangue Seco will have turned into a sewer for the titanium factory? Have you ever wondered why no country in the world wants an industry like that within its borders?"

Tieta didn't reply, only gazed out over the majestic land- and seascape opening before her eyes. Yes, her beginnings were here. She had pastured goats on the Agreste sandhills and learned the facts of life on the Mangue Seco dunes. Was it her home? It was her beginning, yes; but her home was São Paulo; the immense, bustling, polluted, lonely metropolis was home to her now. São Paulo was where she made her living, and a very good living too, from the most expensive and exclusive house of pleasure in Brazil, the Lords' Retreat. And the apartments, and the ground-floor boutique—all of them were bringing in more money every month. Why on earth should she get involved in Agreste's problems? Once she was Tieta the goatherd, bleating with desire on the Mangue Seco sand dunes. Now she was Antoinette, the wealthy madam, procuress to millionaires. There was nothing for her to do here at the end of the earth. If Agreste's water and sky and Mangue Seco's beauty were despoiled, that was just too bad.

There was a desperate plea in the Skipper's voice.

"Only you, with your influence and your prestige, can save Agreste."

Tieta's face hardened into the face of Madame Antoinette. She had nothing more to do in Agreste; it was time she went back to São Paulo. She had visited her family, enjoyed the peace and quiet, been generous to her kin and her neighbors, succored the poor, and that ought to be enough. She had nothing else to do here, she repeated to herself.

Just let things happen as they would. She would come back someday, a wealthy, respectable, retired elderly lady, to spend the last years of her life here if that still seemed like a good idea. It was a good place to wait for death; that was what the traveling salesman who was responsible for her beating and expulsion had said. If it weren't for the prospect of seeing her and taking her in his arms in the shady corners down by the river, he had said, he'd stay the hell away from this hole. And he was right. Agreste was a perfect place to wait for death, that was all, with its health-farm climate, its peace and quiet, and its incomparable scenery. She was about to answer the Skipper with a resounding no when a doubt assailed her. Was it possible that the world no longer had a right to the existence of one place, just one, where it was good to wait for death?

"Tieta, if you say no, Agreste's finished and it's all over with Mangue Seco."

Before she could open her mouth, Ricardo spoke up imperatively from the stern.

"Don't you worry, Skipper, Aunt's going to say yes. She won't let them spoil Mangue Seco. Otherwise, why build Inácio's Corral?"

Tieta turned around to look at him. Her boy had grown into a man all of a sudden. She listened in astonishment to the steely determination in his voice.

"I read the story in the paper, Skipper: Barbozinha showed it to me. Aunt won't let them kill off the fish and fishermen, and neither will I. If you think I'll be of any use to you, Skipper, you can count on me."

Of a budding real-estate market in Mangue Seco,
and how Ricardo the seminarian cuts
the Gordian knot.

In Mangue Seco the sun was glorious, the sea vast; the sand dunes and endless palm groves lay apparently in utter peace—more apparent than real, as they soon found out.

While Dona Laura stayed behind at Liberty Hall with Gripa to see to the household arrangements, the Skipper took Ricardo and Tieta to inspect progress on the little house. He smiled at the astonishment of nephew and aunt when they saw the roof already on. The workmen had not taken their customary Christmas break, because of either Tieta's reputation, her money, or the combination of the two; or, more likely, the Skipper's prodding. He had taken over Ricardo's job as overseer and had wanted to give them a surprise. While Tieta lay covered with salve in Agreste and Ricardo stayed behind to take care of her, he had treated the workers to the traditional ridgepole-raising beerfest and had promised them a hefty bonus in the impatient owner's name if the roof was on by New Year's. All they had to do now was pour the concrete floor, paint the walls, fit the doors and windows, and fence the lot, in one corner of which the thoughtful Skipper had driven a tree trunk in which he had carved the singular name Tieta had chosen for her summer cottage. Liberty Hall and the Cozy Corner, Modesto Pires' comfortable dwelling place, were nearby, and Dr. Cáio Vilasboas' veranda-encircled house, to which he had given no name, could be seen at a little distance away from the beach near the riverbank.

As they were discussing the finishing stage of the work with the head stonemason and carpenter, Pedro Palmeira, the engineer, came up to them, sunburned and wearing only trunks, with his young son perched on his shoulders. That cheerful young man looked troubled, though he was usually talkative and fond of a good joke, an ideal vacation companion, always ready to kick a ball around on the beach with the boys and young fishermen or play a hard-fought game of bridge after the siesta with his wife, the Skipper and Dona Laura. His first question, even before he said good morning, revealed why.

"Have you read Giovanni Guimarães's column? What do you think?" He set the child down.

"It looks as if things could hardly be worse, doesn't it?" Skipper Dário replied.

"It sure does. I had a fight with Seu Modesto about it today. He doesn't feel the same way I do; all he can see is that there's a mint of money to be made."

Tieta hid a smile and threw the Skipper a meaningful glance to remind him of the beginning of their conversation in the canoe. The young man went on, scratching in the sand with the stalk of a palm frond:

"It wasn't pleasant. There are certain things I try not to talk about with my father-in-law because we never see eye to eye. Today I couldn't help it, though, and we had a row. It's too bad." He ran to grab his son, who was about to dive into the leftover plaster. "Marta was crying. When Seu Modesto gets mad he says the first thing that comes into his head. And he cares a lot more about money than anything else, including the basic values that are being threatened by pollution from Brastânio. He doesn't give a damn about them."

Tieta blushed in spite of herself. Hadn't her own first thought been of money? Hadn't she proposed to the Skipper that they buy up the land along the river where the company was thinking of building the factory and resell it at a profit? The Skipper had had to remind her of things like peace and quiet, the therapeutic climate, and the people's happiness and well-being before she snapped out of it and remembered those other, more important values—fundamental values, the bearded, worried young engineer called them—such as the right to health, beauty, tranquillity and a good place to wait for death. It was only after Ricardo, her golden boy, her gold-and-diamond boy, had proclaimed his militant solidarity with Agreste's cause and hers as well, that she had made up her mind to take a stand.

"Seu Modesto cut his vacation short and went back to Agreste to poke around in the public registry for old deeds that might give a lead as to who really owns the palm grove."

"It won't be easy to find out. He already tried once, you know, when he bought some land that belonged to the fishermen and was thinking about cutting it up into lots. It's a good thing that idea never got off the ground."

"That's because he didn't pursue it, Skipper. The housing development didn't work out, so he let it drop. But now he says he's not coming back until he discovers who the real owners are," the engineer explained. "As far as he could learn from one of the Brastânio experts who came around before I got here, the ideal place for the factory (there would be two of them, actually, two connecting factories) is a spot a little way downstream from the land he owns along the river. The guy wanted to know who it belonged to so he could tell the board of directors and try to make a deal. Naturally Seu Modesto clammed up like a crab."

"Well, if they've been in town asking around they must already have a pretty good idea that the palm grove either belongs to the fishermen or has no owner. That's what everybody thinks in Agreste."

"Seu Modesto told me he had bought all the land the fishermen owned."

"That's right."

"And now he wants the rest so he can turn around and sell it to Brastânio. By this time he's probably down at the registry giving Dr. Franklin a hard time."

They were so absorbed in their conversation that none of them noticed the approach of the austere Dr. Cáio Vilasboas. During his summer vacation the physician relaxed his habitual formality, shed his stiff collar and spent the day in pajamas. When he had to leave the house he donned the blue duster he wore when traveling in Jairo's *marineti*. He saluted them in passing but did not stop; he was walking toward the beach and appeared to be in a hurry. They looked after him curiously.

"I wonder if he's going to visit a patient?" remarked the Skipper in concern, as he watched the physician turn off toward the fishing village. "I've never seen Dr. Cáio around here before."

The engineer had another explanation.

"Don't you think he may be another one who wants to buy the palm grove from the fishermen? He probably thinks they own it."

"Of course! You've hit the nail on the head. The land rush is on. You know, Dr. Pedro, I was telling Tieta just now in the canoe that we can't just sit back, we've got to do something to stop this juggernaut."

"I couldn't agree with you more, but what? It's like Giovanni Guimarães says: the cacao barons have political clout and so does the Recôncavo, but the people around here think they're going to make a profit by bringing the factory in."

"If Tieta takes up the cudgels, everyone will be on our side."

The engineer nodded and smiled at Tieta.

"That's right, for sure. Seu Modesto tells me the people have put Dona Antonieta right up there on the altar next to St. Anne. And I'm not surprised."

The putt-putt of a speedboat was heard coming down the river.

"That's Pirica's boat," said the Skipper.

The speedboat crested the waves with passengers in it. Skipper Dário, with the unerring eye of an old salt, recognized them.

"What's Edmundo Ribeiro doing out here? Don't tell me . . ."

Sure enough, the tax collector disembarked on the beach with his son Leleu and made straight for the fishermen's hovels, his feet sinking into the sand. The engineer finished the Skipper's sentence for him.

". . . he's come to find out who owns the palm grove. Yessiree, that's why he's here."

"So there's another one. This is getting ridiculous. We've got to do something about it right away."

"But what can we do?" asked the bearded young man. "If this were Salvador you could agitate among the students, go to the newspapers, threaten to hold a demonstration. But here . . ."

The Skipper scratched his head in perplexity. Of course they couldn't stand idly by. But what the devil *could* they do, even if Tieta took the lead and they got the people behind them?

"Yes, what can we do?" Tieta asked in her turn.

Bronzed, barefoot, bare-chested in his bathing trunks, resembling a youthful fisherman more than a Levite in the temple, Ricardo raised his voice again and issued a stern sentence from which there was no appeal.

"The next time those people come around Agreste or Mangue Seco, we'll make them run for their lives."

"What?" exclaimed the Skipper before exploding with enthusiasm.

"Cardo!" exulted Tieta, turning to gaze at her nephew, her boy, a he-goat with a vengeance.

"Put 'er there." The engineer gave the seminarian's hand a hearty shake.

The figures of Dr. Cáio Vilasboas and Edmundo Ribeiro the tax collector passed each other among the scattered half-dozen hovels. That was the beginning of the land rush on Mangue Seco.

In which the boastful author defends himself
from harsh criticism on the pretext of
providing essential information.

Don't think I'm spoiling for a fight; why should I be? I've already taken my stand as a neutral; I'm an objective, cool-headed narrator laying the facts before his readers. Neither is it my intention to remark upon the visible change taking place in young Ricardo's behavior. It is just that once again I bear witness to the influence of a luscious, perfumed—what shall I call it?—a luscious, perfumed honeycomb, an intoxicating black rose. That was all it took to turn ice into fire, lamb into lion, pious seminarian into subversive student roughneck.

The other day my friend and literary comrade in arms, Fúlvio D'Alambert (José Simplício da Silva, banker, in the humdrum mediocrity of bourgeois life; if I've already explained who he is I'll do it again—better be accused of being redundant than of having left something out), told me he was shocked to discover that there are seminaries where the students actually read and analyze Freud and Marx, not to deny and refute their heretical theories and denounce them to the political police (that body having nicely replaced the Holy Inquisition) but quite the contrary, to praise and applaud them. Despite Frei Thimóteo's presence on the faculty, I don't believe the students at the seminary in Aracaju studied Marx and Freud in 1965. That was only yesterday, yet how far in the past it seems already and what transformations the world has witnessed since then! Changes are taking place so fast that time is left behind and the present is reduced to a fleeting moment. Ricardo's encounter with the hippies and his many talks with Frei Thimóteo both contributed to the young man's surprising development, but what definitely made him into another man and turned him inside out was the fragrant black rose, the succulent honeycomb into which the hungry, thirsty wayfarer dived, to emerge reborn.

These images—black rose, honeycomb—are metaphors used by the author on purpose to avoid the real words, some of which, the respectable ones, express nothing. Vagina and vulva, for example, are so ugly they ought to be cuss words; and the others, taboo in polite society, are the very ones that express vigorously, precisely, poetically the warmth, sweetness, grace, eternity and perfection of a woman's cunt: *xoxota, xibiú, boceta.**

My fellow scribbler and critic Fúlvio D'Alambert, to whom I turn over my manuscript chapter by chapter for grammatical corrections, accents in the right place and stylistic advice, has upbraided me harshly for the use and abuse of these terms, for plunking them down in a literary work, debasing the language and disfiguring the sentences in which they appear. Why make a point of repeating obscenities, why return again and again to the forbidden subject with copious references to what he primly calls women's genital organs?

And I ask in my turn: how on earth could I *not* talk about something so important in the life of every man? And why call it by hard, aggressive names that defile its beauty and grace? Why deny it the appealing pet names that spring from the grateful tongues of the people? At the table in the barroom, whenever Aminthas, Fidélio,

---

* All these words mean the same thing, but they imply a certain playful tenderness lacking in the four-letter Anglo-Saxon word.—Translator's note.

Seixas, Barbozinha the poet and the diligent Ascânio begin to discuss higher philosophy and show off their intellectual prowess, Osnar yawns with boredom and protests, "Why waste so much time shooting the bull when you could be talking about the most interesting subject there is: cunt?"

Every once in a while, as Dona Carmosina says—and here I have to agree with that smarty-pants—Osnar says something that does our souls good.

While I'm on the subject of the poolroom gang I'll reply to another objection made by my fussy friend Fúlvio D'Alambert, who has kindly pointed out that my readers have not been informed what three of the four cronies who turn up so often in the pages of this melodramatic screed do for a living. They are apprised of Osnar's enviable circumstances as a citizen who lives off his income and doesn't have to work, but what about the others? Aminthas' bent for humor has been mentioned, and the fact that he raves over pop music and is kin to Dona Carmosina, but none of that describes his trade or source of income. As for Seixas, all my readers have been told is that he has a passel of female cousins; and about Fidélio, who seems to be a slippery sort of individual, they know nothing at all. I agree with the criticism, I admit my error, I deserve a public flogging. My friend Fúlvio D'Alambert was right to draw my attention to such a grave lapse, such a lack of important, not to say basic, information: how do these characters earn their keep? It is economy that conditions human life and actions, as the seminarians learn from Marx. Or is it sex, as they learn from Freud? There's a hell of a lot of confusion there, which I'll take advantage of to provide the missing information and redeem my negligence. Well then, all three of these individuals, Aminthas, Seixas and Fidélio, are civil servants, the first employed by the federal government, the other two by the state. Now that the reader knows the three young men are servants of the nation and the state he will no longer think of them as shiftless, idle, unemployed loafers. Shiftless and idle they may be; unemployed they are not.

And now at last I come to my only real reason for putting this chapter in at all. What I wanted to do was give my readers the names of the five subscribers to *A Tarde*. Here they are: Modesto Pires, Chalita the Arab, Edmundo Ribeiro, Dr. Cáio Vilasboas, and Seu Manuel the Portugee. The sixth copy, as we know, went to Dona Carmosina, courtesy of management. After Giovanni

Guimarães' "Letter to De Matos Barbosa the Poet" exploded in print, the number of subscriptions rose from five to nine, and Dona Carmosina, who always manages to come out ahead, pocketed a fat commission. Fat for Agreste, of course. Everything is relative, as Einstein, whom the Aracaju seminarians do not study either, so aptly remarked.

Of the fair Leonora Cantarelli, lying in a hammock among goats and whales, under an azure sun.

Lovely Leonora Cantarelli, as she lay in a hammock on Perpétua's veranda, received a hasty goodbye kiss from Peto, whose obligation as a poolroom kibitzer, to say nothing of a well-founded fear of punishment for some rash words he had just said, was calling him to the bar, where a billiards tournament among the best cues in town was to begin at five o'clock. Peto never would forego a kiss from his cousin when he went in or out. Leonora was amused by the youngster's guile, precocity, and knowing eyes. Otherwise he was loving and solicitous, always at the beck and call of his aunt and cousin from São Paulo. He worshiped Antonieta, but that did not prevent him from peeking down her low-necked dress and feasting his eyes on however much of her bosom he could see.

After Barbozinha had left for the post office, Peto had stayed to keep Leonora company and tell her about his fishing expeditions. He had gone down the river that morning with Elieser in the motor launch. The fish were biting like anything, great big *carapebas*; the reel and rod Aunt Antonieta had given Cardo turned out to be the best thing on the water. He had come back with his creel full of *carapebas* and pike this big—he showed her with his hands—and taken them to Aunt Elisa. That night they'd eat off fish caught by himself, Peto, king of the fishhook and bait. Aunt Elisa knew how to cook fish all right, they'd all lick their chops. And she was pretty too, the prettiest lady in Agreste; the only one in the running with her was Leonora.

"I'd say my aunt and my cousin are neck and neck. If I had to make a choice, I'd take both."

Perpétua, whose antennae were always out, heard him as she passed and reprimanded him:

"Here, boy, what do you mean by such lack of respect? Is that how you were brought up? Do you want me to punish you?"

Peto lit out before his mother could make up her mind whether to send him to his room to study for an hour or make him go to church with her and listen to the dingdong vesper sermon; the champions were gathering in the bar. Peto winked at Leonora, stole his kiss, and by the time Perpétua came to get him—"Where's that limb of Satan?"—he had hightailed it out the door. Perpétua stopped grumbling about her younger son to give instructions to Aracy to scour the silver with sand to make it gleam. As long as the girl was there she was making use of her for a general spring cleaning, and everything in the house shone like new.

"That boy'll be the end of me. Ricardo doesn't give me any trouble, but that Peto—I don't know who he takes after. You'd think he was Tieta's boy." She clapped her hand over her mouth in horror. What if the little minx tattled to her stepmother?

"Oh, no, he's a fine boy," Leonora said sweetly.

"You just close your eyes to his foolishness out of the goodness of your heart." She disappeared into her private oratory.

Alone again, Leonora went back to the works of De Matos Barbosa, lent her by the author. Two were poetry and the third contained philosophical maxims. The loan had been accompanied with many admonitions. She must be very careful of the books, because he had only those volumes and the edition had long been out of print. One of them was worth a fortune today, and no one who had a copy wanted to sell it. A limited number of copies had been privately printed. The volume, illustrated with ten woodcuts by Calasans Neto, some in color, some in black and white, had been financed by the poet's friends and sold by subscription when an embolism had threatened to end his life, or worse, to leave him mute, blind or paralytic in a wheelchair. The direct sale of the book had brought in enough to pay for medicine and a private room at the hospital. As for doctors, he had had the best medical attention free of charge. There was no one in Salvador who did not know and appreciate De Matos Barbosa the poet and his gentle lunacy.

When he handed Leonora the old volumes, leafing through the beautiful edition of *Poems from Agreste* with her and lingering over the illustrations, Barbozinha had philosophized a little about life and the whims of fate. That was the last book he had been able to publish. Once out of danger but weakened by the hemorrhage, halting in voice and step, he had retired from public life and gone into voluntary exile on his placid native ground, far from the bookshops, the lively cafés and evening gatherings, the stories in the papers, the success and fame that might have been his. While his star was declining, that of the young engraver Calasans Neto (half-breed Calá was a ball of fire, the poet assured Leonora earnestly) had risen to glorious heights, borne on the backs of those first goats and whales, carved in wood eleven years ago to embellish Barbozinha's poems about Agreste's sandhills and the dunes of Mangue Seco—those whales, rising unexpectedly from the sea and gliding up the Real River, those goats skipping on the rocks like coquettish young girls. Today he was famous all over Brazil and his work was shown in New Orleans and London. "Yes, ma'am, yes, my dear friend. That's life, isn't it? Some going up the ramp, others going down," he remarked without bitterness. Having lived so many lives in so many different reincarnations, these crests and troughs of life affected him very little, especially since his soul brother Giovanni Guimarães, *A Tarde*'s star reporter, had lifted him out of his obscurity and placed the standard of the struggle against pollution in his hands.

In two nights of inspired fury he had composed five Poems of Damnation, branding with the red-hot iron of poetry the putrid face of the peddlers of death. He had hoped to read them to Tieta, eternal one and only muse of his published works, whose arm and heart had sustained him when lightning struck and the bard found himself buried beneath the humiliation of his paean in verse to Brastânio, that abject product of the error into which he had wandered in Ascânio's company. Both of them were innocent victims of perfidy. He would take this occasion to thank the charming sylph for having fed her copy of the *corpus delicti* to the purifying flames, quenching for all time the memory of that infamy; he had already burned the original to ashes.

Not finding Tieta, who had ungratefully neglected to tell him she was going back to Mangue Seco, he recited two of the five poems of redemption to Leonora. He felt that the other three were unfit to print in a newspaper or a magazine or for tender ears to hear. To Tieta, a widow, an old and intimate friend and his permanent muse, he would have had the courage to recite them, but not to

Leonora. He, De Matos Barbosa, catching fire from the creative impulse of his glorious predecessor Gregório de Matos, had laid about him in rough and vigorous language and rained blows on the heads of Brastânio's board of directors. Here and there among the verses, four-letter words glittered like rough black diamonds, to use Barbozinha's metaphor.

Peto, clattering up the steps to the porch with the noisy heartiness of the triumphant fisherman, hastened the bard's departure for the post office to mail off his poems and a long letter to Giovanni Guimarães. Before doing so, however, he intended to read both to his friend Carmosina. That good lady, spinster though she was, could hear any amount of bad language without being shocked.

And so off they had gone; first the poet, pipe unlit, step slow, heart ablaze; then the impudent but affectionate boy in his gauche but touching precocity. Leonora gazed at the woodcuts of goats and whales, rocks and hillocks, the girl with her shepherd's crook, and a strange blue sun rising over the river, a fantastic and extravagant touch on the part of the artist. That blue sun did not surprise her, though; it had a familiar air. Ever since she had arrived in Agreste, Leonora had felt surrounded by a diaphanous light in shades of sky blue, an unreal, magic world where there was no room for either evil or misfortune. Her lips murmured the two stanzas of Barbozinha's repudiated poem, the ones in which the poet called Ascânio Trindade the Captain of the Dawn.

The Captain was under siege. He had had no rest for two days and two nights; his wild look and bloodshot eyes were sure signs of insomnia. That first night he had hardly said a word. Circling the plaza with Leonora, he had taken the girl's hand and caught it between his own as if mutely seeking support and reassurance. The story in the paper had literally made him ill. Little by little, perhaps because she made no comment and asked no questions, he began to tell her what was on his mind. Giovanni Guimarães had taken the lid off something real, there was no doubt about that, he said; there must be some truth to what he said. But though he, Ascânio, was not prepared to make a statement of his own, he was almost certain that the angry reporter's diatribe was grossly exaggerated, for what obscure reasons Ascânio couldn't say. Titanium processing was bound to cause a certain amount of pollution; all industries polluted, some more, some less. What he found hard to believe was that ghastly prediction of mortal danger to the flora, the fauna, the river and the sea. At any rate, before taking a stand they ought to wait until the journalist's accusation was either confirmed, refuted, or placed in proper perspective by qualified experts. Leonora lifted his hand and kissed it. Ascânio was right, they ought to wait. Maybe it would all turn out to be just a tempest in a teapot.

Last night had been even harder. Ascânio usually managed to find two or three good reasons during the day to go to Perpétua's house, either asking permission to come in for a moment or calling Leonora to the window for a few words, a smile, a kiss, she standing at the living-room window, he on the sidewalk. Yesterday, though, he had not appeared all day. Leonora had heard from Dona Carmosina about the violent argument that had taken place at the post office that morning. A little while after that the Skipper had come with Dona Laura to pick up Mama and Ricardo, but he had said nothing about the incident. Of Ascânio there had been no sign.

He came at the usual time after supper, unsmiling and grave. Leonora was waiting for him in the doorway. Ascânio wouldn't come in, not even to wish Perpétua good evening. They crossed the square to the little park, where flirtatious girls and young men were walking two by two. After a heavy silence, he asked, "Have you heard?"

"About the argument? Yes."

"It was awful. I lost my head and insulted the Skipper, a person a lot older than I am, a man I respect. But he accused me of being dishonest."

"The Skipper? I thought it was Carmosina."

"She just blew up and cussed me out; that isn't important. But the Skipper said I had lied, that I knew all the time about the project for the factory and fooled everyone and never let on. He thinks that proves I'm unworthy of my trust. I don't know if that's true or not, but the rest of it is: I did lie, I did hide what I knew, I did try to keep everyone else in the dark. But I swear I only did it for the good of Agreste. Dr. Stefano—you know who he is—asked me to keep it a secret because nothing was decided yet and if the word got out it might spoil everything. As far as I'm concerned, Agreste's best interests come before everything else."

Just as she had done the day before, Leonora lifted Ascânio's hand to her lips and kissed it. The youth smiled such a sad smile that she realized how deeply hurt and upset he was. And so, right there under a tree in the plaza, without a thought for the other couples nearby, she stopped, took his face in her two hands and kissed Ascânio on the mouth, so that he and everyone else would know that she was with him all the way.

Lying in the hammock, admiring the woodcuts, the haughty goats and peaceful whales and the great blue sun that was both real and a dream, Leonora counted the minutes. Ascânio had sent Leôncio with a message that morning: he had a very busy day ahead of him, what with the problem of paving that street at the edge of town, but he would come by to see her sometime during the day if he could find the time. Leonora was in on the festive plot, the ceremonies planned in honor of the Joan of Arc of the *sertão*. Barbozinha's stanzas fluttered on her lips.

The cathedral bell clanged out five in the afternoon. Threats and dangers bristled around the Captain of the Dawn. Was it only around him or around both of them, around Ascânio's and Leonora's courtship and the blue sun of Agreste? Where were Captain Ascânio's pride, his enthusiasm, his certainty of winning out in the vanguard of progress, toppling the walls of backwardness, lighting fires of hope in the lifeless town and in Leonora's breast? Now she saw him drooping, moody, sad, almost beaten. Triumphant or defeated, she loved him just the same.

Just at that moment he swooped onto the veranda without asking permission, his old, proud, enthusiastic, victorious self. He carried a bundle of newspapers and was full of the news that Mud Lane was about to be paved and the street sign reading "Antonieta Esteves Cantarelli" had arrived.

Of the paving of a street, a street sign and a newspaper headline; a chapter all in flashbacks, in which Ascânio Trindade resumes his threatened role as leader.

We now find Ascânio Trindade at the edge of town between the marketplace and the bend of the road in a wrangle with the foreman, Esperidião do Amor Divino, about the paving of the street along which the electric power line was to enter Agreste, just as the much-delayed *marineti* sounded its frightful honk and hove into view in a cloud of dust, a familiar yet somehow always surprising, even resplendent apparition. When he put his foot on the brake, Jairo caught sight of the county clerk. Amid squeals and explosions the *marineti* shook, jumped up in the air, danced, threatened to skid, shake loose, break in two, and finally quieted down. The motor's indomitable old heart went on throbbing erratically. Jairo was not fool enough to turn it off; there was no guarantee it would ever start up again. It had already given him a hard time that day.

Up until the moment when Jairo proved not only that the vehicle had brakes but that they were far better than anything manufactured nowadays, Ascânio had had an extremely hard day. His life had been a nightmare ever since he had clapped eyes on Giovanni Guimarães' column. After his talk with Dr. Mirko Stefano (Doctor Magnifico, as his executive secretary called him, that girl who had headed the battalion of "experts" and come back dressed as Santa Claus) and before that column exploded into print, Ascânio had fashioned for himself a splendid dream castle of intimations of a sensational future for Agreste and himself. Progress would follow the chimneys of the factories built on Mangue Seco as night followed day: a wide paved road, maybe even a two-lane highway; a model town in the coconut grove for workers and employees; a model hotel in Agreste several stories high; a prosperous, wealthy community. Brastânio, the pioneer, would blaze the trail for other industries, all eager to benefit from the peerless facilities the community afforded. And at the head of it all, beckoning them onward, was that resourceful, versatile, enterprising administrator and statesman with a head full of plans and the know-how to carry them out—none other than Ascânio Trindade, mayor of Sant'Ana do Agreste, who was soon to marry the beautiful, virginal—no, not virginal; the beautiful, innocent, appealing heiress from São Paulo, Leonora Cantarelli. Sometimes he prolonged their engagement, that delightful period when desire tantalized and, little by little, gained ground throughout the body; sometimes he wished them married right away, and pictured her in their home and with child, her angelical air maturing with the waxing of her belly.

It was a castle built of cards, and the explosion flattened it and the young man's self-confidence together. Without warning he found himself shaken by a whirlwind like the storms that sometimes descended on Mangue Seco, uprooting coconut palms, splintering the fishermen's cabins to bits, stirring the ocean to its depths, raising incredible whirlpools of sand, changing the position and height of the dunes. When the storm was over and peace returned, the landscape had changed; it resembled what had been but was another, different scene.

Ascânio refused to take Giovanni Guimarães' dire predictions of the evils deriving from the titanium-dioxide industry at face value. His skepticism was bolstered by the fact that the reporter was a layman, unqualified to give a scientific verdict. And yet, what if his accusations were true? Maybe he had consulted physicists and chemists. The story exuded self-assurance, as if the writer were absolutely sure of his facts. Well, not all of them. Hadn't Dona Carmosina herself, that passionate partisan, found one gross error in it, the color of the smoke? If Giovanni was mistaken about that, he might be mistaken about all the rest. But what if he were right about everything but the color of the smoke? What if that industry really was a mortal threat to the fish, and thus the fishermen's livelihood? On the other hand, it was true that people nowadays had a mania for seeing pollution everywhere and blaming the factory chimneys for all the misfortunes of the world.

What stand should he take? That was the question. If it could be proved that Giovanni Guimarães had exaggerated, the decision was easy. If, on the other hand, the experts backed him up, what should Ascânio do? Break with Mirkus the Magnificent and take back his promise of smoothing the way for the installation of Brastânio in the community, or face the threat of pollution head on in the conviction that the economic transformation of the area and the wealth to be derived from industrialization were more important to Agreste's future than a handful of fishermen on Mangue Seco, more important than clear water and a beautiful river? What should he do? Which side should he be on? Should he give up all his statesmanlike plans and his dreams of engagement and marriage to buy time for a faultless climate, simple beauty and sluggish placidity? What good did a cloudless sky, limpid water, beauty and peace do anyone, after all? A good place to wait for death; with the passing of time the traveling salesman's *bon mot* had been repeated so often it had become a worn-out cliché. Wouldn't it be better in the long run to sacrifice a few fishermen (and incidentally put an end to the smuggling at the mouth of the Real River, which had held out against the sporadic incursions of the police for nearly a century) and accept the risk of contaminating the water, in exchange for future wealth, opportunities and progress on the march? The fishermen on Mangue Seco were few, and all of them were smugglers, but those in Saco across the bar were numerous, sober and hardworking. There was no getting around it, the killing of the fish and the contamination of the water would affect the whole mouth of the river delta and the ocean itself. Good God, it was enough to drive a Christian or a Marxist mad, this contradictory universe in which so many conflicting interests were at stake. Ascânio, exhausted, nervous and at the end of his rope, tried to quash this last disturbing argument by reminding himself that since Saco and its beaches were in the state of Sergipe, the fate of the fishermen who lived there was no concern of his; the community he managed was in another state. To his credit, he was not convinced.

The proof that he was not was a decision he had made at the courthouse that morning with respect to the paving of Mud Lane at the city limits, in time for the christening of the hydroelectric plant's powerline. It was high time the work got underway; in less than a month the pylons would reach Agreste and Tieta's Light would go on. Ascânio squared his shoulders and decided to ignore Mirko Stefano's glittering promises and go back to his modest original idea of paving the street with stones. After all, stones abounded in the river and on the hills, the only really cheap thing in Agreste besides mangoes and cashew fruit. He would just have to appeal to the community's prosperous citizens once again, go down his list and be a public beggar for the umpteenth time.

Feeling uncharacteristically irascible and grouchy after making his decision, he endured a long and difficult argument with Esperidião over how long the project would take and how much it would cost. Ascânio hoped for a fast, cheap piece of work; Esperidião found the county clerk's miserly offer unreasonable, especially considering the press of time. He would have to find a lot of men who were willing to work far into the night, and even then he couldn't guarantee to get the job done by the stipulated date. In the end they went out to the edge of the town for a better look at the site.

They had just worked out a compromise of sorts when Jairo

braked his *marineti*, smothering the skinny, feisty Espiridião do Amor Divino in a cloud of dust. Turning his head so he could breathe, the foreman yelled:

"All this talk about pollution, as if that goddam *marineti* hadn't been giving us all black lung for the last twenty years!"

Jairo, rested and in fine fettle despite the fact that he was three hours late because the temperamental motor was in a rebellious mood and had stalled several times that day, stepped out of the bus with two packages.

"Two items for you, Ascânio. This one's for Canuto." It was a fat package, still in its original wrappings, addressed to Canuto Tavares from a business firm in Bahia.

Ascânio took the package and felt it.

"I know what this is." He turned to Esperidião. "It's the street sign. I didn't think it would be ready this soon."

"And here's one Miroel gave me down at the bus station and told me was urgent. It looks like it might be important; it came in on the through bus from Salvador to Aracaju, and the bus made a special stop in Esplanada just to leave it off. Here you are. How's that for service?"

He laughed, handed over the parcel and stood waiting, impatient for Ascânio to open the packages. As Ascânio had thought, the first one contained the new street sign with Dona Antonieta's name in white letters on a blue background. Jairo and Esperidião came closer to have a look. Ascânio had ordered it from Bahia through Canuto Tavares' good offices. The lapsed postal employee was a kind of agent for Agreste in Esplanada and had often obliged Ascânio before.

One passenger was in a hurry and in no mood to put up with any nonsense. Dona Preciosa, the grammar-school principal, got up and sounded the *marineti*'s amazing horn, frightening the birds. That Jairo was just impossible. Here they were, hours and hours late, and he had nothing better to do than get off the bus for a chat, just when they were finally on the home stretch. The other package, addressed to Ascânio Trindade, Dynamic Mayor of Sant'Ana do Agreste, with URGENT in red capital letters, contained several newspapers and a letter. As the sound pollution from the horn put the sand-diver lizards to flight, Ascânio unfolded one of the papers and his face relaxed. His irritability, fatigue and resentment fell

away as he read a headline in bold type on the front page—BRASTÂNIO
UNMASKS AN IMPOSTOR—and took in at a glance that the unmasked
impostor was none other than *A Tarde*'s columnist, Giovanni
Guimarães.

Dona Preciosa appeared at the door of the *marineti* and raised
the acid, threatening voice which had reduced generations of trou-
blesome children to obedient silence. The wart on her neck quivering, she called out, "Are you fixing to stand there talking very much
longer, Jairo?"

"No, ma'am, we're as good as on our way." It was Ascânio who
replied as he strode toward the *marineti*, followed by Jairo and
Esperidião, carrying his newspapers as reverently as if they were
gold, precious stones or a cure for death.

Of the arguments in favor.

Giovanni Guimarães' arguments were unanswerable, so Barbozinha
the poet had told Leonora. There was nothing more to say, said
Dona Carmosina and the Skipper; *A Tarde*'s columnist had crossed
every *t* and dotted every *i*. The publishers and editors of other
newspapers did not agree, and the proof lay before Ascânio Trindade on the mayor's desk. There were copies of two newspapers
from the capital in which the negative views the columnist had
expressed in his "Letter to De Matos Barbosa the Poet" were demolished, or at least subjected to a thoroughgoing review, harsh criticism, and a disagreeable confrontation with the weighty arguments
of noted scientists and responsible businessmen.

One of these papers had printed the screaming headline that
had caught Ascânio's eye. Taking a seat in the *marineti* and excitedly rereading it, he took in the full measure of the harsh treatment
meted out to Giovanni. He was denounced as an impostor, no less.
The paper took no notice of the journalist's fame or the general
esteem in which he was held.

A long editorial in 12-point black type sang the praises of
Brastânio in glowing terms that put the tributes in Barbozinha's
excoriated poem to shame. Just as the state government was about to
complete work on the Aratu Industrial Center, thus creating the

conditions for a surge of new life in Bahia, the location in the *Boa Terra* of an industry like Brastânio, of fundamental importance to the country's development, was the most auspicious news of the year that was coming to an end, a splendid Christmas present for the people of the state, the article declared. It was not too much to say that Bahia had hit the jackpot, having been so fortunate as to be chosen by the distinguished board of directors of this corporation as the site for a capital investment on a hitherto unheard-of scale for a private venture. Naturally there were those who raised the cry of pollution, but "the naysayers we have always with us, opposing progress and prophesying doom. Their voices are scattered and of doubtful origin, and they serve doubtful masters too. If simple curiosity leads us to examine the political biographies of these croaking birds of ill omen, we soon find a suspicious ideological slant made in Moscow," etc. The whole editorial was in the same vein. Giovanni Guimarães was not mentioned by name, but it was obvious who was meant.

He *was* mentioned by name, however, in an interview in the same newspaper with one of the "dynamic directors of Brastânio (Brazilian Titanium Industry, S.A.), the rapidly rising young executive Dr. Rosalvo Lucena, a nationally known economist, a graduate of and later professor at the Getúlio Vargas Foundation, and a Ph.D. in Business Administration from Boston University." The bearer of all these distinguished titles began by poking fun at Giovanni, "an entertaining columnist with no scientific background at all, who ought to stick to what he knows best—the trivial events of everyday life, whatever he finds on the police blotter, and winning and losing soccer teams—all favorite subjects of his—and not go off half-cocked in public on subjects about which he knows absolutely nothing. When he does that, he ceases to be a columnist and becomes an impostor, trying to arouse public opinion against a highly patriotic enterprise which will contribute to Brazil a saving in foreign currency, a broader work market and good hard cash. As to the alleged mortal peril that Brastânio's factories would represent, a danger existing only in the mind of this hack journalist, it may be more instructive to read the opinion of a technical expert of whose qualifications there can be no doubt: Dr. Karl Bayer, whose name will be familiar to all who take an interest in environmental problems." In a three-column spread in the middle of the page, Ascânio saw a photograph of "the dynamic Dr. Rosalvo Lucena, the distinguished scientific expert Herr Karl Bayer and the affable Dr. Mirko Stefano talking to the editor of this paper during a visit to the newsroom."

In an exceedingly learned-sounding essay which was in its very opacity all the more convincing, the distinguished scientific expert gave a crushing reply to the skeptics by answering three questions he had made up himself, reporters being too ignorant about ecology to ask the right ones. With a reckless expenditure of elmenite, chloride, Australia, catalyzers, vanadium pentoxide, necton, plankton, and effluents, he proved beyond doubt that all these alarming rumors about the danger of pollution, the killing of fish and the contamination of water were nothing but "despicable demagoguery." Who, in the face of all that science, could doubt it?

In the other newspaper, which was no less enthusiastic about the installations of Brastânio, that "industry of national salvation, destined to be a prime factor in the reconstruction of the economy of Bahia," Aristóteles Marinho, an engineer from the State Bureau of Industry and Commerce, had lent his pen to the corporation's cause. There was no danger whatever, this expert declared in plain language shorn of scientific terms and effluents, a modest contribution compared to that of the German Bayer. It was not without importance, nonetheless, for it showed the thinking of the state government, which (so the engineer claimed) after making a thorough study of the matter and taking the vital interests of the population into account had concluded that "the industry to be located in Bahia by Brastânio is not only perfectly harmless but vital to the state." In conclusion, the engineer reassured his readers that they need lose no sleep, for their ever-vigilant government would never allow the land, water and air of Bahia to be contaminated. He meant both the state and national governments, "united indissolubly in the defense of their natural resources and the health of their people."

The newspapers (there were several copies of each) were accompanied by a note from Dr. Mirko Stefano addressed to his dear friend Dr. Ascânio Trindade, informing him that Brastânio had contracted for a transportation company to make a survey and submit a plan for the widening and paving of the fifty kilometers of road between Agreste and Esplanada. The same company would pave the street at the edge of the town at Brastânio's expense, just as he had promised. The road machinery and workmen would be arriving in a few days. He made no mention of the newspapers or Giovanni Guimarães.

Reflections of the author concerning names and experts.

Weary of the constant effort of maintaining my unblemished reputation as a prudent and objective storyteller and keeping clear of polemics when summarizing and transcribing the widely varying opinions expressed in newspaper columns, editorials, feature stories and interviews, I will here take the liberty of reflecting briefly on the surnames and methods of those renowned scientific experts whose opinions have the force of law. My only intention in doing so is to preserve the reader from confusion.

In these parlous times when books are a luxury instead of a staple of life like bread and water (which also cost a fortune, incidentally; nothing comes cheap these days but vexation and grief), I cannot allow any reader who has spent good money to buy his copy of this entertaining fat novel—and every novel worth its salt should be both—to draw any wrong conclusions, as he very well might if he were not enlightened on a significant point regarding the eminent scientist who granted an interview to a newspaper in Salvador, a summary of the profound contents of which was included in the previous chapter. Since the interview was long and weighted down with physics, chemistry, ecology and such, it did not seem advisable to reproduce it in its entirety. Let us skip this detail, however, and pass on to the distinguished gentleman's family name, with which these reflections are primarily concerned. Bayer is the illustrious surname in which Herr Professor Karl rejoices.

A famous name, an illustrious name, and one which for that very reason can easily give rise to misinterpretation and its dangerous consequences. Therefore I hasten to point out that, as far as I can determine, the professor is not a member of the great German family that owns industrial and chemical plants in the four corners of the earth. Nationality in this case means capital, both social and revolving capital; in the age of multinational enterprise it is money, not birth or blood, that determines nationality.

When I came across Herr Professor Karl Bayer laying down the law in the previous chapter, I shouted hallelujah, here's my chance for literary immortality and prizes, preferably in cash, at the thought of the honor heaped on my humble novel by the presence of one of the world's great men, a Bayer no less, among the humble folk of Agreste. When I launched into this faithful account of Tieta's mishaps and adventures, I expressed a hope that somewhere in this poor narrative there would appear, to the greater glory of its dirty-minded author, one of the magnates who really own Brastânio. One of the bosses, mind you, not a bootlicker like the Magnificent Doctor, the Ph.D. in Business Administration, His Excellency the Governor, or the Parliamentarians Young and Old. They all earn salaries, they're all well up the ladder and they're all well paid, some of them in foreign currency, for what they do, but none is a Big Boss. My heart beat faster when I read the name Bayer in the story lead. Here, I thought, is one of these legendary kings of industry at last. Well, I was wrong, he's just another stooge, a reputable enough expert and a German but not one of *the* Bayers. It's just one of those odd coincidences.

If I take pains to clarify this point, it is because I read somewhere that the real Bayers are associated with the titanium-dioxide industry in more than one country. The transcription of the interview with this obscure Bayer is more than likely, therefore, to suggest a hidden and unsavory motive on my part; i.e., to insinuate that certain predatory German capitalists are major stockholders in Brastânio. Not at all; it so happens that Brastânio claims to be patriotic and Brazilian through and through, and I have no reason to doubt their corporate word. I neither ratify nor rectify it. I merely wish to point out from the sidelines that the Bayer who gave the interview is a Karl Nobody, a mere respected technical expert and nothing more; he isn't even a shareholder. Whether those other Bayers, who own half the world, have money and a say in this business or not, I don't know and don't care. Anyone rash enough to put his head in the lion's mouth can go and find out for himself; not this old party.

Having steered the reader away from a possible source of confusion, I would like to add a word or two before returning to my story about how these formidable experts, who are paid their weight in gold, really operate. My word is worth very little, of course. I'm a layman in scientific matters, even more of a layman than Giovanni Guimarães, whose good intentions got us all into this mess in the first place; but for all that, I may be able to throw light on a curious fact about the awesome expertise of these gentlemen, whose opinions, as I said before and will shortly prove, dictate laws and cause governments to change their course.

Herr Professor Bayer stated categorically that there was absolutely no danger of pollution. With that he liquidated the last remaining scruples of certain government officials who had appeared to be uneasy at Brastânio's purported tendency to contaminate the environment. Not that the expert's positive assurance should be taken for inflexibility; there's a right time and place and amount for everything in this world. Tomorrow Herr Bayer may change his mind and say exactly the opposite of what he said today, and that is precisely where the greatness (and the great good fortune) of these remarkable experts lies.

What brings me to this conclusion is the reported arrival in Brazil of another eminent, infallible expert, this one under contract to a multinational corporation with headquarters in the United States to negotiate a high-risk drilling contract in a new oilfield. The enthusiasm with which this emissary swears that measureless reserves of the coveted black gold lie just under the surface of Brazilian territory is unbounded. Yet this is the same competent specialist who, when hired by a former Brazilian government to determine once and for all whether there was petroleum in Brazil or not, stated even more categorically, peremptorily and explicitly than the peremptory Bayer in the case of Brastânio, that there was not. On that occasion, after months of exhaustive surveys, investigation, drilling and dinner parties, he swore on his word of honor that there were no underground oilfields in Brazil at all; not a single drop of oil anywhere, on land or sea, and that any statement to the contrary was the work of subversive agitators in the pay of Moscow and should be sternly repressed. He pocketed his kingly fee and, if I am not mistaken, was decorated for his services to Brazil into the bargain. His word became law and several people were sent to prison on the strength of it, among them a certain professional writer named Monteiro Lobato, a stubborn, irresponsible Brazilian who saw oil where no oil was. After all, the nonexistence of Brazilian petroleum had been proved, and proved conclusively, in the report by Mr. . . . what was that wise guy's name again?

My readers can see his name for themselves in the papers, where he is again being quoted admiringly, this time affirming exactly the opposite: that there is indeed petroleum under Brazilian territory and within its offshore limits. This time his fellow countrymen are paying the bill. The expert is American by birth and money, and American is one of the best things to be these days.

Maybe one day our Herr Professor Bayer too will change his mind, who can say? As for those other Bayers, the magnates, it's no concern of theirs whether the titanium-dioxide industry pollutes or not. Whatever it does, it does it a long way from where they live, in a place called Bahia which they've never even heard of. The lethal smoke, black or yellow, doesn't ever reach their nostrils. All they have to do is rake in the profits from the capital invested and the tips paid to the Excellencies and the wise guys.

Of death and a shepherd's staff.

Old Zé Esteves died of joy, Tieta concluded when she heard the account of his last moments. He had keeled over dead, still laughing, when he went back to the corral with Jarde Antunes and his son Josafá after closing the deal for purchase of their land and flock. He had done nothing to deserve such an easy death, as his son-in-law, in whose house the wake was being held, murmured confidentially in the ear of his friend Osnar.

"He was a mean old coot. Threw away everything he had, but he never hung his head and never stopped telling everybody else where to get off. It was going to live on Easy Street so sudden that did him in, Tieta giving in to every crazy notion he had, and then the goats. It was just too much for him."

They were talking out on the sidewalk, the living room being full to bursting. Through a window they could see Tonha sitting next to the coffin, as silent and obedient to her husband's wishes as she had been during all their married life. Astério Simas looked at his mother-in-law and finished what he had to say.

"Mean and hard. Nobody around him had any say but him, not

even Perpétua." He corrected himself. "Nobody but Antonieta. They say she talked back to him from the time she was so high."

On the other side of the casket, Perpétua touched a handkerchief to her dry eyes and heaved her bosom in make-believe sobs, while in the kitchen Elisa, with Dona Carmosina's help, made sandwiches and coffee to ease the night along.

It had happened on the way to Rocinha, on Jarde Antunes' land, a bumpy hillside covered with tufts of thin grass and prickly pear, steep and with outcroppings of stone, a wild, harsh landscape suited to the feet and eyes of Zé Esteves, the native son. Zealous Jarde was up with the sun every day to see to his animals and the manioc field. His piece of land adjoined Osnar's, whose manioc, corn, beans, goats, sheep and workmen were managed by his friend and overseer, Lauro Branco. Lauro cheated him on the accounts, no doubt, but he kept him from losing any sleep over the farm. One thing compensated for the other, and to Osnar's way of thinking, his peace of mind was cheap at the price.

As Josafá, a husky, crafty-eyed *caboclo*, listened to his father discussing the herd and the billygoat and realized how painful the final decision had been, he wondered, not for the first time, how men like Jarde and Zé Esteves could be so attached to a piece of dry wilderness where there was nothing but bald knobs of hills and wild goats. Josafá, like almost all the other young men in Agreste, had left his parents' adobe house in his teens and headed south. His first job was sweeping out Seu Adriano's grocery store in Itabuna. In ten years he was Adriano's partner and had fulfilled his lifelong ambition of buying a cacao plantation; a small one producing fifteen thousand pounds a year, but a good beginning. Now that was really worth something; cacao was a rich man's crop. Planting cacao was like planting gold dust and harvesting bars of gold twice a year. Manioc and goats were sheer drudgery, only fit for a poor man.

Josafá was a good son, though, and every year at Christmas and New Year's he visited his parents. His mother had died two years before, and ever since then he had been trying to persuade Jarde to sell his land and flock and come to Itabuna to live with him. If he couldn't be happy anywhere but in the country, let him give his son a hand on the cacao plantation in the rich groves of Itabuna. His father was reluctant to exchange his home for anyplace else, even if it meant settling down in a fertile land of cacao instead of

manioc, and cattle instead of goats. On this trip, however, Josafá
got wind of the transformations about to take place in Agreste and
armed himself with such good arguments that Jarde could find nothing to say, especially when Josafá pointed out that he owned half
the property, having inherited it from his mother. He didn't like to
use that argument, but he was determined not to lose this only
chance of having a sizable sum of money to invest in another plantation. The older man yielded, since he had no choice.

When he heard from Astério, who had it from the horse's
mouth in the Azores Bar, that Jarde's land was for sale, Zé Esteves
set out at once to walk the three miles to Jarde's place on foot. The
price seemed reasonable to him, but there was a catch; he'd have to
pay cash down. Back in Agreste, Zé Esteves counted the money in
his treasure cache over and over. He had been accumulating this
nest egg for close to twelve years, beginning with the very first
check from his wealthy daughter in São Paulo. He had more than
half of what he needed to pay for the land already, but where was
he going to get the other half?

He stumped back to Jarde and Josafá with a proposition: he'd
make a big down payment now and pay the rest in monthly installments. Josafá wouldn't hear of it; he needed all the money now and
wasn't interested in installments. Why didn't Zé Esteves ask his
daughter for the money? It was chickenfeed to her, he assured Zé.
At this point old Jarde quietly went out, leaving the two of them to
work it out, and went to watch his goats in the sunlight. He'd gladly
live his last days among those bald hills if he could, with the ornery
critters he loved.

Zé Esteves scratched his head. Asking his daughter for the
money was easier said than done. In the short time she had been in
Agreste, Tieta had already bought Dona Zulmira's mansion, one of
the best houses in town, where he and Tonha were going to live like
lords, and was having a lot of repairs done on it which, in Zé
Esteves' opinion, could very well have been left off—who in
Agreste had ever thought of having a house with two great big
bathrooms? Then she had bought a lot on Mangue Seco and was
building a cottage. All of those things had cost plenty, and she had
paid cash. Tieta would spend whatever she had to to live in comfort.
She wanted the best of everything, just went full steam ahead and
hang the expense: furniture, household utensils, bathtubs all the way

from Bahia. Bathtubs! What the hell for? What would those crazy southerners think up next?

When Tieta wanted something she didn't fool around; she just went ahead and bought it. But Zé Esteves somehow didn't think she'd want a hillside planted with manioc, parched hummocks and prickly pear, and rocks for goats to jump around on. Josafá gave him until the following day to make up his mind. Seeing no other solution, Zé Esteves bolted down his lunch and hired Pirica to ferry him down the river to Mangue Seco.

"Over here, Father. What's got into you all of a sudden?" Tieta took him to see the nearly completed cottage, which Ricardo, paintbrush in hand, was helping to whitewash. When his grandson asked for his blessing the old man thought to himself, "The young pup's wide awake now; nobody'd take him for the same churchmouse he was when he came home for the holidays."

While they watched the work in progress, Tieta tried to draw him out.

"How is the work on the house coming along? You'd better give Liberato a push, the way Cardo did with the men here. They're looking lively, I can tell you. I want to spend a night in our house in Agreste before I leave."

"You ain't fixing to leave now, I hope?"

"Yes, I am, just as soon as the electricity comes in and the party's over. That's all that's holding me back. I came for a month, and just think, it's been almost two."

"Well, you can't clear out before the party, child. After all, it's you who's bringing the light to Agreste, and we're all mighty grateful."

Tieta sensed undertones of nervousness and hesitation in her father's flattering words.

"All right, Father, tell me what you came for."

"I have a thing to talk over with you."

"Go right ahead; I'm all ears."

"Not here," he said in a low voice, glancing at Ricardo, the workmen and Skipper Dário, who had gone back to read in the hammock at Liberty Hall after greeting him when he arrived.

"Come on then, let's see if my father's legs are still strong enough to climb a dune."

The brief bathing suit revealed a dark new bruise on the inside of her thigh, which she explained away by saying she had hurt herself with a two-by-four there at the house, where she and Ricardo were helping with the work to set the men a good example. Ricardo laughed up his sleeve when he heard her. It was a good thing the bathing suit covered her behind and her stomach and her crotch. He remembered his aunt's words between cries: "I'll have to go around in long pants here on the beach because of you, you nut!"

Tieta, too, hid a smile as she told how the two-by-four had got away from her. That beloved two-by-four and those voracious lips and teeth! Ah, the joys of love on the beach; youth, sand and the foamy caress of the waves. Oh, my own fallen angel, will I have the will power to tear myself away from your arms when it's time to go?

Father and daughter ascended the dunes in silence under the sultry heat of early afternoon, her thoughts on the sublime pranks of Ricardo, his on trying to find the right words in which to phrase his plea. He came out with it at last.

"Daughter, I have a favor to ask you."

"Ask me then, Father. You know I'll do you any favor I can."

"It's a thing I want more than anything in the world, but you've been so good to me and have made me so happy, it seems like I'm ashamed to ask you for anything else."

"Oh, Father, don't talk that way. You never were one to beat around the bush. The only time you didn't speak up and ask for something you wanted was when you could take it without asking. Come on, what is it you want?"

The violent, spellbinding, infinite landscape opened out before them as they rose step by step. The souls of father and daughter had been tempered by that ocean, their hide scored by the sand-laden wind like a knife blade. The shepherd's staff, useless in the shifting sand, impeded rather than aided Zé Esteves in his climb. It was a real effort for the old man. He was not as tough and agile as in the days when he had clambered up the dunes after girls and run and jumped on the rocky hills to grab and mount nannygoats in heat when the pretty young woman he had brought from the cleared land to be his wife wasn't enough for him. Still he advanced uncomplainingly under the scorching summer sun, his mind fixed firmly on the thing he wanted and the hoped-for response.

When they reached the top and had gazed for a minute over the breathtaking panorama before them, they sat down on a palm branch. With some difficulty Tieta found a position that would conceal another even bigger bruise. Luckily the wind had swept away the imprint of their bodies on the sand, and the traces of their nocturnal grappling down on the beach had been washed away to sea. Just think, Father, your daughter and grandson coupled in shameless lust. Just like you, Father, when you lay down with the nannygoats.

"Daughter, as you know, I've been raising goats all my life, but things didn't go very well after you went away. I guess it was God's way of punishing me"—he scratched his head, where the sand was encrusted like hard black cottonseeds—"for my wickedness in turning you out of house and home. That must have been it."

"Father, please don't talk about that. Nobody remembers it anymore, so don't you fret about it either."

"Well, I was punished for it. I lost everything I had, and if you hadn't come along and rescued me I'd be a beggar in the streets today, because if I had to depend on Perpétua I'd starve to death, and Elisa doesn't have a penny to her name. You gave me everything I have, but there's one thing that would make me even happier before God calls me to Abraham's bosom; besides the joy of seeing you, which I didn't deserve—"

"Father, will you quit all this bowing and scraping? It doesn't suit you and you don't have to butter me up. Just tell me what that great joy is that you're hankering for so much, and I'll see you get it, if I can."

"Oh, you can, all right, Daughter, but I don't know if you'll want to. It's this way: I'd trade the rest of my life for a little patch of land and a couple of goats. Just a pair of them, or three or four, half a dozen would be too many, and I'd be busy and happy the rest of my days."

"If I understand you rightly, Father, you'd like to own a few acres of land and a little flock of goats again, is that it?"

"And a billygoat, a great big he-goat like Inácio. You remember him? There never was a billygoat to match him in Agreste."

"Do I remember? I'm calling my beach house after him: Inácio's Corral. He never would mind anybody, not even you, Father, but he'd come when I called him and eat out of my hand. So that's it. You want to raise goats on your own land the way you used to. Well, we can think about it. Or do you already have something special in mind and want to sign a contract?"

"Ain't no way to hide anything from you, child; you were born with brains like me. Elisa's foolish, like Tonha. And Perpétua's sneaky. She'd try to cheat her own father. . . ."

The old man laughed his hoarse, hollow tobacco laugh, sly and conspiratorial. The sand raked over them, burying itself in Tieta's curly hair and Zé Esteves' kinky wool.

"Every month I put away part of the money you sent. I'd set aside just enough to eat and pay the rent, saving up all the time with the idea of buying a little patch of land and a pair of goats. I have enough saved up now to pay more than half of what Josafá's asking for Jarde's land and the breeding goats. But he wants it all right now. He won't give me credit for a penny." He added, to encourage her, "I reckon he'd go down a little on the price if he saw the money in my hand."

"How much do you need, Father?"

Tieta thought of her suitcase, stuffed full of bills when she got off the bus and now nearly empty. She had made large outlays of cash in Agreste. She had bought one house and was building another; she had bought furniture, ordered bathtubs, toilets and mirrors from Bahia, and had given money away to everybody and his brother. A piece of land, a flock and a ram to gladden old Zé Esteves' heart during his last years on earth would be money thrown away. Hadn't she already guaranteed his comfort in his old age, hadn't she pulled him out of the hole he was living in and installed him in a comfortable house, a mansion by Agreste's standards? He was taking advantage of her. Tieta didn't like being taken advantage of and she didn't like pouring money down the drain.

There was anguish in the old man's suppliant face as he waited for her answer on the Mangue Seco dunes. In his hands was the staff he had wielded in the days when he possessed a large flock and imposed his will on his daughters, striking them on the back and legs with the rawhide strap and that goad. Tieta felt his distress and yearning and remembered Felipe's explaining to her, when he bought her expensive gewgaws to satisfy her whims and vanity, how much deeper and more satisfying the joy of giving was than that of receiving. Felipe had taught her the singular pleasure there is in making others happy. Modesto Pires would cash a check for her if she needed money; the owner of the tannery had told her he would be glad to do so anytime.

"All right, Father. Go ahead and close the deal."

Zé Esteves could not say a word. He winced painfully; such intense happiness was like the sharpest pain. He picked up his staff, rose to his feet with an effort and made his way down the dune, his daughter smiling contentedly by his side at seeing him too overcome to speak. They walked together down the beach to where Pirica's launch was waiting. Before getting into it the old man tried to kiss his daughter's hands, but Tieta wouldn't let him. The sound of the departing motor was muffled by another, louder one: a helicopter, coming in from the sea, hovered over the coconut palms, flying so low they could see three people in the cockpit. One of them was reconnoitering the area through binoculars.

Back in Agreste, Zé Esteves did not even stop at home, nor at the new house to see how the work was going, nor at the bar to tell them about the helicopter. He went straight from the dock to the Rocinha road and trudged out to Jarde's land for the third time that day, leaning heavily on his stick, for the climb up the dunes had left him weak in the legs and short of breath.

Before getting down to business he told Jarde and Josafá about the apparition of the flying machine and the men with binoculars spying out the land around the coconut grove on Mangue Seco. Josafá listened attentively but made no comment. Jarde said:

"It's those fellows from the factory that kills all the fish. Ain't you heard?"

Zé Esteves didn't answer; he was intent on beating Josafá down a little on the price. Once the details were settled (he would send Pirica out to Mangue Seco again that afternoon with a message for Tieta about the money) he went off in high good humor with Jarde and Josafá to look at the goats in the corral. They had had a few swigs of *cachaça* while they talked to ease Zé Esteves' weariness and cheer Jarde up a little.

In the corral he admired the father of the flock again, a fine young ram of imposing proportions and good loud bleat, who went by the name of Seu Mé. Josafá pulled the animal nearer by the horns so that Zé Esteves could take a better look at him. As he praised the he-goat's sexual organs, as imposing as the rest of him, the new owner laughed aloud for pure joy, the happiest man in the world. So happy it took his breath away; the joy was too much for him, and his heart failed under its weight.

He was still laughing when he toppled over on the ground, one hand pointing to the billygoat's balls. That was what Jarde told Astério Simas when he delivered his father-in-law's corpse.

The wake was at its height and Astério's little parlor was full, with more clusters talking out on the front walk, when Tieta, escorted by Ricardo, Skipper Dário and Dona Laura, came in from Mangue Seco, where a message had been sent.

"He was clowning around and he up and had a stroke. He didn't feel a thing," explained Astério, repeating to his sister-in-law the details he had heard from Jarde and Josafá.

"He died of joy, then," Tieta said.

At that time she didn't know that Brastânio had had a part, though indirectly, in old Zé Esteves' death. Her brother-in-law cleared a pathway for her through the crowd, and she went to the coffin and embraced Tonha. Her sisters came over to her and someone woke up Peto. Leonora, too, approached the family group and kissed her beloved Mama.

To her Agreste relatives, Zé Esteves' death was an emancipation, but Tieta had renewed her acquaintance with her father only a month before. She had not seen him for twenty-six years, had not been wronged by him in any way since that long-ago beating and expulsion, and had found his quirks and crotchets amusing now. It brightened her day to see him shuffle in, chewing tobacco, cantankerous and spoiling for a fight, still spunky, still full of plans and crafty ambition, still able to laugh and joke and flourish his shepherd's staff with his old insouciant impudence. She recognized herself in the old man. Father and daughter were very much alike.

Astério wore a long face, Elisa cried and sobbed, Perpétua wiped her eyes with her black handkerchief and beseeched high heaven to assuage her inconsolable filial grief. Tieta neither wept nor raised her voice. She lightly stroked her father's dark, stony face with her hand. Of the three sisters, she was the only one who had lost something precious, the only one bereft. She and Tonha, poor hapless Tonha.

He had died laughing at the ram, so happy with his new goats and the piece of land he had regained. Tieta picked up the shepherd's staff lying forgotten in a corner of the room and went outside, where the talk was lively, as was fitting and proper at a self-respecting wake.

In which Zé Esteves is buried, ridding this otherwise agreeable and exciting novel of his boorish, overbearing presence.

Zé Esteves' funeral was a proof of Tieta's popularity. If the old man had turned up his toes before the wealthy widow and prodigal daughter had come back from São Paulo, it is doubtful whether half a dozen people would have bothered to escort him to his last resting place.

But since Tieta had come back, the funeral was a great occasion. Father Mariano said mass at Elisa's house before the coffin was taken away, praying to God in His infinite mercy to receive that soul into His bosom. Mercy was what Zé Esteves needed, thought the priest as he tried to make his eulogy sincere. He cast about for some praiseworthy trait of the deceased to eulogize, and finding none, he praised his daughters, all three of whom possessed rare virtues: Perpétua's devotion as a pillar of the parish and an exemplary Catholic mother, Elisa's deportment as a modest and devoted wife, and the excellent attributes of Antonieta, "whose husband, thanks to his exceptional merit, had been singled out by the Vatican to receive a title from the hands of the Father of Christendom, His Holiness the Pope." This reflected glory shone on Antonieta, whose fruitful visit had bestowed on Agreste a priceless gift, the light of Paulo Afonso, as well as new electric wiring for the Cathedral. As if that were not enough, she had shown high heroism and love of her neighbor when she had thrown herself into the flames, risking her life to save a poor old woman from a horrible death. The good Father's listeners almost broke into applause as he eloquently extolled the virtues of the Esteves sisters, Mrs. Batista, Mrs. Simas, and Mrs. Cantarelli, and the last-named lady's heroic deeds.

The townspeople turned out en masse. Besides Astério, the town notables served as pallbearers: Barbozinha the poet, Modesto

Pires, the Skipper, Dr. Vilasboas, Osnar and Ascânio Trindade. Ascânio had called to present formal condolences in the name of his sponsor, Colonel Artur de Figueiredo, the Mayor, who had stayed behind on Tapitanga Plantation. The death and burial of anyone younger than sixty years of age left him quite unmoved, but it did upset him when anyone older passed away. He sent his regrets and excuses to the three sisters and Astério, promising to present his condolences in person at a later date.

The pages of the newspapers sent by Dr. Mirko Stefano were sticking out of Ascânio's pocket. He fully intended to rub the Skipper's nose in them and make him swallow his insulting accusation of dishonesty. "Rub his nose," "make him swallow it," were only a manner of speaking. His intentions had nothing to do with physical violence, only with moral redress. All the while he was carrying the casket along and helping to place Zé Esteves' body in the ground, Ascânio Trindade puffed out his chest and proudly bore aloft the haughty captain's plume of the Agreste musketeers, the D'Artagnan of the Dawn.

*Of haste and greed for profit, a chapter in which
property values in the coconut grove go up.*

When they got back to the house and even before they had changed their clothes, in a hurry though Tieta was to get that hot black dress off, Perpétua paused in her lamentations long enough to say, "It's time we had a talk about the inheritance."

"Inheritance?" Tieta cried. "The old man didn't leave anything."

"Oh, didn't he? That's what you think. Every single month he put away most of the money you sent him, all but a little bit he needed to buy groceries and pay the rent. Nobody ever saw the rest. He never spent a single penny on a present for me or Elisa or the boys. Didn't you even notice how he used to come visiting around lunchtime or suppertime? He must have left a pile of money squirreled away somewhere."

More than ten years' savings—no, twelve—must indeed add up to a respectable amount. What had he intended to do with all that money? Perpétua grew angry in the telling and the subject made her disagreeable voice even more strident.

"I asked him more than once what he was planning to do with all that money and he'd tell me it was none of my business. I told him he ought to put it in the savings bank or let Seu Modesto manage it for him so it would bring in some interest. He never would do it, though; he didn't trust any human being, much less a bank. I don't think he wanted it for anything at all but just kept it back out of meanness"—she lowered her voice—"God forgive me."

"Perpétua, for pity's sake! The old man hasn't been in his grave an hour! Before we start thinking about his faults, we ought to remember he was our father."

Perpétua backtracked, not wanting to annoy Tieta.

"You're right. Father Mariano told me the same thing, that I lacked the gift of compassion. It's my duty to weep for him, I know. But I can't help it. When I think of the hard time he gave us . . . You know as well as I do."

"Yes, I know, but I'm sorry he's dead just the same. He was my father. He had his faults and his good points. He did have some, you know. He looked at life straight in the eye and when he wanted something he fought for it."

"You call those his good points? Heaven help us! Anyway, he's dead and I'm not sorry. Getting back to what I was saying, we'll have to find out where he kept that money hidden. Mother Tonha may know. Once we find it, we can take our part of it to pay for the wake and the funeral expenses—you weren't here, so I had to pay for everything—and for seventh- and thirtieth-day masses. The rest we'll divide between Mother Tonha and the three of us. Half for her, half for us. Anyone who wants to have more masses said can pay for them out of her own pocket."

Afraid she had shocked the wealthy sister and generous aunt, she offered a splendid cast-iron proof of filial love. "I'll have three more said myself, one in my name and one each in the names of the two boys. And every year as long as God spares me, I'll have a mass celebrated on the day of his death." She could not resist adding, "I think that's better than inventing good qualities Father never had."

Tieta was worn out and had had enough of the dispute. It was just a waste of time to argue with Perpétua; there wasn't any argument that could make her change her mind. She got up to leave the room.

"I'm going to get these clothes off and bathe and go to bed. I'm tired out."

Pirica had brought Astério's message to her the night before on the dunes, where she was playing wild games with Ricardo. It was a lucky thing the Skipper had shouted for her and she had shouted back. After giving her the bad news Pirica remarked, "I brought him out here and back in the boat just a little while ago. He was mighty pleased with himself, even gave me a little something extra."

She had spent the rest of the night at the wake accepting condolences, repeating the same words over and over and listening to tales about Zé Esteves in his days of prosperity, some of them droll and some pretty rough. When morning came it was time for the funeral, stuffed into that tight dress made for the São Paulo climate. Then there had been the walk to the cemetery, the prayers over the corpse, the people filing by to pay their respects, and the melancholy return. Tieta longed to go to sleep and forget everything and everybody, even Ricardo. She suddenly felt like a stranger in Agreste. One of the ties that bound her to her birthplace had been broken, and for the first time since she had come she wished she were back in São Paulo.

As she was undressing to take a shower, fall into bed and sleep until morning, Perpétua called out from the dining room that Jarde and Josafá were there to see her right away on urgent business. Tieta threw on a robe and took them out on the porch, Perpétua hovering nearby.

They sat down. Jarde twirled his hat on his hand and lowered his eyes, dazzled by the sumptuous vision of the Paulista's bosom, only half concealed by the lace of her negligee. Finally Josafá spoke up.

"Dona Antonieta, we're mighty sorry to bother you at such a time, but it's urgent and we can't help it, Father and I."

"Is it about the sale of your property?"

"Yes, ma'am, and the flock. Seu Zé Esteves said he had talked to you, ma'am, and that you'd pay the rest."

"Yes, but he's dead."

"That's why we're here, ma'am. The thing is, when he came back from Mangue Seco he asked us to come down on the price, which we did because we were in a hurry to close the deal, and then he gave us a deposit to seal the bargain, more than half." He reached into his trouser pocket, took out a packet of money tied with a faded pink ribbon and laid it on a chair near Tieta. "Here's the money Zé Esteves left us on trust. He wouldn't even take a receipt. . . ."

"Why, the old fool!" thought Perpétua when she heard this piece of folly. She had crept closer as soon as she heard what the conversation was about. So that's what he had been scrimping and saving for all those years.

Jarde had trouble keeping his mind on what they were saying; his eyes kept wandering to the open neckline of the robe. Tieta pulled herself together. She had to be careful not to show any of those dark bruises on her breasts, her thighs or her belly. She had marks all over her body from Ricardo's lips and teeth. Right there and then, just back from the funeral, talking business and catching Jarde staring at her bosom, she felt a chill of pleasure down her spine. Desire mingled with weariness in a pleasant tingling lassitude.

Josafá went on, "So we came to bring you the money. It's a crying shame Zé Esteves had to go and die on us, he wanted that land and the goats so bad. He just about clapped his hands for joy when he saw Seu Mé."

When Tieta looked uncomprehending, he explained, "Seu Mé's the ram of the flock, and a mighty good one, too."

He got to his feet, a fine figure of a *caboclo*, and Jarde awkwardly followed suit. Josafá said regretfully, before offering his hand in farewell, "It was bad luck for us too, for Seu Zé Esteves to up and die like that. We were all set to make a sale and now we're back where we started. We're thinking of offering it to Seu Osnar. His land's right next to ours, but it's a great big piece of property, almost as big as Colonel Artur's. If Seu Osnar ain't interested, then we'll have to step lively to find a buyer, and that ain't easy when folks are in a hurry. You know how it is, ma'am. . . ."

"But why are you in such a hurry, Seu Josafá? It was doing things in a hurry that made the old man's heart give out."

"We need the money, Father and I, so we can hire a lawyer in Itabuna, Dr. Marcolino Pitombo. There ain't a lawyer can touch him when it comes to lawsuits over property rights."

"Are you mixed up in a lawsuit down there?"

"Not there, here. I want to bring Dr. Marcolino to Agreste, and that's why I need the money so bad and why I want to sell the land and the flock. I own a little something in Itabuna, but I need all the money I can get my hands on so I can hire me the best lawyer I know and bring him up here."

"Here? What for, if you don't mind my asking?"

"Well, ma'am, you know the coconut grove on Mangue Seco, where you bought a piece of the land that belongs to Seu Modesto Pires, or anyway Zé Esteves told me so. You know who owns the rest of that land that runs from Quebra Pedra to Seu Modesto's property line? The land that company wants to buy to put up the factory? Well, it belongs to us—to my father and your servant here."

"It does? The coconut grove? But I thought nobody really knew who the owners were. The Skipper was saying so only the other day."

"If other people have rights there, that I can't rightly say. Maybe they do. But if they do they'd better shake a leg and get a lawyer like I'm doing to prove they have a right to it, because I'm going to prove I do. That inheritance goes a long way back, Dona Antonieta, and it's all written down in the land-office registry. It's just that my pappy and my grandpappy before him never paid it any mind. Why should they, when the palm grove was more swamp than dry land? I didn't think about it either, until I came back here a few days ago. My pappy here was telling me about the factory and then it kind of dawned on him that that land belongs to us. So I put my ear to the ground and heard about those engineers prowling around. And Seu Zé Esteves told me only yesterday there was a helicopter flying around over the palm trees. He said you and him saw it plain as day."

"We saw it, all right. And you're right; you are going to have to act fast, because there are lots of important people interested in that palm grove."

"Well, there's bound to be, ain't they, with the Germans wanting to buy?"

"Germans?"

"That's what I heard down in Itabuna. They've been poking around down there too, sounding people out, looking for a place to put a factory on the Cachoeira River; but there was a big stink about it and there still is, because they say that factory or whatever it is kills off all the fish, the shellfish and all, and stinks up the air something terrible. Why, I even signed a paper against the idea those people had of setting up business down there. But I'm all in favor of it here. This is a good place for one of those factories. Farming here ain't worth a damn, and goats are a varmint nobody can kill off."

"Maybe the goats can hold out. But the fish will be poisoned and die, and then there won't be any more fishing."

"Aw, Dona Antonieta, how many fishermen are there on Mangue Seco? Ten or twelve bums who make their living smuggling. When the factory comes in they'll have to go to work for a living like everybody else."

"Well, at Saco people fish for a living. And there aren't just a dozen or so of them."

Josafá laughed knowingly, flashing his teeth and his shrewd eyes, as he repeated the argument that had occurred to Ascânio Trindade but that he hadn't had the nerve to use.

"The people at Saco? Let the Sergipanos worry about the folks who live in Saco. Saco's on the other side of the state line, so that's Sergipe's problem. All I want to do is sell my land to the Germans. And I've got a paper that says I can."

They were talking standing up. Jarde's eyes were irresistibly drawn to the lace at the opening of her negligee. What pretty skin and what nice round she-goat tits she had. Josafá put his hand in his inside jacket pocket, took out a billfold and extracted a piece of yellowing paper which he held out to Tieta. It was an ancient letter in faded ink, and in it there were references to some land along the riverbank near the ocean, belonging to the Antunes family.

"My pappy and I are the only family by the name of Antunes in Agreste, as far as I know. I went to the civil registry to see about it, and Dr. Franklin told me that my great-grandfather's name, Manuel Bezerra Antunes, is written down there in the deed. As soon as this factory business came up a lot of people started saying they were the owners. That's why I'm going to hire me a lawyer and put in my claim just as quick as I can, and that's why I want to bring in Dr. Marcolino. Nobody can hold a candle to him when it comes to who owns what land. He started out as Dr. Basílio's lawyer, did you know that?"

"I don't know who Dr. Basílio is."

"He's a real big man down in the southern part of the state who went and cleared the land, a fine man with guts. He got in a fight over some land that not even bullets could settle. Well, didn't Dr. Marcolino, who was just a spring chicken at the time, straighten out the whole mess and win the fight in court, fair and square as can be? Just think what he can do now he's an old man who's spent his whole life on such quarrels over land. I want to bring him up here, that's why I have to sell the land and the goats. After that I'll make a deal with the Germans, sell 'em the palm grove and buy me a cacao plantation with the money."

"I see."

Before shaking the hand that Josafá held out and touching Jarde's fingertips, Tieta stood lost in thought for a second and inquired, "Did you say that land of yours is next to Osnar's?"

"It surely is. The boundary line runs right between his land and ours."

"Listen, Seu Josafá. If you can't find a buyer by tomorrow morning, come back here and we'll talk about it."

"If you're thinking of buying it, I won't look for anybody else."

"Seu Josafá, I came straight in from Mangue Seco when I heard that Father had died; I didn't get a wink of sleep last night and I just got back from the cemetery. I don't like to rush into a thing like this without thinking it over. But don't let me hold you back. If you find a buyer, go ahead and sell. If you don't, then come see me tomorrow morning early and I'll let you know what I've decided."

"Since it's you, Dona Antonieta, I'd rather wait and not talk to anybody else until you give me your answer. As far as I'm concerned, the only one higher up the totem pole in Agreste is St. Anne. They told me about the electric light in Itabuna and I could hardly believe it. I say it's a miracle. And when I got here I heard about the fire, God be praised!"

The handshake the frank, plain-speaking *caboclo* gave her was strong and warm. Jarde just touched her fingertips, lowering his eyes. So rich, such a heroine, almost as good as a saint, and what a fine figure of a woman.

Perpétua saw them out. When she came back she was spoiling for a fight.

"So that's why the old man hid all that money away, to buy land and goats with. Ridiculous, at his age!" She picked up the packet of money and hefted it in her hand. "He lived like a beggar, cadging meals at other folks' houses, and had that money hidden all the time. And you were going to pay the rest and give him that land! Whatever for?"

"Because when he wanted something he wanted it so bad, Perpétua, just like me. And just like you, too. We're all alike. And I miss him."

"Is that why you're going to buy Jarde's flock and his land? Or are you going to go in with him and Josafá on the palm grove? That's it, isn't it?"

Tieta left the question hanging and went to her room. Watching her as she walked away, stepping firmly with swaying haunches, not caring what anybody thought, Perpétua remembered her father in his prime. The wild young she-goat and the fierce billygoat both sprang from the same demon-goat stock and both delighted in feeding on iniquity. The three of them were alike, Tieta had said. Perpétua shook her head; she did not agree. Maybe all three of them were ambitious, obstinate, and as hard as the stony hills of Agreste, but that was all they had in common, and she was not like the other two at all. She was a lady, a proper widow who lived to serve God. In her devoted breast she yearned for no one but for the Major, that unforgettable fount of virtue, so handsome in his dress uniform or his yellow-striped pajamas.

Her thoughts still on the Major, all at once she jumped. What about the gold Omega watch Tieta had brought from São Paulo as a present for her father? Both watch and watchband were gold and worth a good deal. She had seen Astério take the watch off the old man's wrist and had forgotten to mention it. They'd have to sell it and divide up whatever it brought, unless Tieta wanted to keep it to remember her father by. In that case, she could pay the widow's and orphans' share.

She thought of her gallant Major again, with his handsome military bearing. A good watch like that would have looked so well on his strong wrist, with his dress uniform or his yellow-striped pajamas. What a man he was in those pajamas! She would never see his like again.

Of the rites of death and the afflictions of life.

As the afternoon was waning that December 31st, Tieta, rested and refreshed, dressed soberly, and after a talk with Osnar at home and another with Modesto Pires at the tannery, picked up Dona Carmosina at the post office and set off for Elisa's house. From the counter where he lingered in case a tardy customer showed up to make his lást purchase of the year, Astério saw them go by and guessed they were going to keep Elisa company and comfort Mother Tonha. He glaced toward the Azores Bar. Today he would be cheated of his customary pastime. One good thing at least: the pool championship finals which would crown the Golden Cue of 1965 had been postponed because of the death of old Zé Esteves, father-in-law of one of the four semifinalists—Astério Simas, José da Mata Seixas, Ascânio Trindáde, and Fidélio Dórea A. de Arroubas Filho. It would have to happen on the last day of the year. They had planned a commemorative beer party to toast the champion, too. Astério had held the scepter for three years now, after wresting it away from Ascânio Trindade, whose obligations at the courthouse kept him away from the pool table almost every afternoon. And lately he had made himself so scarce a soul in Purgatory was saved every time he picked up a cue and chalk; as if his job weren't enough to keep him away from his favorite sport, he was going steady. Astério sighed. The contest put off, the party forgotten—the old man was a devil even after he was dead. Even from the grave, he persecuted Astério and spoiled his fun.

Elisa threw herself into her sister's arms in a new outpouring of woe. Death must be honored and the sentiments of the dear departed's relatives proclaimed with weeping, lamentations, moaning and groaning, visible and certifiable signs of grief. That was the only proper way to show respect for the dead, in public displays of affection and loss. Above and beyond one's personal sorrow and pain were the obligatory rituals of death, from black funeral garb to the wailing of professional mourners.

Silent and apathetic in a corner of the room, suddenly old beyond her years, Mother Tonhà sat with reddened eyes. For all his despotism, Zé Esteves had been all she had. He had taken her from the house of her parents, who were just poor farmers, and after a tumble in the bushes had married her—he, a man of property, a city gentleman who owned land and flocks. They had been married by both priest and judge when he could easily have left her to her fate with a full belly, as happened in Agreste with impunity and all too often.

Silent, obedient Tonha had lived in the shadow of her husband for almost thirty years. Suffering insults, curses, ill treatment, but with his companionable warmth to keep the cold away, his rude hand to sustain her, and every so often a kiss, a caress, the randiness and fire of an old goat who was incorrigible until the day he died. Zé Esteves liked to boast of his exploits in bed, and if anyone called his wintry vigor into doubt he would appeal to Tonha.

"Am I lying, woman? You tell him!"

And he'd wink and laugh his thick smoker's laugh and spit out a black wad of tobacco. Tonha would lower her eyes and smile fleetingly, half ashamed to assent.

The arrival of Tieta and Dona Carmosina set the machinery of affliction in motion again, plunging the parlor into gloom. Tonha got up and burst out crying when she saw them. Elisa went over to them and flung herself first into the arms of her sister, then into those of her friend and protector. Tonha said over and over in a plaintive singsong, "Oh, what'll I do now, what'll I do?"

Tieta clasped her stepmother in her arms in silence, then settled her back in her chair and sat down beside her at the table.

"Now, Mother Tonha, don't you fret. You won't want for anything. You'll go and live with Elisa and Astério, and every month I'll send you a little something so you can make ends meet."

Tonha tried to kiss her hand, just as Zé Esteves had before embarking in Pirica's boat on the road to his death. Tieta couldn't have been a better daughter to her if she had been her own natural child. And they hadn't even lived in the same house very long, two years at the most. They were both adolescents then, and the same age.

"When I was throwing my things together into a bundle after the old man kicked me out, you gave me money," Tieta reminisced. "Did you think I'd forgotten that? If it hadn't been for you and Dona Milu I would have gone out to face the world without a plugged nickel to my name."

The two women had been the same age that early morning when Tieta went away in the cab of a truck. Tieta called her *vosmicê* and Mother then because the cantankerous old man made her. Now she did it of her own accord, and they were no longer the same age, the São Paulo Comendador's spectacular, blooming young widow and the old, worn-out, fragile, long-suffering widow of the ruined breeder of goats, shrinking in the desolation of her black sateen dress.

"Now pay attention, we have things to talk about."

Tieta plunked the packet of money Josafá had brought her down on the table, minus Perpétua's share and the cost of the funeral expenses and masses to be said. Elisa's sobs dried up at sight of the money, and Tonha eyed it wonderingly.

"It's the old man's savings," explained Tieta.

Tonha recognized the pink ribbon the packet was still tied with.

"Oh, mercy, I'd forgotten all about it. You found it inside the mattress, didn't you? He made a hole in the cloth and every month he put in some more, and he tied that ribbon around it and wrapped it up in newspaper. He made me swear by my sainted mother's soul never to say a word about it to anybody. He took it out every day to make sure it was there, and he'd wake up and count it in the middle of the night."

"Father took it out himself before he died. I'll explain that in a minute, but first I want to give you your part."

"My part?"

"Half of what he left is yours, the wife's part. The other half belongs to his children, Perpétua, Elisa and me. I've already paid Perpétua back for the funeral expenses: the coffin, the gravediggers, the priest, the soft drinks and sandwiches and things for the wake. And I've given her her part too, and this is what's left." With all the attention to detail of one accustomed to keeping accounts and managing credits and debits, she informed them exactly how much the nest egg amounted to, what the expenses had been, how the money was divided, how much should go to Tonha and how much to each sister. She counted the bills, dirty and worn-out from handling, and gave one part to the widow, saying, "This money's yours, Mother Tonha. Don't you give it away to anybody else. Keep it safe in case you ever need it in a hurry. After we sell the watch there'll be a little more."

She divided the rest into two little piles, her share and Elisa's, and left it lying on the table, ignoring her sister's outstretched hand.

"Just a minute, Elisa. First I want you to listen to what I have to say. When Father died he had just made a deal with Jarde Antunes to buy Jarde's land and flock of goats. Now that property isn't very big, but from what I hear it's well kept up and yields a pretty good living. It's right next to Osnar's. The old man asked me to give him enough to make up the difference because he was hankering for a piece of land and a few goats. I don't think he cared so much about making a profit; it was just for his own satisfaction. He loved those animals and he loved to feel important."

"That he did," chimed in Dona Carmosina, who had kept quiet until then. It came as no surprise to her that Zé Esteves had stashed away money.

"Did you know about it, Elisa? About his buying the land?"

"Astério told me. Jarde told him."

Tieta reached out and stroked her sister's hair. She'd give anything if that black mane were hers.

"Well, then, listen. The price that Jarde and Josafá are asking for the property is really too good to pass up. They need cash right away. Even Seu Modesto Pires thought it was cheap, and Osnar said I ought to close the deal and not try to bargain." She assumed an executive air, as of one used to handling money and making business deals. "This is my plan: we'll take both parts, yours and mine, I'll chip in the rest, and we'll buy it for you and Astério. You'll have clear title to it. That way you won't have to go on scrimping and saving and counting every nickel. With the store and the goats you'll have plenty and to spare. The property turns a good profit, and it's next to Osnar's, too. For Astério, what could be better? I'm helping Perpétua's boys and I want to help you and Astério, too. Now that the old man is dead, you can move into the house when it's finished and live with Tonha. That was what I wanted to say." In her voice was the satisfaction that came from the joy of giving, from doing what she could to give her sister and brother-in-law a better life.

"Anyone would be lucky to have a sister like you, Tieta. You're simply tops! You don't find a heart of gold like yours every day in the week." Dona Carmosina was deeply touched; her good opinion of her friend was growing day by day.

Elisa said nothing, nor did she raise her eyes. She was too over-come to express the gratitude she felt, no doubt. Without looking up, she made an effort to speak, stammering with nervousness.

"Carmosina's right; we don't deserve your goodness, Tieta. Before I met you I always thought of you as a kind of fairy god-mother, and that's what you really are." She lifted her head and looked at Dona Carmosina, seeking support for what she was about to say. "And I do thank you for what you're offering to do for me and Astério, buying the land and giving us the house to live in and all." A pause to gather her breath and courage. "But I can't accept it. I want to ask you for a different kind of favor. I talked to Carmosina about it once so she could tell you."

Tieta's face clouded over. She knew what it was Elisa wanted.

"You don't need a go-between to talk to me. Tell me what it is you want." She had turned remote and cold.

Elisa raised fearful eyes to her rich and powerful sister. Then she took the plunge and her voice rang out in the room.

"There's only one thing I want: to go to São Paulo with you. I want you to take me there and help Astério find a job, and let me—"

Tieta interjected brusquely before she could finish. "So you want to go to São Paulo. To do what, will you kindly tell me that? Put horns on your husband? Walk the streets?"

A sob burst from Elisa's breast and tears started from her eyes. She trembled as though she had been slapped and hid her face in her hands. Those sobs, those tears, had nothing in common with the ritual mourning tears she had shed earlier. These were sincere and genuine tears forced from her by a cruel and unexpected blow, a real disappointment, a broken dream. Her head with its disheveled hair sank down on her arms on the table, and she keened softly like a child.

Tieta got up and went over to this sister twenty-five years younger than herself. She pulled her gently to her feet, took her in her arms and comforted her, kissed her face, wiped away her tears, caressed her hair and called her "Lisa, honey" in a gentle, sweet, maternal voice.

"Don't cry, Lisa honey, I'm telling you no for your own good. São Paulo's no place for you two. It would be bad for you and worse for Astério. Someday, I promise you, next time I need a holiday and want to take a trip, I'll send for the two of you and take you with me. You know when I promise something I don't go back on my word. But what you have got to do now is help your husband in the store, because he's going to need more time for the livestock." Her voice was steely again. "And don't you ever say a word about going to São Paulo ever again."

Dona Carmosina, unable to hold back her feelings, wiped her eyes with a little embroidered handkerchief. Tonha looked on dumbly, wondering why they were all making so much fuss. Tieta left Elisa and went over and embraced her with a farewell admonition.

"You be careful of your money. Don't you lend it or give it away to anybody. Not even Elisa or Astério or Perpétua, not even if they ask you. They won't need it." She beckoned to Dona Carmosina. "We'd better be going, Carmô."

Still choking on her disappointment, Elisa embraced Tieta again, intending, perhaps, to risk one last plea in spite of her sister's curt prohibition, but she did not have time. Steps were heard in the hall and Astério entered the room. He wondered at his wife's desperation, which built to a crescendo of convulsive sobbing and crying when he appeared. What could be the cause of such impassioned weeping, such heartfelt laments? It wasn't because the old man was dead, that was for sure.

"What's the matter?" He had heartburn already.

Dona Carmosina had an explanation for him:

"Elisa's crying because she's so happy and grateful. Tieta's going to buy a farm for the two of you."

Of Tieta's face reflected in the mirror on New Year's Eve.

Old Zé Esteves's funeral, the argument with Perpétua about the inheritance and the subsequent petty squabble about the watch, and the poignant scene with Elisa were all reflected in Tieta's face as she sat before the mirror removing her makeup, all alone in the silent house and street. The rest of the family had gone to the Te Deum mass at the cathedral. The world of Agreste, so simple and unruffled on the surface, was turning out to be harder to deal with and more roiled with passion than the notoriously wicked world of prostitutes, crooks, bullies, pimps, gigolos and madams in which she had lived ever since she had gone off in the cab of that truck twenty-six years ago. It was easier to hold her own and keep her footing at the Lords' Retreat, where the feelings of those around her were out in the open like their bodies. Here she ran into sham, deceit and falsehood everywhere she turned. Not a single one of them ever said all that he was thinking or showed his hand completely; they all had something to cover up, out of selfishness or fear or just because they

were poor. It was a universe of play-acting and hypocrisy, a con-
tumacious struggle fueled by mean ambition and narrow self-
interest.

At nine o'clock when the churchbells rang curfew for most of
the population, the generator went off as usual; but tonight it would
come back on at eleven and light up the town to help church and
state usher in the New Year with a Te Deum mass and fireworks.
When Modesto Pires' daughters were still unmarried and came
home on holiday from their convent school in Bahia, the tannery
owner had always given a New Year's Ball. Now it was only in
Zuleika Cinderella's establishment that a party lasted until dawn.
The party didn't begin until after the Te Deum and the fireworks,
for the girls, daughters of God and good citizens all, went to church
and then to the plaza to give thanks to the Lord and clap enthusiastically as lame Leôncio, aided by young Sabino, set off a blaze of
pyrotechnics—skyrockets, mortars, firecrackers—ending the modest marvel with a spectacular shower of silver stars.

Visitors gathered on the porch after supper, Colonel Artur da
Tapitanga, Dona Milu, Dona Carmosina, Barbozinha the seer-bard,
and of course Elisa and Astério, a disgruntled Peto in shoes and
socks and clean clothes, and Ascânio Trindade, who haunted the
place so constantly he had long since ceased to be thought of as a
visitor. By the light of the acetylene lamps they reminisced about
the old man. The Colonel and Dona Milu rummaged in their memories for anecdotes, and Dona Carmosina elaborated on them with
intelligent comments. When the main topic of conversation had
been exhausted they turned to the weather. That is, they discussed
the pregnancy of Sátima Farath, the daughter of Seu Abdula and
Dona Soráia, relentlessly feudal Levantines who had kept their attractive only daughter jealously under lock and key, only to discover that, thanks to the September rains, she was four months on
the way to being a mother. And her imminent marriage to Licurgo
de Deus, the humble, dusky man of all work in the Faraths' small
notions store, who brought nothing with him to the marriage but
his dark manly beauty, ringing laugh and gentle ways; yes, that
unexpected wedding was a happy event to look forward to that
summer. Exercising to the full that subtle art of talking about other
people's business, they mentally scrutinized the notions store, speculating as to whether the main event had taken place on top of the
counter or under it, in a jumble of buttons, needles, thimbles and

ribbons; settled the state of the Faraths' finances and expressed satisfaction at young Licurgo's good luck to be eating raw *kibe* off a gold plate. Dona Carmosina's graphic image ended the argument as to where the deed had taken place. The subject of pollution and Brastânio was on the tip of the postmistress's tongue more than once, and on the acting mayor's as well, but it was too polemical for the occasion. After all, they had called in the first place to offer their condolences, and besides, it was New Year's Eve. They all left for church as soon as the light came back on. Tieta begged off. She was anxious to be alone; she had never imagined that her father's death would hit her so hard.

All alone on New Year's Eve in an empty house! If anybody had told her, she would not have believed it. As long as Dona Olívia was alive, Felipe had always come to see Tieta and bring her a gift, usually an expensive jewel, before joining his wife and children to see the New Year in. After his wife's death they saw it in together in some fancy nightclub where Carnival reigned after the congratulations and "Happy New Years," the effervescence of toasts in champagne and the renewed fondness of each for the other.

Only a year ago the night had begun in the traditional way in an elegant *boîte*. They talked about business and recalled the early days of their long-lasting liaison, which was, as Felipe said, irrevocable. As his gift that year he presented her with the title to a large shop on the ground floor in the Monteiro Lobato Building (a tribute from the financier to the São Paulo writer he had known and admired), a vast structure located on one of the busiest downtown streets. How could she get the most out of it? Should she rent the shop or set up her own chic, exclusive boutique? The boutique would be more profitable, of course, if she could manage the business herself. But where would she find the time, since the Retreat kept her running all day? She'd better rent the space, Felipe advised, and pocket a sizable profit every month with no work or worry.

Touched by his generosity, Tieta recalled the day she had met him just after he returned from Europe. Madame Georgette had said to her the day before, "Tomorrow you'll meet *le vrai patron du Nid, Monseigneur le Prince Felipe*." Felipe, too, remembered that day well. Madame Georgette had informed him that she had "*une petite mulâtresse*, the kind you like, a little shepherdess, fresh, unspoiled, tender but as wild as a young goat." Recalling this, he teased her as they danced, threatening to set up housekeeping with some young girl, telling her an old crock like him needed a youngster to warm his bones. Old crock nothing! He was as tough as he had ever been, as hard-muscled and as good in bed, as strong as a horse. When he kissed her at midnight, he spoke of the incurable, irremediable, marvelous adventure their liaison was.

"What if I told you you're the only woman I've ever really loved?"

After that their conventional New Year's Eve became meaningful and turned into an unforgettable night of love. As soon as the shouted congratulations and best wishes were over, he took her hand and led her away. Although Dona Olívia had been dead and buried for six years, this was the first time Felipe had invited Tieta to visit the mansion on Avenida Paulista. She was conducted from room to room under the sparkling, many-faceted crystal chandeliers, treading on soft Persian carpets, her eyes dazzled by the gold and silver ornaments, the art objects scattered about the dark, gleaming furniture, the paintings by modern masters—Picasso, Chagall, Modigliani—names she'd learned from her wealthy clients at the Retreat, who never spoke of them without alluding to their astronomical worth and thus reducing their beauty to a good investment. Here was a different kind of wealth; heavy, noble, almost solemn, and unknown to Tieta. Accustomed though she was to luxury and to hobnobbing with the great men of politics and high finance, she felt awed by this sort of wealth. Now that she had glimpsed the splendor of the other side of Felipe's life, she understood less than ever why he should have become so attached to a goat girl.

The servants had been given this festive night off, and the mansion was as empty as Perpétua's house tonight, where Tieta had lain long ago with Lucas and now lay with Ricardo. Felipe had shown her the wine cellar, the bottles with their famous labels all in rows, and had chosen the champagne—"not mere champagne, but *le meilleur champagne du monde, ma belle*"—and set the bottle to chill in a silver ice bucket. Then he fetched the glasses, of the finest and rarest Bohemian crystal. Thus laden, they entered the bedroom, where they drank and made love on the double bed. A good wine springing from old stock, Felipe made up in refined knowledge what he lacked in youthful ardor. Tieta, intimidated at first, soon recovered her aplomb and with it an unfamiliar emotion: for the first and only time in her life, she felt married.

Only then, lying beside Felipe in the big colonial bed in the mansion belonging to the Camargo do Amaral family, did she realize the true meaning of the feeling that bound her to the millionaire and papal Comendador. Only a little while before, this liaison of theirs in which selfish interest, friendship, understanding, pleasure and desire were mingled had struck her as absurd. Now, lying on Dona Olívia's fine cambric sheets, she finally understood the meaning of the word "love," worn out by repetition and cast aside in the stress of passion and desire. But this love was exclusive and unique.

She had wanted so many and such different kinds of men! Those passions had been flames darting up, sometimes lingering, sometimes dying quickly, but all of them shallow, if insatiable while they lasted, whether they were kindled in the man-hungry girl giving herself in the hollows along the riverbank or atop the dunes on Mangue Seco, the strumpet on her way south to São Paulo, or Felipe's kept woman. All those years she had been his private property, her expenses paid by him, his pajamas under her pillow and his slippers beside the bed. Her giddy head had been turned by any number of different men during those years, but none of them had kept her from being a tender mistress, companion and friend to the powerful man in his fifties. Felipe was forty-nine when she met him and looked forty, and he had aged in her arms.

Had Felipe ever suspected that his protégée was fancy-free? Tieta had never received a man in the Nid d'Amour again (not that Madame Georgette would have allowed such a lack of respect), nor at the Lords' Retreat after the day he expressed his wish to keep her exclusively for himself. Her off-and-on love affairs were conducted in apartments, pieds-à-terre or cheap hotels. Despite all her precautions, Felipe was certainly shrewd and experienced enough to know when she burned with desire; it surely must have shown in her glittering eyes, her nervous gestures and her tigerish lovemaking, for the harder she had fallen for someone else the greater the skill and ardor with which she gave herself to him, as if she wanted to make up to him for her infidelity.

Felipe had never shown that he had the least suspicion. In the last months of his life, however, when signs of age began to mark his well-cared-for face and threaten his equanimity and pride, Tieta saw, or thought she saw, a trace of sadness in the Comendador's eyes when he saw her so vibrant and overflowing with desire. She, in turn, endeavored to keep her waywardness in check so as not to hurt him. Or was it that she was so fond of her protector that she really felt less wayward?

After Felipe died she felt so alone and lost that she had actually broken the oath she had made when she left Agreste behind (that she would never again set foot in the place) and had come seeking strength and comfort and a renewed interest in life in the bosom of her family. Back to the place where she had been born and raised, herded goats on the sandhills and learned that life was hard, had become a woman on the sand dunes under the weight of a peddler who reeked of garlic and onions. She had longed to breathe pure air, and see cloudless night skies, and bathe in the moonlight. She had fled from São Paulo and its polluted air, the Retreat's degrading commerce in human flesh, and Felipe's absence, his unworn pajamas and his cast-off slippers.

On this other New Year's Eve, such a contrast to last year's, alone before the mirror in her elder sister's house, Tieta asked herself if it had been worth her while to come.

Yes, it had, in spite of all the pretense and hypocrisy, the plotting and jangling disharmony of the Esteves family concealed under a cloak of humdrum placidity. Ricardo alone would have made a much harder journey worthwhile. He was so innocent, so honest, so free of malice and guile; all of a piece. There was nothing ambiguous about him in word, thought or deed. He was her boy, her golden boy. This was the first time in her life she had wanted an adolescent, almost a child. Her preference had always been for older men, and here she was dying and being reborn for love of a boy.

He was in church now, her divided boy who belonged half to her and half to God, dressed as an altarboy in his black cassock, white surplice and red stole and enveloped in a cloud of incense, that fallen angel of hers. That witch of an Edna, riding on her husband's horns like a broomstick, was stretching out her greedy neck this very minute, biting her lips and yearning for that beautiful cherub. Well, the old hag could go on eating her heart out, because Ricardo wouldn't even notice she was about to jump out of her pants. He had no eyes, no laughter on his lips, no other thought in his head except for his smart, lucky aunt, who had deflowered her virgin nephew and was teaching him all about the best things in life.

He would come home with Perpétua and Leonora after the Te Deum and the fireworks. At the thought of her *soi-disante* stepdaughter Tieta shook her head. She was worried about her.

She had brought the girl with her to give her a respite from her joyless life, clear her lungs out with Agreste's health-giving air, and teach her sad lips how to smile. Had that been a good idea? It certainly seemed that way; the girl was so happy she was like a different person. But now what? She simply had to fix things so that Leonora and Ascânio would make up their minds to go to Catherine's Basin or find themselves a hiding place under the willows. The day of their departure was not far off, and Leonora needed and deserved, just once in her life, to lie with a man for love, not because it was her profession or because she couldn't help it. That was a problem Tieta would have to solve, and soon. Next week Inácio's Corral would be ready for occupancy. That would be a perfect excuse to get the couple to Mangue Seco, where, as Ricardo could have told them, the overwhelming beauty of the magical night and the sky and the sea would shipwreck whatever scruples and shyness they still felt.

Before that happened, though, she would have to persuade Ascânio to give up this wretched plan of letting that titanium-dioxide factory have a free hand to poison Agreste's clean air, veil its clear sky with a dirty pall and ruin the sea and the river for fishing. So the fishermen were smugglers. They always had been, but there were no bolder sailors anywhere than on Mangue Seco when it came to braving the fierce sharks and the fiercer waves. Immense pity and boundless tenderness suddenly swept over her and she forgot the stings and falsehoods and family lies. Poor Agreste, its people were so dear to her! All of them loved her, every one, good and bad. They had made a heroine and a saint out of her, and all the time she was nothing but a low, vile whore; worse still, she made a living, and a good one, too, out of other whores.

Before the mirror Tieta was primping and scenting herself for Ricardo. She hadn't had him the night before; in the hall between the study and the bedroom the memory of the father and grandfather, newly dead and buried, had lain like a barrier. Tonight she expected him, though. Cunts don't stay in mourning long, she had whispered to him in the hall.

When she went back to São Paulo, Felipe wouldn't be there anymore. No one could talk so well, no one liked to laugh as he did, no one knew so much or was such a rare mixture of caution and boldness. She fled from that final absence to take refuge in the temporary absence of Ricardo. Her young man would soon come looking for her in the bed that had sheltered Dona Eufrosina and Dr. Fulgêncio, Perpétua and Major Cupertino. Both couples had made love there, and so had she and Lucas; and it was there that the young doctor had revealed to her the ultimate refinements of pleasure, the absurd and nonsensical rules of the ypsilon Y. Nothing, however, could compare to the nights of Tieta and Cardo, the fiery young nephew and the blazing bonfire of the aunt in her prime.

He would come home right after the Te Deum and the fireworks, and then he would impatiently wait in his hammock until Perpétua and Leonora were in bed and asleep before he crossed the hall in one stealthy stride and come to nestle in her arms. Tieta went to the open window over the alley where she could hear the distant murmur of prayers, though the cathedral was not visible from there. The people of Agreste were giving thanks to God. She ought to be giving thanks herself, but she never had been one for masses and prayers; in fact, she wasn't religious at all. Father Mariano, with calculated flattery, had said that she, Tieta, widow of a Papal Comendador, was an integral part of the Church and Rome. Through Felipe, Father? But he hadn't been her husband, only the man who kept her; their relationship was an illicit one. Maybe Ricardo was her link with the Church, her Levite in the temple, a child of God and her beloved boy. Their liaison was sinful, too, Father; everything about Tieta was spurious and false.

She turned back to the mirror and scrutinized her usually cheerful face. She was down in the mouth tonight. Who was she, of all people, to accuse others of hypocrisy and sham? She, the widow Antonieta Esteves de Cantarelli, was nothing but a fabrication, an intricate hoax assembled piece by piece. There had once been a Tieta in Agreste who herded goats and was a goat herself, a she-goat in heat. In São Paulo there was a rich and famous madam called Madame Antoinette, a Frenchwoman from Martinique. But Antonieta Esteves Cantarelli didn't exist.

Did she really not exist, was she no use to anyone? Ricardo, having taught her to scorn the profit to be made from a good investment in land around the palm grove and fight instead to protect Agreste's unpolluted climate, sky and water, had breathed life and reality into Antonieta Esteves Cantarelli by giving her a cause and a banner to unfurl. He was her boy. She smiled at her reflection in the mirror, no longer dispirited and tired.

She stripped off her nightgown and lay down in her skin on the bed to wait, dressed in nothing but the purple marks of Ricardo's lips and teeth and the faint vestiges of the burns. She would be asleep by the time he came in; she would wake up in his arms and they would see the New Year in together—a little late and without champagne, but those were unimportant details compared to their boundless affection and desire. They would light fires before daybreak to greet the New Year, and in homage to it would perform the double ypsilon Y. Double, not single. To follow its crazy rules to the letter, crazy, ridiculous rules that were nonetheless strict and unchangeable, took a skilled and experienced older woman and a pleasure-hungry boy. Or vice versa: a battle-scarred veteran and a tender green recruit. Either way, they had to be mad for each other or it wouldn't work.

*In which a new character makes her appearance;
another prostitute, in a novel that's
full of them already.*

At the same time that Tieta lay down nude in her bed to fall asleep waiting for him, Ricardo caught sight of Maria Imaculada for the first time through a cloud of incense smoke and was startled. She was so young, surely not more than fifteen. She wore a pale-blue organdy dress and a white sprig of cape jasmine in her crisp curly hair. Her figure was full, her eyes were two black coals, and her lips were smiling—smiling at him.

During the festive Te Deum mass, whose pomp and chanting and gaily colored vestments were very much to the seminarian's taste, Ricardo felt himself lapped in the admiring and covetous glances of at least three interesting women. In the front row near the altar, one on the right side and one on the left, were Cinira and Dona Edna.

From a pew on the right, Cinira, hovering on the verge of irrevocable spinsterhood, turned up her eyes and parted supplicating lips when Ricardo advanced with the thurible in his hands, as if the divine vision made her faint. In the front row at the left, kneeling on the narrow rail beside her unlikely but legal husband Terto, Dona Edna, skinny and fidgety but by no means the old hag of Tieta's scornful insults, bit her lip, stared at him hungrily with her gimlet eyes and even risked a wave. Oh, if she could just get him alone in a corner of the sacristy and cover him with kisses! Ricardo passed before the altar, stopping left and right before the *demi-vièrge* and the adulteress and sending a wave of aromatic incense like a wordless message in the direction of each.

He would have liked to walk down the nave to the back benches where Carol, contrite and demure, followed every step and gesture of the unattainable acolyte before the altar. Now that Modesto Pires had returned to Mangue Seco and the bosom of his family, she had to be doubly discreet. The entire population of the town kept her under surveillance in the exciting expectation of a misstep by the rich tannery owner's concubine. Since he could not very well go to where Carol was, Ricardo held the incense burner aloft and shook it in the air, smiled at her and offered her a fragrant cloud of white smoke. Had she understood the meaning of the gesture? Probably so, for she lowered her eyes and placed her open hand on her heart in her heaving bosom.

Ricardo scanned the cathedral nave, almost completely full, with a preponderance of seated and kneeling women. The men, dressed in their Sunday best, all stood at the back of the church, except for a few unusually jealous or devoted husbands who had posted themselves near their wives. Terto, for instance, thus demonstrated to the incredulous that he actually was the happy consort of the appetizing Dona Edna. Perpétua and Peto knelt side by side before the altar on fancy genuflecting stools bearing metal plaques inscribed with their owners' names—Dona Perpétua Esteves Batista and Major Cupertino Batista—to keep alien and unworthy knees from touching those hallowed cushions. Peto felt neither contrition nor satisfaction at the honor of kneeling in his father's place. He wanted to stand with the men at the back of the church, or better yet, in the vestibule where the conversation was lively, Aminthas distilling his poison and Osnar boasting of his own rascality.

Ricardo could not help smiling at the sight of his little brother scratching himself and squirming, with an expression of infinite boredom on his face. He scrutinized the benches where the women were praying and recognized Zuleika Cinderella standing against the wall near the back; he had met her sometimes in the street or shopping. None of the half-dozen prostitutes around her had the courage to sit down, but formed a compact group by themselves. Then Ricardo's eyes fell on Maria Imaculada and he recognized her as none other than his Aunt Antonieta as a girl, as if St. Anne had miraculously restored her to eager adolescence and the days of trysts by the riverside in the shade of the weeping willows. She had the same open countenance, sparkling eyes, full but slender body, black serpentine ringlets and greedy mouth.

And she was looking at him and laughing. As Father Mariano blessed the congregation, Ricardo lifted the thurible once more, taking a step forward to offer the unexpected apparition a gift of incense.

When mass was over, everyone trooped down to the boat basin, where Leôncio and Sabino had the skyrockets and the firewood ready to be lit. Ricardo lingered in the sacristy to take off his surplice and stole and help Vavá Muriçoca and Father Mariano tidy up and put away the religious objects. The Father wondered why Dona Antonieta had not come to the Te Deum mass. Ricardo explained that she was not feeling well and was still in a state of shock from her father's death.

"What a generous, distinguished person she is, a pillar of the Church," remarked the priest. "Be sure to take the Lord's blessing to her, from me."

Holding out his hand for the seminarian to kiss, he thought of something else.

"You haven't been to confession lately; why is that?"

"I've been at Mangue Seco all this time, so I go over to confess at Saco with one of my teachers at the seminary who's spending the summer there."

"Which one?"

"Frei Thimóteo."

"You're in good hands then, a saint's hands."

At the corner of the public square, half hidden in the shadow of a mango tree, Maria Imaculada was waiting. Ricardo was not surprised, for he had sensed that she was near and had looked around in the hope of seeing her when he left the sacristy. When they stood face to face, both smiling, she asked, "Are you free now, honey?"

"I have to meet my mother and my cousin down by the dock."

"I'm going down there, too."

The plaza was empty except for the priest retreating back on his way to the parish house. Vavá Muriçoca had left in a hurry, not wanting to miss any of the fireworks. They started in the direction of the river. As soon as they left the street and were plunged in darkness she held out her arms to him. Ricardo caught her to him and they clung together in a kiss. Her kisses tasted like his aunt's, but the perfume was different, a wildwood smell. Ricardo touched her breast and molded it in his hand. Someday, when it was fully formed, it would be just like Tieta's; now it was unripe fruit, a young she-goat's tit. Their two mouths parted in a sigh, only to melt together again, and she became softer and more fragile in Ricardo's arms.

They walked on a few steps more and saw the first fireworks rise into the sky and burst into stars. His mother and Leonora would be waiting.

"I'll have to go."

"Stay with me just a little longer, honey."

The girl offered her parted lips.

"Kiss me again, honey."

Their mouths were hungry and thirsty; their tongues mingled. Ricardo's hand dropped from the button of her breast to her new young haunches, prows of a prideful ship on her maiden voyage; the day they reached port they would be as majestic as his aunt's. Rockets went off and exploded into fire.

"I really do have to go now. How can we see each other again?"

"I'll meet you tomorrow, honey, as soon as the light goes out."

"Where?"

She laughed mischievously.

"You can't go to Dona Zuleika's 'cause you're fixing to be a priest, so I'll wait for you right where I did tonight."

In their farewell kiss under the fiery flowers in the sky, prolonged by reluctance and longing, the girl's teeth bit the seminarian's lip and made him cry out.

"Did I hurt you, honey? I'm sorry, Ricardo."

"You know my name?"

"Yes, I do, but you don't know mine." She laughed again, a triumphant little laugh.

"Well, what is your name?"

"Maria Imaculada, honey."

"Happy New Year, Imaculada."

He ran off and left her as a happy New Year began. Turning around at the bend in the road, he was just in time to see her bathed in a shower of silver light. "Goodbye, honey, see you tomorrow."

Of the importance of Antunes as a last name and Astério's promotion to the rank of major.

"I'm your best customer these days, Dr. Franklin," Tieta said jokingly as she greeted the public notary that January 2nd afternoon. She had brought Astério with her, and they were to meet Jarde and Josafá at the notary's.

"You don't mean to say you've come to find out if you're part owner of the palm grove, too? Half the people in town have been in here this week asking to look at the old books. I finally had to lock them up in the safe to keep the pages from being torn out. I've never seen anything like it in all my years as a notary."

"You're not as far off the mark as you might think, Dr. Franklin. No, I didn't come to see if my name's in your books, but I am buying property that belongs to the Antuneses, old Jarde and his son Josafá, for my sister and brother-in-law, and the reason they're selling it is this business of the coconut grove."

Dr. Franklin knew all about it. He nodded and smiled at Astério. Now there was a lucky stiff, with a millionaire sister-in-law giving him land and goats. More power to him! That was the way of the world. Some people were born with a caul, with their rear end pointing up at the moon, and those people never had to worry about where their next meal was coming from; it would be served to them off a silver plate with a silver spoon. As for the rest of us—well, we all know how the rest of us muddle along.

"That's right, the name Antunes is written down in the books. I told Josafá that but I also warned him he's got plenty of company."

"Well, Dr. Franklin, I never heard of any other Antuneses here in Agreste but me and my father and my sainted mother, God bless her."

Josafá's powerful voice boomed from the doorway, cutting the notary short. He came into the office with Jarde in tow.

"We have a paper, we showed it to you, and you were the one who told us our name was in the books. I sent a wire to my lawyer in Itabuna yesterday morning just as soon as Dona Antonieta gave me her word. I got Dona Carmosina out of her house on New Year's Day to send it. That's the way I am; I work fast, like we all do down on the coast, not the slowpoke way you all do things here. Down there, if a fellow goes to sleep on the job, he'll find his cacao plantation's been stolen out from under him before he wakes up. I sure hope they bring that factory in. That'll make folks around here wake up and hustle whether they want to or not."

"It was lucky for you Dona Antonieta honored the promise old José Esteves made. If she hadn't, you would have had a devil of a time finding a buyer, and even if you had it isn't likely he'd have been in as much of a hurry as you are. And you couldn't have done a blessed thing about it."

The notary took off his spectacles, wiped them clean with a handkerchief with the unhurried motions of a man who has all the time in the world, and went on with his homily. "I'm going to tell you something, my friend. It may be true that if that industry we've all heard so much about comes in here, this little registry, which must have less business than almost any other in the state, may pick up some and bring me in a little cash which I badly need. Still and all, I'd rather those Brastânio people stayed out of here. I read about it in *A Tarde*, in that letter to our poet, and it gave me gooseflesh. And before that I'd heard about the pollution those titanium factories spew out; the Skipper told me what happened in Italy, Italy or France, I don't remember which. Just give me our easygoing rhythm, slow and sure, clean water, good fishing, and our own way of doing things." He put his spectacles back on, held up his hand to forestall a reply, and indicated that the subject was closed. "Let's get down to business. Bonaparte, come here and write down what I tell you. . . . Deed for the purchase and sale of the property called . . ."

"Vista Alegre," murmured Jarde and was silent again. In the registry he lacked even having the consoling sight of Dona Antonieta's opulent bosom under the lace of her open kimono.

Josafá fished in his pocket for a little blue notebook, dictated measurements, boundaries, dates and numbers, and handed over the certified copies of the inventory of Dona Gercina da Mata Antunes's belongings, her sole property consisting of Vista Alegre, a corn, manioc, and goat-breeding farm. Dr. Franklin's son Bonaparte, a squat, bigheaded tub of lard and a public notary, took the documents and wrote everything down. Dr. Franklin told them to come back in three days for the payment and signing of the document. "Fortunately or unfortunately, my dear Josafá, Bonaparte can't draw up a contract as fast as you all do down on the coast." Tieta left a down payment, for which Josafá had a receipt ready. The daughter knew just what she was doing, not like her dotty old father who left money with other people and wouldn't take a piece of paper to prove it. Tieta put away the receipt and turned to the notary.

"You won't need me anymore. The title will be in Astério's and Elisa's names, and they're the ones who'll sign. I'm going straight back to Mangue Seco tomorrow to put one last coat of whitewash on the little place I'm building out there."

"I heard about it. Bonaparte spends a lot of time out at Mangue Seco and he told me that of all the miracles you've accomplished in the short time you've been here, and there've been a good many, the biggest of all was getting your summer cottage built as fast as you did. I'll never know how you got those lazy beachcombers to work almost as fast as Josafá's friends down in Itabuna."

"Itabuna, Dr. Franklin? You mean São Paulo. Dona Antonieta's a jet-propelled lady!" Josafá laughed his hearty laugh.

"It's all thanks to my nephew Ricardo. He took over and lit a fire under those men. He's worth his weight in gold, he and my good friend Skipper Dário."

It was just as well that Bonaparte was not worth his weight in gold; it would have amounted to a considerable sum. He wasn't a bad sort of boy, though; it was just that he wouldn't and couldn't run. But then, the notary wondered, why on earth should he have to?

Osnar strode laughing into the office at the head of the pool-hall gang, Aminthas, Seixas and Fidélio, with Seu Manuel added on for good measure.

"Well, well, well, where's the big landowner? Captain Astério, now that you're a proprietor of land and goats I promote you to Major."

They surrounded their friend and companion, the champion of the Golden Cue. Would he be able to keep the title this time around? Jarde and Josafá took their leave, and Josafá shook Tieta's hand.

"Dona Antonieta, I want you to know it's been a real pleasure to make your acquaintance. If there's one person in Agreste who's straight as a die, it's you. You play fair and square, and I take my hat off to you."

"You never said a truer word," agreed Dr. Franklin. "Dona Antonieta sets an example of kindness and integrity to us all. But before you go, Josafá, I want you to hear the answer to a question I'm going to ask our friend Fidélio here." He took off his spectacles and turned to the young men around Astério. "Fidélio, what's your real name?"

"Fidélio de Arroubas Filho."

"Your whole name, please."

"Fidélio Dórea A. de Arroubas Filho."

"And what does the A stand for?"

"Fidélio Dórea Antunes de Arroubas Filho."

"Thank you very much." The notary turned to Josafá, who was waiting in the doorway, and pointed with his spectacles. "You see, Josafá? Another Antunes. And he's not the only one. Dona Carlota Alves—you know, the grammar-school principal—doesn't sign her name that way, but she's an Antunes on her mother's side."

Josafá seemed unshaken. He let out the hearty laugh of one who has nothing to fear.

"Those Antúneses who don't even use the name . . . they ain't the same kind as my father and me, Jarde and Josafá Antunes. It's our only name and we're proud of it!"

Not wanting to reveal his trump card, he fought down the urge to extol the fame and cunning of the lawyer whom he had wired and was confidently expecting, Dr. Marcolino Pitombo, the greatest specialist in land disputes in the cacao country, famous in Itabuna and Ilhéus since time immemorial, when Uruçuca was still called Água Preta and Itajuípe was a miserable little village called Pirangí, and a man was liable to lose his life if he had a funny look in his eye. Dr. Marcolino Pitombo always won his case, by hook or by crook.

Josafá was a smart man from the coast and he was sure Dr. Marcolino would come, for out of consideration for the attorney's advanced age and birthplace, he had reserved a seat on the plane from Ilhéus to Aracaju and back. Agreste was closer to the capital of Sergipe than to Salvador, and that way he would not have to come so far by road, only from Aracaju, where Josafá would meet him and bring him the rest of the way. Dr. Marcolino surely would not refuse to receive his fee, plus such proofs of special consideration and an unexpected expense-free visit to his hometown.

Live-wire Josafá had thought of everything. Jarde thought of nothing but his goats, Seu Mé especially, and Dona Antonieta's half-glimpsed teats, all precious to him and all lost forever.

In which, with the coming of progress, a poster
appears in Agreste; with a brief note on the
composition and behavior of the pool-
championship claques.

Ascânio Trindade had not after all had the opportunity to rub the Skipper's nose in the erudite arguments of Herr Professor Karl Bayer or make him swallow his insults and offer reparation. The overwrought naval man, with Dona Laura in tow, had gone straight from Zé Esteves' burial to his canoe. He intended to see in the New Year with the Mangue Seco fishermen and do full justice to the savory shark and ray-fish fry with which the fishing folk paid him back for Christmas dinner. These courteous rituals of friendship called for punctilious observance.

While he bided his time and waited for another chance to show the interviews and editorials to the Skipper, Ascânio tried to think how he might best unmask *A Tarde*'s columnist in the eyes of the townspeople, who had not yet recovered from the shock of the "Letter to De Matos Barbosa the Poet" and the ensuing flood of rumors launched by the diabolical Dona Carmosina and by Barbozinha atop his pinnacle of glory. Not even Zé Esteves' death and the pomp of a first-class funeral had diminished the echoes of the tocsin sounded by Giovanni Guimarães.

Those who had met the journalist during his warmly remembered visit to Agreste unquestioningly took his part and sallied forth to catechize the rest and arouse public opinion against Brastânio. Ascânio cudgeled his brains for a way to reach the townspeople and put before them the articles, the statements, the newspaper stories that would get things off to a fresh start by showing how exaggerated Guimarães' column was and reduce this problem of the titanium-dioxide factory to its true proportions. No ominous peril hung over them, just run-of-the-mill pollution. But what the hell *was* titanium dioxide, anyhow? He had read the interview with Professor Bayer over and over and he still didn't really know. All he knew was that it was an important product, essential to Brazilian development, and that ought to be enough. He must open people's eyes to the truth, make them see the advantages of having Brastânio in Agreste and what it would mean in terms of wealth and progress to Agreste and to Brazil. But how?

To make everyone read the newspapers one by one would take much too long. To leave them at the Azores Bar for the customers to read didn't solve the problem either, because only one sector of the townsfolk, intellectually weighty but numerically small, would read them there, not to mention the risk that the papers would disappear or be torn or destroyed. Should he hold a meeting in the public square for a sort of collective reading and learning session? It was a tempting idea but rather impracticable, and there were pitfalls, too. Hearing the name Brastânio, the poor people (and others, too, if experience was any guide) might think the company was giving out toys again. When none were forthcoming, they would be disappointed, and the whole idea would backfire.

Finally, remembering his college days, he decided to put up a poster at the courthouse. For the first time in several years of a badly paid sinecure, Lindolfo the county treasurer proved really useful. Making skillful use of his battery of colored pencils, he copied the most important quotations from the interviews and editorials in eye-catching letters on a backing sheet to which he had glued the clippings themselves, the whole topped by a headline running across the sheet of cardboard: BRASTÂNIO MEANS WEALTH AND PROGRESS FOR AGRESTE! As a finishing touch to this work of art he drew an enormous factory in the middle of a crowd of happy citizens waving festive banners. As a border around this central scene were pictures symbolizing the great benefits that would accrue: skyscrapers, model houses for workers, a magnificent hotel, a movie theater as good as any in the capital, and a luxurious ultramodern bus. Lindolfo's mural, rather obvious and primitive but designed to appeal to his customers' tastes, took up the bottom of the cardboard; between it and the headline praising Brastânio were pasted the clippings that told the story.

The wall newspaper was hung in the first-floor room where the Town Council met whenever Colonel Artur da Tapitanga took a notion to call a meeting. He had better take a notion soon, for the councilmen would have to approve Brastânio's request for a permit to build a factory within the city limits. Ascânio took it for granted that the corporation would do so; he took it for granted that the results of the survey would be favorable. If Brastânio didn't intend to come in, why would the directors hire a road-building firm to submit a plan for widening and paving the road between Agreste and Esplanada?

Since the Skipper was gone, Ascânio had rubbed the postmistress' nose in the interviews and stories, and not even Dona Carmosina's insolent retort after reading the newspapers could shake his confidence, enthusiasm and high good humor. He had been in a state of euphoria ever since the arrival of Mirko Stefano's letter and enclosed clippings. Finding no arguments with which to refute the Herr Professor's scientific knowledge and the newspaper owners' patriotism, Dona Carmosina had fallen back on a scornful and categorical statement: "Why, that's nothing but paid propaganda. You can see it a mile away. Only a fool or a barefaced liar would claim it's anything else."

In his enthusiasm, the fiery and progressive Ascânio forgot his self-control and covered Leonora with kisses when he showed her the newspapers and the plaque that read "Antonieta Esteves Cantarelli Street." That is, he covered her with kisses in a manner of speaking; he sprinkled four or five kisses on her cheeks, which was as far as his unbridled passion permitted him to go. Even that was a lot for one who kept himself constantly in check so as not to be taken for the same kind of cynical villain who had deceived and seduced her. Seeing him so happy and excited, like a man reborn, Leonora was tempted to run out into the street to shout hallelujah and greet the lovers' rising sun.

Ascânio's newfound optimism and exuberance were reflected in his brilliant championship pool. Although he was badly out of practice, having neglected the green baize table altogether lately, he was cutting a fine figure and was one of four to reach the semifinals. He had beat Osnar in a sensational game while Fidélio, a calm and crafty player, was winning over the impulsive Leleu. Only Astério,

Seixas, Fidélio, and Ascânio were still in the running, and Leonora
was invited to attend the final matches.

"Come and root for me," said Ascânio. "Everybody has a
cheering section but me."

It was true that the ladies were expected to turn out in unusually large numbers for the tournament finals. Only on very exceptional occasions did women invade the usually male territory of Seu
Manuel's Azores Bar. The presence of ladies and young girls obliged
the men to watch their language and gestures, which they were not
accustomed to doing, and transformed the habitually raffish place
into something quite different. On the occasion of the annual billiards championship, however, the dispute for the Golden Cue, it
had become a tradition for a charming parade of wives, sweethearts,
fiancées, relatives and admirers of the contending rivals to troop
into the bar.

Elisa, for instance, never failed to go, dressed in the height of
fashion, with an assumed air of indifference and remoteness, as if it
were only her wifely duty to encourage Astério that brought her
there. The truth was that she was eager for the chance to breathe
the sinful atmosphere of the bar, where interspersed among the
bottles lining the wall hung the pages of a calendar of naked women
—blond, Nordic, brunette, Oriental, and Afro-Brazilian, one for
each month—a gift from Aminthas to his friend Manuel, "Lusitanian widower, libertine, and aesthete," the dedication read. Sergeant Peto laid them all one by one when he jerked off, and,
according to Osnar, so did Seu Manuel.

Seixas' cousins trooped in, a cheerful and gaily colored throng.
Dona Edna would not have dreamed of missing a single match, even
now, when her two champions were both out of the running: young
Leleu, who acted as if he were her husband, and Terto, who, as we
know all too well, did not act like a lawful wedded husband but was
one. Now that both men had been beaten, Dona Edna couldn't make
up her mind which of the four semifinalists to choose for her favorite. Maybe she'd pick Astério just to get that stuck-up Elisa's
goat—so la-di-dah, putting on airs like the queen of the ball in her
secondhand dresses out of the rubbish bin.

Some of the other female onlookers were just as fickle. Most of
them, however, were unshakably loyal to Fidélio. That gentleman
rejoiced in a lively claque of maidens of all ages, from Dona Carlota
(Antunes) Alves' pupils to the spinster Cinira. Taciturn, monklike,

and with all those admirers! A surprising sort of fellow, that Fidélio A., or rather Antunes.

Ascânio invited Tieta too, but she refused the invitation. Now that the business of Jarde's and Josafá's property was settled there was little to keep her in Agreste. Next day she was going back to Mangue Seco no matter what. The only reason she wasn't leaving early in the morning was that she had promised Dona Milu to go to lunch with her. As soon as lunch was over she intended to brave the early-afternoon glare and heat in Elieser's motor launch and take Ricardo with her for the final touches on Inácio's Corral, the painting and floor-laying.

"Pool tournament? No, my dear, I prefer sea-bathing and moon-bathing on the Mangue Seco dunes." She stretched her limbs in pleasurable anticipation of those delights. "Besides, I want to get some good out of my little grass shack before I leave."

"Before you leave? Surely you're not thinking of leaving before the power line comes in? You don't mean you've forgotten!" High spirits loosened Ascânio's tongue. "I'm getting a surprise ready for you."

"A surprise? Tell me what it is, then."

"I'm sorry, Dona Antonieta, but I can't. I think it'll please you, though."

What would please her most would be for him to shake a leg and take Leonora to bed. She'd just have to give him a little shove in the right direction.

"When the shack is finished in a few days I'll send for Nora to stay there with me."

"You mean she'll be staying out at Mangue Seco?" Ascânio grew pale and his voice shook. Euphoria and enthusiasm suddenly vanished.

It was just as Tieta had foreseen. During the weekend at Mangue Seco she'd get out of that boy's overheated brain the fatal idea of ruining the coconut grove by bringing in an industry rebuffed with horror everywhere else in the world and a mortal threat to Agreste's water and good climate. In return she would plunk him down in Leonora's bed, the most sumptuous bed in the world, the Mangue Seco dunes, still untouched by pollution.

"You come, too. The Corral's not very big, but we can manage to find room for the nannies and the billygoats."

In which God answers a sacrilegious prayer.

The God of Lovers, Ricardo's current favorite, came to his rescue luckily, or it seemed as if He had, at least. But in a very violent way and, if one jumped to conclusions, a cruel and unjust one. Almost immediately, however, the wisdom shown by Providence in choosing one move rather than another became apparent. Just as in the popular refrain quoted by Dona Milu when Tieta was turned out of house and home: God writes straight with crooked lines.

The hard-pressed apprentice of manhood and the priesthood racked his brains for a solution to the pickle he had got himself into. He would somehow have to find a plausible excuse for running first to Maria Imaculada's girlish arms and then to Tieta's delightfully mature ones, and he couldn't see how. He was trapped.

The night before, after he and his mother and Leonora had come back from watching the fireworks and silence reigned through the house, he had crossed the hall and touched his aunt's naked body. With his first kisses Tieta awoke and took him in her arms, clasping him around the waist.

"My billygoat!"

"My little nanny!"

As he said that he was thinking of another little nanny who had said, "Honey, kiss me again," of her swooning voice when she called him honey, and the faint feeling it gave him. He would have liked to say to Tieta, "I met you today, Aunt, the way you used to be when you were a sassy little girl, hiding in wait for me under a mango tree in the dark. I hope you'll forgive me, but I just have to know what you tasted and smelled like when you were a goat girl, with no French perfume, no creams and lotions, no wigs, negligees, gold necklaces or diamond rings; when you smelled of cape jasmine and wore a sky-blue organdy dress."

That night as they belatedly welcomed in the New Year, Ricardo knew for the first time the singular pleasure of possessing one woman while thinking of another. That was even better than the double ypsilon Y performed by Tieta (with his cooperation, of course) when the first light of morning stole in through the window. There were three of them in Dona Eufrosina's and Dr. Fulgêncio's double bed: he, Tieta and Maria Imaculada.

How could he get himself out of the house in time to meet his girl when the lights were out at nine? Even if guests stayed late and the evening's conviviality was prolonged, on what pretext could he get himself out of the house? His mother held him to a strict schedule. He thought of a thousand excuses and invented dozens of reasons to go out, but none of them would hold water. Time was passing and he didn't know what to do. He was almost desperate enough to tell a lie. He had lied to his aunt once already that morning; she had noticed the tooth mark and questioned him about it. He had bitten himself on the lip, he said, when he covered her with kisses and bites at the climax of the ypsilon Y.

As bad luck would have it, no callers had come except for the faithful Ascânio, who was out walking Leonora around the plaza, and Barbozinha the seer, who was telling fibs to Tieta and Perpétua out there on the porch. Ascânio would bring Leonora back on the stroke of nine, and then he and Barbozinha would go off together down the street. Perpétua would retire to her nightly devotions. Leonora, after waving one last goodbye from the doorway, would kiss Tieta goodnight; and then his aunt, after a toilette that would be prolonged until her sister and stepdaughter fell asleep, would lie down to enjoy a pleasant night in Ricardo's company.

He glanced at the clock. Nine o'clock was only half an hour away and no good getaway story had occurred to him yet. He was in a fever of frustration. In a little while Maria Imaculada would be out waiting for him behind the trunk of the mango tree. Flinging down the Portuguese grammar he had buried his face in to think better, Ricardo raised his thoughts to God in a despairing, impious plea. "Help me, Lord God, in my time of tribulation!"

No sooner was the boon asked than granted. There were steps on the sidewalk and Father Mariano's voice was heard calling his name.

"Ricardo! Oh, Ricardo! Are you asleep?"

Perpétua ran to welcome the Father, curious to know what brought him and what he wanted with Ricardo. "I've come on a sad errand, my dear daughter, to give Extreme Unction to old Belarmina, Seu Cazuza Bezerra's widow." A faithful parishioner and nearly a hale and hearty ninety, she had come down with an ordinary head cold a few days before, but just now she had had a dizzy spell and had taken an unexpected turn for the worse. Since Dr. Cáio was away on his summer vacation, Seu Aloísio Melhor the pharmacist, though his sole link with the medical profession was purely commercial, had been called in as pinchhitter. When he saw her lying in bed and couldn't find her pulse, the druggist sent an urgent message to the parish priest to attend the old lady who was dying without the air of the sacraments. Vavá Muriçoca had burned his hand setting off firecrackers the night before, so the Reverend had come to summon Ricardo for this act of Christian charity; he would be helping a poor old woman make her peace with God before she died. "Thank you, Lord!" He offered up silent but heartfelt gratitude as he hurriedly pulled his cassock on over his shorts. After all, Dona Belarmina had already lived for almost a century.

She was destined to live a few years more, it seemed, for the sight of the priest and the seminarian carrying the holy oils for Extreme Unction gave her such a fright that her flu and fainting fit were cured on the spot. She leaped nimbly out of bed in her cotton nightgown with tiny blue flowers embroidered around the neck, and just to prove how healthy she was the spry old devil did a few dance steps and stuck out her tongue at the pharmacist. Senile she might be, but moribund she was not.

The power was going off when the pharmacist, the priest, and Ricardo left Dona Belarmina's house. The old lady saw them out the door.

"Seu Aloísio, next time you want to put a hex on somebody, you go do it to your mother!"

As he walked the Father back to church to put away the chrism and the holy water, Ricardo caught sight of Maria Imaculada behind the mango tree, and he knew she saw him. He escorted Father Mariano to the parish house and heard him bolt the door. Only when he saw Ascânio and the poet walking off down the Rua da Frente did he walk over to where the girl was standing.

"You look so fine in your cassock, honey."

Ricardo felt lightheaded and happy. God had given him a watertight excuse and no one was the worse for it. Father Mariano had been routed out at night, but that was all, and anyhow it was part of his job.

Maria Imaculada had on a black skirt and print blouse instead of blue organdy, but she wore cape jasmine in her hair as she had the night before and the same clear, fresh laughter bubbled from her lips. They kissed each other several times on the way to the river-bank. Seeing him hesitate, she took his hand and led him to the best hiding place of all under the weeping willows in Catherine's Basin. There she lay down, undid her blouse and pulled up her skirt. She had nothing on underneath but her skin, shivering as a breeze wandered over it.

"Come here quick, honey, I'm cold."

Ricardo pushed up his cassock and unbuttoned his shorts. Maria Imaculada laughed.

"Are you going to sanctify me, honey?"

They walked back to the plaza together, Ricardo laughing for no reason, touching her face, kissing her eyes, burying his hand in her curly hair, putting the spray of cape jasmine in the pocket of his cassock. They said goodnight next to the mango tree.

"Tomorrow I'll meet you here again, honey. Same time, same place."

"Tomorrow I'm going to Mangue Seco."

"Will you be there long, honey?" Her voice was anxious.

"I'll be back on Saturday; we have a date."

"You be sure and come back or I'll be so unhappy I'll die."

"I'll come back, don't you worry. See you Saturday, Imaculada."

"Don't go off so fast, honey. Kiss me one more time."

At the height of the kiss an indistinct form appeared in the plaza. Ricardo tore himself away and Maria Imaculada melted into the darkness. Goatstink, staggering drunk, was coming back from the riverbank. Muttering and belching, he kept his voice down instead of bellowing as he usually did, not out of respect for other people's sleep but because he too had his protégés.

"That's right, little priest, have yourself a good lay and long live God the Father."

In which the author informs and indoctrinates the reader concerning regional susceptibilities and famous names in the world of belles-lettres

*and the arts, no doubt in the hope of being classed
with them, with a mention in passing of the
forthcoming election for mayor of Agreste.*

At this critical juncture, when he still lacked a definitive reply to
the questions raised by the announcement of the imminent installation of a Brastânio factory in the Mangue Seco palm grove, Ascânio
Trindade still maintained that the threatened livelihood of the Saco
fishermen was no problem of his, arguing to himself that this settlement was on the left bank of the mouth of the Real River and was
therefore in the state of Sergipe. Josafá had followed the same
provincial line of reasoning in his conversation with Tieta—"Let the
Sergipanos yell and scream their heads off."

They did yell and scream. In a front-page story, *A Tarde* called
the attention of its readers to a burning issue which was dealt with
in more detail on the inside pages. The issue was pollution, and the
theme was taken up in several stories. One said that mayoralty elections had been called in Sant'Ana do Agreste, another quoted a
telegram from Seu Raimundo Souza, mayor of Estância in the
state of Sergipe, and a third was an interview with "Carybé, the
world-famous artist who has done so much for the international
reputation of Brazil."

Concerning the elections there was a brief italicized paragraph
in the "Political News" column: "Rumors are circulating to the
effect that the favored treatment shown by the Election Tribunal in
setting a date in the near future for the election of a new mayor in
Agreste was in response to a maneuver on the part of Brastânio, in
whose interest it is to place a man they can trust in the highest post
in the community where they intend to install the notorious and
universally condemned titanium-dioxide plant."

The telegram from the mayor of Estância seethed with indignation. "Brastânio's ignoble plot to locate its factories on Mangue
Seco poses an unconscionable threat to the southern coast of Sergipe, to the valiant, honest fishermen and all the law-abiding, hardworking people of Saco. It promises ruin to the rich piscatorial
fauna of the neighboring ocean and rivers, the Piauí and the Piau-
tinga, which meet to form the Real River a little above Estância,
and violent changes in the ecology and economy of the neighboring

townships in both Sergipe and Bahia, sister states whose voices and strength should be as one in the defense of their environment."

If the mayor of Estância had not been famous for his perfect breeding, one might have thought that by calling the Saco fishermen honest he was covertly contrasting their honest toil to the illegal smuggler's calling plied by the little colony of so-called fishermen on Mangue Seco. In the same way, noting how the mayor stressed the fact that Brastânio's plans threatened the ecological balance of both states and appealed to the fraternal feeling which ought to unite at least the neighboring states of our ramshackle federation, one might come away with the impression that the author of the telegram was replying with a stinging rebuke to Ascânio Trindade's unworthy thought and Josafá Antunes' unfortunate words. There was no way the popular and capable mayor of Estância could have known, of course, about Josafá's cynical remark, still less Ascânio's desperate, though unarticulated, argument of last resort. We will have to lay the blame for these insinuations, if such indeed they were, at the door of the old recurring complaints of the Sergipanos, unfair or not, that the Bahianos are colonialists at heart.

While quoting from the vigorous protest of the worthy mayor of Estância in *A Tarde*'s columns, I would like to take this opportunity to pay public tribute to his merits. I understand he owns a traditional pollution-proof cigar factory, really a craft shop, where the tobacco leaves are rolled on the thighs of skilled female workers and thus acquire a distinctive aroma and taste. You never know; maybe if I speak well of him as I'm doing now, he'll think to send me a few boxes of his superb product, a precious gift indeed these days when royalties are so meager.

As for the interview with the painter whom the newspaper eulogized in fulsome, flowery language as a remarkable and world-famous artist (and I can vouch for it, the paper did no more than justice to the magnificent oeuvre of Carybé), it was the second in which this "distinguished citizen of Bahia and the owner of a charming rustic summer cottage in Arembepe" had given his views on the subject of Brastânio. He began by quoting from his first interview in which, anticipating Giovanni Guimarães, he had indignantly condemned Brastânio as "a monstrous threat to Arembepe Beach and the entire seacoast of Bahia and to its hard-working people, its fish and marine life and the maternal spirit of the sea." This reference to the Afro-Brazilian sea-mother spirit showed how closely the

artist is identified with the *candomblé* worshippers, in whose ceremonies he holds the rank of either *babalorixá* or *iaô*. In the second
interview he congratulated himself and the people of the city of
Bahia for the fact that Brastânio, bowing to a riptide of protest from
all over the country, including such well-known admirers of the
beauties of Arembepe as the writers and journalists Rubem Braga
and Fernando Sabino, had apparently dropped its initial plan to
"turn Arembepe into a lethal sewer." That was no mean triumph,
but the battle against the corporation must not end there; it must be
fought on other fronts to prevent "this murderous industry from
invading Bahia or any other part of Brazilian territory."

This was flinging down the gauntlet with a vengeance, and
public response was assured, given the fame and popularity of
Carybé. Protests against the installation of a factory in Arembepe
were already coming thick and fast, even though so far no one had
raised his voice in defense of Agreste, the Real River, the Mangue
Seco coast and the neighboring townships except Giovanni Guimarães, the mayor of Estância, and De Matos Barbosa (in two
poems published in *A Tarde*'s literary supplement).

Not surprisingly, Arembepe had innumerable champions ready
to defend its tranquil beauty, many of them as famous as the illustrious painter quoted above. After all, it not only boasts fine,
abundant fishing and spectacular scenery, but the picturesque fishing village with its gaily painted houses had been featured in the
newspapers of the south, used as the scene for a movie and, as
Skipper Dário remembered, was for a time known as the hippie
capital of South America.

By a strange coincidence, Carybé is the same shabby character
who appeared in this novel once before when I described the
underhanded (and successful) purchase, at a ridiculous price, of the
wooden image of St. Anne, a priceless work by a seventeenth-
century "saintmaker," from poor naive Father Mariano.

The sum he offered had seemed enormous at the time to the
unsuspecting priest, and he had yielded the worm-eaten saint to the
scoundrel trickster without a murmur. Poor backlands priest! He
was overcome with remorse years later when Dona Carmosina
showed him some pictures of the restored image (taken from various angles in a Rio magazine, where it was described as "a major
piece in the artist Mirabeau Sampáio's remarkable collection").
Only then did he realize how he had been tricked, and ever since

that day the secret has been kept between him and the postmistress as silent as the grave. Although no friend of the church and a self-proclaimed agnostic, skeptic and atheist, Dona Carmosina promised to destroy her copy of the magazine and forget the incident out of pity for the artistic ignorance of a humble priest buried away in the wilderness.

While I am on the subject, Dona Carmosina's reply to Ascânio Trindade's poster at the courthouse was another, bigger and even more spectacular one. In addition to quotations, in huge block letters, from such articles as Giovanni Guimarães' column, there were macabre illustrations: yellow fumes issuing from Brastânio's chimneys, a frightful stain of sulfur dioxide hiding the blue sky (gaseous effluents) and a stream of dead fish in a filthy sewer flowing with the lethal refuse of ferrous sulfate and sulfuric acid (liquid effluents). Dona Carmosina knew all there was to know about titanium dioxide and how it was produced. Mangue Seco's luxuriant coconut grove would be reduced to a few emaciated palm trees where a wretched handful of beggars was slowly being asphyxiated.

As a work of art it was just as primitive and rudimentary as Lindolfo the treasurer's and at least as effective, for the artist had used watercolors and not just a set of colored pencils. This was the handiwork of Seixas, an amateur artist who painted in a modest way when pool and his cousins permitted—and the office, let us hasten to add, where he checked in faithfully every day, on the sly, so the gang wouldn't pull his leg. It was no secret, of course, to Dona Carmosina.

Dona Carmosina's mural, in the center of which were Giovanni Guimarães' column, the local poet Barbozinha's two laureate Poems of Damnation, and a portrait of the famous adoptive Bahiano Carybé, was strategically placed between the two doors to the Areopagus and was much more widely read and commented upon than Ascânio Trindade's in the council room. There was no comparison between the number of people who frequented the two public buildings. No one ever went to the courthouse unless necessity brought him there. Necessity might take one to the post office, too, but many people went there for pleasure—to chat, to hear the town notables engage in erudite discourse, or to find out what was going on in the world: the few happy events, the many misfortunes, the innumerable perils to human life.

FIFTH EPISODE

※ ※ ※

Of a Blue Sun and a Black Moon,
or
God's Rival

WITH HUGE MACHINES: STREET, MUDFLATS, BEACH AND CRABS
SMOTHERED IN A TIDE OF ASPHALT, TOGETHER WITH A
DAZZLING VISION OF THE FUTURE; IN WHICH WE WATCH THE
EDUCATION OF A LEADER IN THE CAUSE OF PROGRESS AND A
TOAST IS DRUNK TO FRIENDSHIP AND GRATITUDE; IN WHICH
A MASS MOVEMENT EXPLODES WITH IMPETUOUS FORCE IN
MANGUE SECO, AGRESTE IMPORTS LAWYERS AND FORENSIC
PLOYS AND SOME SECONDARY CHARACTERS BECOME
IMPORTANT; WITH THE SEXUAL INITIATION OF A VIRGIN BOY,
REVELATORY DREAMS AND FAMILY REVELATIONS, RASH
AND RECKLESS ACTS, THE GNASHING OF TEETH AND A WORD SAID
IN GERMAN, AND IN WHICH TIETA CHOKES ON LOVE,
LOSS AND DEATH.

*Of the rapid paving of the road by which the
electric power lines will come to Agreste, or
rather the street along which Tieta's light will
come as the rhythm of the town quickens.*

What had so far been columns in the newspapers, jawing on street
corners and perplexing, unidentified apparitions which puzzled even
Barbozinha, hand in glove though he was with the supernatural, all
came down to earth with a bang the morning the heavy road machinery of the Bahian Engineering Projects Company (BEPC) appeared in Agreste and gravely, majestically crossed the Rua da
Frente. With their cavernous roaring sound and outsize eccentric
forms, they were the very exemplar of progress on the march.

Young Sabino, tongue hanging out and eyes starting out of his
head, ran ahead of them full speed from Tapitanga Plantation,
where he had been taking his ease and comfort with the corrupt,
docile nannygoat Negra Flor, the flower of Colonel Artur de
Figueiredo's flock. In the form of the gentle, compliant animal the
youth possessed all the Agreste women who haunted his adolescent
dreams: Elisa, his boss's wife; Carol, the big shot's mistress; Edna,
who was married to Terto but might as well not have been; two of
Seixas' cousins, the slightly cross-eyed girl and the busty one (the
rest of them weren't worth looking at), and little Aracy, whose
fanny he liked to rub up against when she walked by—a variegated
nosegay enhanced by the coming of the exotic and sensational
Paulistas. Sabino did his best to respect Dona Antonieta, but could
he help it if it was as good as a movie to see through the gauzy
clothes and carelessly unbuttoned kimonos she wore when he knelt
for her blessing? The boy was completely out of breath when he
reached Astério's store, where Osnar was talking crops and animal
diseases with his new fellow landowner and neighbor. The words

burst out of Sabino's mouth: "There's tanks coming up the road with cannons and everything."

First a large jeep went tearing past the store. Then came the slow, ponderous machines and a truck carrying men in overalls and helmets, with thick work gloves on their hands. These were nothing like the Paulo Afonso Power Plant vehicles that sometimes brought engineers and workmen to town to check the calculations for the light poles.

Next appeared a powerful machine with a front blade like a snowplow, one of those motorized graders that scrape the ground and flatten the road, then a steamroller, and finally a chemical asphalt sprayer. Osnar jumped up in excitement from the chair where he was perched, waved goodbye to Astério, and loped off toward the courthouse, lured by the faint hope that Elisabeth Valadares, Betty to her colleagues, Bebé to close friends, might have come in the jeep. Osnar had missed her by seconds on Christmas Eve. He had run into the square just in time to catch a glimpse of her in the helicopter, dressed in a Santa Claus suit and waving to the crowd. He had waved back and the redhead had looked as if she recognized him and thrown a kiss.

Although the whole Brastânio business disturbed him because he knew it would upset the town's peaceful routine, so precious to one who had no intention of leaving and only wanted to be left alone, Osnar did not associate Betty with the tide of pollution. She was efficient, seductive, poised, and he chose to think of her as victimized by the system. While waiting for her to return he had made a rash resolution and was ready to carry it out right there if by some lucky chance the executive secretary had come along with the group in the jeep. He would tell her the story of the Polish whore.

The famous history of Osnar's Polish whore was, experience had shown him, the master key that unlocked all cunts; it simply never failed. Fortified with this certainty, Osnar strode toward the square. Maybe someday the shit factory really would come to Mangue Seco, but before everything rotted, Bebé, hailed Queen of Agreste, her heart and nether regions aquiver with the exciting details of that extraordinary tale, might very well want a fling with a strong, sturdy, stiff, healthy, unpolluted, mouthwatering backwoods prick.

He came up in time to see a fellow in khaki jump out of the jeep, portfolio in hand, and head for the front entrance of the courthouse, leaving two others behind in the vehicle. Behind them the giant machines panted in and out with their savage, stony breath. Of Betty there was no sign. And the jovial con man, the fast-talking polyglot who gave orders to the well-endowed redhead, had not come either. Osnar retired crestfallen to the bar to exchange sour remarks about Brastânio with Seu Manuel.

"They used to send eye-filling broads for us to look at, at least. Now it's just guys and no dolls."

"And those great hulking machines." Manuel pointed to the vehicles. "What do they do? What are they for?"

"To fuck up our lives, Admiral, mark my words."

At the courthouse the man who had gotten out of the jeep handed Ascânio a letter from Dr. Mirko Stefano in which Mirkus the Magnificent, with many compliments for his "delightful friend Ascânio Trindade," presented Dr. Remo Quarantini, chief engineer of the Bahian Engineering Projects Company (BEPC) and leader of the brigade of technicians who were going to Agreste to make a survey and proposal for straightening, widening and paving the road. While they were at it, they were bringing along equipment and workmen to pave the street into town, thus honoring the promise Brastânio had made to the community through his, Mirko's, intervention. At the end of the letter he invited his esteemed friend to visit Bahia at his earliest convenience for an important conference with some of the corporation board members to discuss the installation of the titanium-dioxide industry in the area. He had good news for Ascânio and wanted to deliver it personally. Before closing with cordial best regards, he informed him that Brastânio, which did not wish to be a burden on the city budget, would pay the expenses of his trip. "Until soon then, my dear friend; I'm counting on your visit. Ask Dr. Remo to bring you back with him, and get him to tell you some of those hilarious stories of his. Besides his other talents, he has a fantastic sense of humor."

No one could have told from looking at Dr. Remo that he had a fantastic sense of humor; he was bald and taciturn, with a long, blond, scraggly beard and the face of a man who has eaten shit and didn't like it. Ascânio wished him a warm welcome in the name of the authorities and townspeople, nevertheless, placed himself at his disposal and advised the engineer that he intended to accompany him back to Bahia and was looking forward to hearing some of those hilarious stories of his. While these niceties were taking place inside the courthouse, a crowd of openmouthed idlers were inspecting the caterpillar trucks. Peto, who was almost as interested in roadbuilding and machines of all kinds as he was in the mysteries of sex, described the use of each one and called them by their technical and colloquial names.

Sprayer, leveler, and steam roller were for laying down roadways and paving them, he explained. Not with rough jagged stones like the ones with which Ascânio's grandfather had paved Cathedral Square, Front Street and the Market Square (thenceforward known as Colonel Francisco Trindade Square) in more prosperous times, but with black asphalt, a paving surface unknown except to those who had traveled at least as far as Esplanada. Peto, a veritable globe-trotter, was one of them; he had gone with Perpétua to the neighboring town three times and once to Aracaju. Yes, things were really beginning to happen in Agreste. It wasn't just idle talk any more.

The engineer questioned Ascânio about the road. He apologized for speaking his mind, but that mule track didn't even deserve to be called a wagon road. It was nothing but a trail, and a rough trail, narrow and pitted with ridges, quagmires, humps, ditches, craters. In plain language, a shithole. They would have to rebuild it entirely, maybe even lay a whole new roadbed, and that would be one hell of job. Ascânio gave him what information he could, but only Jairo, who owned the *marineti* and knew the road like the palm of his hand, could tell him everything he wanted to know, and not until he got in from Esplanada.

A sneer came over Dr. Quarantini's sullen countenance. They had passed that remarkable vehicle outside of Esplanada. It was so old and broken down that even the heavy machines going in first gear had left it behind. Yes, the man who drove that heap of scrap iron back and forth would have to know that ditch that called itself a road like the palm of his hand. Ascânio warned him not to fool around with Jairo; the *marineti*'s owner had been in a bad mood ever since he had seen the poster at the courthouse with the drawing of the magnificent passenger buses envisioned for that new road the engineer was planning to build.

While they were on the subject he asked for a minute of the engineer's precious time to show him the wall newspaper before they went to look at the piece to be paved, which he had just gone over, of course, coming into town. The bearded engineer vouchsafed the poster another one of his wry smiles. Ascânio was not sure whether it was a tribute to Lindolfo's dubious artistic vocation or to the enthusiasm displayed in the mural for Brastânio and its progressive effluents. The visitor made no comment on either the drawing or the upbeat slogan in bright colored letters, but merely said, "Let's have a look. The sooner we get started the better."

The engineer was in a hurry. With the exception of the calm and unflappable Mirko Stefano, everyone who had anything to do with progress seemed to have a horror of wasting time; they were always impatient, always on the go. As the baldheaded man led the way to the jeep, Ascânio realized that he'd have to hustle if he wanted to keep up. In these years away from the capital he had grown used to the slow wheeling of time in Agreste.

Jeep, truck and equipment rolled back down the street, trailed by a growing, gaping crowd. They stopped at the edge of the town and engineers, overseers and workmen jumped out. Ascânio, the two head engineers and the company inspector walked the few blocks to be paved, the future Rua Antonieta Esteves Cantarelli.

"Is that all?" Dr. Quarantini turned to the foremen. "Don't bother to set up the tents; after all, we can take care of this little job today. I thought it was a big deal." Then, addressing Ascânio, "OK, pal, let's get to work. Maybe you could do me a favor and rustle up some grub for the men and a few bottles of beer, OK? Where do we eat? Is there a decent restaurant around here? It sure doesn't look like it. . . ." A resigned flop of the hand. "Whatever you've got'll be fine."

"Don't worry, I'll take care of it. What time do you think you'll start back?"

"Late afternoon. We'll try to finish up before dark. How about it, Sante?"

Sante, a powerful mulatto biting on a stubby cigar, nodded. "Sure." He turned to the men. "Let's get this show on the road."

Yellow sawhorses were set up to stop traffic, the curious onlookers were shooed away, and the great machinery went into action. Elbowing one another behind the barriers under the glaring sun, the townspeople avidly watched the progress of the work. The steam shovel produced oohs and ahs from the crowd, and the steamroller still more as it rolled back and forth on the hundred-yard stretch, pressing the loose soil and transforming it into a solid roadbed for Rua Antonieta Esteves Cantarelli, a short street but a paved one now, the first beneficiary of the progress Brastânio would bring.

And to think there were people who badmouthed big business, Ascânio marveled, indignant at the ingratitude of the world. As his eye wandered over the crowd of bystanders, he could see that the prevailing sentiment was awe. Caloca, owner of the Elite Bar, a dive in the Beco da Amargura where *cachaça* was sold, summed up the general mood. "Hot damn, but those motherfuckers work fast!"

Agreste's presumptive mayor, his heart thumping a victory march, withdrew to attend to his affairs. First he stopped at Dona Amorzinho's boardinghouse and ordered food for the work brigade. He and three others would come back to the pension for lunch, but the workmen would eat where they were. Would she make them up a good mess of black beans and roast kid? "And don't charge them anything, the county's footing the bill." Next he hurried to Perpétua's house to tell Leonora the news and inform her of his unexpected business trip to the capital. Would she realize how important that trip was? That it might make all the difference between a love affair with no future, an insubstantial dream, and the thrilling reality of engagement and marriage? He would bring Brastânio's official request to invest in Agreste back with him, but that wasn't all. The horizon opening out before him was much wider than that.

That day at noon, in Ascânio's company, the two engineers and the supervisor enjoyed the best lunch of their lives: juicy clams fried, boiled and poached with eggs, fish stew cooked in bright-yellow palm oil, chicken and brown gravy, roast kid, jerky with milk mush; desserts of exotic-tasting fruit: jackfruit, acid carambola, currant, gooseberry, guava; cashew nuts and genipap raisins; plummy, refreshing drinks squeezed from hog plum and ambarella. The glum chief engineer ate so heartily and so well that his sallow face took on a healthy flush. Leaving his partner in charge of the paving job, he stretched out in a hammock to sleep until late afternoon, waking up in time to see the job finished.

When Jairo's *marineti* honked at the curve as the workmen were still smacking their lips over their beer and black beans (and Dona Amorzinho's beans, not just any old beans), the first layer of gleaming black tar had just been laid over the flattened earth. The men took away the barriers to make way for the puffing vehicle and saluted it with a chorus of whistles and wisecracks—junkheap! jalopy! war surplus! and then yelled, "Get a horse!" and booed loudly as it passed.

Ascânio came back about six, arm in arm with Leonora and carrying a suitcase. The job was just about done. The gooey black asphalt glittered in the sun. The chemical car squirted a top coat of fine asphalt from a pipe. Antonieta Esteves Cantarelli Street was ready to be christened.

Caloca went up to Ascânio with a request that made everyone laugh.

"Hey, Mr. Ascânio, why don't you ask them to pave my alley while they're at it? It'll only take a minute."

Chief Engineer Remo Quarantini, still half asleep, gave the signal to hit the road. God, that lunch! Ascânio said goodbye to Leonora, kissing her on the cheek in front of everybody. As he left her with Dona Carmosina in the front row of bystanders, he could not resist a mild taunt at his friend and adversary.

"See, Miss Smartypants?"

He didn't wait for an answer. The engineer was already in the jeep and blowing the horn. From now on they'd all have to pick up a foot; lazy days were over. Lazy days or leisure days?

In which we learn what happened to the equipment on the road, or Jairo the jubilant.

That's life for you. The dog catches the rabbit one day and the rabbit gets away the next, or he laughs best who laughs last. Shortly after the generator was turned off and the cathedral bells, rung by Vavá with his hand still in bandages, pealed out on the stroke of nine, there was an insistent clapping at the humiliated Jairo's door.

There stood the driver's sidekick, one of the team of workmen who had been so quick to boo and scoff. He needed Jairo's tools and Jairo's precious help, too, if he would come. Two of the machines had broken down on the road; only the steamroller was still on its way to Esplanada. As for the jeep and the truck with the workmen, they had taken the lead outside of Agreste and should be approaching Bahia by now. The young fellow had walked all the way and was parched with thirst. He sure would be grateful for a glass of water. "Sorry to bother you."

"Where did it happen?"

"Not far from here, five or six miles. You know that steep grade where there's a broken-down cattle guard? Well, it broke down sure enough when the steam shovel tried to cross it and got stuck in the mud. The other one didn't even get that far before it went haywire."

Winners can afford to be generous. Jairo magnanimously offered to help.

"All right, let's go have a look. I don't expect it's anything much. We'll have 'em on the road again in no time."

He went out to the garage, patted the *marineti* and whispered words of affection and trust.

"Come on, Flying Saucer, let's go pull the rich folks out of the mud. They called you a jalopy and a junkheap, didn't they? Well, now it's our turn. We'll show 'em, won't we? Don't you go back on me now. Come on, you sexy little critter, show 'em what you've got."

The sexy little critter came through with flying colors. They rattled along at quite a respectable rate of speed and the motor did not miss even once. "That's a good little bus you've got," remarked the driver's helper as the vehicle went its way, serenely indifferent to craters, mudholes, bumps and dizzying drops, and all to the sound of music, for, incredible as it seemed, even the Russian radio worked that night.

Jairo, who was not only obliging but a tip-top mechanic, had the vehicles in working order fairly soon. It was a little past midnight when he stood up, wiped his hands on a wad of waste, and without waiting to be thanked climbed into his *marineti*, turned on the motor and drove off with a fine volley of backfire from the exhaust.

"Thank you, Star of the *Sertão*. Home at last, my little chickadee."

Of the headaches of a nouveau riche.

The hustle and bustle increased; Agreste was on the move. In the case of Astério, promoted from humble shopkeeper to nouveau-riche and from captain to major, the responsibility belonged to his rich São Paulo sister-in-law and, if Brastânio had anything to do with it, it was only indirectly and by chance. However it had happened, he was living life to a faster beat.

He had routinely spent his mornings and afternoons at the store waiting on an occasional customer, selling a few yards of cloth, a man's shirt, a woman's skirt, a dozen buttons, needles and thread—notions, trifles. There had been all the time in the world to chew the fat with his friends, especially with the indefatigable Osnar, hear the latest gossip, extract the juice out of all the little things that happened, laugh over stories of "Agreste's vibrant night life," as Aminthas called it, and keep fully informed about Zuleika Cinderella's new recruits. Several days before, they had told him about a brand-new one, a kid who hadn't turned fifteen yet, but had an ass on her that was well on its way to being the greatest ass Agreste had ever seen. She came from Saco and her name was Maria Imaculada.

In the hours of the early afternoon, siesta time, he would leave young Sabino to watch the store and indulge in long practice sessions in the poolroom at the bar. Now there weren't enough hours in the day, what with the store, the land, and the work on Tieta's house.

Every morning he went to Vista Alegre to see how the flock and the planting were coming along under the care of Menininho, Lauro Branco's son. That had been arranged by Osnar.

"Major, you're gonna be cheated anyhow, whoever you put in there; so you're better off being cheated by our good friend Lauro, who won't rob you blind and is a very hard worker, all kidding aside. Menininho can plow up a storm, he knows goats backward and forward, and he's got Lauro to keep him in line. If you keep an eye on what's going on, like I do, it'll all work out just fine."

Then he'd run from the shop to Dona Zulmira's old house to see how the last stages of the work were coming along. Old Zé Esteves used to take his stand there from morning to night, getting in Liberato the foreman's way and making life hell for the workmen. Now it was up to Astério to see that the work didn't bog down when the end was in sight. The bathrooms were all finished, and they were the best in Agreste, too, with showers, bathtubs, and the fanciest toilets ever seen in those parts. The painters had begun work and the house would soon be ready for occupancy. Astério was anxious to move in as soon as possible, even if the work wasn't finished. He saw two advantages: they could stop paying rent, and when they were living in the house the work would go faster. He had already told Elisa to start packing up their things.

Old Zé Esteves's death had opened the way to prosperity for them. Manioc, goats, land . . . If you own land you own a piece of the world, his father-in-law had said, lamenting his lost patrimony. And now they had a brand-new house, not their property but theirs to use, and one of the best in town; a worthy setting for Elisa's beauty and elegance.

He was worried about Elisa. She went around moping and crying when she didn't think he was looking. No one would have thought she had had so many blessings heaped upon her, such proofs of sisterly love as Agreste had seldom seen. Tieta was open-handed, more than generous, prodigal with her bounty, and yet Elisa went around with a woebegone face and a chip on her shoulder. Astério had not seen a smile on her face since the day after the old man was buried, when Tieta announced that she was buying Vista Alegre in the couple's name. More than once Astério had asked her what was wrong and why she was so sad, and Elisa had told him there was nothing the matter, she wasn't sad and he was not to worry about her. She had not even laughed when he confided to her that Osnar intended to make the same proposition to the executive secretary of that guy from Brastânio, "the red-headed dame with the silver streak in her hair, remember?" that he had made to the Polish whore. "Can you imagine that?"

It was unbelievable what a crushing blow the old man's death had been to Elisa. As long as he was alive Astério had never seen the least sign of any deep love between father and daughter. He had seen fear all right; Elisa couldn't hide what Astério was vaguely aware of—that the main reason she had married him was to get away from her father's tyranny, the prison that was home, the never-idle shepherd's staff and leather strap. Even after his daughters were married, the old man imposed his will on them and on his sons-in-law too. Astério had never heard him pronounce one tender word or show affection, not even to comfort Elisa when Toninho died. At the Major's wake, when the bereft Perpétua was in tears and inconsolable, Zé Esteves had taunted her, "You'll never hook another man, so forget it. A fool like that comes along once in a lifetime, and not always then."

He was always accusing Astério of dishonesty because he had

once taken one of Tieta's checks to pay off a pressing debt. Years went by and the old ogre still hurled the old accusation in his daughter's face and accused his son-in-law of trying to swindle him, threatening to have him thrown in jail if he ever tried such a trick again.

Lord, but some people were hard to understand! He'd thought Elisa would finally be able to breathe free of fear now, fear of her father and fear of being poor. She ought to be happy now that her sister's gift had solved the money problems that had made their life a burden, besides giving them a fine new residence, the status of a well-to-do couple, and a prominent place in Agreste society. Instead Elisa was inconsolable, as if she had lost her last chance of happiness when she lost her father.

Astério was not much of a psychologist despite the fact that his billiard caroms were awesome demonstrations of intellect, perfectly calculated to a tenth of an inch. Some of his strokes were true works of art, but the complex behavior of human beings and their sulks, crying spells and fits of bad temper upset him and made him feel helpless. Maybe Dona Carmosina, who was so clever and well read, could understand and explain them, but not he. Or maybe Tieta could; nothing got by her.

When he and Tieta had discussed Elisa's expressed desire to move to São Paulo, his sister-in-law had counseled him to keep his wife on a short rein like old Zé Esteves; she had even talked of his using the quincewood staff.

For all her kindness and her heart of gold, Tieta talked just like the old man sometimes. Raise his voice against Elisa? Keep her on a short rein? How could he, when she was such a good, devoted wife, who kept her house so spic and span and was so stylish and beautiful besides?

When he thought of his wife's virtues Astério was touched. What was so bad about a daughter's crying and being unhappy when she had lost her father? She would get over it in time. Sooner or later she'd go back to being his Elisa again and assume the old distant, rather snobbish, slightly melancholy air that became her so well. She was the prettiest, most stylish woman in town. She had been poor but now she was a landowner, and whoever owned land owned a piece of the world; the old man had hit the nail on the head, confound him. And she was the owner of a royal ass besides.

Astério had been told there was a certain Maria Imaculada whose ass might someday grow to be . . . That was just foolishness. Nature could work prodigies, but she'd never make another ass like Elisa's.

In which a last toast is drunk to friendship and gratitude.

As he caught sight of the imposing figure of Dr. Baltazar Moreira, full-fledged attorney with a law office in Feira da Sant'Ana, black briefcase under his arm, sweating copiously as he trundled down the street, Aminthas asked mockingly, "Has Agreste been chosen as the site for a legal convention? You can't go out of the house these days without tripping over a lawyer."

Osnar rested his cue, calculating the number of points Fidélio was ahead of him. Seeing no hope of overtaking and beating him, he donned the mantle of hierophant customarily assumed by Barbozinha.

"Vultures don't come around unless they smell carrion. It's gonna stink around here before long."

The championship finals had been put off again because of Ascânio's trip to the capital, and the Golden Cue finalists had to be satisfied with friendly games for rounds of beer. Seixas, standing up for a better look at Fidélio's, his rival's, game, put in a word.

"It's about time it started to stink. We can't start smelling oil, sulfur, and chemical gases soon enough for me. It's the stink of prosperity. What do you say, Fidélio?"

"What are you asking me for?" said Fidélio, taken aback.

"You're an Antunes, aren't you? One of the palm-grove heirs. We all heard Dr. Franklin say so in his office. What are you trying to do, hide your wealth? Here you are, a millionaire partner of Brastânio, all set to pollute Mangue Seco. Why, I'll bet one of those lawyers out there came to town on your account, or am I wrong? Which one was it? Come on, loosen up, tell your pals all about it."

Fidélio suspended his cue and answered seriously, as if he saw nothing funny in his opponent's gibes, "I don't need a lawyer." He squinted at his cue and retreated into his habitual reserve.

"I'll take the case if you want me to." Seixas persisted in his raillery, taking no notice of his friend's long face. "To begin with,

I'd advise you to set up housekeeping with Dona Carlota. She's another candidate for the coconut grove, so it would be a marriage with common property, Antunes joining forces with Antunes. And besides, you'd be getting a genuine antique cunt that belongs in a museum."

Fidélio concluded the game with a fine carom and a flourish and tried to put an end to the teasing, which he plainly did not enjoy.

"I don't need a lawyer and I don't need advice from anyone, so you just keep your nose out of my business. I know what you're trying to do; you want to get me all riled up and nervous so I'll lose when it's our turn to play. And I won't stand for that."

Seixas was stung. "I was pulling your leg, that's all I was doing. I don't have any intention of doing anything else. I don't have to pull that kind of stuff to beat you; I've won from you plenty of times before. And I won't stand for you calling me a cheater."

Osnar hung up his cue and put a stop to the argument.

"What the hell are you talking about? Come on, both of you, cut it out and let the carrion rot someplace else. I said there's gonna be a stink and that isn't all. But anyone who wants to argue about that crap had better do it a long way off. Our crowd has nothing to do with it. How many years have we been friends?" He changed the subject. "If you all swear not to let on to Astério, I'll tell you about a little surprise party I'm planning for one of these days."

Seixas was still muttering and Fidélio said nothing. Osnar went on, "Did you know that Sergeant Peto turns thirteen in just a few days? Zuleika and I are fixing to give him a high old time next Saturday to celebrate his birthday."

"Zuleika? How'd she get in on this?" exclaimed Seixas, a trace of hurt feelings still in his voice. "You celebrate a kid's birthday at home with Coke and soda pop and cake and candy and all that junk. It's the living end. If Dona Perpétua gives a party I'll have to go and take Zelita, my eleven-year-old cousin. She'll love it."

Osnar smiled gratefully at Seixas. Now the conversation was taking a turn for the better. He was sick of listening to arguments about pollution and the factory, which was all people talked about in Agreste lately. Not even the steadily advancing pylons of the São Francisco Valley Authority, the subject of so much enthusiastic comment only a week before, could distract people's attention from the problem that had riven the town ever since Brastânio had sent in the Bahian Engineering Projects Company to pave old Mud Lane (soon to be rechristened Antonieta Esteves Cantarelli Street), and they'd done it in the twinkling of an eye. The plans were no secret any more; several people had seen the street sign in Ascânio's hand and everyone knew about it. Only Tieta, blissfully summering on Mangue Seco, was unaware that she was soon to be officially immortalized. Of all the projects brewing down at the courthouse, this was the only one to meet with unanimous approval and applause. For the rest, discord reigned and the town was divided.

Battles were joined and insults traded in the formerly peaceful streets. Arguments for and against the installation of the factory were hurled back and forth. Should the company be allowed to come in or not? Should it be hailed with joy or repulsed with indignation? Did it signify life or death? Part of the population was still undecided, not knowing which of the two murals to believe, the one at the courthouse, attesting to the utter harmlessness of the titanium-dioxide industry and promising all manner of marvels, or the one at the post office, which warned shrilly that Brastânio was a deadly threat to sky, land, sea, a threat to the whole region, and that the titanium-dioxide industry would bring a thousand misfortunes in its train. Titanium dioxide: the name suggested all sorts of fascinating, menacing mysterious things.

There were some eclectics who mingled allegations from both sides. That is, while they did not dispute the veracity of many of the statements about the tremendous pollution caused by the controversial industry, they nevertheless did not think that it should be forbidden in Mangue Seco's coconut grove or anywhere else in Sant'Ana do Agreste. These people did not see how there could be progress without pollution and cited the examples of the United States, Japan, Germany and São Paulo—four colossi to be reckoned with.

This highly intellectual debate was soon carried beyond the limits of the Areopagus, the Azores Bar, Zuleika's cathouse and the cathedral, the four cultural centers of Agreste. (The last-named specialized, of course, in liturgical questions, at which the church-mice were all experts who more than once put Father Mariano in his place.) It was argued in every shop, grocery store, marketplace, house and streetcorner, even in Caloca's dive in the Beco da Amargura—argued heatedly, sometimes passionately. The first serious fallings-out began to occur, precursors of all that were to follow. Two men employed in the tannery, Nighthawk and Carioca (who owed his nickname to having lived for several years in Rio and having pretensions to being a man of learning), actually came to blows when Nighthawk called Carioca pestiferous and the injured man accused him in turn of being medieval, a terrible insult to Nighthawk, who was not a man of learning and didn't know what it meant. Titanium dioxide became a watchword for both good and evil. As always with mystical symbols, no one knew anything about this fearsome totem, not even what it looked like or whether it was a gas, a liquid or a solid. Being a divinity, it was probably all three. As a gas, it infected the air; as a liquid, it poisoned the water; as a solid, it would crush the population under its oppressive weight. Osnar was right; the whole town stank of titanium dioxide. Well, it had better not stink up their daily socializing in the bar over a beer or at the green baize tables! He smiled gratefully at Seixas. Friendship was precious to Osnar and he was determined to save it from pollution. He tapped his companion's knee affectionately with his long, thin hand.

"I'm telling you the Sergeant's going on thirteen. Don't you know Brazilian citizens reach their sexual majority at thirteen? Were you a retarded child? Oh yes, some are retarded, some of us are precocious, and the rest are normal. Yours truly here was a good example of a precocious kid. I got a head start on all of you before I was twelve, and that was the beginning of the meteoric career to which you can all bear witness."

Laughter all around cleared the air and cordiality reigned again. Fidélio's voice regained its normal serenity.

"Who'd you do it with the first time? With her?"

Seixas forgot their wrangle and his annoyance.

"Of course it was with her, Fidélio; who else do you think? Remember the two of us? Both the same day, you rascal, but you stole a march on me and went in first."

Fidélio corrected him in the interest of historic truth.

"Now tell it like it was. You asked me to go in first because you were scared as the dickens."

They smiled reminiscently, and Seixas softened.

"You're right, I was so scared I was shitting in my pants. Even after you came out and told me everything was hunky-dory I could hardly get ahold of myself. But as soon as I went inside she made me feel right at home and everything was fine."

"How many of us do you think she's broken in in her time?" mused Aminthas. "There's nobody like her for showing a greenhorn the ropes. She's got such nice manners; she knows just what to say and do. I know guys who've gone to hookers the first time and it made a terrible impression on them; it was so different from what they expected that it took them months to get over it and start enjoying themselves. Some of them never did. But with her, you start off on the right foot from the very beginning."

"I propose a toast," said Seixas, his good humor restored.

"Let's have a round of *cachaça*, Admiral, so we can seal a pact and drink a toast to the woman who brought us into the world for the second time," called out Osnar. While they waited to drink to friendship and gratitude, he returned to the subject of Peto's initiation. "What do you say we give the Sergeant a party he'll never forget? It's been a long time since we really tied one on, and it's high time we did. All anyone talks about in Agreste these days are nasty things like money and pollution."

Seu Manuel brought the rum and wanted to know who that mother was who had all those kids and how she had brought them into the world twice.

"She gave us the light of understanding, Admiral." These were mysterious words to the good Lusitanian, but he was soon enlightened. Osnar lifted the thick cheap glass, inhaled the odor of pure white rum and declaimed, "To the health of Zuleika Cinderella and her narrow doorway, by which we went in as children and came out as men. And to our friendship that no titanium shall rot."

Osnar too has his flashes of genius, at which times, whether by chance or necessity, he rightfully usurps the predestined Barbozinha's privileges as seer and poet.

A chapter in which Agreste imports legal procedures from more progressive climes and there is some theorizing about money and power.

First of the lawyers to arrive and the only one to stay for some time, lodging at Dona Amorzinho's boardinghouse and making the acquaintance of the townspeople (the other two went back and forth between Agreste and Esplanada), was Dr. Marcolino Pitombo, a charming, distinguished-looking, dapper elderly gentleman, from the legendary, wealthy and progressive land of the cacao. He wore a white linen suit and a real panama hat, smoked Suerdieck cigars and carried a gold-headed cane.

Josafá Antunes had met him at the airport in Aracaju and rented a car to take him from the capital of Sergipe to the wilds of Agreste. This thoughtful gesture was doomed to partial failure, since the automobile, for all its showiness and modernity—Josafá had picked the shiniest, flashiest car from the taxi rank in front of the hotel—broke down less than halfway from Esplanada to Agreste with a fused motor. Had it not been for the providential arrival of Jairo and his *marineti* (lately dubbed the Samaritan of the Highway by its proud owner), which enabled the distinguished lawyer and his client to finish their journey sedately and in safety, Aminthas would have had a perfect excuse to perpetrate one of his execrable puns on a motor fused and Josafá confused.

Josafá was afraid the old gentleman would lose his temper and go back where he came from, abandoning the cause. Dr. Marcolino, however, proved to have a splendid sense of humor and was fascinated by Jairo's vehicle; he wanted to know all about it, listened attentively to the Russian radio, and praised its sound and personality. When they finally reached the edge of town and rolled over that short but magnificent piece of paved road, he applauded, "Bravo, my friend! Motors today are worthless." He shook Jairo's hand. "And so are men's characters."

Comfortably settled in the best room at Dona Amorzinho's boardinghouse, with the right to use the proprietress's porcelain chamberpot, a very rare honor indeed, Dr. Marcolino was soon esteemed in Agreste for his age, his polished manners and his urbane wit. People admired his Ilhéus origin, his reputation, his cordiality and his cane, on the gold knob of which was carved the head of a serpent, fitting symbol of the subtle lawyer's guile and venom. It was well known that he had formidable powers of corruption. When the townspeople saw him strolling down Front Street (Colonel Artur de Figueiredo Street; when *will* people learn the new names?) on his way to the Bureau of Records, they felt a throb of pride; no doubt about it, their town was getting rich and civilized. The presence of a prominent legal consultant like Dr. Pitombo was living proof of it.

In the office, with the notary's help, he examined the books and pored over old documents, even scrutinizing them with a magnifying glass in search of nonexistent erasures. He made a point of personally going out in the motor launch to have a look at the disputed land, and while he was there see Mangue Seco, of whose beauty he had heard as a child in Aracaju. He gazed at it in awe.

"Why, it's even more wonderful than I had been led to believe. There isn't an artist in the world who could create such a landscape, only God."

When his initial reconnaissance was done, he shut himself up with Josafá for a private talk in his room at the boardinghouse.

"Who are the other claimants, the other Antuneses?"

"There're only two as far as I know. One's a schoolteacher; she runs the Ruy Barbosa Grammar School."

"Married? A widow?"

"She's an old maid, must be fifty at least. The other one's a young fellow who works at the tax collector's office."

"A young man? What about his parents?"

"Both dead. His father in Rio and his mother here, years ago, when he was a child. He was raised by an aunt, his father's sister. He's an Antunes on his mother's side."

"Oh, yes, I recall now, the notary told me. Are you thinking of working out a settlement with the other two?"

"Only if there isn't any other way. But it's up to you. That's why I asked you to come here, Dr. Marcolino, because I wanted your advice."

"I know that, but I also need to know the way your mind is running so I can act accordingly."

"Dr. Marcolino, I sold some land and goats, property that my father and I owned here, just so I could hire you to help me clear my title to the coconut grove. I want to sell it to Brastânio and put what I get into cacao. If I can get it all, so much the better. We ought to try for the big brass ring, or anyway that's what I think. Settlement, agreement? Not unless there isn't any other way."

"There always is another way. Back where we come from it would be a whole lot simpler. It's going to be harder here. There's only one records office in town, and the notary wasted no time telling me in a joshing way, but letting me know what was what, that he isn't taking any bribes. And it looks as if the most surefire argument of all"—he pulled the trigger of an imaginary gun—"can't be used here. Too bad; that would nip the trouble in the bud."

Josafá laughed heartily.

"It can't be used down south either, Dr. Marcolino. That was in the old days. And it's never been used up here."

"Well, that's a pity. There's nothing quite so effective as a last resort." A gleam of malice crept into the tired, innocent blue eyes. "What the devil does a backwoods notary know about bribes?" He answered his own question. "Nothing, three times nothing. Do you think he's incorruptible?"

"Dr. Franklin? Yes sir, I do. In fact, I'd be ready to swear he is."

"What about his son, the beer barrel? I'm just asking you in case we need him. It's always good to know."

"I don't know anything about the son. He was only a kid when I left town."

"We'll find out; there'll be time enough for that. Now I'll tell you my opinion and explain my plan, but first I want to ask you one more question. Is there a surveyor in town?"

"I don't know of any in Agreste. There's bound to be one in Esplanada, though."

"That's what I thought. All right, now listen carefully. By tomorrow we'll have all the documents that prove your rightful ownership to the land. I've already told the notary I want a transcript of the old deed and asked him to notarize your father's documents and yours. Now I'm going back there and offer Fatty a little kumshaw on the side. That way we'll have the transcript sooner, and we'll also learn if our young clerk is agreeable to the idea of pocketing a little something extra. At his age and fat as he is, he ought to welcome a bit of extra cash to spend on girls. As soon as we have those documents we'll hotfoot it to Esplanada, where you'll find a surveyor and bring him back with you to survey the palm grove. I'll stay there to spy out the lay of the land, talking to my colleagues, studying the reactions of the judge and prosecuting attorney; just getting the feel of things, you know, to have some idea of what we can expect. When you get back with the survey I'll file a brief for possession of the whole area. By that time I'll have softened them up enough so they'll be working for me."

"For the whole thing? Terrific! That way, by the time those

half-assed Antuneses wake up to what's going on we'll be miles ahead of them. Just imagine, sir, they haven't even brought in a lawyer, either one of them, the old maid or that bum who doesn't have a thing on his mind but the pool championship."

Dr. Marcolino gazed at the fiery litigant with shrewd blue eyes and answered coolly, before his client's enthusiasm could run away with him, "If they haven't brought one in, they will; make no mistake about that. Try to get it into your head that they have as much right to the land as you do; that is, if they really are descended from Manuel Bezerra Antunes. I'm going to claim the whole area for you, but I don't have much hope of our getting it if they bring in a counterclaim, and they will. Even if the initial verdict is in our favor, as I trust it will be, we ought to be prepared for the more than likely eventuality of having to divide up the land your great-grandfather registered at the land office. The really important thing is to find out which piece of it we want most."

"I don't follow you."

"You will, but first I want you to answer a question. Does anyone here know exactly where in the grove the factory is to be built?"

"Ascânio must know. Ascânio Trindade, the county clerk, the one who's sweet on the São Paulo heiress. I told you about him, remember? He's a shoo-in for mayor, but he's as good as mayor already; he's Colonel Artur's fair-haired boy."

"I remember, all right. From what you say it looks as if he's Brastânio's man in Agreste. He's the one who's pushing so hard for the factory, isn't he?"

"Ascânio wants to see Agreste get ahead. That's why he jumped into this fight with both feet. You could call him a hero, I guess."

The old man's innocent-looking eyes lit up with malice.

"A hero? Well, my dear Josafá, your hero is our man. What we've got to do is get him to tell us and nobody else where that factory's going to be built; the exact spot. That piece of information is the key to everything else. We'll probably . . . no, we'll certainly have to grease that civil servant's palm of his and grease it well to pay for the exclusive right to that information. We may even have to pay him a commission."

"Sir, are you suggesting that we buy that information from

Ascânio? And pay him off so he won't give it to the others?"

"I think I made my meaning clear, son."

"It won't work, sir. Ascânio isn't that kind. I'm pretty sure we can get the information, though, and without paying a nickel for it. All we have to do is ask him. But as for getting him to give it to us and keep it from the others, for money—nothing doing. If we come to him with a proposition like that he'll get mad and we'd only make things harder for ourselves."

The lawyer's weary, gentle eyes rested on his client with something akin to pity.

"No one would ever take you for a man who's been living down south, friend Josafá."

"Ascânio's an honorable man, sir."

"How do you know? How can you be so sure of what you say? You've been out of Agreste a mighty long time to be going around vouching for the integrity of people you hardly know, haven't you? You seem to think everyone in Agreste is incorruptible. The notary, and now this young fellow. How do you *know*?"

"Well, I come back at least once a year to see my old man, and I pick up things. And I never heard anyone say a word against Ascânio."

"It's the facts that count. Let's have a look at them. We're dealing with an individual who's willing to play Brastânio's game, and it's a dirty game, my friend. And as if that weren't enough, he's a fortune hunter running after a rich Paulista. Forgive me for saying so, but if you're holding him up as a model of integrity you seem to have picked a mighty poor example."

"But he really is in favor of progress—"

"Let's admit for the sake of argument that he is, and that he used to be as honest as people say and you repeat. It's quite possible that he was, once. But, son, don't you see that the minute he got mixed up in this business, he knocked his integrity into a cocked hat whether he meant to or not? If he were made of steel he'd rust, but he's made of flesh and blood, so he rots. How much do you think Brastânio is paying him? If they were offering him a trifling sum it wouldn't be hard for him to refuse. But this is big money we're talking about, old fellow, very big money. I want you to introduce me to this Ascânio. I'll sound him out cautiously and then act accordingly."

"Ascânio's in Bahia to discuss the factory deal. The man sent a jeep for him."

"What man?"

"Some big wheel in Brastânio. Another reason he went, they say, is to see about getting the Election Tribunal to set a date for the election. At least that's what I've heard around town."

"Well, there you are then. It's clear as daylight and here you are trying to sell me a bill of goods about an incorruptible man! Brastânio whistles and your hero goes running off. It's as plain as the nose on your face that they're pulling strings to get him elected mayor, and you tell me the fellow's above playing footsie. Come on now, Josafá!"

His assurance shaken by the attorney's reasoning, Josafá thought for a moment and then admitted ruefully, "Well, sir, now that I think about it maybe you're right; the guy may be putting on an act, pretending to be honest while he fills his pockets. I recall reading something in the paper about the Brastânio directors trying to get the election put forward. It could be. . . ."

"With the exception of St. Francis of Assisi, son, I never knew of anyone who could hold out against the power of money, much less against power pure and simple. The yen for power makes crooks of us all. I've seen plenty in my day. Saints and sinners, when it comes to power they'll sell their own mothers, children, neighbors, and God. Not to mention their fathers; that goes without saying."

"Well, I'll be . . . You never know, do you? I always thought Ascânio was as straight as a die."

"Maybe he was. Now to get back to our battle plan, I'm assuming that in all that enormous sandy stretch of coconut grove, Brastânio's only interested in one little piece where the factories will be built. Do you follow me? And that piece, my friend, is the only part that's worth anything, but the resale value of that part will be plenty. For that one small piece, Brastânio will pay whatever the owner asks. And the rest of the grove, however big and beautiful it is, won't be worth a plugged nickel. Land that's located in the vicinity of a titanium-dioxide industry is worth literally nothing. It's valueless for other industry, or for building summer cottages, or for anything else. Nobody would take it if you gave it away. The only spot that interests us is the future factory site, that one spot and none other."

"Sir, are you trying to say that this factory is as bad as people claim?"

"Whatever they're saying, it's everything they say and worse. I read up on it when Brastânio was thinking about setting up a factory down there."

"I heard about it. In fact, I signed a paper saying we didn't want it there."

"A petition to the President of the Republic. It was drafted by me, and I can tell you without false modesty that it was unanswerable. It's coming out in the papers as paid ads in Bahia and down south." His satisfied expression clouded over. "I feel sorry for the people here in this pretty place. It'll be the end of Mangue Seco and a blot on God's masterpiece." He made a helpless gesture. "But I'd rather have it here than down there."

There was no denying that, and this time Josafá nodded his assent.

"Do we agree on what to do, then?" the lawyer went on.

"Let's go over it again." He counted on his fingers. "First, get the documents and measure the palm grove; second, file our claim and while we're waiting for a decision, have a little talk with our wide-awake friend down at the courthouse. You leave him to me. I'll fix it so that when the other heirs wake up and start bringing in their lawyers, we'll have a legal claim already filed and we'll be in a very good position to negotiate, listen to what the others propose and set our own conditions. And the one condition we'll set, my friend, is ownership of that little piece of the coconut grove where Brastânio's going to build its rotten factory. Is that understood?"

Josafá rubbed his hands. He had hit the bull's-eye when he hired Dr. Marcolino Pitombo. It had cost him plenty in fees, air fare, and a luxury-class taxi (and the goddam car had broken down, it had a pretty paint job and that was all), but the wily lawyer he had imported from Ilhéus was worth any expense, even the money thrown away on the taxi. He had made a smart investment with the capital he had raised with the sale of the manioc slopes and bare goat pasture. You had to be an old stick-in-the-mud with no ambition in life and halfway over the hill like Jarde not to understand and rejoice in what a very wise investment it had been. His father, sitting on a bed in a boardinghouse far from his goats, was dwindling away to nothing before his eyes, as if he were being poisoned by the noxious gases from the titanium dioxide. Josafá had heard that people who inhaled them turned yellow and listless and kept getting unhappier and yellower all the time until they soon turned into walking skeletons and then into dead ones. It was too bad, but what could he do?

In which a heretofore minor character steps off Jairo's marineti *claiming to be an Antunes and an heir, and reference is made to Fidélio's secret aspirations and a plot concocted by Aminthas.*

Optimistic Josafá was mistaken when he said the other parties had not hired lawyers. That very afternoon, or rather that very evening —the carburetor had clogged up—the *marineti* debouched two more attorneys, who took the last two vacant rooms at Dona Amorzinho's boardinghouse. It now resembled the congress of jurisprudence about which Aminthas had joked.

With Dr. Franklin the only lawyer in Agreste, and he a public official who did not practice, the simultaneous presence in town of three legal experts, that longtime rarity in the community, was patent proof of the thorny problems that might spring from the mere possibility of the installation of polluting or nonpolluting industries in a poor and backward community. "There are no nonpolluting industries, you idiot!" You see? You can't avoid an argument.

As if to demonstrate those who defended progress at any cost were right, land values immediately skyrocketed; not everywhere, of course, but at least on the river around the Mangue Seco palm groves, the place where the Brastânio industrial complex would presumably be built. The speculation had its origin in a wave of rumors to the effect that more factories would come in and make a reality of the "hub of industry" to which Ascânio Trindade had referred in a historic speech in the newly refurbished Tannery Square— Modesto Pires Plaza, when *will* people learn the new names?

The disputed ownership of the palm grove, which had already brought Dr. Marcolino Pitombo into town with his gold-headed cane, canny shrewdness and urbane charm, soon brought the swaggering Dr. Baltazar Moreira and gallant Dr. Gustavo Galvão, who had all the girls in town sighing over him.

The stout, heavy-jowled Baltazar Moreira, with his oracular voice and haughty profile, had been called in from Feira de Sant'Ana by Dona Carlota Antunes Alves, as she had begun to sign her name. By Dona Carlota we really mean Modesto Pires, with whom she had formed an association, her modest means not permitting any high-flying dealings with the law. The Ruy Barbosa Grammar School, where the children of the well-to-do were taught the rudiments of learning, brought in just enough for her to live on, and the prudent teacher had no intention of risking the loss of her home to pay a lawyer. Friends had cited the example of Jarde and Josafá, who had sold their land and flock, but she wasn't impressed. However, when Modesto Pires sought her out she entered into an agreement with the owner of the tannery as to expenses and profits. If they did make a profit the usurer would get the lion's share, but meanwhile he would pay all the expenses. It was an advantageous deal for Dona Carlota either way; that swampy land in the palm grove had never brought her in a penny. She had not even known that part of it might be hers. It was Dr. Franklin, out of feelings of gratitude to the patient teacher who had managed to teach Bonaparte his ABCs and multiplication tables and endowed him with that extraordinary calligraphy, who informed her of the fact and showed her the old deed. If he hadn't done so Dona Carlota would still have been in the dark.

As for Dr. Gustavo Galvão, a flashy young lawyer from Esplanada who affected sport shirts and long sideburns, he got off the bus with Canuto Tavares, his client. To everyone's surprise, the skilled mechanic and lapsed telegraph operator turned out to be another descendant of Manuel Bezerra Antunes. Not even Dr. Franklin, for all his tireless investigation into the family of the celebrated Antunes who had signed the deed, had stumbled across Canuto Tavares. Tavares was a perfectly good Antunes connection nevertheless; a direct descendant, in fact, and a double one, the scion of a union between Pedro Miranda Antunes Tavares and Deodora Antunes do Prado, who were cousins. His father was dead, but his mother was living with Canuto's brother, who managed a shoe store in Bahia.

As to the evasive Fidélio, another Antunes with a watertight claim, according to Dr. Franklin, where was his lawyer? At the time of the incident with Seixas, he had told the truth when he said he didn't have one. He already had an adviser, though, and a good one. Owing, perhaps, to a similarity in musical tastes and to Fidélio's admiration for Aminthas' sarcastic intelligence, the latter was his favorite among the little band of five close friends who had spent most of every day together all their lives, playing pool in the bar, imbibing beer or white rum, laughing at the same silly jokes, going down to Zuleika's and dancing to the victrola with the girls. Astério had virtually abandoned this favorite old haunt after his marriage. He sneaked over there once in a great while on a Sunday afternoon when vice got the better of him, to cheat on his wife with a promising piece of tail, but should that really be called cheating? Against his will and his principles, it was Elisa's ass he thought about when he climbed on top of some jutting rear at Zuleika's.

Dona Carmosina, who had read Dumas in her distant youth, dubbed them the Agreste Musketeers. Her cousin Aminthas, the cynical skeptic, was Aramis. Still, Fidélio knew that beneath the caustic wit of that eternal doubter was a loyal friend who would counsel him well. And so it was Aminthas to whom he turned when his Antunes surname began giving him trouble. He had already lost sleep over it and missed a date with Ritinha, although pleasure with Ritinha was double; she was roly-poly and good in bed, and Fidélio knew besides that when he was with her he was planting horns on two assholes at once: Chico Sobrinho and Lindolfo. One put on airs, the other was a two-bit Don Juan.

The trouble began when Seixas, the tax collector's assistant, sought him out with a message from his boss, Edmundo Ribeiro, who had a proposition to make. Knowing that Fidélio was poor and lived on such a miserable salary that if an aunt had not given him free room and board, he wouldn't have earned enough to cover his pool bets and sprees at Zuleika's, and that a legal battle was therefore out of the question, the tax collector offered to buy his property rights in the coconut grove. The offer was good only if Brastânio turned out to be interested in the area, of course. Seixas, anxious to please the good-natured, benevolent boss who let him keep such easy office hours, had advised his friend to accept the offer; had pressed him to do so, in fact, and was at a loss to understand why Fidélio kept saying no. Later, when Seixas learned there were others who were interested, that Modesto Pires had proposed a partnership and Dr. Cáio Vilasboás had offered to buy the land immediately, cheap but in cash, he interpreted Fidélio's apparent lack of interest ("I'm fed up with this inheritance business; I don't want to hear any more about it") as a clever ploy to pit the rivals against one another so that he could then sell out to the highest bidder. Seixas was hurt. Of course his friend had a right to look after his own interests by taking advantage of the law of supply and demand, but why try to cover it up and not tell Seixas the truth? If he had come right out and told his friend what he was up to, Seixas would have been able to hold out some hope to Seu Edmundo Ribeiro of negotiating on a different basis instead of being presented with a flat negative. As we can see, his attempt to provoke Fidélio in the bar had not been accidental. Even among the Agreste Musketeers the Brastânio gases were infiltrating their insidious poisons, altering ties of friendship formed in childhood and strengthened with time.

Fidélio, who was almost abnormally reserved by nature, was not in the habit of discussing his affairs with anyone, and so far he had had little cause to regret it. Without fanfare he had beat all his partners at pool one after another and now stood a very good chance of capturing first place in the tournament and wresting the coveted Golden Cue away from Astério. Without bragging or playing the Don Juan, he somehow managed to lay all the sexiest women; by the time the others discovered an interesting prospect, Fidélio had invariably got in ahead of them. This time, though, there was no help for it; he'd have to tell Aminthas what was preying on his mind and ask for advice. He went to his friend's house and listened in silence to part of a rock tape. Before Aminthas could put on another one he stopped him.

"There's something bugging me and I need your advice."

"OK, tell me about it."

"The other day you offered to make a bet with anyone in the bar that that damned factory won't ever be built here. Can you be sure of that or were you kidding as usual? I want the straight dope."

"Why do you want to know?"

"I've got personal reasons for wanting to know. It looks as if I own part of the palm grove—at least Dr. Franklin says so, and he ought to know. All kinds of other people are putting in claims: Josafá, Dona Carlota, and now Canuto Tavares, every one of them out to get his part and let the devil take the hindmost. I want no part of that game, but not a day goes by that somebody doesn't proposition me to sell my share. That is, Seu Modesto doesn't want to buy, he wants to go into partnership with me, same as he has with Dona Carlota. But Seu Edmundo Ribeiro and Dr. Cáio do, and Dr. Cáio's offering to pay cash down."

"Um-hmn. So you want to know which is the best deal? If you'll give me the details, I'll—"

"All I want to know is whether the goddam factory's coming into Mangue Seco or not. You said you were positive it wasn't."

"Now I see what you're driving at. You want to know because if the factory comes in, you'd do a lot better to hold out and sell your part directly to Brastânio, right?" He held up one hand to keep Fidélio from interrupting. "And if it doesn't come in, you sell now to that ass Dr. Cáio, pocket the cash and leave him stuck with the swamp, right?" Aminthas knew he was clever and liked to show off.

"Wrong. You've got it backward."

"I have? Then I haven't understood a word you've been saying."

"If I could only know for a fact, or at least be as sure as you seem to be, that the factory will never be built, then yes, I might sell to Dr. Cáio. God knows I need the money, you have no idea how much I need it. But I won't sell unless I'm sure."

"Why not? Are you holding out for more, like I said? Is that your idea?"

"No. My idea is not to sell at all. I don't want the factory to come in and mess everything up." He took a deep breath; talking so much was hard work. "I wasn't born here, you know. I was born in Rio, but my mother brought me back here as a kid after my father died down there. Poor Dad, all he ever thought about was saving enough so he could come back here to live, and he didn't have time." He stopped again, thinking of his father, exiled in Rio, who had not had much to say for himself either. "I don't ever want to leave except on vacation, but I do want to visit Rio and São Paulo and see what the south is like if I ever get a chance. I mean go and come back. That's why Dr. Cáio's money would come in so handy. But I'd rather lose a fortune than let those sons of bitches mess up Mangue Seco. When I'm out there I don't feel like a poor dumb civil servant. I feel like a man who owns the world."

Aminthas put another tape on the machine. It was an old Bra-

zilian favorite by Dorival Caymmi, "Does the Fisherman Know
He'll Come Back When He Puts Out to Sea?" He turned down the
volume, but the melody persisted in the background. Strangely
enough, he was moved.

"Well, for whatever my opinion's worth, I don't think the
factory will ever be built here. For that to happen there'd have to be
no other place in Brazil that offered more. There's nothing here for
them; they'd have to build from the ground up. That's why I don't
think they'll come in. But at the same time, I've got to admit that
for that very reason Agreste may be the only place in Brazil that
would *let* them come in. Look, Fidélio, that goddam titanium industry is the end. Osnar said it: it stinks. It stinks and it rots everything it touches."

"You mean—"

"I mean that if you think the way Osnar and I do, don't sell.
Instead of going to Rio, go to Zuleika's; there's plenty to see there,
too. She's got a new girl, a little kid named Maria Imaculada."

"I know. She's a honey fuck."

Aminthas turned up the recording a little so they could listen to
the tale of fish and the sea and the fishing rafts braving the storm.

"Listen, Fidélio, do you really mean what you just said? Are
you ready to fight?"

"Yes, I do. Yes, I am."

"All right, old pal, then listen. I know a way we can take this
fucking factory and tell the lawyers to shove it up their asses. It's
this way."

He explained the idea that had just occurred to him. What
Fidélio had said about Mangue Seco had put it into his head; that
and Caymmi's poem about the sea, the great source of life where
men rise above the elements. Fidélio heard him in silence. When his
friend stopped speaking, all he said was, "I always knew you had
brains and guts. Only thing is, the Skipper's out at Mangue Seco."

"No, he's in town. I saw him today with Carmosina at the
Areopagus."

"Good. I'll go see if I can track him down."

He left in better spirits, though with a trace of lingering yearning, a sense that he was about to give up the only chance he would
ever have to fulfill a cherished secret plan that he had never revealed
to anyone, not even Dona Carmosina. It was a many-faceted project
and therefore a costly one, out of the question for someone trying

to live on a civil servant's ridiculous salary, hardly more than the minimum wage.

Fidélio's dream was a trip to the great cities of the south: Salvador, Rio de Janeiro, São Paulo. It would be a pleasure trip, of course, but with certain specific objectives. The most important of these was to buy himself the best set of drums he could find and a manual that would teach him how to play them. Someday he might even be as good as Xisto Bom de Som, Colonel Artur da Tapitanga's son-in-law. Whenever the drummer turned up with Célia and the two kids to pay his father-in-law a visit and incidentally rustle up some cash, Fidélio haunted the fazenda day and night. Once when the musician came for a longer stay than usual and brought his drums, the "Itapuã's Kings" clarinetist and electric guitarist had landed in jail for possession of pot, and Xisto had let Fidélio try out the flashy percussion drums after giving him a few pointers. "You got a feel for it, man," he had told him encouragingly. With the bundle Dr. Cáio was offering he could bring back a fine set of drums and give some meaning to his life. He'd really be somebody if he had those drums.

While he was down there he'd go to the shows and see his idols, Caetano and Gil and Vinícius de Morais. And to wind it all up with a flourish, he would find out once and for all whether certain exciting but inadmissible details about Osnar's famous Polish whore were accurate or not. It was well known even in Agreste that the cathouses in Rio and São Paulo were bursting at the seams with Polacks. With a pocketful of cash Fidélio could certainly afford one, maybe even more than one, and put old Osnar in the shade. He'd be able to laugh knowingly when his friend started to brag, "If you haven't laid a Polack, you don't know dames."

That was the way Osnar always began, and it always got attention. But things would be different if he ever got to make that trip. Osnar could boast all he wanted to, and Fidélio would be laughing up his sleeve.

In which the word "Ja" is pronounced.

"The latest report we've received is quite pessimistic."

Angelo Bardi's voice revealed no trace of uneasiness or fear. Cordial, affable, but accustomed to giving orders, he had retained the slight Italian accent of an immigrant's son from the working-class district of Bras. A handsome, well-groomed man in his fifties, neither fat nor thin, Angelo Bardi had the knack of inspiring confidence. Rosalvo Lucena, Ph.D. in Business Administration and aggressive, rising junior executive as the papers called him, looked like an earnest young graduate student as he listened attentively to the other man. Angelo Bardi looked like exactly what he was, a tycoon, a man at the top.

They were sitting at one end of a large conference table in the air-conditioned, soundproof room at the headquarters of Brastânio. Mirko Stefano was there, and an elderly man with a crew cut and lusterless eyes presided at the head of the table.

Mirko opened his mouth to speak. There was a knock at the door and Betty came into the room, followed by an office boy carrying a tray with coffee, sugar, three other sweeteners, cups and spoons. She served them with quick, graceful movements, smiling as if she were delighted to be in the presence of such distinguished men. The crew-cut man rested his dull gaze on the executive secretary's pert breasts and the long line of her legs.

Betty, preceded by the boy, left the room in silence, feeling the rich weight of those lackluster eyes on her hips as she shut the door. Only then did Mirkus the Magnificent translate what Bardi had said. A top PR man sometimes had to be an interpreter on occasions like these, when the conference was too confidential for outsiders.

"There's no reason to panic," Angelo Bardi went on. "But at the same time we ought to recognize that there's a lot of resistance to be overcome. They seem to be having trouble making up their minds. As long as we don't back down, though, I think we'll end up with the right place, the place we know is ideal. Maybe—"

The man with the lackluster eyes cut him short with a gesture and a glance at Mirko, who translated Bardi's last speech word for word. Those were his orders: to translate word for word. At another gesture the magnate went on with what he was saying. PR director, successful executive, magnate, big boss; that was the pecking order.

"All these objections may just be a delaying tactic to get more money out of us, although personally I think there is some real opposition, especially at the state level."

He waited for the translation before going on. Even in Mirko's bland voice the other language sounded rude and harsh to Latin ears used to the sonorous plasticity of the Italian tongue.

"One more good hard push ought to do it. By that I mean money. Hopefully, that will be enough to put us where we want to be."

While he listened to the translation, the dull-eyed man stared at each of the three men in turn and a sudden steely light came into his eyes. He pronounced a few words which Mirko translated. "Where we have decided is where it must go."

How can you translate blows with fists, rocks and shrapnel? The light went out in the dim eyes.

"Yes, we all agree on that," Angelo Bardi said. "Nevertheless, we ought to be prepared to follow up on our contingency plan. We've already decided the cacao zone doesn't really interest us. As for the Real rivermouth area, in spite of the drawbacks cited in the reports, the lack of an infrastructure—"

The crew-cut man made another gesture. Bardi and Mirko obeyed, one stopping short, the other taking up fluently and precisely where he had left off. Rosalvo Lucena listened with such an air of intelligence that anyone would have thought he understood the German translation. The São Paulo magnate continued.

"As I was saying, the Real River area, while it lacks an infrastructure, should not be left out of our calculations entirely. They've already given us the green light. We know we can build the factory there; there are no serious objections."

For a gifted man who had made it to the top after coming from the bottom, or lower than the bottom, from Bras, Angelo Bardi was singularly ungifted at languages. Besides the Italian he had learned at home he spoke French (who doesn't?) with the usual bad accent, and had sweated to acquire the rudiments of English. You had to if you wanted to talk to the Americans; they didn't speak anything else. Their attitude was, why should they? Let the other bastards grapple with English grammar. Angelo Bardi had grappled not only with the grammar but with his skinny nymphomaniac teacher, Miss Judy. German? Have a heart, that he'd never learn. He smiled at the thought that before long he would be dealing with the Japanese.

"For my part, I think there are two reasons why investing a little more along that line might not be a bad idea. First, we may end up having to build the factory on the Real River as a last resort if we lose out at the other location. Second, because it will be a very useful diversionary tactic. While they're talking about Agreste, and not many are, they won't be thinking about . . ."

He left the sentence unfinished; Mirko could add the last word when he translated. It was such a pretty word, Arembepe, worth writing a poem about. But with Von So-and-So sitting there at the head of the table it had an implacable sound.

In two languages Mirko asked the three directors, "Does this mean I can get my little project under way?"

Angelo Bardi answered for himself and Rosalvo Lucena, who said nothing but smiled an approving and competent smile.

"It's all right with us, but the final decision is up to him. The fellow's here in town, isn't he?"

"Yes, he came in last night, and he's staying at the same hotel we are and He is." You could hear the capital letter when Mirko Stefano respectfully pronounced the word "he." His voice went back to normal. "It's a good hotel, and that always helps."

After hearing a word-for-word translation of Mirkus the Magnificent's question and the two Brazilians' opinion, He of the crew cut, He of the lackluster eyes, gave his assent.

"*Ja!*"

*In which the author, not satisfied with his
usual imbecility, shows off his doltish
vanity as well.*

It's too much for me, I simply must interrupt my story to ask my readers if they heard what I heard in that noble tongue. Harsh as it sounded to the delicate ears of Angelo Bardi, accustomed to *la dolce vita*, it sounds like music to the ears of an unpublished author whose fate it is to write about narrow-minded, prejudiced small-town folk, rough backwoodsmen and fishermen of dubious ethics. It echoes and resounds like a heroic Wagnerian trumpet call, a summons to the conquest of the world. To think that one of the great men of Europe, the head of a multinational company, a hero of our time, no less, should deign to step down from the clouds of grandeur where he habitually gives orders and makes fateful decisions to give an order and make a decision in the humble pages of my book! True, he didn't say much, but he listened closely, and what little he did say was final. With that one word he blasted hesitation and banished doubt.

Forgive me, but I simply can't keep it to myself; this is a red-letter day on which these poor pages have been honored, and I feel as if I had arrived at last. I'll surely be able to find a publisher now that such a personage graces my book, especially if the great man should reappear in another chapter, with his superb crew cut and the magnificent light of his lackluster eyes. If that should happen, the publisher may even pay me royalties; not that I have any claim to them, I'll be happy enough just to see my little volume in the windows of the bookstores. With a high heart, banners unfurled, bugles and trumpets blowing, I salute him and eagerly await his return.

This was my sole object in interrupting the story, to communicate my joy so that my readers may share it. Now that I've interrupted, though, I'll just take this opportunity to reply to one or two new imputations made by my friend and colleague Fúlvio D'Alambert.

This time he wonders what has happened to Tieta, who seems to have disappeared from these pages. Am I forgetting that her name figures in the title, right at the top of the page? By abandoning her I'm abandoning the most elementary rule of fiction. A main character can't be relegated to the background, Fúlvio D'Alambert admonished me.

It isn't my fault Tieta's not around these days, it's hers. While the arguments about Brastânio rage in Agreste and the town is infested with lawyers, while Dona Carmosina collects signatures for a plaintive petition to the authorities protesting vigorously and with a note of panic against the construction of a titanium-dioxide factory in the community, while Skipper Dário, going against long-standing habit, gives up his summer sojourn on Mangue Seco to help the postmistress persuade the doubtful, Tieta lolls on the beach, taking her ease and given over to debauchery. That is a strong word, I know, but what other word can I use to describe the illicit relations between an aunt in her forties (she's forty-four, practically fifty) and a minor who happens to be her nephew?

Even if Osnar does state categorically that Brazilian citizens attain their sexual majority at thirteen, is there any reason why that vagabond's questionable moral values should prevail over the current standards of Christian Western morality? I am told, incidentally, that the Orientals, if by Orientals we mean Socialists, are extremely puritanical and allow no such liberties either on their beaches or in their books. There's nothing to tell about Tieta these days except her tender, lewd, voracious, lyrical debauchery. She's been a little out of it lately, but that doesn't mean her name is not mentioned often in Agreste. As the Skipper soon found out, everyone wanted to know what Dona Antonieta Esteves Cantarelli's position was in the debate swirling around the proposed titanium-dioxide plant. Once again the Skipper realized how important an influence Tieta's words and actions could have on the uncertain majority. The stalwart sailor intended to have a serious talk with Tieta as soon as he went back to Mangue Seco. "My dear friend," he would say, "it's high time you took the lead in the campaign to stop this heinous crime from being committed."

Well, there you have my explanation and my news. You're welcome. Ah! I was forgetting one last quibble, the last so far from Fúlvio D'Alambert, that pedantic critic who permits no author to nod.

His objection stems from the description, some pages back, of Dr. Marcolino Pitombo's arrival in Agreste. When reporting the esteem expressed by him for Jairo's *marineti*, I wrote that after listening attentively to the sound of the Russian radio, the attorney had praised that appliance's strength of character, without explaining—and therein lay my error—the reason for the praise. What kind of strong character can a radio have to deserve such admiration from an illustrious lawyer, one of the most learned people to appear in these pages? It is Fúlvio D'Alambert's opinion that I left my readers up in the air.

Well, if that's so it's easily remedied, and here's the explanation. Having been told that it was a Soviet radio, made in the USSR, the elderly jurist's curiosity was aroused by an odd coincidence. When this radio was broadcasting music from Third World countries— Brazilian sambas and *batuques*, tangos, boleros, rumbas, or Paraguayan *guaranias*—the sound was fairly decent. When the songs were French, German, Italian, English, or from anywhere in the developed countries, the sound was bad. It became totally unintelligible, an intolerable succession of ear-splitting blasts, when the radio stations insisted on broadcasting contemporary rock music or any other sound from the United States.

In its exile, crossing dusty, stony, crater-pitted roads in the wilds of the Bahian backlands, at the service of the last remaining *marineti* in the universe, the radio remained faithful to strict anti-imperialist principles. Considering the present political state of the world, this might be called excessive sectarianism.

But what perfection, what clarity, what purity of sound when an Ilhéus radio station played "Orchi Chornya" on its program of "Memorable Melodies." The old Russian favorite evidently stirred the radio to the depths of its being, reminding it of its origin and transporting it back to the nostalgic romance of the steppes. No stereophonic sound could equal that Soviet radio as the melody soared over the Bahian wilderness. An indomitable character indeed!

Episode No. 1 of Ascânio Trindade's stay in the capital, or the education of a leader in the cause of progress: the swimming pool, the industrial park, and Patricia, also called Pat

It was not until his third and last day in the capital was drawing to a close and a final talk with Mirkus the Magnificent had produced a feeling of warmth heightened by brandy that Ascânio Trindade got rid of a vague feeling of discomfort, of being dependent on others and not entirely his own man. He couldn't pin the feeling down and there was no apparent reason for it, except that everything about the visit was totally strange to him. Suddenly he found himself a guest in a luxury hotel, rubbing elbows with people from an alien, insidious, disconcerting world with which he had had no previous contact at all.

On the first day he had begun to think that Mirko Stefano had summoned him urgently for no other reason than to offer him drinks and girls around the swimming pool. The jeep had deposited him at the hotel the night before, wearier if anything from Quarantini's funny stories than from the rough, jolting ride. The driver, following orders no doubt, had driven him straight to the big hotel, where he was handed a message from Mirko telling him to go right up to the suite reserved for him and that they would see each other the next day.

They finally did meet the following day shortly after noon, just as Ascânio was about to go to lunch after a wasted morning. After waiting some time in his room for a call, he had wandered around the lobby and the adjacent boutiques, the art gallery and antique shop, admiring tapestries by Genaro, a ceramic mural by Carybé, and fiberglass sculptures by Mario Cravo; idly watched the tourists in their Bermuda shorts and gaudy shirts; glanced into the bar; and occasionally ogled the swimming pool, where beautiful women in provocative two-piece bathing suits were sunbathing and displaying their charms.

Then Mirko sprang out of one of two official-looking black cars toward which bellboys and doormen converged to dispute the baggage and the tips. Three other passengers got out and disappeared into one of the elevators as if by magic, carrying their briefcases and hand luggage. Mirko remained in the lobby and was on his way to the reception desk when he caught sight of Ascânio and advanced toward him with open arms, apologizing effusively for having left him to his own devices for so long.

"It's been a terrible day. The São Paulo airport was closed in and the plane didn't take off until nine o'clock, the time it was due here! Come right this way."

Mirko shook hands and waved to people as he went, with a word here and a smile or a pat on the back there. Three men had joined them by the time they reached the pool. One of these, who was blind in one eye, inquired in a conspiratorial hiss, "Who'd you come with?"

"Dr. Bardi."

"Yeah, him and who else? I saw a bunch of other guys at the reception desk."

Now that was a lie. The new arrivals had not stopped at the desk but gone directly up in the elevator. Ascânio had been watching them the whole time. Mirko smiled at the blabbermouth and stroked his face lightly, in an almost feminine gesture.

"Naughty boy."

All the girls in the pool or around it—or at least it looked that way—belonged to Mirkus the Magnificent (or to Brastânio, rather; no individual is rich or powerful enough to own such a varied collection of beauties, but a great corporation may). A bevy of them came running to the table as soon as he sat down. The three hangers-on stared at Ascânio curiously, waiting for news or an introduction, but as Mirko forgot to introduce him, accidentally or on purpose, they soon turned to pleasanter things, whisky and girls. They drank like troopers and propositioned the girls in a way that was much too gross for Ascânio's taste. All three were reporters, Mirko afterward informed him. The girls actually seemed to enjoy the filthy language and earthy propositions.

The party didn't last long. Mirko, protesting that he was terribly busy, stood up to go, leaving the women and the newly opened, nearly full bottle of Scotch to the avid reporters.

"I'll have news for you tomorrow or the day after. Remember, not a word before then. Nobody's here in Bahia and all's quiet in the city and on Wall Street," he told them pleasantly.

"What if *A Tarde* jumps the gun?" the one-eyed reporter challenged him.

"So much the better. You'll be first with the scoop and first to print a retraction."

He took Ascânio's arm and steered him toward the elevators, signaling to one of the girls to accompany them.

"Today I'll be in a meeting all afternoon. All I am authorized to tell you is that this is a decisive meeting of the board of directors. We'll have to put off our talk until just before dinner. But I'm leaving you in good hands." They had reached the elevator. He turned to the girl. "Take good care of him, Pat. Someday you'll be proud of having been Ascânio's guide in Bahia."

Patricia smiled and took Ascânio in hand without delay.

"Shall we have lunch here at the hotel or would you rather go to a restaurant? I'll just slip on my caftan and be right back."

Patricia was a blonde, but not like Leonora. Verses about ripe wheat were inappropriate for her hair, and Barbozinha would not have compared her to a sylph. She was attractive, certainly, but with none of the other girl's unique, incomparable beauty or the innate good breeding that only a good family and social standing can give, the distinction of the daughter of a millionaire and papal Comendador, born in a golden cradle and educated in the best finishing schools; in short, the flower of São Paulo society, her elegance and gentle upbringing revealed not only by good taste in dress but in her every gesture, her lovely manners, her daintiness, her infinite charm. There was something common about Patricia's obvious good looks, and in her very eagerness to please there was a hint of things bought and paid for, a too-professional touch.

After lunch in the luxurious hotel's fancy restaurant, Patricia left him, suggesting that he take a nap; she had an appointment herself but would be back at three to take him sightseeing or shopping, whichever he preferred.

That afternoon Patricia drove Ascânio around Bahia in her Volkswagen. He had not set foot in the city for more than seven years. New avenues cut through it, another hugged the coast, and the old town was swarming with people; the population seemed to have doubled. Bahia had changed beyond belief in those few years. Where was the sleepy old place he had known as a university student, the Bahia that lived in its past glory, its historic tradition as the mother cell, the cradle of Brazilian nationality, and all those other rhetorical phrases; the capital of an economically backward, agro-pastoral state? Máximo Lima, decrying Bahia's stagnation and decadence, had vociferated in their law-school days, "We don't even have a brewery, and pretty soon we won't even have any ruins to show off!"

He would have to look up Máximo while he was here and find out what he thought about the fateful transformation that would soon reach all the way to far-off Sant'Ana do Agreste. That was why he had come, to be a witness to the great decision.

After they had driven for a while along the new avenues, Patricia, either obeying orders or of her own accord, turned in the direction of the highway and drove him out to the Aratu Industrial Center. All Brazil was ringing with the news of that great enterprise, held up as an example of brilliant planning from the ground up by a team of specialists under the direction of the celebrated city planner Sérgio Bernardes. It was a hotbed of novel plans and projects. Some of the newly built plants were already in production, while many others were still in the early stages of construction.

Ascânio had driven by Aratu the night before but had seen nothing but tall chimneys and boxy structures looming up vaguely in the dark, still night. Now he could really see them; the chimneys belching smoke, the structures being transformed before his eyes, with all the confusion and uproar of a battlefield. For miles around, huge billboards extolled a variety of products that were already emerging or would soon emerge from the Aratu Industrial Center. Giant machinery and hundreds of men excavated and removed tons of earth, raised walls of brick and concrete, and soldered and welded shiny metal as if driven by demons.

The Volks came to a stop at the side of the road. Ascânio, still open-mouthed, felt the pressure of Patricia's thigh against his own and tore his eyes away from the chimneys. The girl smiled at him.

"The petrochemical plant is a little farther on, going toward Camaçari. It's colossal, isn't it." It was a statement, not a question.

They drove back along the coast. Along the beautiful, once-deserted oceanfront were hotels, restaurants, club bars, nightclubs and luxurious modern residences one after another, a whole glittering new panorama to Ascânio. They stopped at a bar, where thirsty Patricia gaily called for beer (made in Bahia with Danish know-how, it's the best in the world, said his well-informed guide) and bought a pack of American cigarettes. By the time Ascânio took out his wallet to pay for it, she was already holding out a bill to the cashier. She ignored the protests of the young man, whose masculine self-esteem was wounded.

"Machismo is out, baby, and anyway Brastânio's paying the tab."

They walked over to the beach, sat down on the sand and exchanged kisses.

"Baby, you're yummy."

Mirko Stefano kept his promise to call before dinner; it was only a rapid phone call but extremely cordial. Mirkus the Magnificent was still busy busy busy, *pardon, mon cher ami*. He wouldn't be able to meet with Ascânio until the next day, but Pat would look after him until then. He asked how the afternoon had gone, and Ascânio told him they had been to see the industrial center and the impression it had made on him.

"Golly, it's big! I knew it was important, but when I saw it I just couldn't believe my eyes. It's great!"

"Isn't it? And only yesterday there was nothing there but weeds—worse than the Agreste beaches. Just think what the Mangue Seco palm grove is going to look like before long. Well, run along now and make the most of your evening, because we'll be very busy tomorrow. Be downstairs at ten o'clock sharp so I can introduce you to some friends of mine."

Particia had left Ascânio at the door of the hotel and gone home to change for dinner. When she returned she looked so glamorous that he felt slightly ill at ease in his badly cut, threadbare blue suit, the work of Seu Miguel Rosinha, who had been cutting and tailoring Colonel Artur da Tapitanga's coats and trousers for more than forty years. As they went out Patricia warned him to forget any funny ideas he might have about paying for anything because it was all on Brastânio. They dined at a restaurant overlooking the ocean, then at Pat's suggestion went on to a nightclub where they danced cheek to cheek until after midnight. In both places he was shocked at the amount of the bill. If he had had to pay for all this he wouldn't have had enough money and would be in a fine fix.

Patricia parked the car in front of the hotel and went up with Ascânio in the elevator. In his room she asked him to pull down the zipper of her dress, a long greenish-mauve gown with appliqués of white lace. She was completely naked underneath; the filmy panties hid nothing. She had a beauty mark near the top of her thigh.

Pat took a shower and got into bed to wait for him. It's all on Brastânio, thought the apprentice executive.

Of the campaign for signatures on a petition
and how it was put in jeopardy by Tieta's absence.

The petition drafted by Dona Carmosina, with constructive criticism from Aminthas, did garner some signatures but far fewer than the prime movers had hoped for and expected. Skipper Dário came in from Mangue Seco expressly to help. He walked the streets, petition in hand, putting his prestige and popularity on the line. His presence won over a few adherents who had ignored the problem or knew little about it. They listened to their distinguished neighbor's earnest explanations, remembered his medal and citations, and took the pen he held out.

"All right, Skipper, I'll sign if you want me to."

There were others, however, who did not sign but slipped away when they saw him coming. These people understood the controversial significance of the paper, but they either avoided the Skipper or refused to sign because they were convinced of the advantages of having a big factory in the neighborhood. The passionate arguments against pollution didn't faze them. They hoped, without knowing quite how, to obtain some advantage, some profit from the coming of Brastânio. The word "progress" had to mean a better life.

The great majority, as always, consisted of people who didn't know and didn't want to have to make up their minds. The petition's harsh, uncompromising language about rot, crime, death and corruption was pored over, reread, analyzed, and called into question.

"Is it really as bad as that? That poster down at the courthouse says different."

The Skipper argued patiently and courteously with the doubters. The postmistress, on the other hand, was ready to explode when she met with resistance, doubtful looks and timid questions.

"If you want to live in a rotten filthy pigsty, you can!"

"Now, Dona Carmosina, don't get mad. The thing is, some folks say one thing and some say just the opposite. Take you, now, ma'am; you have as much book learning as anybody in this town and you ought to know what you're talking about. The Skipper too, he's seen the world and he says the same thing. But you take Ascânio now, he's always done his best for Agreste and we know he wouldn't let us down, and he says just the opposite. And so does Seu Modesto Pires, and Dona Carlota, the children's teacher. She gets just as riled up as you do, ma'am, only she's on the other side."

Over and over the Skipper and Dona Carmosina heard the same words from the undecided: "Well, I don't rightly know. . . . If I could just be sure what Dona Antonieta thinks about it all. . . . She knows what's what if anybody does. Whatever side she's on, that must be the right one."

In vain Dona Carmosina swore by Tieta's adherence to the cause and Skipper Dário expostulated that he had just returned from Mangue Seco where she was his house guest and that he knew exactly what she thought. They wanted to hear her say it.

"She's hasn't come right out and said so, and I'm going to wait until she does."

The two campaign leaders met at the post office to review the results of their labor and count the number of signatures obtained. There were not enough to justify the statement in the petition to the effect that the entire population of Agreste repudiated the nefarious plots of the titanium-dioxide industry. They began to feel discouraged.

The petition had been Dona Carmosina's idea. She was a woman of action. Jawing about it in the streets and fighting it out in posters would get them nowhere. Overcoming his innate skepticism, Aminthas agreed and helped draft it. The Skipper waxed enthusiastic, made some rough calculations, and concluded that if they could get at least a thousand signatures out of a population of nine thousand, counting children and the vast illiterate majority, it would be fair to claim that almost everyone capable of thinking about the problem at all had come out against Brastânio. Unfortunately they had collected only slightly over a hundred names after working like dogs, and none of the really important people had signed. The tradesmen expected more business to come their way when the factory was installed and so they hung back. Father Mariano made it clear that he was neutral; he did not feel it his place as parish priest to take sides in such a touchy matter. He did have a suggestion, though.

"I don't see Dona Antonieta Cantarelli's signature here. Her name ought to be at the top of the list, Skipper, if you really want people to sign."

Barbozinha wrote poem after poem (he already had enough for a book he intended to publish in Bahia, *Poems of Anathema*) and deluged Giovanni Guimarães with letters, but at collecting signatures he was a flop. Not so Dona Milu, who proved to have a rare talent and zest for the task and had beat everyone else hollow so far. The little band found an unexpected ally in Osnar, who lay in wait for patrons at the bar and did a creditable amount of arm-twisting. The result of all their labors was exactly 116 names, thirty-seven of them brought in by Dona Milu. Compared with the thousand they had hoped for, it was a defeat. The Skipper shook his head worriedly.

"My dear Carmosina, I just don't know. Either Tieta makes up her mind to lead this campaign, or I'm afraid we won't get very much further. I'm going back to Mangue Seco tomorrow and I'll try to persuade her to give us a hand. I know it won't be easy. The Corral's just ready to move in, and she's going to want to get some good out of that house that's taken so much work and cost her so much money to build. And besides, she asked me to take her stepdaughter back out with me. I'll rouse Leonora and Laura out bright and early tomorrow and go plead with Tieta to come back, even if it's just for a few days, so she can let everybody in town know she really is against the factory and tell them that if Brastânio comes in she'll never set foot here again."

Dona Carmosina agreed with the Skipper that the success of the campaign depended on Tieta.

"I'll go out there Sunday and back you up. Between the two of us I think we can get her to come."

"It's downright shameful the way people are beginning to think that Brastânio's going to make everybody rich, what with all these lawyers in town and the records office always crowded. The price of land's gone up in Rocinha, imagine!"

"You know, I got to thinking over all this business of the lawyers and the heirs to the land around the palm grove and I'm beginning to think it has its good side; as long as they're fighting among themselves the plant won't be built. And by the time it's all settled—"

"Don't deceive yourself, my good Carmosina. It won't take those lawyers any time at all to come to an agreement; you'll see. The heirs will get together and name Modesto Pires, who's the smartest of them all, to negotiate the sale of the grove to Brastânio. And there won't be a thing we can do about it."

"Well, in that case, neither can Tieta."

Someone came up the post office steps and stood bashfully in the doorway: Fidélio. No one had asked him to sign the petition. They all knew he was one of the heirs to the land the Brazilian Titanium Company, S.A., was planning to build on and therefore one of the few who stood to make a real profit.

"Hello, Dona Carmosina. Hello, Skipper. I'd like to have a word with you, sir, if you have time."

"If it's private I'll go on inside," offered Carmosina, bursting with curiosity.

"It is private, but not to you, ma'am." He knew he should have asked Aminthas to come with him. A man of few words by nature, how on earth was he going to explain something as complicated as this? He hoped the Skipper wouldn't be annoyed. "It's about this business of the palm grove. I'm one of the few who stand to inherit, as I think you already know."

Dona Carmosina leaned over the counter to hear better.

*Episode No. 2 of Ascânio's stay in the capital,
or the education of a leader in the cause of
progress: ambition, idealism, whisky and Nilsa
with the big bazoom.*

Ascânio, who had been on the lookout since nine-thirty, went over
to the group as they left the elevator. One of the men walked
quickly by him and disappeared into a black limousine. Ascânio
never knew who he was or even whether he was a member of
Brastânio's board; all he remembered about the man afterward was
that he wore his hair in an old-fashioned crew cut. Mirko Stefano
introduced him to the other two at the elevator door. They had just
time to make it to the airport, so the handshake was a brief one.

"Dr. Angelo Bardi, chairman of our board of directors."

The tycoon, for that was clearly what he was, held out his hand
and smiled.

"So this is our man? Fine, fine." The approving smile grew
broader and he turned to Mirko. "You take good care of him, now.
Let's get those little problems cleared up, the election business, for
one. I telephoned São Paulo yesterday. The president of the Election Tribunal has probably received a telegram by now." He shook
Ascânio's hand again. "Pleased to meet you. So long."

The other one, a young man ("Dr. Rosalvo Lucena, another
member of our board of directors and a real brain," Mirko said),
said he'd like to have a talk with Ascânio when he got back from
the airport and they had more time. They were all going out there,
including Mirko. Ascânio accompanied them to the door and saw
them off in the two powerful black cars.

He found himself once again at loose ends in the luxurious
lobby. Tourists were departing to visit the churches and Gallows
Square or to spend their money at the Model Market in noisy,
motley bands of frightful old women, arthritic elderly men, middle-
aged ladies with roving eyes and wide-eyed, dazzled young girls.
Ascânio buried himself in one of the huge leather armchairs and

read the hotel prospectus from cover to cover. It told him in five different languages that the design (this word was left in English) for his armchair and the other hotel furniture were the exclusive creation of one Lew Smarchewski. Ascânio had never heard of him but was impressed by the artist's name and the word "design." After a quick glance around he stuffed the prospectus in his pocket to show at the Areopagus. He had not spent much time at the post office lately. Why should he? Just to hear Dona Carmosina bawl him out? Patricia, who had left him about eight, after coffee and a shower, appeared just as he was about to pick up a newspaper. She was hanging on the arm of one of the three characters who had been lapping it up with Mirko around the pool the day before, and this time he was introduced.

"Dr. Ascânio Trindade, a friend of Dr. Mirko's, Ismael Julião, the big bad columnist who makes the fat cats shake in their boots," she said mockingly, then abruptly turned serious. "My fiancé."

Ascânio, who had been about to shake the fellow's hand, almost dropped it. Fiancé? She must be kidding. But Pat laid her head romantically on the shoulder of her scraggly bearded boyfriend, ran her fingers through his unkempt hair and, as if she could tell Ascânio didn't believe her, confided, "We're going to be married in a month or so."

"Two months, honeychild. Not till after Carnival," said Ismael. "Honeymoon and Carnival don't mix."

"Carnival's more fun when you're on your own," agreed Pat. "He swings with the Internationals and I go around with the Jacú Boys."

Ascânio didn't get it and she didn't explain. Instead she said coaxingly, "Why don't you go put on your trunks and relax in the pool with us? Mirko won't be back before noon, even if he comes here right from the airport. You never know with him."

"*Je suis l'imprévisible!*" The reporter mimicked the affected voice of the PR man.

"Too bad I didn't bring my trunks," said Ascânio, not eager to accept the invitation.

"Oh, that doesn't matter. They rent bathing suits here; come on and I'll show you where." She winked at her boyfriend. "I'll meet you at the diving board, sugar."

"Is he really your fiancé?" Ascânio still thought his leg was being pulled.

"Of course he is. I already have my wedding gown. Doctor Magnifico brought it all the way from Laïs Modas in Rio, and is it ever gorgeous! You ought to see the wreath."

"You mean you're getting married with a wreath and veil?" The exclamation came out so spontaneously he couldn't hold it back.

Pat was not insulted. She laughed good-naturedly.

"Yes, my dear, I plan to march down the aisle with a veil, wreath and orange blossoms to the sound of the 'Wedding March,' I love it! Baby, you're just an old fuddy-duddy. But you're an adorable fuddy-duddy all the same. Ismael's adorable too, don't you think? Nobody could find fault with that beautiful hunk of man, hmm?" She bit her lip as she praised her boyfriend's physical attributes. "And he's really with it, too, not an old stick-in-the-mud like you. This is 1966, baby, hadn't you heard out there where you come from? You ought to bring your calendar up to date."

Ascânio was a fine swimmer, and once he was diving and splashing in the pool he began to relax in the company of Patricia and Ismael, Christmas choice of the sprightly social columnist Dorian Grey, Jr. for Engaged Couple of the Year. That girl was right, he needed to relax some; he had felt tense and insecure ever since the jeep had left him at the door. He slowly began to unwind and feel a little more at ease. Around the pool it was as if they had all known each other for years. One group was playing with an enormous plastic beach ball and Ascânio joined in; he had a nice talk with a young couple from Rio who had fallen in love with Bahia, and talked to several other strangers. Sometimes, it was true, there were peculiar words, even whole sentences, that he couldn't get the gist of, but no one seemed to notice; they treated him as an equal, just as if he were an attractive, wealthy young man on holiday and part of their world.

Ismael climbed out of the pool and lay down on a chaise longue. Patricia swam near Ascânio, flirting with him and teasing him, splashing water on him, grabbing him by the legs and shoulders, jumping on his shoulders, wrestling with him and diving under him. It was a very pleasant morning.

"Here's Mirko with Dr. Lucena," Pat told him.

Ismael Julião stood up, sauntered over to say hello, served himself a double Scotch and went back to the poolside, glass in hand. Patricia gave her sweetheart an affectionate hug. Ascânio had gone running off to change and was back on the double in a coat and tie. At a gesture from Doctor Magnifico he sat down at their table.

Rosalvo Lucena (of whose university degrees and business titles Pat had whispered to him while they were still in the water, since it was part of her job to keep him informed) impressed Ascânio Trindade very much. He felt insignificant in the presence of this young technocrat who exuded self-confidence and authority. Lucena was not much older than he was, yet he had already made a name for himself as a hard-driving executive on the way up. Ascânio was soon as tense and unsure of himself as he had been before his swim. Now here was a real leader, a success in the business world, the kind of fellow who might properly aspire to Leonora Cantarelli's hand. Lucena possessed all the right qualifications, the right titles and the right place in the world. He had diplomas written in Latin and English, and at thirty years of age he was already on the Brazilian Titanium Company's board of directors. Fantastic! Notwithstanding the status gap that separated them, Rosalvo Lucena seemed pleasant and interested and could not have been more considerate and cordial.

"Mirko's said very fine things about you. He told me how hard you were trying to bring progress to Agreste. I hope we can be of real help in putting your ideas to work. I'm in charge of all the technical and economic problems involved in setting up our two integrated plants, so I look forward to the pleasure of seeing your fair city for myself before long, not to mention that beach I've heard so much about. It looks very much as if we're going to locate our industrial complex in your part of the world. One of our teams should be arriving there just about now, and they've been given precise directives. We've gone into Phase Two of the project now."

"You mean they'll be there today?"

"They left here this morning in two large, very fast speedboats, so they're probably there already. They're prepared to camp out on the beach for a few days, or however long it takes them to survey the possible factory sites, pick a residential area for the technical and administrative personnel and for the workers, and so on. This is a tremendous undertaking, you know. Choosing exactly the right spot is very important. It looks as if it's going to be a place where there's a sort of lake and a creek, right in the middle of the grove." He smiled complacently. "I've never been there, but I know Agreste and Mangue Seco as well as if I'd lived there all my life. I know all about the place, including the smuggling. Did you know it was one of the oldest smuggling points in the northeast? We'd like to work in close collaboration with you and the other municipal authorities."

"Well, you can certainly count on my support at least. The Brastânio plant at Mangue Seco will be the redemption of Agreste."

At this fine phrase Doctor Magnifico could not refrain from applauding Ascânio in both English and French.

"Wonderful! Fine! *Une trouvaille!* I might have said that myself. Better write it down, old boy; one of these days you're going to have to say it again."

"Yes, we hope to be very useful to your part of the country," went on the earnest young executive. "We intend to give ample support, in every sense of the word, to whatever initiatives you take to raise the economic and cultural level of Agreste. Unfortunately, the development gaps in Brazil between one region and another are still much too great; islands of poverty and backwardness still persist. We must change that as quickly as possible; we must even out those differences, which are stumbling blocks to our national development." He tapped Ascânio's thigh in a friendly way. "Men like you are a priceless community asset. As idealists we feel an obligation to help you in every way we can. After all, you're an idealist yourself, and we share the same high ideal: progress!"

These brilliant considerations, almost a speech, were expressed with beguiling naturalness, in a conversational tone which was nonetheless persuasive, as Lucena carelessly fondled a blonde and a brunette, both in bikinis, who were perched on the wide arms of a comfortable modern chair, another of Lew Smarchewski's exclusive designs. The even flow of his assured, well-modulated voice and clear pronunciation did not change as he drew the waiter's attention to the inferior quality of the whisky which had been brought in a fancy green-tinted bottle, all wavy, wobbly curves. Having poured himself a drink and tasted it, Lucena gave vent to polite but sincere indignation. "What do you know, phony Scotch! Isn't that the limit?" He called Doctor Magnifico's attention to the outrage. "It never fails. Liquor that comes in a cut-glass bottle that looks like a fancy piece of sculpture but doesn't have a label is never any good; that beautiful cut glass is just bait for the yokels." The young technocrat included among his many and varied talents a thorough knowledge of sublime Scotch whisky, to his mind the only true nectar of the gods. Mirko disagreed; he liked whisky well enough, but he preferred a fine French wine any day, and nothing could compare with the best champagne. What was friend Ascânio's opinion? Friend Ascânio didn't have one; he knew nothing about whisky and next to nothing about champagne. Rosalvo Lucena returned the green bottle and his full glass to the waiter.

"Throw this vile stuff away, friend, and bring another glass. And tell the barman to save this bottle for some drunk who can't tell fake Scotch from the real thing. I want Scotch, not this vomit-making brew. Bring me a bottle of Chivas Regal, a sealed one, so I can look at it and open it here. And tell him I intend to complain to the *maître d'* about this lack of respect."

Ascânio was filled with admiration at the easy self-assurance with which the other man talked about national development and spurned the false whisky, and his admiration knew no bounds when he next heard Rosalvo remark, "Look, Mirko, look at your friend Ismael lapping it up over there! That one can stomach anything. It's disgusting!"

He can stomach anything, all right, thought Ascânio. Horns on his head before he was even married. He was bound to know about his fiancée's little diversions on the side; maybe they were even in cahoots. He was worse than disgusting, he was an insect!

The barman hurried over anxiously, with a new bottle in his hand and humble excuses on his lips. "If I had known it was for *your* table, sir . . ." Affable, generous Rosalvo Lucena accepted the apology and sent the barman away with the promise to say nothing to the *maître d'* after all.

Ascânio plucked up his courage and congratulated the executive on how superbly he had demolished Giovanni Guimarães, the feature writer for *A Tarde*, in that illuminating interview of his. It had been very useful in setting those people right who had been so impressed by the "Letter to De Matos Barbosa." He explained that Giovanni had visited the town a few years before, had made many friends there and enjoyed a certain amount of prestige. First inspecting the bottle of Chivas before nodding approval, opening it and serving himself, Doctor Magnifico, Ascânio and the girl who preferred Scotch to Campari, Rosalvo answered, "Giovanni? Not a bad chap at all. He's intelligent, has a good sense of humor and writes well. But he'll never be anything but a provincial hack writer with his little bureaucratic post and his reporter's salary. He just doesn't have it in him. What he lacks is ambition and idealism." He sipped his drink and poured himself another. "Now *this* is what I call Scotch." He looked at Ascânio thoughtfully and tapped him on the leg again to emphasize the importance of what he was about to say. "Without idealism and ambition, old fellow, you won't get anywhere at all. You need a high ideal to amount to something in life, to be a mover and shaker. And ambition greases the wheels. Ambition is the mainspring of the world."

As soon as he finished speaking he drank down a long swig of Scotch, rolling it around on his tongue with the self-satisfaction of an expert. The barman smiled behind the counter as he shook the cocktail shaker, thinking how much appearances were worth. For the merely vain there was the twisted cut-glass green-tinted bottle, a sign of special consideration; for the conceited and arrogant there was the plain bottle from the United Kingdom, sealed and unopened, a sign of still greater respect. Two different bottles for two kinds of men, both filled with the same ersatz Scotch from the hotel's own stock. The only difference was the price. How much discrimination and refinement could you expect from a whisky swiller, anyway? None, to the barman's way of thinking.

During the brief hour in which they sat drinking and exchanging ideas at the edge of the pool, enjoying the pleasing sight of women's bodies seen through the blue, transparent water, Ascânio was introduced to a good many men, all apparently important, who stopped to say hello to Rosalvo Lucena and have a word with Mirko, which was sometimes whispered in his ear. Not to speak of the girls, some of whom surely worked for Brastânio at least some of the time, since Mirko asked them to run various errands—telephone calls, a reservation at Chez Bernard's for six people for dinner that night, Dorival Caymmi records to be bought at one of the shops. When introducing Ascânio, Doctor Magnifico did not mention his real job or where he came from but praised him as "a dynamic leader with a great future before him and an important role to play in this state, perhaps a national role as well. A real leader of men."

Those were pleasant words to hear. They soothed him like a lullaby while strengthening his backbone and giving him a pattern for his life. Idealism and ambition, the successful young executive had said. Ascânio had always been an idealist, and as for his ambition, it was growing by leaps and bounds at the edge of the swimming pool.

What with the sunny morning, the friendly atmosphere, the lovely women, the intelligence of his tablemates, the expensive liquor—now *this* was real Scotch—he no longer felt quite so humble beside Rosalvo Lucena. Lucena was saying goodbye; he had a luncheon date with someone very high up in the state government.

"I'll see you in Agreste one of these days."

"I'll look forward to seeing you there."

He caught a murmured warning from Mirko Stefano as Lucena stood up to leave. "He's hard as nails, so watch out. A lot is riding on this. Be sure and tell him that what he ordered is on its way."

Doctor Magnifico lingered awhile, relishing his whisky, with a growing circle around him. Although he still had *une journée terriblement chargée* before him, as he said, he seemed to be in no particular hurry to get back to it. He delighted in his surroundings: the cloudless day, the people strolling to and fro between the bar and the pool, the vision of all those half-clad bodies, the girls offering themselves, the idle gossip and adulation of the greedy reporters. After a while he got up, signed the check and made an appointment with Ascânio for four o'clock that afternoon. Pat would escort him to company headquarters.

"We have a lot to talk about. Bye-bye."

At last, thought Ascânio. It was about time they had that talk; it was his whole reason for coming. Pat came up to him with another girl, a slim brunette with a spectacular bust.

"This cute trick is Nilsa, baby. She's just been appointed your secretary. I can't take you around today, it's Ismael's day off. All he has to do is hand in his column at the paper and the rest of the day is his." She glanced affectionately at her fiancé, who was walking back to the pool after helping himself to the dregs of the whisky. "You understand, don't you, baby? Nilsa can do anything I can do. I know you'll like her and she'll like you."

Nilsa said very little, laughed a great deal, and missed no chance to show off her fine bosom. She suggested a cold buffet lunch, which was quicker and wouldn't weigh on their stomachs. That day there wasn't any nap; she went right up to his room with him. As he stripped off his shorts and feasted his eyes on Nilsa's round swollen breasts and the thick black hair of her lower belly, Ascânio thought that all things considered, the postponement of the talk which was his sole reason for coming to the capital had its compensating features. If he hadn't been missing Leonora so much, he wouldn't have minded staying on a few more days.

Of a controversial incident at Mangue Seco, a chapter in which we learn of a vigorous mass movement by the workers (so to speak) and the people, which provides this novel with an essential ingredient of militancy and social agitation it has heretofore lacked.

"We'll run them off the beach if they ever come around here," Ricardo, the young seminarian, had threatened, meaning anyone from Brastânio, in a conversation with Tieta, the Skipper, and Pedro Palmeira the engineer. The threat had earned him a hearty handshake from the engineer. And Ricardo had kept his promise. There he was in his cassock, along with Tieta, who was having a whale of a good time. She felt as if she had been transported back to her early youth when she used to scramble down the hills, leaving her flock in Inácio's care to go out to the dunes with some man and mingle with the fishermen.

Ricardo had not been able to keep his promise to the letter, however, since the first envoys from Brastânio after his impetuous vow had merely flown over the beach and the palm grove in a helicopter on the fatal day of Zé Esteves' death, armed with binoculars and movie cameras. Although he longed to fly, Ricardo was not yet endowed with wings, even if the women of Agreste thought him an angel of the Lord, especially those with a propensity for the incomparable sport in which Tieta had an advantage over the others since it was she who knew her nephew's celestial attributes best. Of course, you never could tell. Maybe someday the Lord would grant him that prerogative reserved for angels and archangels as a reward for the sincerity of his vocation.

The handshake had marked the beginning of a growing friendship between the seminarian and the engineer. The twelve-year difference in age did not keep them from forming a deep brotherly attachment as they kicked a soccer ball around with the boys from the fishing village, sailed out on deep-sea fishing expeditions beyond the bar (Ricardo had finally wrested his new rod and reel away from Peto) and in long hours of talk, sometimes with Frei Thimóteo at Saco. Before going to work at Petrobras and moving to Bahia, where he had had the good luck to meet Marta and win her for his wife, and consequently the bad luck to meet Modesto Pires and have him for a father-in-law, Pedro had been an active university radical in Rio de Janeiro. "Do you have any idea what it's like, Cardo? When you think of a reactionary and a bigot, think of my father-in-law. Some people don't know their ass from their elbow, if you'll pardon the expression, but Seu Modesto doesn't know his head from a thousand-cruzeiro bill." Pedro loved to recount the heroic escapades of his days as a student agitator. He was still as interested in student politics as ever, although he had had to stop taking an active part in them after he graduated, married and became a father. He kept track of what was happening, signed protests, and sent money to help out. From Pedro Ricardo learned that even seminarians sometimes joined the demonstrators and were involved in fights with the police.

The two initiated an educational campaign among the proletarian masses, as the dogmatic engineer and former drafter of manifestoes called them; that is, eighteen or twenty fishermen's families, rough sailors toughened by the ever-blowing wind, with athletic sons skilled at swimming, fishing and beach soccer. One of these, Budião, was already a crack soccer player. One of the directors of the Sergipe Football Club had seen him play in Saco's scratch team in Estância and asked him to come to Aracaju. But people born on Mangue Seco don't emigrate; they can't live away from the mountainous breakers and the howling wind.

The engineer preached his ideological best. The grave problems of imperialism, internal colonialism, pollution, mortal threats to the maritime fauna and the fishing industry itself; the presence of a majority of foreign shareholders in the titanium-dioxide industry (which was really an obstacle and not a stimulus to national development, since it channeled immense profits abroad and left the Brazilian people worse off than they were before)—none of this, sad to say, made much of an impression on the token mass to which he addressed himself with such pathos, fervor and goodwill. It impressed Ricardo, though. What a fantastic summer vacation he was having! Walls crumbled before him and roads opened out. God was illuminating his spirit with a vengeance.

God so illuminated Ricardo that the only argument to make a crack in the general indifference was his contention that dumping the fill on which to build the factories and workers' houses would be the end of the mudflats and with them the crabs. The news of the probable extinction of the crabs, which were the basis of the villagers' diet (the women caught them in the palm grove while the men mended their sails and smoked their clay pipes), sparked a lively debate, which was cut short when old Jonas, whose word was law to the rest, remarked skeptically, "How're they gonna cover up all the mud and all the crabs? There ain't money enough in the world to do that."

They nodded but listened politely to the explanations of the Skipper, who reinforced the seriousness of the threat with plain words: "Who? Well, some heartless bastards after easy money want to build a factory in the palm grove to make poison, and that poison is worse than strychnine. It kills everything it touches, including crabs."

"Crabs ain't that easy to kill, Skipper. I never heard of a poison that could kill a crab. It'd have to be some poison!"

What finally decided them to help Ricardo and the engineer run off the Brastânio people next time they came back was a conversation that Jonas, Isaías and Daniel, the three acknowledged leaders of the little community, had with Jeremias in his schooner outside the bar one lowering dawn. The *compadre* Jeremias, who had a godchild in every one of the fishing families, told them with a heavy heart that their age-old livelihood and that of their ancestors, the *compadres* and godchildren, their wives, brothers and sisters, their aunts and their grandmothers, plus a good many people scattered in the nearby towns, including Elieser, was about to come to an end. The schooners and ships would have to land their merchandise someplace else. If the factory was built on Mangue Seco—and it sure looked like it would be, because people were fighting it everywhere else while here no one lifted a finger to stop it—that meant no more smuggling. It wouldn't be safe anymore. Mangue Seco would lose its one great advantage: isolation. A deserted beach at the end of the world was ideal for landing contraband goods and hauling them away. Once the plant was in operation it would be too much of a risk.

That threat decided them. As an afterthought they asked the *compadre* if it was true that that business, whatever it was, turned out a poison strong enough to kill crabs. Jeremias had a deep scar on his face and he spoke without taking his pipe out of his mouth. There wasn't a better man in the world and only the Skipper was as good, but the ties that bound the people of Mangue Seco to the two men were different. The Skipper was a fast friend; the *compadre* was one of them. They had risked life and freedom together.

"Does it kill crabs? You won't have a crab left to throw in the cooking pot. That titanium's as bad as the plague. It even kills freshwater turtles, and they're mighty hard to kill."

Jonas, the eldest of the three, reassured him.

"Don't you fret, *compadre*, we ain't gonna let 'em come in here. If we can give the police a run for their money, it won't be hard to scare off those shit-spitters."

Isaías, the middle one, seconded him.

"The engineer and the young priest told us we ought to teach 'em a lesson. Well, we will. Don't you worry none, and don't change your course. You won't find a better place than this."

Daniel, the youngest, spoke up.

"*Compadre*, don't forget your new godchild's christening next month. I never thought that stuff would kill the crabs. I know the Skipper ain't a man to tell a lie, but I had my doubts even so. There ain't nothin' to worry about, *compadre*. This place, this sand and this piece of water belong to us and nobody else but God. They can do anything they want to with the rest, but nobody's gonna set foot on Mangue Seco who don't respect our rights."

It was up to Jonas to say the last word. He raised the stump of his arm.

"Have a safe journey, *compadre*, and be sure you come back. We won't let you down."

"Then I'll be back next month, *compadres*; now I can go easy in my mind. Regards to the womenfolk and a blessing for my godchildren."

It was an ugly night. The wind was howling, the sea was angry, and so were they. Kill the crabs? Like hell they would. The schooner vanished into the darkness and the boats cut through the waves and sharks. They were the only ones who dared pass through those breakers, as their fathers and their grandfathers had done, bent on the same forbidden errand. They unloaded the merchandise onto the beach in silence and stowed it safely away to wait for Elieser and their other partners.

The team from Brastânio reached Mangue Seco at the end of a long, unpleasant voyage through choppy, dangerous seas. At the mouth of the Real the waves towered into billows and the wind made eddies in the sand, transforming the topography of the beach. The weather was so bad that the Saco fishermen had not gone out that day. By the time the strangers crossed the sandbar, some of them, the women especially, were starting to panic.

They had come in two powerful streamlined motor launches, with everything aboard they could possibly need, from five large tents to an abundance of canned food, mineral water and soft drinks, and bead necklaces from the Model Market to give to the natives. Tired and nervous as they were, and out in such disagreeable weather, nevertheless, when they saw the splendid panorama of Mangue Seco before them—the sight of the tall dunes breasting the furious ocean, the wide beach stretching for miles on each side of the peninsula and the palm grove bordering both banks of the river as far as the eye could see—they felt how insignificant they were and decided the trip had been worth it.

They stopped the motors at some distance from the beach. One of the passengers jumped into the water, which was up to his waist, and waded in to shore. He walked over to the palm huts half buried in the sand and addressed Isaías, who was industriously mending a sail that had a rip in it from the storm the night before.

"Hey, you! You and the others too!" The others were very busy doing nothing, seated in a wide circle talking and smoking. "Come help us unload some things. Hurry up!"

Isaías looked at him without answering. Old Jonas stood up.

"Say, young fellow, are you from the factory?"

Struggling to keep his footing in the wind but mindful of his status, the gallant pioneer assented. "We're from Brastânio, yes. Don't just stand there, man! Come on, we're in a hurry."

Jonas scrutinized the two motor launches anchored off the beach, pitching like toys in the rough seas, and estimated the number of passengers there might be. How many women? The women were a problem. The old fisherman scratched his sparse beard. He could recall times when the police had more guts—usually at the beginning of a new administration, with all the politicians breathing fire about law enforcement and swearing they'd put a stop to this smuggling business once and for all. No one had said anything like that for a long time, or if they had, they hadn't done anything about it. But when you came right down to it, where could you find any soldiers or secret police who'd be willing to risk their necks coming out to Mangue Seco?

The fishermen had a method they used as a last resort, but they hadn't had to use it for a long time. The younger ones only knew about it from hearsay; now they were going to have some fun. It was the peddler who used to enjoy it the most; he had taken part in more than one of these punitive expeditions.

"Get the boats ready, Isaías. Daniel, round up the men. Budião, you run and tell Dona Tieta they're here. Tell Cardo, too, and the engineer. And step on it, 'cause the man's in a hurry." He turned to the emissary. "You can go on back now, we'll be with you in a minute."

As he watched Brastânio's stalwart march off, bent over against the wind, Jonas thanked his lucky stars that the Skipper had gone to Agreste on business. Skipper Dário was a real pal who closed his eyes to clandestine nocturnal goings-on and pretended he didn't know about the schooners, freighters and speedboats and what kind of cargo they unloaded. Still, in spite of his friendship for the people of Mangue Seco and the determination with which he opposed the poison factory, he might object to the planned operation, and that would create a real problem.

They hadn't had to carry out one of these jobs since that business with the sergeant. The police had never come back after that, and it was just as well. Now they had no choice, but when they decided to do it Jonas warned them all to be very careful. Tieta, the future priest and the engineer would have to stay on the beach; they couldn't afford to be mixed up in this.

Not even Tieta, ready for anything though she was. Back when Jonas was the youngest of the three leaders of the village, many, many years ago, and Tieta was a tomboy who herded goats on the Agreste hills, she used to come out to the beach sometimes and climb the dunes, but never alone; she always had some man with her. She had round heels all right, but how could she help it when she was so pretty? Well, she had come back from São Paulo twice as good-looking as when she went away. She was a knockout now and no mistake. As a girl she had always gone around with older men. Now she was fulfilling her obligation as an aunt by teaching her nephew to be the right kind of priest.

Once when she came out for some fun on the beach, Tieta had landed in the middle of an ugly fight. Two soldiers, several secret police agents and the Estância chief of police were trying to seize the goods and arrest the old man who was the fence in Estância. The dude who was with her turned yellow and just about dropped his teeth when he saw the ruckus. He hightailed it back to the boat and rowed back out to sea as fast as he could go, leaving his girl in the lurch like the sorry little coward he was. Tieta didn't care; she took one look and laughed, and jumped into the fight with her shepherd's staff flying until the fishermen drove off the police. You should have seen her crack that staff of hers across the chief of police without a bit of respect for his revolver or the whistle he used to give orders with, a great novelty then. Tieta hadn't been born on Mangue Seco but she deserved to have been. Maybe he ought to take her along after all to see to the women.

Except for the fellow who had come ashore to round up some porters, none of the Brastânio staff got out of the boats. They were a fairly large group, about twenty people, four of them women: a cartographer, two secretaries and the team leader's wife, a robust, romantic and extremely jealous lady who had joined the caravan so as not to leave her husband at the mercies of those ants-in-the-pants secretaries, and also in the hope of a swim at Mangue Seco. That was what all of them wanted. Every one of those well-paid specialists had joined the team in the agreeable hope of combining business with pleasure and taking time off from work to enjoy the fabulous beach everyone in the company was talking about. Once they got over their fear after crossing the bar, their spirits picked up.

"Won't this be glorious when the sun comes out?" Kátia, the leader's wife, exclaimed happily.

They were about to have the surprise of their lives. It took them some time to realize exactly what was going on. The first thing they saw was surrealistic. A woman came running from away off through the coconut palms, wearing trousers and a black rubber sou'wester like the kind sailors wear, with a long staff in her hand. They couldn't hear what she was shouting because of the wind, but the upraised stick seemed threatening. She was followed by a priest and a bearded man. Then came the fishermen: old men, young men and boys. Soon afterward their surprise turned to fear and then to terror.

When he took a good look at the launches and counted four women, Jonas decided he'd better take Tieta along.

"You come with us, Dona Tieta. Don't be afraid none."

"Jonas, you ought to know me by now."

"Sorry, ma'am, I take it back."

Ricardo was about to follow his aunt, and the engineer too, but Jonas barred the way.

"No, you two better stay here. If Seu Modesto found out about this he'd raise hell, Dr. Pedro. You wait right here, we'll take care of this." To Ricardo he said, "God won't like what we're going to do, *meu padrezinho*." It was not a suggestion but an order; this stern elder was not the good-natured Jonas who had joshed the seminarian crossing over to Saco.

Pedro nodded and walked off. For the sake of Marta and the children he had to try to get along with his father-in-law. But Ricardo answered back in a voice as firm as Jonas's, "Who told you God doesn't like it? God sends thunderbolts when He has to. I'm going even if nobody else does."

Jonas scratched his chin.

"Well, come on then, if you're so set on coming, but don't say I didn't warn you. Maybe you'll turn out to be the right kind of priest-teacher after all."

They put out in the fishing boats, some of the men carrying coils of rope. When they were close to the launches they jumped into the water and subdued the passengers and the two sailors in each launch with what seemed incredible rapidity to those who had only seen them lounging indolently on the beach and knew nothing of their nocturnal exploits. They were favored by surprise. The outsiders were too scared and startled to put up much of a fight. Jonas took command of one launch, Isaías the other.

"All the women in that launch there," ordered Jonas. "Dona Tieta, you keep an eye on them. Ricardo, come with me."

The rope was used to bind the men's wrists and tie them all together in two lines, one in each boat. Stupefied, the Brastânio men protested, expostulated and demanded explanations. Their questions were as useless as their arguments, reasoning and threats. No one paid the slightest attention. Of them all only the young electronics expert, wanting to impress the secretary he had his eye on and show

her how brave he was, made a lunge at Isaías. He was restrained by
Budião and the soccer-team left end, Samu (who was not much of
a dribbler but had a powerful kick), and tied to the others. They
were taken up on deck and guarded by the younger men, so they
could see and feel the danger up close. At a sign from Jonas the
launches slowly got underway, with the fishing boats escorting
them.

Instead of taking the traditional route across the bar where the
surf, though very high and spectacular on a day of unsettled
weather like this, was not really dangerous, they headed for the
great combers in the wake of the smuggling route. This was the
course they followed when they rendezvoused with the schooner,
the one they had followed with the captive policemen. One sergeant
had been so terrified he lost his wits, escaped from their restraining
hands and threw himself into the water. The sharks had instantly
torn him to bits and the blood was soon washed away by the waves.
For this reason Jonas had ordered that the men be tied together in
two groups, one in each launch, and had placed the four women
under Tieta's threatening staff.

"Don't any of you make a move, nannygoats, or you'll get a
drubbing."

Screams and weeping, cries for help and pity for the love of
God rose from the launches. Indifferent to the commotion, the
fishermen guided the boats through the towering waves and crossed
the most dangerous patch, where they rise to an immense height and
break with fury against the dunes. All of them were drenched when
the boats reached a place that only those born and bred there could
reach. They and the sharks.

They lifted their oars, silenced the motors and stopped still at
the door of death. Motorboats and fishing boats whirled, rose and
fell and threatened to capsize or be swamped. It was all the fishermen at the wheels could do to hold them in precarious balance. And
all the time the giant waves threatened to fling the boats against
those stony mountains of sand. The passengers looked death in the
face. More than one kind of death, for leaden forms drew near like
shadows under the turbulent water. Suddenly one of them, looking
even bigger than it was, sprang into the air not two yards from the
launch under Isaías' command. Everyone screamed in unison and
the women wept. Three more sharks leaped up together, and then
two more, and another—how many were there? The monstrous

mouths opened greedily, revealing pointed, voracious, sinister teeth. Jonas was missing an arm, and no one had to be told how he had lost it. How long did they remain there, face to face with death? It may have been only a few minutes, but to them it was eternity, a space and time of bottomless, infinite fear.

Kátia shrieked to her husband, "I want to die with you!" and fainted in Tieta's arms. Some of the men vomited, and the bowels of at least two of them turned to water with fear. Even the bravest of them learned the lesson.

Launches and fishing boats came to life again, broke through the great waves and headed for open water. The sharks followed them hopefully for a time and then disappeared. Rain pelted down and the clouds started to lift. Before relinquishing the launch and swinging down into the fishing boat, Jonas raised the mild but authoritative voice of a prophet with few pretensions.

"Don't ever come back here, and tell the others not to come either."

The rain washed the sky and quieted the waves, and the night fell soft and warm, a perfect night for carefree talk, happy memories and a quiet celebration. Sitting on the sand around the huts they quaffed *cachaça*; no reference was made to what had happened. Only the engineer laughed contentedly to himself at seeing his trust in the masses vindicated. For a moment he had had his doubts.

Daniel brought out the accordion. Budião, who could dance as well as he could kick a soccer ball, showed off some fancy steps with Zilda, his betrothed. The engineer and Marta took a twirl. What a shame seminarians couldn't dance; silly, too. Ricardo gazed at the sky, now cloudless and sprinkled with stars, and felt that the roads of the world were open before him. He knew something of good and evil now, he had crossed the breakers to the other side of damnation and learned what desire was. With Tieta beside him, he felt the urgent call of her flesh fly to him and surround him even as he listened attentively to what Jonas was saying. Perhaps because she would not be in Agreste much longer, only until the new power line came in, his aunt wanted him with her all the time, night and day.

Jonas and Tieta were reminiscing about old times, telling stories of scuffles with the police, names, details. "That peddler had guts, remember him, Dona Tieta? Now that was a man." In the shadow of the dunes Tieta saw the peddler's form and inhaled his strong smell of onion and garlic on the salt air. He had been shot down in Santa Luzia Village, standing up to the soldiers.

Episode No. 3 of Ascânio Trindade's stay in the capital, or the education of a leader in the cause of progress: elections, tribunal, enemies of Brazil, foreign agents, art, and Betty, Bebé to close friends.

At Brastânio headquarters—spectacular, a whole floor with smoked-glass windows, in one of the modern buildings in Lower Bahia, a constant springlike temperature, and a goddess in a wig at the switchboard—Ascânio Trindade met up with an old acquaintance. When the Greek goddess announced him and invited him to take a seat, Betty appeared in a doorway before he could do so. Displaying efficiency and a good memory, she welcomed him effusively.

"Hi there, luv! Welcome to our little workshop. Come right this way, Dr. Stefano's expecting you. And how's Mr. Handsome?"

"Mr. Handsome?"

"That beanpole, that funny one who oozes charm."

"Oh! You mean Osnar. He'll be fit to be tied when I tell him I saw you."

"Tell him I send him a kiss and miss him to death." She made a sign to Nilsa to wait where she was.

On a glass table in Mirko Stefano's office was a large colored drawing. Ascânio recognized features of Mangue Seco; the dunes, the mouth of the river and the palm grove. Part of the grove had disappeared. In its place was an imposing cluster of tall factories with a chimney which emitted little puffs of clean smoke. Between the factory and the dunes were a couple dozen very comfortable-looking houses, with verandas and gardens, for the managers, engineers and technicians. On the other side going toward Agreste was what looked like a small town, with hundreds of gay little houses in twos, all alike, where the workers would live. Then there was a modern marina, almost a port, with big motor launches. Ascânio was dazzled by this vision of the future. Doctor Magnifico's affected voice brought him back to the present.

"Do you see that house a little away from the others, the one closest to the beach? That's mine. That's where I plan to relax when I can get away. I adore Mangue Seco; it's the prettiest place in the world. And now it will become a wealth-producing center besides. *C'est ça.*"

He sat down at his desk, waved Ascânio to a chair facing his and rubbed his hands with satisfaction.

"I asked you to come to Salvador to give you the good news in person, my dear Ascânio. May I call you that? Let's not stand on ceremony."

"Yes of course, Dr. Mirko."

"No doctor, no mister. Your friend Mirko Stefano, and your admirer. But to get back to our news. Brastânio has definitely decided to install its titanium-dioxide plant in Sant'Ana do Agreste. Did you know that this enterprise is one of the most important to be planned and carried out in this country in the last twenty years, from the point of view of national development and the balance of payments? A most distinguished enterprise!"

The mannered voice was categorical. The statement was a crushing reply to all doubts, attacks and opposition.

"The decision was made at a meeting of the board of directors which didn't end until late yesterday afternoon. But since I knew ahead of time what the decision would be, I went ahead and asked you to come so that we could confer and synchronize our watches, *c'est bien nécessaire.* I trust the waiting hasn't bored you."

"Oh, no, not at all, I've enjoyed it very much. All I can say is thank you very much."

"*Rien, mon cher.* We'll make our decision public in a few days. As soon as we can iron out a few minor difficulties with the state government, which Dr. Lucena is taking care of now, we'll go to Agreste to submit a formal presentation to the Town Council and request authorization to carry out our plans. I ought to tell you that I fought hard for your township. I really took a liking to Agreste, especially the beach. Other communities with far better infrastructure have tried to win favor by offering various advantages, including tax exemption. But that isn't what we're after. For a pioneer undertaking like this, Brastânio prefers an area that's farther off the beaten path, a neglected area where we can act as a lever to bring in progress. As you put it so aptly, Brastânio will be the redemption of Agreste. It's going to cost us a little more, but we will have attained our principal objective, which is to serve."

He pressed a button which rang a little bell on top of his desk, then stood, walked over to Ascânio and held out his hand.

"As mayor of the town of Sant'Ana do Agreste, or the mayor's representative, please accept my warmest congratulations."

Ascânio stood up and gave the other man an *abrazo*; a handshake seemed too cold. Betty appeared, followed by the office boy bearing a red acrylic tray with crystal goblets and a dark bottle of champagne. Seeing there were only two glasses, Doctor Magnifico ordered a third and the boy hurried off to bring it. Plainly in his element, Mirko said as he fussily uncorked the bottle, "Dom Pérignon. You know it, surely."

Although tempted to say he did, Ascânio admitted ruefully, "No, I've never had any. Once I tried another kind called Widow something . . ."

"Veuve Clicquot."

The cork gave the usual festive pop and Doctor Magnifico poured, handing one of the glasses to Betty.

"Betty and I were the first to set foot in Agreste. We were the pioneers."

"Some people thought you were Martians, strange beings from outer space," Ascânio told them.

They laughed as they remembered how they had amazed the inhabitants of Agreste. Betty had a good memory.

"Mr. Handsome asked me whether I was a Martian or a Polack. He's so funny."

"They're good people," concluded Mirko Stefano, raising his glass. "Let's drink to a prosperous Agreste and to the brave man at the helm, my friend Ascânio Trindade. Chin-chin."

They touched goblets in a toast with a faint ringing of crystal, like Leonora's laughter. If she were here now she'd be so proud she'd start reciting that verse from Barbozinha's poem about Ascânio Trindade, Captain of the Dawn. Betty went up to him and kissed him on both cheeks with a "Congratulations, luv," then left them alone.

Mirko served them both another glass, sat down on the edge of the desk, waved Ascânio to a chair and began expatiating on Brastânio's plans.

"We'd like for you to be in office, if possible, by the time we come in with our proposition. We did all we could to set forward the election date. Dr. Bardi took a personal interest, the Election Tribunal put it on the agenda, and yesterday Dr. Bardi telephoned to friends in São Paulo to make sure the resolution would come up for discussion at today's session—the tribunal only meets once a week, you know. Everything was OK, everything fine. Well, wouldn't you know the presiding judge took a notion to have a heart attack and kick the bucket this morning of all times? As a result, today's session was canceled and they won't be holding another one until next week. You can go back easy in your mind, though; a week from now we'll have a firm date."

He served them again, daintily; champagne was one of the few things that merited his full respect and esteem. He admitted to being a real connoisseur.

"I drink Scotch with friends or in a bar or at parties, but what I really love is champagne." He pronounced it the French way, not with a vulgar Brazilian accent. "As Rosalvo told you, a team of experts has gone to Mangue Seco, while we're going right ahead and preparing all the necessary documents for the official request to the state government and then to the local authorities in Agreste for permission to begin work. We intend to hire workmen from all over the area, including Sergipe. Very soon we should have the final estimate for straightening and asphalting the road between Agreste and Esplanada. Things are being accomplished, *mon vieux*."

He held his goblet pensively up to the light.

"Some people rise up in protest against implanting a titanium-dioxide industry in Brazil because it pollutes. Their reasons vary, though they're often pretty murky; but the foreign agents who are leading this anti-Brazilian campaign have been successful in hoodwinking many honest people who oppose us out of fear. Now I'm not going to tell you the titanium-dioxide industry doesn't pollute. It does, of course, just as any industry pollutes, maybe a little more than some. And yet you never hear anyone come out against a textile mill or a factory that makes household appliances. But when it comes to basic industries like this one, the people who have an interest in keeping us underdeveloped and dependent come up with the most ridiculous lies. For example, they say we'll destroy the river and ocean life. That's sheer fantasy. We'll put in underwater pipelines to carry the contaminated industrial waste several miles out to sea where it can't possibly do any harm. I'm putting together a portfolio for you which will completely clarify the problem of this so-called lethal titanium-dioxide pollution and put it in proper perspective. That will give you plenty of ammunition to show up the liars and open the eyes of those who've been taken in or have been trying to block progress by waving the shibboleth of pollution. Why, if those people had their way, São Paulo would still be a little two-bit provincial capital today. You've seen the Aratu Industrial Center. You wouldn't believe the fight those idiots put up, old chap! And behind the idiots, pulling the strings, were the enemies of Brazil." He did not clarify which enemies he meant, having had no opportunity to take Ascânio's political pulse. If he was a right-winger he'd think of the Soviet Union; if a leftist, of the United States.

The phone rang. It was Betty. After a moment Doctor Magnifico hung up.

"Time for me to go to the judge's funeral. I can't get out of it. You see the kind of things you make me do?" He laughed in a friendly way. "We'll finish our conversation tomorrow at the hotel, in my suite, where we won't be interrupted."

Ascânio opened his mouth and then hesitated.

"Was there something you wanted to say?" said Mirko encouragingly. In his mind was a hopeful surmise that maybe Ascânio would ask for money.

Ascânio pointed to the drawing on the table, that glowing vision of the future.

"It would be dandy if I could take that plan back with me. Lindolfo made me a drawing for the poster I put up at the courthouse, but this is a painting, a work of art. It's magnificent!"

Betty was summoned by telephone and told to bring Rufo with her. And so Ascânio renewed his acquaintance with not only the luscious redhead with the streak in her hair—today it was a blue streak—but the Christlike youth with hair to his shoulders who had made the drawing. Ascânio congratulated him warmly, told him he was a fine artist and thanked him on behalf of Agreste. Mirko promised to have the masterwork delivered to the hotel the next day, conveniently rolled in a tube, together with the portfolio of "ammunition."

For dinner that evening Nilsa chose a restaurant at the Solar do Unhão, a lovely colonial mansion next to the Museum of Modern Art, at which there was an important exhibit opening of photos, engravings, paintings, and a variety of objects. The patio was full of cars.

After dinner Nilsa took him to see the exhibit, and Ascânio had another shock. What in the world kind of garbage was this? He had expected to see landscapes, artistic nudes, still lifes, beautiful pictures, and here he was gaping at ridiculous, immoral photographs, engravings of churches squeezed out of shape, and some crazy stuff like bric-a-brac made with bits and pieces of discarded objects. The artist had even used a latrine.

"You call him an artist?"

"Yes I do," declared Nilsa, "and he's very famous too, not just in Bahia but all over Brazil. Surely you must have heard of Juárez Paraiso!"

Nilsa pointed to a tall bearded mulatto in a circle of fawning admirers. He was standing in front of the exhibit poster, a huge photograph of a woman's naked bottom, for God's sake!

"See that man next to Celestino the banker? That's Carybé. He's always being interviewed and saying the most awful things about Brastânio, but the old guy's a cool cat just the same. He only paints black women."

She accompanied Ascânio back to the hotel, hung around his neck in the deserted lobby and gave him a hearty goodbye smack.

"I can't stay tonight. I have to be home early, and it's already after ten. My parents are so strict! They keep me in a straitjacket."

A straitjacket. Ascânio realized that words he thought he understood had other meanings here. Strict, art, engaged. Other values and another world he was watching from the doorway just before he crossed the threshold. Why did that indefinable uneasiness persist, as if he were not entering that world of his own volition but were being led? He missed Nilsa's presence in the empty room; her big bosom was a haven. The phone rang.

"Hello!"

"Is that you, luv?"

"Ascânio Trindade here."

"Why didn't you come over and talk to me at the exhibit, luv?"

He recognized the swooning voice of Betty, Bebé to her close friends.

"I didn't see you. I'm sorry. Can I do anything for you?"

"You sure can, luv. I'm down here at the desk and I'm coming up. Leave the door open for me."

*In which an unexpected heir appears and
Barbozinha is commissioned to write a poem.*

At about the same time the Mangue Seco fishermen were scaring off the Brastânio experts with the help of Tieta, Ricardo and Pedro Palmeira's sound ideological spadework, the various parties with an interest in the palm grove were gathering in Dr. Franklin's office. The notary had called the meeting at the request of Dr. Baltazar Moreira. Twice postponed because of Dr. Marcolino Pitombo's trips to Esplanada, it was now finally taking place.

The postprandial meeting was attended by the three attorneys and their clients. There were Dr. Marcolino Pitombo, flanked by Jarde and Josafá Antunes, the old man hunched over in a chair, the young one standing up proudly and looking triumphant; Dr. Baltazar Moreira, rushing to offer the best chair to Dona Carlota Antunes Alves, who sat in murmured confabulation with Modesto Pires; and Dr. Gustavo Galvão, in a coat and tie for once, advising Canuto Tavares to take it easy. As time passed and Fidélio, who had also been summoned as an Antunes and heir presumptive, did not come, it was decided to call the meeting to order in his absence. He was a strange sort of litigant, still with no lawyer to look after his interests.

This odd behavior prompted an opening comment from Dr. Marcolino: "That fellow's playing a pretty clever game if you ask me. He's waiting for us to come up with a solution before he shows his hand. You can write that down verbatim."

Pencil in hand, the robust Bonaparte, who had asked to act as secretary and take minutes at the meeting, was about to jot down these remarks on a sheet of foolscap when the lawyer stopped him.

"Don't bother including that in the minutes, son."

Bonaparte put down his pencil obediently. Although the attorney contradicted himself every five minutes—"Write down what I'm saying; no, don't put that in the minutes"—he was a nice old coot and didn't mind parting with a little change, which was more than those other skinflints were willing to do.

"And that being the case, I really wonder whether it's worth having our discussion without him," went on Dr. Marcolino, to whose interest it was to postpone the meeting until after the county clerk came back and he had had a chance to have a talk with him and find out exactly where Brastânio planned to build.

"Well, I see no reason why we should wait around for him. I propose that we discuss the problem before us without waiting any longer for this young man, who strikes me as rather irresponsible," declared Dr. Baltazar Moreira from atop his double chin, smiling now at Dona Carlota, now at Modesto Pires.

"That boy is supposedly a civil servant, a functionary at the civil registry. Since he has very little to do he spends his day at the bar when he's not at home listening to the noise young people today call music. I doubt very much that he'll show up. I sent someone to sound him out a few days ago about the land and he didn't even answer. I'm not saying he's a bad young fellow, just lackadaisical," remarked the tannery owner.

"All right then, the meeting's called to order," said Dr. Franklin, trying to gain time. "Since you asked for this meeting, Dr. Baltazar, would you please begin by telling us your reasons?"

"Why, certainly. Having given this complex matter considerable thought, I have arrived at the conclusion that an agreement among all the interested parties, that is, all the presumptive heirs and descendants of Manuel Bezerra Antunes, is absolutely essential if we are to settle the matter amicably by putting in a joint claim, without disputes among ourselves."

"That sounds like a very sensible idea," seconded Dr. Galvão, who already knew all about Dr. Moreira's proposal, having talked with him in private the day before. He quoted the argument his colleague had used to persuade him. "After all, why are the heirs, after ignoring the land entirely all these years, only now taking up the cudgels in defense of their own interests to make sure they get their share of the inheritance? Why, because they expect a valuable offer to be made for that land, from none other than Brastânio. That is a matter of public knowledge, is it not?"

Dr. Baltazar Moreira took advantage of the rhetorical question to continue his own remarks. The idea had been his, after all, and here was this young pup just out of law school trying to look clever at his expense, when all he had been asked to do was second the motion.

"Dr. Galvão is right. It's very important that we present a united front to the prospective buyer and that we all be entirely in agreement. If we begin to fight among ourselves the litigation may go on for years, and since Brastânio can't wait that long they'll take their business elsewhere."

"And for that very reason," put in Dr. Marcolino Pitombo, "it's no use our discussing the matter unless all the heirs are present. How do we know this young man's opinion? How can we be sure what he thinks?"

From the office doorway, where he had been silently listening without their noticing his presence, Skipper Dário de Queluz spoke up.

"I can tell you what he thinks right now, gentlemen. Good afternoon, Dr. Franklin. Do you mind if I take part in the debate?"

They all turned around to stare at him. The Skipper was neither a lawyer nor an Antunes. What was he doing there, anyway, and why did he want to take part? Dr. Pitombo knew the Skipper's opinion of Brastânio, knew that he was adamantly opposed to the production of titanium-dioxide in the community and was going around showing people the petition signed by the mayors of Ilhéus and Itabuna and printed in newspapers in the south. What the Skipper didn't know, luckily, was who had drawn up that petition. The lawyer essayed a smile that was cordial, surprised and knowing, all at the same time.

"The pleasure is ours, Skipper. But may I ask you first what brings you here?"

Dr. Franklin, too, smiled faintly. He had drawn up the sales option himself, not wanting to leave such an urgent matter in Bonaparte's hands, nor in his head for that matter. Bonaparte was pretty thick with Dr. Pitombo and had been coming home at all hours of the night, always a bad sign. Skipper Dário de Queluz smiled too.

"Why, as an heir. Fidélio Dórea Antunes de Arroubas Filho

has given me an option on the sale of his part of the palm grove, which has been registered by the notary here." He turned to Dr. Franklin.

"That is correct. The deed was notarized this morning," confirmed the notary.

"And I can tell you now, gentlemen, that for my part I have no intention of selling my rights to the land, nor of entering into an agreement, nor of forming a partnership. Nothing, three times nothing! Now that you are all aware of that fact, if you'll excuse me I'll be getting back to Mangue Seco. Good day, gentlemen."

On his way to pick up Dona Laura and Leonora he stopped at the bar, where the poolroom gang, amid cheers and guffaws, was treated to a blow-by-blow account.

"They must be racking their brains this very minute to find some way of disinheriting Fidélio. But Franklin told me—in fact he told all of us this morning—that of all those who stand to inherit, Fidélio's in the most direct line, he and Canuto Tavares. Isn't that so, Fidélio old chap?"

Even Seixas, despite the disappointment this news was bound to cause the tax collector, laughed as much as the rest. Another who joined in the merriment was Barbozinha, who came in just then with news.

"The paper says the date for the mayoralty elections here is going to be set today."

The Skipper knew that already; Dona Carmosina had shown him a brief paragraph on the editorial page of *A Tarde* to the effect that Brastânio was interested and had put pressure on the Election Tribunal. He took his leave until the beginning of the following week, when he hoped to bring Tieta back with him.

The poet took a seat and ordered a rum cocktail with lemon. His throat was bothering him and there was nothing like rum to clear it out.

"What about the election?" he asked. "What do you all think?"

"You're my candidate," said Osnar.

"For mayor? God forbid! You must be out of your mind."

"No, for sponsor at Peto's male initiation rites on Saturday. And we'd like to ask you to write a poem for the occasion."

Barbozinha's face darkened. Were his friends pulling his leg again over those blasted verses he had written for Brastânio? "No, Sir Poet, none of that! We only want Peto to have the best of everything and give him a day to remember: Zuleika Cinderella, a fabulous supper, music, flowers and some verses to immortalize the happy event." Barbozinha's face cleared at once. That was a new subject, rather risqué but one which might, handled properly, make a sonnet that would be a nice blend of naughtiness and innocence. Yes, he would go right to work on it, but he wanted to collect his royalties in advance.

"Make it another rum, Manu, and charge it to the sonnet."

Final episode of Ascânio Trindade's stay in the capital, or the education of a leader in the cause of progress: the engagement ring.

Dr. Mirko Stefano's suite, which was always kept reserved for him even when he was away for long periods in the south, was no cold, anonymous hotel room in which to spend a few days in impersonal comfort. The stamp of an expansive, civilized man—a bon vivant, as he called himself—was in every cubbyhole and bibelot.

Punctually at nine Ascânio pushed open the half-closed door in time to hear the end of a sentence in Doctor Magnifico's affected voice.

". . . your fault. I told you you'd have to butter him up."

Ascânio saw the worried expression on the face of Brastânio's public-relations director, who was wearing only a black silk robe of Oriental cut that resembled a judo champion's kimono as he sat talking with Rosalvo Lucena before a tray with the remains of coffee, papaya and grapefruit juice. Both serious faces relaxed; both men smiled.

"Sorry I didn't knock. The door was open."

There was a brief moment of indecision, during which Ascânio had time to observe the two Brastânio bigwigs and compare their styles. Rosalvo Lucena, all set for a busy morning at the office, was nattily dressed in the casual elegant executive style his position called for: gray slacks and blue blazer, with a cheerful matching shirt and tie. He didn't have to dress in serious suits like Dr. Bardi; he wasn't a magnate yet. Mirko Stefano, as he lounged comfortably barefoot in his Japanese robe, looked less like a businessman than like one of those mature television actors women go wild over. Two men who counted, in Ascânio's opinion. He liked Mirko but he wanted to be like Rosalvo.

"No, I'm glad you came in. I left the door open on purpose." Mirko pointed to an armchair. He would have to remind the waiter to close the door whenever he went in or out. Service in these new hotels left much to be desired.

Before taking his leave Rosalvo Lucena repeated to Ascânio, who eagerly drank in every word, the arguments he had used to no effect at lunch the day before with the top-ranking state government official. The whole region would benefit if the factory was installed; there would be two-lane highways, a new job market, skilled labor, technical training, a school for the workers' children, medical services, workers' housing, business opportunities, and well-paid jobs for specialists.

And all this would take place in a fallow zone, heretofore the preserve of a privileged few, transforming it into a center vital to the region's economy. He naturally suppressed any reference to the sore point of proximity to the capital city. It would hardly do to discuss this aspect of the question with the representative of far-off Agreste, although it was the main reason his distinguished luncheon companion had refused to budge. ("You'll build there over my dead body!") On the other hand, Rosalvo dwelt on the lack of infrastructure around Mangue Seco and the enormous expense that providing it would entail, an expense which, however, Brastânio would be only too glad to assume out of patriotic duty.

"Patriotic duty, my foot," thought Rosalvo, as he recited his carefully prepared text to Ascânio, all agog with admiration. If the Elderly Parliamentarian's demarches were unsuccessful, which they very well might be despite Dr. Bardi's optimism, they would have no other option but to start from scratch. It was a hell of a prospect. He smiled at Ascânio.

"I was talking about you to a top official in the state government yesterday, someone with plenty of political clout. I told him you were a man to watch."

Knowing that Ascânio was going back that afternoon, Lucena took his leave. "I guess I won't be seeing you again until I go to Agreste. Have a good trip and win that election. Has the date been set, Mirko?" He thought he would get a little of his own back from Mirko.

"Not until next week. The presiding judge dropped dead yesterday. Heart attack. I went to the funeral."

Rosalvo Lucena's polite smile turned into a derisive laugh.

"Each of us has his own cross to bear, old boy."

He waved goodbye from the door, avenged, and banged it shut hard enough to make sure it was really closed and remind Mirko that it had been unwise to leave it open. He enjoyed reminding Mirko that everyone was careless sometimes.

"What will you have to drink?" asked Doctor Magnifico, after he had digested the rebuke.

"Don't go to any trouble, thanks, I've just had breakfast."

"So have I. There's nothing like getting the day off to a good start after breakfast with a drop of Napoleon, *une fine, mon cher,* wait and see."

He picked out a bottle from a collection on top of a table. What the devil is Napoleon, *een feen,* wondered Ascânio, who realized that he had a lot to learn. The round big-bellied glasses enlightened him; they were brandy snifters, of course. He had never imagined, though, that the golden liquid in the bottom should be warmed with the hands, or rather with one hand, since with the other Doctor Magnifico covered the mouth of the glass to keep the aroma from escaping. Ascânio copied the gesture awkwardly. Mirko took his hand away, held the glass to his nostrils, and inhaled the fragrance, *quelle délice!* When Ascânio followed suit, the potent fumes went up his nose and made his head swim. He compounded the *faux pas* by gagging and coughing after downing the contents at a gulp. God, but it was powerful! Delicious, though. Of all the drinks he had been offered in the past few days, including the champagne, he liked the brandy best. Mirko served him again without comment or laughter; he had neither seen nor heard. This time Ascânio savored it in small sips as the master bon vivant had done.

"You know, Ascânio, I'm called upon to deal with a lot of different people in my work, and they're a pretty motley crew. I get along with everyone, that's the way I am and it's my job. Every so often, though, I run across someone who stands out from the crowd by reason of his talent, strength of character, a certain quality, a certain moral fiber. I know men and I seldom make a mistake; I can tell which ones are worth cultivating after only one or two meetings. Your personality impressed me the very first time we talked at the Agreste courthouse. Now there's a real man, I said to myself, *un vrai homme*. At that time we hadn't decided on Agreste; quite the contrary, we had set our sights on the southern part of the state, in an area between Ilhéus and Itabuna on the Cachoeira River, where there's a highway, a seaport, all the facilities, and the local authorities promised us the moon. At that very moment I made my mind up. If we don't go into Agreste, I thought, I'm going to invite that fine young man to come and work with us at Brastânio. He has what it takes."

He inhaled the brandy, savoring the double pleasure to nose and palate. Ascânio thanked him modestly.

"That's mighty nice of you."

"If he stays in this decaying town, I said to myself, his flame will flicker and go out, and we mustn't let that happen. I'm going to invite him to give us the benefit of his talents wherever we decide to go. Now, since the decision has fortunately been in Mangue Seco's favor, I think that being mayor of a wealthy, powerful industrial town might be the first step toward a brilliant political career for a rising young statesman."

What with the brandy fumes and the inspiring words, Ascânio felt he was already on his way. Doctor Magnifico picked up the bottle again; it was hardly the hour for it, but circumstances gave him no choice. Ascânio could choose between a career in either politics or business, for if, after a term as mayor of Agreste, he decided he wanted to go into private business instead, the invitation was still on; there would always be an executive position open to him at Brastânio. The world was full of intelligent, hardworking men, but the born leaders were few and far between.

Thinking that the right moment had arrived, he added invitingly, "For that very reason I want to tell you that I—that we—are at your service. If you need anything, you have only to ask. Don't keep it to yourself and don't be bashful; consider us your friends."

"The confidence you have in me is reward enough. I hope I can live up to it."

"What about the election campaign? Brastânio would be honored to pay your expenses."

"Thanks, but that won't be necessary." At last he had found something to boast about. "There won't be any campaign. I'll be the only candidate, it's in the bag. You see, my godfather, Colonel Artur de Figueiredo, has already said that's the way it's going to be, and everyone agrees. I'm not just bragging when I tell you I'll be unanimously elected. So I won't need any help, thanks all the same. It's better that way anyhow; nobody can say I have personal motives for being in favor of Brastânio. Later on, if things work out and my dream comes true, I may ask for your help. But not now."

That last talk, the longest and most intimate they had had yet, went beyond business and politics and touched on Ascânio's private life.

"You mentioned a dream. I love to dream, what's yours?"

Unused to alcohol and in a slight state of euphoria from the cognac and the esteem and admiration shown by Mirkus the Magnificent, Ascânio took him into his confidence, told him Leonora's name, described her beauty in glowing terms and bemoaned her fortune, which had so far been an insurmountable obstacle to their union. Now, though, things were looking up. Once he was mayor of a prosperous industrial community and the road to success lay open before him, maybe he would find the courage to speak.

Mirko Stefano, also known as Mirkus the Magnificent, was obviously touched. He poured out one more drop of *fine Napoléon* for a toast.

"Ascânio, my dear fellow, besides all your other good qualities you're a man of integrity. Now I want you to promise me something, that the first thing you do when you get home is to ask that girl to marry you. No one proposes to a girl these days; just tell her you two are getting married. Why not have the ceremony the day you take office?" He lifted the round-bellied snifter in which the brandy glowed like a golden coal. "Here's to the future happiness of the bride and groom."

They were still drinking to the bride and groom when the telephone rang. Mirko answered.

"Yes, of course it's still on. I'll have someone take him over there in five minutes."

He hung up and explained to Ascânio, "That was a reporter, a friend of ours, the one who wrote that interview with Dr. Lucena that you liked so much. He'd like to hear what you have to say about Agreste and the prospects Brastânio would open up for the region. If you have no objection, we have none either. It would be a way of beginning to make yourself known."

"Of course I don't mind. It'll be a pleasure."

"Good, then I'll call and have somebody take you over there. Why don't you meet me at the pool when you come back, and we can have lunch together."

As Ascânio was about to leave, Mirko reminded him, "Don't forget to repeat that beautiful expression you used yesterday, 'Brastânio will be the redemption of Agreste.' I envy you that phrase, *mon vieux.*"

In the paper's city room the reporter, who turned out to be the one-eyed individual who had been so hot for information the first day, remarked when he heard the beautiful phrase, "It was Mirko who handed you that pitch for the headline, wasn't it?"

Far from feeling offended, Ascânio was proud.

"No, it's mine, but he said he wished he had thought of it himself."

"You've got to hand it to the old fox, nobody can beat him at his own game. He really had me fooled about that German the other day, me and everybody else, but *A Tarde* got on his tail and broke the news." He shrugged. "Anyway, even if he had given me the straight scoop it wouldn't have done me any good. He would have had a word with the man in there"—he pointed to a door over which a sign said *Editor*—"and they would have hushed the story up. If you've got it, you've got it."

All of this was so much Greek to Ascânio, and he didn't care to be enlightened. A photographer took pictures as they talked. After he had answered two or three questions and managed to work in the famous phrase, the reporter said he had enough.

"That'll be fine, just leave the rest to me. If you'll let me hitch a ride, I'll have a look at the femmes around the pool and soak up some of old Mirko's Scotch."

In the car he asked inquisitively, "Tell me, pal, are the broads who go to that beach of yours worth a gander? Do a lot of dames from São Paulo go there?" His one eye shone lewdly. "Because around here, pal, the lady tourists from São Paulo get off the airplane wagging their tails."

Ascânio felt like belting him a right to the jaw.

"You find tramps and honest women everywhere, as far as I know. The Paulistas I know are decent women."

The journalist took alarm at these fighting words.

"Hey, pal, I didn't mean to insult your folks. I was talking about the kind of dame who comes up north looking for action. Don't get me wrong."

Betty and Doctor Magnifico took him to the railroad station in one of the big black cars after lunch. Ascânio would stay overnight in Esplanada in Canuto Tavares' house, and, God and Jairo's *marineti* willing, before one o'clock the next day he would be with Leonora and would tell her he loved her and wanted to marry her. Betty snuggled tenderly against him as they walked to the bus and gave him her arm. She seemed to have enjoyed the night she had spent with him, although to the best of his recollection most of the initiative had been hers. No matter what Osnar might think, you didn't have to sleep with a Polack to know what a sexy woman was like.

Before giving him a farewell *abrazo*, Mirko Stefano, PR director for the Brazilian Titanium Company, S.A., took from his pocket a little black velvet pouch stamped in gold letters with the name of the Casa Moreira, a famous and expensive firm of jewelers and antique dealers.

"Brastânio takes the liberty of offering the engagement ring for you to put on your sweetheart's finger tomorrow. I hope to have the pleasure of meeting her in a few days when I make another visit to Agreste."

In the bus Ascânio's curiosity overcame him and he undid the cord, opened the little pouch and drew out a tiny casket. Inside was a rosette of diamonds set in an antique gold ring with the letters L and A engraved inside. It was a beautiful and valuable piece of jewelry in the best of taste, worthy to be Leonora's engagement ring.

Of how Brastânio's board of directors is reminded of an old proverb.

In Rosalvo Lucena's office at Brastânio, the leader of the team sent to Mangue Seco was making his report and threatening to quit. This man, known around the office as "Old Unflappable" for his mild disposition and serenity in dealing with the toughest professional problems, not to speak of his wife's violent fits of jealousy, seemed to have turned into a different man overnight. His famous sang-froid was gone, his voice and hands were trembling as he recounted his story.

"At the head of that horde of assassins was a madwoman laying about her with a stick. She was the one who kept an eye on the women in the launch. Mr. Lucena, I swear I thought we were done for. I prepared to die and gave up my soul to God."

"Well, what kind of a crazy broad was she?"

"Oh, she wasn't bad-looking at all, but you should have seen her running down the beach and shouting: 'Get out! Get out of here, you murderers!' The woman, the priest and the bearded guy were together. The priest was just a kid, I doubt he's said his first mass yet. The bearded fellow reminded me of an engineer I know, but I couldn't be sure because he stayed on the beach. He couldn't have been who I thought he was. The rest of them were a ragged, shabby-looking bunch, a gang of criminals."

"How many of them were there?"

"How many? I don't know. At least thirty, counting the kids. They were like people from the Stone Age. They made us stand right by the rail and look out. God, it was awful! It gives me goosebumps to think about it."

One of the secretaries, who had taken a week's leave of absence to get over the shock, confided to Doctor Magnifico beside the swimming pool, "You know, there was one of them, the one who held back Mário José and gave him a shove"—she meant Budião—"who was real cute. It wasn't a bit of use smiling at him, he wanted us out of there. He would have killed us." She shuddered. "And that woman pointing to the sharks with her great big pole. I closed my eyes so I wouldn't see them."

The team leader knew he'd never be the same man again, but in spite of his trauma he wanted to be fair.

"No, they didn't mean to kill us, I finally realized that—only give us a good scare. But they made it plain that if we ever went back there they wouldn't stop at threats. It's my opinion, Mr. Lucena, that nothing can be built out there at all unless you send the police in first. Police, did I say? You'd have to send in the army to clean out that rats' nest and eliminate every last one of that band of desperadoes. They told us they were going to throw us to the sharks. Kátia fainted. She's still in bed and she swears she'll never go swimming in the ocean again."

The other secretary, poor thing, a pretty, quivering bundle of nerves and a whirlwind in bed, couldn't sleep a wink for three nights. Every time she dozed off she saw the sharks leaping up around the launch. The whole thing made such a deep impression on her that she joined the Hare Krishnas.

The team leader ended by saying, "If you intend to ask me to go back to Mangue Seco, Mr. Lucena, I may as well hand in my resignation right now."

Rosalvo Lucena and Mirko Stefano listened to the whole dreadful story, the lamentations and all the awful details, without turning a hair; they had not risen as high as they had in a big company like Brastânio for nothing. These violent reactions did not really surprise them; they were the first but they would certainly not be the last. They asked the victims of the lurid incident to say as little about it as possible. Silence, they warned them, was the best policy. The news leaked out nevertheless and found its way into the press.

A Tarde presented it in a sympathetic light, as a vigorous display of popular wrath against the threatened contamination of Mangue Seco Beach, which, with its beauty and delightful climate, was a patrimony to be guarded at all costs. The story was bylined by no other than Giovanni Guimarães. As if that were not enough, he sent a congratulatory telegram to De Matos Barbosa the poet. In another newspaper, the incident was cited as proof of how far the subversion by foreign agents had extended its dangerous tentacles and how it was actively impeding national progress in the most distant corners of Brazil.

The story also rated a headline and an editorial in the weekly magazine edited by the combative Leonel Vieira and out of which that notoriously venal journalist made a very good living. The editorial referred to the importance of the titanium-dioxide industry but stressed the drawbacks of producing it in Agreste, the least of which was its high chemical content of pollutants. It promised to return to the subject in its next issue with new information straight from Agreste, where a reporter from the wide-awake weekly would soon be on the spot.

But why send a reporter all that way? Mirkus the Magnificent would be glad to tell his friend Leonel Vieira everything he wanted to know about the titanium-dioxide industry and throw in a check, whisky and young ladies besides. He even managed to lay the editor's ideological qualms to rest. As we know, far-leftist principles were valuable coin to the dauntless Vieira in radical-chic circles. He did return to the subject, just as he had promised his readers, and provided them (he hadn't many) with a splendid example of journalistic integrity. When the new information reached him he had the civic courage to stand up in public and confess that he had been wrong in defaming Brastânio, whose establishment in the state of Bahia would make a great contribution to progress, the economic independence of Brazil and the formation of a working proletariat in Bahia.

Mirko Stefano and Rosalvo Lucena—Doctor Magnifico and the Ph.D.—drew up a balance sheet of work accomplished so far. President Angelo Bardi, in repeated telephone calls from São Paulo, informed them that there were roadblocks in Brasília. It was the Bahian authorities who were causing most of the trouble. They had been quite ready to yield when it was a question of Agreste and Mangue Seco, unsung, unchampioned places nobody had ever heard of; but when it came to Arembepe, which was right under their noses and already a bone of contention, they dug in their heels. No one had come to Agreste's defense, so far, except for Giovanni Guimarães, an unknown poet and half a dozen fishermen. In Arembepe it was quite a different story. Nationally known artists and writers, tourists and hippies were taking their places in the trenches; but weighing far more in the balance than all this miscellaneous folklore was the prestige of the development firms that owned vast and valuable subdivisions which were already for sale in the area. With Brastânio spewing out noxious fumes, those high-priced lots would soon be worth exactly nothing and this lucrative business would come to a halt.

Although he still had confidence that the new subsidy placed at the disposal of the Elderly Parliamentarian would have a salutary effect, President Bardi sent an urgent telegram to applaud the precaution agreed on at the last meeting at Mirko's suggestion. It was very important, he said, not only because it diverted the attention of the press and the public but because there was a real possibility that Mangue Seco might be the only option open to them in the end. He therefore recommended that an experienced lawyer be sent to Agreste to study the lay of the land on which, if they were driven to the wall, the factories would be built. Apparently no one knew who the palm grove belonged to, and it was time to clear the matter up, just in case.

Mirko Stefano, who knew his way around Bahia very well, reminded Lucena that there was a professor at the law school, a certain Dr. Hélio Colombo, who might be the very man, less for his title and academic position than for the sagacity he had shown in other cases as muddled as this one. But would Dr. Hélio Colombo, head of a department and senior partner in a prestigious law firm, agree to go all the way to Agreste? Rosalvo was afraid he might send a junior partner instead. Mirko assured him that if the right fee was offered Dr. Colombo would go all the way to Hell and back, let alone Agreste. They would put a car at his disposal, and a secretary too, to make the trip more fun and "take notes." During these informal discussions the two Brastânio directors allowed themselves a certain freedom of expression. Doctor Magnifico actually neglected his snobbish little phrases in several languages and quoted instead, à propos of the incident at Mangue Seco and its repercussions in the press, a good old Brazilian (or rather Portuguese) proverb to the effect that when our neighbor gets a thrashing, our own back gets a rest. While the press was up in arms about Mangue Seco, Arembepe was forgotten.

The two executives and the shaken expert were in unanimous agreement on one point. If they did have to build the plants on Mangue Seco, the first thing that would have to be done was to clean out the rabble that infested it and wipe out that den of smugglers and outlaws. It would have to be a fine-tooth-comb operation from which not a single criminal thug or subversive would escape, beginning with that young priest. "The Church is becoming a hotbed of subversives, Mirko!" Rosalvo Lucena figuratively closed the balance book. "And don't forget the kids. Aprígio told me the young boys were the worst of all, actually stirring up the sharks, and naked besides. Big as life and not a stitch of clothes on. Lombrosian degenerates, Aprígio called them."

Doctor Magnifico smiled a broad and kindly smile. "Don't worry, Rosalvo, old chap. The boys and the sharks won't last long if we go into Mangue Seco. The poison gas will just wash them away."

*In which Ascânio Trindade makes Barbozinha's
poems come to life and embarks on the golden trail
of a comet, an atrociously romantic chapter—
worse than romantic; pallid and speechless.*

The moon was sailing on the other side of the world or lying at the
bottom of the ocean; in the black night the dunes were white bridal
gowns sprinkled with stars reflected from the Mangue Seco sky.
So Barbozinha had written in one of his *Poems from Agreste*, in
memory of a rendezvous with Tieta. "A train of star-white foam,
fine sand for your bridal gown and a wreath of stars, oh wanton
bride, rose shorn of its petals, black, secret moon"—old-fashioned
verses, ideal for recitation at old-time soirées. Leonora had read
them during those troubled days when Ascânio was half-mad with
distress and their dream had threatened to crumble into ruins. To
illustrate this poem Calasans Neto had thrust a black moon into
the gulf of the sea and laid a road of stars along the dunes for
his beloved. A blue sun and a black moon for Leonora's days and
nights.

Pirica's outboard motor could be heard coming up the river.

"Mama, it's him, my heart tells me so." Leonora jumped up and
ran to the door of Inácio's Corral.

She had come out the day before with the Skipper and Dona
Laura in obedience to a message from Mama asking her to come
help put the house in order. Although she was allergic to the smell
of fresh paint, Tieta was in such a hurry she had moved in as soon as
the doors were painted green. She showed each room off proudly.
"It's just a little bitty house but it's cute, isn't it?" Living room, two
bedrooms, a bathroom; it was cozy and had every comfort. There
was even an icebox that ran on kerosene. Money had been no object; Tieta had sent away for the best-quality goods. A few friends
were coming over on Sunday for lunch and a swim. The rites of
death, so severe in Agreste, would not allow a housewarming; it was
too soon since Zé Esteves had been buried and consigned to God's
keeping. God's or the devil's?

Tieta went over to the door and put her arm around Nora's waist.

"Make the most of it this time, Nanny. I'll go over and chew the fat for a while with the Skipper and Dona Laura. If you're as much in love as you say you are, then grab your billy by the horns and wiggle your hindquarters, 'cause it's getting close to time for us to leave. Watch out you don't climb the same dune as Pedro and Marta; they're up there at it right this minute. They don't miss a night."

She left Leonora standing there and vanished in the direction of Liberty Hall, where the Skipper's acetylene ship's lanterns burned brightly. She leaned on the shepherd's staff, which she had kept beside her since the old man died. Ricardo had gone back to Agreste, and she felt deprived. Saturday and Sunday morning belonged to God. After he confessed in the afternoon with Frei Thimóteo at Saco it was total abstention, not so much as a kiss for old time's sake, until he came back on Sunday after mass. That Saturday, though, he had gone earlier than usual, leaving at dawn in Jonas' canoe. He had to be in Agreste in time for Peto's birthday mass and to give him the presents Tieta and Leonora had sent; besides, he had promised to help Father Mariano in some kind of ceremony, Tieta wasn't sure what; religion was not her strong point. Tieta was beginning to chafe at the restrictions of the partnership between herself and Holy Mother Church to share Cardo's time between them. Her possessive desire was at its height and she wanted him with her every minute, knowing what a short time was left her to be with her boy. She had never been so smitten in her life before. This was the passion of an old nannygoat for a kid still smelling of milk. Oh, if St. Anne would only consent to let her monopolize his time for those few days, less than a month, in exchange for some improvement in the cathedral! Trafficking with Heaven was becoming a habit in the Esteves family, as we have already seen. Although her merits could not be compared to Perpétua's, Tieta would have been willing to pay dearly for the right to those last few Saturday nights, those brief hours in which Ricardo fulfilled his obligations as a Levite in the temple.

As Tieta's footsteps died away, Ascânio's approached. Leonora waited, trembling with excitement—"You awaited me, pallid and speechless," Barbozinha the seer had written in his poem to Tieta. Ah, poets knew all that was hidden and revealed! If Ascânio would have her for his servant or his mistress she'd never leave Agreste; Mama would have to go back alone. She knew how to take care of a house even if she was a whore. She was fanatically tidy, could cook fairly well and had taken care of her own clothes since she was a little girl. She had washed and starched Cid Raposeira's things and mended his shirts and trousers. It was time Rafa got some rest; Ascânio had said himself that his old wet-nurse was getting senile and forgetful and snoozed the whole day along. His form appeared among the palm trees, carrying a great long tube.

"Nora!"

"Ascânio, darling!"

The tube rolled on the ground as they exchanged a tight embrace and ardent kiss; no more shy pecks for them. A river of stars rolled in the Milky Way, Barbozinha the seer's stars, lighting the way to the dunes. Leonora gave Ascânio her arm and glanced toward the great white mass of the dunes.

"Let's go for a walk!"

"Let's put this away. I'll show it to you later." He picked up the tube and handed it to Leonora, who took it into the house. They kissed again before starting out for their walk among the stars.

In the *marineti*, hours before, Ascânio had crowed, "It won't be long before this cart track is one of the best roads in Bahia and all of Brazil. A paved two-lane road, practically a highway."

The passengers were impressed and asked for details, which he was glad to provide. The Bahian Engineering Projects Company— "the one that paved Mud Lane, remember?"—was about to turn in a final estimate for Brastânio's OK. Ascânio was returning from the capital with Progress in his black leather briefcase, a stylish and expensive one, and in that long, thick metal tube. The briefcase was a present from Rosalvo Lucena, who had left it with a nice note at the hotel reception desk. It contained all the thorough documentation put together by Doctor Magnifico. In the tube was the precious drawing by Rufo the decorator. Ascânio's voice took on newfound vigor and clarity; every syllable was enunciated distinctly, every word well chosen and correct. They all sensed a change in the energetic young county clerk with the limited sphere of action and the impractical dreams. He had been transformed into a hardheaded, dynamic executive. In the capital, rubbing shoulders with those gifted, greathearted men, he had grown more mature.

Perhaps because the news of the road's being paved was not to

its liking, Jairo's *marineti*, called the Mule of the Mudholes by slan-
derous tongues, broke down in earnest. It was the romantic hour of
twilight when they pulled into Agreste at last. At the door of Perpétua's house Ricardo the seminarian, in his cassock, with a gold
watch on his wrist and a jade ring on his finger, smilingly informed
him that Cousin Leonora was on Mangue Seco. Without even taking
his leave Ascânio ran off to look for a ride.

They walked in silence toward the dunes, hand in hand, laughing companionably at nothing. Studying her face in the shadows,
Ascânio tried to compare her to Pat, Nilsa, Betty. Impossible! Not
only because Leonora was infinitely more beautiful, but above all
because of the vast moral gulf that separated her from those piranhas. Piranhas, that was what the reporter, Ismael Julião, had called
the females gathered around the swimming pool, as if he weren't
engaged to one of them. He was a repulsive individual; Mr. Lucena
was right.

Leonora's face reflected purity, nobility and honorable sentiments. You could tell at a glance that she came from a family of
high principles and gentle breeding. Those other women—what else
could they be, poor things, but what they were, piranhas, not to use
the vulgar word that fit best. At no time during those hectic days
and nights had it occurred to Ascânio that he was betraying Leonora by going to bed with Pat, Nilsa and Betty. In Agreste he went
to Zuleika Cinderella's at least twice a week to discharge his energy
in whichever woman was available. Lying with a harlot was not a
betrayal of the beloved, the chosen wife. Trulls, piranhas, prostitutes were all the same. Love and bed were two different things and
one had nothing to do with the other, just as Leonora had nothing in
common with those wanton women from Bahia, the three he knew
and all the others, including Astrud. Yes, Astrud was no different
from Pat, Nilsa and Betty; she was worse, because she was a hypocrite. Well, Astrud could never fool him now. Ascânio was a lot
smarter now than he had been before and he could tell the difference.

Still smiling, still holding hands, they started the climb up the
tallest dune, their feet sinking into the sand. Leonora tripped over a
palm branch, tottered, fell and tried to stand up. Ascânio picked her
up in his arms. How light she was, winged, sylphlike. Poets were
always right. He carried her up the slope, Leonora snuggling close
to his chest, her face against his, their breaths crossing and mingling.

When he set her on her feet at the top, they kissed before the shadowy, sparkling gulf. Up there on a night of full moonlight she had grazed his cheek with her lips when Ascânio had told her how Astrud had betrayed him. On this moonless night the landscape was even vaster and darker, more dense with mystery. When their lips came apart she reminded him in her clear crystal voice, "The coast of Africa's out there. I hadn't forgotten, it's just that the moon I ordered for tonight didn't come. St. George isn't my pal."

They sat down to gaze at the sea hammering in fury, trying to break down and penetrate the land. For such overwhelming emotion she could only summon a tremulous little laugh. Ascânio was too happy to speak, although he had worked out exactly what he would say and had chosen every word.

"Did everything go well?" Leonora asked.

"Just fine. I'll tell you all about it some other time." He took the plunge.

"Now I want to talk to you about something else, about us."

Leonora interrupted him, suddenly distressed, her eyes infinitely sad as she gazed out over the ocean, the ringing crystal of her voice muted.

"Ascânio, there's something I want to tell you first, something I *have* to tell you."

He quickly covered her mouth with his hand. Anything but that. He knew what Leonora wanted to tell him and he couldn't let her do it. It would be unbearable to hear the story from her lips. If the wound must be reopened again just when it was barely healed, he must be the one to make the sacrifice.

"No, don't tell me, I already know."

"You do? Who told you?"

"Dona Carmosina. Dona Antonieta told her so she'd pass it on to me, to see if I'd give you up."

"You mean she told you everything?" The first tears began to flow.

"Yes, she did. She told me how that no-good fiancé of yours abused your innocence. You remember the time I went off to Rocinha? That was after she told me. But the plan didn't work. I don't care what happened. You're as pure as the Virgin Mary as far as I'm concerned."

The tears ran down Leonora's face as she wept in silence. Ascânio wiped them away with kisses.

"All I ask is that we never talk about this again, not a single word. All right?"

Leonora nodded. She had been about to tell him something else—the truth; but now, after what she had just heard, how could she muster the courage to speak? She burst into sobs, which Ascânio smothered with a kiss.

Where was that distant sound coming from? From the next dune, dimly glimpsed in the shadows? There was nothing to be seen, but the sounds were more and more distinct: soft moanings and fragments of sentences blown on the wind. "Oh, Pedro, honey. . ." Ascânio peered into the darkness.

Leonora smiled a little and seized this excuse to break the vicious circle of misunderstandings. "It's just the engineer and his wife. Mama told me they come up here every night."

"It's enough to make you want to be married," said Ascânio jealously.

"Ascânio, whatever happens, don't ever think I wanted to fool you. I never had another love in my life. Before I met you I didn't know what love was."

When he bent over to kiss her gratefully, Leonora clasped him in her hands and unexpectedly caught him with her legs, pulling him down to lie on top of her. "Take your billygoat by the horns and wiggle your hindquarters," Mama had told her. Ascânio made one attempt to get up; he was afraid of losing control and taking advantage of so much innocence and trust, afraid he would do for love what the deceiver had done out of vile calculation. But she clasped him to her, all along her length. He could feel her breasts, her warm belly, her thighs, and could hardly contain himself. Leonora murmured, "Forgive me for not being what you thought I was. Take me, I'm yours. Or don't you want me any more?" Her tears began to flow again.

"Not want you!"

The sighs coming from the neighboring dune grew more intense. The strong wind abetted them by lifting the hem of Leonora's dress, and she opened herself to him. Facing the coast of Africa, Ascânio took her, and in place of the lost hymen he touched the golden trail of a comet. For the first time in her life Leonora gave herself for sheer love with no admixture of any other sentiment, pure or ignoble. She wept and she laughed. She had been a motherless kid, a little nannygoat whipped and defeated by life. At the end of the world, facing the coast of Africa, she became as totally and happily a woman as any other woman was or ever would be. The blue sun and the black moon were hers.

The moans of love spiraling upward from the two dunes mingled. White sand for a bridal veil and a wreath of stars, wanton bride, rose unfurled. Leonora's strength melted away. On the horizon the blue sun was born while the black moon sank into the depths of the sea. Her tears were dried, her laughter was kindled. "Oh, love, now I can die happy!"

In which the author heaps praise on an unexpected object—and has his own good reasons for doing so, no doubt.

Much has been said about patriotism and patriots in this novel. In this connection, it is high time I made amends for a grave injustice which must be corrected before I usher my readers into the liveliest (and only) bawdy house in Agreste, the one owned and managed with such efficiency and tact by Zuleika Cinderella.

Praise has been heaped, and justly so, on the abnegation of Skipper Dário de Queluz in relinquishing a glorious career aboard a naval vessel out of love for the beauty, climate and tranquillity of Agreste. Laud has been sung to the poems dedicated by the laurel-crowned seer Gregório Eustáquio de Matos Barbosa to his native place, whose landscape so inspired him; note has been taken of the significance of his return to Agreste, worn by illness but bearing with him the priceless patrimony of fame and success, the memory of illustrious friendships, the trophies of his printed volumes. Much has been made of Ascânio Trindade's loyalty to the poor, backward community which he longs to make wealthy and progressive. After his father died he could have gone back to law school and then headed south in search of greener pastures but did not; even the board of directors of Brastânio recognized his abilities. Worthy names and deeds from the past have been recalled.

Yet nothing has been said of the dedication, the unconditional devotion to Sant'Ana do Agreste, of Zuleika Rosa do Carmo, or Cinderella, to whom the township owes so much. Not only did her name not figure on the list of tried and true patriots; her appearances in the voluminous pages of this scandalous novel have been rare and almost in passing. She has been seen in church once, surrounded by her girls, on New Year's Eve, and the four friends drank to her health in the bar (without Astério, because he wasn't there and is happily married); and that's all. This is a great injustice for which I now wish to make amends.

If Cinderella had not stayed in Agreste and turned a deaf ear to the numerous advantageous offers she received, where would *joie de vivre* hide its head in this godforsaken burg? Where would the young men, and those not so young, turn except to the goats? To a handful of filthy streetwalkers, lost women peddling themselves in the darkest, lost corners of the Hollow and in Bitter Alley.

My inclusion of Zuleika's house on the list of cultural centers in Agreste has drawn sharp fire from Fúlvio D'Alambert, as one might expect from such a stickler for literature and morality. I ask you, though, where else can the hillbillies who come in to market from Rocinha's farms and plantations on Saturdays come in contact with city life and pick up a little culture? Where else can they count on finding perfume and charm, music and dancing, flirting and compliments, lively talk, singing, poetry reading, and a genuine tango with all the flourishes, not to speak of the theory and practice of sexuality, a science that is so in vogue in our time?

The days and nights in Agreste, especially the nights, would be a whole lot drearier and lonelier than they are if Zuleika had been tempted by greed or lured by high living to leave in search of fame and fortune, for which she certainly has all the necessary attributes, moral and physical. If she had, daily life in Agreste would not have jogged along as pleasantly as it did for so long and discord would have been sown long before Brastânio appeared on the scene. Zuleika Cinderella truly scatters joy and blessings among the people; it is not going too far to say that she is responsible for the marital harmony in more than one household. If it were not for her hardworking girls, many a husband would have left home by now in search of more enlightened climes.

Zuleika has been turning down inviting propositions for years from madams in Esplanada, Mata de São João, Caldas do Cipó, Dias D'Ávila, Feira de Santana, Jequié, Itabuna, Aracaju and Salvador, all of them tempting, for she was always an alluring, quicksilver girl. She was nicknamed Cinderella because she began life in the kitchen on Tapitanga Fazenda, where Colonel Artur exercised his patriarchal rights before she was fourteen years old. After she was a grown woman with her own establishment she still had many offers to transfer her executive abilities to more advanced and populous centers where she might have made a fortune.

But our Zuleika, like the Skipper, Barbozinha and Ascânio, turned out to be a patriot through and through. She would never hear of leaving Agreste, where she knew she was indispensable as well as loved. Was not the delicate task of initiating boys of good family almost invariably left to her? Conscientious fathers entrusted to Zuleika Cinderella's capable hands the sexual future of their sons and heirs, placing them under her care by one circuitous route or another through relatives and friends, imploring her to look after them and see that they were well and truly initiated into the state of manhood. She did the same thing sometimes for lower-class boys, out of kindness or because she wanted to. She was small in stature, but no one had a bigger heart.

When Osnar was eleven and a cousin took him to her, she had just turned twenty and was already a famous specialist. By the time our story takes place she was a fine-looking woman in her fifties, and if she had ever counted up the boys who had left their virginity with her she could have boasted of a record. Her boisterous, girlish exuberance had given way to a stately serenity, but her freedom from restraint was unchanged and her kindness even greater. She still exulted in the splendid body and irresistible sensuality of her youth; even the marks of smallpox were fading on a face that was always ready for a party.

If there were any justice in the world and if the townspeople of Agreste were not so hidebound, hypocritical and prejudiced, Zuleika and her model establishment would have been declared a public asset long ago. Life, however, is just one injustice after another. I'll leave this truism as it stands, adding one more cliché to all the others piling up in the rambling pages of this penny novel.

Peto's Espousals.

None of them had ever seen him so well-scrubbed, serious and dressed up, but strangely enough nobody pulled his leg or teased him but Seu Manuel.

"Ho there, Peto! Are you going to your first communion? Aren't you a little old for that? Or is this your wedding day?"

Osnar interrupted the well-meaning chaffing of the Portuguese.

"Why Admiral, don't you know today's the Sergeant's birthday? You might offer him a Coke, at least."

"His birthday? Well, well, well, hearty congratulations and many happy returns, my boy. Order anything you like."

Sloppy Peto really did look like another boy. For once, every hair on his head was in place; he had used a whole tin of brilliantine and the peculiar odor rose above the stink of cigarettes and cigars. He had on a watch, "a little remembrance from your loving Aunt Antonieta," and a new shirt that was a real novelty in those parts; stamped on the cloth in red and blue were the names of the great cities of the world, "with best wishes and a kiss from Cousin Leonora." The gifts had been delivered by his brother at the birthday lunch. His shoes were shined and he had on his first long pants; his mother had finally given in on that point. Even when he rooted for his Uncle Astério in a friendly game against Seixas, Peto did so with a little more restraint and no childish squealing.

As Seu Manuel began to light the lamps, when the cathedral bells pealed out the nine fatal strokes and the lights went out, Osnar made a sign and Peto unobtrusively slipped out to wait in the plaza. If anyone noticed, he pretended not to see, and there was no break in the conversation. In case Uncle Astério came looking for him later, Aminthas was to say that he had already gone home.

In a few minutes Osnar joined him in the square and said to buck him up, "It's OK, Sergeant, don't be scared."

"Who's scared? I'm as cool as a cucumber."

Osnar smiled in the darkness. They all said the same thing. He had sworn he wasn't scared either when he had gone with his cousin Epaminondas, God bless him, and all the time his heart was thumping like a fire engine.

Before setting off on their own they saw people coming out of the moviehouse, the only place in town that was lit up until a little after nine; it had its own generator.

"Hmmn, the Father went to the movies today," said Osnar, catching sight of a cassock.

"That ain't the Father, it's Ricardo. He went with Mother. It's a dumb movie all about religion or something. I ain't sorry I missed it."

In order to stick close to Osnar, Peto was skipping a movie for the first time in three years. To judge by the praise heaped on it at lunch by Father Mariano (Peto made a wry face) he wasn't missing anything. To Peto's way of thinking, a movie without either gun-slinging or half-naked women or both was no movie at all. He could see it at the matinee tomorrow anyway.

They took the opposite path out of town, toward Jaqueira, where, discreetly hidden among trees in its own plot of land, stood Zuleika Cinderella's establishment.

Saturday was a special day there, the busiest day of the week. From late afternoon to early evening it was full of farmers who had been to market. They would enter the big room, go upstairs or sit down to wait for the woman of their choice, order a beer or a brandy and count their money over once or twice—sometimes only a few coins tied in one corner of a handkerchief. Some men always went back to the same girl, others liked variety. The rural customers stayed until about seven, never later than seven-thirty. When the movie got out around nine or nine-thirty the young fellows from town began to arrive. Saturday was party day, a night to go to bed late, dance to the victrola, drink up and celebrate. Between seven-thirty and nine-thirty were a couple of empty hours when the girls had supper, rested, or went to the movies.

The room was almost empty when Osnar and Peto came in. Two women were talking at one of the tables; Leleu was whispering at another with a bleached blonde he had a crush on. A young girl was just leaving as they entered the room.

"Good evening, Seu Osnar. You're Peto, ain't you? I've heard about you."

"Where are you off to, Maria Imaculada?" in a reproachful voice.

"I'm just going out for a little while, Seu Osnar. I'll be right back, don't you fret."

In the front room Osnar went over to Neco Suruba, the immemorial white-haired waiter who had started on the job as a youngster.

"Where's Zu?"

One of the women answered for him.

"Dona Zuleika's taking a bath. She won't be long."

She and her companion smiled at Peto and inspected him from

head to foot. They knew that reek of brilliantine. The farmers used the same brand, a cheap, strong one that came in little tins.

"Did you get what I ordered?" Osnar asked.

"Sure did, sir, it's in the icebox," answered Neco. Modesto Pires' and the whorehouse were the only places in town besides the bar to have refrigerators run on kerosene.

As soon as they sat down at the table with the two women, Zuleika Cinderella came into the room and with her a good smell of toilet soap and cologne that softened the powerful brilliantine a little. Her high heels made her look taller than she was. She had straight Indian hair and a curving, voluptuous body; she was wearing a costume ring and bracelet and a loose, low-cut, hydrangea-blue dress with white pockets; everything about her was spanking clean and ready for action. She went straight over to Peto, and her smile was a gift from Heaven.

"Hello, Peto, make yourself at home. Would you like a drink? Congratulations on your birthday. I have a present for you." She winked at him.

As Peto refused the offer of a drink, she held out her hand and nodded invitingly. Osnar and the two women looked on, and Leleu's blonde turned around to watch. Peto stood up, feeling the curiosity all around him. Osnar ordered a beer.

When she had closed the door of her room Zuleika took a lantern that was hanging on the wall and placed it on the night table so that she could see better. Peto stood awkwardly before her, looking down. They were about the same height.

"My goodness, you're a handsome boy! I've seen you in the street I don't know how many times, and thought to myself, 'Now when is that boy coming to see me?'" What gentle ways she had. "I told Osnar, 'You be sure and bring him here to celebrate his birthday.'"

She unbuttoned Peto's brand-new shirt.

"What a lot of names of cities. Paris, Rome. That's where the Pope lives. Was it a birthday present?"

Peto nodded and almost said, "My cousin gave it to me," but caught himself in time. Zuleika slid her hand under the open shirt, stroked his chest and thin ribs, came closer and kissed Peto behind the ear before she kissed him on the mouth. When she took her lips away, Peto tore off his shoes. Zuleika Cinderella helped him out of his shirt and long pants. Peto caught them so they wouldn't fall on the brick floor and get dirty; after all, they were his very first long trousers. Zuleika shook her feet to get rid of her shoes, leaning against Peto as she did so; then let her hand run down his body, opened his shorts, touched his balls and played with them a little.

"What a pretty pigeon!" She took it in her hand and caressed it slowly, at the same time offering her mouth for a kiss.

She turned her back to him.

"Pull down the zipper of my dress, honey."

As the zipper came down her naked body appeared before his eyes. With a shrug of her shoulders the dress was off and Peto could see all of her. Gosh, but she was pretty!

"You think I'm pretty?"

"I sure do."

"Do you want to do it?"

"I sure do."

"Come on then."

She got on the bed and made room for Peto. They were lying down face to face. He reached out his hand awkwardly and touched her breast. It was smaller than his aunt's, bigger than Leonora's, different from both of them, rounder; it looked like a corncake just out of the oven. Zuleika sighed as he touched her; each advance, each timid caress, was ambrosia to her.

"Tell me, is this really the first time?"

"With a woman it is."

"You mean you've been fooling around with another boy?"

"No, just a goat."

"It was Black Flower, wasn't it?"

"Yep, it was her."

That confounded, shameless she-goat. Peto was the third boy lately to tell her about that goat. Black Flower had gotten in ahead of her again.

"Well, it's different with a woman. I'll show you."

She changed her position. Now she was lying on her back with her legs spread. Peto's eyes rested on the furrow of black hair. Zuleika Cinderella's hand sought him.

"Come on, my little he-man, bring that pretty pigeon and take your little wife."

She kissed him tenderly, caressed him gently, made him mount her, lifted her buttocks so that he could embrace her, thrust her tongue in Peto's ear and murmured, "Hmmm, that's nice! You know, I could really fall for you."

She crossed her legs over the boy's back.

"Come on now, put it in me."

Holding him firmly between her thighs, she kissed him on the face and mouth, wriggled her hips and offered him her breast; "Here's a pretty pacifier, made especially for growing pigeons to bite and kiss." She must see to it that he learned to love the taste so that he would be really and truly a man; that was why he had been entrusted to her. At the same time Zuleika, old Cinderella, was drunk with pleasure as she savored every drop of the boy's virginity. Life and eternity could hold no pleasure to compare with this.

"Are you coming? I am."

It was a victory each time the initiate came at the very moment she did, both crying out at once, dying and being born again at the same time.

Wild applause rang out as Peto, a proud and happy boy, left the bedroom and entered the hall. It was a full house; every table was taken. There were the poolroom gang, Seu Barbozinha, Chalita the Arab with a half-grown girl on his knees, and young Sabino, his partner, who went halves with him on Black Flower and whom Zuleika had initiated the week before for her own pleasure, without anyone's paying for it. Osnar had paid for Peto, and royally, too, and the other men had gone in together to pay for the party.

The women came up to him one by one and kissed him on the mouth. The bleached blonde called him sweetypie, another her coconut candy, and the little new one who had gone out and come back called him brother-in-law; each one crazier and prettier than the last. Peto sat down next to Aminthas, reeking of brilliantine and female.

Osnar struggled with the champagne cork—domestic champagne, of course; this is just Zuleika Cinderella's house in Agreste, not Madame Antoinette's Retreat in São Paulo. The poet stuck out his chest, cleared his throat, took a sheet of paper out of his pocket and declaimed, in the ensuing total and respectful silence, a splendid "Sonnet to the Wedding Feast," composed especially for the occasion. Then Neco Suruba brought in the birthday-wedding cake.

Zuleika Cinderella, still floating on a sea of pleasure, demanded a copy of the sonnet, told the girls to put a tango on the victrola, and swung off in her blue dress with Barbozinha, faces pressed together, thighs entwining in those intricate, elaborate steps. Peto, who was already in love and wildly jealous, followed every turn and movement of the dance.

Of how Ricardo the seminarian, putting his vocation to the acid test, flings caution to the winds.

As he put away his alb and stole on Sunday after mass, Father Mariano watched Ricardo as he moved about the sacristy giving orders to Vavá Muriçoca and freely expressing his opinions about the inventory the archdiocese had ordered.

"You didn't take communion today, Ricardo. Why not?"

"I sinned last night, Father, and there was no time to confess. I had an argument with Seu Modesto Pires, and I guess I lost my temper and insulted him."

"You insulted Seu Modesto Pires? *You?*" The incredulous priest shook his head.

His protégé had been transformed by his holidays at Mangue Seco. When he had come back after exams he was still a boy, though physically developed, a smiling and affable youngster with nothing on his mind more serious than fishing and soccer, when he wasn't at his homework or helping out in the cathedral. And now he had suddenly turned into a great strapping youth, still smiling and affable but with a different air somehow. Now he took an interest in serious things; he thrilled with indignation at the idea of a titanium-dioxide plant's being built in Agreste, he boldly argued with Modesto Pires and even dared to criticize him. What bug could have bitten him?

"I told him what I thought about that factory and those who are in favor of it, Father. I committed the sin of anger."

What he told the priest was a lie, of course. He had, it was true, exchanged words with Modesto Pires, but he hadn't gone so far as to insult him. He had admittedly shown him a lack of respect, not so much in the heated conversation in the street as in a more discreet way at the movies. Just thinking about it gave him a pleasurable thrill of gooseflesh. He had committed sins that made communion impossible, but he had committed them the evening and the night before and they were sins of the flesh committed in the steeple, in the darkness of the movie theater, and on the bluffs along the river. The priest sensed that a great change had occurred but could not guess how the rhythm of his pupil's life had altered. Ricardo was caught up in a whirlwind, putting his vocation to the test by walking down a road of light and shadows. Ah, Father, don't ask what bug it was that bit him!

"Have you confessed to Frei Thimóteo? Is he still your spiritual guide?"

"Yes, Father. He's spending the summer at Saco."

"And how is that saintly man? Still ailing?"

"He says that being on the coast has done him good."

"God preserve him, he's a luminary of the Church."

Father Mariano was only repeating what he had heard in Aracaju and Salvador. Everyone praised the friar's virtues and wisdom even if they disagreed with his ideas. Ricardo agreed enthusiastically and seconded the praise, knowing it was deserved. Frei Thimóteo had revealed the existence of problems and realities about which Father Mariano had never said a word, no doubt because he had never thought much about them. The friar had given him a new understanding of the duties of a priest, which were by no means limited to the churchly obligations that Agreste's parish priest carried out so punctiliously. He had brought Ricardo closer to God.

At the seminary the young man had conjured up a terrible, abstract God, detached from life and men, whom one was obliged to serve so as not to suffer the pangs of Hell for all eternity. Frei Thimóteo's God was part of life and understood men's problems. He was a real, familiar being and a lovable one. The words of the prayers had sounded hollow, droningly repeated in the seminary, but now the Franciscan had taught him what they really meant. "Most loving heart of Jesus," for example; as the old monk had said, it meant that God is love and peace. When Ricardo accused himself of being unworthy to go on aspiring to the priesthood because he had sinned, the friar had counseled him, "You still have plenty of time to test your vocation before you decide. If the world is too much with you, choose another walk of life and serve God as a humble Christian. You won't be any the less worthy because you don't wear a cassock and say mass. If your vocation does thrive and you feel it as an inner urge, then keep your cassock, fulfill your destiny and the law of God. But don't ever be afraid; don't run away and hide, and never deny what you are. The heart of God is loving."

Ricardo had spoken to Frei Thimóteo about Pedro the engineer, materialist and atheist, who harangued him about social injustice, the crimes of capitalism and the bourgeoisie, and the need to transform society.

"He serves God too, if he thirsts after justice and wants men to be happy." The old man smiled. "Even those who say they don't believe in God may serve Him if they love men and work for them. Why don't you bring your friend here? I'd like to meet him."

Ricardo lived hours of exaltation at Saco listening to the conversation between the engineer and the friar. Pedro, impulsive, frank and enthusiastic, denied the existence of God and the soul in inflamed speeches. The Franciscan, who had come out of the anxious tumult of the world to meditate in a monastery cell, spoke quietly and used poetic imagery. Yet Ricardo discovered a likeness and a kinship between the two, points of convergence and common objectives, their concern for human beings. He tried to thread a path through all these contradictions and coincidences. He was willing to submit his vocation to all the necessary trials and not refuse to argue or to act. He would decide when it was time, but not before he had cleared up all his doubts.

Sitting beside Jonas on that fearful night of the sharks, he had realized how hard it is to command, especially if the price of duty is cruelty and violence. Jonas was a good-hearted, jolly man, but at the crucial moment the fisherman's face had turned stern and unpitying. Which were the roads that led to joy and justice? When he saw the panic-stricken men and women and the sharks on the surface of the water, when he saw his aunt, Jonas, Daniel, Isaías, Budião, people of whose goodness he had firsthand knowledge, risking death to defend life, Ricardo shook off the bridle and seized the bit in his teeth, determined to gallop his own unfettered way.

Day by day he was eagerly storing up a rich confusion of words, ideas and events in his heart. It had all begun with his aunt's arrival only a month and a half ago. Ricardo had waited at the bus stop for an elderly lady, a grandmother rather than an aunt, the weeping, black-garbed widow for whose health he had prayed, kneeling on kernels of corn to fulfill a vow. And lo and behold, a goddess had stepped off the bus; the spitting image of a saint and a nannygoat with full teats, as dirty-mouthed Osnar had put it, at one and the same time. A saint and a nannygoat; how could that be? Well, it was.

So very much had happened to him between that first night on the dunes with Tieta, when he had gone up to Heaven and gone down to Hell, and the stormy afternoon among the waves and sharks when he had threatened the terrified Brastânio employees and fulfilled his stern duty as a citizen. A tremendous obligation! Then he had seen Maria Imaculada for the first time at the Te Deum mass when the weight of many women's eyes had been on him as he opened the gates of the new year. One link had broken and another had been forged, the first in a chain. So many experiences had come his way in such a short time—the exaltation of life and the terror of death.

There were other experiences that were easier to bear, delightful, in fact! The path of his testing wound among women. His aunt had lit a bonfire in his breast, and now it was spreading to others. How could he ever put it out? Tieta wasn't enough; Maria Imaculada wasn't enough. The live coals flared up whenever Ricardo caught sight of a pair of eyes that were moist with desire or the hint of a smile. And he couldn't, wouldn't, refuse. Why run away, after all that had been vouchsafed to him to see and do?

He had come in from Mangue Seco that morning because of Peto's birthday, thinking all the time that he would have the whole night free for Maria Imaculada. Perpétua had limited the celebrations to a lunch to which she had invited no one but Father Mariano, Elisa, Astério, and Mother Tonha. She complained of Tieta's and Leonora's absence to the Father, but that was just talk. Had they been in Agreste Perpétua would have felt obliged to invite a whole crowd of people, beginning with that hateful Carmosina, and a pretty penny it would have cost her. Things had worked out much better this way. Tieta and Leonora had sent their gifts with Ricardo instead of coming. The rich aunt had given fresh proof of her generosity and love for her nephews; Peto's watch was the subject of encomiums and a little homily from the parish priest.

"A kingly present indeed, Dona Perpétua. Dona Antonieta is openhanded and adores her nephews. Your sons' future is assured. I have no doubt they will be"—he lowered his voice as Elisa and Astério approached—"privileged heirs."

Perpétua's eyes lighted up. "I hope God is listening, Father, may He bless your words." As soon as her sister came back they would have a serious talk about the children's future. Tieta had no heirs in the direct line, and when it came to choosing between nephews and stepchildren, she certainly ought to give preference to those in whose veins her own blood ran, to Esteves blood. That prissy Leonora was the real danger, with her Mama this and Mama that. She was more like a daughter than a stepchild. Perpétua counted on the Lord to help her just the same; He always paid up. They had made a bargain, and the time was drawing near for the Lord to fulfill His part.

When lunch was over and the Father took his leave after a few minutes' chat, Ricardo went out with him. He had not lied when he told Tieta he had an appointment with the Reverend Father. He had promised to help him with the inventory of parish property the archdiocese had requested. The Cardinal was concerned at the outbreak of thefts in the churches and the loss of valuable images and rich religious objects, sometimes abetted, as the murmured accusations had it, by conniving priests and sextons. Father Mariano flushed as he remembered that wormeaten wooden image of St. Anne he had sold, no, traded for a handful of cruzeiros, practically given away to that heathen painter, that pharisee who had pretended to be so pious. For all that he had put every penny of the money back into the cathedral, Father Mariano could not quite get rid of a feeling of guilt.

Back in the sacristy, Father Mariano, who was indifferent to the heat and had drunk deep of Rio Grande wine like a priest worthy of the name, pointed to the chests of drawers and said to Ricardo, "You'll find the vessels there and the antiques in the belfry. Our dear custodians will take out each ornament, one at a time, while you note them down on this sheet of paper. I've already made a list of the other things. Now I'll go home and finish reading my breviary and come back in a little while."

Ricardo knew those breviary readings on the couch; they never lasted more than five minutes. The Father's siesta was another matter entirely; it often lasted until time for the Angelus. As for Vavá Muriçoca the sexton, you could never count on him before Sunday Benediction, if then. Three of the devout helpers were there, rummaging around in the drawers: Dona Milita, Dona Eulina and the latter's niece Cinira, one foot in the old maid's charity barrel and the other in the air, ready to be lifted higher to make it easier. Make what easier? Oh, come now!

While her elders took out the ornaments one by one, Cinira, seeing Ricardo there waiting, asked him with languishing eyes if he didn't want to begin by making a list of the jumble of antiques up in the belfry. She would be very glad to help him. According to the circular from the archdiocese, the antiques were the most precious property of all and should be given careful attention and precedence. "Yes, indeed, Dona Cinira, that's a good idea."

"Just Cinira. I'm not an old lady to be called Dona."

"Let's go then, Cinira."

So they did. She went first, he following her with paper and pencil. High, steep stone steps led to the steeple. Ricardo admired Cinira's strong thighs covered with an exciting bluish fuzz and slowed down to get a better view. In the tiny, stuffy belfry there was hardly room for them to move. When Cinira bent over to pick up something—an old candlestick, a broken statue, a cast-off poorbox—she would bump into Ricardo. They were constantly touching, intentionally or not. At each movement one of them bumped up against the other, and suddenly—how did it happen?— they found themselves embracing, mouth to mouth. Cinira sighed and went limp, and Ricardo held her up. It was she who guided the seminarian's hand to her private parts, then raised one foot and placed it on the poorbox, forming a propitious angle with her leg. Following her custom in Plínio Xavier's grocery store, it was only when she moaned and stifled a cry that she thrust her arm under his cassock to ask a blessing of the Father-Teacher.

They separated in silence and finished making a short list of useless things. On the stairs going down, she held out her lips for a goodbye kiss. That was the beginning of the marathon.

Since he had an hour or so of free time before his date with Maria Imaculada, Ricardo took his mother to the movies. It was very seldom that Perpétua went to the movies, only once in a blue moon when the film was recommended by the Holy Office, like this one, the story of an American nun who had recently been canonized. Father Mariano had praised it emphatically at lunch.

"Be sure not to miss it, Dona Perpétua. It's a most remarkable film, a real lesson in virtue. I saw it in Salvador in the company of Canon Barbosa of Conceiçao da Práia Cathedral."

The theater was already full when they went in. There were

only two empty seats, one to the right of Modesto Pires (the one habitually reserved on Saturdays for Dona Aída), and the other two rows back, to the left of Carol, whose maid acted watchdog at her right. That seat almost always stayed vacant. No self-respecting woman would have taken it, and while the men would have liked to they didn't quite have the nerve to stare down the Moneybags Pires' displeasure and the talk of the town.

Perpétua settled down next to the tannery owner, who courteously stood up to let her by. Ricardo sat down next to Carol, whose distant, indifferent gaze did not flicker. Modesto Pires watched him out of the corner of his eye. A seminarian wasn't really a man, so there wasn't any danger. It was much worse when some stranger from out of town came in and rushed to sit down in the providentially vacant seat next to the glorious mulatto girl. With the worst intentions, of course.

The lights went out and the program began with a newsreel that was several months old. Ricardo felt the toe of a shoe touch his foot. It nudged him again, harder this time, and their two shoes were touching, side by side. Then their legs. He felt a soft pressure, a gentle warmth, tiny fearful movements that were delicious torture. Carol shifted imperceptibly in her seat, her eyes on the screen; their knees were touching. The "Events of the Week" were over, the lights went on, and when Modesto Pires craned his neck around he saw Carol shrinking into the corner of her seat nearest her companion, away from the youth in the cassock. When the movie came on they began again, little by little, slowly, slowly, foot, leg, knee. Halfway through the film Carol let her fan drop, bent over to pick it up, and ever so shyly, ever so boldly, slipped her hand under Ricardo's cassock and stroked his leg, giving him gooseflesh all over. What nameless pleasure, what measureless desire, how novel and exciting! Yet it was almost nothing, a delicate holding back, a subtle, timorous, ever-so-gentle touch. With Cinira it had been violent, almost fierce.

As soon as the film was over, Carol got up, followed out of the theater by her maid, without a single glance right or left, while Modesto Pires walked a block or two with Perpétua and Ricardo. He complained of being all alone in Agreste, far from his family, keeping an eye on that business of the coconut grove that was going to drag on forever, it seemed. All their efforts to come to an agreement had been stymied, thanks to the wiles of Josafá's foxy lawyer and that crazy fool Fidélio, who had given up his rights—and to whom, did they think? To the Skipper, of all people.

"It's ridiculous, Dona Perpétua. There are actually people in this town who are against bringing in a great industry which will make us all rich. And the Skipper's one of them! You'd never know he'd seen as much of the world as he has."

Perpétua raised her eyes to heaven in mute concurrence with her eminent fellow citizen, but Ricardo rashly butted into the conversation.

"Rich? It'll bring pollution, that's what. And misery."

Modesto Pires frowned and raised his voice at such impudence.

"Young man, I advise you not to interfere in matters that are none of your concern."

For two different but equally powerful reasons, Carol and the engineer, Ricardo could not stomach the owner of the tannery just then.

"If they come to pollute Mangue Seco we'll kick them out, you can be sure of that." He did not add that they had already done it, nor how; he had sworn to keep the secret.

"Oh!" Modesto Pires all but fell over with astonishment.

Perpétua could not believe her ears.

"Ricardo, what are you saying? Show respect to Seu Modesto."

"But Aunt—"

"You hush your mouth!"

"These young people today have no idea of proper values, Dona Perpétua. Even seminarians. I never would have thought it." Modesto Pires went off to assuage his ruffled feelings in Carol's bed.

Perpétua began to give Ricardo a tonguelashing, but he cut her short by explaining, with inward laughter, that he had done nothing but repeat his Aunt Antonieta's own words. She was even more worked up about the factory than the Skipper. Perpétua, in a quandary as to which source of wealth to risk offending, decided to stay neutral, but she warned her son not to argue with people to whom respect was due because of their age and their social position. And speaking of his aunt, had Tieta ever mentioned taking him back with her to São Paulo, by the way? His aunt? Why, yes, come to think of it, she had. Ricardo did not enlighten his mother as to when. Naked in bed, fainting in his arms, she had murmured in a swooning voice, "I'm just crazy enough to take you back to São Paulo with me, my own little billygoat!"

Hardly had Perpétua blown out the lamp when Ricardo opened his bedroom window and jumped out. Maria Imaculada was waiting for him next to the mango tree.

"You took so long, honey, I just about gave you up. And tonight I'm in a hurry, too."

"Why are you in a hurry?"

They were expecting her at the house. Dona Zuleika wanted all the girls to be there for a party, which had probably begun already. She laughed slyly.

"A family party, honey. You'd be the first one there if you didn't wear a cassock. I've got to hurry, honey, sure enough."

Ricardo had come from Mangue Seco in happy anticipation of spending the night with Maria Imaculada. He would have a whole night free, without having to go running back to Tieta. He had thought of a daring plan; he would get her to jump through the window into his bedroom and possess her at his leisure in the same wide bed, on the same fluffy lamb's-wool mattress where he took his pleasure with his aunt when they were in Agreste. In the extreme youthfulness of her body, in the reckless behavior of the mischievous, gentle, fearless little girl, he had found that other Tieta, the adolescent goat girl who had run after goats and men on the sandhills and gullies; the girl who was still remembered in Agreste in spite of the respect due to the rich Paulista, the widow of the papal Comendador, with prestige and money to burn. This was the willful, eager goat girl who had defied prejudice to live her life without shackles, without reins, without fear, until she was whipped and driven out of the town.

He had dreamed about the girl all week, seeing in Tieta's present opulence the budding form of Maria Imaculada. Here he had looked forward so much to taking his delight with her until daybreak, and he had come all the way from Mangue Seco only to find that she was busy and had to go back for a party. Party be damned!

He had just time enough to lie down on top of Imaculada under the weeping willow trees, feel her new breasts, her round hips, the curve of her belly, with a heavy heart and no delight, angry at the party and Zuleika's customers, jealous of the man who would take his girl to bed. On that festive Saturday both Perpétua's sons, both Tieta's nephews, learned how bitter jealousy can taste; felt like yelling and biting their knuckles and smashing men's faces and slapping women around.

He took her eagerly and angrily, holding back the tears.

"You're too much for me tonight, honey. You're gonna kill me if you give me any more."

She adjusted her skirt and ran off laughing, flinging back at him, "Tomorrow I can stay with you all night if you want, but not tonight, honey."

Ricardo lost his head and said he would meet her the following night at the same time, when the lights went out, under the mango tree. It was a crazy thing to do because he had promised his aunt he'd go back to Mangue Seco right after mass on Sunday. Tieta was waiting impatiently, and she was the mistress of every minute and every move he made. All he had left were his seminarian's obligations, his commitment to the church. It was a lucky thing for him that the inventory was not quite finished. It was a flimsy excuse but it would have to do.

He sent a note by Dona Carmosina. It wouldn't be fair to leave poor Father Mariano to cope with this emergency all by himself; he'd have to stay and help him with the inventory. It was urgent, the Cardinal had given them a deadline. But he'd be with her first thing on Monday without fail. He signed it, "Your nephew who adores and longs for you, Cardo."

Of a piquant dialogue in Pirica's boat between a lovelorn woman and another even more so.

At the boat basin, Dona Carmosina and Elisa took their seats in Pirica's motorboat. Poor Ricardo, a slave to his churchly duties, had stayed behind to help Father Mariano with the inventory. The other guests would go out later with Astério in Elieser's motor launch: Barbozinha, Osnar, Aminthas, Seixas and Fidélio, noble Fidélio. "What a fine thing that boy has done, Elisa!" Dona Milu would be one of the party too if the baby she was bringing into the world came in time. Astério had risen at the crack of dawn to go out to Vista Alegre. He spent every Sunday morning out there going over the accounts. But where were the others? "Listen, child, the others are still asleep. They're tuckered out after the wild night they've had. That must have been quite a party. And you'll never guess what they were celebrating."

"Oh, tell me about it, Carmô!"

That Carmô! It was only nine o'clock in the morning and she already knew all about the events of the night before and the wicked deeds the bohemian crew had perpetrated at dawn. As the boat pulled away from the wharf and Pirica busied himself with the motor and the rudder, Dona Carmosina described the outrageous goings-on during Peto's initiation party at Zuleika Cinderella's house.

"Peto? But he's just turned thirteen, he's only a child!" Elisa could not believe her ears.

"That's right. Brazilian citizens reach their sexual majority at thirteen, according to Osnar." Dona Carmosina laughed with relish; that Osnar was inimitable, but alas, it was no use her sighing over him. "Aminthas stopped by to tell us the launch would bring them out in time for lunch. He was just coming back from the party, can you imagine, at six-thirty in the morning? He told me all about it. Zuleika's a specialist, you know; she's had first crack at every boy in Agreste." She said this with jealousy and greed.

Elisa had been so glum and out of sorts that Dona Carmosina tried in every way to make her smile and take some interest in what was going on in town. This piquant topic had finally succeeded in riveting the attention of Astério's lovely, melancholy wife, who took advantage of this chance to satisfy her longtime curiosity.

"Astério too?"

"All of 'em, as far as I know."

"Well, Astério isn't that kind. Oh, he sometimes tells me things about the others that he hears down at the bar, but that's all. You can be sure he was never one to go to that sort of place."

"Astério? You mean you didn't know?" Dona Carmosina answered her own question. "How could you, if I never told you and nobody else would have dared? Well, it's time you knew; your husband was a famous playboy."

"A famous playboy? Astério? Oh, Carmô, you don't expect me to swallow that."

"No? Well, you'd better try. He was famous inside that house and out of it, honey. And it wasn't just for quantity, but for quality. You know what his nickname was when he was a bachelor?"

"No, what?" There was a new vivacity in Elisa's face and voice. Curiosity had finally broken through her crust of bitter indifference.

"Now don't get mad! Your little hubby was known as 'Old Maids' Ass Comforter'! Suggestive, isn't it?"

"What?" Elisa didn't know whether to laugh or be shocked. "Comforter? But why? For heaven's sake, Carmô, what on earth do you mean?"

Dona Carmosina scanned her friend's and protégée's face suspiciously with her little eyes. Was it possible that Elisa really was ignorant of Astério's nickname, inclinations and sexual prowess, or was she just playing innocent?

"Don't tell me you don't know your own husband's sexual preferences. You've been married to him more than ten years."

"His preferences? I swear I don't know what you're talking about. If you mean those things people say some men and women do, I can tell you right now he never does them with me. When he does anything at all, it's always the same old thing, the babymaking way. There's a special name for it, isn't there?"

"Mommy and Daddy, the missionary position. Osnar says it's for creeps. That Osnar . . ." She liked to repeat his name, the constant rhyme in her poems.

Elisa's voice took on an aggrieved, querulous note.

"Even so, it's only once in a while when he feels like it."

"Well, if you didn't know before, you know now, child, your husband was famous for . . ." Although they were alone and Pirica was concentrating on the steering, she put her mouth close to Elisa's ear to inform her of Astério's vaunted predilections.

"In the behind? Lord's sake! I never knew that." She was galvanized by the shock of that incredible revelation, like a navigator gone astray who suddenly glimpses a distant, unknown shore. "I never dreamed of such a thing. I just can't believe it."

On nights when they had intercourse her husband's hand would timidly graze her hips at the moment of climax; only now did Elisa understand the significance of that hesitant gesture. Dona Carmosina was tempted to tell her that when their engagement was announced the townfolk had unanimously attributed Astério's passion to Elisa's sumptuous, undulating hindquarters. She refrained from doing so; her aim was to cheer her friend up and help her get over her disappointment, not provide her with fresh reasons for hating Agreste. She returned to a lively description of Peto's party.

"Aminthas told me it was a party to remember. Barbozinha, who ought to have more sense at his age, wrote a sonnet in praise of Zuleika the cradle-snatcher. You've got to hand it to Barbozinha, he's a real poet; he can take any subject and make a poem of it." There was a note of envy in her praise. Dona Carmosina worked hard and lost sleep over every line she wrote, while Barbozinha rhymed bashful boy with pagan joy, virgin shame with prick aflame, the very first time (Peto's) with cunt sublime (Zuleika's), as easy as falling off a log.

Elisa, however, was not to be distracted from her surprise at the revelation of her husband's peculiar fault, or virtue.

"A playboy, and not even normal. Well, you'd never know it from the way he acts at home."

"You're his wife and Astério respects you. That's the way a decent husband acts."

The disdainful moue that expressed Elisa's scorn and rejection of such backwoods habits was enough to convince Carmosina that Astério had never taken Elisa from behind as he most certainly had a hankering to do. The unwritten law engraved inside every man was stronger than desire. Your wife was the mistress of your house and the mother of your children, the one with whom you fulfilled your marital duties with restraint and respect. If it was unbridled pleasure and refinements you craved, you could always find them at Zuleika's house. No wonder Elisa felt frustrated and dreamed of going somewhere else. Customs were different in a civilized place like São Paulo, where the feudal code no longer prevailed. You never could tell; maybe there Astério would learn that a wife is a woman just like any other, that what she wants in bed is male lust, not husbandly respect. And if he didn't learn . . .

Tieta was wise, though; she could divine the most secret intentions, and she was defending the harmony of Elisa's and Astério's home like the good sister and sister-in-law she was. Elisa would just have to resign herself and take what joy she could in the comfortable new house she would move into next day and the security of the Vista Alegre land and flocks. She ought to try to recover her sense of proportion and stop bemoaning her fate. She might follow Carmosina's example, for one.

Carmosina had much weightier reasons than Elisa for feeling lovelorn, frustrated and bitter, for hating men and life. She had not even tasted the limited pleasure vouchsafed by respectful husbands to wives; not even that. She had neither husband not fiancé nor sweetheart nor lover. She was an untouched virgin through and through. She had never heard sweet nothings, never been propositioned. Nobody wanted her, no one had ever beseeched or seduced her. And yet she hadn't given way to despair; she had learned to live with her loneliness and her empty heart. She loved life, she had friends, she knew how to laugh. Elisa came out of her silent pouting.

"What was that nickname again? 'Old Maids' . . .' "

" '. . . Ass Comforter.' The word is that Astério loved the tail off a whole passel of old maids behind the counter of his store. Between the counter and Zuleika's he must have been kept pretty busy consoling everybody he could find."

He had not consoled Carmosina; he had always treated her with deference. Not that he couldn't have; there were plenty of opportunities. Alas, Carmosina, with her meager hips, withered buttocks and bony ass, had never kindled Astério's lust, neither his nor anyone else's. People said Osnar was clever with his tongue, but she only knew about it from hearsay. Despite this unjust treatment, though, she had not lost her relish for life.

She had succeeded in making Elisa laugh, forget her disappointment, take pleasure in their idle conversation and pull herself out of the well she had fallen into. But she, Carmosina, was suddenly overwhelmed with a vast feeling of loneliness as she sat in Pirica's boat, an absence of hope. There was no hope of a man any longer for her. She would go on defending Agreste against pollution, even so, and go on burning the candle over her notebook and dictionary at night in search of new rhymes for desire, love, passion, Osnar.

Wanting to change the subject, she trotted out another exciting topic. "Fidélio has certainly showed his true colors, hasn't he? Thanks to him, those Brastânio bandits and their ilk won't be able to buy the palm grove. He doesn't care about the money; he refused some good offers and deeded his rights to the Skipper. He's a jolly good fellow, and good-looking, too!"

Of crabs paved over with asphalt.

Ricardo had failed her just when she needed his comforting presence most, just when victory tasted of disaster and all seemed lost. Only in the young man's greedy tenderness could Tieta have found consolation for the disappointments of a frustrating day, a Sunday of disillusionment and aborted plans. Brastânio cast an ominous shadow over the housewarming of Inácio's Corral and polluted it.

Zé Esteves's death had already reduced the planned celebration to a genteel gathering, lunch for a few intimate friends, a dip in the ocean and some good talk; but Tieta was still looking forward to a memorable day. After the stormy weather had cleared, the sun came out and beamed on Mangue Seco in all its splendor. Never had the landscape been finer, the air so pure, the peace so utter and complete. During all her years of exile, Tieta had dreamed of owning just enough land on the Mangue Seco dunes to build a cabin for herself to rest in. Felipe's death had only hastened the project. She had come back in her distress to search for her beginnings, for the little goat girl and the hot-blooded, eager adolescent. In less than two months she had walked down all the old roads and byways; had even been able to fight the good fight at the fishermen's side and cross the shark-filled ocean face to face with death. There had been gnashing of teeth, moans of desire, nights in heat astride the dunes. She had not only built her little grass shack, she had built joy and tenderness into it; four hands had plastered mud, sand and caresses together to make the adobe. She wanted the housewarming at Inácio's Corral to be a day of pure and simple joy, with friendship that day and fiery passion that night, as a sign that her journey had been successful, that the little goat girl, beaten and anathematized and driven out of town, had returned in triumph, under a sign of peace.

There was precious little joy, friendship was subjected to severe strains, and she spent the night alone. The only ones who were as happy as they should have been were Leonora and Ascânio.

Leonora had come back in exultation from the dunes and fallen into Tieta's arms, laughing and crying.

"Do you want to see a happy person, Mama? Just look at me. I took your advice . . . and if today were my very last day on earth it wouldn't matter."

"Don't be silly. What is it Barbozinha says? People don't die of love, they live on it. Go back to Agreste with Ascânio and make the most of these last few nights. You'll find some first-class nooks on the riverbank, but be careful you don't get caught. I'm an honest widow woman, don't forget, and you come from a good family. Just make the most of your chance, little one, and store up all the loving you can, so you have something to be homesick for later. You don't know what a good feeling that is. It's exactly what you need."

Leonora was radiant all day Sunday because, when Ascânio took Rufo's drawing out of the metal tube and laid it on the table, she was still asleep and knew nothing of his argument with Tieta.

Ascânio, too, had lain down in a state of bliss in the hammock strung on the porch for Ricardo. As he tried to get to sleep he thought about what had happened on the dunes. The certainty of being loved by the loveliest and most perfect of women made him feel invincible, as if he could conquer the world and lay it at Leonora's feet. He awoke with the sun and ran down to the beach for a swim, laughing to himself. He asked at the village for news of a team of experts who, Mr. Lucena had told him, should have come to Mangue Seco several days ago. There were a good many of them; they couldn't have come and gone unnoticed. Strangely enough he could get no information about them at all. Jonas puffed on his clay pipe and gestured toward the ocean with the stump of his arm.

"The weather warn't fit for a dog to be out in. Nobody come around here. They must have lost their bearings or headed back, one."

"Maybe they're over at Saco."

"Maybe so."

As he walked back he saw Tieta standing in the doorway of her cottage. He was counting on bringing Leonora's stepmother to look more kindly on his matrimonial plans by christening Antonieta Esteves Cantarelli Street one of these days soon; but he could enlist the millionaire widow in Brastânio's cause right now, today, this very minute, by showing her Rufo the decorator's work of art to admire. Living in São Paulo, the widow of an industrialist and a shareholder in more than one factory herself, Dona Antonieta could hardly fail to respond to that "dazzling vision of the future," as he mentally termed the showy colored drawing. The help of Leonora's stepmother was essential to his plans; she would bring the whole town along with her, and Dona Carmosina and the Skipper would be left talking to themselves. As for Barbozinha the seer, who paid any attention to poets, anyway? Tieta's angry reaction was a shock.

"How dare you show me this garbage the very day of my housewarming on Mangue Seco? All those projects and blueprints are good for is to pull the wool over gullible people's eyes." Her gaze swept over the panorama of buildings, chimneys, houses and paved roads. "It's horrible! If you really care anything about Agreste, Ascânio, and I think you do, you'd better wash your hands of this mess and start thanking God for what we've got. It may not look like much but it's a lot."

"Why, ma'am, how can you say a thing like that, when you were the one who got them to put in the electricity?"

"Electricity's one thing, pollution's something else. You're smart enough to figure out for yourself that if that industry could get permission to set up in business anywhere else in Brazil, they wouldn't come all the way out here to this godforsaken place. And if you're counting on me to help you help them do it, you can think again. I'm agin' it."

Ascânio tried to put up an argument, repeating phrases he had heard from Doctor Magnifico and Rosalvo Lucena, but Tieta cut him short.

"You're wasting your breath trying to persuade me. I like you a lot, Ascânio, but I like Agreste a whole lot more, and I love Mangue Seco."

"My way of loving Agreste is different, Dona Antonieta"—his voice rang with the decisive executive accents of Rosalvo Lucena— "I'm a county official; I have a responsibility to the public—"

"Well, you stick to your responsibility and I'll stick to my guns. And keep your pictures and your speeches for Agreste. Today's a special day for me; I don't want any bickering or arguments, I just want everyone to have a good time. You go on and take Leonora for a walk. She hasn't been to Saco yet, she hasn't even seen much of Mangue Seco. Show her everything; make the most of your time before it's too late. Time's getting short, Ascânio." She thought of Ricardo and murmured, "Mighty short."

And so a truce was declared for the last time; but their faces did not clear. Tieta could see the steel and concrete landscape of that drawing in her mind's eye: the factory buildings, the chimneys, the fine houses of the technical and administrative personnel, the not-so-fine houses for the workers, and off by itself near the dunes a luxurious dwelling, reserved, no doubt, for the factory manager. The coconut palms had been replaced by reinforced concrete; the mudflats had disappeared under the asphalt paving of the road to Agreste. The fishing huts were gone, the settlement no longer existed; instead of canoes there were flatboats loaded with vats and containers. The crabs and the fishermen were extinct.

Ascânio rolled up the euphoria and self-satisfaction with which he had initiated his morning sermon on the merits of Brastânio back in the tube, together with the controversial vision of the future. When she had said the time was getting short, had Dona Antonieta been referring to the construction of the factory, with the inevitable changes it would bring to the Mangue Seco landscape, or to her own imminent return with her stepdaughter to São Paulo? Hydroelectric pylons had already reached municipal territory. Dona Antonieta was right; there was a lot to be done and not much time to do it in.

Tieta was fixing breakfast when she heard the sound of Pirica's motorboat. Leaving the guest to his own devices, she ran out to the beach to meet Ricardo, calling as she left, "Leonora's awake now; she'll take care of you."

Carmosina and Elisa got out of the boat. Ricardo hadn't come. Tieta read the message from her "nephew who adores you and misses you," crumpled up the paper and threw it on the sand. She made an effort to join in Carmosina's bubbling high spirits as she spilled out a detailed account of the sensational events of Peto's birthday party and initiation at Zuleika's establishment the day before. At any other time the news would have sparked a leisurely conversation between the two old chums, interspersed with laughter and *doubles entendres*. Today it was all she could do to show a little interest.

"Oh, so they deflowered the young limb of Satan? High time, too. He was always trying to get a peek up our skirts."

What did she care what had happened to Peto? What mattered was the other boy, the one she had initiated on the dunes, her own boy who was in the cathedral sacristy that very minute jotting down a list of images and vestments. Why couldn't he have left the inventory to the priest and the pious old ladies? How could he stay away on Housewarming Day at the Corral, the house the two of them had built, mixing the adobe for the walls with their own hands? Didn't he know that the new bed, with its lamb's-wool mattress, was waiting to be initiated too? Tieta had never thought she would be jealous of temples, altars, ceremonies and prayers. It was too ridiculous! She let Carmosina drag her off to Liberty Hall to find the Skipper.

Dona Laura was seeing about lunch in the kitchen, and Elisa offered to help her. Out on the veranda, Carmosina and the Skipper urged Tieta to return to Agreste immediately to help collect signatures on the petition against the Brastânio project. The Skipper, who had been awake since five o'clock that morning, had seen Ascânio in the fishing village and knew he was inquiring about a crew of Brastânio experts who were due in any day. He had said there were a lot of them. The invasion was about to begin.

"I asked Ascânio as a favor, and now I'm asking you, to try not to talk about the confounded factory today and ruin my party."

"All right, we'll promise not to talk about it if you'll promise to come back to Agreste. We need you there," said the Skipper.

"Give me a few more days in my little grass shack, at least. It cost me enough money and enough trouble to put it up."

"There's not a minute to lose, Tieta. We won't get anywhere at all unless you take the lead. It all depends on you."

"All of what? You all are making me feel like a criminal. Who do you think I am, anyway, and why do you think I can keep the damned factory from coming in?"

"Who are you? You're what Modesto Pires says you are, the new patron saint of Agreste. Under God, the people only trust in you," said Carmosina sententiously.

"Nobody loves Mangue Seco more than I do. I hardly set foot in Agreste all summer when I can stay out here." There was a hint of reproach in the Skipper's voice. "But precisely because I love it so much, I'm willing to stay in town as long as I have to. If anything can be done to prevent this crime it'll have to be done there, not here."

"Who says so, Skipper?" Tieta gazed at her two friends in

silence, then lowered her voice. "If anything worthwhile's been done at all it was here on Mangue Seco. I shouldn't say anything about it, I promised I wouldn't. But you're sure to hear about it sooner or later anyway."

"Hear about what?" Carmosina prodded her impatiently.

"That team of experts Ascânio's been looking for . . ."

They listened dumbfounded to the thrilling adventure. Carmosina put her hand on her heart to stop its wild beating.

"Oh, I feel palpitations. I'm all over gooseflesh."

Skipper Dário, stickler for law and order, merely said, "Please forget you ever told me."

Tieta tried to smile, but her heart wasn't in it. She thought of the drawing on the table and the assurance in Ascânio's voice. "We're definitely going ahead with this, Dona Antonieta." What use was it to go back to Agreste and blather about Brastânio? Tieta knew she had no way on earth of keeping the titanium-dioxide industry away from the palm groves of Mangue Seco. Important issues were argued and decided at a much higher level, and no one else's opinion counted for a hill of beans. How many times had Felipe, by dint of clever maneuvering, wealth and prestige, managed to go over everyone's head, get around the law and ignore the best interests of everyone else, the majority? In the hush of reserved suites at the Lords' Retreat, meetings were held to petition for building permits, approve factory sites, license concessions, every imaginable kind of favor and business deal. Oh, Skipper, what earthly good will it do to grind out news stories, petitions, indignant sonnets, protests from poor devils in Agreste? Not even the sharks in the angry sea, Carmô, not even they can change the fact that it's all up with the crabs and the fishermen, all up with Mangue Seco. All we can do now is make the most of what few precious days are left. She opened her mouth to say all this, then shut it again. Why make her friends unhappy on a red-letter day? That wouldn't do any good either. She promised she would go to Agreste at the earliest possible moment.

Osnar, Aminthas, Seixas and Fidélio disembarked from Elieser's motor launch at lunchtime, dead on their feet. As soon as they had eaten they crawled into the shade of the palm trees and went to sleep. Barbozinha was even more weary; he was no longer up to riotous drinking and dancing all night. He had brought the original manuscript of *Poems of Damnation* to read aloud but he did not even take them out of his pocket; he could see the atmosphere was not propitious.

"Why didn't Ricardo come with you?" demanded Tieta as Astério came up with Elisa. Of all her guests he was the only one in fine fettle and high good humor, having slept well and feeling pleased with life and himself.

"He was over at the church with the Father and the custodians, doing I don't know what, but he looked mighty busy. I went over there to see if Perpétua was coming. She said she wasn't, but to tell you that one of these days she'll come out with Father Mariano to christen the house. Speaking of houses, I wanted to let you know that Elisa and I are moving into the other house tomorrow."

He thought it was better not to wait until all the work on Dona Zulmira's old house was completed. The painting and cleaning up could be done with them in the house to make sure Liberato didn't dawdle. Astério thanked his sister-in-law and benefactress again.

"Wouldn't you like to move into the house yourself?" he asked. "Or would you rather just stay where you are at Perpétua's?"

"Oh, I guess I'll just stay where I am. I'm allergic to fresh paint. I've got an upset stomach just from the smell of the door and window here at the Corral; imagine what it would be like in a big house like that. Anyway, it's not worth the trouble of moving just for those last few days I'll be spending in Agreste. Next time I come I'll stay with you." If she moved out of Perpétua's house, how could she manage to sleep with Ricardo those very last nights?

Downcast and silent, scratching at the sand with a palm stem, Elisa listened apathetically without joining in. Tieta was annoyed at her sister's moody silence.

"What about you, Elisa, don't you have anything to say for yourself? Aren't you happy? What's eating you?"

Elisa flinched.

"Of course I'm happy, Sis. Why shouldn't I be?"

"Well then, why are you wearing that long face like a funeral?"

"Poor Elisa, she's been this way ever since the old man died. She just can't seem to get over it," Astério apologized for her.

Tieta looked from her sister to her brother-in-law. For the second time that Sunday she opened her mouth, then thought better of it and closed it again. She felt sorry for the poor devil, and the truth was usually cruel. It would only hurt him and leave a wound.

What a bloody Sunday. Nothing was turning out right. Her house-warming was more like a wake than a party.

When it was time to go home and the guests were about to embark, Leonora, seeing Tieta standing on the shore with a serious face, let go of Ascânio's arm and ran over to her.

"I'll stay with you, Mama, I don't want to leave you all by yourself."

The reply was withering.

"Why not? Who's gong to bite me?" Her voice softened immediately and she touched the girl's blond hair, wet with salt spray. "Don't be silly, little nanny. You go along and have a good time. Don't you worry about me. Ricardo'll be here in a little while, as soon as he finishes helping the Father. He's all the company I need."

The Skipper and Dona Laura took their leave next.

"Tieta, I'll be waiting for you in Agreste. Come as soon as you can."

The boats cut through the surf on the bar and went off up the river. The women of the fishing settlement, hauling panniers boiling over with crabs, stalked along the edge of the water. A vast night was coming on.

God's rival.

Ricardo's absence hurt her all over, from her toes to the tips of her ringlets, in every last muscle, inside and out. She needed him, and there was nothing to be done.

She had thought she would never again feel such longing, such desire gnawing at her flesh, such pain crushing her chest so that she could hardly breathe. She had felt that way once before many years ago, when Lucas ran away from Agreste without telling her beforehand or leaving a forwarding address. When she turned up for the party in the bed that had belonged to Dona Eufrosina and the late Dr. Fulgêncio, bubbling with high spirits and eager for the soft warmth of the wool mattress, she had found the bedroom window shut on the alley and on her hungry, dazed adolescent passion. Defeated and baffled, she had lingered there peering between the venetian blinds trying to make out the shadow of a man's form; putting her ear to the boards to catch the sound of breathing. How long had she stood there next to the window in the warm night before she dragged herself off, sick at heart, to suffer through her first bout of loneliness, riddled with desire, wanting him so much and he not there? It had never happened again. After that she had always been the one not to show up, to miss a date, to stay away, to shut doors and windows: the doors to her body and the windows to her heart.

White cambric sheet, lamb's-wool mattress ordered from Estância, wide bed frame suitable for wild battles in bed, smell of fresh paint—everything was brand spanking new and ready to be broken in. Tieta was wakeful all during that long, endless night, listening to the wind on the dunes and the crash of the breakers, alone again and lonely, wanting what she couldn't have. Ricardo had forgotten her and traded her in for the esoteric pleasure of prayers, ceremonies and sacristy chores. He was her two-timing lover, and half his heart belonged to God.

She couldn't imagine Ricardo sleeping with another woman. She knew nothing of Maria Imaculada and swallowed whole the scrawled excuse in the note Carmosina had delivered, the tale of the parish inventory. Women prowled around the seminarian, she knew that and had seen it for herself. Dona Edna was so brazen she didn't even try to hide her game, that nymphomaniac, that tenth-rate whore! In affairs of the bedroom, however, Tieta felt that she was on safe ground.

No man, not even the most fickle womanizer, had ever left her for another woman. Lucas had been the only one who had broken with her first. She had left the others, every one of them, as soon as she sensed the first signs of satiety, to avoid the dreary sequence of quarrels, pleas, accusations, lies and unhappiness that went with the end of a romance. At the very first telltale symptom, Tieta would leave without warning so as to preserve the memory of the affair intact and miss him, the more the better. Flames, passions, crushes, hasty or prolonged, romantic or licentious love affairs, every one of them was a passing adventure, but that did not mean that each of them in turn was not the one and only, exclusive, definitive, immortal love.

Ricardo was her one and only love, definitive, immortal; she had never had another love and never would. She needed him imperatively that minute; she must have him immediately! Desire tore at her flesh and her hurt pride. Although it never occurred to her that Ricardo might be in someone else's bed, Tieta felt none the less abandoned and insulted. Empty and needing him, she wore away the longest night of her life, the night on which she should have felt most happy and fulfilled.

When she dropped off at last she had a dreadful nightmare. Under a black sky on a rotting sea, now a cemetery of fish and crabs, floated the ruins of Inácio's Corral and the fishermen's huts. On the farthest line of the horizon she could see Ricardo as a glorious archangel, and she stretched out her arms to him, trying to escape from death. But he flew off indifferently on the trail of God, leaving her doomed to struggle in vain. Where the paradisiacal splendor of Mangue Seco had been, there had sprung up a São Paulo landscape of factories, slums, concrete, iron, steel, smoke and death.

EPILOGUE

🐎 🐎 🐎

Of the Pollution
of the
Terrestrial Paradise
by Titanium Dioxide,
or the
Shepherd's Staff

CONTAINING A DETAILED, ABSORBING AND TOUCHING ACCOUNT
OF THE PAULISTAS' LAST DAYS IN AGRESTE, IN WHICH WE
LEARN OF HUMAN AMBITION AND THIRST FOR POWER AND OF
HOW POWER CORRUPTS, WITH REFERENCES TO THE PRESENT
REIGN OF CORRUPTION; IN WHICH TEARS FLOW AND
LAUGHTER BREAKS OUT, SOME OF IT SARDONIC, AN ABUNDANT
HARVEST OF HORNS IS SOWN AND REAPED, AND THE JOYS
AND SORROWS OF LOVE ARE PROCLAIMED, AND SO WE COME
TO THE END OF OUR STORY AT LAST, WITH THE RIGHT TO
A FANTASTIC JOURNEY IN JAIRO'S MARINETI WITH
MUSIC BY THE RUSSIAN RADIO AS A BONUS.

⤜ ⤜ ⤜

Of an illustrious personage.

The passage of the imposing, perspiring bulk of Dr. Hélio Colombo through the streets of Agreste brought matters to a head. Events thereafter succeeded one another at a dizzying speed, throwing the once peaceful town into confusion and alarm.

The stay of that illustrious personage was notably brief. He was in Agreste for only a few hours, during which only a few citizens made the great legal consultant's acquaintance and learned the motives that brought him to that unlikely place. This in no way detracts from the historic consequences of his journey, for in Dr. Colombo's interview with Ascânio Trindade in the latter's office lies the key to all the subsequent confusion, rashness, violence and despair. Those were tumultuous days; in less than two weeks the people saw so many and such momentous events take place that they might well have thought the end of the world was approaching and the Blessed Possidônio's prophecy come true at last.

The unwonted sound of a car stopping in front of his office brought Dr. Franklin to the door in time to recognize the famous professor and his driver in the arduous task of jointly trying to extract his corpulent frame from the back seat of the car. The notary's eyes opened wide. "Well, God bless the coconut palms!" This time it was no shyster lawyer from Esplanada or Feira de Sant'Ana, no old backwoods attorney from the cacao country who had ventured to brave the precarious roads of the *sertão*. Before the notary's gaze, amid much puffing and panting, rose the vast humanity of Dr. Hélio Colombo, 250 pounds of sagacity and experience. Dr. Franklin, bursting with curiosity, came forward to shake his hand effusively.

"Welcome to Sant'Ana do Agreste, honored teacher! Dr. Franklin Lins, notary public and your humble servant. To what do we owe the honor of your distinguished visit?"

The dean emeritus of the Federal University of Bahia Law

School and senior partner of the largest legal firm in the state took the outstretched hand but left his affable colleague's curiosity unsatisfied. He made no sensational declaration worthy of his fame, no hint of the events that were about to shake the town and county to their roots. Instead he puffed and groaned, "Thank you, my dear colleague. I'm afraid I'll never be the same again after this safari. I have dust in my very soul, and I don't think I'll ever get it out."

He shook out his jacket, yards and yards of the finest English cashmere, wiped his sweat-stained countenance and stared gloomily around. Those scoundrels at Brastânio would pay dearly for this. And that was no vain threat. A legal consultant's fee didn't normally cover this sort of thing. Damn Mirko's eyes anyway, insisting he come out in person to have a look at the problem himself and see what could be done, promising to send along an attractive secretary to enliven the journey and praising the beauty of the place. No attractive young lady had turned up at the appointed time, the place was a dump, and as for "highway"—God! that last stretch of road! . . . He intended to get his own back for every inch of that road, every last pothole, every jounce; and for the missing secretary, the sweat, the dust, the thirst, the extreme discomfort.

After they had shaken hands Dr. Franklin ventured another question.

"If you don't mind my asking, sir, do we owe the honor of your visit to our pleasant climate, or was it some professional matter that brought you to Agreste? But do come in."

"Please tell me first, my dear colleague, whether there is such a thing as cold beer to be had here in this place?" He looked as if he doubted it. "If by some miracle there is, please tell me where to find it. I'm literally dying of thirst."

"At the bar."

"Show me the way."

"Come in and sit down, sir. I'll send out for beer."

He turned to shout for Bonaparte and caught his son behind the door, ears flapping.

"Run to the bar and bring a few bottles of beer. Make sure it's really cold. Instanter! I want you to run down there so fast it'll make your head swim."

The rotund Bonaparte, slow by nature but sensing that a new day was dawning, rose to the occasion nobly. He tore off down the street followed by the driver and came back panting in a jiffy. It was not just that he was an obedient son; he didn't want to miss a detail of the eminent lawyer's visit, seeing him the object of so much bowing and scraping. What professional interest could have brought the famous legal consultant to Agreste but the palm grove to which so many people were heirs, and who else could Dr. Colombo's client be but Brastânio? Bonaparte was a devoted friend and loyal accomplice. Dr. Marcolino had contributed generously toward the young clerk's modest vices: cigarettes, rum fizzes and girls. Now Bonaparte would have a chance to reciprocate.

Of rare and precious things.

While his wife was apologizing for not serving a special lunch worthy of her famous guest, Dr. Franklin tried to probe a little.

"For you, sir, there are obviously no difficult problems. But this affair of the palm grove is the devil of a tangle, isn't it? If it weren't for Fidélio's stubbornness, or rather the Skipper's . . . Do you see any way out of it, sir?"

Dr. Hélio Colombo suspended his fork full of food in the air.

"My dear lady, if your family eats this royally every day, what would one of your special lunches be like? Why, ma'am, this is a veritable feast."

That was the only pleasant memory of his journey the great lawyer retained: that abundant table and the exquisitely cooked meal. The juicy clams, the bouillabaisse, the crab stew, the roast kid! By the time dessert came, the great man's irascible temper had mellowed into the kindliest feelings toward the couple and their lumpish, inarticulate son. The boy had the face of a nincompoop, but he might not be as doltish as he looked. Sincere in his praise of the food and his thanks to the lady of the house, he picked his words carefully when he addressed his indiscreet host.

"The problem . . . hmmm . . . I'm beginning to form an opinion, but it's too early yet to say for sure. I want to mull over a few things before I make up my mind."

Dr. Franklin wasn't fooled. The lawyer had picked his brains, asked him for a blow-by-blow account of the case, riddled him with questions, pored over the old books and examined the newly drawn-up deeds, leaving not one loose end. He had shaken his great head and asked Bonaparte to draw up certificates to take with him. At last he had smiled shrewdly, and then Dr. Franklin was sure that the Master had found the solution. For there was a solution that would cut the knot of the impasse and benefit Brastânio, and if a humble backwoods notary like himself had discovered it, how could it escape the experienced eye of the great lawyer? His guest's reserve seemed only natural. Why should he lay his hand out on the table and reveal his trump cards?

Dr. Colombo sighed with pleasure as he tasted the first spoonful of ambrosia. Incomparable! Before the delicious taste had worn off he took over the questioning, seeking information on Agreste's leading citizens.

"This candidate for mayor, what sort of fellow is he?"

"An honest young man."

A shadow of doubt flickered in Dr. Colombo's eyes and disappeared.

"I mean the young fellow who's Brastânio's candidate, name of . . ." He fished a piece of paper out of his pocket and read what he had written. "Ascânio Trindade. He went to Salvador not long ago."

"He's the one. I didn't know he was Brastânio's candidate."

"In a manner of speaking he is. I call him that because this young man has shown himself to be a farsighted administrator and has come out publicly in favor of Brastânio's moving into the community. It's only natural that Brastânio should take a favorable view of his candidacy. That's all I meant."

The convincing explanation did not set Dr. Franklin's mind at rest. He was more and more worried lately; he had been hearing surprising things about Ascânio. People said he had changed after his visit to the capital, that he was talking tough and boasting and bossing people around. Dr. Marcolino Pitombo had insinuated that he was a fortune hunter. As far as Dr. Franklin could ascertain, Ascânio really had set his cap for that wealthy girl from São Paulo, Dona Antonieta Cantarelli's stepdaughter. How much truth was there in all this gossip? Talking about other people's business had always been the chief amusement of the town, but now, with all this hot debate over the titanium industry, the gossip had taken on an ugly cast. The stories were no longer gently funny or spicy, but cynical and pitiless. Maybe Ascânio hadn't changed. Maybe he was still the straight, honest young man he had always been, carried away by the possibility of great progress for the community if the factory was built. Having been a friend of Ascânio's father, the late Leovigildo, the notary knew the boy was an enthusiast and a hard worker. When Colonel Artur da Tapitanga had put forward his name for mayor to fill the vacancy left by Dr. Mauritônio Dantas' death, Dr. Franklin had applauded his choice, along with everyone else in town. Now suddenly Ascânio was Brastânio's candidate and Professor Colombo seemed to have valid reasons for casting doubt on his honesty.

Accepting another generous helping of ambrosia, the illustrious professor inquired, "As I understand it, this boy is certain to be elected, isn't he? There's no one else in the running, am I correct?"

"Ascânio's the only one so far. If you want to be technical about it there is no candidate yet because the election date hasn't been set."

"You're mistaken, my friend. An election date has been set. It was decided at yesterday's meeting of the Election Tribunal."

Gooseflesh ran down Dr. Franklin's spine. He had read a reference to Brastânio's interest in the mayoralty election in Agreste in a Salvador paper, which implied that Brastânio was putting pressure on the Election Tribunal to set the date. In the old days no one ever bothered about elections in that lost little township, the immemorial preserve of Colonel Artur da Tapitanga. Now another political force was rearing its head, so powerful that it could hire Professor Hélio Colombo himself, invincible in court and apparently invincible at table, and bring him to Agreste.

Bonaparte, who knew when he was beaten, withdrew from the competition and crossed his knife and fork. The distinguished professor was a worthy adversary; dauntless, he attacked the strawberry guava paste, "a sweetmeat as rare and seldom met with these days as an honorable man, my dear notary."

Of Agreste's reputation.

Rufo's colorful drawing hung in a place of honor at the entrance to the courthouse, where the "dazzling vision of the future" attracted many curiosity seekers who shook their heads in admiration at the decorator's artistic talent but differed as to its content. "Wonderful!" exclaimed some enthusiastically: Ascânio was a first-rate mayor who was going to pull Agreste up by its bootstraps and transform the whole community. Other, cooler heads repeated the Skipper's and Dona Carmosina's arguments. If that industry was such a great boon to humanity, why should it come into an area that was so poor and far away and so lacking in resources? It was said to rot the water and poison the air. It was in the papers. The rest of the world didn't want it. It had been banned in São Paulo and Rio. They had tried to build one of those plants between Ilhéus and Itabuna and the people had risen up in arms. Either Ascânio's being hoodwinked, or . . .

Or what? Ascânio was a right-thinking man, his life was an open book, he was an honest citizen, above suspicion or any hint of wrongdoing—

Whoa there! Nobody's hinting anything, but it's public knowledge that he has his eye on that rich girl from São Paulo, the Comendador's heiress and Dona Antonieta's stepdaughter. What penniless suitor to the hand of an heiress, practically a beggar in this case, could help losing his head around those big corporations where money flowed like water? It would certainly do Ascânio no harm if the factory were built in the township. Who could deny the evidence?

The arguments grew more bitter. The readers of newspapers from Salvador, heretofore limited to the privileged subscribers to *A Tarde*, increased in number. Chalita, always looking for ways to diversify his sources of income, ordered several copies of each of the various daily papers from the capital. If the owner of the movie theater had formed any judgment of his own on the titanium affair he was not advertising the fact; he simply offered for sale all arguments pro and con and pocketed the meager profits. The Brastânio polemic, fed on news and rumors and malicious gossip, spread like the proverbial wildfire.

Ascânio's grandiloquent interview was read and remarked upon. "Brastânio will be the redemption of Agreste; wealth and progress for the north coastal region of the state." The girls admired his two-column photograph with admonishing uplifted finger, the very picture of a young political leader with a bright future before him, the people's candidate for mayor, as the reporter said. The brief but starchy editorial which constituted *A Tarde*'s retort to those statements caused an equal sensation. Under a headline reading "The people's choice, or Brastânio's?" it labeled Ascânio a "playboy bumpkin, Brastânio's guest at a luxury hotel." As for the wealth and progress announced by this "droll and lightminded person," what they amounted to was pollution and misery, according to the responsible opinion of the Sergipe intellectuals who had signed a petition in support of the telegram sent by the mayor of Estância. These included such well-known figures as the painter Jenner Augusto, the writer Mário Cabral, Professor José Calasans and the journalist Junot Silveira.

Shock and incredulity greeted the confused accounts of threats made on the lives of a team of Brastânio experts who had been prevented from landing at Mangue Seco. By the indignant population united in defense of their environment, applauded Giovanni Guimarães. By foreign agents in the hire of godless Communism under the command of a Russian woman, none other than the notorious Bolshevik Alexandra Kolontai, whose presence in Brazil had been revealed by informed sources, according to the paper in which Ascânio's interview had appeared.

This ample coverage reached a climax when the date set for the election was made public. Why is this election being held so soon? asked A Tarde's commentator, and supplied the answer: because Brastânio's in a hurry. Whatever the differences of opinion regarding titanium dioxide, the townspeople were all proudly in agreement on one thing: never before had Agreste been showered with so much attention from the press. Doctor Magnifico's vanity was no less touched. Angelo Bardi made a telephone call from São Paulo to congratulate him.

Of unwonted and troublesome scruples of conscience.

As he listened to Professor Colombo, Ascânio was assailed by the very same sensation he had felt in Bahia the week before, a vague feeling of discomfort, as if he were not walking on his own two feet but were being led and confronted with accomplished facts when it was too late to do anything about them; as if he had to carry out decisions made by others behind his back. Yet his natural urge to resist, to demand an explanation and not to let himself be led around by the nose, to stop and figure out the whys and wherefores of what was happening to him, remained unexpressed. He felt ill at ease, but he listened and kept quiet.

Brastânio's power was made evident once more when the eminent Professor Hélio Colombo was ushered into his office at the courthouse. Ascânio had not taken any of Professor Colombo's courses, but he, like all his classmates, had dreamed of clerking in his law office after graduation. Here was the Master in person, restored by a hearty lunch and a good nap, describing and then solving the palm-grove dilemma that had caused Ascânio so many headaches. After he had divulged the good tidings he bore of the election date having been set, and even before the young man had finished saying how much he admired him, the eminent lawyer started to clarify the muddle caused by Fidélio and dictate Ascânio's future course.

Metal tube and leather briefcase in hand, an engagement ring in his pocket and his chest puffed out with ambition and requited love, Ascânio had sprung exultantly down from Jairo's *marineti*. The Brazilian Titanium Company's decision to choose Sant'Ana do Agreste as the site for its factories had already changed the township and with it the prospects of its future mayor. He had counted on winning over Leonora's stepmother by means of Lucena's arguments and Rufo's fairy-tale drawing. All the other side would be left with were the Skipper's speeches, Dona Carmosina's expletives and Barbozinha's poems, most of which were still unpublished—much sound and fury, signifying nothing.

His euphoria had been short-lived. Tieta's indignant negative reaction was a nasty blow. After that he had found plenty of reasons for apprehension and vexation: obstacles, injustices, doubts and rankling wounds.

Down at the post office, Dona Carmosina had flung the option granted the Skipper by Fidélio in his face, getting her own back for the "See, Miss Smartypants?" with which he had taken his leave of her when he drove off in the jeep. Now she taunted him in turn.

"I'll be interested to see how your friends are going to build that factory in the grove after this. It's lucky there're still a few honest people in the world."

Ascânio made no reply but left Dona Carmosina talking to

herself. He wanted to avoid an argument that might lead to a break with the old friend who was getting harder and harder to talk to these days. What she told him, however, proved to be more than idle words. He could not answer the postmistress' question as to when Brastânio would be able to build in the palm grove. Questions of land ownership tended to drag on interminably in the courts, and this one was just beginning; the judge in Esplanada had not even moved to grant a title of possession claimed by Dr. Marcolino on behalf of Jarde and Josafá Antunes.

Dr. Hélio Colombo pooh-poohed this obstacle and informed Ascânio that he could have found a perfectly good solution without having to make that frightful journey whose only redeeming feature had been the notary's magnificent lunch, over which he was still licking his chops. Bonaparte snored away the torpid afternoon in the office with them, huddled on a bench. By his side were the certificates and a can of strawberry guavas in syrup, a present for the Master. Dr. Colombo eyed the sleepyhead indulgently. Let the boy have his rest; he had given up his nap to write out the certificates in time. He was a lunkhead but a nice one.

"Be sure you keep absolutely mum about this talk of ours," he warned Ascânio. "Mirko told me I could place full confidence in you."

There was a perfect solution to their problem and a very neat one. As soon as Ascânio was elected mayor he could expropriate all the land around the palm grove under the right of eminent domain. Where would he get the money to reimburse the owners? Why, the expropriated land would be sold to Brastânio, of course. There would be enough of a profit on the deal to pay the owners and have money left over for the county coffers. And it would all be perfectly legal.

"What if the heirs refuse?"

"How can they refuse? They aren't even recognized as heirs. By expropriating the land at a reasonable price you're making them a gift."

"What about the Skipper? He won't make a deal at any price."

"There's not a thing he can do about it if it's a case of eminent domain. He can take it to court afterward if he wants to, but he'll be wasting his time and his money. Don't worry about him, just go ahead. I'll take care of everything. Right after you take office I'll send someone from my office, one of my own clerks, with the expropriation decree all drawn up with all the whys and wherefores. All you have to do is sign it."

All you have to do is sign it. What a strange, uncomfortable feeling that gave him. He put his hand in his pocket and touched the little box with the engagement ring inside. When would he put it on Leonora's finger? There wasn't much time. What else could he do now but just plow ahead? Besides, by conniving to bring Brastânio to Mangue Seco he was only furthering the interests of the community and the public. When he stopped to think about it, he didn't see why his conscience should bother him at all.

A sample of the mortifications of a would-be leader and husband, or character under stress.

He was young, healthy, virile and in love. No, the phrase is too tame; he was madly in love and he knew that his love was returned, knew it beyond the shadow of a doubt. He had had indisputable, heavenly proof of it, the greatest proof of all; his beloved had opened her legs and given herself to him, asking for nothing in return. Since he was poor and she was rich he had never dared to speak of marriage; he had neither proposed nor promised anything. Leonora's gesture on the dunes was a proof of infinite love.

How to explain, then, that the hero of our story, this gallant and virile young man in the pink of condition, whose splendid good health and sexual potency had been so recently put to the test on the fat of the land in Bahia, not only did not take advantage of the situation but actually tried to avoid, or at least postpone, another blissful night of love with Leonora? Didn't he have at his disposal the most desirable and heretofore unattainable of women, the one he wanted to spend his life with and who loved him equally ardently? Where was such a flagrant, absurd contradiction ever before seen? What reason could there be for such lunacy? Can such a benighted idiot exist in this world, even in a back end of nowhere like Agreste?

When they disembarked on Sunday, Ascânio walked Leonora to Perpétua's door. Taking her hands in his, his voice and looks overflowing with tenderness, he said, "I'm going home now, so I'll say goodbye for today. You get some rest. You must be tired; you hardly got any sleep at all. I'll stop by tomorrow on my way to the courthouse to say hello, if I may."

Ascânio certainly might—anything he wanted; she only wished that what he wanted was to take her down to one of the coves along the river that night. She wasn't really as tired as all that, and even if she were, where could she happily rest with no trace of sadness except in his arms? She said nothing, however, feeling intimidated, hoping that Ascânio would be bold enough to take the initiative. Make the most of him, nanny; build up your stock of memories, time's getting short, Mama had warned her. That Sunday night, veiled in prejudice and scruples, would be wasted.

He came nearer to kiss her goodnight. Leonora clasped her arms around his neck, her bosom swelling. Their bodies clung together, their thighs met, they were flooded with warmth from the long, desperate, heartfelt kiss of lips, tongues and teeth. Ascânio freed himself and fled up the street under the dim light of the old street lamps.

Instead of taking him home his steps led him to Zuleika Cinderella's, where a smiling Maria Imaculada welcomed him.

"Seu Ascânio! I've been waiting for you so long. . . . I'm glad you came."

Taking the pretty, sprightly girl did not relieve Ascânio, only proved to him that it was Leonora alone who could fully satisfy him and make him invincible, the master of the world.

In order to deserve her again he would have to wait. Leonora's gesture, a proof of infinite love, was equally a proof of boundless trust. She was so pure and innocent that not even her painful earlier experience had made her doubt the sentiments and character of her present suitor; she had placed herself in his hands because she thought they were clean and honest. The enamored youth was consumed with desire, but he controlled himself; his behavior must be worthy of Leonora's trust.

He kept the engagement ring in his pocket. As soon as Dona Antonieta came back to Agreste he would seek her out for a frank talk and they would have it out. "I love your stepdaughter," he would tell her, "and I want her for my wife. I'm poor but I've learned to be ambitious. Believe in me, I'll be somebody someday." Once he was accepted as Leonora's fiancé, with the ring on her finger and the wedding date set, well, then maybe. . . . Any sooner, and he would be vilely taking advantage of her.

Dona Antonieta had refused him her support in his campaign for Brastânio. How would she react to a proposal of marriage? She seemed to view their love affair with indulgence, perhaps because she thought it was just a summer flirtation. There was a wide gulf between flirtation and marriage. What would he do if the omnipotent stepmother said no?

Ascânio violently rejected the very thought of never again holding Leonora's warm, vibrant body in his arms. Now that he had touched and known it, he could no longer live without possessing it. But he would have to wait. It wasn't easy to be a man and try to do the right thing.

Of happy days.

The days that followed the frustrated Sunday housewarming of Inácio's Corral and the painful night when Ricardo had abandoned her for God were the happiest of Tieta's holiday and among the happiest of her life.

When she had planned her return to Mangue Seco she had dreamed of recovering the beauty and peace she remembered. She had had the incredible luck to be granted a burning passion to boot, of a kind new to her broad experience of love. For once she was not the spoiled nannygoat waiting to be courted and won and finally submitting to the powerful call of the all-conquering male. Now suddenly she was snatched back to the scene of her early youth, a she-goat with swollen teats, brimming over with irrepressible desire, and she had seduced and conquered a kid who was barely weaned, thrown him down on the dunes and raped him. Transcending the beauty and peace she had found were the boy's timidity and lust. As if that were not lunacy enough, he was her nephew and a seminarian besides. What a crazy, ridiculous, incomparable adventure it was to dispute each precious minute with God.

Those days of fulfillment, of passion decanted into one immortal love alone, when her very existence was unthinkable without the presence of the beloved, would have been perfect had they not been coming to an end. She was tempted to take Ricardo with her to

São Paulo, but she knew that she could not and should not. Sooner or later the spell would be broken and the shadow of satiety and tedium would chill their desire. For that very reason she could not bear to waste a single moment of their unparalleled good fortune as long as their love was immense and seemed eternal. Trips to Agreste were forbidden, the altar boy's duties suspended, the Levite's obligations in the temple annulled. The seminarian shed his cassock and went around practically nude in brief trunks.

Tieta had no intention of keeping the promise she had made to Dona Carmosina and the Skipper; she intended to stay on Mangue Seco right up until the day the power line came in, and the day that was celebrated would be the day before they left. She would say her goodbyes at the ceremony. So long folks, until we meet again, I'll miss you all, it's been more wonderful than I can say.

She saw no reason to be a martyr. There was nothing she could do to stop the factory from being built, and her presence in Agreste would only be a futile waste of time and effort. So she lived her gay and carefree days to the full, chatting with Pedro and Marta or Jonas and the fishermen; moaning and laughing in Ricardo's arms atop the dunes, by the edge of the water, in the hammock, in the bed, on the sand, in the whitecaps, in the shell of the canoe, at night, at early dawn, at dusk, at daybreak. The crescent moon stabbed the dunes and shone in through the window of the Corral.

She wanted nothing but to stay there forever, grow old there and wait for death, with no worries or commitments. Why did she have to leave Paradise? Because she had to get back to São Paulo, resume command at the Retreat, make money and invest it well. Besides, before very long Mangue Seco would be only a sad and rotting landscape of concrete, smoke and debris. Better not think about that but just enjoy it while peace and beauty and love were all around her.

The days of plenitude began on Monday morning when Ricardo finally came back. Tieta was ready for him.

"If what you wanted was to ruin my party, you did it. Why did you bother to come at all?"

"But Aunt, you told me there wouldn't be a party."

"Since when am I Aunt again? Are we surrounded by people, or what?"

"I'm sorry, but I never saw you so mad. Father Mariano kept me because of the inventory. The Cardinal—"

"The Cardinal can go to hell for all I care, along with the priest and all his ilk. What time did you finish the damned inventory?"

"Right at vespers."

"Well, why didn't you come on then?"

"It was dark by the time vespers were over, and it just didn't occur to me"—what didn't occur to him was a good excuse—"so I said the rosary with Mother, and after that I went to bed. And I dreamed"—he lifted his eyes to Tieta—"I dreamed of you all night. And what dreams!"

Precisely because he hadn't given her an excuse, Tieta believed him.

"If you ever do that to me again, I'll show you what's what! From now on you're not going anywhere, to say mass or anything else. No more God for you until I leave." Her voice became gentle. "Did you really dream about me?"

"Yes I did. I dreamed you were a young girl again, younger than I am, before you went away. Just the way you said you were, just exactly, a cute little tomboy." Well, it was true, wasn't it? All Maria Imaculada lacked was a shepherd's staff.

"All right, little billy, you come and tell me all about it."

In which the fair Leonora Cantarelli finally
makes the acquaintance of the nooks
along the riverbank.

Leonora understood Ascânio's feelings, in a way. In her hard life she had never known a man like him and she was afraid of hurting him, disillusioning him, losing him. She felt intimidated and lacked the courage to fight for the little time she had left.

First the boy had thought she was a virgin, the chaste girl of good family and delicate breeding, a wealthy heiress waiting for a match in keeping with her social standing. Then Mama had made up that story of a fiancé who turned out to be a heel and was unmasked before he could get his hands on her millions, but not before he had had his way with her. She had thought that would turn Ascânio's bashfulness to boldness by putting in his way a modern girl from São Paulo with no provincial prejudices and no more maidenhead to lose. That should have been enough to transform this dismal, platonic, backwoods love affair into a flaming, lyrical passion, a grand way to spend the summer. Mama had brought her on this trip to cure her chest and her heart. "Up there in the *sertão* you'll breathe fresh air and learn what a pleasure a romantic love affair can be, the kind you long for and remember all your life. Do you know what it's like listening to poetry while you hump? Well, little nanny, in Agreste you'll find out." Pure air for lungs weakened by big-city pollution, sentimental feelings for a heart scarred with violence. "And you can stock up on nostalgia for the lonely days to come."

Mama's plot had been only partly successful. Ascânio still went on thinking of her as a naive young girl of good family, all the more worthy of protection and respect because she had suffered and been betrayed. Yes, my love, I have been betrayed, and I've suffered more than you can ever know. But oh, I'm not an innocent girl from a good family who deserves your respect. The secret was not hers and she could not open her mouth and say, "Why don't you hurry up and take me to bed? I ask nothing from you in exchange, I deserve nothing; I'm only a hustler, a whore. A nobody. Besides all the johns—they don't even count—I've had other men before you, but not until here and now in Agreste have I known what love ought to be like. I love you, I want to be yours and I want you to be mine, for a day or an hour!

She couldn't tell him the truth, but nothing prevented her from holding out her arms to him and begging him to take her down to the riverbank and throw her down in the darkness, in the shade of the willows. Grab your billygoat by the horns, Mama had told her. Leonora had followed her advice on the dunes, and it had turned out well.

They trod the old familiar lovers' path around Cathedral Square, exchanging tender looks, swift squeezes of the hand and fleeting kisses; seeing time go by and Ascânio hanging back and another precious night about to be irrevocably lost, Leonora conquered her fear, swallowed her inhibitions, and said firmly, "Why do we always stick around the plaza? I feel like going down to Catherine's Basin. It's such a pretty walk."

"Yes, it is. We'll go down there one of these days."

"Why don't we go right now?"

"There isn't anyone to chaperon us."

"What do we need a chaperon for? I want to go with you, just the two of us."

"All by ourselves?" He stroked her cheek. "Agreste isn't São Paulo, Nora. By tomorrow everybody would be talking about you."

Ascânio, thinking the subject was closed, went back to discussing his administrative plans and the prospects that Brastânio's coming opened for the community. Leonora listened absently with half an ear, Mama's words echoing antiphonally with his. "Grab your goat by the horns, little nanny." Finally she broke in and stopped short.

"Ascânio, do you really love me?"

"Can you possibly doubt it?"

"Then why are you running away from me? Or didn't you enjoy it?"

"Running away from you? Didn't I enjoy it? Don't ever say that again. I love you and I don't want people to talk about you, don't you understand?"

Leonora smiled gently but did not give in.

"Yes, I understand; that's what I thought. Let them talk. I don't care a bit, it won't hurt me." She caught his hand. "Take me down to the river, love. There or anywhere you like, my lord."

Ascânio felt perspiration breaking out all over his body. Thoughts and feelings came all in a rush and he couldn't make sense of them, try as he might.

Of how a holy man came to disturb the peace.

Ricardo had gone out in the canoe with the engineer and Budião to fish. Tieta was lying in the hammock when she heard footsteps in the sand. She raised up and saw a stranger approaching. Although she had never met him she recognized Frei Thimóteo, wearing a straw hat and smiling. Tieta ran to throw a dress on over her bathing suit and came back just in time to ask the Franciscan for his blessing.

"Dona Antonieta Cantarelli? Everyone talks about you so much I didn't want to go without making your acquaintance. I'm delighted to meet you."

"Oh, I've been anxious to meet you too, Father. My nephew Ricardo says you're a saint."

"Saint?" He laughed in amusement. "I'm just a poor sinner. Is Ricardo around? I haven't seen him much lately."

"He's been in Agreste helping Father Mariano, but now he's back here. He's just gone fishing. He won't be long."

"He's a good boy. God will show him the right road, I have no doubt. I'd like to stay and tell him goodbye if you don't mind. My holiday's over, and I'm going back to São Cristóvão tomorrow."

"Please do; make yourself at home. Let me go get you a chair."

The friar refused the chair and sat down beside Tieta on the porch railing. His agility belied his white hair. He remarked as he gazed up at the dunes, "São Cristóvão is a beautiful old town, and the men who built it did honor to the Lord . . ."

"I haven't been there, but I've heard about it."

". . . but nothing can compare to Mangue Seco. This place is privileged. It's so incredibly beautiful—a gift of God to men. I know you've done what you could to keep a crime from being committed, the crime of building a titanium-dioxide plant here."

Tieta blushed. She didn't deserve this praise. The Skipper had been urging her to go back to Agreste, and here she was with her nephew, living the life of Riley.

"But I haven't done anything, really. Skipper Dário's always begging me to go back to Agreste to give him a hand, but I can't seem to pick up a foot and go; I just want to enjoy this wonderful place while I can. Carmosina tells me I'm selfish, but I ask you, Frei Thimóteo, what use would it be to go back to Agreste to get people all worked up and tell them they ought to protest and sign a petition against the factory? The factory's going to be built anyway in the end no matter what I do; me, or Carmô, or the Skipper. Am I wrong?"

"Yes, Dona Tieta, I think you are. Will you let me call you that? The protests from Agreste may not be enough by themselves to keep the factory from being built, but they may help. But whether they help or not, we ought to do everything within our power to prevent this crime, without worrying too much about whether or not we'll succeed." He paused briefly before going on. "When you got into the boat with Jonas and the fishermen, ma'am, you didn't ask whether it was worth the trouble."

Taken by surprise, Tieta tried to explain. "That was because I remembered the old days when I was a tomboy and loved a good fight—"

"I'm not judging or accusing; what other way do they have to protest? But you have many other ways of helping without having recourse to violence. The people of Agreste need to be enlightened, and a word from you would be enough to convince the undecided. God has entrusted us with the stewardship of these precious things and it is our bounden duty to preserve them. If we don't, we're no better than the criminals ourselves. Those industries are lethal. Forgive me for speaking out this way, Dona Tieta, but you asked my opinion. . . ."

In the infinite peace of the afternoon, the friar's soft, fervent voice and his timid, encouraging smile disturbed Tieta. She couldn't answer—what could she say? Just then Ricardo appeared. When he saw the friar the seminarian left the engineer and came running.

"You here, Frei Thimóteo? What a grand surprise!"

"I came to tell you goodbye, my boy, and so I had the pleasure of meeting and talking with Dona Tieta. I'm going back to the monastery tomorrow."

The engineer came up with a creel full of fish.

"Marta and I have our bags packed, too; this is our next-to-last day. We won't see Mangue Seco again for another year, if everything hasn't rotted by then. When I think about it I could—"

"That's what we were talking about, Dona Tieta and I. A great crime is being planned, a very great crime."

Ricardo walked with the friar to the canoe. As Frei Thimóteo blessed him, he said, "What a nice person your aunt is. I know how much you love her and are going to miss her. Why don't you come and spend a few days with me at the monastery after she goes?"

That night in bed Tieta remarked à propos of the visit, "Do you think he suspects anything?"

"He never let on if he did."

"He knew about the business with the boats, he told me so; but he didn't scold me for it. He's a funny kind of a friar. He made me feel uncomfortable."

"Why?"

"Oh, this business of people having bounden duties to fulfill. I don't want to leave this place until the electricity comes in and I have to go away for good."

Felipe used to say that the first thing you had to do if you

wanted to live a happy life was suppress your conscience. "That
conscience of yours is going to get you into trouble one of these
days," he warned her whenever she was worried about one of the
girls at the Retreat. Tieta clasped Ricardo to her breast, trying
to forget the friar's words and not seeing the flash of hope in the
boy's eyes.

Of a mysterious correspondent.

How could such a breach of confidence have taken place? Professor
Hélio Colombo had told no one about the expropriation project
except the young candidate for mayor. Ascânio Trindade, in turn,
had every good reason not to let a word of his conversation with the
lawyer transpire. Nevertheless, a few days later *A Tarde* printed a
"Letter from Agreste" with an account of the eminent jurist's brief
visit to Agreste on retainer for Brastânio. Nothing was left out: the
morning spent at the registry office poring over books and deeds;
the afternoon meeting in Ascânio Trindade's second-floor office at
the courthouse, at which he had ordered the future mayor to expropriate the whole vast coconut grove and resell it, all or in part, to
the Brazilian Titanium Company, S.A.; and the obedient civil servant's immediate acquiescence. Expropriation by eminent domain
was the solution found by the lawyer to secure his client's right to
the area regardless of the intransigence of one or two of the heirs,
who were adamantly refusing to do business with the controversial
corporation out of a firm conviction that the contaminating effluvia
from the titanium industry might cause irreparable damage to the
region. The correspondent had used the verb "ordered" and the adjective "obedient." Copies of the paper were passed from hand to
hand.

The identity of the mysterious correspondent was never precisely known. When Dr. Hélio Colombo recalled his few hours in
Agreste, the awful trek out there and back over that mule track, the
dust, the thirst, the abundant table, the flavor and size of the clams,
the golden hue and incomparable taste of the ambrosia, he marveled
at the deceptive simplicity of people from the interior. You took
them for dumb hillbillies, gaping hicks, and they were laughing up

their sleeves and making fools of you all the time. City slickers didn't stand a chance against their wiles. The professor recalled the notary's open curiosity and eager questions during lunch. And he thought he had pulled the wool over his eyes! He could hear Fatty snoring, see his expressionless full-moon face and doltish air as he lay there lost to the living in that room at the courthouse after so obligingly trotting in with the certificates and the can of strawberry guava preserves. Father and son, what a pair!

Of a toast in violet liqueur.

Dona Carmosina's depression deepened when she realized that when her neighbors wracked their brains over the identity of the anonymous, well-informed correspondent, the first one they thought of was her. Aminthas even came by to congratulate her.

"Cuz, I take off my hat to you. How'd you ever find out?"

She hadn't found out anything! It was no thanks to her the story had leaked out; she hadn't even known about Professor Colombo's visit. She was out of it entirely and very cross. Besides being plunged in gloom by the news itself, by seeing the trump card that Fidélio's noble gesture had won for them snatched away, she found herself ignored and shunted aside. She had always known everything that was going on in Agreste almost before it happened; now she was taken by surprise. It was nothing less than an affront. Dona Carmosina's little eyes turned opaque.

"I read it in the paper, just like you did. And to think I laughed in Ascânio's face . . . Well, there's no help for it now. I've lost face, I'm discredited, and there isn't a thing I can do about it."

Crushed and drooping, the Skipper joined them, flinging on the counter the sheets of signatures gathered for the petition. Tieta was right; petitions would get them exactly nowhere. He had just talked to Dr. Franklin at the notary's office and found the story to be accurate. Even acting on behalf of a presumptive heir, there was no way he could prevent the act of expropriation by eminent domain. Any action in the courts would have to be subsequent to the expropriation, and what good was that? They might as well forget about the grove; it was lost. A cloud of desolation settled over the post office. Only Aminthas was still his jaunty self and tried to tease his friends into good humor.

"The ship hasn't gone on the rocks yet, Skipper! Carmô, where's your true grit? I never saw anybody throw in the sponge as quick as you two. You'd think that factory was really going to be built, the way you all carry on."

"Well, isn't it? They bring in a lawyer like Hélio Colombo, invite Ascânio to the capital—"

"The playboy bumpkin," laughed Aminthas.

"—to make sure they've got him in their pocket, they set a date for the election, and you still wonder what they're up to?"

"It looks pretty bad, I admit. We'll have to go on the assumption that it's true, anyhow."

He abruptly changed the subject as curious idlers from the bar and the local shops began sauntering in, eager to sniff out what they were talking about. Agreste was all agog these days, and the news of the imminent expropriation had aroused uncommon interest. Chalita, the first to arrive, leaned against the doorpost and picked his teeth.

"Good morning, gentlemen and lady."

"Good morning, Pasha of the Poor." Aminthas was unfazed. "As I was saying, Carmô, you'll never get me to admit that anyone can take the place of the Beatles. I'll stop by your house after lunch with the record and prove to you I'm right. See you then, Skipper."

As he went out he met Edmundo Ribeiro coming in.

"What do you think of this news?" he asked. "Do you reckon it's true? The way things are going, Agreste won't be recognizable in a couple of years."

At Dona Carmosina's house, where Dona Milu was serving homemade marmalade, Aminthas struck an orator's pose.

"My noble fellow do-gooders, answer me this. Before he can expropriate the land Ascânio has to be elected, doesn't he?"

"The date of the election has already been set."

"I know that; I read the papers and I hear what people say. But as far as I know, our rustic playboy hasn't been elected yet."

"He's as good as elected," retorted the Skipper.

"Maybe he is and maybe he isn't. It all depends."

"It all depends on what? Are you trying to say he may *not* be elected?"

Discouragement and frustration showed plainly in Skipper Dário's voice. Dona Carmosina listened in silence.

"I may be trying to say just that. Why not? Depending on the circumstances, I might even be willing to go out on a limb and bet he won't be."

"How could he not be? He's the only candidate, Colonel Artur's candidate."

"Well, if he wasn't the Colonel's candidate, or, failing that, if he wasn't the *only* candidate—"

"Are you trying to say . . ." interrupted Dona Carmosina, beginning to be interested.

"I'm saying that all it takes is another candidate who can do better than Ascânio, either with the Colonel or at the ballot box."

"Yes, I see what you're getting at. But it won't work. The Colonel is Ascânio's godfather, and he trusts him. The day of Mauritônio's funeral he said Ascânio was going to be the new mayor and everybody agreed. I don't see why he should change his mind."

"Well, I'm not so sure. The old man's pretty well over the hill, so nobody's thought to ask him what he thinks about this factory coming in. I for one don't know whether he's for it or against. It wouldn't hurt to go out and talk to him and try to persuade him. Then if he still backs Ascânio, we can go straight to the people."

"Ascânio's still unbeatable at the ballot box."

"Is he? He may have been once, Carmô, but he isn't now. Everyone used to think of him as a hardworking, honest fellow; there weren't any two minds about Ascânio, and everybody wanted him for mayor. But now a lot of people think, fairly or unfairly, that he's sold out to Brastânio and has his eye on Leonora's money. Just between us, I think Ascânio's been duped. But the best thing people who don't know him as well as we do have to say is that his head's been turned. Don't you see, Carmô? The feeling isn't unanimous any more. We all used to follow Ascânio's lead and be ready to vote for him anytime. Well, he wouldn't get my vote today."

"Nor mine," assented the Skipper.

"I don't know who can give him any competition, even so."

"Cousin, where are your eyes?"

"Who then? Tell me!"

"Why, none other than the sterling citizen, that illustrious son of Agreste, an officer in our glorious navy, Skipper Dário de Queluz!"

"Me? Are you crazy? I'm no politician and I never will be."

"All the better! Politicians aren't much in demand these days;

the military are running things now, aren't they? Skipper, to your
post!"

"Me? Never!"

Aminthas ignored him.

"It won't be easy, but I think we can win, if . . ."

"If?"

"If we can count on Dona Antonieta's help. With St. Tieta of
Agreste beside us to wheedle votes for the Skipper, it'll be a
cinch."

"I won't agree and that's final," the Skipper began again, standing up to make his refusal more emphatic.

Dona Carmosina whirled around on him, all fired up again and
on the warpath.

"What do you mean you won't agree? This is a test of your
patriotism!"

Dona Milu poured out tiny glasses of violet liqueur. The occasion called for a toast, and the old lady had been a fighting ward
boss in her day.

"Skipper, your health! I'll begin campaigning for you this very
day. I already have a slogan for you: 'Down with pollution.'" Dona
Milu took a sip of the liqueur and smacked her lips.

A chapter of memorable events in which
Ascânio Trindade fumbles a speech and a
carom—first part: the speech.

Between Dr. Hélio Colombo's visitation and the news of it in a
Bahia paper, Ascânio Trindade almost lost his temper twice. The
first time he lost the thread of his speech, the second time he missed
a carom.

The incident of the speech took place at a rally to hail the
coming of the power line to Agreste. When the chief engineer got
out of the jeep and ran up the courthouse steps, Ascânio Trindade
was sitting alone in his office, ruminating sheepishly on a couple of
recent decisions that had been made behind his back by others
without his having a chance to argue or even open his mouth. Yet
he found them both highly satisfactory.

Making light of his scruples, trampling on local bigotry and backwardness, Leonora transported him to Paradise—that is, to Catherine's Basin—every night. Putting finis to an intricate problem, the famous lawyer had ordered him to expropriate the land around the palm grove as soon as he took office as mayor. He had meekly agreed to both solutions, since both were advantageous to him. And yet he felt a persistent twinge of uneasiness, as if, by passively agreeing to such courses of action and actively going along with them, he were doing something reprehensible. When he analyzed these actions he found nothing dirty or dishonest about them. Why, then, this uneasiness and doubt? There was only one explanation; he just didn't have it in him to be a leader. He was always getting bogged down in scruples, in provincial reluctance and qualms; he hesitated and hung back when the moment called for bold and decisive action. Professor Colombo and Leonora represented the advanced, open-minded thinking of the great metropolis. Surprising Leonora, so fragile and so spunky, so timid and so bold. . . .

The voice of the chief engineer broke in upon his ruminations.

"Do you want to watch the first pole set up? I'd like to call in that rich dame too, the one who bosses the federal government around. That way I'll finally get to meet her."

Delighted at the news, Ascânio jumped up and put on his jacket.

"She's out at Mangue Seco. You'll meet her the day of the party. Can we set a date right now?"

"Sure. Let's say Sunday two weeks from now."

Ascânio counted up; that was exactly seventeen days away. By setting the date for the festivities, the engineer had determined the day the Cantarellis, widow and heiress, would start back for São Paulo. Ascânio shivered. They had told each other over and over how little time they had left, but now the vague words crystallized into a fatal deadline. Eighteen days from now the purest and fairest of women would leave Agreste aboard Jairo's *marineti*.

The news spread quickly and the townspeople gathered around. The cathedral bells pealed merrily in Vavá Muriçoca's party-loving hands. Father Mariano appeared on the church porch. Thanks to the grace and good works of a devout parishioner, a generous lamb in the Lord's flock, a papal Comendadora of peerless merit, new electric wiring had been installed in the church, whose facade, covered with a network of colored light bulbs, awaited electricity from the

Paulo Afonso Falls. Father Mariano quickened his pace to catch up
with Ascânio and the chief engineer.

Workmen with spades and shovels dug a hole for the first pole
in old Mud Lane, the future Dona Antonieta Esteves Cantarelli
Street. People swarmed out of every lane and street. The last skeptical holdouts yielded to the evidence; in another two weeks Agreste
would be hooked up to the Paulo Afonso Power Plant. That was the
kind of energy it took to power industries—strong, bright light
twenty-four hours a day, not feeble flickers from a generator that
was on only three hours a day, when a fuse didn't blow. Tieta's
Light. The benefactress' name, pronounced with awe and admiration, was on every tongue. They all felt proud of the wealth and
importance, the prestige and power of their fellow townsperson,
patroness of the city and county, their favorite prodigal daughter.
To her and her alone were thanks due for that miracle, a truth
proclaimed by the chief engineer himself.

An incredible miracle he had called it, from atop a kerosene tin.
Ascânio, seeing dozens of townspeople pressing around the engineers and workmen, admiring the work and all ready to clap, sent
Sabino in search of a box or a drum. Such a solemn moment in the
life of Agreste should not be allowed to pass unnoticed. Once his
tribune and assembly were assured, he invited the chief engineer,
"dauntless chieftain of this epic battle for progress, to whom we
wish to express our deep gratitude," to say a few words. The engineer, who was no orator, limited himself to four quick sentences.
He congratulated the local people but wouldn't take any credit; he
and his outfit were just carrying out orders from the company,
orders that had, he admitted, seemed ridiculous when given. The
extension of an electric power line to Agreste was "a genuine honest-
to-goodness miracle." All the credit should go to the influential lady
who had done it, and whom he had not yet had the pleasure of
meeting. When he stepped down he was introduced to some of the
influential lady's relatives: her sister Perpétua, her nephew Peto,
and her stepdaughter Leonora, whom he stripped with practiced
and covetous eyes. She was first-class material, that little dish.

Leonora thought Ascânio should have had his share of the
gratitude and applause. He had fought for it with such dogged
desperation, had suffered rebuffs, but had persevered through thick
and thin. True, he hadn't been able to accomplish much, but that
didn't mean he hadn't tried.

Ascânio did get a big hand when he took the engineer's place on the drum, particularly when he thanked Dona Antonieta Esteves Cantarelli, to whom the people of Agreste would always be grateful. If he had only stopped there, he would certainly have had his share of the public gratitude toward those responsible for power lines, lampposts, light bulbs and light. Ascânio's mistake was in trying to take advantage of the occasion to get in some propaganda for Brastânio. With an imperious gesture he pointed to the ground and asked, "Who do we have to thank for the pavement we're standing on, the asphalt that covers the mud that used to be a permanent fixture here on the edge of town? Who sent the machines, the technicians, the workmen? Brastânio, whose presence in the county will mean the redemption of Agreste," he answered himself, repeating the hackneyed phrase he had used in the interview. Applause and bravos mingled with shouts and boos. Public opinion was sharply divided.

"Down with pollution!" bawled Dona Carmosina.

Ascânio paid no attention and went on speaking as earnestly and eloquently as before, until an anonymous falsetto voice, obviously disguised, rose out of the hubbub: "Ain't you ashamed, you playboy bumpkin! We know you sold out!"

Ascânio choked in the middle of a sentence. Unable to spot the son of a bitch—"Show your face and repeat that if you're a man"—his self-assurance wavered, his fluid speech faltered. When he stepped down from the oil drum, applause and *vivas* broke out, but they were hailing not Ascânio but the pole the workmen had just set in the ground. A marvel of the twentieth century—a lofty concrete post with arms branching out for the light bulbs. Snazzy.

Second half of the chapter of memorable events,
during which Ascânio Trindade loses his
eloquence and fumbles his carom—
the poolroom affair.

The setting for the incident in the poolroom was of course the Azores Bar, where the tournament finals were finally taking place. They were late this year; the Golden Cue should have been proclaimed in December. Everything was out of step and out of tune in Agreste lately. Routine and harmony were giving way to improvisation and wrangling. Mistrust and short tempers were becoming the rule, and a war seemed about to break out any minute.

The presence of ladies young and old, the crème de la crème of Agreste, lent a festive character to the tournament finals. This was always the occasion for a parade of elegant toilettes, as if the Best-Dressed Woman were being chosen along with the Golden Cue. The ladies went there to cheer their champions on, of course, and to breathe the excitingly sinful atmosphere of the bar, but above all they went to show off their get-ups, each more elaborate than the last. Elisa, modeling southern fashions courtesy of Tieta, had been head and shoulders above the other women in past years. Astério, too, had always defeated his opponents with ease. Between them the couple monopolized the applause; he had been the champion three years in a row, while she reigned absolute as queen of the fair. Things had changed. What with his preoccupation with goat-breeding and manioc-planting, Astério had neglected his training, while Seixas and Fidélio spent hours at a time practicing caroms. As for Elisa, she had a rival worthy of her elegance and beauty, the lovely Paulista Leonora Cantarelli, on holiday in Agreste.

The first game was won by Fidélio and lost by Seixas, on points and by audience acclaim. Seixas' female cousins had recruited friends and schoolmates to swell the ranks of their cousin's supporters. Aloof, unsociable Fidélio had recruited no one, but fans appeared of their own accord and in surprising numbers. There were actually some instances of desertion from Seixas' hosts, clear proof if any were needed that local custom was going to the dogs. Even his prettiest cousin, the nearsighted girl, caught the turncoat fever. Throwing self-respect to the winds, the false wench leaped shamelessly to her feet to applaud a sensational stroke by the enemy. What were things coming to?

Dona Edna, both of whose champions, the faithful Terto (tame and a cuckold but a very good husband just the same) and the voluble Leleu, had been knocked out of the running early on, could not conceal her pique at having been knocked out of the running herself by Elisa and Leonora. She had plenty of flair and good taste; what she lacked was money or a generous sister. To make up for it, everywhere she went, as soon as her come-hither eyes had swept over all the men in the room, she began talking a blue streak and needling everyone in sight. Her tongue excelled at more than one art, not least at distilling venom; her stiletto cut as deep as a scalpel. If she was taken to task she defended herself by explaining that however mercilessly she raked other people over the coals, they said even worse things about her. During the tournament, not even Peto was safe from Dona Edna's sweet looks and bitter teasing—a grown-up Peto in long pants and shoes with his hair combed.

"My, Peto, what's got into you all of a sudden? I declare, you've turned into a man."

Her languid, provocative gaze and the tip of her tongue grazing her lips set the boy on fire. He was a cute little devil, greasy kid stuff and all. The one who gave Dona Edna the hots, though, was the other one, his brother, that young priest who was just at the right stage, the heavenly mass-server. From Peto Dona Edna's gaze traveled to Elisa, whom she loathed in dead earnest since the conceited thing had gone to live in one of the best houses in town, for which she paid no rent, making her habitual air of a martyred madonna even more intolerable than before. Dona Edna had come in a fighting mood; she was determined both to get Elisa's goat and to harass that prissy little hypocrite Leonora. She wasn't sure which of the two she despised the most.

"Elisa, would you mind if I root for your hubby, dear? Don't worry, I won't take him away from you, not even a little bitty piece." She laughed provocatively.

Whatever the motives were that had led Dona Edna to bestow the privilege of her ardent support on Astério, truth impels me to say that it was to her the three-time champion owed his victory, just when he had rested his cue and was about to concede defeat.

In contrast to the brilliant match between Fidélio and Seixas, in which one master stroke followed another, the game between Ascânio and Astério dragged out tediously. They were evenly matched, it was true, but only because they were playing equally badly. Both showed lack of practice; both were on edge and so off their form that they badly disappointed their public and the bettors.

As the monotonous contest wore on, Elisa pretended not to hear Dona Edna's condescending remarks about hand-me-down elegance and her fond words of encouragement to Astério, as if he were her husband or her lover. The better to ignore her, Elisa concentrated on every move of the match. She didn't understand much about pool but she could see that Astério was playing a lousy game. If he somehow managed to beat Ascânio, who was playing just as badly as he was, he would certainly lose to Fidélio, whose display of skill had been applauded by the public. Men were so funny. Fidélio had lived peacefully in his little corner all this time, overlooked by all and sundry. Now all of a sudden this palm-grove business had transformed him into one of the most talked-about people in town. Now people were saying that his usual moroseness was really a way of concealing his cleverness and guile, and that he was an inveterate libertine besides. Yes, men were unpredictable, all right. If Dona Carmosina hadn't told her all those stories about Fidélio, Elisa never would have believed he was a Don Juan. And Astério! What about those tastes and predilections of his? It looked as if Edna, the floozy with the sucked-in tail, was wasting her time; she just wasn't Astério's type.

Osnar abruptly flung away his cornhusk cigarette when he saw Astério, on whom he had bet heavily, throw away his last chance to win. The game was running down; Astério needed three more points and Ascânio only one. For a three-time champ who held a record for caroms the difference meant very little as it was his turn to play, but he had gotten flustered and thrown away his chance, leaving the ball perfectly placed for Ascânio to score. All he had to do was calculate the force of the stroke with some precision and he would have the point he needed to win. Astério laid aside his cue; it was a bad day and there was nothing he could do about it. He felt a cramp in his stomach, the first since he had come into possession of Jarde's land. He had thought he was cured.

Ascânio gazed at the pool table, smiled triumphantly at Leonora, rubbed chalk on the cue and strolled up to the table, considering the game as good as won. The silence in the room was broken by Dona Edna's shrill voice.

"Osnar, you're the president of the Catherine's Basin Club; is it true what everybody's saying?"

Ascânio bent over the edge of the green baize, placed his cue in position and drew back his arm before shooting a carom.

"They say there's never been so much traffic on the riverbank, and all new faces, foreign faces . . . that the foreigner doesn't miss a night. . . ."

The cue jumped, barely touching the ball and leaving it in position for Astério. As Dona Edna's voice echoed through the bar, Ascânio lost his carom and the match.

*Of the first victory of the ecological candidate,
in which the reader is granted the treat of
beholding Skipper Dário de Queluz
in summer whites.*

"Good Lord, what's happened? Look at him, Cardo." Tieta pointed at Skipper Dário de Queluz sitting in the bow of his beached canoe and putting on his white socks and shoes before stepping ashore.

"You'd think today was the seventh of September," replied the seminarian, no less astonished.

Once a year on September 7, in honor of Independence Day, Skipper Dário took his dress uniform out of the closet, shook out the mothballs, put it on and attended the patriotic ceremony at the grammar school in all his splendor. The rest of the year he wore a sport shirt and trousers in town and shorts and a jersey on the beach. Why in the name of wonder was he dressed in uniform, gold braid glittering in the Mangue Seco sun? Tieta had never seen him dressed up like this. He looked different, commanding and austere; he imposed respect. Something very serious must have happened to make the Skipper put on his dress tunic and flaunt his navy medal of merit besides. Tieta and Ricardo ran to meet him.

"Where's Laura? Is she all right?" asked Tieta, concerned.

"Yes, she's fine; she sent her regards. She stayed in Agreste because I'm going right back. I came out to talk to you, Tieta." His voice was stern. "It's a private matter, and it's serious."

Ricardo eyed his aunt in alarm. Did the talk have anything to do with them? He was about to walk away when the Skipper stopped him.

"You don't have to go, Ricardo, you're not a child. But I'm warning you: none of what we say must get out. This is confidential."

The uniform imposed formality and distance; his manner was self-assured, almost haughty. They walked back to the Corral, where Tieta served coconut milk, a favorite of the Skipper's—

"There's nothing like it for the bowels, dear friend!"—and put the kettle on the fire to brew some coffee.

"The election date's been set, Tieta."

"Well, we knew it would be, didn't we? Carmô told me the papers were speculating about it."

Skipper Dário informed her of Dr. Hélio Colombo's visit; that he was a famous attorney and professor at the law school, a brain out of the top drawer, and that he had been sent to Agreste by Brastânio. And did they know why? he asked, in a sepulchral voice, eyes flashing with indignation as if he were revealing some monstrous conspiracy or sinister plot—which indeed he was. He was seeking to unmask and foil the vile machinations of an abominable cabal. Ricardo listened closely, eyes wide with indignant solidarity. Tieta still had not grasped the reason for the uniform or for the dramatic emphasis and heroic attitude assumed by the Skipper.

"Have you any idea, my friend, what Ascânio's first act will be after taking office? You don't? Well, I'll tell you. First he'll expropriate the land around the palm grove, and then he'll turn around and sell it to Brastânio. That's why I'm here, Tieta. I've come for you."

Tieta, still nonplussed, forced a laugh.

"Is that why you put on your uniform? Are you going to take me off to jail?"

The naval officer did not echo her joke or her playful tone.

"Don't try to be funny, Tieta; this is too serious. The only means of heading off the catastrophe and saving Agreste is to keep Ascânio from being elected."

"But how do you intend to do that?"

"By electing someone else."

"Who?" Her voice changed as she was assailed by a sudden suspicion. "You don't mean to say that you and that nutty Carmô have picked on me—"

"You'd be the ideal candidate if you didn't live in São Paulo." The Skipper took off his cap, wiped away the perspiration, and scratched his head. "You know me, Tieta, and you know I'm a man of my word. I retired from the navy and came back here to Agreste because I wanted to live with my wife in peace and quiet for the rest of my life in this little piece of Paradise. You know I have no other ambitions; I'm happy the way I am." He spoke in the old cordial way, as simply and unpretentiously as if he had doffed his uniform.

"Of course I know that; everyone does. I feel the same way in São Paulo sometimes. There're days when I feel like giving it all up and coming back here for good. That's why I bought me the house and land. Someday I'm going to do just what you did."

"With a titanium-dioxide industry here in full blast, you'd better forget it. Our Paradise will turn into a garbage dump, just like what happened in Italy. We have a very special problem on our hands, Tieta." He turned formal again, his voice grave, his gestures vigorous, his stare belligerent and accusing. "So special that I'm willing to accept the honor made to me by a group of public-spirited friends and put myself in the running. And if my candidacy is to be anything but an empty gesture, it's essential that you consent to take charge of the campaign. Everyone knows the public will support whomever you do, so it all depends on you. The reason I've come here is to call upon you, in the name of Agreste's future, to enlist in a sacred cause."

Tieta listened, looking thoughtfully at her friend's taut face. Poor Skipper, he was leading a lost battalion. Out of sheer love for Agreste's climate and Mangue Seco's wild beauty he had thrown away an honorable career and shed a uniform to come back and wait for death, hoping to enjoy many long years of health and tranquillity. But that's all over, Skipper. It won't do a bit of good to take your uniform out of the wardrobe and pin your medal on your chest.

"Do you really think people in Agreste have anything to say about whether the factory's built here or not? I don't. I know how those things work. They're decided behind the ordinary fellow's back, they don't ask for our opinion. And you're going to come down off your dunes, you're—"

"I'm going to do my duty. It's our obligation, mine and yours, everyone's who knows what that factory would mean. If I had to fight on all alone . . . I told you once, if you remember, that I'll fight to my last breath to keep pollution out of Agreste."

"Yes, I remember."

Ricardo broke in impulsively.

"I'm sorry, Aunt, but the Skipper's right. Frei Thimóteo said we ought to go ahead even without knowing whether we can accomplish anything. Pedro thinks so too."

Tieta could see the friar's frail figure and the engineer's frank, open countenance and hear the gentle, fervent voice of the religious man and the vibrant, passionate voice of the atheist, both speaking of crimes and obligations, breaking into her *dolce far niente*, making her feel like the lowest of all lazy, useless, no-account women. Now here came the Skipper, all splendiferous and solemn, commanding her to do her duty. Felipe, a wise man, had alway said that to live well the first thing you had to do was get rid of your conscience. The catch in that philosophy was that there were times when you couldn't.

The kettle was boiling. Tieta made coffee and put the cups on the table where Ascânio Trindade had unrolled Rufo's brightly colored drawing, his dazzling vision of the future. Tieta's gaze darkened again as she remembered the molten asphalt smothering the mangroves and the boxy little houses built on the ruins of the fishing village. Shacks, crabs, fishermen, adolescent dreams, passionate days and nights, all buried in the rot of titanium dioxide. No goat girl would ever run up those dunes again.

Of how Perpétua, devoted mother, swallows camels and grits her teeth.

The unexpected return of Tieta, inspired by civic duty to cut short her idyllic season in the sun (things happen in this world that even God could never have thought of), was hailed with enthusiasm and fulsome flattery by Perpétua, who had been ready to go to Mangue Seco for a serious talk with her sister about her sons' future. It was high time to dot the i's and cross the t's on her carefully matured plans for Cardo and Peto—preferably signed and sealed at the registry in black on white.

She welcomed her son and her sister with open arms and an effusiveness foreign to her nature.

"God bless you, son, and keep you on the right road and deserving of your aunt's protection." No one would have recognized in her the cool and distant Perpétua of the old days, now opening

ness you're back. I've been missing you so much I couldn't stand it.
Peto too. He adores you, you know. He never stops talking about
you. Just ask Leonora."

"It's true. Peto's a darling," responded Leonora, still puzzled by
the abrupt change in Tieta's plans.

"We have a lot to talk about before you go, Sister. I'm going to
miss you all so much, I don't even want to think about it." She
trampled on her best feelings and extended the flattery to her sister's
stepdaughter. "You too, Nora."

"Please don't remind me of sad things, Dona Perpétua."

The hussy's lament forced Perpétua to shake her head in
feigned pity, her voice hissing affectionate reproach, "Tieta, did
you know this silly girl is sweet on Ascânio? . . . Pretty and rich as
she is, she could have any sweetheart she wanted in São Paulo, and
she wastes her time fooling around with a poor country boy. I don't
say he's a bad young man, but he don't have a penny to his name.
He's no match for her, I've told her so a thousand times."

Oh, she was so concerned about Leonora's happiness. Perpétua
gritted her teeth and choked down her desire to give the shameless
minx what-for, coming in late every night with cheeks on fire and a
crumpled dress from God knew where. Where? From rolling
around on the riverbank night after night, that's where; everybody
was talking about it. Perpétua swallowed her indignation and disgust. Her children's future demanded praise, smiles and silence, and
she would pay the price. When it was time for an accounting, the
Lord Almighty, with whom she had made a solemn bargain, would
credit her with all the camels she had swallowed and all the many
times she had gritted her teeth. As she did now, welcoming her son
and her sister from Mangue Seco, sunburned, smelling of salt air and
exuding health and satisfaction.

"Whoever marries Ascânio will be a happy woman, Dona
Perpétua. He's a wonderful man."

"Go along with you! He's just a poor devil."

"Well, Perpétua, I'm mighty glad to find you in such a good
humor. I've been thinking of staying on here a little longer. I was
planning to go the day after the celebration, but now I guess I'll stay
a few more days."

Tieta went into the bedroom to unpack her things, and Leonora went with her. Perpétua turned to her son. Before going into
action she would have to find out from him whether his aunt had

said anything about taking him to São Paulo, whether she had made him any promises and if so, what, and whether she had by any chance hinted at adopting him. Why, when she had set a firm date for going, had she decided to stay after all? But Ricardo hastily dropped his bundle of clothes and books and took his leave with the pretext of asking the Father's blessing and offering his services to the Skipper.

"The Skipper?" said Perpétua in surprise.

"I'm going to be working for the Skipper until the end of vacation."

"What are you talking about?"

"Aunt'll explain, Mother. I can't stop now; I don't have time."

And he was out the door without a by-your-leave. Through her astonishment Perpétua recognized the tone, the look, the laugh, the impudence; they had been familiar to her for years. Tone, look, laugh, impudence—she was seeing Tieta as a girl Ricardo's age, ignoring her father's commands, violence, shouts and punishment, the leather strap and the staff. A rebel with her own strong will.

"God help us!" groaned Perpétua, one hand in the pocket of her black skirt, touching her rosary beads.

Of buzzards in a clumsy ballet.

Lawyers and heirs trotted through Agreste's short and empty streets in a jerky, disjointed ballet of meetings, whispered conferences, spats and disagreements patched up, from Dona Amorzinho's boarding house to the registry, from the registry to Modesto Pires' office at the tannery and from there to the courthouse. One day they stood shoulder to shoulder, a united little band, combatants in the same uncertain cause, allied in the determination to get as much as they could from the land inherited from a vague great-grandfather. The next day it was every man for himself, each skulking about and trying to get in ahead of the others, guerrillas intent on shady deals and dirty tricks, every one trying to grab the best piece for himself. A cloud of buzzards around the carrion, was how Modesto Pires described them.

peccable in his white suit and panama hat, armed with his cane and his good-natured smile, he showed no irritation or surprise when Josafá Antunes raved and blustered at a story in *A Tarde* about Professor Colombo's visit and his collusion with Ascânio to expropriate the palm grove. This controversial gambit had thrown the aggrieved heirs into a tizzy. Dr. Marcolino's equanimity was unshaken.

"A master stroke! Exactly what I would have done if I were a corporation lawyer. I take my hat off to Professor Colombo; he's done it again. Didn't I tell you, Josafá, that that boy, the young man who's running for mayor, is a stalking horse for Brastânio? And he's a fool into the bargain." He disclosed, with some satisfaction, "I already knew about it."

"You did? How's that?"

"I heard about it the same day it happened, from our peerless Bonaparte. Remember how I've been giving him a little bit here and a little bit there? It's been money well spent."

He had been analyzing the problem for days, working out a new plan of action, which he now proposed to his clients, or rather to one of them, Josafá. Old Jarde, shut up in the boarding house, no longer took any interest in the things of this world. Josafá listened with drooping spirits. He wasn't happy at all with the way things were going. It looked as if the judge in Esplanada was never going to establish his claim to the title. The money he had got from the sale of his farm was dribbling away, and Josafá was afraid that whatever compensation the county might pay would not even cover the amount he had already spent. He had dreamed of multiplying the sum in one daring gamble, but it was beginning to look as if he'd be lucky if he came out even.

"We have to be realistic. Professor Colombo's gambit has left us very little room for maneuver."

Dr. Marcolino could see only one loophole that might get them a better price for the land and at the same time avoid any more expense; to try to enter into direct agreement with Brastânio by which the rights to the inheritance of the legendary Manuel Bezerra Antunes would be ceded directly to the company. Once the rights were transferred, it would be up to Brastânio to establish title. That meant that the heirs would have to join forces, however. With the threat of expropriation hanging over their heads, young Fidélio's stubborn intransigence no longer made any sense.

Josafá found the idea tempting, particularly since it held out the prospect of settling the matter without further delay and thus stopping the drain on his finances, including Dr. Marcolino's fees and living expenses. Not that he didn't do his legal counsel justice; he was a smart lawyer who knew all the angles, but he was honest with his clients. If he hadn't been, he would have tried to prolong his well-paid holidays as long as he could, letting the cause drag on in the courts as long as Jarde and Josafá still had money to spend.

And those were memorable, golden days indeed for Dr. Marcolino. In Agreste he put on weight and a healthy color, found that he was free of the cramps in his hands and arms that had given him such cause for alarm, and made friends with the townspeople. In the bar he talked amicably with Osnar and Aminthas and played backgammon with Chalita; at the post office he read the papers and exchanged ideas with Dona Carmosina, a very well-informed person indeed, to whom he did not conceal his true opinion about the titanium-dioxide industry; in the church porch he argued religion with Father Mariano and admitted that he was a freemason; and finally, he fell into the habit of dropping in at Zuleika Cinderella's establishment late in the afternoon. The climate of Agreste, as has been explained too many times, really does work wonders.

As he explained his idea, Dr. Marcolino was overcome with pity and rage. That infernal factory would put an end to this marvelous climate and this happy life.

"Seu Josafá, I tell you we're all conniving at a crime. This profession of mine is the devil—"

"Crime nothing, sir. This place has nothing to lose, it's half dead already. The factory may make things better; you never know."

Of reasons hard to explain or to understand.

Once alone with Tieta in the bedroom, Leonora gave vent to her grief and gladness.

"Oh Mama, I don't know how to thank you for having brought me here. It's been so wonderful. . . . Can we really stay a little longer?" She caught Tieta's hand, kissed it and laid her face against it with tender gratitude.

"It looks that way; maybe as long as a few weeks more, I don't know exactly yet. But nanny, don't you think of parting until you climb on board the *marineti*. Until then you just make the most of the time you've got and forget you'll ever have to leave."

"If I only could—"

"Don't think about it anymore, I tell you. Tell me about the riverbank."

"Mama, you can't imagine how hard Ascânio was to convince. He wouldn't hear of going there; I had to drag him. He's afraid I'll be talked about and called a scarlet woman. Poor Ascânio, I can't help feeling guilty. The other day playing pool at the bar he lost a match to Astério because he thought Dona Edna was talking about me in a remark she made to Osnar."

"She probably was, the barefaced bitch."

"To tell the truth, I wouldn't be surprised. We're awfully careful, though, especially Ascânio. Mama, do you know what I wish? I wish I could spend a whole night with him, just one at least before I go. In a real bed, on top of a mattress, without any clothes on, without being in a hurry or having to whisper because we're afraid somebody'll come. But I don't know of any good place."

"You don't? What about his house? He lives by himself, doesn't he?"

"Well, not really. There's Rafa."

"The servant? That old, broken-down, deaf, almost blind woman? Nannygoat, nannygoat, I don't know how you ever got along without me."

"Do you think he'd go for that? He has so many scruples! Oh, Mama, I just can't resign myself to leaving. I'm going to miss him so much I think I'll die!"

"Missing somebody's just like love, Nora. You don't die of it, it helps you to live."

Leonora did not confine herself to the story of her love and their nightly excursions to the sheltering riverbank, the murmured poems, the smothered sighs. She related some disagreeable episodes, too. What with this business of the expropriation of the palm grove, Ascânio hadn't had a minute's peace. What she regretted most of all was the rupture with Dona Carmosina. Ascânio had tried his utmost to head off that unfortunate outcome and had even stopped going to the post office so as not to hear her taunts and biting jests. But when he learned that Carmosina had gone running off to Tapitanga

Fazenda with the sole object of getting him in trouble with his godfather and protector, Ascânio couldn't take it any longer. His erstwhile friend had said every bad, terrible thing about Brastânio she could think of, read newspaper clippings, criticized the support the company's plans were getting from the county, had even used the words "breach of public trust." She had got the Colonel so riled up that he had called his godson on the carpet and demanded an explanation of why he had gone to Bahia and what all this talk about expropriation meant. Ascânio was so hurt and indignant he had not listened to Leonora's pleas but had written a letter—"Such a sad letter, Mama, I couldn't help crying when he read it to me"—to the troublemaker, breaking off relations and putting an end to a friendship "which I thought was above any differences of opinion we might have." Dona Carmosina, no mean letter writer herself, had replied in kind to his accusations of slander and intrigue in a missive no less dramatic in style and content. "You have thrown away my tried and true friendship, tested at crucial moments in your life, on the Brastânio dump heap."

"What an awful fight, Mama. They were all such good friends before. And I like Carmosina so much too. I feel just terrible about it."

Tieta stroked the girl's fair hair.

"You don't know yet why I came back from Mangue Seco."

"I wondered why, Mama. I thought you weren't coming back till the day of the party."

"Well, that's what I thought too. If you're happy here, just think how happy I was out at Mangue Seco. Tasting Paradise, I was, with my archangel watching over me. Well, I gave it all up and came back."

"But Mama, why?"

"Because I couldn't help it. I tried my damnedest not to come, but I came back just the same. And the worst of it is that I know it won't do a bit of good in the end. It wasn't Mama who came back, Nora. It was Tieta, the goat girl who used to get mixed up in fights with the police on the fishermen's side. I can't explain it, really, but if I hadn't come I don't think I ever would have had the nerve to set foot here again."

Leonora was not sure she understood either. Tieta rose and walked over to the window, gazing down at the alley. Poor Leonora!

"I've come back to knock Ascânio out of the running, by fair means or foul."

"Oh, Mama! What are you doing to me?"

"This doesn't have a thing to do with your affair. Don't get mixed up in this fight. You're not from Agreste, you're only here on a visit, and none of this is your concern. You just look out for your man if you love him as much as you say you do. He's going to need it."

In which the carrion begins to stink.

Beside himself with anger, Modesto Pires bellowed, "You flock of buzzards!"

Canuto Tavares, twice an Antunes, stood up to the owner of the tannery.

"And the filthiest buzzard of us all is you! Sharper! Shylock!"

Drs. Baltazar Moreira and Gustavo Galvão, who had been hand in glove until now, were trading insults.

"Cheater! Hypocrite! Scoundrel!"

"Stupid, primitive illiterate!"

Dr. Franklin, whose office was the scene of the row, tried to calm the tempest.

"Gentlemen, gentlemen, please calm down!"

He was afraid they would suit their actions to their words. Dona Carlota the schoolmistress, who was used to being treated with respect, threatened to have conniptions. Dr. Marcolino seized on the maiden lady's hysterical outburst to beg for peace and quiet.

"Let's hear what Dr. Baltazar has to say, since he's already taken the initiative and talked to the people at Brastânio."

"Yes, I did, and I don't need anyone's permission to act in defense of my clients' interests as I think best. If you'll listen I'll tell you what I found out, but I want to make it clear that I feel in no way obligated to do so."

The uproar began when Dr. Baltazar interrupted Dr. Marcolino, at whose request they had gathered in the notary's office, in the middle of an explanation.

"The measure proposed by my colleague has already been

taken by me, on my own initiative. There's no point going on the same errand twice."

On his own initiative! That is, on behalf of Dona Carlota and Modesto Pires, behind the others' backs and without their knowledge! Treachery, a stab in the back! Dr. Marcolino, still smiling, succeeded in pouring oil on the waters, to the keen disappointment of young Bonaparte, who was partial to shoot-'em-ups and had had high hopes of being treated to a scene of fisticuffs between Canuto and Modesto Pires. Daily life in Agreste was getting wilder all the time. Dr. Marcolino proposed that the epithets be withdrawn on both sides. Dona Carlota, still quivering with indignation, pulled herself together under the kind ministrations of the notary.

Insults, threats, fainting fits—anyone would think Dr. Baltazar had snitched all Brastânio's gold for Dona Carlota. Far from it; the results of the lawyer's approach to the company's board of directors had been nil. To begin with, when he had told them he represented the heirs to the palm grove they had sent him to Dr. Colombo's office. He said nothing about the long and humiliating wait in the outer office; instead he stressed the courtesy with which the great lawyer had received him. He had cordially but categorically stated that Brastânio's interest in Agreste at the moment was still purely theoretical, since the state government had yet to make a pronouncement on the plant. There was, of course, a possibility that the industry would be installed in Agreste, but until the authorities had made their decision it would be highly improper for Brastânio to enter into agreements, discuss prices or buy up land, in Agreste or anywhere else. They couldn't very well go over the government's head and jump the gun on an official decision that was still pending, could they? And besides, how could they deal with people who were not yet juridical entities, would-be heirs without a leg to stand on as yet? Before proposing agreements they ought to make sure their own claims were recognized, because when it came down to it the company would make no deals except with heirs proclaimed as such in a court of law. As for the alleged expropriation, he declared he knew nothing about it and it was probably only idle speculation in the press.

"In any case, if the county is thinking of expropriating the area with a view to driving up property values, that's the county's problem, not ours."

With this statement, which was clearly false, Professor Colombo had taken leave of his esteemed colleague. Dr. Baltazar ended his account by affirming in a conciliatory tone that he had intended all along to advise the other heirs of what had transpired. There ensued a meditative silence, which was presently interrupted by Canuto Tavares.

"Well, it looks like we're up the creek without a paddle."

Not at all, said Dr. Marcolino, who urged a general reconciliation with a view to joint action to be taken vis-à-vis the future mayor. Expropriation might be a perfectly good solution if it was handled right. There was no use trying to head it off; it was perfectly legal and all they could do was try to make the best profit from it they could. What did his esteemed colleagues think?

At last they went bustling off down the streets of Agreste in the heat of the afternoon. In the registry, Dr. Franklin pinched his nostrils and murmured, "There's a very bad smell around here."

"I thought for sure Canuto would sock Seu Modesto in the jaw," complained Bonaparte. "That would have been great, wouldn't it, Dad?"

"I don't want to think about it."

*In which the reader learns of the existence
of a still-clandestine electoral committee.*

Ricardo became the indispensable handyman for the hardworking team laboring clandestinely in the backyard of the Skipper's bungalow, which had been transformed into electoral committee headquarters—clandestinely because only a few conspirators were in on the secret. The Skipper had agreed to Tieta's request not to take to the hustings until she had a chance to speak to Ascânio and Colonel Artur.

Ricardo lent a hand with the carpentry work and painting, went to his Uncle Astério's shop to buy cloth and acted as liaison between the conspirators, circulating between the post office, the bar and Dona Milu's house, not forgetting his sacred obligations to the church. In church he met Cinira again, still studying to be a churchmouse; they climbed the steps of the churchtower, she in front and he behind, gazing. As he rushed around town taking shortcuts, he found himself in alleys and back lanes and sometimes in the arms of Maria Imaculada, all coquetry and complaints: "Honey, I thought you'd never turn up." At night, before retiring to Tieta's bosom, he conferred with the chiefs of staff—Dona Carmosina, Aminthas and the Skipper—thrilled to be in on all the campaign plans. Devoted and tireless in the surging energy of his seventeen years, he shirked none of his duties as a citizen and a man. He had a tool for every job.

Taking a piece of calico into the deserted yard one day at siesta time, Ricardo heard a low "psst!" that seemed to be for him. He looked around but could see no one. There was another, louder summons from the other side of the fence.

The bungalow yard bordered on that of the house in which the secluded and coveted Carol, submissive but not resigned, languished unseen. This circumstance assured the peace of mind of Modesto Pires, to whom an unjust Providence and the power of wealth had granted exclusive rights over the captive beauty. No better neighbors could have been found. The Skipper's incurable monogamy was public and notorious; even Osnar had lost all hope of ever taking him to join the merry company at Zuleika's house. Furthermore, Carol had the deepest feelings of gratitude and devotion for Dona Laura. The ladies of Agreste avoided any contact with the rich man's mistress, all but Dona Laura de Queluz, born and bred in the liberal south. Dona Milu also spoke to Carol and treated her like a human being, but Dona Milu didn't count. As a widow advanced in years and a midwife besides, she was above local mores, beyond good and evil.

An ornamental fence decked with blue and yellow flowering vines separated the two yards, and Carol sometimes peeked at the neighboring yard through the chinks in the fence. It was almost always quiet and peaceful, even when the owners of the house were in town. Sometimes Gripa the maid went out to pick lemons there. Early in the morning the Skipper did gymnastics, which, along with sea bathing at Mangue Seco, were enough to keep him fit and trim. To admire him was a platonic pleasure which could lead to nothing, for the reasons already explained. The Skipper's integrity and the girl's gratitude reduced the spectacle to one of sheer esthetic delight.

After this, picture Carol's surprise when she noticed an unusual stir and bustle on the other side of the fence. She kept her eyes peeled and soon saw an odd collection of material being brought in;

planks, laths, cloth, cardboard and paint, and a sensational group of people to work with it all. There were the gallant barroom boys— Aminthas, who winked and waved; Seixas, who sighed so deeply when he passed beneath her window; Fidélio, the best-looking of the four, but cagey and reserved, biding his time until the right opportunity came along; and fresh, funny Osnar. Suddenly they trooped into the yard with Dona Carmosina, unrolled cloth and cardboard, hammered and mixed paint, while the Skipper gave orders. Seu Modesto had commented one night not long ago that everybody in Agreste seemed to have gone crazy.

The excitement of our luscious, forbidden Carol reached its peak when she glimpsed through the flowering vines the unexpected, angelic figure of young Ricardo, with his light feet and his hairy legs. On lonely, unhappy nights she dreamed of him and cuddled her pillow, pretending it was him, and now here he was, so close she could reach out and touch him. Seu Modesto was right; Agreste had charms it had never had before.

"Psst!" she said again. Ricardo came over and put his face in the opening, his head crowned with flowers.

Of banzo *blues, diagnosed by Osnar.*

At Dona Amorzinho's boardinghouse old Jarde Antunes, the hardworking farmer and jovial goat breeder of old, was pining away. He spent most of the day lying on the bed, down in the dumps, taking no interest in anything. Josafá tried to cheer him up from time to time.

"Just a few more days, Pa, and we'll sell the land, pocket our cash and be on our way to Itabuna. And that's where you'll see what fertile land is like, and fat cattle, every kind of eye-filling livestock —cacao country, Pa! Not these scorched little dried-up checkerboards we have here. Just be patient a little while longer."

The old man's gaze never left the ceiling boards.

"Are you feeling sick, Pa? Do you want me to call the doctor?"

"Ain't no need. I ain't sick."

Josafá was a good son. He spent hours either describing the great cacao plantations and opulent grazing land of southern Bahia, or telling his father about how their claim was going, the comings and goings of the lawyers, Modesto Pires' sharp deals and foxiness, and his doubts about Ascânio. He could not even be sure the old man was listening.

"Do you hear me, Pa?"

"Yep, Son, I hear you."

As the afternoon grew hotter Jarde would close his eyes and fall into a torpor in the breathless heat, indifferent to everything around him, or almost everything. Once in a while he would put on his sandals and shuffle across the street to Astério's store to ask for news of Vista Alegre and his goats, especially Seu Mé. The news was always good, and that put new life into Jarde and sometimes even made him smile. He would discourse with Astério and Osnar about goats and their ways; there was no animal wild or domesticated, he maintained, that compared to the goat. As for Seu Mé, not even Colonel Artur da Tapitanga owned a superb male like that. "Yep, he's a fine hunk of he-goat all right," Osnar agreed.

When he took his leave old Jarde visibly drooped again into melancholy. As he stood up he was livid, skin and bones, unsteady on his feet, eyes fixed on the ground. Astério felt so sorry for him that he urged the old man to walk out with him to the farm the next morning. Jarde refused with a despondent gesture and a feeble voice.

"What for? Just to feel bad looking at what don't belong to me no more? Just take good care of the critters, that's all I ask."

And he would shuffle back across the street with dragging steps.

"He's got the *banzo*," was Osnar's diagnosis.

"*Banzo*? queried Astério. "I never heard of anybody around here getting *banzo*. They used to call it the nigger blues."

"That's right. It should have gone out with slavery, but it looks like the factory's brought it back. What do you bet we have an epidemic?"

Of the last touches in the education of a leader, or how Ascânio gets a bellyful.

Leaders are forged in the thick of the battle, winning out over hardships and adversity, or so Ascânio had read in a book called *Trajectory of Leaders, from Tiradentes to Vargas.* Now that he was being given a chance to prove it in the flesh, his personal experience was beginning to bear out the truth of the statement. In the thick of the battle, bearing up under injuries, disappointments, insolence and threats, Ascânio was changing, maturing and reformulating his scale of values. His ambition was growing by leaps and bounds ("A man who lacks ambition will never get ahead," the successful Rosalvo Lucena had taught him) and he was tougher than before, convinced of the rightness of his actions and determined to go as far as he had to. According to the author of the biographical sketches, a mysterious force almost always sustained the leader in combat: a star guided his steps, a sun lighted his path. Exactly. In the case of our young leader from Agreste, that mysterious force came from Leonora Cantarelli, his star, his sun, his inspiration and his quest.

It was from her that he drew courage and strength. A leader had to endure a great deal if he wanted to overcome and to rule. Were it not for her loving encouragement renewed night after night, how could he have stood his ground and confounded lawyers and heirs? Separately and together they filed up and down the steps of the courthouse, bugging him all day long. The well-brought-up Ascânio would never have used such a crude verb in the old days, but he had had a bellyful and was now letting fly with bad language right and left.

Whether alone or in groups, they always ended up in his office, pestering the life out of their candidate and trying his patience to the limit. They wanted decisions, promises, guaranteees. Was he going to expropriate the land or not? The whole palm grove or just part of it? On what basis would compensation be determined? By experts? Who were they? Although he had left law school in his second year, Ascânio parried the lawyers' questions and the pressure put on him by the heirs. Getting sore wouldn't help at all, he knew. He couldn't tell them all to go fuck themselves, although he longed to do just that. Consideration and respect were owed to Modesto Pires and Dona Carlota, Canuto Tavares was a friend of his, and he needed them all more than ever now that it looked as if the election would no longer be a foregone conclusion in which the will of the people coincided happily with that of Colonel Artur da Tapitanga.

Turning a deaf ear to warnings, hints and innuendoes, Ascânio managed to pacify and appease them all while promising nothing. Once so strict, he was learning to be flexible. Given Fidélio's intransigence, there was really no other solution to the problem of the factory site but expropriation. If there was one he'd be very glad to hear it; maybe you, sir, as a lawyer . . . And expropriation would of course benefit the heirs. The county government had no wish to act to anyone's detriment; the installation of this industry should bring wealth to all citizens, at least that was Ascânio's point of view. Why didn't they concentrate on legalizing their claims? That way, when the time came, if Fidélio still held out it would be a simple matter for them to come to an agreement with the county on the details. He navigated skillfully among heirs and lawyers, trying not to disagree too strongly with anyone who might support his candidacy in the future. With all his caution he had a brush with Dr. Marcolino Pitombo, of all people.

"Another word, sir, and I'll have to ask you to leave this room." A leader has to know how to be firm at the right time.

The wily attorney, in Josafá's presence and in the middle of a confused conversation, had referred à propos of nothing to "Adequate compensations in case . . ." Ascânio, his pride stung, stopped Dr. Pitombo before he could finish the sentence. Undefined insinuations floated in the air. Was this an attempt at a bribe? His indignant reaction had no effect on Dr. Marcolino. As placid and smiling as ever, the lawyer said diplomatically that his esteemed friend was unusually thin-skinned these days; that, no doubt, was why he misinterpreted words said in all innocence—would he please calm down? The explanation was accepted, and what had been said was declared unsaid.

As they left the building Josafá reminded his impulsive attorney of a previous conversation.

"Didn't I tell you Ascânio was a straight shooter, Dr. Marcolino? He cut you off good and proper."

"I admit I was wrong, but only when I said he was stupid. That young man is neither stupid nor honest. He may have been honest once, before he was put in the way of such a good thing. My dear Josafá, I've told you before that every man has his price. Ours was too low, that's all; we can't expect to compete with Brastânio. Professor Colombo passed this way before we did, don't forget."

Ascânio never knew of this particular conversation, but other, varied speculations as to his motives did reach his ears. His character and integrity were the subject of passionate arguments, just as those of all leaders were. Never had he imagined that the redemption of Agreste ("Brastânio will be the redemption of Agreste," the headline on his poster at the courthouse still proclaimed) would cause him so much mortification and annoyance. In spite of Dr. Marcolino's excuses, the attorney's specious phrases and the insidious word "compensations" still hummed in his ears, together with the insulting aside flung in his face at the improvised rally when the first electric light pole was set up: "Brastânio stooge! You've sold out!" He had refused Dr. Mirko's offer of help in the election campaign for that very reason, to remain above any shadow of suspicion; but it had all been for nothing, they accused him just the same.

As one troubled day succeeded another, he became used to ambiguous situations which had once seemed intolerable to him. When he had heard the aside he had been fighting mad and dared the coward to show himself and repeat the insult if he had the guts. At the Golden Cue finals in the bar he had been furious when he heard Dona Edna's sly allusion to Catherine's Basin. Now he didn't care what they said. A leader should be above such petty vexations, especially when there were really serious problems to worry about beside which the anonymous aside, the lawyer's unfinished sentence and Dona Edna's coarseness were as nothing.

Dona Carmosina, the bosom friend who had sustained him in the blackest hour of Astrud's treachery and watched over his love affair with Leonora as benevolently as a fairy godmother, had behaved in an unheard-of, not to say abominable, way: she had tried to set old Colonel Artur, to whom Ascânio owed both his present and his future political posts, against him; and what was worse, she had succeeded.

The landowner, his mind poisoned against Brastânio, had summoned him to the plantation and told him he wanted no filth in Agreste. Ascânio tried to rebut the assertions and arguments of the postmistress, whose passionate opposition, he insisted, was owing to her friendship with Giovanni Guimarães, by repeating things he had heard Mirko Stefano and Rosalvo Lucena say and inveighing against the enemies of progress in Brazil. The Colonel heard him out with half-closed eyes and a weary expression but was not convinced; he came back at him with the stories in O Estado de São Paulo about the verdict of the Italian judge. O Estado de São Paulo didn't lie and never made a mistake. He raised his eyes and looked at his godson.

"It was me who made you a candidate after Mauritônio died. But now people are going around saying you're some factory's candidate."

"I owe everything to you, Godfather. But I don't care if they do say I'm Brastânio's candidate; that's nothing to be ashamed of. On the contrary, it's an honor because we share the same ideal, to bring progress to Agreste. Whatever people may say and do, they won't be able to break me. I'm seeing this through. I want to thank you, sir, for all you've done for me, but Godfather, please don't ask me to change my mind." A leader is tempered on the field of battle.

He had hardly recovered from that difficult interview—painful, too, for his godfather was visibly wasting away—when he was dealt another blow, the worst one of all. Dona Antonieta Esteves Cantarelli, Leonora's stepmother, Distinguished Citizen of Agreste and Joan of Arc of the *sertão*, came back from Mangue Seco and sent word that she would like to see him. Just the two of us for a talk, she said. Ascânio was terrified. Tieta had probably found out what was going on between him and Leonora on the riverbank; the murmured gossiping whispers going around town must have reached her ears. Well, he wouldn't deny it; he would seize the opportunity to confess his deep and honest affection and tell her his intentions were honorable. Though poor, he was able and ambitious and would surely find his place in the sun. Here was a way to settle the matter once and for all. He put the engagement ring in his pocket. Whatever Dona Antonieta's reaction was, he had no intention of giving up Leonora. He was ready for anything.

Leonora's name was not mentioned once during their talk, nor was their affair. Dona Antonieta informed him that it was the Brastânio business that had brought her back to Agreste. She and some friends of hers were against the installation of Brastânio factories in the county, as Ascânio knew, and were ready to fight for their convictions. However, they did not want to go any further without giving him a hearing, and that was why she had requested this meeting. She respected him and believed he was honest. Honest but naive; he was being taken in by unscrupulous businessmen, a breed she understood very well. Ideally, Tieta and her friends would like to throw their full support behind Ascânio's candidacy. In order for them to do so, he would have to change his present stance for one of opposition to the lethally contaminating titanium-dioxide industry. If he was willing to do that, all would be well. It was up to Ascânio to choose between them and Brastânio. She wasn't asking for an answer right off the bat, but she would like one fairly quickly; there wasn't much time left.

"Thank you, ma'am; I'm grateful to you for coming to talk to me before going any further, but I'm not grateful to the others. Everyone in town knows the Skipper plans to run for mayor. And Carmosina—"

"All you have to do is say yes and they'll all be on your side, including me. I represent the others, too. You think about it and then let me know."

"There's nothing else for me to think about, Dona Antonieta. The last thing in the world I wanted was to displease you, ma'am. You ask me to do anything at all and I'll come running. But please don't ask me to be a turncoat. Even if I have to fight on all alone to bring progress to Agreste, even if you never forgive me and become my enemy—"

"Whoa, there! Hold your horses! Who said anything about enemies? I have nothing to forgive or not forgive you. You think one way and I think differently, that's all. We'll see who wins in the election, but that doesn't mean we're enemies. You're just a kid, you're drowning in a glass of water. Felipe was against everything Dr. Ademar stood for, but they got along fine. Don't confuse politics with friendship."

They parted protesting they were friends, but Ascânio felt resentful and bitter. He had hoped Tieta would keep out of this fight and stay at Mangue Seco until the day the new light was turned on as she had said she would do. As it was he hadn't even mentioned his planned tribute, afraid she would take it the wrong way and think of the street sign as a kind of bribe. Bribe, that unpleasant word, seemed to hang in the air.

After supper Ascânio came to pick up Leonora at Perpétua's door as usual. They walked around the plaza waiting for the tired generator to go off so that they could take one of the byways down to a dark nest under the willows. He told Leonora about the difficult talk he had had. She already knew about it; Mama had told her.

"Are you going to be the next one to ask me to change my mind and throw in the sponge? After my godfather and Dona Antonieta, you're the only one left," he said bitterly.

"All I'm asking you to do is love me." She kissed his hand in her submissive gesture of tenderness and devotion. "Mama told me I wasn't born here and to keep out of it. Maybe it's selfish of me, Ascânio, but I can't help being glad, because with this hitch in her plans Mama's put off our going back to São Paulo. She was all set to leave the day after the party, but now she wants to stay and help the Skipper. My grandmother always said that everything in the world has a good side."

Come to think of it, that's true, Ascânio thought. If his talk with Dona Antonieta had upset him, the meeting with his godfather had frightened him. The Colonel was very fond of his godson. He had been willing to give him his daughter in marriage, he had gotten him an administrative post, and he had announced Ascânio's candidacy for mayor when Dr. Dantas died. He had not withdrawn his support despite Carmosina's intrigues, but he was not convinced of Brastânio's merits, either. If the Skipper ran, surely that would annoy the Colonel enough to forget his demands and throw all the weight of his prestige behind Ascânio's campaign. Colonel Artur da Tapitanga wasn't used to having any of his plans opposed; there had been no opposition in the county for many, many years.

And that was fortunate indeed, for otherwise Ascânio would be obliged to ask Brastânio to cover his campaign expenses. There weren't very many, but there were some, and the piddling sum of money it would take was more than he had. He wouldn't like having to ask the industrialists for help on this occasion; his pride was at stake. He had told Mirko he didn't need their help, that he was as good as elected already. But he had said he might welcome their support later on. By later on he had meant after the election, the inauguration and the expropriation, when the factory complex built on Mangue Seco was producing wealth and prestige for Agreste, and everyone would understand and do justice to the leader forged in struggle and adversity. Yes, even Dona Carmosina and Dona Antonieta. Once the rectitude of his intentions was proved beyond a doubt, he would be free to accept any offer of assistance Brastânio might make to help him run for state office. Leonora Cantarelli's husband could hardly limit his aspirations to the post of mayor of Agreste, and Colonel Artur de Figueiredo's prestige, even if the old political boss should live that long, was not enough to elect a state deputy.

Of how the old caudillo, Artur da Tapitanga, lost his candidate.

On a wooden bench on the veranda of his plantation house, Colonel Artur de Figueiredo sat by himself warming his bones. Goats browsed and munched nearby and the corral was only a little way off. He was roused from his doze by a woman's voice calling lustily at the gate. Old age was a terrible thing; your legs buckled under you, the food lost its taste in your mouth, sounds were weak and far away to your deaf ears, and people and things moved in a fog to your dull eyes. He had some difficulty in recognizing the visitor who was approaching, picking her way across the yard among chickens, guinea fowl and ducks.

"Who goes there?"

"A friend, Colonel!"

The voice sounded familiar. He stood up, leaning on his cane, and narrowed his eyes to see better.

"Is that you, Tieta? God be praised! I was going to send you a message but they told me you were out at Mangue Seco."

When she was closer Tieta realized how much the octogenarian had gone down in little more than two weeks. When he had gone to see her on New Year's Day after Zé Esteves's death he was still a vigorous, jolly old man parading his memories; full of sly sallies, urging her to come out to the plantation to see Branding Iron, his ram, the father of the flock, unrivaled in history. Now he looked ancient and pitiful, bent over his stick. He spoke with an effort, his eyes had no luster, he was all skin and bones.

One thing he had kept, though, was his willfulness, together with certain old habits and interests, public and private. When he hugged Tieta, he felt of her abundant flesh with tremulous hands, alas for old times!

"Come and sit down, child; I want you to explain to me what's going on in Agreste."

Tieta laughed mischievously, alluding to his fumbling hands.

"Time goes by, Colonel, but I see you haven't lost your sense of touch."

When she was a young goat girl she used to run away when she saw him coming. If he caught her he'd run his hand over her breasts and legs.

"I've lost my taste for just about everything else, but not for women. I'm just like an old billygoat that ain't good for much any more but still likes to go around sniffing at the nannygoats' tails." He thumped with his stick on the ground and called out, "Merência!"

The servant, a shapeless, humpbacked woman with white kinky hair, so old it was impossible to tell her age, peered out from the doorway and recognized Tieta.

"You're Tieta, ain't you? You a blonde these days or are you wearin' a toupée?"

"Yes, Merência, it's me. I'll be in to see you in a little while."

"Don't just stand there, woman. Why don't you fix us some coffee?"

"How old is Merência anyway, Colonel?"

"She must be nigh on a hundred if she ain't that already. She was a rambunctious young gal when I was born. Now Tieta, I want you to tell me what's going on and tell it to me right. I never heard such foolishness in all my born days."

"What kind of foolishness, Colonel?"

"Take my godson Ascânio now, my right arm in the county government; he seems to have lost his good sense somewhere along the line over this famous industry that wants to get a foot in the door out on Mangue Seco. That's what they tell me, anyway. Ascânio seems to think that's all this township needs for the money to start rolling in. He's been down in the state capital to talk with those investors, and I tell you he swears by 'em. When he told me about it the first time it sounded like a fish story to me, but I kept my mouth shut 'cause I don't pretend to understand these times we're living in. There's things going on I think the devil himself would be hard put to it to explain." He paused and changed the subject. "Now tell me this. How'd you get 'em to run the Paulo Afonso electric power all the way to Agreste? They've been clear out here putting up the lines. Not even the devil can explain a thing like that." Here was a flicker of sly humor in the dull eyes and rheumy voice. "For you to boss those São Paulo politicians around like that, I just don't know. . . ."

Tieta laughed and threw more wood on the old man's fire.

"Oh, I have my ways and means, Colonel, I have my secret weapons."

"I know you do. You ain't been Christian folks since you was a little gal." His eyes swept over Tieta's bust and hips. "The Lord did well by you in the way of bread and milk. I hope you keep the gifts He gave you. I bet your departed husband was a nice, good-tempered man. . . . Did you say he was a count?"

"A Comendador, Colonel."

"They're all the same. Those monarchists are a tame bunch, born to wear horns. But let's backtrack a little bit. Now the next one to come along is Dona Carmosina, another fine person. She trots out here with a pile of newspapers under her arm, the newspapers I subscribe to but she's the one who reads 'em, and she wades right in quoting me stories from the *Estado de São Paulo* and *A Tarde*, both of 'em responsible papers, where it says that industry's a calamity and a ruination, and the only reason they're putting it here is because nobody wants it anyplace else. And I got to thinking those people might be winding Ascânio around their little finger; he's still a spring chicken and it ain't hard to bamboozle him. So I sent for him to come out here and we had a talk about the stories and the filth and all that pollution business. When the mayor's job fell vacant, I told Ascânio to be sure and keep the town clean, since he couldn't bring the good times back again, and the first thing I hear is he's bringing in a factory nobody wants. He told me the factory would bring back the good old days and make Agreste rich again; that all that song and dance about pollution's nothing but a tall tale invented by folks who don't want Brazil to get ahead, who are against the government and take orders from Russia, like that fellow Giovanni who came around and got so thick with Carmosina. But I showed him where the *Estado de São Paulo* was giving it to that industry hot and heavy, and I never heard of *Estado de São Paulo* having anything to do with Russia; the *Estado* knows what it's talking about, it ain't the kind of newspaper to make things up. That kind of stopped him in his tracks for a minute, but then he asked me to believe him when he said he was only doing it for Agreste's good. And I do believe him there. Ascânio's a good boy, but those people may be pulling the wool over his eyes. You got it all figured out, I know, and I want you to tell me what's what."

Tieta heard him out without interrupting. The old man spoke

deliberately, breaking his sentences off in the middle because he was short of breath. He barely touched the coffee Merência had brought. From time to time a goat ran through the yard and the Colonel raised his eyes to look.

"That's why I came, Colonel, to see you and to talk about all this. I like Ascânio and think he's honest too. But he's always dreaming about the old days when you and his grandfather ran things, and he thinks Brastânio can bring back the kind of prosperity there was back then. Well, that's where he's wrong. If this were a textile mill or a shoe factory, everyone would be in favor of it. But what Brastânio wants to make is titanium dioxide."

"And what the dickens might titanium dioxide be? Carmosina tried to explain it to me when she came out, but she talks too highfalutin for me to understand."

"Colonel, I won't lie to you. I don't know exactly what it is and that's the truth. All I know is that it's the worst-polluting industry in the world. It would ruin our fine climate, stink up the river and the ocean, and there'd be no more work for the fishermen."

"You mean it kills the fish?"

"Colonel, it kills everything, even goats."

"Goats too?"

"Colonel, that's why I'm here: to tell you that if Ascânio won't tell that Brastânio where to get off we intend to run Skipper Dário for mayor."

Colonel Artur da Tapitanga quivered with indignation, as if Tieta had struck him in the face. His eyes flashed dangerously; his voice, with a supreme effort, turned violent.

"Who's we? Who has the nerve to talk about running somebody else without consulting me?"

"Nobody, Colonel, don't get your hackles up. Nobody's running yet. The Skipper and I and Carmosina and some other friends of ours want to ask for your permission first. That's what I'm here for. You're Ascânio's godfather and political patron. We're not against Ascânio, just against the titanium-dioxide factory. All Ascânio has to do is turn his back on those people and say he'll have nothing more to do with them, and the fight'll be over before it begins. But if he doesn't want to do that, Colonel, then he leaves us no other choice but to fight him if we don't want Agreste turned into a garbage can like the paper says."

The old man rested his chin on his cane. Nothing remained of his anger. The fire in his eyes had died out. He repeated slowly in a low voice, "A garbage can. . . . That's right, Carmosina read that to me. I've already talked to Ascânio, I tell you. I called him out here days ago. And you know what he answered? That he was honored to be that company's candidate, that he was going to see this thing through come hell or high water, and that nobody was going to stop him from giving Agreste a push on the road to progress."

The fleshless hand reached for Tieta's hand and touched her fingers, covered with rings and precious stones.

"Listen to me, child. You're talking to a useless old billygoat who's been put out to pasture. The poor old varmint thinks he's still the king of the barnyard, but he ain't no such thing; even the new little kids can kick him around. Colonel Artur de Figueiredo the Big Boss is dead. I ain't picking any more candidates or bothering my head about any more elections. Don't you see, child? There's those big investors from the factory on one side, and they ain't even from around here. On the other side there's you, Tieta, a little barefoot gal I knew back when she herded goats and now she's covered with diamonds. The old Colonel don't count anymore." His voice was weary and bitter.

In her sympathy for him, Tieta stroked his hand affectionately.

"Colonel, don't say that. If you leave Ascânio on his own, no factory in the world can elect him. You're the big man around here, and you're still the boss. And I'll prove it to you. If you ask me to or order me to, I'll stop the Skipper from running this very day. I won't go against you, not even to save the goats."

A faint smile appeared on the old caudillo's withered lips.

"I don't believe you when you say that titanium kills the goats, Tieta; you're just saying that to fool me. But I'm not asking you or ordering you to do anything. I don't want to fool with it anymore. Everybody can just act according to his lights. Ascânio thinks he's doing the right thing; well then, let him do it. You, Carmosina, the Skipper and I don't know who else, think the opposite. If I still had any use for money I might have gone in with the foreigners to bring that factory in here; people do worse things than that for money. And if I still got any fun out of living I'd back your side all the way; the worst man in the world can do a noble thing once. But I ain't got nothing left to win or lose in the world, Tieta; I've even lost my taste for ordering other folks around. But I'm mighty grateful to you just the same for what you said to me and being thoughtful of an old man. Those words of yours have put honey on my lips now it's almost time for me to die."

"Colonel, there's a favor I'd like to ask you before I go."

"You can ask me for anything you want."

"I'd like to have a look at Branding Iron, that famous billygoat of yours. I want to compare him with Inácio, a ram that belonged to my father, old Zé Esteves."

"I'll have somebody take you out to the corral."

"Won't you come with me? Come on, get up and give me your arm."

They went down the veranda steps together.

"You ain't no Christian woman, you're the devil in female form." A deep sigh. "If I was only ten years younger now, if I could only be a spry seventy-five again, you wouldn't be a widow woman long, I wouldn't let you."

Of civic zeal and divine justice.

On Saturday the city awoke to find itself in the middle of a full-fledged electoral campaign. A VOTE FOR SKIPPER DÁRIO DE QUELUZ IS A VOTE AGAINST POLLUTION! read four banners placed strategically at points where people tended to gather. One was right in front of the courthouse. Signboards urged everybody to show up the next day, Sunday, at about five in the afternoon, after the movie matinee and before Benediction, at a big rally to launch Skipper Dário's campaign for mayor. The candidate would speak and De Matos Barbosa the poet would recite his *Poems of Damnation*.

Banners and signs had been put together in the Skipper's back-yard by the efficient team whose civic zeal the lovely Carol had greeted with such joy and hope. At Dona Milu's house, brainy Carmosina and Aminthas drafted a sort of manifesto to the people outlining the reasons for the Skipper's candidacy. The flyer, printed in Esplanada on yellow paper, would be distributed to all and sundry in Agreste that Saturday and Sunday. Sensational events were to take place on Saturday, following days of underground agitation.

Praise be to agitation! In all these comings and goings Ricardo was becoming more than ever the man with a tool for every trade.

From the other side of the yard the oppressed concubine languished at the siesta hour. The two young people exchanged vows and promises between the vines and made their plans; the slaveowner would be spending the weekend on Mangue Seco with his wife and grandchildren. In the churchtower at eventide Cinira, one foot in the grave of spinsterhood, the other uplifted to facilitate matters, gazed out over the tranquil town. From behind the mango tree Maria Imaculada waited for him at nine o'clock sharp, when the light went off and the lovers' lanes to the river bluffs were open for business. "Hurry up, honey, hurry up, we don't have much time." At home Tieta waited impatiently. As for Dona Edna, she bided her time. After all, no one's made of iron, not even a young seminarian fanatically ready for action.

On Friday, though, the generator went off without interrupting the tasks of the Skipper's devoted partisans, and Ricardo did not run to meet Maria Imaculada as usual. The girl had been told beforehand and had agreed to sacrifice her moment of pleasure to the cause for one night. Fidélio, Seixas, Ricardo, Peto and Sabino worked most of the night hanging banners and placards under Aminthas' direction and Osnar's supervision. Osnar, averse to any kind of physical labor—"I save up my strength for hard work in bed"—gave orders and bossed everybody around. The Skipper directed the work with a grave face, preoccupied with the heavy responsibility of preparing his speech for the rally. Goatstink had offered his moral support to the militant environmentalists from the first, but having pinched an almost full bottle of rum out from under Osnar's nose, had gone off somewhere and not come back.

They all ended up at Zuleika's for a celebratory fishfry at which the worthy Osnar was host, all but the Skipper, who was incorruptible, and Ricardo, who was a seminarian. However, that young man was in no hurry to retire. Owing to the happy coincidence of Modesto Pires' departure for the beach and the bosom of his family, a door in the sleeping town just happened to be closed but not locked, awaiting the coming of the valiant doer of justice.

All during those hectic days the prevailing atmosphere was one of mistrust and clashing opinions; but when certain facts came to light and Modesto Pires' horns were publicly assumed, there was unanimous agreement and no one criticized the authors of the deed.

Authors, yes, but that in no way detracts from the glory of Ricardo's feat in being the first to cross the heretofore invulnerable barriers of respect for the powerful and fear of despotic vengeance to see that justice was done. Divine justice, in the words of the people. All Agreste had been waiting for this auspicious event to occur ever since the owner of the tannery had imported Carol's many charms from the wilds of Sergipe to enrich the patrimony of Agreste but then made the gesture almost meaningless by selfishly claiming exclusive rights.

Goatstink, back in the hope of more *cachaça*, found the plaza empty. Wending his way through deserted alleys in the first glimmer of dawn, he caught sight of the shadow of the robust Samaritan as he crossed the threshold of the slave cabin to proclaim abolition. Goatstink, an enemy of tyranny and private property, called out to his meager public of two mongrel dogs and a bitch, "Blessed be the Lord and divine justice be done! Hop to it, priest-boy!"

Of how the high old times come back and fists fly in the marketplace.

"You'll see high old times again when the factory comes in," Ascânio Trindade had promised Colonel Artur de Figueiredo. Events proved him right before many days had passed; it was not even necessary for the factory to come in for the Agreste market-place to recapture a hustle and bustle worthy of the liveliest days of yore. It was all so lively, in fact, that Possidônio the Prophet, convinced that Judgment Day was at hand, flung down his begging bowl and threw himself wholeheartedly into the salvation of sinners by letting fly with his redeeming rod and staff.

Vendors coming early into the marketplace (Colonel Francisco Trindade Plaza; people are stubborn and refuse to learn) found that some new touches had been added, including a banner strung between two poles stuck in the ground proposing the Skipper for mayor and a signboard inviting everyone to come to the rally. This sign, nailed to a post right in the middle of the plaza, was the same shape and size as one on the front of the moviehouse announcing a sensational shoot-'em-up for that weekend. "A knock it to 'em, sock it to 'em show!" promised the sign.

The banner and the placard aroused little interest at first. The countryfolks' curiosity was directed to something bigger and more spectacular, the brand-new light poles of the Paulo Afonso Power Company, gigantic, impressive, fearfully modern. Two of them were already standing, and the marketgoers craned their necks to try to see the light bulbs. An admiring little crowd was exclaiming over a third, still lying on the ground.

Only a few of the more literate took the trouble to spell out the words on the banner, and fewer still showed any interest in the placard; most could not read. Market day, then, began in the normal way, until Ricardo and Peto started passing out the flyers. Then it turned into a free-for-all.

Gumercindo Saruê, who milled manioc flour in small quantities and sold it at the market, gaped witlessly at the posts, hardly noticed the banner and did not even see the placard. A huge man and a bully, he had been arrested one rumsoaked Sunday for chasing after two boys with his scythe. The boys' mother, Siá Jesuína, a widow and virago, did not rest until Saruê was in "prison." (Agreste's jail, almost permanently empty, was a room at the rear of the court-house with bars on the windows.) When Ascânio heard about it he left his game of pool, soothed the irate mother, opened the door of the hoosegow and told Gumercindo to go in peace.

"You can count on me for anything, Doc, as long as I'm alive," the grateful giant had sworn on that occasion.

These were not vain words, as we shall see. By now Ricardo and Peto had appeared in the marketplace and begun to distribute the prospectus drafted by the indignant Dona Carmosina in col-laboration with the sardonic Aminthas. While the signs and banners merely announced that the Skipper was a candidate, with only a brief reference to pollution, the leaflet explained the reasons for the campaign which could be the salvation of Agreste, a Paradise threat-ened with corruption. It quoted parts of Giovanni Guimarães' column, came down hard on Brastânio, "a multinational business out to enrich foreigners at the expense of the people's misery," and equally hard on Ascânio, "who uses his official post to play the dirty game of these criminals, who won't rest until they turn Agreste into a garbage dump unless we stop them." It was an obligation of all right-thinking citizens to keep this "playboy bumpkin, this cat's-paw of the merchants of death," from being elected.

Ricardo did his duty out of pure idealism, while Peto expected to be paid for his work by Osnar, one of the financial backers of the Skipper's candidacy; but both brothers, the altruistic one and the mercenary one, conscientiously carried out the task entrusted to them, handing out the flyers to each buyer and seller, one at a time. Sabino, obliged to stay behind the counter at the store, took no part in the doings at first.

When Peto came to Gumercindo Saruê's sacks of flour he handed one leaflet to the seller and another to his customer, Dona Jacinta Freire, a pious old busybody. Gumercindo, thinking it was publicity for that day's movie, let the paper fall to the ground. Dona Jacinta, though, interrupted her purchase to read it aloud and the miller had no choice but to listen. When he heard Ascânio's name he pricked up his ears and asked what it was about. Dona Jacinta was only too glad to oblige him. She pointed to the signboard in the middle of the plaza, then to the banner, and read the insults over again in a fruity warble, relishing each word.

"You mean they want to keep Dr. Ascânio from being elected?" demanded Gumercindo incredulously.

"They want Skipper Dário to be mayor instead. This says that Ascânio—"

Saruê was a man of action. He looked around for the kid who had given him the paper with the rotten pack of lies in it and saw him a little farther on, resting from his exertions as he sucked on a lollipop. Gumercindo took out after Peto and reached for the bundle of flyers, managing to grab some, which he angrily tore up, and holding out his hand for the rest.

"Come on, kid, hand over that bunch of crap!"

Now Peto, as we know, was pretty quick on the trigger himself. Suiting words to action, he let fly at Gumercindo with a kick on the shin while insulting his mother.

"Hey, *compadre*, what's going on?" asked Nhô Batista, another farmer from Rocinha, when he saw his friend, blind with rage, trying to collar the boy.

"They're trying to keep Dr. Ascânio from being elected!"

The news ran around the marketplace like a powdertrain; that is, it was rapid and deadly and immediately caused a commotion. Most of the farmers, almost all of whom came from the Rocinha district, held Ascânio in great esteem. Those who lived around the river and the seacoast and brought in fish, shellfish, and sea and land crabs swore by the Skipper. Though numerically in the minority, they were feared and respected. Some of them were said to be smugglers, with a tradition of resisting authority.

It was the miller's pursuit of Peto around the marketplace, with spectacular lunges and much knocking over of merchandise, that started the fracas. Peto managed to escape by turning some hogs loose at the feet of Saruê and his partisans. As he lit out for the bar to bring in reinforcements, the last thing he saw in the confusion was leaflets fluttering in the wind and Ricardo being seized by a group of men. The bar was full of men and they all came running.

Such a lively market day had never been seen; it beat June 4, 1938, all hollow. That was when the vaunted Corporal Euclides attempted the public castration of a guitarist named Ubaldo Capadócio, who had dishonored his bed by seducing his wife Adélia. Capadócio escaped by the skin of his teeth that day. The banner and placards were not so lucky; even the movie poster, prophetically announcing a knock-it-to-'em sock-it-to-'em, was destroyed. The fishermen, not realizing at first what the trouble was, were slow to join in; but when they found out the Skipper had been insulted, they turned the fight into a battle royal.

And a battle royal it was, on every front. Many of the participants had no notion what the fight was about, but no one stayed out of it. Considerable damage was done; sacks and sacks of flour, beans, rice and corn were overturned, fruits and vegetables were trodden on and squashed under foot, slabs of jerky were flung to the ground, fish were waved about as weapons, and crabs scuttled under the feet of the champions. Possidônio the Prophet, proclaiming the end of the world once again, laid about him indiscriminately with his shepherd's rod, indifferent to politics—all of them were sinners and all of them were damned.

Not even Ascânio, who came running from the courthouse, was able to calm the tumult. Neither was the Skipper, called away from drafting his speech, nor Father Mariano, whose intercession did, however, keep the Skipper and Ascânio from coming to blows.

But when Tieta, alerted by Sabino and brandishing old Zé Esteves' staff, rushed into the midst of the people like St. Anne herself, and shouted, "Stop the fight!" everyone made way for her and calm gradually returned; too late to rescue the banner and the placard but in time to gather up what was left of Ricardo, and just in time, too. No sooner had she picked up her glorious nephew and led him away with black-and-blue marks all over his face and legs than into the plaza from different directions came young Maria Imaculada, pious Cinira, aspiring Edna and liberated Carol, all four with fire in their eyes. Ricardo had his electorate, too; not many of them, but choice.

Of Tieta decked out in horns.

Perpétua was awakened by Tieta's screaming. She thrust her black skirt on over her nightgown, picked up the kerosene lamp and opened her door just in time to see Ricardo running down the hall taking a drubbing without saying a word, and God in Heaven, he was naked as the day he was born! Behind him in hot pursuit, beside herself, scorning caution, and flinging restraint, decorum and the conventions to the wind, his aunt ran after him as far as the street door, the shepherd's staff thwacking on her nephew's ribs—Zé Esteves' staff, the very one that had given Tieta a lesson when Perpétua told her father about the traveling salesman.

Ricardo tried to turn back to put his trousers on, but the fury behind him, in a paroxysm of jealous rage, raised her staff and hit him in the face, that perfidious angel face, just as Zé Esteves had hit her one long-ago dawn. She had had an angel face, too. She barred the corridor and let fly with the staff, threatening her false lover's heavenly, treacherous balls and divine, false prick. With a bound Ricardo gained the street and saved his precious jewels. Before he had half recovered from the shock, he found himself in the public square wearing nothing but bruises, slashes, shame and a jade ring, and heard the door slam violently and a furious voice yelling, "Get out of my sight!"

There was Tieta, decked out in horns! She had gone looking for him down by the river. When the generator went off at the appointed time she was lying in wait; she witnessed the meeting behind the mango tree and followed the liar and the little hoyden in the darkness to Catherine's Basin. Subjecting her pride to a severe test, she posted herself to listen in order to drink her indignation to the full and sweat out her jealousy drop by drop. She was one open wound, disgraced, covered with mud, abject, ridiculous, cuckolded. She heard the laughter and lost count of the sighs, felt how long the silent kisses lasted, and learned the thousand nuances the word "honey" can have: kiss me again, honey; bite me; put it in me, honey; don't go away, honey, make it last longer; oh, honey!

As soon as she had returned from Mangue Seco she had begun to suspect the existence of another rival besides God, a rival who was human and female. She sharpened her ears and picked up hints here and there, but it seemed so impossible that she wanted to make sure for herself. Well, now she had seen, she had heard, she had done everything but join in. It was true, all right. She had let herself be fooled. She, Tieta, so vain and so sure of herself, was no smarter than the silliest, most credulous of her girls.

Back in her bedroom she stripped and anointed herself, just as she did every night, and waited for him so that the final sparks of passion would be extinguished when he touched her with hands still warm from the girl's body and nothing was left but humiliation and anger.

It had never happened to her before. Lucas had run away because he was afraid he was becoming too attached to her, not because of another woman. She had had to come back to Agreste for a man to do that. A man? A kid who was barely weaned, dressed in innocence, fear and a cassock, a boy whose flower of virginity she had gathered one night on the dunes by moonlight.

Of the dialogue between the two sisters concerning family matters, a rather sordid chapter in which a quantity of dirty linen is washed and the shit hits the fan.

Naked, blossoming out with horns (and she didn't know the half of it, at that), Tieta faced her sister. She had undressed to wait for that skunk in order to savor every last ingredient of betrayal, sink to the nadir of vileness, and feel her despair turn to hatred when he reached out his hand, still hot from the other girl's warmth, and touched her body. And that was how it had happened.

Her opulent, belligerent, splendid nudity, her thrusting arrogant breasts, long thighs, high-strutting ass and thick black mat of hair were adorned with nothing but horns, except for the staff she still held. Seeing her so shameless and in such a rage, Perpétua decided to postpone the difficult confrontation and not demand an explanation just then. A conversation made up of subtle hints and *sous-entendus* calls for serenity and a calm mind. It did not seem advisable to try to start one at a moment when her hotheaded sister felt so wounded in her pride. When it came to settling accounts, Tieta might very well decide to charge old grievances and defamations to her own account.

Perpétua thought she would close her bedroom door, try to go back to sleep and draw a veil over what she had seen, but she did not withdraw quite quickly enough. Tieta saw the flickering light of the lamp and guessed that her sister was watching.

"What are you sneaking around spying on me for?" she cried in a fresh burst of anger.

Since she was discovered, Perpétua stepped forward and came into view.

"What's going on here? What does this mean?"

There was no scandalized fury in her sibilant voice, only shock. There was still time to save appearances and cling to a last shred of decency. Perpétua, willing to cooperate, left the way open for any halfway satisfactory version of the night's events: Ricardo had been self-willed and disobedient lately, he wasn't coming home on time, he deserved scolding and punishment. As for the nudity of the two persons concerned, that could be explained by the summer heat or simply left out as a minor detail. If appearances could be preserved, negotiation would be easier. But Tieta was much too angry to care. Spurning this last chance to save face, she threw the shit at the fan with both hands.

"It means that lowdown son of yours had the gall to put horns on me with a barefaced little whore, something no man ever did to me before in my life."

Perpétua smothered a cry with her hand. She took another step forward and leaned against the chest of drawers.

"You mean you and Cardo . . . Oh my God, how horrible!" Her stern face was contorted with shock and repugnance, but again she covered her mouth with her hand. Neighbors in Agreste were light sleepers; how many might have been awakened by all the commotion Tieta was making and be lying in their beds listening?

Dragging the heavy burden of betrayal and her abundant collection of horns, Tieta went back in her room and sat down on the bed in an indecent posture with her legs doubled under her. Her indignation and wrath, still unabated, were now directed at her sister.

"Don't come in here and try to play innocent and pretend you didn't know. You knew, all right."

"What do you mean by saying that? Have you gone crazy? I welcomed you into my home with open arms, thinking you'd changed, but you haven't changed one bit, you're the same depraved woman you've always been. This time you've led an innocent, god-fearing boy astray and ruined him for life. He was going to be a priest and now he's eternally damned. . . ." The afflicted mother choked back a sob of panic. "And you have the nerve to tell me I knew about it. Get thee behind me, Satan!" Since there was no way of patching up the situation, she would have to brazen it out and take the offensive.

"Didn't know! You liar!" Tieta's fingers tingled with the desire to strike the hypocrite across the face and belabor her with the staff as she had done to her disgusting son. "Who was it who sent her boy out to Mangue Seco at night when she knew I was crazy for him? You were out to get my money, do you think I didn't know? But you forgot to tell him I'm not the kind that likes to wear horns. I don't know why I don't knock your teeth in!"

Lamp in hand, backed against the wall with cold sweat breaking out on her forehead, Perpétua struck back in kind.

"You're making all that up to avoid responsibility and pretend it wasn't your fault." Her voice was belligerent, her finger accusing. "You can't lead an innocent boy astray from the sacred road of priesthood and destroy his vocation without—"

"Without paying for it, is that it? All you think about is money. And all you used to think about was finding a man who was willing to lay you, wasn't it?"

"I never had those kinds of thoughts, I'm not wicked like you."

"Why did you promise your son to God, then, if it wasn't to get a man to fuck you? You're not like me because you're worse. All this was a plot of yours to get money out of me. When you gave up your room and put him in the bedroom facing mine, you knew what you were doing. I should have smelled a rat."

"That's a lie! I never thought any such thing."

"And later on, when you saw I had my eye on him, you played it for all it was worth, didn't you?"

"It's no use your trying to flimflam me. What I want to know is how you intend to make it up to my boy. And I want to know right now."

"Make it up to your boy? Make up to him for what? He was a big booby who might have ended up queer if I hadn't come along and made a man of him. As if you really thought a priest has to be a virgin."

"He was a boy without a single fault, a boy who always treated his elders with respect and only thought about his schoolwork. Now he's not the same boy any more, he's taken the bit between his teeth. You're a bad influence on him. He's just the way you used to be, confound you! You've abused him. Do you mean to sit there and deny it?"

"You want me to pay for your son's maidenhead, don't you?"

She got up from bed, her lascivious body an affront, and walked over to the wardrobe, swinging her hips. She unlocked the suitcase where she kept her money, raised the top, took out a handful of bills and flung them at her sister.

"Here, this is for your son's virginity. It was worth it, too; I had my fill. Go on, pick it up, you miserable pimp. You make me sick."

Perpétua set down the lamp, came into the room, squatted down and began picking up the money. Her nasal voice from floor level was softer, more conciliatory. "What you ought to do is adopt both boys."

"Adopt them? As my sons?" Tieta, perched on the bed again, watched Perpétua on all fours, sweeping the money into piles and picking it up. "So that's what you want. They'll be my sole heirs then, won't they? I'd be the mother of a man I've slept with, but that doesn't matter, does it? You're too much."

As she watched Perpétua crawling about, reaching under the bed in search of a stray cruzeiro note, her withered breasts swaying under her nightgown, her topknot coming undone and the loose hair falling over her sour, pious face, her witchlike ugliness and eyes kindling with avarice, a feeling of admiration and pity mingled with Tieta's anger. The woman was a she-devil, but she'd do anything for her cubs.

"And to think you had a man who loved you, wanted you, slept with you and gave you children. If I didn't know it was true I wouldn't believe it."

Then she remembered a crazy idea she had had, a grotesque image that had once crossed her mind of Perpétua, lying on top of that bed on the fluffy lamb's-wool mattress, tangling with her husband when they were fooling around—a ghastly vision! All at once her anger disappeared and she began to laugh.

"If you'll tell me something, I promise to put you in my will."

Perpétua looked up quickly, a covetous, suspicious, curious expression on her face.

"All I want to know is this. At the crucial moment, if you know what I mean, did you and the Major make love in the missionary position or did you try some variations? Did he like a good suck?"

At the thought of her sister attempting the ypsilon Y with her husband, Tieta was shaken by an attack of uncontrollable laughter. She tried to stop and couldn't; her merriment overflowed into a wild fit of laughter. She could just see Perpétua clinging to the Major's clapper—and it must have been a good one, judging by his son's. As she laughed, her horns dropped off, every one of them, those planted by Maria Imaculada down by the river and the others that she never knew about.

"Respect the dead, you wicked, evil woman!" Perpétua rose to her feet in a passion, hands clutching at the bills, eyes starting out of her head as she glared over at the bed, smelling the old smells and seeing every movement again.

There was the sound of a key in the lock and light footsteps coming down the hall. Perpétua tried to pull herself together and thrust the money into her skirt pockets so that other shameless hussy, coming back from sinning (she came in later every night), would not realize what had happened. When she saw light and heard movements and laughter from the bedroom, Leonora went in.

"Oh, hello, Dona Perpétua. What's so funny, Mama?"

Mama was still helplessly laughing at the comic vision she had conjured up. As soon as she could get the picture of the virile and passionate Major taking off his yellow-striped pajamas out of her head, Perpétua explained, "We were just having a little chat, the two of us, and some foolishness I said struck Tieta as funny." She picked up the kerosene lamp. "We can finish our talk tomorrow, Sister."

If Tieta thought she had closed the book on the affair with a few *contos de reis*, she had another think coming or she didn't know her big sister. What Perpétua wanted and was determined to get was a signed and notarized document, nothing less. She left the room, then swooped back to pick up a bill lying next to the wardrobe. There were probably more scattered around. She would come back tomorrow before Aracy swept out the room.

Tieta was still laughing when Leonora launched into a tale of woe.

"Oh, Mama, Mama! Poor Ascânio. He's just desperate, poor man."

Of Beelzebub's slipper, the city's eye and tongue.

At daybreak Goatstink opened his eyes in the gutter where *cachaça* had laid him low the night before. "Gutter" is a sensational manner of speaking; actually he had gone to sleep in the doorway of the moviehouse, comfortably sheltered against wind and rain. He scrambled to his feet and shambled off toward the Hollow. As he crossed Cathedral Square he saw movement at the door of Terto's house. He stopped to see who was leaving so early and in such a hurry when he could have taken his time. Terto, that fond, devoted husband, was addicted to lying abed in a hammock on the porch, sleeping the heavy, dreamless sleep of all good cuckolds content with their lot; those who like themselves the way they are, as a young contemporary author might put it.

When she met Goatstink roaming the streets and alleys of the town at ungodly hours of the night, missing nothing and blabbing about everything he saw, Amélia Dantas (now Régis), nicknamed Mel, ex-First Lady of the Township, had dubbed the beggar Beelzebub's Slipper. To Barbozinha, Goatstink was the city's eye. He had an eye in his ass, Aminthas added. He had seen so much that almost nothing could surprise him anymore. He couldn't help being surprised, though, when he saw that the individual wearing an old pair of trousers belonging to Terto was Ricardo the seminarian. Dona Edna in her nightgown was hanging on the boy's neck and giving him a passionate farewell smack. Terto's trousers were much too tight for him; why was the young priest wearing them? He had been in his cassock when Goatstink surprised him on his way to the river with that little tomboy from Zuleika's cathouse. He had been wearing slacks and a sport shirt when he crossed Carol's forbidden threshold four nights ago. Goatstink had seen him in his cassock only yesterday, climbing the steps of the belfry to console the restless spinster. Not to speak of . . . Goatstink, hush your mouth.

Goatstink the town crier set off again, with words of revelation and good counsel: "Lock up your asses, folks, the Heavenly Dove is on the loose in Agreste!"

Of a shepherdess and a young goat.

Ricardo crossed the public park in the middle of the square as quickly as those tight pants would let him and knocked at the back door. Aracy burst out laughing when she opened it, Seu Cardo looked so funny. Oh, but he was handsome, though. Maybe he would notice her someday, God willing.

Ricardo went in, put on his cassock and had his suitcase almost packed when he sensed that someone was watching him and looked up. It was Perpétua, dressed for church in her black garments, rosary in hand. She looked menacing, ready to accuse and punish, eyes flashing, indignation and revulsion written on her face. In a terrible voice, but speaking low so as not to wake the two accursed women, she said ominously, "What do you think you're doing, you heretic?"

"I'm going to take the *marineti* to Esplanada in a little while."

"Take the *marineti*? Who gave you permission?"

"No one, Mother. I'm going to Esplanada to catch the Aracaju bus and get off at the road to the monastery at São Cristóvão."

"Have you gone out of your mind? Have you forgotten you have a mother to make up your mind for you? Do you think you're over twenty-one? You unpack your things and get some sleep now. I'll want an explanation in the morning, so be prepared."

"I'm going to spend a few days with Frei Thimóteo at the monastery. He invited me to go. After Tieta . . . after my aunt leaves, I'll come back."

"You're going nowhere. You do what I tell you."

She knew she wouldn't be obeyed, that she would never be able to order him around again. She was the older sister but she had never been able to boss Tieta around, either. Tieta had never obeyed her.

"Mother, I've told you I'm going to São Cristóvão. I'm not over twenty-one but I'm a man now, can't you see that? Don't try to stop me; I don't want to have to run away. Don't worry, I'll be back."

"You don't even act like my boy anymore. You're just like her. She was the shame of this house; she spent all day with the goats and all night sinning, and you're doing your best to take her place. Aren't you afraid God will punish you?"

For the first time since the Major's death she felt the urge to weep.

"My God's changed too, Mother. He's not like yours anymore. My God forgives, He doesn't punish."

"But you can't just go away like this before we've settled things. That woman lured you from the right road, she perverted you, she's kept me from keeping my promise. She'll have to make up to us somehow for the evil she's done. She brought sin to this house and dragged you to perdition."

"No, Mother, I was blind and she taught me to see. I don't know whether I'm going to be a priest or not; it's too soon to tell. But I swear to you that if I'm not ordained it'll be because God doesn't want me to be. As soon as I'm sure, I'll let you know. But I'll keep on studying anyhow, so don't worry about that."

"Do you swear you're going to the monastery?"

"I've already said so, Mother. And I want to tell you that Aunt Tieta was good to me, better than I deserve. I can never repay what I owe her."

He picked up his suitcase and smiled tenderly and serenely at his mother.

"Your blessing, Mother."

"Oh, my God!" The martyr raised her eyes to Heaven.

As he turned to go, Ricardo saw Tieta in her bedroom doorway, the beloved body dressed in a ray of new morning light.

"Goodbye, Aunt . . . Tieta!"

"Goodbye, Cardo. You can call me Aunt. Tell that friar of yours I'm back in Agreste and I'm going to raise an almighty rumpus."

The street door closed after Ricardo. Without a glance at her sister, Tieta went back inside her room. The goat girl was proud of her nephew. He was exactly like her; Perpétua was right. A wild young billygoat running free on the hills, head high, heir to her own rebellious nature. What was past was past. It had been a crazy whim, but she would miss him so!

Of facts and rumors, a chapter in which Chalita the Arab expresses a vague hope.

The ten days that shook Agreste, Aminthas called them, paraphrasing the forbidden author John Reed, whenever he referred to that brief and tumultuous period. He himself had had a part in shaping the nightmare, pulling invisible strings that set in motion some of the most serious events, although the major share of responsibility was generally attributed to Dona Carmosina.

"Just look what you've got us all into, Carmosina," said Edmundo Ribeiro the tax collector accusingly, taking a seat at the post office. "Something new every day! A fight, a scandal, a ruckus—"

"When it isn't two or three. Before you get through talking about one hot piece of news the next one comes along. Things really are interesting these days," chimed in Chalita the Arab from where he sat in the doorway. "Everybody's gone crazy, it looks like. Where's it all going to end, that's what I wonder."

Dona Carmosina disclaimed responsibility.

"Me? Why me? You'll all be accusing me of having invented titanium dioxide next. We were all here peacefully minding our own business until that came along."

"If you weren't all the time reading the newspapers and telling people what you read . . ." The tax collector pointed to the posters, which now covered the wall in the room. ". . . You all could sell Agreste with impunity," retorted Carmosina.

The tone and language of conversations in Agreste had changed. Rudeness had taken the place of the old cordiality, the good humor, the polite rituals that had made their talk, the community's principal entertainment and one that was free to all, a refined pleasure. Instead of sly *doubles entendres*, there were out-and-out insults.

"Whoa there!" protested Edmundo Ribeiro. "I'm not selling anything."

"That's because you couldn't get a toehold in the palm grove, not because you didn't try. But that gang of pirates has your support, or did you think we didn't know?"

"Know what?"

"That you signed a pledge to contribute to Brastânio Trindade's campaign for mayor."

"Brastânio Trindade! That's a good one," laughed the Arab. There was nothing like a good talk with intelligent people like Dona Carmosina, confound her. "What's he doing in Esplanada, by the way?"

"Has Ascânio gone to Esplanada?" asked Dona Carmosina, concerned. "When?"

"Today. He told me he'd be back tomorrow."

Jairo's *marineti* departed and arrived in front of the movie theater next to Chalita's house, and the Arab never failed to supervise the departures (on the dot) and arrivals (unpredictable) of the vehicle and to notice who the passengers were.

"I wonder what he's cooking up this time. You say he'll be back tomorrow? Then he's not going anyplace but Esplanada. He wouldn't have time to go to Salvador and back. He doesn't know where to turn. He thought the election was in the bag, but the rally took the wind out of his sails."

"Well, I still think he'll be elected," remarked the tax collector. "The Skipper has prestige, I don't deny that, but you know how these things are. Ascânio's acting mayor, and what's more important, he's Colonel Artur's choice. And when it comes to prestige, it's the Colonel who's really got it."

"You mean he was the Colonel's choice. Don't you know the Colonel won't have anything to do with Dr. Dioxide's campaign?"

"Dr. Dioxide, ho, that's a good one!" chortled the Arab, squirming with laughter.

"Seu Edmundo, will you tell me just one thing? Was it out of sheer generosity that Modesto Pires headed that contribution list, the one you signed, or was it after your candidate came back from Tapitanga empty-handed, with his tail between his legs? Do you know what the Colonel said when Ascânio asked for money to finance his campaign? He told him to ask Brastânio for it. Don't try to tell me you didn't hear about it."

"Yes, Carmosina, I did. But you hear so many things these days you can't go around believing all of them. For all I know, it may be true that the Colonel told Ascânio he wouldn't help him; the old miser's getting more feebleminded every day. But it's also true that he hasn't told anyone not to vote for Ascânio. Am I lying? If I am, tell me so."

"Colonel Artur's told everyone who's gone to see him about it that each person should vote the way his conscience dictates. He's no more feebleminded than you or I, and it wasn't because he's a miser that he wouldn't give Ascânio money. What's more, the only reason the Colonel doesn't come right out in support of the Skipper is that he's sorry for his godson. But you ask Vadeco Rosa what he heard at Tapitanga, and don't forget Vadeco's on the Town Council and has plenty of votes in Rocinha. He told me himself. He went out to get his instructions, and the Colonel told him to throw his support either way he liked, that he had no orders to give and no candidate for mayor because he had retired from politics."

"Maybe so, but Ascânio still has the folks in Rocinha eating out of his hand, beginning with Vadeco."

"They used to eat out of his hand. Not anymore. Vadeco was mighty crestfallen after he had a talk with Tieta. In Rocinha everybody was thinking Ascânio was going to buy up all the land in the township at a fantastic price after he was elected. When they found out he only intends to expropriate the land around the coconut grove they felt they'd been had. Did you know that Tieta's campaigning from door to door? We're holding a rally out in Rocinha next week and she's going to speak."

"No doubt about it," admitted the tax collector, "Dona Antonieta's your trump card; she's the only one that scares me. You can tell the Skipper doesn't really want to run, and I know who made him."

"You mean me, don't you? I'll have you know I feel honored by the accusation."

"Poor man, the minute he has a breathing spell he hotfoots it back to Mangue Seco. He's on the beach right now, isn't he?"

"To make sure he has the people's votes out there. But he's coming right back."

"Votes on Mangue Seco? There must be less than a dozen. But Tieta now, she might tip the scales if she sees it through to the end. . . . It's a funny thing, though, in spite of being so dead set against Ascânio for mayor, she doesn't seem to mind his making love to her stepdaughter. And while we're on the subject, Carmosina, that's what I call a real hot love affair."

Dona Carmosina let the subject drop; she didn't want to discuss Ascânio's private life. Leonora was a darling. But now that the tax collector had turned the conversation from political topics into other, more pleasant channels, she would very much like to know . . .

"What, Carmosina?"

"If it's true what people are saying—that Modesto Pires has taken on a partner."

"At the tannery?"

"No, Seu Edmundo. In Carol's bed."

It was Chalita the Arab who answered, voluptuously stroking his big mustache.

"Not just one. I know of two at least." His covetous eyes flashed briefly. "I'm just waiting for a company to be set up, so I can buy a little stock in it myself."

Of the final conversation concerning the fate of water, fish and men, in which Brastânio selects a new director and—horrors!—whisky with guaraná is served on the sophisticated premises of the Lords' Retreat.

Among the carefully chosen group was a long-legged, slender young woman distinguished from the rest by her elegance of bearing. More than slender, she was downright skinny, a *haute-couture* fashion model and very much to the taste of the magnate Angelo Bardi. She had been brought there especially for him; the management of the Lords' Retreat knew the tastes of its best clients and did everything possible to satisfy their whims. Dr. Mirko Stefano was happy to see the undulating, mischievous redhead who looked like Betty among the girls; at their last meeting His Excellency had confiscated her, leaving Doctor Magnifico vaguely frustrated. The Elderly Parliamentarian had not been forgotten, either; there was a little girl so childish in face and manner that she was sometimes passed off as a virgin, successfully. In honor of the new gentleman, whom she had been cautioned to treat with the utmost deference, Tieta's assistant, not knowing his inclinations, had called in three girls of different types, all ravishing—*il n'aura que l'embarras du choix.* While they served the mighty lords with Scotch, the six beauties displayed their charms to advantage. Only one wore as much as a bikini, and the skinny one flaunted a filmy veil that showed off her bones. In her sober, well-tailored suit, the stocky manager resembled a headmistress at a girls' boarding school.

The stiff man with the receding hairline glanced at the naked girls out of the corner of his eye, endeavoring to overcome his shyness at finding himself in such a place for the first time. He had gone to brothels in his youth and on one special occasion he had been to an illicit hotel in Botafogo, in Rio de Janeiro; then he had married. There was no danger of his being spotted; he was incognito and not in uniform, just one of the fellows out on a spree. As the redhead served him he tore his eyes away and remarked, "I'd like my Scotch with *guaraná.*"

With *guaraná*? Sweet and sticky *guaraná*? There was a shocked silence. The bony girl next to Bardi smothered a giggle. That rare and precious brand of Scotch was served nowhere in São Paulo but the Jockey Club and the Lords' Retreat. In England they drank it straight, without ice. But the Elderly Parliamentarian, a lord if there ever was one, followed through with true British phlegm and intrepid adulation. "Scotch and *guaraná*, that's a Brazilian drink and very much in style. I'll have mine that way too."

It took all kinds, thought the manager. Recovering from the sacrilege, she fought down her repugnance and ordered, "*Guaraná*, and hurry!"

Dr. Angelo Bardi changed the subject by asking for news of his dear friend, whom he hadn't seen in some time.

"And our dear Madame Antoinette, isn't she ever coming back?"

"She's still in France. She was going to board the ship when her father died, the general. A heart attack, poor man."

"A general?" He of the receding hairline and the sidelong glances at the girls overcame his shyness and showed a sudden interest.

"Yes, Madame Antoinette is the daughter of a French general and a native of Martinique." The manager repeated this lore with the air of a history teacher giving a class.

"How's that?" The receding hairline was shocked.

"Like Napoleon Bonaparte's Empress Josephine, you know," said Doctor Magnifico helpfully.

"Ah! A historic figure! Very interesting." Now he felt a little more at ease. He splashed more *guaraná* into his glass.

"Is there anything else you'd like?" As there was not, the manager said, "Come on, girls!" and marched out, leading her eye-filling platoon.

The Elderly Parliamentarian set down his glass.

"Well, here we are, and we can celebrate at last. It was a very knotty problem and it took a lot of fancy footwork. I'm not trying to make it seem harder than it was, but if it hadn't been for the timely assistance of our friend here . . . The hardliners were turning up their noses and the authorities in Bahia had dug their heels in. Let it be anyplace but Arembepe, they said, and they wouldn't budge an inch. But they finally had to stop being pigheaded and bow to the arguments presented by our distinguished advocate here."

"National development is our first priority. Sentimental considerations certainly cannot be allowed to prevail, much less irrelevant details of location. I've been up there personally and I saw how absurd the allegations were. My opinion is based on firsthand study of the problem. I'll give you a quick rundown of the factors I took into account and my conclusions." The distinguished advocate cleared his throat with a long swig of Scotch and *guaraná*.

Without waiting for them to acquiesce he went ahead with his quick rundown, which turned out to be almost a lecture. Angelo Bardi listened with half-closed eyes as if every word were precious. The Elderly Parliamentarian appeared to drink in the lecturer's words, with an occasional approving nod of assent. Doctor Magnifico adopted an attitude of rapt but discreet attention, wondering what he had done to deserve punishment like this. None of them dared interrupt.

At Bahia at that very moment, Rosalvo Lucena heard the good news in the secretary's office; new high-level surveys had led to a fresh appraisal of the problem. Powerful reasons of an economic, social and political nature had determined the location of the titanium-dioxide industry in Arembepe, and the state government obediently did an about-face, backtracked, submitted and approved Brastânio's request. As the authoritative, metallic voice fell silent in the Lords' Retreat, Bardi the magnate applauded.

"It's a good thing we still have farsighted statesmen who are capable of routing subversion and making the supreme national interest prevail over local prejudice. Congratulations, my illustrious friend."

The Elderly Parliamentarian set down his glass with its sickening mixture of whisky and *guaraná*.

"My dear Bardi, just one last detail before we go our separate ways. When will the assembly vote to enlarge Brastânio's board of directors?"

"Oh, immediately. As soon as we're back in Salvador tomorrow we'll convoke the assembly." He turned to the author of the report, who was regaling himself with whisky and *guaraná*. "It's with the greatest pleasure that we welcome Dr. Gildo Veríssimo aboard. We've heard great things about his managerial skills."

"It's not because he's my son-in-law," agreed his illustrious friend, "but competence is his middle name. He'll be a fine addition to your board of directors."

"Well, I guess that winds it up," said the Elderly Parliamentarian.

Angelo Bardi rang a little silver bell and the manager returned, conveying the girls. The stiff man with the receding hairline, distinguished advocate and illustrious friend, leaned toward Doctor Magnifico and inquired in a low voice, "Are all the expenses taken care of?"

"Why, of course."

"All of them? Including—?"

"Including."

"Then tell her"—he pointed to the manager—"that I want that girl with the fiery red hair."

There goes my redhead again, thought Mirko. Lost for the

second time. It was just one of those things in the life of a PR man, one of those many disappointments. But his profession had its compensations, too. It was worth anything—redhead, blonde, or brunette—;just to know that Agreste was no longer on the map, that never again would he have to jounce over that mule track or endure the equatorial heat, the dust, the mud, the discomfort, the warm beer, not to mention the bandits and the sharks on that deserted coast, the squalor and dangers that surrounded and threatened him out there.

At no time, when he thought of Agreste and Mangue Seco, did he give a single thought to Ascânio Trindade. For Dr. Mirko Stefano, Agreste and its poor and unsophisticated people had ceased to exist.

*In which the author reappears, just when we
thought we were rid of the bore.*

I had every intention of not interrupting my narrative once we arrived at the epilogue of this monumental novel (yes, monumental; count the pages). Having taken no sides in the battle going on in Agreste, I hoped to remain on the sidelines as a neutral spectator. Now, instead, I find myself obliged to defend myself once more from criticisms leveled at the form and content of my work by the merciless though fraternal Fúlvio D'Alambert. I am beginning to suspect that some less worthy sentiment, such as envy, dictates these quibbles of his just as I am coming to the end of this literary undertaking. He never thought I'd actually finish it.

I won't prolong this aside by commenting on a quantity of minor faults in grammar and syntax with which he reproaches me but will cite just one as an example. D'Alambert has harsh words for the way I used the verb "gaze." Ricardo climbs the stairs to the churchtower with Cinira, "she in front, and he behind, gazing." "To gaze" is a transitive verb and takes an indirect object, or so Fúlvio tells me; anyone who gazes should have something to gaze at. According to Fúlvio, I've concealed the target of the seminarian's jubilant contemplation from my readers.

Now I wonder if my readers really need a direct or indirect

object to tell them what the landscape was that was being gazed at by the young man. What other object could there be on that dark narrow staircase but the old maid's thighs and bum? Besides, although these details of the pious, aging virgin's anatomy were enough to excite an adolescent, they were not of a quality to interest most of my readers.

A more serious accusation has to do with the breakneck pace of the final part of the story. Up until now events have been few and far between. The action takes pages and pages to develop as a leisurely, exaggeratedly detailed account, with much trivial repetition and a crying absence of literary economy, for five interminable episodes. In the epilogue the pace speeds up abruptly, the illusion of fictional time and space is broken, and narrative balance is lost.

According to Fúlvio, the author is all at once in so much of a hurry that he leaves the reader in ignorance of certain important and interesting facts, skipped over in passing. As examples he mentions the rally in Cathedral Square and the question of Modesto Pires' partners in Carol's Caresses, Ltd. We know about Ricardo, but who are the others?

If the tempo of the story has picked up, it isn't my doing. It's the events themselves that are coming too thick and fast. So many things have happened in such a short time that to keep up I have to ignore those of lesser importance, however colorful or amusing they are.

Take the rally. It was held the day after the fight in the marketplace and attracted a large audience. Barbozinha the seer was the first to mount the rostrum; that is, step to the front of the platform and raise his voice (in the literal sense of the word, for since there was no microphone or loudspeaker available, the orators had to rely on the strength of their lungs). The bard had his unconditional admirers, especially among the old maids, who loved to hear him recite love poems with one arm extended, eyes raised to heaven, and tremolos in his voice as he enunciated the rich rhymes, describing the romantic and sensual emotions of false or eternal love. Most of Barbozinha's muses had been girls from Salvador's whorehouses, fancies from his bohemian days of dalliance. As he explained, however, in *Poems of Damnation*, he had tuned his patriotic lyre to express feelings of civic indignation. He was applauded when he had finished, but his fans shouted for some famous verses he had recited at parties dozens of times: the *Ballad of the Sad Troubadour*. Had it not been for the forceful opposition of Dona Carmosina ("This is a political rally, my dear fellow!") the poet would be up there on the platform yet, reciting the *Dark Elegy of the Rua São Miguel*, the *Poem to Luciana's Lips*, the *Sonnet Written on Isadora's Breasts* and other *pièces de résistance*.

Dona Carmosina came out of her first political meeting remarkably well. Constantly heckled by asides from Ascânio, she got the better of him every time with her sharp tongue and nimble wit. The only interruption that nearly stopped her in her tracks was a rude remark rather than an aside, and it did not proceed from Ascânio but from Goatstink, although he was so drunk he couldn't stand up. Hearing Dona Carmosina declare that she spoke "in the name of the mothers of families concerned with the future of their husbands and children," the beggar protested, "Aw, no you don't . . . old maids can't speak for married women. They don't know their cunt from their asshole!"

This remark drew laughter from the crowd, a good part of which was more interested in hearing an exchange of insults and accusations than in the grave matters being debated or the facts about the pollution problem and the level of the threat from titanium-dioxide effluents, all of which Dona Carmosina had at her fingertips. Machiavellian and given to petty chicanery she may be, but I'll never deny that she's smart and has plenty of guts.

In short, the political rally, a novelty in a town in which agitation and propaganda had never featured in local elections, Colonel Artur de Figueiredo being the one who did all the thinking and told everybody how to vote, turned into a party and was deemed a success; so much so that Ascânio Trindade resolved then and there to hold one of his own the following Saturday in the marketplace. He chose that locale because it was officially called Colonel Francisco Trindade Plaza in honor of his grandfather, the mayor of many achievements, and because he could count on the market-goers' support. He knew he would need money to combat the Skipper's campaign with a rally, banners and flyers of his own, but that was no problem; he was the Colonel's candidate, after all. His godfather had never let him down. This time he did let him down, as we all know, and Ascânio was obliged to turn to Brastânio. That was why he had gone to Esplanada to call Doctor Magnífico.

The Skipper spoke last and presented the platform on which he hoped to be elected.

He asked that there be no heckling or comments from the audience, fearful of losing the thread of the impromptu remarks he had memorized with such difficulty during sleepless nights of oratory to Dona Laura's critical applause. He began by saying that he had sacrificed the calm and repose which were justly his after a life devoted to his country (*applause*) to don the glorious uniform of the Brazilian Navy once again (*prolonged applause*) and place himself at the service of the people of Agreste (*much applause*). Although dressed as a civilian on the rostrum, his heart was in uniform and he had taken his place in the trenches (*loud applause and cries of "Bravo! Show 'em, Skipper!"*). He was accused of being an enemy of progress, but that was a vile slander. He was against false progress, yes; against the progress that makes no contribution to the community's well-being but only pollutes, befouls, contaminates, and fills the pockets of the industrialists of death (*cries of "Hear! Hear!" and "That's a lie!—Brastânio will redeem Agreste!"*). No one welcomed genuine progress more than he, the kind of progress that would benefit not a few sharp operators but the entire population, the kind that was symbolized by the lights of the São Francisco Valley Authority (*loud applause*), a victory which "the people owe entirely to our honored, influential fellow citizen, Dona Antonieta Esteves Cantarelli, our own beloved Tieta" (*applause, bravos, vivas, "Viva Tieta! Viva! Vivooo!"—an ovation that drowned out the speaker's last words*). An apotheosis.

As for the rumored partners of Modesto Pires, industrial partners with no capital, Pires being the silent partner who put up all the money, there is not much I can say about them. Should Ricardo the seminarian be thought of as a partner, in the loose sense of the word? I don't think so. All he did was open the way to the liberalization of a private firm with no outside shareholders, much less partners. Had he stayed on in Agreste he would certainly have occupied an important place in the company, Carol's Caresses, Ltd. Maybe when he comes back?

As for other partners, the only one I know of for sure is Fidélio, this year's champion of the Golden Cue. Yes, I know; the outcome of the billiards tournament, a relatively important event, has not been duly recorded in the tumultuous pages of this novel. There isn't really much to tell. Fidélio beat Astério in the finals, but it was a hard-fought game, disputed point by point and stroke by stroke. As usual, the rebel heir to the coconut grove was applauded by a numerous feminine claque, while Astério had only a melancholy Elisa who hardly cared whether he won or lost. Someone or something kept Dona Edna away, and Leonora did not show up either. After Ascânio was eliminated, she had no reason to go to the bar just to hear whispers and snide remarks.

More than one of Fidélio's admirers had reason to believe that the new champion might dedicate his victory to her. He chose, however, to push ajar an unlocked door (Modesto Pires was still out at Mangue Seco) and celebrate it with Carol. For lack of funds—Agreste is so poor!—the Golden Cue was an abstract title without a trophy attached to it, or even a cheap plaque. Carol, with the practical skill of rich men's mistresses in small towns, turned the abstraction into a tangible object in no time and endowed the Golden Cue with form, weight and flavor. It was while they were engaged in this meritorious labor that the slaveowner surprised them. Summoned hastily to town by the alarming rumors regarding the Colonel's unexpected political neutrality, he tore himself away from Dona Aida's loving but flabby arms and came back to see what was really going on. He found out, too; more than he might have wished.

Since Modesto Pires is one of Agreste's fiercest guardians of public morality and Fidélio the most closed-mouthed man in town, it is not surprising that we are still in ignorance of the tenor of the conversation that gave birth to the partnership. If indeed it began with fighting words, it must have ended in harmony and concord, for several witnesses saw Fidélio leave by the street door, calm, decently dressed and smiling to himself. Contrary to what everyone thought would happen, Carol was not bundled off in Jairo's *marineti* to the wilds of Sergipe; she was seen in the shops that very afternoon spending money like water. Those were expensive horns Modesto wore; golden horns, as befitted so wealthy and virtuous a citizen. A good many people would like shares in his company, but I don't think there's much hope for Chalita. This corporation is a limited one though not anonymous.

Having analyzed the current political situation, Modesto Pires fulfilled his civic duty by pledging a modest amount toward Ascânio Trindade's campaign in the hope of recovering his investment, with interest, after the election.

One last detail and I'll be off, this time for good. Fúlvio D'Alambert is concerned about the verisimilitude of my characters; he thinks I sometimes lack a sense of proportion when shaping the clay from which these humble country folk are created. As an example of this deficiency he cites the seminarian Ricardo, whose physical endowments are so wildly exaggerated they amaze even Goatstink.

The stricture only reveals how little he knows about daily life in those dead little towns, with their eager, sex-starved women condemned by the scarcity of men to a life of boredom and radio serials. On the other hand, I don't know what the sexual capacity of my dear readers may have been at eighteen, but I find nothing abnormal in the feats of this fiery, impulsive adolescent, this invincible warrior. Besides, as my readers have certainly perceived before now, Levites partake of the glorious nature of archangels.

Of the polluted Calvary on Agreste's longest night—first station of the cross: reviled by telephone.

The *marineti* was stranded out on the highway that sultry afternoon and the passengers were sweltering as they waited and hoped for the motor to start up again. Father Mariano pulled Ascânio into the shade of the vehicle; he was perspiring under his cassock, never having adopted the modern fashion of slacks and sport shirt in vogue among priests in the capital.

"My dear Ascânio, I just don't know. This election is a toss-up. If Colonel Artur decided to lend a hand it would be a battle of titans, with him on one side and Dona Antonieta on the other. But our Comendadora's managed to get the Colonel to stay out of the race, and that's nothing short of a miracle." He shook his head with a compassionate look in his eyes, as if to say that it was all up with Ascânio. "When I was telling the Auxiliary Bishop about the new wiring in the cathedral, I said to him, 'We have a saint in Agreste, a flesh-and-blood saint who works miracles.' "

Ascânio bit his tongue so as not to answer. What could he say? She was Leonora's stepmother. Saint? She was Old Nick incarnate, a sworn enemy of his aspirations for mayor and his plans of engagement and marriage. Every time he brought the subject up, Leonora turned evasive and reticent. It was impossible to doubt that the girl was in love with him; after all, what greater proof could she give him? What could be the trouble, then, but her stepmother's categorical refusal to let her marry anyone but the millionaire she deserved? Tieta had become Ascânio's nightmare, his hex, the evil genius who caused him to stumble at every step he took. Only two days ago Vadeco Rosa, who owned a few dozen votes, had come to talk to him, scratching his head sheepishly.

"The way I look at it, a candidate needs a strong sponsor who can pull in the votes, somebody like Colonel Artur or Dona Antonieta. If you can get the Colonel or Dona Tieta to back you, you can have my votes."

Sworn enemy, evil genius, black-winged jinx, Ascânio's nightmare; Comendadora, saint, Skipper Dário's sponsor. The talk with the well-intentioned Father Mariano only added to Ascânio's woes. The trip to Esplanada had left him worried and discouraged enough. He had felt this way once before—wounded, ill-used, humiliated and belittled—when he had gone to Paulo Afonso in a last-ditch effort to bring hydroelectric power to his community and the big bosses had laughed him to scorn. And then, with two simple telegrams, Dona Antonieta had succeeded where he had failed. Everything always came back to her.

And now it was even worse; he was not just downcast but fearful and gnawed with suspicion. It was nothing he could put his finger on, but he hadn't liked the way the Brastânio people had talked to him over the phone. Betty worried him the most; she had been her usual friendly, flirtatious self when he made his first call the day before and distinctly curt, distant and impatient the second time. Ascânio had come away with a flea in his ear.

He had called Salvador four times to try to talk to Doctor Magnifico and explain that he was in a pickle and needed Brastânio's help in the campaign after all. He thought Mirko might already know about it; A Tarde had published the news that the Skipper was running. The day before, the operator had told him Dr. Stefano was away and transferred him to Betty. The executive secretary said that Mirko had gone to São Paulo but would be back in Bahia that night. She suggested that he call again the next day. She was as nice and sweet as could be, calling him Mr. Sexy in her sexy voice and asking for news of the good-looking hunk of man. (That was Osnar.) So far, so good.

Next morning Ascânio called the hotel first and after identifying himself learned that Dr. Stefano had come back the night before but had gone to the office early. Then he called Brastânio. Every one of these calls took a ridiculous amount of effort and interminable waiting; luckily the Esplanada telephone operator was a friend of Canuto Tavares and did her very best to help him. When he asked to speak to Dr. Mirko Stefano and explained that he was Ascânio Trindade from Sant'Ana do Agreste but calling from Esplanada, he was told to wait a moment while the call was transferred to Dr. Stefano's office. The moment was prolonged for several minutes, Ascânio praying all the time that he wouldn't be cut off. The anonymous voice finally came back on the line. Dr. Stefano was away on a business trip and wasn't sure when he would be back. Ascânio asked to speak to Betty. There was another long delay, at the end of which the same voice told him the secretary was busy and couldn't speak to him just then. Half an hour later Ascânio tried again and after much pleading was put through to Betty, but this time she was impatient and brusque. She told him Mirko was still in São Paulo. Oh, they had said at the hotel that he had returned the night before? Well, they didn't know anything about it in the office; he hadn't come in and they didn't expect him. Should he try again later? Not that day, anyway. Why didn't he write a letter? Oh, it was important and urgent? Well, she was sorry, but there was nothing she could do. She was about to hang up; she had no time to chat. He tried to keep her on the line—"Listen, Betty, please"—but she was in such a hurry that she hung up before he could finish the sentence. It was all mighty peculiar, and he had a glum feeling he'd been given the brushoff. He wrote a letter, begging for an urgent reply, and put it in the mail.

That afternoon the *marineti* broke down three times. Jairo had to call on his entire repertory of fond nicknames and filthy words. Night was falling when they pulled into Agreste. Chalita greeted them with a sad piece of news; old Jarde Antunes was dead. He had gone to lie down after lunch, closed his eyes and never opened them again.

"By the time they realized what had happened the body was cold. They're sitting up with him there at Dona Amorzinha's boardinghouse."

*Of the polluted Calvary on Agreste's longest
night—second station of the cross: the
engagement ring and the cup of hemlock.*

He wanted to take a bath before going to the wake. Sitting on the
doorsill puffing on her pipe, Rafa informed him, "You've got company."

"Inside the house? Who is it?"

"Some tootsie. She just walked in."

Leonora? Who else could it be?

Leonora had been trying to convince him for days that they
should go to his house; she was tired, no doubt, of their risky,
uncomfortable nightly forays to the riverbank. But Ascânio wanted
his beloved to cross the threshold of his family home for the first
time as Mrs. Ascânio Trindade, in broad daylight, coming as a wife
from the altar. Only after their relationship had been sanctified by
the laws of man and God did he want her to lie in the rosewood bed
where his parents had slept.

And here Leonora was presenting him with a *fait accompli*.
Rising from the bed where she had been lying, she threw her arms
around his neck and offered her mouth to be kissed.

"The bus took so long to get here! Mama went to the wake and
I came here to wait for you. Darling, forgive me if I did wrong. I've
missed you so much I couldn't stand it."

"Neither could I. I couldn't wait to get back. But you
shouldn't—"

"Oh, Ascânio, why not?" She silenced his reproach with a
kiss.

They kissed again and again; the kisses became longer and more
ardent. Ascânio felt Leonora tremble as she pressed against him. He
would have liked to take a bath to wash away the dust and cares of
the journey, but she made him sit down on the bed and stroked his
weary face.

"You're sad, my darling. Didn't things work out the way you
wanted them to?"

Ascânio laid his head on Leonora's shoulder.

"No. I couldn't get through to Mirko. He's not in Bahia, at least that's what they told me. Some cock-and-bull story that makes me wonder what their game is."

He did not only wonder; he was feeling offended, morose, and dreadfully low in his mind. Leonora covered his face with kisses, trying to comfort him. Ascânio took the girl's hands in his.

"You're all I have in the world, Nora. Nobody else."

As he touched her fingers he remembered the engagement ring, an offering from Brastânio in happier days of trust and good comradeship between him and the company directors. It was in the pocket of his other suit. He got up to get it.

"This is for you."

He had intended to make a little ceremony out of the ring-giving, with her stepmother, the family, and a few friends present at their formal engagement. Never mind; he would dispense with ceremony and protocol. For Leonora rightfully to enter his house they should at least be engaged. Besides, he deserved a little happiness to make up for the way those Brastânio people had treated him like dirt.

He placed the token on the ring finger of Leonora's right hand, the proper finger for an engagement ring. Once, years before, he had put his ring and his trust, his promise and his heart, into the hands of an unworthy sweetheart. He had paid dearly for his mistake, had been destroyed by her betrayal, had thought he was dead to love. But then one day the impossible had happened: from Jairo's *marineti* had stepped the fairest and purest of women, the one who was now his betrothed.

"I brought you this from Bahia; it's an engagement ring. I wanted to save it for a special occasion, but I don't see how I can ever talk about this with your stepmother. Nora, will you marry me?"

Leonora stared at the ring that fitted her finger so well. It looked like an antique. Poor Ascânio, thinking she was a girl from a good family. That token must have cost him a good deal.

"Let's not talk about it," she murmured in a broken voice.

"About what?"

"About engagement and marriage. Isn't it enough that I belong to you?"

Ascânio turned pale and his unsteady hand dropped the hand of the girl.

"Won't you have me? I should have known. Why should you want to marry me, rich as you are?"

"I love you, Ascânio. You're everything in the world to me. I've never loved anyone in my life before. The other men were just mistakes."

"That's what I thought. But if that's so, then why won't you have me?"

"I just can't marry you, that's all, I have reasons. . . ."

"Is it because of your weak chest? In this climate you'll be well before you know it."

"No, I'm not sick. I just can't."

"I know. It's because *she* won't consent, is that it? Her being so important and all, how could she let her stepdaughter marry a nobody, and one who has a mind of his own besides?"

"Mama has nothing to do with this."

"Why, then?"

Leonora covered her face with her hands to hold back the tears. Ascânio was stung; the blood rushed to his face and his wounded heart.

"It's because I'm just a poor devil, a hick, a nobody from noplace. All right to fool around with on a holiday, but that's all. When it's time to marry I guess you'll pick a rich fellow from São Paulo."

"You're mistaken, Ascânio! How can you be so unfair? I do love you. I'm crazy about you. Will you let me be your mistress, or your maid? I can be either one or both, but I can't be your wife."

"But plague take it all, why not?"

"I can't tell you why. It isn't just my secret."

Ascânio held her hand again, stroked her hair and kissed her wet eyes.

"Don't you have any confidence in me at all? Didn't I give you proof of how much I love you, when I found out about what had happened with that other fellow?"

"Darling, all that was a lie. The truth . . ."

"Can't you trust me enough to tell me?"

"I'm not rich, I'm not a Comendador's daughter and I'm not Mama's stepdaughter."

"Huh? Who are you then?"

Between sobs she told him everything. About the sordid slum, the hunger, the squalor, the streets, the Retreat. Ascânio drew away from her and stood up, his face a death mask of horror. How could he have been such a fool? Numbly he listened and drank down the hemlock. This was much worse than the first time, when he had been told in a letter. The slime oozed into the room, covered the bed and rose into a towering wave that was choking him. Pus flowed from the mouth he had thought of as innocent and pure.

At last Leonora fell silent. She raised supplicating eyes to Ascânio, ready to offer herself again as his mistress or servant. Before she could speak, Ascânio let out a heartrending howl, like an animal in its death throes. Leonora understood that it was all over; in her lover's face there was nothing but hatred and disgust. He pointed to the door.

"Get out of here, you whore! If you want a man, go out and walk the streets."

Although Rafa could not have heard a word of what they said inside the house, when Leonora, frantically weeping, rushed past her into the darkness, the old woman spat black saliva and muttered, "Nasty little tramp."

Of the polluted Calvary on Agreste's longest night—third station of the cross: the saint divested of her tunic and her halo.

There were plenty of neighbors to watch over Jarde's corpse, but the animation that should prevail at a good wake was missing. Despite the excellent refreshments prepared by Dona Amorzinho and the rivers of beer and *cachaça* that Josafá had brought from the bar, the atmosphere was only lukewarm. There were no bursts of laughter, either in the front room where Jarde reposed or from the group standing out on the sidewalk. Grave themes predominated in what desultory conversation there was. Tieta chatted rather primly with Father Mariano, who inquired after Ricardo. "Oh, so Frei Thimóteo has invited him to the Franciscan monastery at São Cristóvão? That nephew of yours, my dear Dona Antonieta, is destined to be a luminary of the Church, thanks to the help of God, his mother's example, the teachings of Frei Thimóteo and his aunt's generosity." The Reverend Father plied that estimable lady with incense and crowned her charming head with a halo. She was such a prominent figure, such a pillar of the Church, such a symbol of the most illustrious virtues. As this tunic of praise was flung over her, Tieta smiled a modest smile. Ah, if the good Father only knew what the maternal example had been and what virtues had been inculcated by the aunt! It was a good thing for Ricardo that he still had God's help and Frei Thimóteo's teachings, at least.

Osnar's way of thawing out the chill and seeing that the deceased was honored in a proper way was to tell Dr. Marcolino Pitombo and fat Bonaparte the oft-repeated story of the Polish whore. It was new to the lawyer, and though certainly not to Bonaparte, he relished it as much each time; Osnar always embroidered the tale a little differently.

Jarde's slight form reposed in the coffin, his face like wax. Josafá, in a chair beside him, received condolences. Lauro Branco, the overseer at Osnar's fazenda, the neighboring plantation to Vista Alegre, had come in from the country to take leave of his old friend.

"I came to tell him goodbye from me and the goats," he explained to Josafá. "I sure hope he finds a great big herd up in Heaven. They were what he liked best of all."

The cathedral bell clanged nine, the streetlights went out and the irregular throbbing of the old generator ceased. The day was for families, the night was for lost souls. Dona Amorzinho lit the lamps. Suddenly a figure rushed out of the darkness. Was the man drunk, ill or in pain?

Even in the dark they all saw immediately that something was very wrong with Ascânio Trindade. Osnar broke off his story in the middle.

"Hey, Captain Ascânio, what's the trouble?"

Barbozinha's Captain of the Dawn, haggard and wild-eyed, entered the room. When he saw Tieta sitting next to the priest he extended one arm, pointed at her and cried out in a hoarse, sepulchral, terrible voice, each word costing him an effort.

"Do you know what that woman is? You all think she's a widow, a factory owner, the head of a family, don't you? Well, she's not; she's the madam of a whorehouse in São Paulo. That's where all her money comes from. The other one told me so. I asked her to marry me and she said, 'I can't, I'm a prostitute.' She works in a whorehouse run by that disgusting hypocrite over there who passes herself off as a saint. Two tramps and a clown!"

Of the polluted Calvary on Agreste's longest night—fourth station of the cross: condemned to live.

Over and over Tieta begged Eliezer to hurry. The moonlight shone on the river and on the form of the woman straining forward as if she could make the boat go faster by doing so.

Peto, in the plaza, had told her which way Leonora had gone. Crying so hard she could scarcely speak, his cousin had sent him to find Pirica and had gone off in the motorboat. Leonora was probably at Mangue Seco by now.

Eliezer called her attention to a light on the water and a distant sound; it was the other boat coming back. At a signal from Tieta, Pirica turned down his motor and the two boats bobbed in the water side by side.

"Where's Leonora?"

"She stayed out there. I asked her if she wanted me to wait and she said no, that she was planning to stay for a few days. What's happened to her? She couldn't stop crying; it's enough to break your heart."

At Mangue Seco Eliezer beached the launch on the sand and jumped out with Tieta. They saw a group of people at the other end of the beach in the moonlight next to the towering dunes. The night was infinitely soft and beautiful and the water was calm. Tieta ran down the beach, followed by Eliezer.

Jonas looked up.

"She threw herself off the dunes, climbed up there without anyone seeing her. Lucky for her Daniel and Budião had gone out fishing. They heard a body hit the water and Budião pulled her into the canoe."

Leonora was lying on the sand struggling as two women held her down, beseeching them to let her die. Tieta bent over her.

"You fool!"

Leonora turned her head when she heard Tieta's voice.

"I'm sorry, Mama. Tell them to let go of me. I just want to die, and no one's going to stop me."

Tieta knelt down, pulled Leonora to a sitting position and slapped her several times. Her hand fell heavily, with anger, on one side of the girl's face and then the other. The fishermen did not try to stop her, and Leonora made no effort to defend herself. Skipper Dário, to whom word had been sent, came running down the beach. Tieta broke off the punishment and tried to lift the girl to her feet.

"Come on, let's go."

"What is it, Tieta? What on earth has happened?" The Skipper helped Leonora to her feet as he spoke.

"Nora had a fight with Ascânio and tried to drown herself." She held out her hand in farewell. "Tell Dona Laura goodbye for me, Skipper."

"Goodbye? But why?"

"I'm going back to São Paulo tomorrow."

"But what about the campaign, Tieta? Don't abandon us like this!"

"I can't be of use to you any longer, Skipper. But you keep the boat on course and save the crabs if you can."

In the launch Tieta warned Leonora, "If you say another word about dying, I'll break every bone in your body."

Mangue Seco faded into the distance, its water and its dunes draped in moonlight. Tieta gazed back at it with dry eyes.

There were some who observed the two women through chinks in the curtains as they came up from the landing and crossed the square—Dona Edna, for instance—but at Perpétua's house the doors and windows were barred. Tieta's and Leonora's suitcases, sacks and shopping bags had been flung helter-skelter on the sidewalk.

*Of the polluted Calvary on Agreste's longest
night—fifth station of the cross:
a passion and an errand.*

Dona Milu and Dona Carmosina busied themselves with Leonora, changed her wet clothes and put her to bed. In the old midwife's house there was an unwonted bustle of tisanes and home remedies: lemon verbena tea for her nerves, eggnog to warm her and help her recover her strength. Sabino came in with their hand luggage; the larger pieces were already stowed aboard the *marineti* in the garage.

"I'm going out for a little while," Tieta announced.

Dona Milu was concerned.

"Out where? What are you up to now?"

"Don't be afraid, Mother Milu, I'm not looking for a fight."

In the apparently sleeping houses the inhabitants were wide awake and on the lookout. Rays of light filtered out between the cracks in the doors and beams. Every so often a word spoken a little more loudly could be heard in the street outside. Even Jarde's wake was animated now. The bar was full of men arguing. Osnar's voice was bitter. "The goddam factory isn't even here yet and it's already made the whole town rotten."

Windows were cracked open as Tieta passed. She crossed the town and walked through the alleys, headed for the bluffs along the river, walking unhurriedly, saying goodbye, perhaps. Saying goodbye and recruiting; her wanderings were not aimless. Madame Antoinette, *voilà!* knew what she was about.

Of the polluted Calvary on Agreste's longest night—sixth station of the cross: Lent and hallelujah.

"You know what they're saying? That she runs a cathouse in São Paulo." Astério rushed in early from the bar in a state.

Elisa sat up in bed, her breasts bouncing out of the transparent shortie nightgown passed down from Tieta and half her rear end showing. Astério looked away. He had fearful news to tell. This was a night of disgrace and affliction. There was no place in it for congenial marital duties, much less for the depraved thoughts he was thinking.

"You don't mean it! A cathouse?"

"That's right; a whorehouse, a bawdy house."

"What else did you find out?"

"They're over at Carmosina's now, and tomorrow they're leaving for São Paulo."

"What? Tieta's going back to São Paulo tomorrow?"

She sprang out of bed, threw on a dressing gown, another of Tieta's hand-me-downs, put on her sandals and started for the door. At first Astério was disturbed, then he was touched. Elisa wanted to say goodbye to her sister in spite of everything. They owed her plenty, let the old cats say anything they liked. He wanted to tell her goodbye himself. Whatever else she was, she was a good sister and a generous relative.

"Are you going to see her now? I'll go with you."

Elisa looked back from the doorway.

"I'm going with her, that's what."

"Going with her? To São Paulo, you mean?" he asked uncomprehendingly.

Elisa went off without answering. Dona Milu lived nearby. When she heard Astério following her she quickened her steps, breaking into a run when she saw Tieta about to go into the house.

"Tieta! Sister!" she called.

Tieta waited in the doorway, unmoving, a scowl on her face, a cold, austere look in her eyes. Elisa held out her arms beseechingly.

"Take me with you, Sister, don't leave me here alone!"

"Haven't I already told you—"

"I want to be a whore in São Paulo. I don't care."

Astério listened in bewilderment, that stabbing pain in his stomach again. Tieta turned from her sister to her brother-in-law. She sympathized with him, the booby.

"Astério, when are you going to make your wife toe the mark and teach her to respect you? I told you what you ought to do. Why didn't you do it?"

"Sister, for the love of God, don't leave me here." Elisa knelt down before Tieta.

"Take her away and do as I told you, Astério. It's now or never." She looked at her sister for a moment and felt sorry for her. "You keep the house. If you need anything just let me know."

Elisa threw off any last vestige of restraint and self-respect.

"Take me with you, Mama. I want to go to work in your whorehouse."

Tieta looked at her brother-in-law as if to say, "Well?" Astério shook off his perplexity, his stomachache and his prejudices, tore the blindfold from his eyes and seized his wife by the arm.

"Come on, get up. We're going home."

"You let me go!"

"Get up! Didn't you hear me?"

He slapped her face hard. Tieta nodded approvingly.

"Thanks for everything, Tieta. We'll be seeing you."

He gave the stunned Elisa a shove in the direction of their house, one of the best in town. Tieta had bought it to come back to and wait in for death to come slowly someday, and now her sister and brother-in-law would have the use of it for a long time.

He pushed her into the bedroom. Elisa tried to escape.

"Don't you touch me."

He struck her a blow that sent her reeling onto the bed. Her nightgown was twisted up around her neck and her haunches swam before Astério's clouded gaze.

"You want to be a whore, don't you? Well, you can start being one right now." He reached out and tore off the scrap of nylon, feasting his eyes on her buttocks after such a long fast. "The first thing I'm going to do is put it up your ass!"

A shudder ran over Elisa's body and her eyes opened wide. Was it repugnance, fear, shock, curiosity or eager expectation she felt? She was a soap-opera heroine torn by conflicting emotions.

Oh, for the love of God! She placed the steep, narrow entry in position like a submissive wife and bent her shoulders under the weight—and felt fire and honey inside her, a hard pole bursting into bloom. Elisa cried hallelujah for the Golden Cue.

Of the polluted Calvary on Agreste's longest night—seventh station of the cross: Barbozinha the Cyrenean offers himself in holocaust.

Tieta had just gone to bed when Barbozinha knocked frantically at Dona Milu's door and called out, "It's a friend!"

A friend indeed. Tieta came out of the guest room, where Leonora had finally dropped off. Barbozinha caught her hand and brought it to his lips. He looked pathetic, and his voice, which had never been the same after his embolism, could not rise above a strained whisper.

"I've heard you're going to leave us, Tieta. Is it true?"

"Yes, we're going back to São Paulo tomorrow."

"Is it because of what they're saying? Well, go if you want to. But if you'll stay and do me the honor . . ."

"What honor, Barbozinha?"

"The honor of being Mrs. Gregório Eustáquio de Matos Barbosa. . . ."

"Are you proposing marriage? To pick me up out of the gutter?"

"I know very well I'm not the young man I used to be; this old carcass isn't worth much, but I have an honorable name—"

"—and can still dance a tango like nobody's business." Tieta laughed, a frank, merry laugh of pure contentment that filled her eyes with tears.

"No, poet, it just wouldn't do. I'm too fond of you to put horns on you, and besides, you wouldn't like it. When I'm an old lady I'll come back for good and we'll get married. Until then, you look after that carcass of yours and write me some more poems."

She kissed him on both cheeks and finally let the tears flow as they would.

Of the news that brought relief.

"That sure is a neat little gadget!" said the Arab admiringly. "The years go by but it never misfires."

He meant the Russian radio. It was just after dawn and Jairo was tuning up the *marineti*'s motor with Sabino's help in front of the moviehouse where he waited for his passengers; they all knew he always left on the dot. He smiled complacently and indulged in a little boasting.

"I had an offer to trade it in for a new one—Japanese—but I didn't take it."

The announcer of the *Morning News Parade*, a popular news program from the capital, asked his audience to listen for a special announcement after the commercials. The broadcast was perfectly clear with no static, fully justifying Chalita's flattering praise. Dr. Franklin Lins, a towel over his shoulder, joined the group. Every day at that hour, before the *marineti*'s departure, the notary went down to the river for a swim.

The announcer's well-modulated voice warned them again: "Attention, everybody! Now for the news. Yesterday afternoon the Brazilian Titanium Company, Brastânio, was given permission by the government to build two interconnecting factories in Arembepe to produce titanium dioxide. With the aim of starting up this large-scale, controversial industrial project as soon as possible, the company will begin construction immediately on a large area already purchased by government authorization." A volley of loud reports saluted the announcement. Considering the origin of the venerable radio, it was not too farfetched to take this as a protest.

"Did you all hear what I heard?" demanded Dr. Franklin.

"Hey, isn't that the same factory Ascânio wanted them to build out at Mangue Seco?" The Arab's eyes kindled. As if the events of the night before had not been stirring enough, here was this news on top of it. It promised to be an exciting day.

"You mean they're not putting it here after all?" Jairo looked up from his inspection of the motor.

"No, they're going to build it in Arembepe instead, right outside the capital. That was one of the places they were talking about," explained the notary.

"Well, I'll be damned!"

Dr. Lins took a deep breath and adjusted the towel on his shoulder.

"Well, now we can breathe fresh air again." He lit a cornhusk cigarette and strolled off toward the river, blissfully at peace.

In which Tieta waves goodbye.

It was a light day, not many passengers. Tieta said goodbye to Dona Carmosina.

"Sorry for all the trouble we gave you, Carmô."

Leonora, head bent, a tear-drenched handkerchief in her hand, took refuge in the bus and sat huddled on a bench. Peto came running across Cathedral Square with old Zé Esteves' shepherd's staff, Tieta's inheritance.

"Here, Aunt, you forgot this." In a low voice he added, "I'm going to miss you."

Farewell to lovely visions of bosoms and thighs! He climbed into the bus to talk to Leonora and was greeted with choked sobs.

"Goodbye, Cousin," he said.

Peto dashed off home again, leaving an unforgettable memory of his special brand of kindness and a pronounced odor of cheap brilliantine.

Tieta the goat girl, holding her staff, sat down next to Leonora and just let her cry. It was too soon to try to make conversation. Jairo walked down the aisle to collect the fares. Tieta paid for three.

"The two of us and that little nannygoat back there."

She pointed to Maria Imaculada, who was sitting on a bench at the back of the bus, clutching her tin trunk. Jairo took his seat at the wheel and put the key in the ignition. Still four minutes to go. Tieta was in a hurry.

"Let's hit the road, Jairo, and we'll see if this contraption can get us as far as Esplanada."

Jairo consulted his watch.

"We can go all the way to São Paulo if you say the word. No distance is too great for the Empress of the Highways. And you'll hear music all the way."

He turned the dial of the Russian radio. Tieta waved goodbye to Dona Carmosina standing on the sidewalk. The *marineti* rolled away so smoothly that it might have been an airplane gliding down the runway. Floating over rocks, tree stumps, and rough places, it rose above the muletrack and crossed the sky of Agreste.

And so ends my tale about the return of the prodigal daughter to her birthplace and all that happened there during her brief stay.

On the street signs, an author's note.

Well, here we are; one way or another we've reached the end by hook and by crook and it's time to write finis. In all good adventure novels, Fúlvio D'Alambert reminds me, the author is expected to say a little something about what happened to the characters after the story ends. I don't intend to do that. I'll leave it to the imagination and conscience of my readers to decide the fate of my characters and the moral of the tale.

As a sop to the critics and in the hope of gaining their goodwill, I will simply add that Agreste is slowly recovering. Skipper Dário de Queluz has shed his candidate's uniform and is enjoying every summer day on Mangue Seco to the full to make up for the days misspent on dirty politics. As for Ascânio Trindade, the last time we saw him he was crying on Dona Carmosina's shoulder.

There was a big celebration when the Paulo Afonso power was turned on. Old Mud Lane, the street going out of town, was renamed after the then director and president of the São Francisco Valley Authority. The presiding authorities unveiled a handsome dark-blue enamel sign which was ordered from the capital and had come in record time. Rua Deputado . . . what was that fellow's name again?

The blue street sign didn't last long. Someone stole it one night and nailed a wooden sign in its place, made by an anonymous artisan's hand, which read: TIETA'S LIGHT.

An anonymous artisan's hand. The people's hand.

THE END

Bahia, London, Bahia—1976–1977